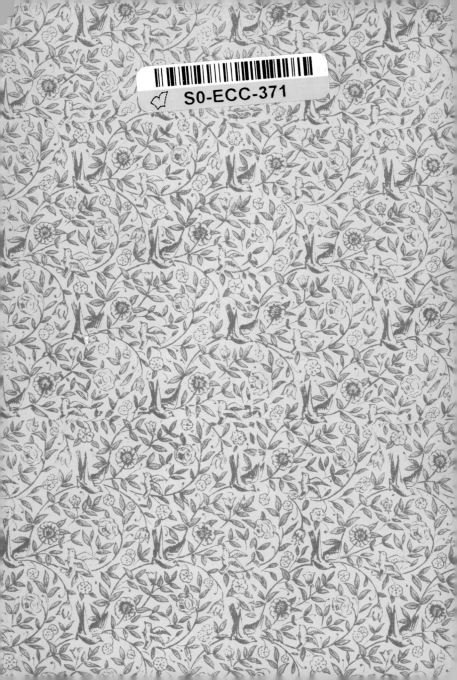

THANKSGIVING.

THE
ADVENTURES OF PHILIP
ON HIS WAY THROUGH THE WORLD;

SHEWING

WHO ROBBED HIM, WHO HELPED HIM, AND WHO PASSED HIM BY:

TO WHICH IS NOW PREFIXED

A SHABBY GENTEEL STORY.

BY

WILLIAM MAKEPEACE THACKERAY.

WITH ILLUSTRATIONS BY F. WALKER AND THE AUTHOR.

CHICAGO AND NEW YORK:
BELFORD, CLARKE & COMPANY,
PUBLISHERS.

ADVERTISEMENT.

WHEN the "Shabby Genteel Story" was first reprinted with other stories and sketches by Mr. Thackeray, collected together under the title of "Miscellanies," the following note was appended to it :—

It was my intention to complete the little story, of which only the first part is here written. Perhaps novel-readers will understand, even from the above chapters, what was to ensue. Caroline was to be disowned and deserted by her wicked husband : that abandoned man was to marry somebody else : hence, bitter trials and grief, patience and virtue, for poor little Caroline, and a melancholy ending—as how should it have been gay ? The tale was interrupted at a sad period of the writer's own life. The colors are long since dry ; the artist's hand is changed. It is best to leave the sketch, as it was when first designed seventeen years ago. The memory of the past is renewed as he looks at it—

die Bilder froher Tage
Und manche liebe Schatten steigen auf

W. M. T.

LONDON, *April 10th,* 1857.

Mr. Brandon, a principal character in this story, figures prominently in "The Adventures of Philip," under his real name of Brand Firmin ; Mrs. Brandon, his deserted wife, and her father, Mr. Gann, are also introduced ; therefore the "Shabby Genteel Story" is now prefixed to "The Adventures of Philip."

CONTENTS.

A SHABBY GENTEEL STORY.

THE ADVENTURES OF PHILIP.

A

SHABBY GENTEEL STORY.

CHAPTER I.

AT that remarkable period when Louis XVIII. was restored a second time to the throne of his fathers, and all the English who had money or leisure rushed over to the Continent, there lived in a certain boarding-house at Brussels a genteel young widow, who bore the elegant name of Mrs. Wellesley Macarty.

In the same house and room with the widow lived her mamma, a lady who was called Mrs. Crabb. Both professed to be rather fashionable people. The Crabbs were of a very old English stock, and the Macartys were, as the world knows, Country Cork people; related to the Sheenys, Finnigans, Clancys, and other distinguished families in their part of Ireland. But Ensign Wellesley Mac, not having a shilling, ran off with Miss Crabb, who possessed the same independence; and after having been married about six months to the lady, was carried off suddenly, on the 18th of June, 1815, by a disease very prevalent in those glorious times—the fatal cannon-shot morbus. He, and many hundred young fellows of his regiment, the Clonakilty Fencibles, were attacked by this epidemic on the same day, at a place about ten miles from Brussels, and there perished. The ensign's lady had accompanied her husband to the Continent, and about five months after his death brought into the world two remarkably fine female children.

Mrs. Wellesley's mother had been reconciled to her daughter by this time—for, in truth, Mrs. Crabb had no other child but her runaway Juliana, to whom she flew when she heard of her destitute condition. And, indeed, it was high time that some one should come to the young widow's aid; for as her husband did not leave money, nor anything that represented money, except a number of tailors' and bootmakers' bills, neatly docketed, in his writing-desk, Mrs. Wellesley was in danger of starvation, should no friendly person assist her.

Mrs. Crabb, then, came off to her daughter, whom the Sheenys, Finnigans, and Clancys refused, with one scornful voice, to assist. The fact is, that Mr. Crabb had once been butler to a lord, and his lady a lady's-maid ; and at Crabb's death, Mrs. Crabb disposed of the " Ram " hotel and posting-house, where her husband had made three thousand pounds, and was living in genteel ease in a country town, when Ensign Macarty came, saw, and ran away with Juliana. Of such a connection, it was impossible that the great Clancys and Finnigans could take notice ; and so once more widow Crabb was compelled to share with her daughter her small income of a hundred and twenty a year.

Upon this, at a boarding-house in Brussels, the two managed to live pretty smartly, and to maintain an honorable reputation. The twins were put out, after the foreign fashion, to nurse, at a village in the neighborhood ; for Mrs. Macarty had been too ill to nurse them ; and Mrs. Crabb could not afford to purchase that most expensive article, a private wet-nurse.

There had been numberless tiffs and quarrels between mother and daughter when the latter was in her maiden state ; and Mrs. Crabb was, to tell the truth, in nowise sorrow when her Jooly disappeared with the ensign,—for the old lady dearly loved a gentleman, and was not a little flattered at being the mother to Mrs. Ensign Macarty. Why the ensign should have run away with his lady at all, as he might have had her for the asking, is no business of ours ; nor are we going to rake up old stories and village scandals, which insinuate that Miss Crabb ran away with *him*, for with these points the writer and the reader have nothing to do.

Well, then, the reconciled mother and daughter lived once more together, at Brussels. In the course of a year, Mrs. Macarty's sorrow had much abated ; and having a great natural love of dress, and a tolerably handsome face and person, she was induced, without much reluctance, to throw her weeds aside, and to appear in the most becoming and varied costumes which her means and ingenuity could furnish. Considering, indeed, the smallness of the former, it was agreed on all hands that Mrs. Crabb and her daughter deserved wonderful credit,— that is, they managed to keep up as respectable an appearance as if they had five hundred a year ; and at church, at tea-parties,

and abroad in the streets, to be what is called quite the gentle-women. If they starved at home, nobody saw it; if they patched and pieced, nobody (it was to be hoped) knew it; if they bragged about their relations and property, could any one say them nay? Thus they lived, hanging on with desperate energy to the skirts of genteel society; Mrs. Crabb, a sharp woman, rather respected her daughter's superior rank; and Mrs. Macarty did not quarrel so much as heretofore with her mamma, on whom herself and her two children were entirely dependent.

While affairs were at this juncture, it happened that a young Englishman, James Gann, Esq., of the great oil house of Gann, Blubbery and Gann (as he took care to tell you before you had been an hour in his company),—it happened, I say, that James Gann, Esq., came to Brussels for a month, for the purpose of perfecting himself in the French language; and while in that capital went to lodge at the very boarding-house which contained Mrs. Crabb and her daughter. Gann was young, weak, inflammable; he saw and adored Mrs. Wellesley Macarty; and she, who was at this period all but engaged to a stout old wooden-legged Scotch regimental surgeon, pitilessly sent Dr. M'Lint about his business, and accepted the addresses of Mr. Gann. How the young man arranged matters with his papa the senior partner, I don't know; but it is certain that there was a quarrel, and afterwards a reconciliation; and it is also known that James Gann fought a duel with the surgeon,—receiving the Æsculapian fire, and discharging his own bullet into the azure skies. About nine thousand times in the course of his after-years did Mr. Gann narrate the history of the combat; it enabled him to go through life with the reputation of a man of courage, and won for him, as he said with pride, the hand of his Juliana; perhaps this was rather a questionable benefit.

One part of the tale, however, honest James never did dare to tell, except when peculiarly excited by wrath or liquor; it was this: that on the day after the wedding, and in the presence of many friends who had come to offer their congratulations, a stout nurse, bearing a brace of chubby little ones, made her appearance; and these rosy urchins, springing forward at the sight of Mrs. James Gann, shouted affectionately, "*Maman! maman!*" at which the lady, blushing rosy red, said, "James, these two are yours;" and poor James wellnigh fainted at this sudden paternity so put upon him. "Children!" screamed he, aghast; "whose children?" at which Mrs. Crabb, majestically checking him, said, "These, my dear James, are the daughters of the gallant and good Ensign Macarty, whose widow you yesterday led to the altar. May you be happy with her, and may these blessed children" (tears) "find in you a father, who shall replace him that fell in the field of glory!"

Mrs. Crabb, Mrs. James Gann, Mrs. Major Lolly, Mrs. Piffler, and several ladies present, set up a sob immediately; and James Gann, a good-humored, soft-hearted man, was quite taken aback. Kissing his lady hurriedly, he vowed that he would take care of the poor little things, and proposed to kiss them likewise; which caress the darlings refused with many roars. Gann's fate was sealed from that minute; and he was properly henpecked by his wife and mother-in-law during the life of the latter. Indeed, it was to Mrs. Crabb that the stratagem of the infant concealment was due; for when her daughter innocently proposed to have or to see the children, the old lady strongly pointed out the folly of such an arrangement, which might, perhaps, frighten away Mr. Gann from the delightful matrimonial trap into which (lucky rogue!) he was about to fall.

Soon after the marriage, the happy pair returned to England, occupying the house in Thames Street, City, until the death of Gann senior; when his son, becoming head of the firm of Gann and Blubbery, quitted the dismal precincts of Billingsgate and colonized in the neighborhood of Putney; where a neat box, a couple of spare bedrooms, a good cellar, and a smart gig to drive into and out from town, made a real gentleman of him. Mrs. Gann treated him with much scorn, to be sure, called him a sot, and abused hugely the male companions that he brought down with him to Putney. Honest James would listen meekly, would yield, and would bring down a brace more friends the next day, with whom he would discuss his accustomed number of bottles of port. About this period, a daughter was born to him, called Caroline Bradenburg Gann; so named after a large mansion near Hammersmith, and an injured queen who lived there at the time of the little girl's birth, and who was greatly compassioned and patronized by Mrs. James Gann, and other ladies of distinction. Mrs. James *was* a lady in those days, and gave evening-parties of the very first order.

At this period of time, Mrs. James Gann sent the twins Rosalind Clancy and Isabella Finnigan Wellesley Macarty, to a boarding-school for young ladies, and grumbled much at the amount of the half-years' bills which her husband was called upon to pay for them ; for though James discharged them with perfect good-humor, his lady began to entertain a mean opinion indeed of her pretty young children. They could expect no fortune, she said, from Mr. Gann, and she wondered that he should think of bringing them up expensively, when he had a darling child of his own, for whom he was bound to save all the money that he could lay by.

Grandmamma, too, doted on the little Caroline Brandenburg, and vowed that she would leave her three thousand pounds to this dear infant ; for in this way does the world show its respect for that most respectable thing prosperity. Who in this life get the smiles, and the acts of friendship, and the pleasing legacies ?—The rich. And I do, for my part, heartily wish that some one would leave me a trifle—say twenty thousand pounds—being perfectly confident that some one else would leave me more ; and that I should sink into my grave worth a plum at least.

Little Caroline then had her maid, her airy nursery, her little carriage to drive in, the promise of her grandmamma's consols, and that priceless treasure—her mamma's undivided affection. Gann, too, loved her sincerely, in his careless, good-humored way ; but he determined, notwithstanding, that his step-daughters should have something handsome at his death, but—but for a great BUT.

Gann and Blubbery were in the oil line,—have we not said so ? Their profits arose from contracts for lighting a great number of streets in London ; and about this period GAS came into use. Gann and Blubbery appeared in the *Gazette;* and, I am sorry to say, so bad had been the management of Blubbery, —so great the extravagance of both partners and their ladies, —that they only paid their creditors fourteenpence halfpenny in the pound.

When Mrs. Crabb heard of this dreadful accident—Mrs. Crabb, who dined thrice a week with her son-in-law ; who never would have been allowed to enter the house at all had not honest James interposed his good nature between her quarrelsome daughter and herself—Mrs. Crabb, I say, proclaimed James Gann to be a swindler, a villain, a disreputable, tipsy, vulgar man, and made over her money to the Misses Rosalind Clancy and Isabella Finnigan Macarty ; leaving poor little Caroline without one single maravedi. Half of one thousand five hundred pounds allotted to each was to be paid at marriage, the other half on the death of Mrs. James Gann, who was to enjoy the interest thereof. Thus do we rise and fall in this world—thus does Fortune shake her swift wings, and bid us abruptly to resign the gifts (or rather loans) which we have had from her.

How Gann and his family lived after their stroke of misfortune, I know not; but as the failing tradesman is going through the process of bankruptcy, and for some months afterwards, it may be remarked that he has usually some mysterious means of subsistence—stray spars of the wreck of his property, on which he manages to seize, and to float for a while. During his retirement, in an obscure lodging in Lambeth, where the poor fellow was so tormented by his wife as to be compelled to fly to the public-house for refuge, Mrs. Crabb died; a hundred a year thus came into the possession of Mrs. Gann; and some of James's friends, who thought him a good fellow in his prosperity, came forward, and furnished a house, in which they placed him, and came to see and comfort him. Then they came to see him not quite so often; then they found out that Mrs. Gann was a sad tyrant, and a silly woman; then the ladies declared *her* to be insupportable, and *Gann* to be a low, tipsy fellow: and the gentlemen could but shake their heads, and admit that the charge was true. Then they left off coming to see him altogether; for such is the way of the world, where many of us have good impulses, and are generous on an occasion, but are wearied by perpetual want, and begin to grow angry at its importunities—being very properly vexed at the daily recurrence of hunger, and the impudent unreasonableness of starvation. Gann, then, had a genteel wife and children, a furnished house, and a hundred pounds a year. How should he live? The wife of James Gann, Esq., would never allow him to demean himself by taking a clerk's place; and James himself, being as idle a fellow as ever was known, was fain to acquiesce in this determination of hers, and to wait for some more genteel employment. And a curious list of such genteel employments might be made out, were one inclined to follow this interesting subject far; shabby compromises with the world, into which poor fellows enter, and still fondly talk of their " position," and strive to imagine that they are really working for their bread.

Numberless lodging-houses are kept by the females of families who have met with reverses: are not " boarding-houses, with a select musical society, in the neighborhood of the squares," maintained by such? Do not the gentlemen of the boarding houses issue forth every morning to the City, or make believe to go thither, on some mysterious business which they have? After a certain period, Mrs. James Gann kept a lodging-house (in her own words, received "two inmates into her family"), and Mr. Gann had his mysterious business.

In the year 1835, when this story begins, there stood in a certain back street in the town of Margate a house, on the door of which might be read, in gleaming brass, the name of Mr. GANN. It was the work of a single smutty servant-maid to clean this brass plate every morning, and to attend, as far as possible, to the wants of Mr. Gann, his family, and lodgers ; and his house being not very far from the sea, and as you might, by climbing up to the roof, get a sight, between two chimneys, of that multitudinous element, Mrs. Gann set down her lodgings as fashionable ; and declared on her cards that her house commanded "a fine view of the sea."

On the wire window-blind of the parlor was written, in large characters, the word OFFICE ; and here it was that Gann's services came into play. He was very much changed, poor fellow ! and humbled ; and from two cards that hung outside the blind, I am led to believe that he did not disdain to be agent to the " London and Jamaica Ginger-Beer Company," and also for a certain preparation called " Gaster's Infants' Farinacio, or Mothers' Invigorating Substitute," — a damp, black, mouldy, half-pound packet of which stood in permanence at one end of the " office " mantel-piece ; while a fly-blown ginger-beer bottle occupied the other extremity. Nothing else indicated that this ground-floor chamber was an office, except a huge black inkstand, in which stood a stumpy pen, richly crusted with ink at the nib, and, to all appearance, for many months enjoying a sinecure.

To this room you saw every day, at two o'clock, the *employé* from the neighboring hotel bring two quarts of beer ; and if you called at that hour, a tremendous smoke and smell of dinner would gush out upon you from the " office," as you stumbled over sundry battered tin dish-covers, which lay gaping at the threshhold. Thus had that great bulwark of gentility, the dining at six o'clock, been broken in ; and the reader must therefore judge that the house of Gann was in a demoralized state.

Gann certainly was. After the ladies had retired to the back-parlor (which, with yellow gauze round the frames, window curtains, a red silk cabinet piano, and an album, was still tolerably genteel), Gann remained, to transact business in the office. This took place in the presence of friends, and usually consisted in the production of a bottle of gin from the corner cupboard, or, mayhap, a *litre* of brandy, which was given by Gann with a knowing wink, and a fat finger placed on a twinkling red nose :

when Mrs. G. was out, James would also produce a number of pipes, that gave this room a constant and agreeable odor of shag tobacco.

In fact, Mr. Gann had nothing to do from morning till night. He was now a fat, bald-headed man of fifty ; a dirty dandy on week-days, with a shawl waistcoat, a tuft of hair to his great, double-chin, a snuffy shirt-frill, and enormous breast-pin and seals : he had a pilot-coat, with large mother-of-pearl buttons, and always wore a great rattling telescope, with which he might be seen for hours on the sea shore or the pier, examining the ships, the bathing-machines, the ladies' schools as they paraded up and down the esplanade, and all other objects which the telescopic view might give him. He knew every person connected with every one of the Deal and Dover coaches, and was sure to be witness to the arrival or departure of several of them in the course of the day ; he had a word for the ostler about "that gray mare," a nod for the "shooter" or guard, and a bow for the dragsman ; he could send parcels for nothing up to town ; had twice had Sir Rumble Tumble (the noble driver of the Flash-'o-lightning-light-four-inside-post-coach) "up at his place," and took care to tell you that some of the party were pretty considerably "sewn up," too. He did not frequent the large hotels ; but in revenge he knew every person who entered or left them ; and was a great man at the "Bag of Nails" and the "Magpie and Punchbowl," where he was president of a club ; he took the bass in "Mynheer Van Dunk," "The Wolf," and many other morsels of concerted song, and used to go backwards and forwards to London in the steamers as often as ever he liked, and have his "grub," too, on board. Such was James Gann. Many people, when they wrote to him, addressed him James Gann, Esq.

His reverses and former splendors afforded a never-failing theme of conversation to honest Gann and the whole of his family ; and it may be remarked that such pecuniary misfortunes, as they are called, are by no means misfortunes to people of certain dispositions, but actual pieces of good luck. Gann, for instance, used to drink liberally of port and claret, when the house of Gann and Blubbery was in existence, and was henceforth compelled to imbibe only brandy and gin. Now he loved these a thousand times more than the wine ; and had the advantage of talking about the latter, and of his great merit in giving them up. In those prosperous days, too, being a gentleman, he could not frequent the public-house as he did at present ; and the sanded tavern parlor was Gann's supreme enjoyment. He was obliged to spend many hours daily in a dark, unsavory room in an alley off Thames street; and Gann hated books and business, except of other people's. His tastes were low; he loved public-house jokes and company; and now being fallen, was voted at the "Bag of Nails" and the "Magpie" before mentioned a tip-top fellow and real gentleman, whereas he had been considered an ordinary vulgar man by his fashionable associates at Putney. Many men are there who are made to fall, and to profit by the tumble.

As for Mrs. G., or Jooly, as she was indifferently called by her husband, she, too, had gained by her losses. She bragged of her former acquaintances in the most extraordinary way, and to hear her you would fancy that she was known to and connected with half the peerage. Her chief occupation was taking medicine, and mending and altering her gowns. She had a huge taste for cheap finery, loved raffles, tea-parties, and walks on the pier, where she flaunted herself and daughters as gay as butterflies. She stood upon her rank, did not fail to tell her lodgers that she was "a gentlewoman," and was mighty sharp with Becky the maid, and poor Carry, her youngest child.

For the tide of affection had turned now, and the "Misses Wellesley Macarty" were the darlings of their mother's heart, as Caroline had been in the early days of Putney prosperity. Mrs. Gann respected and loved her elder daughters, the stately heiresses of 1,500*l.*, and scorned poor Caroline, who was likewise scorned (like Cinderella in the sweetest of all stories) by her brace of haughty, thoughtless sisters. These young women were tall, well-grown, black-browed girls, little scrupulous, fond of fun, and having great health and spirits. Caroline was pale and thin, and had fair hair and meek gray eyes; nobody thought her a beauty in her moping cotton gown; whereas the sisters, in flaunting printed muslins, with pink scarfs, and artificial flowers, and brass *ferronnières*, and other fallals, were voted very charming by the Ganns' circle of friends. They had pink cheeks, white shoulders, and many glossy curls stuck about their shining foreheads, as damp and as black as leeches. Such charms, madam, cannot fail of having their effect; and it was very lucky for Caroline that she did not possess them, for she might have been rendered as vain, frivolous, and vulgar, as these young ladies were.

While these enjoyed their pleasures and tea-parties abroad, it was Carry's usual fate to remain at home, and help the servant in many duties which were required in Mrs. Gann's establishment. She dressed that lady and her sisters, brought

her papa his tea in bed, kept the lodgers' bills, bore their scoldings if they were ladies, and sometimes gave a hand in the
kitchen if any extra piecrust or cookery was required.   At two
she made a little toilet for dinner, and was employed on numberless household darnings and mendings in the long evenings, while her sisters giggled over the jingling piano, mamma
sprawled on the sofa, and Gann was over his glass at the club.
A weary lot, in sooth, was yours, poor little Caroline ! since the
days of your infancy, not one hour of sunshine, no friendship,
no cheery playfellows, no mother's love ; but that being dead,
the affections which would have crept round it, withered and
died too.   Only James Gann, of all the household, had a good-
natured look for her, and a coarse word of kindness ; nor, indeed, did Caroline complain, nor shed many tears, nor call for
death, as she would if she had been brought up in genteeler
circles.   The poor thing did not know her own situation ; her
misery was dumb and patient ; it is such as thousands and
thousands of women in our society bear, and pine, and die of ;
made up of sums of small tyrannies, and long indifference, and
bitter wearisome injustice, more dreadful to bear than any
tortures that we of the stronger sex are pleased to cry *A*ℓ! *A*ℓ!
about.   In our intercourse with the world (which is conducted
with that kind of cordiality that we see in Sir Harry and my
lady in a comedy—a couple of painted, grinning fools, talking
parts that they have learned out of a book,)—as we sit and
look at the smiling actors, we get a glimpse behind the scenes
from time to time ; and alas for the wretched nature that
appears there !—among women especially, who deceive even
more than men, having more to hide, feeling more, living more
than we who have our business, pleasure, ambition, which
carries us abroad.   Ours are the great strokes of misfortune,
as they are called, and theirs the small miseries.   While the
male thinks, labors, and battles without, the domestic woes
and wrongs are the lot of the women ; and the little ills are so
bad, so infinitely fiercer and bitterer than the great, that I would
not change my condition—no, not to be Helen, Queen Elizabeth, Mrs. Coutts, or the luckiest she in history.

Well, then, in the manner we have described lived the Gann
family.   Mr. Gann all the better for his " misfortunes," Mrs.
Gann little the worse ; the two young ladies greatly improved
by the circumstances, having been cast thereby into a society
where their expected three thousand pounds made great
heiresses of them ; and poor Caroline, as luckless a being as
any that the wide sun shone upon.   Better to be alone in the

world and utterly friendless, than to have sham friends and no sympathy; ties of kindred which bind one as it were to the corpse of relationship, and oblige one to bear through life the weight and the embraces of this lifeless, cold connection.

I do not mean to say that Caroline would ever have made use of this metaphor, or suspected that her connection with her mamma and sisters was anything so loathsome. She felt that she was ill-treated, and had no companion; but was not on that account envious, only humble and depressed, not desiring so much to resist as to bear injustice, and hardly venturing to think for herself. This tyranny and humility served her in place of education, and formed her manners, which were wonderfully gentle and calm. It was strange to see such a person growing up in such a family; the neighbors spoke of her with much scornful compassion. "A poor half-witted thing," they said, "who would not say bo! to a goose;" and I think it is one good test of gentility to be thus looked down on by vulgar people.

It is not to be supposed that the elder girls had reached their present age without receiving a number of offers of marriage, and been warmly in love a great many times. But many unfortunate occurrences had compelled them to remain in their virgin condition. There was an attorney who had proposed to Rosalind; but finding that she would receive only 750*l.* down, instead of 1500*l.*, the monster had jilted her pitilessly, handsome as she was. An apothecary, too, had been smitten by her charms; but to live in a shop was beneath the dignity of a Wellesley Macarty, and she waited for better things. Lieutenant Swabber, of the coast-guard service, had lodged two months at Gann's; and if letters, long walks, and town-talk could settle a match, a match between him and Isabella must have taken place. Well, Isabella was not married; and the lieutenant, a colonel in Spain, seemed to have given up all thoughts of her. She meanwhile consoled herself with a gay young wine-merchant, who had lately established himself at Brighton, kept a gig, rode out with the hounds, and was voted perfectly genteel; and there was a certain French marquess, with the most elegant black mustaches, who had made a vast impression upon the heart of Rosalind, having met her first at the circulating library, and afterwards, by the most extraordinary series of chances, coming upon her and her sister daily in their walks upon the pier.

Meek little Caroline, meanwhile, trampled upon though she was, was springing up to womanhood; and though pale, freckled thin, meanly dressed, had a certain charm about her which some people might prefer to the cheap splendors and rude red and white of the Misses Macarty.   In fact we have now come to a period of her history when, to the amaze of her mamma and sisters, and not a little to the satisfaction of James Gann, Esquire, she actually inspired a passion in the breast of a very respectable young man.

CHAPTER II.

HOW MRS. GANN RECEIVED TWO LODGERS.

IT was the winter season when the events recorded in this history occurred ; and as at that period not one out of a thousand lodging-houses in Margate are let, Mrs. Gann, who generally submitted to occupy her own first and second floors during this cheerless season, considered herself more than ordinarily lucky when circumstances occurred which brought no less than two lodgers to her establishment.

She had to thank her daughters for the first inmate ; for, as these two young ladies were walking one day down their own street, talking of the joys of the last season, and the delight of the raffles and singing at the libraries, and the intoxicating pleasures of the Vauxhall balls, they were remarked and evidently admired by a young gentleman who was sauntering listlessly up the street.

He stared, and it must be confessed that the fascinating girls stared too, and put each other's head into each other's bonnet, and giggled and said, " Lor ! " and then looked hard at the young gentlemen again.   Their eyes were black, their cheeks were very red.   Fancy how Miss Bella's and Miss Linda's hearts beat when the gentleman, dropping his glass out of his eye, actually stepped across the street, and said, " Ladies, I am seeking for lodgings, and should be glad to look at those which I see are to let in your house."

" How did the conjuror know it was our house ? " thought Bella and Linda (they always thought in couples).   From the very simple fact that Miss Bella had just thrust into the door a latch-key.

Most bitterly did Mrs. James Gann regret that she had not

on her best gown when a stranger—a stranger in February—
actually called to look at the lodgings. She made up, however,
for the slovenliness of her dress by the dignity of her demeanor ;
and asked the gentleman for references, informed him that she
was a gentlewoman, and that he would have peculiar advantages in her establishment ; and finally, agreed to receive him
at the rate of twenty shillings per week. The bright eyes of the
young ladies had done the business ; but to this day Mrs. James
Gann is convinced that her peculiar dignity of manner, and
great fluency of brag regarding her family, have been the means
of bringing hundreds of lodgers to her house, who but for her
would never have visited it.

"Gents," said Mr. James Gann, at the "Bag of Nails" that
very evening, "we have got a new lodger, and I'll stand glasses
round to his jolly good health ! "

The new lodger, who was remarkable for nothing except
very black eyes, a sallow face, and a habit of smoking cigars in
bed until noon, gave his name George Brandon, Esq. As to
his temper and habits, when humbly requested by Mrs. Gann to
pay in advance, he laughed and presented her with a bank-note,
never quarrelled with a single item in her bills, walked much,
and ate two mutton-chops per diem. The young ladies, who
examined all the boxes and letters of the lodgers, as young
ladies will, could not find one single document relative to their
new inmate, except a tavern-bill of the "White Hart," to which
the name of George Brandon, Esquire, was prefixed. Any
other papers which might elucidate his history, were locked up
in a Bramah box, likewise marked G. B. ; and though these
were but unsatisfactory points by which to judge a man's character, there was a something about Mr. Brandon which caused
all the ladies at Mrs. Gann's to vote he was quite a gentleman.

When this was the case, I am happy to say it would not unfrequently happen that Miss Rosalind or Miss Isabella would
appear in the lodger's apartments, bearing in the breakfast-cloth,
or blushingly appearing with the weekly bill, apologizing for
mamma's absence, "and hoping that everything was to the
gentleman's liking."

Both the Misses Wellesley Macarty took occasion to visit
Mr. Brandon in this manner, and he received both with such a
fascinating ease and gentleman-like freedom of manner, scan-
ning their points from head to foot, and fixing his great black
eyes so earnestly on their faces, that the blushing creatures
turned away abashed, and yet pleased, and had many conversations about him.

"Law, Bell," said Miss Rosalind, "what a chap that Bran don is! I don't half like him, I do declare!" Than which there can be no greater compliment from a woman to a man.

"No more do I neither," says Bell. "The man stares so, and says such things! Just now, when Becky brought his paper and sealing-wax—the silly girl brought black and red too—I took them up to ask which he would have, and what do you think he said?"

"Well, dear, what?" said Mrs. Gann.

"'Miss Bell,' says he, looking at me, and with such eyes! 'I'll keep everything: the red wax, because it's like your lips; the black wax, because it's like your hair; and the satin paper, because it's like your skin!' Wasn't it genteel?"

"Law, now!" exclaimed Mrs. Gann.

"Upon my word, I think it's very rude!" said Miss Lindy; "and if he'd said so to me, I'd have slapped his face for his imperence!" And much to her credit, Miss Lindy went to his room ten minutes after to see if he *would* say anything to her. What Mr. Brandon said, I never knew; but the little pang of envy which had caused Miss Lindy to retort sharply upon her sister, had given place to a pleased good-humor, and she allowed Bella to talk about the new lodger as much as ever she liked.

And now if the reader is anxious to know what was Mr. Brandon's character, he had better read the following letter from him. It was addressed to no less a person than a viscount; and given, perhaps, with some little ostentation to Becky, the maid, to carry to the post. Now Becky, before she executed such errands, always showed the letters to her mistress or one of the young ladies (it must not be supposed that Miss Caroline was a whit less curious on these matters than her sisters); and when the family beheld the name of Lord Viscount Cinqbars upon the superscription, their respect for their lodger was greater than ever it had been:—

"MARGATE, *February*, 1835.

"MY DEAR VISCOUNT,—For a reason I have, on coming down to Margate, I with much gravity informed the people of the 'White Hart' that my name was Brandon, and intend to bear that honorable appellation during my stay. For the same reason (I am a modest man, and love to do good in secret), I left the public hotel immediately, and am now housed in private lodgings, humble, and at a humble price. I am here, thank heaven, quite alone. Robinson Crusoe had as much society in his island, as I in this of Thanet. In compensation I sleep a great deal, do nothing, and walk much, silent, by the side of the roaring sea, like Calchas, priest of Apollo.

"The fact is, that until papa's wrath is appeased, I must live with the utmost meekness and humility, and have barely enough money in my possession to pay such small current expenses as fall on me here, where strangers are many and credit does not exist. I pray you, therefore, to tell Mr. Snipson the tailor, Mr. Jackson the bootmaker, honest Solomon-son the discounter of bills, and all such friends in London and Oxford as may make inquiries after me, that I am at this very moment at the city of Munich in Bavaria, from which I shall not return until my marriage with Miss Goldmore, the great Indian heiress; who, upon my honor, will have me, I believe, any day for the asking.

"Nothing else will satisfy my honored father, I know, whose purse has already bled pretty freely for me, I must confess, and who has taken the great oath that never is broken, to bleed no more unless this marriage is brought about. Come it must. I can't work, I can't starve, and I can't live under a thousand a year.

"Here, to be sure, the charges are not enormous; for your edification, read my week's bill :—

'George Brandon, Esquire,
             'To Mrs. James Gann.

	£.	s.	d.
A week's lodging	1	0	0
Breakfast, cream, eggs	0	9	0
Dinner (fourteen mutton-chops) . . .	0	10	6
Fire, boot-cleaning, &c.	0	3	6
	£2	3	0

'Settled, Juliana Gann.'

"Juliana Gann! Is it not a sweet name? it sprawls over half the paper. Could you but see the owner of the name, my dear fellow! I love to examine the customs of natives of all countries, and upon my word there are some barbarians in our own less known, and more worthy of being known, than Hottentots, wild Irish, Otaheiteans, or any such savages. If you could see the airs that this woman gives herself; the rouge, ribands, rings, and other female gimcracks that she wears; if you could hear her reminiscences of past times, 'when she and Mr. Gann moved in the very genteelest circles of society;' of the peerage, which she knows by heart; and of the fashionable novels, in every word of which she believes, you would be proud of your order, and admire the intense respect which the *canaille* show towards it. There never was such an old woman, not even our tutor at Christchurch.

"There is a he Gann, a vast, bloated old man, in a rough coat, who has met me once, and asked me, with a grin, if my mutton-chops was to my liking? The satirical monster! What *can* I eat in this place but mutton-chops? A great bleeding beef-steak, or a filthy, reeking *gigot à l'eau*, with a turnip poultice? I should die if I did. As for fish in a watering-place, I never touch it; it is sure to be bad. Nor care I for little sinewy, dry, black-legged fowls. Cutlets are my only resource; I have them nicely enough broiled by a little humble companion of the family (a companion, ye gods, in *this* family!), who blushed hugely when she confessed that the cooking was hers, and that her name was Caroline. For drink I indulge in gin, of which I consume two wine-glasses daily, in two tumblers of cold water; it is the only liquor that one can be sure to find genuine in a common house in England.

"This Gann, I take it, has similar likings, for I hear him occasionally at midnight floundering up the stairs (his boots lie dirty in the passage)—floundering, I say, up the stairs, and cursing the candlestick, whence escape now and anon the snuffers and extinguisher, and with brazen rattle disturb the silence of the night. Thrice a week, at least, does Gann breakfast in bed—sure sign of pridian intoxication; and thrice a week, in the morning, I hear a hoarse voice roaring for 'my soda-water.' How long have the rogues drunk soda-water?

"At nine, Mrs. Gann and daughters are accustomed to breakfast; a handsome pair of girls, truly, and much followed, as I hear, in the quarter. These dear creatures are always paying me visits—visits with the tea-kettle, visits with the newspaper (one brings it, and one comes for it); but the one is always at the other's heels, and so one cannot show oneself to be that dear, gay seducing fellow that one has been, at home and on the Continent. Do you remember *cette chère marquise* at Pau? That cursed conjugal pistol-bullet still plays the deuce with my shoulder. Do you remember Betty Bundy, the butcher's daughter? A pretty race of fools are we to go mad after such women, and risk all—oaths, prayers, promises, long wearisome courtships—for what?—for vanity, truly. When the battle is over, behold your conquest! Betty Bundy is a vulgar country wench; and *cette belle marquise* is old, rouged, and has false hair. *Vanitas vanitatum!* what a moral man I will be some day or other!

"I have found an old acquaintance (and be hanged to him!), who has come to lodge in this very house. Do you recollect at Rome a young artist, Fitch by name, the handsome gaby with the large beard, that mad Mrs. Carrickfergus was doubly mad about? On the second floor of Mrs. Gann's house dwells this youth. His beard brings the *gamins* of the streets trooping and yelling about him; his fine braided coats have grown somewhat shabby now; and the poor fellow is, like your humble servant (by the way, have you a 500 franc billet to spare?)—like your humble servant, I say, very low in pocket. The young Andrea bears up gayly, however; twangles his guitar, paints the worst pictures in the world, and pens sonnets to his imaginary mistress's eyebrow. Luckily the rogue did not know my name, or I should have been compelled to unbosom to him ; and when I called out to him, dubious as to my name, 'Don't you know me? I met you in Rome. My name is Brandon,' the painter was perfectly satisfied, and majestically bade me welcome.

"Fancy the continence of this young Joseph—he has absolutely run away from Mrs. Carrickfergus! 'Sir,' said he, with some hesitation and blushes, when I questioned him about the widow, 'I was compelled to leave Rome in consequence of the fatal fondness of that woman. I am an 'andsome man, sir—I know it—all the chaps in the Academy want me for a model ; and that woman, sir, is sixty. Do you think I would ally myself with her ; sacrifice my happiness for the sake of a creature that's as hugly as an 'arpy? I'd rather starve, sir. I'd rather give up my hart and my 'opes of rising in it than do a haction ₃o dis*hhh*onorable.'

"There is a stock of virtue for you! and the poor fellow half-starved. He lived at Rome upon the seven portraits that the Carrickfergus ordered of him, and, as I fancy, now does not make twenty pounds in a year. O rare chastity! O wondrous silly hopes! *O motus animorum, atque O certamina tanta!—pulveris exigui jactu*, in such an insignificant little lump of mud as this! Why the deuce does not the fool marry the widow? His betters would. There was a captain of dragoons, an Italian prince, and four sons of Irish peers, all at her feet ; but the Cockney's beard and whiskers have overcome them all. Here my paper has come to an end ; and I have the honour to bid your lordship a respectful farewell.

"G. B."

Of the young gentleman who goes by the name of Brandon, the reader of the above letter will not be so misguided, we trust as to have a very exalted opinion. The noble viscount read this document to a supper-party in Christchurch, in Oxford, and left it in a bowl of milk-punch ; whence a scout abstracted it, and handed it over to us. My lord was twenty years of age when he received the epistle, and had spent a couple of years abroad, before going to the university, under the guardianship of the worthy individual who called himself George Brandon.

Mr. Brandon was the son of a half-pay colonel, of good family, who, honoring the great himself, thought his son would vastly benefit by an acquaintance with them, and sent him to Eton, at cruel charges upon a slender purse. From Eton the lad went to Oxford, took honors there, frequented the best society, followed with a kind of proud obsequiousness all the tufts of the university, and left it owing exactly two thousand pounds. Then there came storms at home ; fury on the part of the stern old "governor ;" and final payment of the debt. But while this settlement was pending, Master George had contracted many more debts among bill-discounters, and was glad to fly to the Continent as tutor to young Lord Cinqbars, in whose company he learned every one of the vices in Europe ; and having a good natural genius, and a heart not unkindly, had used these qualities in such admirable manner as to be at twenty-seven utterly ruined in purse and principle—an idler, a spendthrift, and a glutton. He was free of his money : would spend his last guinea for a sensual gratification ; would borrow from his neediest friend ; had no kind of conscience or remorse left, but believed himself to be a good-natured devil-may-care fellow : had a good deal of wit, and indisputably good manners, and a pleasing, dashing frankness in conversation with men.   I should like to know how many such scoundrels our universities have turned out ; and how much ruin has been caused by that accursed system which is called in England "the education of a gentleman."   Go, my son, for ten years to a public school, that "world in miniature ;" "learn to fight for yourself" against the time when your real struggles shall begin. Begin to be selfish at ten years of age ; study for other ten years ; get a competent knowledge of boxing, swimming, rowing, and cricket, with a pretty knack of Latin hexameters and a decent smattering of Greek plays,—do this and a fond father shall bless you—bless the two thousand pounds which he has spent in acquiring all these benefits for you.   And, besides, what else have you not learned?   You have been many hundreds of times to chapel, and have learned to consider the religious service performed there as the vainest parade in the world.   If your father is a grocer, you have been beaten for his sake, and have learned to be ashamed of him.   You have learned to forget (as how should you remember, being separated from them for three-fourths of your time ?) the ties and natural affections of home.   You have learned, if you have a kindly heart and an open hand, to compete with associates much more wealthy than yourself ; and to consider money as not much, but honor—the honor of dining and consorting with your betters—as a great deal.   All this does the public-school and college boy learn ; and woe be to his knowledge !   Alas, what natural tenderness and kindly clinging filial affection is he taught to trample on and despise !   My friend Brandon had gone through this process of education, and had been irretrievably ruined by it— his heart and his honesty had been ruined by it, that is to say ; and he had received, in return for them, a small quantity of classics and mathematics—pretty compensation for all he had lost in gaining them !

But I am wandering most absurdly from the point ; right or wrong, so nature and education had formed Mr. Brandon, who is one of a considerable class.   Well, this young gentleman was established at Mrs. Gann's house ; and we are obliged to enter into all these explanations concerning him, because they are necessary to the right understanding of our story— Brandon not being altogether a bad man, nor much worse than many a one who goes through a course of regular selfish swindling all his life long, and dies religious, resigned, proud of him-

self, and universally respected by others ; for this eminent
advantage has the getting-and-keeping scoundrel over the extravagant and careless one.

One day, then, as he was gazing from the window of his
lodging-house, a cart, containing a vast number of easels, port-
folios, wooden cases of pictures, and a small carpet-bag that
might hold a change of clothes, stopped at the door. The
vehicle was accompanied by a remarkable young fellow—dressed
in a frock-coat covered over with frogs, a dirty turned-down
shirt-collar, with a blue satin cravat, and a cap placed wonderfully on one ear—who had evidently hired apartments at Mr.
Gann's. This new lodger was no other than Mr. Andrew Fitch ;
or, as he wrote on his cards, without the prefix,

ANDREA FITCH.

Preparations had been made at Gann's for the reception of
Mr. Fitch, whose aunt (an auctioneer's lady in the town) had
made arrangements that he should board and lodge with the
Gann family, and have the apartments on the second floor as
his private rooms. In these, then, young Andrea was installed.
He was a youth of a poetic temperament, loving solitude ; and
where is such to be found more easily than on the storm-washed
shores of Margate in the winter ? Then the boarding-house keepers have shut up their houses and gone away in anguish ; then
the taverns take their carpets up, and you can have your choice
of a hundred and twenty beds in any one of them ; then but one
dismal waiter remains to superintend this vast echoing pile of
loneliness, and the landlord pines for summer ; then the flys
for Ramsgate stand tenantless beside the pier ; and about four
sailors, in pea-jackets, are to be seen in the three principal
streets ; in the rest, silence, closed shutters, torpid chimneys
enjoying their unnatural winter sinecure—not the clack of a
patten echoing over the cold dry flags !

This solitude had been chosen by Mr. Brandon for good
reasons of his own ; Gann and his family would have fled, but
that they had no other house wherein to take refuge ; and Mrs.
Hammerton, the auctioneer's lady, felt so keenly the kindness
which she was doing to Mrs. Gann, in providing her with a
lodger at such a period, that she considered herself fully justified in extracting from the latter a bonus of two guineas,

threatening on refusal to send her darling nephew to a rival establishment over the way.

Andrea was here then, in the loneliness that he loved,—a fantastic youth, who lived but for his art ; to whom the world was like the Coburg Theatre, and he in a magnificent costume acting a principal part. His art, and his beard and whiskers, were the darlings of his heart. His long pale hair fell over a high polished brow, which looked wonderfully thoughtful ; and yet no man was more guiltless of thinking. He was always putting himself into attitudes ; he never spoke the truth ; and was so entirely affected and absurd, as to be quite honest at last : for it is my belief that the man did not know truth from falsehood any longer, and was when he was alone, when he was in company, nay, when he was unconscious and sound asleep snoring in bed, one complete lump of affectation. When his apartments on the second floor were arranged according to his fancy, they made a tremendous show. He had a large Gothic chest, in which he put his wardrobe (namely, two velvet waistcoats, four varied satin under ditto, two pairs braided trousers, two shirts, half-a-dozen false collars, and a couple of pairs of dreadfully dilapidated Blucher boots). He had some pieces of armor ; some China jugs and Venetian glasses ; some bits of old damask rags, to drape his doors and windows ; and a rickety lay figure, in a Spanish hat and cloak, over which slung a long Toledo rapier, and a guitar, with a ribbon of dirty sky-blue.

Such was our poor fellow's stock in trade. He had some volumes of poems—" Lalla Rookh," and the sterner compositions of Byron : for, to do him justice, he hated " Don Juan," and a woman was in his eyes an angel ; a *h*angel, alas ! he would call her, for nature and the circumstances of his family had taken sad Cockney advantages over Andrea's pronunciation.

The Misses Wellesley Macarty were not, however, very squeamish with regard to grammar, and, in this dull season, voted Mr. Fitch an elegant young fellow. His immense beard and whiskers gave them the highest opinion of his genius ; and before long the intimacy between the young people was considerable, for Mr. Fitch insisted upon drawing the portraits of the whole family. He painted Mrs. Gann in her rouge and ribbons, as described by Mr. Brandon ; Mr. Gann, who said that his picture would be very useful to the artist, as every soul in Margate knew him ; and the Misses Macarty (a neat group, representing Miss Bella embracing Miss Linda, who was pointing to a pianoforte).

"I suppose you'll do my Carry next?" said Mr. Gann, expressing his approbation of the last picture.

"Law, sir," said Miss Linda, "Carry, with her red hair!—it would be *ojus.*"

"Mr. Fitch might as well paint Becky, our maid," said Miss Bella.

"Carry is quite impossible, Gann," said Mrs. Gann; "she hasn't a gown fit to be seen in. She's not been at church for thirteen Sundays in consequence."

"And more shame for you, ma'am," said Mr. Gann, who liked his child; "Carry *shall* have a gown, and the best of gowns." And jingling three and twenty shillings in his pocket, Mr. Gann determined to spend them all in the purchase of a robe for Carry. But alas, the gown never came; half the money was spent that very evening at the "Bag of Nails."

"Is that—that young lady, your daughter?" said Mr. Fitch, surprised, for he fancied Carry was a humble companion of the family.

"Yes, she is, and a very good daughter, too, sir," answered Mr. Gann. *Fetch* and Carry I call her, or else Carryvan—she's so useful. Ain't you, Carry?"

"I'm very glad if I am, papa," said the young lady, who was blushing violently, and in whose presence all this conversation had been carried on.

"Hold your tongue, Miss," said her mother; "you are very expensive to us, that you are, and need not brag about the work you do. You would not live on charity, would you, like some folks?" (here she looked fiercely at Mr. Gann) "and if your sisters and me starve to keep you and some folks, I presume you are bound to make us some return."

When any allusion was made to Mr. Gann's idleness and extravagance, or his lady showed herself in any way inclined to be angry, it was honest James's habit not to answer, but to take his hat and walk abroad to the public house; or if haply she scolded him at night, he would turn his back and fall a-snoring. These were the only remedies he found for Mrs. James's bad temper, and the first of them he adopted on hearing these words of his lady, which we have just now transcribed.

Poor Caroline had not her father's refuge of flight, but was obliged to stay and listen; and a wondrous eloquence, God wot! had Mrs. Gann upon the subject of her daughter's ill-conduct. The first lecture Mr. Fitch heard, he set down Caroline for a monster. Was she not idle, sulky, scornful, and a sloven? For these and many more of her daughter's vices Mrs.

Gann vouched, declaring that Caroline's misbehavior was hastening her own death, and finishing by a fainting-fit. In the presence of all these charges, there stood Miss Caroline, dumb, stupid, and careless ; nay, when the fainting-fit came on, and Mrs. Gann fell back on the sofa, the unfeeling girl took the opportunity to retire, and never offered to smack her mamma's hands, to give her the smelling-bottle, or to restore her with a glass of water.

One stood close at hand ; for Mr. Fitch, when this first fit occurred, was sitting in the Gann parlor, painting that lady's portrait ; and he was making towards her with this tumbler, when Miss Linda cried out, " Stop! the water's full of paint ;" and straightway burst out laughing. Mrs. Gann jumped up at this, cured suddenly, and left the room, looking somewhat foolish.

" You don't know Ma," said Miss Linda, still giggling ; " she's always fainting."

" Poor thing ! " cried Fitch ; " very nervous, I suppose ! "

" Oh, very ! " answered the lady, exchanging arch glances with Miss Bella.

" Poor dear lady ! " continued the artist ; " I pity her from my hinmost soul. Doesn't the himmortal bard of Havon observe, how sharper than a serpent's tooth it is to have a thankless child? And is it true, ma'am, that that young woman has been the ruin of her family ? "

" Ruin of her fiddlestick ! " replied Miss Bella. " Law, Mr. Fitch, you don't know Ma yet ; she is in one of her tantrums."

" What, then, it *isn't* true ? " cried simple-minded Fitch. To which neither of the young ladies made any answer in words, nor could the little artist comprehend why they looked at each other, and burst out laughing. But he retired pondering on what he had seen and heard ; and being a very soft young fellow, most implicitly believed the accusations of poor dear Mrs. Gann, and thought her daughter Caroline was no better than a Regan or Goneril.

A time, however, was to come when he should believe her to be a most pure and gentle Cordelia ; and of this change in Fitch's opinions we shall speak in Chapter III.

CHAPTER III.

A SHABBY GENTEEL DINNER, AND OTHER INCIDENTS OF A LIKE NATURE.

MR. BRANDON'S letter to Lord Cinqbars produced, as we have said, a great impression upon the family of Gann ; an impression which was considerably increased by their lodger's subsequent behavior : for although the persons with whom he now associated were of a very vulgar, ridiculous kind, they were by no means so low or ridiculous that Mr. Brandon should not wish to appear before them in the most advantageous light ; and, accordingly, he gave himself the greatest airs when in their company, and bragged incessantly of his acquaintance and familiarity with the nobility.   Mr. Brandon was a tuft-hunter of the genteel sort ; his pride being quite as slavish, and his haughtiness as mean and cringing, in fact, as poor Mrs. Gann's stupid wonder and respect for all the persons whose names are written with titles before them.   O free and happy Britons, what a miserable, truckling, cringing race ye are !

The reader has no doubt encountered a number of such swaggerers in the course of his conversation with the world— men of a decent middle rank, who affect to despise it, and herd only with persons of the fashion.   This is an offence in a man which none of us can forgive ; we call him tuft-hunter, lickspittle, sneak, unmanly ; we hate, and profess to despise him. I fear it is no such thing.   We envy Lickspittle, that is the fact ; and therefore hate him.   Were he to plague us with the stories of Jones and Brown, our familiars, the man would be a simple bore, his stories heard patiently ; but so soon as he talks of my lord or the duke, we are in arms against him.   I have seen a whole merry party in Russell Square grow suddenly gloomy and dumb, because a pert barrister, in a loud, shrill voice, told a story of Lord This or the Marquis of That.   We all hated that man ; and I would lay a wager that every one of the fourteen persons assembled round the boiled turkey and saddle of mutton (not to mention side-dishes from the pastry-cook's opposite the British Museum)—I would wager, I say, that every one was muttering inwardly, " A plague on that fellow ! he knows a lord, and I never spoke to more than three in the whole course of my life." To our betters we can reconcile ourselves, if you please, respecting them very sincerely, laughing at their jokes, making allowance for their stupidities, meekly suffering their insolence; but we can't pardon our equals going beyond us. A friend of mine who lived amicably and happily among his friends and relatives at Hackney, was on a sudden disowned by the latter, cut by the former, and doomed in innumerable prophecies to ruin, because he kept a footboy,—a harmless little blowsy-faced urchin, in light snuff-colored clothes, glistening over with sugar-loaf buttons. There is another man, a great man, a literary man, whom the public loves, and who took a sudden leap from obscurity into fame and wealth. This was a crime; but he bore his rise with so much modesty, that even his brethren of the pen did not envy him. One luckless day he set up a one-horse chaise; from that minute he was doomed.

"Have you seen his new carriage?" says Snarley.

"Yes," says Yow; "he's so consumedly proud of it, that he can't see his old friends while he drives."

"Ith it a donkey-cart," lisps Simper, "thith gwand cawwaige? I always thaid that the man, from hith thtile, wath fitted to be a vewy dethent cothtermonger."

"Yes, yes," cries old Candour, "a sad pity indeed!—dreadfully extravagant, I'm told—bad health—expensive family—works going down every day—and now he must set up a carriage forsooth!"

Snarley, Yow, Simper, Candour, hate their brother. If he is ruined, they will be kind to him and just; but he is successful, and woe be to him!

*　　　*　　　*　　　*　　　*

This trifling digression of half a page or so, although it seems to have nothing to do with the story in hand, has, nevertheless, the strongest relation to it; and you shall hear what.

In one word, then, Mr. Brandon bragged so much, and assumed such airs of superiority, that after a while he perfectly disgusted Mrs. Gann and the Misses Macarty, who were gentlefolks themselves, and did not at all like his way of telling them that he was their better. Mr. Fitch was swallowed up in his hart as he called it, and cared nothing for Brandon's airs. Gann, being a low-spirited fellow, completely submitted to Mr. Brandon, and looked up to him with deepest wonder. And poor little Caroline followed her father's faith, and in six weeks after Mr. Brandon's arrival at the lodgings had grown to believe him the most perfect, finished, polished, agreeable of mankind

Indeed, the poor girl had never seen a gentleman before, and towards such her gentle heart turned instinctively. Brandon never offended her by hard words ; insulted her by cruel scorn, such as she met with from her mother and her sisters ; there was a quiet manner about the man quite different to any that she had before seen amongst the acquaintances of her family ; and if he assumed a tone of superiority in his conversation with her and the rest, Caroline felt that he *was* their superior, and as such admired and respected him.

What happens when in the innocent bosom of a girl of sixteen such sensations arise ? What has happened ever since the world began ?

I have said that Miss Caroline had no friend in the world but her father, and must here take leave to recall that assertion ; —a friend she most certainly had, and that was honest Becky, the smutty maid, whose name has been mentioned before. Miss Caroline had learned in the course of a life spent under the tyranny of her mamma, some of the notions of the latter, and would have been very much offended to call Becky her friend ; but friends, in fact, they were ; and a great comfort it was for Caroline to descend to the calm kitchen from the stormy back parlor, and there vent some of her little woes to the compassionate servant of all work.

When Mrs. Gann went out with her daughters, Becky would take her work and come and keep Miss Caroline company ; and if the truth must be told, the greatest enjoyment the pair used to have was in these afternoons, when they read together out of the precious, greasy, marble-covered volumes that Mrs. Gann was in the habit of fetching from the library. Many and many a tale had the pair so gone through. I can see them over " Manfrone ; or the One-handed Monk "—the room dark, the street silent, the hour ten—the tall, red, lurid candlewick waggling down, the flame flickering pale upon Miss Caroline's pale face as she read out, and lighting up honest Becky's goggling eyes, who sat silent, her work in her lap : she had not done a stitch of it for an hour. As the trap-door slowly opens, and the scowling Alonzo, bending over the sleeping Imoinda, draws his pistol, cocks it, looks well if the priming be right, places it then to the sleeper's ear, and—*thunder-under-under*—down fall the snuffers ! Becky has had them in her hand for ten minutes, afraid to use them. Up starts Caroline, and flings the book back into her mamma's basket. It is that lady returned with her daughters from a tea-party, where two young gents from London have been mighty genteel indeed.

For the sentimental, too, as well as for the terrible, Miss Caroline and the cook had a strong predilection, and had wept their poor eyes out over "Thaddeus of Warsaw" and the "Scottish Chiefs." Fortified by the examples drawn from those instructive volumes, Becky was firmly convinced that her young mistress would meet with a great lord some day or other, or be carried off, like Cinderella, by a brilliant prince, to the mortification of her elder sisters, whom Becky hated. And when, therefore, the new lodger came, lonely, mysterious, melancholy, elegant, with the romantic name of George Brandon—when he wrote a letter directed to a lord, and Miss Caroline and Becky together examined the superscription, such a look passed between them as the pencil of Leslie or Maclise could alone describe for *us*. Becky's orbs were lighted up with a preternatural look of wondering wisdom ; whereas, after an instant, Caroline dropped hers, and blushed, and said, " Nonsense, Becky ! "

" *Is* it nonsense ? " said Becky, grinning and snapping her fingers with a triumphant air ; " the cards comes true ; I knew they would. Didn't you have king and queen of hearts three deals running ? What did you dream about last Tuesday, tell me that ? "

But Miss Caroline never did tell, for her sisters came bouncing down the stairs, and examined the lodger's letter. Caroline, however, went away musing much upon these points ; and she began to think Mr. Brandon more wonderful and beautiful every day.

In the meantime, while Miss Caroline was innocently indulging in her inclination for the brilliant occupier of the first floor, it came to pass that the tenant of the second was inflamed by a most romantic passion for her.

For, after partaking for about a fortnight of the family dinner, and passing some evenings with Mrs. Gann and the young ladies, Mr. Fitch, though by no means quick of comprehension, began to perceive that the nightly charges that were brought against poor Caroline could not be founded upon truth. " Let's see," mused he to himself. " Tuesday, the old lady said her daughter was bringing her gray hairs with sorrow to the grave, because the cook had not boiled the potatoes. Wednesday, she said Caroline was an assassin, because she could not find her own thimble. Thursday, she vows Caroline has no religion, because that old pair of silk stockings were not darned. And this can't be," reasoned Fitch, deeply. " A gal haint a murderess because her Ma can't find her thimble.

A woman that goes to slap her grown-up daughter on the back
and before company too, for such a paltry thing as a hold pair
of stockings, can't be surely a-speaking the truth." And thus
gradually his first impression against Caroline wore away.   As
this disappeared, pity took possession of his soul—and we
know what pity is akin to ; and, at the same time, a corre-
sponding hatred for the oppressors of a creature so amiable.

To sum up, in six short weeks after the appearance of the
two gentlemen, we find our chief *dramatis personæ* as follows :

> CAROLINE, an innocent young woman, in love with BRANDON.
> FITCH, a celebrated painter, almost in love with CAROLINE.
> BRANDON, a young gentleman, in love with himself.

At first he was pretty constant in his attendance upon the
Misses Macarty when they went out to walk, nor were they displeased at his attentions ; but he found that there were a great
number of Margate beaux—ugly, vulgar fellows as ever were—
who always followed in the young ladies' train, and made themselves infinitely more agreeable than he was.   These men Mr.
Brandon treated with a great deal of scorn : and, in return, they
hated him cordially.   So did the ladies speedily : his haughty
manners, though quite as impertinent and free, were not half
so pleasant to them as Jones's jokes or Smith's charming
romps ; and the girls gave Brandon very shortly to understand
that they were much happier without him.   " Ladies, your
humble," he heard Bob Smith say, as that little linendraper
came skipping to the door from which they were issuing. "The
sun's hup and trade is down ; if you're for a walk, I'm your
man."   And Miss Linda and Miss Bella each took an arm of
Mr. Smith, and sailed down the street.   " I'm glad you ain't
got that proud gent with the glass hi," said Mr. Smith · " he's
the most hillbred, supercilious beast I ever see."

" So he is," says Bella.

" Hush ! " says Linda.

The "proud gent with the glass hi " was at this moment lolling out of the first-floor window, smoking his accustomed cigar ;
and his eyeglass was fixed upon the ladies, to whom he made
a very low bow.   It may be imagined how fond he was of them
afterwards, and what looks he cast at Mr. Bob Smith the next
time he met him.   Mr. Bob's heart beat for a day afterwards ;
and he found he had business in town.

But the love of society is stronger than even pride ; and the
great Mr. Brandon was sometimes fain to descend from his
high station and consort with the vulgar family with whom he

lodged. But, as we have said, he always did this with a wonderfully condescending air, giving his associates to understand
how great was the honor he did them.

One day, then, he was absolutely so kind as to accept of
an invitation from the ground-floor, which was delivered in the
passage by Mr. James Gann, who said, " It was hard to see a
gent eating mutton-chops from week's end to week's end ; and if
Mr. Brandon had a mind to meet a devilish good fellow as ever
was, my friend Swigby, a man who rides his horse, and has his
five hundred a year to spend, and to eat a prime cut out of as
good a leg of pork (though he said it) as ever a knife was stuck
into, they should dine that day at three o'clock sharp, and Mrs.
G. and the gals would be glad of the honor of his company.

The person so invited was rather amused at the terms in
which Mr. Gann conveyed his hospitable message ; and at three
o'clock made his appearance in the back-parlor, whence he had
the honor of conducting Mrs. Gann (dressed in a sweet yellow
mousseline de laine, with a large red turban, a *ferronnière*, and a
smelling-bottle attached by a ring to a very damp, fat hand) to
the "office," where the repast was set out. The Misses Macarty were in costumes equally tasty : one on the guest's right
hand ; one near the boarder, Mr. Fitch—who, in a large beard,
an amethyst velvet-waistcoat, his hair fresh wetted, and parted
accurately down the middle to fall in curls over his collar, would
have been irresistible if the collar had been a little, little whiter
than it was.

Mr. Brandon, too, was dressed in his very best suit ; for
though he affected to despise his hosts very much, he wished
to make the most favorable impression upon them, and took
care to tell Mrs. Gann that he and Lord So-and-so were the
only two men in the world who were in possession of that particular waistcoat which she admired : for Mrs. Gann was very
gracious, and had admired the waistcoat, being desirous to impress with awe Mr. Gann's friend and admirer, Mr. Swigby—
who, man of fortune as he was, was a constant frequenter of
the club at the "Bag of Nails."

About this club and its supporters Mr. Gann's guest, Mr.
Swigby, and Gann himself, talked very gayly before dinner ; all
the jokes about all the club being roared over by the pair.

Mr. Brandon, who felt he was the great man of the party,
indulged himself in his great propensities without restraint, and
told Mrs. Gann stories about half the nobility. Mrs. Gann
conversed knowingly about the Opera ; and declared that she
thought Taglioni the sweetest singer in the world.

"Mr.—a—Swigby, have you ever seen Lablache dance?" asked Mr. Brandon of that gentleman, to whom he had been formally introduced.

"At Vauxhall is he?" said Mr. Swigby, who was just from town.

"Yes, on the tight-rope; a charming performer."

On which Mr. Gann told how he had been to Vauxhall when the princes were in London; and his lady talked of these knowingly. And then they fell to conversing about fireworks and rack-punch; Mr. Brandon assuring the young ladies that Vauxhall was the very pink of the fashion, and longing to have the honor of dancing a quadrille with them there. Indeed, Brandon was so very sarcastic, that not a single soul at table understood him.

The table, from Mr. Brandon's plan of it, which was afterwards sent to my Lord Cinqbars, was arranged as follows:—

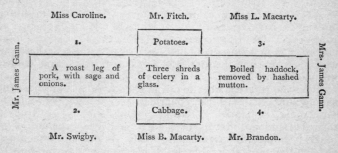

Miss Caroline.	Mr. Fitch.	Miss L. Macarty.

	1.	Potatoes.	3.	
Mr. James Gann.	A roast leg of pork, with sage and onions.	Three shreds of celery in a glass.	Boiled haddock, removed by hashed mutton.	Mrs. James Gann.
	2.	Cabbage.	4.	

Mr. Swigby.	Miss B. Macarty.	Mr. Brandon.

1 and 2 are pots of porter; 3, a quart of ale, Mrs. Gann's favorite drink; 4, a bottle of fine old golden sherry, the real produce of the Uva grape, purchased at the "Bag of Nails" Hotel for 1s. 9d. by Mr. J. Gann.

Mr. Gann. "Taste that sherry, sir. Your 'ealth, and my services to you, sir. That wine, sir, is given me as a particular favor by my—ahem!—my wine-merchant, who only will part with a small quantity of it, and imports it, direct, sir, from—ahem!—from——"

Mr. Brandon. "From Xeres, of course. It is, I really think, the finest wine I ever tasted in my life—at a commoner's table, that is."

Mrs. Gann. "Oh, in course, a commoner's table!—we have no titles, sir, (Mr. Gann, I will trouble you for some more crackling,) though my poor dear girls are related, by their blessed father's side, to some of the first nobility in the land, I assure you."

Mr. Gann. "Gammon, Jooly my dear. Them Irish nobility, you know, what are they? And besides, it's my belief that the gals are no more related to them than I am."

Miss Bella (to *Mr. Brandon, confidentially*). "You must find that poor Par is sadly vulgar, Mr. Brandon."

Mrs. Gann. "Mr. Brandon has never been accustomed to such language, I am sure; and I entreat you will excuse Mr. Gann's rudeness, sir."

Miss Linda. "Indeed, I assure you, Mr. Brandon, that we've high connections as well as low; as high as some people's connections, per'aps, though we are not always talking of the nobility." This was a double shot: the first barrel of Miss Linda's sentence hit her stepfather, the second part was levelled directly at Mr. Brandon. "Don't you think I'm right, Mr. Fitch?"

Mr. Brandon. "You are quite right, Miss Linda, in this as in every other instance; but I am afraid Mr. Fitch has not paid proper attention to your excellent remark: for, if I don't mistake the meaning of the beautiful design which he has made with his fork upon the tablecloth, his soul is at this moment wrapped up in his art."

This was exactly what Mr. Fitch wished that all the world should suppose. He flung back his hair, and stared wildly for a moment, and said, "Pardon me, madam; it is true my thoughts were at that moment far away in the regions of my hart." He was really thinking that his attitude was a very elegant one, and that a large garnet ring which he wore on his forefinger must be mistaken by all the company for a ruby.

"Art is very well," said Mr. Brandon; "but with such pretty natural objects before you, I wonder you were not content to think of them."

"Do you mean the mashed patotoes, sir?" said Andrea Fitch, wondering.

"I mean Miss Rosalind Macarty," answered Brandon, gallantly, and laughing heartily at the painter's simplicity. But this compliment could not soften Miss Linda, who had an uneasy conviction that Mr. Brandon was laughing at her, and disliked him accordingly.

At this juncture, Miss Caroline entered and took the place marked as hers, to the left hand of Mr. Gann, vacant. An old rickety wooden stool was placed for her, instead of that elegant and commodious Windsor chair which supported every other person at table ; and by the side of the plate stood a curious old battered tin mug, on which the antiquarian might possibly discover the inscription of the word "Caroline." This, in truth, was poor Caroline's mug and stool, having been appropriated to her from childhood upwards ; and here it was her custom meekly to sit, and eat her daily meal.

It was well that the girl was placed near her father, else I do believe she would have been starved ; but Gann was much too good-natured to allow that any difference should be made between her and her sisters. There are some meannesses which are too mean even for man—woman, lovely woman alone, can venture to commit them. Well, on the present occasion, and when the dinner was half over, poor Caroline stole gently into the room and took her ordinary place. Caroline's pale face was very red ; for the fact must be told that she had been in the kitchen helping Becky, the universal maid ; and having heard how the great Mr. Brandon was to dine with them upon that day, the simple girl had been shewing her respect for him, by compiling, in her best manner, a certain dish, for the cooking of which her papa had often praised her. She took her place, blushing violently when she saw him, and if Mr. Gann had not been making a violent clattering with his knife and fork, it is possible that he might have heard Miss Caroline's heart thump, which it did violently. Her dress was somehow a little smarter than usual ; and Becky the maid, who brought in that remove of hashed mutton which has been set down in the bill of fare, looked at her young lady with a good deal of complacency, as, loaded with plates, she quitted the room. Indeed, the poor girl deserved to be looked at : there was an air of gentleness and innocence about her that was apt to please some persons, much more then the bold beauties of her sisters. The two young men did not fail to remark this ; one of them, the little painter, had long since observed it.

"You are very late, miss," cried Mrs. Gann, who affected not to know what had caused her daughter's delay. "You're always late !" and the elder girls stared and grinned at each other knowingly, as they always did when mamma made such attacks upon Caroline, who only kept her eyes down upon the tablecloth, and began to eat her dinner without saying a word.

"Come, my dear," cried honest Gann, "if she is late you know why. A girl can't be here and there too, as I say ; can they, Swigby ? "

"Impossible ! " said Swigby.

" Gents," continued Mr. Gann, " our Carry, you must know,

has been down stairs, making the pudding for her old pappy; and a good pudding she makes, I can tell you."

Miss Caroline blushed more vehemently than ever; the artist stared her full in the face; Mrs. Gann said, "Nonsense" and "stuff" very majestically; only Mr. Brandon interposed in Caroline's favor.

"I would sooner that my wife should know how to make a pudding," said he, "than how to play the best piece of music in the world!"

"Law, Mr. Brandon! I, for my part wouldn't demean myself by any such kitchen work!" cries Miss Linda.

"Make puddens, indeed; its ojous!" cries Bella.

"For you, my loves, of course!" interposed their mamma. "Young women of your family and circumstances is not expected to perform any such work. It's different with Miss Caroline, who, if she does make herself useful now and then, don't make herself near so useful as she should, considering that she's not a shilling, and is living on our charity, like some other folks."

Thus did this amiable woman neglect no opportunity to give her opinions about her husband and daughter. The former, however, cared not a straw; and the latter, in this instance, was perfectly happy. Had not kind Mr. Brandon approved of her work; and could she ask for more?

"Mamma may say what she pleases to-day," thought Caroline. "I am too happy to be made angry by her."

"Poor little mistaken Caroline, to think you were safe against three women! The dinner had not advanced much further, when Miss Isabella, who had been examining her younger sister curiously for some short time, telegraphed Miss Linda across the table, and nodded, and winked, and pointed to her own neck; a very white one, as I have before had the honor to remark, and quite without any covering except a smart necklace of twenty-four rows of the lightest blue glass beads, finishing in a neat tassel. Linda had a similar ornament of vermilion color; whereas Caroline, on this occasion, wore a handsome new collar up to the throat, and a brooch, which looked all the smarter for the shabby frock over which they were placed. As soon as she saw her sister's signals, the poor little thing, who had only just done fluttering and blushing, fell to this same work over again. Down went her eyes once more, and her face and neck lighted up to the color of Miss Linda's sham cornelian.

"What's the gals giggling and ogling about?" said Mr. Gann, innocently.

"What is it, my darling loves?" says stately Mrs. Gann.

"Why, don't you see, Ma?" said Linda. "Look at Miss Carry! I'm blessed if *she has not got on Becky's collar and brooch* that Sims the pilot gave her.

The young ladies fell back in uproarious fits of laughter, and laughed all the time that their mamma was thundering out a speech, in which she declared that her daughter's conduct was unworthy a gentlewoman, and bid her leave the room and take off those disgraceful ornaments.

There was no need to tell her; the poor little thing gave one piteous look at her father, who was whistling, and seemed indeed to think the matter a good joke; and, after she had managed to open the door and totter into the passage, you might have heard her weeping there, weeping tears more bitter than any of the many she had shed in the course of her life. Down she went to the kitchen, and when she reached that humble place of refuge, first pulled at her neck and made as if she would take off Becky's collar and brooch, and then flung herself into the arms of the honest scullion, where she cried and cried till she brought on the first fit of hysterics that ever she had had.

This crying could not at first be heard in the parlor, where the young ladies, Mrs. Gann, Mr. Gann, and his friend from the "Bag of Nails" were roaring at the excellence of the joke. Mr. Brandon, sipping his sherry, sat by, looking very sarcastically and slyly from one party to the other; Mr. Fitch was staring about him too, but with a very different expression, anger and wonder inflaming his bearded countenance. At last, as the laughing died away and a faint voice of weeping came from the kitchen below, Andrew could bear it no longer, but bounced up from his chair and rushed out of the room exclaiming,—

"By Jove, it's too bad!"

"What does the man mean?" says Mrs. Gann.

He meant that he was from that moment over head and ears in love with Caroline, and that he longed to beat, buffet, pummel, thump, tear to pieces, those callous ruffians who so pitilessly laughed at her.

"What's that chop wi' the beard in such tantrums about?" said the gentleman from the "Bag of Nails."

Mr. Gann answered this query by some joke, intimating that "per'aps Mr. Fitch's dinner did not agree with him," at which these worthies roared again.

The young ladies said, "Well, now, upon my word!"

"Mighty genteel behavior truly!" cried mamma; "but what can you expect from the poor thing?"

Brandon only sipped more sherry, but he looked at Fitch as the latter flung out of the room, and his countenance was lighted up by a more unequivocal smile.

*   *   *   *   *   *

These two little adventures were followed by a silence of some few minutes, during which the meats remained on the table, and no signs were shown of that pudding upon which poor Caroline had exhausted her skill. The absence of this delicious part of the repast was first remarked by Mr. Gann; and his lady, after jangling at the bell for some time in vain, at last begged one of her daughters to go and hasten matters.

"BECKY!" shrieked Miss Linda from the hall, but Becky replied not. "Becky, are we to be kept waiting all day!" continued the lady in the same shrill voice. "Mamma wants the pudding!"

"TELL HER TO FETCH IT HERSELF!" roared Becky, at which remark Gann and his facetious friend once more went off into fits of laughter.

"This is too bad!" said Mrs. G., starting up; "she shall leave the house this instant!" and so no doubt Becky would, but that the lady owed her five quarters' wages; which she, at that period, did not feel inclined to pay.

Well, the dinner at last was at an end; the ladies went away to tea, leaving the gentlemen to their wine; Brandon, very condescendingly, partaking of a bottle of port, and listening with admiration to the toasts and sentiments with which it is still the custom among persons of Mr. Gann's rank of life to preface each glass of wine. As thus:—

Glass 1. "Gents," says Mr. Gann, rising, "this glass I need say nothink about. Here's the king, and long life to him and the family!"

Mr. Swigby, with his glass, goes knock, knock, knock on the table; and saying gravely, "The king!" drinks off his glass, and smacks his lips afterwards.

Mr. Brandon, who had drunk half his, stops in the midst and says, "Oh, 'the king!'"

Mr. Swigby. "A good glass of wine that, Gann my boy!"

Mr. Brandon. "Capital, really; though, upon my faith, I'm no judge of port."

Mr. Gann (smacks). "A fine fruity wine as ever I tasted. I suppose you, Mr. B., are accustomed only to claret. I've 'ad it, too, in my time, sir, as Swigby there very well knows. I

travelled, sir, *sure le Continong*, I assure you, and drank my
glass of claret with the best man in France, or England either.
I wasn't always what I am, sir."

Mr. Brandon. " You don't look as if you were."

Mr. Gann. " No, sir. Before that —— gas came in, I was
head, sir, of one of the fust 'ouses in the hoil-trade, Gann,
Blubbery & Gann, sir—Thames Street, City. I'd my box at
Putney, as good a gig and horse as my friend there drives."

Mr. Swigby. "Ay, and a better too, Gann, I make no
doubt."

Mr. Gann. " Well, *say* a better. I *had* a better, if money
could fetch it, sir ; and I didn't spare that, I warrant you. No,
no, James Gann didn't grudge his purse, sir ; and had his
friends around him, as he's 'appy to 'ave now, sir. Mr. Brandon, your 'ealth, sir, and may we hoften meet under this ma-
'ogany. Swigby, my boy, God bless you ! "

Mr. Brandon. " Your very good health."

Mr. Swigby. " Thank you, Gann. Here's to you, and long
life and prosperity and happiness to you and yours. Bless you,
Jim my boy ; heaven bless you ! I say this, Mr. Brandon—
Brandon—what's your name—there ain't a better fellow in all
Margate than James Gann,—no, nor in all England. Here's
Mrs. Gann, gents, and the family. MRS. GANN ! " (*drinks.*)

Mr. Brandon. " MRS. GANN. Hip, hip, hurrah ! " (*drinks.*)

Mr. Gann. " Mrs. Gann, and thank you, gents. A fine
woman, Mr. B. ; ain't she now ? Ah, if you'd seen 'er when I
married 'er ! Gad, she *was* fine then—an out and outer, sir !
Such a figure ! "

Mr. Swigby. " You'd choose none but a good 'un, I war'nt.
Ha, ha, ha ! "

Mr. Gann. " Did I ever tell you of my duel along with the
regimental doctor ? No ! Then I will. I was a young chap,
you see, in those days ; and when I saw her at Brussels—
(*Brussell*, they call it)—I was right slick up over head and ears
in love with her at once. But what was to be done ? There
was another gent in the case—a regimental doctor, sir—a
reg'lar dragon. ' Faint heart,' says I, ' never won a fair lady,'
and so I made so bold. She took me, sent the doctor to the
right about. I met him one morning in the park at Brussels,
and stood to him, sir, like a man. When the affair was over,
my second, a leftenant of dragoons, told me, ' Gann,' says he,
' I've seen many a man under fire—I'm a Waterloo man,'
says he,—' and have rode by Wellington many a long day ;
but I never, for coolness, see such a man as you. Gents,

here's the Duke of Wellington and the British Army!" (*the gents drink.*)

Mr. Brandon. "Did you kill the doctor, sir?"

Mr. Gann. "Why, no, sir; I shot in the hair."

Mr. Brandon. "Shot him in the hair! Egad, that was a severe shot, and a very lucky escape the doctor had of it? Whereabout in the hair? a whisker, sir; or, perhaps, a pig-tail?"

Mr. Swigby. "Haw, haw, haw! shot'n in the *hair*—capital, capital!"

Mr. Gann, who has grown very red. "No, sir, there may be some mistake in my pronounciation, which I didn't expect to have laughed at, at my hown table."

Mr. Brandon. "My dear sir! I protest and vow——"

Mr. Gann. "Never mind it, sir. I gave you my best, and did my best to make you welcome. If you like better to make fun of me, do, sir. That may be the *genteel* way, but hang me if it's *hour* way; is it, Jack? *Our* way; I beg your pardon, sir."

Mr. Swigby. "Jim, Jim! for heaven's sake!—peace and harmony of the evening—conviviality—social enjoyment—didn't mean it—did you mean anything, Mr. What-d'-ye-call-'im?"

Mr. Brandon. "Nothing, upon my honor as a gentleman!"

Mr. Gann. "Well, then, there's my hand!" and good-natured Gann tried to forget the insult, and to talk as if nothing had occurred: but he had been wounded in the most sensitive point in which a man can be touched by his superior, and never forgot Brandon's joke. That night at the club, when dreadfully tipsy, he made several speeches on the subject, and burst into tears many times. The pleasure of the evening was quite spoiled; and, as the conversation became rapid and dull, we shall refrain from reporting it. Mr. Brandon speedily took leave, but had not the courage to face the ladies at tea; to whom, it appears, the reconciled Becky had brought that refreshing beverage.

CHAPTER IV.

IN WHICH MR. FITCH PROCLAIMS HIS LOVE, AND MR. BRANDON
PREPARES FOR WAR.

FROM the splendid hall in which Mrs. Gann was dispensing
her hospitality, the celebrated painter, Andrea Fitch, rushed
forth in a state of mind even more delirious than that which he
usually enjoyed. He looked abroad into the street: all there
was dusk and lonely; the rain falling heavily, the wind playing
Pandean pipes and whistling down the chimney-pots. " I love
the storm," said Fitch, solemnly; and he put his great Spanish
cloak round him in the most approved manner (it was of so
prodigious a size that the tail of it, as it twirled over his shoulder, whisked away a lodging-card from the door of the house
opposite Mr. Gann's). "I love the storm and solitude," said
he, lighting a large pipe filled full of the fragrant Oronooko;
and thus armed, he passed rapidly down the street, his hat
cocked over his ringlets.

Andrea did not like smoking, but he used a pipe as part of
his profession as an artist, and as one of the picturesque parts
of his costume; in like manner, though he did not fence, he
always travelled about with a pair of foils; and quite unconscious of music, nevertheless had a guitar constantly near at
hand. Without such properties a painter's spectacle is not
complete; and now he determined to add to them another in-
dispensable requisite—a mistress. "What great artist was
ever without one?" thought he. Long, long had he sighed for
some one whom he might love, some one to whom he might
address the poems which he was in the habit of making.
Hundreds of such fragments had he composed, addressed to
Leila, Ximena, Ada—imaginary beauties, whom he courted in
dreamy verse. With what joy would he replace all those by a
real charmer of flesh and blood! Away he went, then, on this
evening—the tyranny of Mrs. Gann towards poor Caroline
having awakened all his sympathies in the gentle girl's favor—
determined now and for ever to make her the mistress of his
heart. Monna-Lisa, the Fornarina, Leonardo, Raphael—he
thought of all these, and vowed that his Caroline should be
made famous and live for ever on his canvas. While Mrs.
Gann was preparing for her friends, and entertaining them at

tea and whist ; while Caroline, all unconscious of the love she inspired, was weeping up stairs in her little garret ; while Mr. Brandon was enjoying the refined conversation of Gann and Swigby, over their glass and pipe in the office, Andrea walked abroad by the side of the ocean ; and, before he was wet through walked himself into the most fervid affection for poor persecuted Caroline. The reader might have observed him (had not the night been very dark, and a great deal too wet to allow a sensible reader to go abroad on such an errand) at the sea-shore standing on a rock, and drawing from his bosom a locket which contained a curl of hair tied up in ribbon. He looked at it for a moment, and then flung it away from him into the black boiling waters below him.

" No other 'air but thine, Caroline, shall ever rest near this 'art !" he said, and kissed the locket and restored it to its place. Light-minded youth, whose hair was it that he thus flung away? How many times had Andrea shown that very ringlet in strictest confidence to several brethren of the brush, and declared that it was the hair of a dear girl in Spain whom he loved to madness? Alas ! 'twas but a fiction of his fevered brain ; every one of his friends had a locket of hair, and Andrea, who had no love until now, had clipped this precious token from the wig of a lovely lay-figure, with cast-iron joints and a card-board head, that had stood for some time in his atelier. I don't know that he felt any shame about the proceeding, for he was of such a warm imagination that he had grown to believe that the hair did actually come from a girl in Spain, and only parted with it on yielding to a superior attachment.

This attachment being fixed on, the young painter came home wet through ; passed the night in reading Byron ; making sketches, and burning them ; writing poems to Caroline, and expunging them with pitiless india-rubber. A romantic man makes a point of sitting up all night, and pacing his chamber ; and you may see many a composition of Andrea's dated " Midnight, 10th of March, A. F.," with his peculiar flourish over the initials. He was not sorry to be told in the morning, by the ladies at breakfast, that he looked dreadfully pale ; and answered, laying his hand on his forehead and shaking his head gloomily, that he could get no sleep : and then he would heave a huge sigh ; and Miss Bella and Miss Linda would look at each other, and grin according to their wont. He was glad, I say, to have his woe remarked, and continued his sleeplessness for two or three nights ; but he was certainly still more glad when he heard Mr. Brandon, on the fourth morning, cry out,

in a shrill angry voice, to Becky the maid, to give the gentleman up stairs his compliments—Mr. Brandon's compliments—
and tell him that he could not get a wink of sleep for the horrid
trampling he kept up. " I am hanged if I stay in the house a
night longer," added the first floor sharply, "if that Mr. Fitch
kicks up such a confounded noise!" Mr. Fitch's point was
gained, and henceforth he was as quiet as a mouse ; for his
wish was not only to be in love, but to let everybody know
that he was in love, or where is the use of a *belle passion?*

So, whenever he saw Caroline, at meals, or in the passage,
he used to stare at her with the utmost power of his big eyes,
and fall to groaning most pathetically. He used to leave his
meals untasted, groan, heave sighs, and stare incessantly. Mrs.
Gann and her eldest daughters were astonished at these man-
œuvres ; for they never suspected that any man could possibly
be such a fool as to fall in love with Caroline. At length the
suspicion came upon them, created immense laughter and delight ; and the ladies did not fail to rally Caroline in their
usual elegant way. Gann, too, loved a joke (much polite waggery had this worthy man practised in select inn-parlors for
twenty years past), and would call poor Caroline " Mrs. F. ;"
and say that, instead of *Fetch* and Carry, as he used to name
her, he should style her *Fitch* and Carry for the future ; and
laugh at this great pun, and make many others of a similar sort,
that set Caroline blushing.

Indeed, the girl suffered a great deal more from this raillery
than at first may be imagined ; for after the first awe inspired
by Fitch's whiskers had passed away, and he had drawn the
young ladies' pictures, and made designs in their albums, and
in the midst of their jokes and conversation had remained perfectly silent, the Gann family had determined that the man was
an idiot : and, indeed, were not very wide of the mark. In
everything except his own peculiar art honest Fitch *was* an
idiot ; and as upon the subject of painting, the Ganns, like
most people of their class in England, were profoundly ignorant, it came to pass that he would breakfast and dine for
many days in their company, and not utter one single syllable.
So they looked upon him with extreme pity and contempt, as a
harmless, good-natured, crack-brained creature, quite below
them in the scale of intellect, and only to be endured because
he paid a certain number of shillings weekly to the Gann exchequer. Mrs. Gann in all companies was accustomed to talk
about her idiot. Neighbors and children used to peer at him
as he strutted down the street ; and though every young lady,

including my dear Caroline, is flattered by having a lover, at least they don't like such a lover as this. The Misses Macarty (after having set their caps at him very fiercely, and quarrelled concerning him on his first coming to lodge at their house) vowed and protested now that he was no better than a chimpanzee ; and Caroline and Becky agreed that this insult was as great as any that could be paid to the painter. " He's a good creature, too," said Becky, " crack-brained as he is. Do you know, miss, he gave me half a sovereign to buy a new collar, after that business t'other day ? "

" And did—Mr.——,— did the first floor say anything ? " asked Caroline.

" Didn't he ! he's a funny gentleman, that Brandon, sure enough ; and when I took him up breakfast next morning, asked about Sims the pilot, and what I gi'ed Sims for the collar and brooch,—he, he ! "

And this was indeed a correct report of Mr. Brandon's conversation with Becky ; he had been infinitely amused with the whole transaction, and wrote his friend the viscount a capital facetious account of the manners and customs of the native inhabitants of the Isle of Thanet.

And now, when Mr. Fitch's passion was fully developed— as far, that is, as sighs and ogles could give it utterance—a curious instance of that spirit of contradiction for which our race is remarkable was seen in the behavior of Mr. Brandon. Although Caroline, in the depths of her little silly heart, had set him down for her divinity, her wondrous fairy prince, who was to deliver her from her present miserable durance, she had never by word or deed acquainted Brandon with her inclination for him, but had, with instinctive modesty, avoided him more sedulously than before. He, too, had never bestowed a thought upon her. How should such a Jove as Mr. Brandon, from the cloudy summit of his fashionable Olympus, look down and perceive such an humble, retiring being as poor little Caroline Gann ? Thinking her at first not disagreeable, he had never, until the day of the dinner, bestowed one single further thought upon her ; and only when exasperated by the Miss Macartys' behavior towards him, did he begin to think how sweet it would be to make them jealous and unhappy.

" The uncouth grinning monsters," said he, " with their horrible court of Bob Smiths and Jack Joneses, daring to look down upon me, a gentleman,—me, the celebrated *mangeur des cœurs* — a man of genius, fashion, and noble family ! If I could but revenge myself on them ! What injury can I invent to wound them."

It is curious to what points a man in his passion will go. Mr. Brandon had long since, in fact, tried to do the greatest possible injury to the young ladies ; for it had been, at the first dawn of his acquaintance, as we are bound with much sorrow to confess, his fixed intention to ruin one or the other of them. And when the young ladies had, by their coldness and indifference to him, frustrated this benevolent intention, he straightway fancied that they had injured him severely, and cast about for means to revenge himself upon them.

This point is, to be sure, a very delicate one to treat,—for in words, at least, the age has grown to be wonderfully moral, and refuses to hear discourses upon such subjects. But human nature, as far as I am able to learn, has not much changed since the time when Richardson wrote and Hogarth painted, a century ago. There are wicked Lovelaces abroad, ladies, now as then, when it was considered no shame to expose the rogues ; and pardon us, therefore, for hinting that such there be. Elegant acts of *rouerie*, such as that meditated by Mr. Brandon, are often performed still by dashing young men of the world, who think no sin of an *amourette*, but glory in it, especially if the victim be a person of mean condition. Had Brandon succeeded (such is the high moral state of our British youth), all his friends would have pronounced him, and he would have considered himself, to be a very lucky, captivating dog ; nor, as I believe, would he have had a single pang of conscience for the rascally action which he had committed. This supreme act of scoundrelism has man permitted to himself—to deceive women. When we consider how he has availed himself of the privilege so created by him, indeed one may sympathize with the advocates of woman's rights who point out this monstrous wrong. We have read of that wretched woman of old whom the pious Pharisees were for stoning incontinently ; but we don't hear that they made any outcry against *the man* who was concerned in the crime. Where was he ? Happy, no doubt, and easy in mind, and regaling some choice friends over a bottle with the history of his success.

Being thus injured then, Mr. Brandon longed for revenge. How should he repay these impertinent young women for slighting his addresses ? " *Pardi*," said he ; " just to punish their pride and insolence, I have a great mind to make love to their sister."

He did not, however, for some time condescend to perform this threat. Eagles such as Brandon do not sail down from the clouds in order to pounce upon small flies, and soar air-wards again, contented with such an ignoble booty. In a word, he never gave a minute's thought to Miss Caroline, until further circumstances occurred which caused this great man to consider her as an object somewhat worthy of his remark.

The violent affection suddenly exhibited by Mr. Fitch, the painter, towards poor little Caroline was the point which determined Brandon to begin to act.

" My Dear Viscount " (wrote he to the same Lord Cinqbars whom he formerly addressed)—" Give me joy, for in a week's time it is my intention to be violently in love,—and love is no small amusement in a watering-place in winter.

" I told you about the fair Juliana Gann and her family. I forgot whether I mentioned how the Juliana had two fair daughters, the Rosalind and the Isabella ; and another, Caroline by name, not so good-looking as her half-sisters, but, nevertheless, a pleasing young person.

" Well, when I came hither, I had nothing to do but to fall in love with the two handsomest ; and did so, taking many walks with them, talking much nonsense ; passing long dismal evenings over horrid tea with them and their mamma : laying regular siege, in fact, to these Margate beauties, who, according to the common rule in such cases, could not, I thought, last long.

" Miserable deception ! disgusting aristocratic blindness ! " (Mr. Brandon always assumed that his own high birth and eminent position were granted.) " Would you believe it, that I, who have seen, fought, and conquered in so many places, should have been ignominiously defeated here ? Just as American Jackson defeated our Peninsular veterans, I, an old Continental conqueror too, have been overcome by this ignoble enemy. These women have entrenched themselves so firmly in their vulgarity, that I have been beaten back several times with disgrace, being quite unable to make an impression. The monsters, too, keep up a dreadful fire from behind their intrenchments ; and besides have raised the whole country against me : in a word, all the snobs of their acquaintance are in arms. There is Bob Smith, the linendraper ; Harry Jones, who keeps the fancy tea-shop ; young Glauber, the apothecary ; and sundry other persons, who are ready to eat me when they see me in the streets ; and are all at the beck of the victorious Amazons.

" How is a gentleman to make head against such a *canaille* as this ?—a regular *jacquerie*. Once or twice I have thought of retreating ; but a retreat, for sundry reasons I have, is inconvenient. I can't go to London ; I am known at Dover ; I believe there is a bill against me at Canterbury ; at Chatham there are sundry quartered regiments whose recognition I should be unwilling to risk. I must stay here—and be hanged to the place—until my better star shall rise.

" But I am determined that my stay shall be to some purpose ; and so to show how persevering I am, I shall make one more trial upon the third daughter,—yes, upon the third daughter, a family Cinderella, who shall, I am determined, make her sisters *crever* with envy. I merely mean fun, you know—not mischief,—for Cinderella is but a little child : and, besides, I am the most harmless fellow breathing, but must have my joke. Now Cinderella has a lover, the bearded painter of whom I spoke to you in a former letter. He has lately plunged into the most extraordinary fits of passion for her, and is more mad than ever he was before. Woe betide you, O painter ! I have nothing to do : a month to do that nothing in ; in that time, mark my words, I will laugh at that painter's beard. Should you like a lock of it, or a sofa stuffed with it ? there is beard enough : or should you like to see a specimen of poor little Cinderella's golden ringlets ? Command your slave. I wish I had paper enough to write you an account of a grand Gann dinner at which I assisted, and of a scene which there took place ; and how Cinderella was dressed out, not by a fairy, but by a charitable kitchen-maid, and was turned out of the room by her indignant mamma, for appearing in the scullion's finery. But my *forte* does not lie in such descriptions of polite life. We drank port, and toasts after dinner : here is the *menu*, and the names and order of the eaters."

*   *   *   *   *   *   *

The bill of fare has been given already, and need not, therefore, be again laid before the public.

" What a fellow that is ! " said young Lord Cinqbars, reading the letter to his friends, and in a profound admiration of his tutor's genius.

"And to think that he was a reading man too, and took a double first," cried another; "why, the man's an Admirable Crichton."

"Upon my life, though, he's a little too bad," said a third, who was a moralist. And with this a fresh bowl of milk-punch came reeking from the college butteries, and the jovial party discussed that.

CHAPTER V.

CONTAINS A GREAT DEAL OF COMPLICATED LOVE-MAKING.

THE Misses Macarty were excessively indignant that Mr. Fitch should have had the audacity to fall in love with their sister; and poor Caroline's life was not, as may be imagined, made much the happier by the envy and passion thus excited. Mr. Fitch's amour was the source of a great deal of pain to her. Her mother would tauntingly say, that as both were beggars, they could not do better than marry; and declared, in the same satirical way, that she should like nothing better than to see a large family of grandchildren about her, to be plagues and burdens upon her, as her daughter was. The short way would have been, when the young painter's intentions were manifest, which they pretty speedily were, to have requested him immediately to quit the house; or, as Mr. Gann said, "to give him the sack at once;" to which measure the worthy man indignantly avowed that he would have resort. But his lady would not allow of any such rudeness; although, for her part, she professed the strongest scorn and contempt for the painter. For the painful fact must be stated: Fitch had a short time previously paid no less a sum than a whole quarter's board and lodging in advance, at Mrs. Gann's humble request, and he possessed his landlady's receipt for that sum; the mention of which circumstance silenced Gann's objections at once. And indeed, it is pretty certain that, with all her taunts to her daughter and just abuse of Fitch's poverty, Mrs. Gann in her heart was not altogether averse to the match. In the first place, she loved match-making; next, she would be glad to be rid of her daughter at any rate; and besides, Fitch's aunt, the auctioneer's wife, was rich, and had no children; painters, as she had heard, make often a great deal of money, and Fitch might be a clever one, for aught she knew. So he was allowed to remain in the house, an undeclared but very assiduous lover; and to sigh, and to moan, and make verses and portraits of his beloved, and build castles in the air as best he might. Indeed our humble Cinderella was in a very curious position. She felt a tender passion for the first floor, and was adored by the second floor, and had to wait upon both at the summons of the bell of either; and as the poor little thing was compelled not to notice any of the sighs and glances which the painter bestowed upon her, she also had schooled herself to maintain a quiet demeanor towards Mr. Brandon, and not allow him to discover the secret which was laboring in her little breast.

I think it may be laid down as a pretty general rule, that most romantic little girls of Caroline's age have such a budding sentiment as this young person entertained; quite innocent of course; nourished and talked of in delicious secrecy to the *confidante* of the hour. Or else what are novels made for? Had Caroline read of Valancourt and Emily for nothing, or gathered no good example from those five tear-fraught volumes which describe the loves of Miss Helen Mar and Sir William Wallace? Many a time had she depicted Brandon in a fancy costume, such as the fascinating Valancourt wore; or painted herself as Helen, tying a sash round her knight's cuirass, and watching him forth to battle. Silly fancies, no doubt; but consider, madam, the poor girl's age and education; the only instruction she had ever received was from these tender, kind-hearted, silly books: the only happiness which Fate had allowed her was in this little silent world of fancy. It would be hard to grudge the poor thing her dreams; and many such did she have, and impart blushingly to honest Becky, as they sate by the humble kitchen-fire.

Although it cost her heart a great pang, she had once ventured to implore her mother not to send her up stairs to the lodgers' rooms, for she shrunk at the notion of the occurrence that Brandon should discover her regard for him; but this point had never entered Mrs. Gann's sagacious head. She thought her daughter wished to avoid Fitch, and sternly bade her do her duty, and not give herself such impertinent airs; and, indeed, it can't be said that poor Caroline was very sorry at being compelled to continue to see Brandon. To do both gentlemen justice, neither ever said a word unfit for Caroline to hear. Fitch would have been torn to pieces by a thousand wild horses rather than have breathed a single syllable to hurt her feelings; and Brandon, though by no means so squeamish

4

on ordinary occasions, was innately a gentleman, and from taste rather than from virtue, was carefully respectful in his behavior to her.

As for the Misses Macarty themselves, it has been stated that they had already given away their hearts several times; Miss Isabella being at this moment attached to a certain young wine-merchant, and to Lieutenant or Colònel Swabber of the Spanish service; and Miss Rosalind having a decided fondness for a foreign nobleman, with black mustachios, who had paid a visit to Margate. Of Miss Bella's lovers, Swabber had disappeared; but she still met the wine-merchant pretty often, and it is believed had gone very nigh to accept him. As for Miss Rosalind, I am sorry to say that the course of her true love ran by no means smoothly: the Frenchman had turned out to be not a marquess, but a billiard-marker; and a sad, sore subject the disappointment was with the neglected lady.

We should have spoken of it long since had the subject been one that was much canvassed in the Gann family; but once when Gann had endeavored to rally his stepdaughter on this unfortunate attachment (using for the purpose those delicate terms of wit for which the honest gentleman was always famous), Miss Linda had flown into such a violent fury, and comported herself in a way so dreadful, that James Gann, Esquire, was fairly frightened out of his wits by the threats, screams, and imprecations which she uttered. Miss Bella, who was disposed to be jocose likewise, was likewise awed into silence; for her dear sister talked of tearing her eyes out that minute, and uttered some hints, too, regarding love-matters personally affecting Miss Bella herself, which caused that young lady to turn pale-red, to mutter something about "wicked lies," and to leave the room immediately. Nor was the subject ever again broached by the Ganns. Even when Mrs. Gann once talked about that odious French impostor, she was stopped immediately, not by the lady concerned, but by Miss Bella, who cried, sharply, "Mamma, hold your tongue, and don't vex our dear Linda by alluding to any such stuff." It is most probable that the young ladies had had a private conference, which, beginning a little fiercely at first, had ended amicably: and so the marquess was mentioned no more.

Miss Linda, then, was comparatively free (for Bob Smith, the linendraper, and young Glauber, the apothecary, went for nothing); and, very luckily for her, a successor was found for the faithless Frenchman, almost immediately.

This gentleman was a commoner, to be sure; but had a

good estate of five hundred a year, kept his horse and gig, and was, as Mr. Gann remarked, as good a fellow as ever lived. Let us say at once that the new lover was no other than Mr. Swigby. From the day when he had been introduced to the family he appeared to be very much attracted by the two sisters; sent a turkey off his own farm, and six bottles of prime Hollands, to Mr. and Mrs. Gann, in presents; and, in ten short days after his first visit, had informed his friend Gann that he was violently in love with two women whose names he would never—never breathe. The worthy Gann knew right well how the matter was; for he had not failed to remark Swigby's melancholy, and to attribute it to its right cause.

Swigby was forty-eight years of age, stout, hearty, gay, much given to drink, and had never been a lady's man, or, indeed, passed half-a-dozen evenings in ladies' society. He thought Gann the noblest and finest fellow in the world. He never heard any singing like James's, nor any jokes like his; nor had met with such an accomplished gentleman or man of the world. "Gann has his faults," Swigby would say at the "Bag of Nails;" which of us has not?—but I tell you what, he's the greatest trump I ever see." Many scores of scores had he paid for Gann, many guineas and crown-pieces had he lent him, since he came into his property some three years before. What were Swigby's former pursuits I can't tell. What need we care? Hadn't he five hundred a year now, and a horse and gig? Ay, that he had.

Since his accession to fortune, this gay young bachelor had taken his share (what he called "his whack") of pleasure; had been at one—nay, perhaps, at two—public-houses every night; and had been tipsy, I make no doubt, nearly a thousand times in the course of the three years. Many people had tried to cheat him; but, no, no! he knew what was what, and in all matters of money was simple and shrewd. Gann's gentility won him; his bragging, his *ton*, and the stylish tuft on his chin. To be invited to his house was a proud moment; and when he went away, after the banquet described in the last chapter, he was in a perfect ferment of love and liquor.

"What a stylish woman is that Mrs. Gann!" thought he, as he tumbled into bed at his inn; fine she must have been as a gal! fourteen stone now, without saddle or bridle, and no mistake. And them Miss Macartys. Jupiter! what spanking, handsome, elegant creatures!—real elegance in both on 'em! Such hair!—black's the word—as black as my mare; such cheeks, such necks, and shoulders!" At noon he repeated these observations to Gann himself, as he walked up and down the pier with that gentlemen, smoking Manilla cheroots. He was in raptures with his evening. Gann received his praises with much majestic good-humor.

"Blood, sir!" said he, "blood's everything! Them gals have been brought up as few ever have. I don't speak of myself; but their mother—their mother's a lady, sir. Show me a woman in England as is better bred or knows the world more than my Juliana!"

"It's impawssible," said Swigby.

"Think of the company we've kep', sir, before our misfortunes — the fust in the land. Brandenburg House, sir,— England's injured queen. Law bless you! Juliana was always there."

"I make no doubt, sir; you can see it in her," said Swigby, solemnly.

"And as for those gals, why, ain't they related to the fust families in Ireland, sir?—In course they are. As I said before, blood's everything; and those young women have the best of it; they are connected with the reg'lar old noblesse."

"They have the best of everythink, I'm sure," said Swigby, "and deserve it, too," and relapsed into his morning remarks. "What creatures! what elegance! what hair and eyes, sir!— black, and all's black, as I say. What complexion, sir!—ay, and what *makes*, too! Such a neck and shoulders I never see!"

Gann, who had his hands in his pockets (his friend's arm being hooked into one of his), here suddenly withdrew his hand from its hiding-place, clenched his fist, assumed a horrible knowing grin, and gave Mr. Swigby such a blow in the ribs as wellnigh sent him into the water. "You sly dog!" said Mr. Gann, with inexpressible emphasis; "you've found *that* out, too, have you? Have a care, Joe, my boy,—have a care."

And herewith Gann and Joe burst into tremendous roars of laughter, fresh explosions taking place at intervals of five minutes during the rest of the walk. The two friends parted exceedingly happy; and when they met that evening at "The Nails," Gann drew Swigby mysteriously into the bar, and thrust into his hand a triangular piece of pink paper, which the latter read:—

"Mrs. Gann and the Misses Macarty request the honor and pleasure of Mr. Swigby's company (if you have no better engagement) to tea to-morrow evening, at half-past five.
" *Margaretta Cottage, Salamanca Road North,*
        Thursday evening."

The faces of the two gentlemen were wonderfully expressive of satisfaction as this communication passed between them.

And I am led to believe that Mrs. Gann had been unusually pleased with her husband's conduct on that day : for honest James had no less than thirteen and sixpence in his pocket, and insisted, as usual, upon standing glasses all round. Joe Swigby, left alone in the little parlor behind the bar, called for a sheet of paper, a new pen and a wafer, and in the space of half an hour concocted a very spirited and satisfactory answer to this note ; which was carried off by Gann, and duly delivered. Punctually at half-past five, Mr. Joseph Swigby knocked at Margaretta Cottage door, in his new coat with glistening brass buttons, his face clean-shaved, and his great ears shining over his great shirt-collar delightfully bright and red.

What happened at this tea-party it is needless here to say ; but Swigby came away from it quite as much enchanted as before, and declared that the duets, sung by the ladies in hideous discord, were the sweetest music he had ever heard. He sent the gin and the turkey the next day ; and, of course, was invited to dine.

The dinner was followed up on his part by an offer to drive all the young ladies and their mamma into the country ; and he hired a very smart barouche to conduct them. The invitation was not declined ; and Fitch, too, was asked by Mr. Swigby, in the height of his good-humor, and accepted with the utmost delight. "Me and Joe will go on the box," said Gann. "You four ladies and Mr. Fitch shall go inside. Carry must go bodkin ; but she ain't very big."

"Carry, indeed, will stop at home," said her mamma ; "she's not fit to go out."

At which poor Fitch's jaw fell ; it was in order to ride with her that he had agreed to accompany the party ; nor could he escape now, having just promised so eagerly.

"Oh, don't let's have that proud Brandon," said the young ladies, when the good-natured Mr. Swigby proposed to ask that gentleman ; and therefore he was not invited to join them in their excursion ; but he stayed at home very unconcernedly, and saw the barouche and its load drive off. Somebody else looked at it from the parlor-window with rather a heavy heart ; and that some one was poor Caroline. The day was bright and sunshiny ; the spring was beginning early ; it would have been pleasant to have been a lady for once, and to have driven along in a carriage with prancing horses. Mr. Fitch looked after her in a very sheepish, melancholy way ; and was so dismal and silly during the first part of the journey, that Miss Linda, who was next to him, said to her papa that she would change places with him ; and actually mounted the box by the side of the happy, trembling Mr. Swigby. How proud he was, to be sure ! How knowingly did he spank the horses along, and fling out the shillings at the turnpikes !

" Bless you, *he* don't care for change ! " said Gann, as one of the toll-takers offered to render some coppers ; and Joe felt infinitely obliged to his friend for setting off his amiable qualities in such a way.

O mighty Fate, that over us miserable mortals rulest supreme, with what small means are thy ends effected !—with what scornful ease and mean instruments does it please thee to govern mankind ! Let each man think of the circumstances of his life, and how its lot has been determined. The getting up a little earlier or later, the turning down this street or that, the eating of this dish or the other, may influence all the years and actions of a future life. Mankind walks down the left-hand side of Regent Street instead of the right, and meets a friend who asks him to dinner, and goes, and finds the turtle remarkably good, and the iced punch very cool and pleasant ; and, being in a merry, jovial, idle mood, has no objection to a social rubber of whist—nay, to a few more glasses of that cool punch. In the most careless, good-humored way, he loses a few points ; and still feels thirsty, and loses a few more points ; and, like a man of spirit, increases his stakes, to be sure, and just by that walk down Regent Street is ruined for life. Or he walks down the right-hand side of Regent Street instead of the left, and, good heavens! who is that charming young creature who has just stepped into her carriage from Mr. Fraser's shop, and to whom and her mamma Mr. Fraser has made the most elegant bow in the world? It is the lovely Miss Moidore, with a hundred thousand pounds, who has remarked your elegant figure, and regularly drives to town on the first of the month, to purchase her darling Magazine. You drive after her as fast as the hackcab will carry you. She reads the Magazine the whole way. She stops at her papa's elegant villa at Hampstead, with a conservatory, a double coach-house, and a park-like paddock. As the lodge-gate separates you from that dear girl, she looks back just once, and blushes. *Erubuit, salva est res.* She has blushed, and you are all right. In a week you are introduced to the family, and pronounced a charming young fellow of high principles. In three weeks you have danced twenty-nine quadrilles with her, and whisked her through several miles of waltzes. In a month Mrs. O'Flaherty has flung herself into the arms of her mother, just having come from a visit to the village of Gretna, near

Carlisle ; and you have an account at your banker's ever after. What is the cause of all this good fortune ?—a walk on a particular side of Regent Street. And so true and indisputable is this fact, that there's a young north-country gentleman with whom I am acquainted, that daily paces up and down the above-named street for many hours, fully expecting that such an adventure will happen to him ; for which end he keeps a cab in readiness at the corner of Vigo Lane.

Now, after a dissertation in this history, the reader is pretty sure to know that a moral is coming ; and the facts connected with our tale, which are to be drawn from the above little essay on fate, are simply these : 1. If Mr. Fitch had not heard Mr. Swigby invite *all* the ladies, he would have refused Swigby's invitation, and stayed at home. 2. If he had not been in the carriage, it is quite certain that Miss Rosalind Macarty would not have been seated by him on the back seat. 3. If he had not been sulky, she never would have asked her papa to let her take his place on the box. 4. If she had not taken her papa's place on the box, not one of the circumstances would have happened which did happen ; and which were as follows :—

1. Miss Bella remained inside.

2. Mr. Swigby, who was wavering between the two, like a certain animal between two bundles of hay, was determined by this circumstance, and made proposals to Miss Linda, whispering to Miss Linda : " Miss, I ain't equal to the like of you ; but I'm hearty, healthy, and have five hundred a year. Will you marry me ? " In fact, this very speech had been taught him by cunning Gann, who saw well enough that Swigby would speak to one or other of his daughters. And to it the young lady replied, also in a whispering, agitated tone, " Law, Mr. S. ! What an odd man ! How can you ? " And, after a little pause, added, " *Speak to mamma.*"

3. (And this is the main point of my story.) If little Caroline had been allowed to go out, she never would have been left alone with Brandon at Margate. When Fate wills that something should come to pass, she sends forth a million of little circumstances to clear and prepare the way.

In the month of April (as indeed in a half-a-score of other months of the year) the reader may have remarked that the cold north-east wind is prevalent ; and that when, tempted by a glimpse of sunshine, he issues forth to take the air, he receives not only it, but such a quantity of it as is enough to keep him shivering through the rest of the miserable month. On one of these happy days of English weather (it was the very day before the pleasure-party described in the last chapter) Mr. Brandon cursing heartily his country, and thinking how infinitely more congenial to him were the winds and habits prevalent in other nations, was marching over the cliffs near Margate, in the midst of a storm of shrill east wind which no ordinary mortal could bear, when he found perched on the cliff, his fingers blue with cold, the celebrated Andrea Fitch, employed in sketching a land or a sea scape on a sheet of gray paper.

"You have chosen a fine day for sketching," said Mr. Brandon, bitterly, his thin aquiline nose peering out livid from the fur collar of his coat.

Mr. Fitch smiled, understanding the allusion.

"An hartist, sir," said he, "doesn't mind the coldness of the weather. There was a chap in the Academy who took sketches twenty degrees below zero in Hiceland—Mount 'Ecla, sir! *E* was the man that gave the first hidea of Mount 'Ecla for the Surrey Zoological Gardens."

"He must have been a wonderful enthusiast!" said Mr. Brandon; "I fancy that most would prefer to sit at home, and not numb their fingers in such a freezing storm as this!"

"Storm, sir!" replied Fitch, majestically; "I live in a storm, sir! A true hartist is never so 'appy as when he can have the advantage to gaze upon yonder tempestuous hocean in one of its hangry moods."

"Ay, there comes the steamer," answered Mr. Brandon; "I can fancy that there are a score of unhappy people on board who are not artists, and would wish to behold your ocean quiet."

"They are not poets, sir: the glorious hever-changing expression of the great countenance of Nature is not seen by them. I should consider myself unworthy of my hart, if I could not bear a little privation of cold or 'eat for its sake. And besides, sir, whatever their hardships may be, such a sight hamply repays me; for, although my private sorrows may be (has they are) tremendous, I never can look abroad upon the green hearth and hawful sea, without in a measure forgetting my personal woes and wrongs; for what right has a poor creature like me to think of his affairs in the presence of such a spectacle as this? I can't, sir; I feel ashamed of myself; I bow my 'ead and am quiet. When I set myself to examining hart, sir (by which I mean nature), I don't dare to think of anything else."

"You worship a very charming and consoling mistress." answered Mr. Brandon, with a supercilious air, lighting and beginning to smoke a cigar; "your enthusiasm does you credit."

"If you have another," said Andrea Fitch, "I should like to smoke one, for you seem to have a real feeling about hart, and I was a-getting so deucedly cold here, that really there was scarcely any bearing of it."

"The cold is very severe," replied Mr. Brandon.

"No, no, it's not the weather, sir!" said Mr. Fitch; "it's here, sir, here" (pointing to the left side of his waistcoat).

"What! you, too, have had sorrows?"

"Sorrows, sir! hagonies—hagonies, which I have never unfolded to any mortal! I have hendured halmost hevery thing. Poverty, sir, 'unger, hobloquy, 'opeless love! but for my hart, sir, I should be the most miserable wretch in the world!"

And herewith Mr. Fitch began to pour forth into Mr. Brandon's ears the history of some of those sorrows under which he labored, and which he communicated to every single person who would listen to him.

Mr. Brandon was greatly amused by Fitch's prattle, and the latter told him under what privations he had studied his art: how he had starved for three years in Paris and Rome, while laboring at his profession; how meanly jealous the Royal Academy was which would never exhibit a single one of his pictures; how he had been driven from the Heternal City by the attentions of an immense fat Mrs. Carrickfergus, who absolutely proposed marriage to him; and how he was at this moment (a fact of which Mr. Brandon was already quite aware) madly and desperately in love with one of the most beautiful maidens in this world. For Fitch, having a mistress to his heart's desire, was boiling with impatience to have a confidant; what, indeed, would be the joy of love, if one were not allowed to speak of one's feelings to a friend who could know how to sympathize with them? Fitch was sure Brandon did, because Brandon was the very first person with whom the painter had talked since he had come to the resolution recorded in the last chapter.

"I hope she is as rich as that unlucky Mrs. Carrickfergus, whom you treated so cruelly?" said the confidant, affecting entire ignorance.

"Rich, sir? no, I thank heaven, she has not a penny!" said Fitch.

"I presume, then, you are yourself independent," said Brandon, smiling; "for in the marriage state, one or the other of the parties concerned should bring a portion of the filthy lucre."

"Haven't I my profession, sir?" said Fitch, majestically,

having declared five minutes before that he starved in his profession. "Do you suppose a painter gets nothing? Haven't I horders from the first people in Europe?—commissions, sir, to hexecute 'istory-pieces, battle-pieces, haltar-pieces?"

"Master-pieces, I am sure," said Brandon, bowing politely; "for a gentleman of your astonishing genius can do no other."

The delighted artist received this compliment with many blushes, and vowed and protested that his performances were not really worthy of such high praise; but he fancied Mr. Brandon a great connoisseur, nevertheless, and unburdened his mind to him in a manner still more open. Fitch's sketch was by this time finished; and, putting his drawing implements together, he rose, and the gentlemen walked away. The sketch was hugely admired by Mr. Brandon, and when they came home, Fitch, culling it dexterously out of his book, presented it in a neat speech to his friend, "the gifted hamateur."

"The gifted hamateur" received the drawing with a profusion of thanks, and so much did he value it, that he had actually torn off a piece to light a cigar with, when he saw that words were written on the other side of the paper, and deciphered the following:—

"SONG OF THE VIOLET.

"A humble flower long time I pined,
  Upon the solitary plain.
And trembled at the angry wind,
  And shrunk before the bitter rain.
And, oh! 'twas in a blessed hour,
  A passing wanderer chanced to see
And, pitying the lonely flower,
  To stoop and gather me.

"I fear no more the tempest rude,
  On dreary heath no more I pine,
But left my cheerless solitude,
  To deck the breast of Caroline.
Alas! our days are brief at best,
  Nor long I fear will mine endure,
Though shelter'd here upon a breast
  So gentle and so pure.

"It draws the fragrance from my leaves,
  It robs me of my sweetest breath;
And every time it falls and heaves,
  It warns me of my coming death.
But one I know would glad forego
  All joys of life to be as I;
An hour to rest on that sweet breast,
  And then, contented, to die.
                                    "ANDREA."

When Mr. Brandon had finished the perusal of these verses, he laid them down with an air of considerable vexation. "Egad!" said he, "this fellow, fool as he is, is not so great a fool as he seems ; and if he goes on this way, may finish by turning the girl's head. They can't resist a man if he but presses hard enough—I know they can't!" And here Mr. Brandon mused over his various experience, which confirmed his observation, that be a man ever so silly, a gentlewoman will yield to him out of sheer weariness. And he thought of several cases in which, by the persevering application of copies of verses, young ladies had been brought from dislike to sufferance of a man, from sufferance to partiality, and from partiality to St. George's, Hanover Square. "A ruffian who murders his *h*'s to carry off such a delicate little creature as that!" cried he in a transport : "it shall never be if I can prevent it!" He thought Caroline more and more beautiful every instant, and was himself by this time almost as much in love with her as Fitch himself.

Mr. Brandon, then, saw Fitch depart in Swigby's carriage with no ordinary feelings of pleasure. Miss Caroline was not with them. "Now is my time!" thought Brandon ; and, ringing the bell, he inquired with some anxiety, from Becky, where Miss Caroline was ? It must be confessed that mistress and maid were at their usual occupation, working and reading novels in the back-parlor. Poor Carry! what other pleasure had she ?

She had not gone through many pages, or Becky advanced many stitches in the darning of that table-cloth which the good housewife, Mrs. Gann, had confided to her charge, when an humble knock was heard at the door of the sitting-room, that caused the blushing Caroline to tremble and drop her book, as Miss Lydia Languish does in the play.

Mr. George Brandon entered with a very demure air. He held in his hand a black satin neck-scarf, of which a part had come to be broken. He could not wear it in its present condition, that was evident ; but Miss Caroline was blushing and trembling a great deal too much to suspect that this wicked Brandon had himself torn his own scarf with his own hands one moment before he entered the room. I don't know whether Becky had any suspicions of this fact, or whether it was only the ordinary roguish look which she had when anything pleased her, that now lighted up her eyes and caused her mouth to expand smilingly, and her fat red cheeks to gather up into wrinkles.

"I have had a sad misfortune," said he, "and should be very much obliged indeed to Miss Caroline to repair it." (Caroline was said with a kind of tender hesitation that caused

the young woman, so named, to blush more than ever.)   " It is
the only stock I have in the world, and I can't go barenecked
into the streets ; can I, Mrs. Becky ? "

" No, sure," said Becky.

" Not unless I was a celebrated painter, like Mr. Fitch,"
added Mr. Brandon, with a smile, which was reflected speedily
upon the face of the lady whom he wished to interest. " Those
great geniuses," he added, " may do anything."

" For," says Becky, "hee's got enough beard on hees faze
to keep hees neck warm ! "   At which remark, though Miss
Caroline very properly said, " For shame, Becky ! "   Mr.
Brandon was so convulsed with laughter, that he fairly fell
down upon the sofa on which Miss Caroline was seated. How
she startled and trembled, as he flung his arm upon the back
of the couch !   Mr. Brandon did not attempt to apologize for
what was an act of considerable impertinence, but continued
mercilessly to make many more jokes concerning poor Fitch,
which were so cleverly suited to the comprehension of the maid
and the young mistress, as to elicit a great number of roars of
laughter from the one, and to cause the other to smile in spite
of herself.   Indeed, Brandon had gained a vast reputation with
Becky in his morning colloquies with her, and she was ready
to laugh at any single word which it pleased him to utter. How
many of his good things had this honest scullion carried down
stairs to Caroline ? and how pitilessly had she contrived to
estropier them in their passage from the drawing-room to the
kitchen ?

Well, then, while Mr. Brandon "was a-going on," as Becky
said, Caroline had taken his stock, and her little fingers were
occupied in repairing the damage he had done to it.   Was it
clumsiness on her part ?   Certain it is that the rent took several
minutes to repair : of them the *mangeur de cœurs* did not fail
to profit, conversing in an easy, kindly, confidential way, which
set our fluttering heroine speedily at rest, and enabled her to
reply to his continual queries, addressed with much adroitness
and an air of fraternal interest, by a number of those pretty
little timid whispering yeses and noes, and those gentle, quick
looks of the eyes, wherewith young and modest maidens are
wont to reply to the questions of seducing young bachelors.
Dear yeses and noes, how beautiful you are when gently
whispered by pretty lips !—glances of quick innocent eyes how
charming are you !—and how charming the soft blush that steals
over the cheek, towards which the dark lashes are drawing the
blue-veined eyelids down.   And here let the writer of this

solemnly declare, upon his veracity, that he means nothing but what is right and moral. But look, I pray you, at an innocent, bashful girl of sixteen : if she be but good, she must be pretty. She is a woman now, but a girl still. How delightful all her ways are ! How exquisite her instinctive grace ! All the arts of all the Cleopatras are not so captivating as her nature. Who can resist her confiding simplicity, or fail to be touched and conquered by her gentle appeal to protection ?

All this Mr. Brandon saw and felt, as many a gentleman educated in this school will. It is not because a man is a rascal himself, that he cannot appreciate virtue and purity very keenly ; and our hero did feel for this simple, gentle, tender, artless creature, a real respect and sympathy—a sympathy so fresh and delicious, that he was but too glad to yield to it and indulge in it, and which he mistook, probably, for a real love of virtue and a return to the days of his innocence.

Indeed, Mr. Brandon, it was no such thing. It was only because vice and debauch were stale for the moment, and this pretty virtue new. It was only because your cloyed appetite was long unused to this simple meat that you felt so keen a relish for it ; and I thought of you only the last blessed Saturday, at Mr. Lovegrove's, "West India Tavern," Blackwall, where a company of fifteen epicures, who had scorned the turtle, pooh-poohed the punch, and sent away the whitebait, did suddenly and simultaneously make a rush upon—a dish of *beans and bacon.* And if the assiduous reader of novels will think upon some of the most celebrated works of that species, which have lately appeared in this and other countries, he will find, amidst much debauch of sentiment and enervating dissipation of intellect, that the writers have from time to time a returning appetite for innocence and freshness, and indulge us with occasional repasts of beans and bacon. How long Mr. Brandon remained by Miss Caroline's side I have no means of judging ; it is probable, however, that he stayed a much longer time than was necessary for the mending of his black satin stock. I believe, indeed, that he read to the ladies a great part of the "Mysteries of Udolpho," over which they were engaged ; and interspersed his reading with many remarks of his own, both tender and satirical. Whether he was in her company half-an-hour or four hours, this is certain, that the time slipped away very swiftly with poor Caroline ; and when a carriage drove up to the door, and shrill voices were heard crying, "Becky !" "Carry !" and Rebecca the maid starting up, cried, "Lor', here's missus !" and Brandon jumped rather suddenly off the sofa, and fled up the stairs—when all these events took place, I know Caroline felt very sad indeed, and opened the door for her parents with a very heavy heart.

Swigby helped Miss Linda off the box with excessive tenderness. Papa was bustling and roaring in high good-humor, and called for " hot water and tumblers immediately." Mrs. Gann was gracious ; and Miss Bell sulky, as she had good reason to be, for she insisted upon taking the front seat in the carriage before her sister, and had lost a husband by that very piece of obstinacy.

Mr. Fitch, as he entered, bestowed upon Caroline a heavy sigh and a deep stare, and silently ascended to his own apartment. He was lost in thought. The fact is, he was trying to remember some verses regarding a violet, which he had made five years before, and which he had somehow lost from among his papers. So he went up stairs, muttering,

> " A humble flower long since I pined
> Upon a solitary plain——"

CHAPTER VI.

DESCRIBES A SHABBY GENTEEL MARRIAGE, AND MORE LOVE-MAKING.

It will not be necessary to describe the particulars of the festivities which took place on the occasion of Mr. Swigby's marriage to Miss Macarty. The happy pair went off in a post-chaise and four to the bridegroom's country-seat, accompanied by the bride's blushing sister ; and when the first week of their matrimonial bliss was ended, that worthy woman, Mrs. Gann, with her excellent husband, went to visit the young couple. Miss Caroline was left, therefore, sole mistress of the house, and received special cautions from her mamma as to prudence, economy, the proper management of the lodgers' bills, and the necessity of staying at home.

Considering that one of the gentlemen remaining in the house was a declared lover of Miss Caroline, I think it is a little surprising that her mother should leave her unprotected ; but in this matter the poor are not so particular as the rich ; and so this young lady was consigned to the guardianship of her own innocence, and the lodgers' loyalty : nor was there any reason why Mrs. Gann should doubt the latter. As for Mr. Fitch, he would have far preferred to be torn to pieces by ten thousand wild horses, rather than to offer to the young woman any unkindness or insult; and how was Mrs. Gann to suppose that her other lodger was a whit less loyal? that he had any partiality for a person of whom he always spoke as a mean, insignificant little baby? So, without any misgivings, and in a one-horse fly with Mr. Gann by her side, with a bran new green coat and gilt buttons, Juliana Gann went forth to visit her beloved child, and console her in her married state.

And here, were I allowed to occupy the reader with extraneous matters, I could give a very curious and touching picture of the Swigby *ménage*. Mrs. S., I am very sorry to say, quarrelled with her husband on the third day after their marriage,—and for what, pr'thee? Why, because he would smoke, and no gentleman ought to smoke. Swigby, therefore, patiently resigned his pipe, and with it one of the quietest, happiest, kindest companions of his solitude. He was a different man after this ; his pipe was as a limb of his body. Having on Tuesday conquered the pipe, Mrs. Swigby on Thursday did battle with her husband's rum-and-water, a drink of an odious smell, as she very properly observed ; and the smell was doubly odious, now that the tobacco-smoke no longer perfumed the parlor-breeze, and counteracted the odors of the juice of West India sugar-canes. On Thursday, then, Mr. Swigby and rum held out pretty bravely. Mrs. S. attacked the punch with some sharp-shooting, and fierce charges of vulgarity ; to which S. replied, by opening the battery of oaths (chiefly directed to his own eyes, however), and loud protestations that he would never surrender. In three days more, however, the rum-and-water was gone. Mr. Swigby, defeated and prostrate, had given up that stronghold ; his young wife and sister were triumphant ; and his poor mother, who occupied her son's house, and had till now taken her place at the head of his table, saw that her empire was for ever lost, and was preparing suddenly to succumb to the imperious claims of the mistress of the mansion.

All this, I say, I wish I had the liberty to describe at large, as also to narrate the arrival of majestic Mrs. Gann ; and a battle-royal which speedily took place between the two worthy mothers-in-law. Noble is the hatred of ladies who stand in this relation to each other ; each sees what injury the other is inflicting upon her darling child ; each mistrusts, detests, and to her offspring privily abuses the arts and crimes of the other.

A house with a wife is often warm enough ; a house with a wife and her mother is rather warmer than any spot on the known globe ; a house with two mothers-in-law is so excessively hot, that it can be likened to no place on earth at all, but one must go lower for a simile. Think of a wife who despises her husband, and teaches him manners ; of an elegant sister, who joins in rallying him (this was almost the only point of union between Bella and Linda now,—for since the marriage, Linda hated her sister consumedly). Think, I say, of two mothers-in-law,—one, large, pompous, and atrociously genteel,—another coarse and shrill, determined not to have her son put upon,—and you may see what a happy fellow Joe Swigby was, and into what a piece of good luck he had fallen.

What would have become of him without his father-in-law? Indeed one shudders to think ; but the consequence of that gentleman's arrival and intervention was speedily this :—About four o'clock, when the dinner was removed, and the quarrelling used commonly to set in, the two gents took their hats, and sallied out ; and as one has found when the body is inflamed that the application of a stringent medicine may cause the ill to disappear for a while, only to return elsewhere with greater force ; in like manner, Mrs. Swigby's sudden victory over the pipe and rum-and-water, although it had caused a temporary cessation of the evil of which she complained, was quite unable to stop it altogether ; it disappeared from one spot only to rage with more violence elsewhere. In Swigby's parlor, rum and tobacco odors rose no more (except, indeed, when Mrs. Gann would partake of the former as a restorative) ; but if you could have seen the " Half-Moon and Snuffers " down the village ; if you could have seen the good dry skittle-ground which stretched at the back of that inn, and the window of the back parlor which superintended that skittle-ground ; if the hour at which you beheld these objects was evening, what time the rustics from their toils released, trolled the stout ball amidst the rattling pins (the oaken pins that standing in the sun did cast long shadows on the golden sward) ; if you had remarked all this, I say, you would have also seen in the back parlor a tallow candle twinkling in the shade, and standing on a little greasy table. Upon the greasy table was a pewter porter-pot, and to the left a teaspoon glittering in a glass of gin ; close to each of these two delicacies was a pipe of tobacco ; and behind the pipes sat Mr. Gann and Swigby, who now made the " Half-Moon and Snuffers " their usual place of resort, and forgot their married cares.

In spite of all our promises of brevity, these things have taken some space to describe; and the reader must also know that some short interval elapsed ere they occurred. A month at least passed away before Mr. Swigby had decidedly taken up his position at the little inn: all this time, Gann was staying with his son-in-law, at the latter's most earnest request; and Mrs. Gann remained under the same roof at her own desire. Not the hints of her daughter, nor the broad questions of the dowager Mrs. Swigby, could induce honest Mrs. Gann to stir from her quarters. She had had her lodgers' money in advance, as was the worthy woman's custom; she knew Margate in April was dreadfully dull, and she determined to enjoy the country until the jovial town season arrived. The Canterbury coachman, whom Gann knew, and who passed through the village, used to take her cargo of novels to and fro; and the old lady made herself as happy as circumstances would allow. Should anything of importance occur during her mamma's absence, Caroline was to make use of the same conveyance, and inform Mrs. Gann in a letter.

Miss Caroline looked at her papa and mamma, as the vehicle which was to bear them to the newly-married couple moved up the street; but, strange to say, she did not feel that heaviness of heart which she before had experienced when forbidden to share the festivities of her family, but was on this occasion more happy than any one of them,—so happy that the young woman felt quite ashamed of herself; and Becky was fain to remark how her mistress's cheek flushed, and her eyes sparkled (and turned perpetually to the door), and her whole little frame was in a flutter.

" I wonder if he will come," said the little heart; and the eyes turned and looked at that well-known sofa-corner, where *he* had been placed a fortnight before. He looked exactly like Lord Byron, that he did, with his pale brow, and his slim bare neck; only not half so wicked—no, no. She was sure that her—her Mr. B.——, her Bran——, her *George,* was as good as he was beautiful. Don't let us be angry with her for calling him George: the girl was bred in an humble sentimental school; she did not know enough of society to be squeamish; she never thought that she could be his really, and gave way in the silence of her fancy to the full extent of her affection for him.

She had not looked at the door above twenty-five times— that is to say, her parents had not quitted the house ten minutes—when, sure enough, the latch did rattle, the door opened, and, with a faint blush on his cheek, divine George entered. He was going to make some excuse, as on the former occasion; but he looked first into Caroline's face, which was beaming with joy and smiles; and the little thing, in return, regarded him, and—made room for him on the sofa. O sweet instinct of love! Brandon had no need of excuses, but sate down, and talked away as easily, happily, and confidentially, and neither took any note of time. Andrea Fitch (the sly dog!) witnessed the Gann departure with feelings of exultation, and had laid some deep plans of his own with regard to Miss Caroline. So strong was his confidence in his friend on the first floor, that Andrea actually descended to those apartments, on his way to Mrs. Gann's parlor, in order to consult Mr. Brandon, and make known to him his plan of operations.

It would have made your heart break, or, at the very least, your sides ache, to behold the countenance of poor Mr. Fitch, as he thrust his bearded head in at the door of the parlor. There was Brandon lolling on the sofa, at his ease; Becky in full good humor; and Caroline, always absurdly inclined to blush, blushing at Fitch's appearance more than ever! She could not help looking from him slyly and gently into the face of Mr. Brandon. That gentleman saw the look, and did not fail to interpret it. It was a confession of love—an appeal for protection. A thrill of delightful vanity shot through Brandon's frame, and made his heart throb, as he noticed this look of poor Caroline. He answered it with one of his own that was cruelly wrong, cruelly triumphant, and sarcastic; and he shouted out to Mr. Fitch, with a loud, disconcerted tone, which only made that young painter feel more awkward than ever he had been. Fitch made some clumsy speech regarding his dinner, —whether that meal was to be held, in the absence of the parents, at the usual hour, and then took his leave.

The poor fellow had been pleasing himself with the notion of taking this daily meal *tete-à-tete* with Caroline. What progress would he make in her heart during the absence of her parents! Did it not seem as if the first marriage had been arranged on purpose to facilitate his own? He determined thus his plan of campaign. He would make, in the first place, the most beautiful drawing of Caroline that ever was seen. "The conversations I'll 'ave with her during the sittings," says he, "will carry me a pretty long way; the drawing itself will be so beautiful, that she can't resist that. I'll write her verses in her halbum, and make designs hallusive of my passion for her." And so our pictorial Alnaschar dreamed and dreamed.

He had, ere long, established himself in a house in Newman Street, with a footman to open the door. Caroline was up stairs, his wife, and her picture the crack portrait of the Exhibition. With her by his side, Andrea Fitch felt he could do anything. Half-a-dozen carriages at his door, —a hundred guineas for a Kit-Cat portrait. Lady Fitch, Sir Andrew Fitch, the President's chain,—all sorts of bright visions floated before his imagination ; and as Caroline was the first precious condition of his preferment, he determined forthwith to begin, and realize that.

But O disappointment ! on coming down to dinner at three o'clock to that charming *tete-à-tete*, he found no less than four covers laid on the table, Miss Caroline blushing (according to custom) at the head of it ; Becky, the maid, grinning at the foot ; and Mr. Brandon sitting quietly on one side, as much at home, forsooth, as if he had held that position for a year.

The fact is, that the moment after Fitch retired, Brandon, inspired by jealousy, had made the same request which had been brought forward by the painter ; nor must the ladies be too angry with Caroline, if, after some scruples and struggles, she yielded to the proposal. Remember that the girl was the daughter of a boarding-house, accustomed to continual dealings with her mamma's lodgers, and up to the present moment thinking herself as safe among them as the young person who walked through Ireland with a bright gold wand, in the song of Mr. Thomas Moore. On the point, however, of Brandon's admission, it must be confessed, for Caroline's honor, that she did hesitate. She felt that she entertained very different feelings towards him to those with which any other lodger or man had inspired her, and made a little movement of resistance at first. But the poor girl's modesty overcame this, as well as her wish. Ought she to avoid him ? Ought she not to stifle any preference which she might feel towards him, and act towards him with the same indifference which she would show to any other person in a like situation ? Was not Mr. Fitch to dine at table as usual, and had she refused him ? So reasoned she in her heart. Silly little cunning heart ! it knew that all these reasons were lies, and that she *should* avoid the man ; but she was willing to accept of any pretext for meeting, and so made a kind of compromise with her conscience. Dine he should ; but Becky should dine too, and be a protector to her. Becky laughed loudly at the idea of this, and took her place with huge delight.

It is needless to say a word about this dinner, as we have

already described a former meal ; suffice it to say, that the presence of Brandon caused the painter to be excessively sulky and uncomfortable ; and so gave his rival, who was gay, triumphant, and at his ease, a decided advantage over him. Nor did Brandon neglect to use this to the utmost. When Fitch retired to his own apartments—not jealous as yet, for the simple fellow believed every word of Brandon's morning conversation with him—but vaguely annoyed and disappointed, Brandon assailed him with all the force of ridicule ; at all his manners, words, looks, he joked mercilessly ; laughed at his low birth, (Miss Gann, be it remembered, had been taught to pique herself upon her own family,) and invented a series of stories concerning his past life which made the ladies—for Becky, being in the parlor, must be considered as such—conceive the greatest contempt and pity for the poor painter.

After this, Mr. Brandon would expatiate with much eloquence upon his own superior attractions and qualities. He talked of his cousin, Lord So-and-so, with the easiest air imaginable ; told Caroline what princesses he had danced with at foreign courts ; frightened her with accounts of dreadful duels he had fought ; in a word, " posed " before her as a hero of the most sublime kind. How the poor little thing drank in all his tales ; and how she and Becky (for they now occupied the same bedroom) talked over them at night !

Miss Caroline, as Mr. Fitch has already stated, had in her possession, like almost every young lady in England, a little square book called an album, containing prints from annuals ; hideous designs of flowers ; old pictures of faded fashions, cut out and pasted into the leaves ; and small scraps of verses selected from Byron, Landon, or Mrs. Hemans ; and written out in the girlish hand of the owner of the book. Brandon looked over this work with a good deal of curiosity—for he contended, always, that a girl's disposition might be learned from the character of this museum of hers—and found here several sketches by Mr. Fitch, for which, before that gentleman had declared his passion for her, Caroline had begged. These sketches the sentimental painter had illustrated with poetry, which, I must confess, Caroline thought charming, until now, when Mr. Brandon took occasion to point out how wretchedly poor the verses were (as indeed was the fact), and to parody them all. He was not unskilful at this kind of exercise, and at the drawing of caricatures, and had soon made a dozen of both parodies and drawings, which reflected cruelly upon the person and the talents of the painter.

What now did this wicked Mr. Brandon do? He, in the first place, drew a caricature of Fitch ; and, secondly, having gone to a gardener's near the town, and purchased there a bunch of violets, he presented them to Miss Caroline, and wrote Mr. Fitch's own verses before given into her album. He signed them with his own initials, and thus declared open war with the painter.

CHAPTER VII.

WHICH BRINGS A GREAT NUMBER OF PEOPLE TO MARGATE BY THE STEAMBOAT.

THE events which this history records began in the month of February. Times had now passed, and April had arrived, and with it that festive season so loved by schoolboys, and called the Easter holidays. Not only schoolboys, but men, profit by this period of leisure,—such men, especially as have just come into enjoyment of their own cups and saucers, and are in daily expectation of their whiskers—college men, I mean, —who are persons more anxious than any others to designate themselves and each other by the manly title.

Among other men, then, my Lord Viscount Cinqbars, of Christ Church, Oxon, received a sum of money to pay his quarter's bill, and having written to his papa that he was busily engaged in reading for the " little-go," and must, therefore, decline the delight he had promised himself of passing the vacation at Cinqbars Hall,—and having, the day after his letter was despatched, driven to town tandem with young Tom Tufthunt, of the same university,—and having exhausted the pleasures of the metropolis—the theatres, the Cider-cellars, the Finish, the station-houses, and other places which need by no means be here particularized,—Lord Cinqbars, I say, growing tired of London at the end of ten days, quitted the metropolis somewhat suddenly : nor did he pay his hotel bill at Long's before his departure ; but he left that document in possession of the landlord, as a token of his (my Lord Cinqbars') confidence in his host.

Tom Tufthunt went with my lord, of course (although of an aristocratic turn in politics, Tom loved and respected a lord as much as any democrat in England). And whither do you think this worthy pair of young gentlemen were bound? To no less a place than Margate ; for Cinqbars was filled with a longing to go and see his old friend Brandon, and determined, to use his own elegant words, "to knock the old buck up."

There was no adventure of consequence on board the steamer which brought Lord Cinqbars and his friend from London to Margate, and very few passengers besides. A wandering Jew or two were set down at Gravesend ; the Rev. Mr. Wackerbart, and six unhappy little pupils whom the reverend gentleman had pounced upon in London, and was carrying back to his academy near Herne Bay ; some of those inevitable persons of dubious rank who seem to have free tickets, and always eat and drink hugely with the captain ; and a lady and her party, formed the whole list of passengers.

The lady—a very fat lady—had evidently just returned from abroad. Her great green travelling-chariot was on the deck, and on all her imperials were pasted fresh large bills, with the words INCE'S BRITISH HOTEL, BOULOGNE-SUR-MER ; for it is the custom of that worthy gentleman to seize upon and plaster all the luggage of his guests with tickets, on which his name and residence are inscribed, — by which simple means he keeps himself perpetually in their recollection, and brings himself to the notice of all other persons who are in the habit of peering at their fellow-passengers' trunks, to find out their names. I need not say what a large class this is.

Well ; this fat lady had a courier, a tall whiskered man, who spoke all languages, looked like a field-marshal, went by the name of Donnerwetter, and rode on the box ; a French maid, Mademoiselle Augustine ; and a little black page, called Saladin, who rode in the rumble. Saladin's whole business was to attend a wheezy, fat, white poodle, who usually travelled inside with his mistress and her fair *compagnon de voyage*, whose name was Miss Runt. This fat lady was evidently a person of distinction. During the first part of the voyage, on a windy, sunshiny April day, she paced the deck stoutly, leaning on the arm of poor little Miss Runt ; and after they had passed Gravesend, when the vessel began to pitch a good deal, retired to her citadel, the travelling-chariot, to and from which the steward, the stewardess, and the whiskered courier were continually running with supplies—of sandwiches first, and afterwards of very hot brandy-and-water : for the truth must be told, it was rather a rough afternoon, and the poodle was sick ; Saladin was as bad ; the French maid, like all French maids, was outrageously ill ; the lady herself was very unwell indeed ; and poor dear sympathizing Runt was qualmish.

" Ah, Runt ! " would the fat lady say in the intervals, " what a thing this malady de mare is ! Oh, mong jew ! Oh—oh ! "

" It is, indeed, dear madam," said Runt, and went " Oh—oh ! " in chorus.

" Ask the steward if we are near Margate, Runt." And Runt did, and asked this question every five minutes, as people do on these occasions.

" Issy Monsieur Donnerwetter ; ally dimandy ung pew d'o sho poor mwaw."

" Et de l'eau de fie afec, n'est-ce-bas, Matame ? " said Mr. Donnerwetter.

" Wee, wee, comme vous vouly."

And Donnerwetter knew very well what " comme vous vouly " meant, and brought the liquor exactly in the wished-for state.

" Ah, Runt, Runt ! there's something even worse than sea-sickness. Heigh-ho ! "

" Dear, dear Marianne, don't flutter yourself," cries Runt, squeezing a fat paw of her friend and patroness between her own bony fingers. " Don't agitate your nerves, dear. I know you're miserable ; but haven't you got a friend in your faithful Runty ? "

" You're a good creater, that you are," said the fat lady, who seemed herself to be a good-humored old soul ; " and I don't know what I should have done without you. Heigh-ho ! "

" Cheer up, dear ! you'll be happier when you get to Margate : you know you will," cried Runt, very knowingly.

" What do you mean, Elizabeth ? "

" You know very well, dear Marianne. I mean that there's some one there will make you happy ; though he's a nasty wretch, that he is, to have treated my darling, beautiful Marianne so."

" Runt, Runt, don't abuse that best of men. Don't call me beautiful—I'm not, Runt ; I have been, but I ain't now ; and oh ! no woman in the world is assy bong poor lui."

" But an angel is ; and you are, as you always was, an angel,—as good as an angel, as kind as an angel, as beautiful as one."

" Ally dong," said her companion, giving her a push ; " you flatter me, Runt, you know you do."

" May I be struck down dead if I don't say the truth ; and if he refuses you, as he did at Rome,—that is, after all his intentions and vows, he's faithless to you,—I say he's a wretch, that he is ; and I *will* say he's a wretch, and he *is* a wretch—a nasty, wicked wretch !"

"Elizabeth, if you say that, you'll break my heart, you will ! Vous casserez mong pover cure." But Elizabeth swore, on the contrary, that she would die for her Marianne, which consoled the fat lady a little.

A great deal more of this kind of conversation took place during the voyage ; but as it occurred inside a carriage, so that to hear it was very difficult, and as possibly it was not of that edifying nature which would induce the reader to relish many chapters of it, we shall give no further account of the ladies' talk : suffice it to say, that about half-past four o'clock the journey ended, by the vessel bringing up at Margate Pier. The passengers poured forth, and hied to their respective homes or inns. My lord Cinqbars and his companion (of whom we have said nothing, as they on their sides had scarcely spoken a word the whole way, except " deuce-ace," " quater-tray," " sizes," and so on,—being occupied ceaselessly in drinking bottled stout and playing backgammon,) ordered their luggage to be conveyed to "Wright's Hotel," whither the fat lady and suite followed them. The house was vacant, and the best rooms in it were placed, of course, at the service of the new-comers. The fat lady sailed out of her bedroom towards her saloon, just as Lord Cinqbars, cigar in mouth, was swaggering out of his parlor. They met in the passage ; when, to the young lord's surprise, the fat lady dropped him a low curtsey, and said,—

" Munseer le Vecomte de Cinqbars, sharmy de vous voir. Vous vous rappelez de mwaw, n'est-ce pas ? Je vous ai vew à Rome—shay l'ambassadure, vous savy."

Lord Cinqbars stared her in the face, and pushed by her without a word, leaving the fat lady rather disconcerted.

" Well, Runt, I'm sure," said she, " he need not be so proud ; I've met him twenty times at Rome, when he was a young chap with his tutor."

" Who the devil can that fat foreigner be ?" mused Lord Cinqbars. " Hang her, I've seen her somewhere ; but I'm cursed if I understand a word of her jabber." And so, dismissing the subject, he walked on to Brandon's.

" Dang it, it's a strange thing !" says the landlord of the hotel ; " but both my lord and the fat woman in number nine have asked their way to Mother Gann's lodging," for so did he dare to call that respectable woman !

It was true : as soon as number nine had eaten her dinner, she asked the question mentioned by the landlord ; and, as this meal occupied a considerable time, the shades of evening had by this time fallen upon the quiet city ; the silver moon lighted up the bay, and, supported by a numerous and well-appointed train of gas-lamps, illuminated the streets of a town, —of autumn eves so crowded and so gay ; of gusty April nights, so desolate. At this still hour (it might be half-past seven) two ladies passed the gates of "Wright's Hotel," "in shrouding mantle wrapped, and velvet cap." Up the deserted High Street toiled they, by gaping rows of empty bathing-houses, by melancholy Jolly's French bazaar, by mouldy pastrycooks, blank reading-rooms, by fishmongers who never sold a fish, mercers who vended not a yard of ribbon—because, as yet, the season was not come,—and Jews and Cockneys still remained in town. At High Street's corner, near to Hawley Square, they passed the house of Mr. Fincham, chemist, who doth not only healthful drugs supply, but likewise sells cigars—the worst cigars that ever mortal man gave threepence for.

Up to this point, I say, I have had a right to accompany the fat lady and Miss Runt ; but whether, on arriving at Mr. Fincham's, they turned to the left, in the direction of the "Royal Hotel," or to the right, by the beach, the bathing-machines, and queer rickety old row of houses, called Buenos Ayres, no power on earth shall induce me to say ; suffice it, they went to Mrs. Gann's. Why should we set all the world gadding to a particular street, to know where that lady lives ? They arrived before that lady's house at about eight o'clock. Every house in the street had bills on it except hers (bitter mockery, as if anybody came down at Easter !) and at Mrs. Gann's house there was a light in the garret, and another in the two-pair front. I believe I have not mentioned before, that all the front windows were bow or bay-windows ; but so much the reader may know.

The two ladies, who had walked so far, examined wistfully the plate on the door, stood on the steps for a short time, re-treated, and conversed with one another.

"Oh, Runty !" said the stouter of the two, "he's here—I know he's here, mong cure le dee—my heart tells me so." And she put a large hand upon a place on her left side, where there once had been a waist.

"Do you think he looks front or back, dear?" asked Runt. "P'raps he's not at home."

"That—that's his croisy," said the stout person ; "I know

it is ; " and she pointed with instinctive justice to the two-pair. "Ecouty ! " she added, "he's coming ; there's some one at that window. Oh, mong jew, mong jew ! c'est André, c'est lui ! "

The moon was shining full on the face of the bow-windows of Mrs. Gann's house ; and the two fair spies, who were watching on the other side, were, in consequence, completely in shadow. As the lady said, a dark form was seen in the two-pair front ; it paced the room for a while, for no blinds were drawn. It then flung itself on a chair ; its head on its hands ; it then began to beat its brows wildly, and paced the room again. Ah ! how the fat lady's heart throbbed as she looked at all this !

She gave a piercing shriek — almost fainted! and little Runt's knee's trembled under her, as with all her might she supported, or rather pushed up, the falling figure of her stout patroness,—who saw at that instant Fitch come to the candle with an immense pistol in his hand, and give a most horrible grin as he looked at it, and clasped it to his breast.

"Unhand me, Runt ; he's going to kill himself ! It's for me ! I know it is—I will go to him ! Andrea, my Andrea ! " And the fat lady was pushing for the opposite side of the way, when suddenly the second-floor window went clattering up, and Fitch's pale head was thrust out.

He had heard a scream, and had possibly been induced to open the window in consequence ; but by the time he had opened it he had forgotten everything, and put his head vacantly out of the window, and gazed, the moon shining cold on his pale features.

"Pallid horb ! " said Fitch, "shall I ever see thy light again ? Will another night see me on this hearth, or view me, stark and cold, a lifeless corpse? He took his pistol up, and slowly aimed it at a chimney-pot opposite. Fancy the fat lady's sensations, as she beheld her lover standing in the moonlight, and exercising this deadly weapon.

"Make ready—present—fire ! " shouted Fitch, and did instantaneously, not fire off, but lower his weapon. " The bolt of death is sped ! " continued he, clapping his hand on his side. "The poor painter's life is over ! Caroline, Caroline, I die for thee ! "

"Runt, Runt, I told you so ! " shrieked the fat lady. " He is dying for me, and Caroline's my second name."

What the fat lady would have done more, I can't say ; for Fitch, disturbed out of his reverie by her talking below, looked out, trowning vacantly, and saying, "Ulloh! we've hinterlopers 'ere!" suddenly banged down the window, and pulled down the blinds.

This gave a check to the fat lady's projected rush, and disconcerted her a little. But she was consoled by Miss Runt, promised to return on the morrow, and went home happy in the idea that her Andrea was faithful to her.

Alas, poor fat lady! little did you know the truth. It was Caroline Gann Fitch was raving about; and it was a part of his last letter to her, to be delivered after his death, that he was spouting out of the window.

Was the crazy painter going to fight a duel, or was he going to kill himself? This will be explained in the next chapter.

CHAPTER VIII.

WHICH TREATS OF WAR AND LOVE, AND MANY THINGS THAT ARE NOT TO BE UNDERSTOOD IN CHAP. VII.

FITCH'S verses, inserted in a previous chapter of this story, (and of which lines, by the way, the printer managed to make still greater nonsense than the ingenious bard ever designed,) had been composed many years before; and it was with no small trouble and thought that the young painter called the greater part of them to memory again, and furbished up a copy for Caroline's album. Unlike the love of most men, Andrea's passion was not characterized by jealousy and watchfulness, otherwise he would not have failed to perceive certain tokens of intelligence passing from time to time between Caroline and Brandon, and the lady's evident coldness to himself. The fact is, the painter was in love with being in love,—entirely absorbed in the consideration of the fact that he, Andrea Fitch, was at last enamored; and he did not mind his mistress much more than Don Quixote did Dulcinea del Toboso.

Having rubbed up his verses, then, and designed a pretty emblematical outline which was to surround them, representing an arabesque of violets, dewdrops, fairies, and other objects, he came down one morning, drawing in hand; and having informed Caroline, who was sitting very melancholy in the parlor, preoccupied, with a pale face and red eyes, and not caring twopence for the finest drawing in the world,—having informed her that he was going to make in her halbum a humble hoffering of his hart, poor Fitch was just on the point of sticking in the draw-ing with gum, as painters know very well how to do, when his eye lighted upon a page of the album, in which nestled a few dried violets and—his own verses, signed with the name of George Brandon.

"Miss Caroline—Miss Gann, mam!" shrieked Fitch, in a tone of voice which made the young lady start out of a profound reverie, and cry, nervously,—"What in heaven is the matter?"

"These verses, madam—a faded violet—word for word, gracious 'eavens! every word!" roared Fitch, advancing with the book.

She looked at him rather vacantly, and as the violets caught her eye, put out her hand, and took them. "Do you know the hawthor, Miss Gann, of 'The faded Violets?'"

"Author? O yes; they are—they are George's!" She burst into tears as she said that word; and, pulling the little faded flowers to pieces, went sobbing out of the room.

Dear, dear little Caroline! she has only been in love two months, and is already beginning to feel the woes of it!

It cannot be from want of experience—for I have felt the noble passion of love many times these forty years, since I was a boy of twelve (by which the reader may form a pretty good guess of my age),—it cannot be, I say, from want of experience that I am unable to describe, step by step the progress of a love-affair; nay, I am perfectly certain that I could, if I chose, make a most astonishing and heart-rending *liber amoris;* but, nevertheless, I always feel a vast repugnance to the following out of a subject of this kind, which I attribute to a natural diffidence and sense of shame that prevent me from enlarging on a theme that has in it something sacred—certain arcana which an honest man, although initiated into them, should not divulge.

If such coy scruples and blushing delicacy prevent one from passing the threshold even of an honorable love, and setting down, at so many guineas or shillings per page, the pious emo-tions and tenderness of two persons chastely and legally en-gaged in sighing, ogling, hand-squeezing, kissing, and so forth (for with such outward signs I believe that the passion of love is expressed),—if a man feel, I say, squeamish about describing an innocent love, he is doubly disinclined to describe a guilty one; and I have always felt a kind of loathing for the skill of such geniuses as Rousseau or Richardson, who could paint with such painful accuracy all the struggles and woes of Eloise and Clarissa,—all the wicked arts and triumphs of such scoundrels as Lovelace.

We have in this history a scoundrelly Lovelace in the person going by the name of George Brandon, and a dear, tender, innocent, yielding creature on whom he is practising his infernal skill ; and whether the public feel any sympathy for her or not, the writer can only say, for his part, that he heartily loves and respects poor little Caroline, and is quite unwilling to enter into any of the slow, painful, wicked details of the courtship which passed between her and her lover.

Not that there was any wickedness on *her* side, poor girl ! or that she did anything but follow the natural and beautiful impulses of an honest little female heart, that leads it to trust and love, and worship a being of the other sex, whom the eager fancy invests with all sorts of attributes of superiority. There was no wild, conceited tale that Brandon told Caroline which she did not believe,—no virtue which she could conceive or had read of in novels with which she did not endow him. Many long talks had they, and many sweet, stolen interviews, during the periods in which Caroline's father and mother were away making merry at the house of their son-in-law ; and while she was left under the care of her virtue and of Becky the maid. Indeed, it was a blessing that the latter was left in the joint guardianship. For Becky, who had such an absurd opinion of her young lady's merit as to fancy that she was a fit wife for any gentleman of the land, and that any gentleman might be charmed and fall in love with her, had some instinct, or possibly some experience, as to the passions and errors of youth, and warned Caroline accordingly. " If he's really in love, Miss, and I think he be, he'll marry you ; if he won't marry you, he's a rascal, and you're too good for him, and must have nothing to do with him." To which Caroline replied, that she was sure Mr. Brandon was the most angelic, high-principled of human beings, and that she was sure his intentions were of the most honorable description.

We have before described what Mr. Brandon's character was. He was not a man of honorable intentions at all. But he was a gentlemen of so excessively eager a temperament, that if properly resisted by a practised coquette, or by a woman of strong principles, he would sacrifice anything to obtain his ends, —nay, marry to obtain them ; and, consider his disposition, it is only a wonder that he had not been married a great number of times already ; for he had been in love perpetually since his seventeenth year. By which the reader may pretty well appreciate the virtue or the prudence of the ladies with whom hitherto our inflammable young gentleman had had to do.

The fruit, then, of all his stolen interviews, of all his prayers, vows, and protestations to Caroline, had been only this,—that she loved him ; but loved him as an honest girl should, and was ready to go to the altar with him when he chose. He talked about his family, his peculiar circumstances, his proud father's curse. Little Caroline only sighed, and said her dearest George must wait until he could obtain his parent's consent. When pressed harder, she would burst into tears, and wonder how one so good and affectionate as he could propose to her anything unworthy of them both. It is clear to see that the young lady had read a vast number of novels, and knew something of the nature of love ; and that she had a good principle and honesty in her own, which set her lover's schemes at naught : indeed, she had both these advantages,—her education, such as it was, having given her the one, and her honest nature having endowed her with the other.

On the day when Fitch came down to Caroline with his verses, Brandon had pressed these unworthy propositions upon her. She had torn herself violently away from him, and rushed to the door ; but the poor little thing fell before she could reach it, screaming in a fit of hysterics, which brought Becky to her aid, and caused Brandon to leave her, abashed. He went out ; she watched him go, and stole up into his room, and laid on his table the first letter she had ever written to him. It was written in pencil, in a trembling, school-girl hand, and contained simply the following words :—

"George, you have almost broken my heart. Leave me if you will, and if you dare not act like an honest man. If ever you speak to me so again as you did this morning, I declare solemnly before heaven, I will take poison.

"C."

Indeed, the poor thing had read romances to some purpose ; without them, it is probable, she never would have thought of such a means of escape from a lover's persecutions ; and there was something in the girl's character that made Brandon feel sure that she would keep her promise. How the words agitated him ! He felt a violent mixture of raging disappointment and admiration, and loved the girl ten thousand times more than ever.

Mr. Brandon had scarcely finished the reading of this document, and was yet agitated by the various passions which the perusal of it created, when the door of his apartment was

violently flung open, and some one came in. Brandon started,
and turned round, with a kind of dread that Caroline had
already executed her threat, and that a messenger was come to
inform him of her death. Mr. Andrea Fitch was the intruder.
His hat was on—his eyes were glaring ; and if the beards of
men did stand on end anywhere but in poems and romances,
his, no doubt, would have formed round his countenance a
bristling auburn halo. As it was, Fitch only looked astonishingly fierce, as he stalked up to the table, his hands behind his
back. When he had arrived at this barrier between himself
and Mr. Brandon, he stopped, and, speechless, stared that
gentleman in the face.

"May I beg, Mr. Fitch, to know what has procured me the
honor of this visit ? " exclaimed Mr. Brandon, after a brief
pause of wonder.

"Honor !—ha, ha, ha ! " growled Mr. Fitch, in a most
sardonic, discordant way—"*honor !*"

"Well, sir, honor or no honor, I can tell you, my good man,
it certainly is no pleasure ! " said Brandon, testily. "In plain
English, then, what the devil has brought you here ? "

Fitch plumped the album down on the table close to Mr.
Brandon's nose, and said, " *That* has brought me, sir—that halbum, sir ; or, I ask your pardon, that a—album—ha, ha, ha ! "

"Oh, I see ! " said Mr. Brandon, who could not refrain from
a smile. "It was a cruel trick of mine, Fitch, to rob you of
your verses ; but all's fair in love."

"Fitch, sir ! don't Fitch me, sir ! I wish to be hintimate
honly with men of h-honor, not with forgers, sir ; not with
'artless miscreants ! Miscreants, sir, I repeat ; vipers, sir ;
b—b—b—blackguards, sir ! "

"Blackguards, sir ! " roared Mr. Brandon, bouncing up ;
"blackguards, you dirty cockney mountebank ! Quit the room,
sir, or I'll fling you out of the window ! "

"Will you, sir ? try, sir ; I wish you may get it, sir. I'm a
hartist, sir, and as good a man as you. Miscreant, forger,
traitor, come on ! "

And Mr. Brandon *would* have come on, but for a circumstance that deterred him ; and this was, that Mr. Fitch drew
from his bosom a long, sharp, shining, waving poniard of the
middle ages, that formed a part of his artistical properties, and
with which he had armed himself for this encounter.

"Come on, sir ! " shrieked Fitch, brandishing this fearful
weapon. "Lay a finger on me, and I bury this blade in your
treacherous 'art. Ha ! do you tremble ? "

Indeed, the aristocratic Mr. Brandon turned somewhat pale.

"Well, well," said he, "what do you want? Do you suppose I am to be bullied by your absurd melodramatic airs! It was, after all, but a joke, sir, and I am sorry that it has offended you. Can I say more?—what shall I do?"

"You shall hapologize; not only to me, sir, but you shall tell Miss Caroline, in my presence, that you stole those verses from me, and used them quite unauthorized by me."

"Look you, Mr. Fitch, I will make you another set of verses quite as good, if you like; but what you ask is impossible."

"I will 'asten myself, then, to Miss Caroline, and acquaint her with your dastardly forgery, sir. I will hopen her heyes, sir!"

"You may hopen her heyes, as you call them, if you please: but I tell you fairly, that the young lady will credit me rather than you; and if you swear ever so much that the verses are yours, I must say that——"

"Say what, sir?"

"Say that you *lie*, sir!" said Mr. Brandon, stamping on the ground. "I'll make you other verses, I repeat; but this is all I can do, and now go about your business!"

"Curse your verses, sir! liar and forger yourself! Hare you a coward as well, sir? A coward! yes, I believe you are; or will you meet me to-morrow morning like a man, and give me satisfaction for this hinfamous hinsult?"

"Sir," said Mr. Brandon, with the utmost stateliness and scorn, "If you wish to murder me as you do the king's English, I won't balk you. Although a man of my rank is not called upon to meet a blackguard of your condition, I will, nevertheless, grant you your will. But have a care; by heavens, I won't spare you, and I can hit an ace of hearts at twenty paces!"

"Two can play at that," said Mr. Fitch, calmly; "and if I can't hit a hace of 'arts at twenty paces, I can hit a man at twelve, and to-morrow I'll try." With which, giving Mr. Brandon a look of the highest contempt, the young painter left the room.

What were Mr. Brandon's thoughts as his antagonist left him? Strange to say, rather agreeable. He had much too great a contempt for Fitch to suppose that so low a fellow would ever think seriously of fighting him, and reasoned with himself thus:—

"This Fitch, I know, will go off to Caroline, tell her the whole transaction, frighten her with the tale of a duel, and then she and I shall have a scene. I will tell her the truth about those infernal verses, menace death, blood, and danger, and then——"

Here he fell back into a charming reverie ; the wily fellow knew what power such a circumstance would give him over a poor weak girl, who would do anything rather than that her beloved should risk his life. And with this dastardly speculation as to the price he should ask for refraining from meeting Fitch, he was entertaining himself ; when, much to his annoyance, that gentleman again came into the room.

"Mr. Brandon," said he, "you have insulted me in the grossest and cruellest way."

"Well, sir, are you come to apologize?" said Brandon sneeringly.

"No, I'm not come to apologize, Mr. Aristocrat : it's past that. I'm come to say this, sir, that I take you for a coward ; and that, unless you will give me your solemn word of honor not to mention a word of this quarrel to Miss Gann, which might prevent our meeting, I will never leave you till we *do* fight!"

"This is outrageous, sir! Leave the room, or by heavens I'll not meet you at all!"

"Heasy, sir ; easy I beg your pardon, I can force you to that!"

"And how, pray, sir?"

"Why, in the first place, here's a stick, and I'll 'orsewhip you ; and here are a pair of pistols, and we can fight now!"

"Well, sir, I give you my honor," said Mr. Brandon, in a diabolical rage ; and added, "I'll meet you to-morrow, not now ; and you need not be afraid that I'll miss you!"

"Hadew, sir," said the chivalrous little Fitch ; "bon giorno, sir, as we used to say at Rome." And so, for the second time, he left Mr. Brandon, who did not like very well the extraordinary courage he had displayed.

"What the deuce has exasperated the fellow so?" thought Brandon.

Why, in the first place, he had crossed Fitch in love ; and, in the second, he had sneered at his pronunciation and his gentility, and Fitch's little soul was in a fury which nothing but blood would allay : he was determined, for the sake of his hart and his lady, to bring this proud champion down.

So Brandon was at last left to his cogitations ; when, confusion! about five o'clock came another knock at his door.

"Come in!" growled the owner of the lodgings.

A sallow, blear-eyed, rickety, undersized creature, tottering upon a pair of high-heeled lacquered boots, and supporting himself upon an immense gold-knobbed cane, entered the room with his hat on one side and a jaunty air. It was a white hat with a broad brim, and under it fell a great deal of greasy lank hair, that shrouded the cheek-bones of the wearer. The little man had no beard to his chin, appeared about twenty years of age, and might weigh, stick and all, some seven stone. If you wish to know how this exquisite was dressed, I have the pleasure to inform you that he wore a great sky-blue embroidered satin stock, in the which figured a carbuncle that looked like a lambent gooseberry. He had a shawl-waistcoat of many colors ; a pair of loose blue trousers, neatly strapped to show his little feet : a brown cut-away coat with brass buttons, that fitted tight round a spider waist ; and over all a white or drab surtout, with a sable collar and cuffs, from which latter on each hand peeped five little fingers covered with lemon-colored kid gloves. One of these hands he held constantly to his little chest : and, with a hoarse thin voice, he piped out,

"George, my buck ! how goes it ? "

We have been thus particular in our description of the costume of this individual (whose inward man strongly corresponded with his manly and agreeable exterior), because he was the person whom Mr. Brandon most respected in the world.

"CINQBARS ! " exclaimed our hero ; "why, what the deuce has brought you to Margate ? "

"Fwendship, my old cock ! " said the Honorable Augustus Frederick Ringwood, commonly called Viscount Cinqbars, for indeed it was he. "Fwendship and the *City of Canterbuwy* steamer ! " and herewith his lordship held out his right-hand forefinger to Brandon, who enclosed it most cordially in all his. "Wathn't it good of me, now, George, to come down and conthole you in thith curthed, thtupid place—hay, now ? " said my lord, after these salutations.

Brandon swore he was very glad to see him, which was very true, for he had no sooner set his eyes upon his lordship, than he had determined to borrow as much money from him as ever he could induce the young nobleman to part with.

"I'll tell you how it wath, my boy : you thee I wath thtopping at Long'th, when I found, by Jove, that the governor wath come to town ! Cuth me I if didn't meet the infarnal old family dwag, with my mother, thithterth, and all, ath I wath dwiving a hack-cab with Polly Tomkinth in the Pawk ! Tho when I got home, 'Hang it!' thayth I to Tufthunt, 'Tom, my boy,' thaith I, 'I've just theen the governor, and must be off!' 'What, back to Ockthford?' thaith Tom. 'No,' thaith I, 'that *won't* do. Abroad—to Jewicho—anywhere. Egad, I have it. I'll go down to Margate and thee old George, that I will.' And tho off I came the very next day; and here I am, and thereth dinner waiting for uth at the hotel, and thixth bottleth of champagne in ithe, and thum thalmon: tho you mutht come."

To this proposition Mr. Brandon readily agreed, being glad enough of the prospect of a good dinner and some jovial society, for he was low and disturbed in spirits, and so promised to dine with his friend at the "Sun."

The two gentlemen conversed for some time longer. Mr. Brandon was a shrewd fellow, and knew perfectly well a fact of which, no doubt, the reader has a notion—namely, that Lord Cinqbars was a ninny; but, nevetheless, Brandon esteemed him highly as a lord. We pardon stupidity in lords; nature or instinct, however sarcastic a man may be among ordinary persons, renders him towards men of quality benevolently blind; a divinity hedges not only the king, but the whole peerage.

"That's the girl, I suppose," said my lord, knowingly winking at Brandon: "that little pale girl, who let me in, I mean. A nice little filly, upon my honor, Georgy my buck!"

"Oh—that—yes—I wrote, I think, something about her," said Brandon, blushing slightly; for, indeed, he now began to wish that his friend should make no comments upon a young lady with whom he was so much in love.

"I suppose it's all up now?" continued my lord, looking still more knowing. "All over with her, hay? I saw it was by her looks, in a minute."

"Indeed you do me a great deal too much honor. Miss— ah,—Miss Gann is a very respectable young person, and I would not for the world have you to suppose that I would do anything that should the least injure her character."

At this speech, Lord Cinqbars was at first much puzzled; but, in considering it, was fully convinced that Brandon was a deeper dog than ever. Boiling with impatience to know the particulars of this delicate intrigue, this cunning diplomatist determined he would pump the whole story out of Brandon by degrees; and so, in the course of half an hour's conversation that the young men had together, Cinqbars did not make less than forty allusions to the subject that interested him. At last Brandon cut him short rather haughtily, by begging that he

would make no further allusions to the subject, as it was one
that was excessively disagreeable to him.

"In fact, there was no mistake about it now. George
Brandon was in love with Caroline. He felt that he was while
he blushed at his friend's alluding to her, while he grew indignant at the young lord's coarse banter about her.

Turning the conversation to another point, he asked Cinqbars about his voyage, and whether he had brought any companion with him to Margate; whereupon my lord related all
his feats in London, how he had been to the watch-house, how
many bottles of champagne he had drunk, how he had "milled"
a policeman, &c., &c.; and he concluded by saying that he had
come down with Tom Tufthunt, who was at the inn at that very
moment smoking a cigar.

This did not increase Brandon's good-humor; and when
Cinqbars mentioned his friend's name, Brandon saluted it mentally with a hearty curse. These two gentlemen hated each
other of old. Tufthunt was a small college man of no family,
with a foundation fellowship; and it used to be considered that
a sporting fellow of a small college was a sad, raffish, disreputable character. Tufthunt, then, was a vulgar fellow, and Brandon a gentleman, so they hated each other. They were both
toadies of the same nobleman, so they hated each other. They
had had some quarrel at college about a disputed bet, which
Brandon knew he owed, and so they hated each other; and in
their words about it Brandon had threatened to horsewhip Tufthunt, and called him a "sneaking, swindling, small college
snob;" and so little Tufthunt, who had not resented the words,
hated Brandon far more than Brandon hated him. The latter
only had a contempt for his rival, and voted him a profound
bore and vulgarian.

So, although Mr. Tufthunt did not choose to frequent Mr.
Brandon's rooms, he was very anxious that his friend, the young
lord, should not fall into his old bear-leader's hands again, and
came down to Margate to counteract any influence which the
arts of Brandon might acquire.

"Curse the fellow!" thought Tufthunt in his heart (there
was a fine reciprocity of curses between the two men); "he has
drawn Cinqbars already for fifty pounds this year, and will have
some half of his last remittance, if I don't keep a look-out, the
swindling thief!"

And so frightened was Tufthunt at the notion of Brandon's
return to power and dishonest use of it, that he was at the
time on the point of writing to Lord Ringwood to tell him of

his son's doings, only he wanted some money deucedly himself. Of Mr. Tufthunt's *physique* and history it is necessary merely to say, that he was the son of a country attorney who was agent to a lord ; he had been sent to a foundation-school, where he distinguished himself for ten years, by fighting and being flogged more than any boy of the five hundred. From the foundation-school he went to college with an exhibition, which was succeeded by a fellowship, which was to end in a living. In his person Mr. Tufthunt was short and bow-legged ; he wore a sort of clerico-sporting costume, consisting of a black straight-cut coat and light drab breeches, with a vast number of buttons at the ankles ; a sort of dress much affectioned by sporting gentlemen of the university in the author's time.

Well, Brandon said he had some letters to write, and promised to follow his friend, which he did ; but, if the truth must be told, so infatuated was the young man become with his passion, with the resistance he had met with, and so nervous from the various occurrences of the morning, that he passed the half hour during which he was free from Cinqbars' society in kneeling, imploring, weeping at Caroline's little garret door, which had remained piteously closed to him. He was wild with disappointment, mortification—mad, longing to see her. The cleverest coquette in Europe could not have so inflamed him. His first act on entering the dinner-room was to drink off a large tumbler of champagne ; and when Cinqbars, in his elegant way, began to rally him upon his wildness, Mr. Brandon only growled and cursed with frightful vehemency, and applied again to the bottle. His face, which had been quite white, grew a bright red ; his tongue, which had been tied, began to chatter vehemently ; before the fish was off the table, Mr. Brandon showed strong symptoms of intoxication ; before the dessert appeared, Mr. Tufthunt, winking knowingly to Lord Cinqbars, had begun to draw him out ; and Brandon, with a number of shrieks and oaths, was narrating the history of his attachment.

"Look you, Tufthunt," said he, wildly ; "hang you, I hate you, but I *must* talk ! I've been, for two months now, in this cursed hole ; in a rickety lodging, with a vulgar family ; as vulgar, by Jove, as you are yourself ! "

Mr. Tufthunt did not like this style of address half so much as Lord Cinqbars, who was laughing immoderately, and to whom Tufthunt whispered rather sheepishly, " Pooh, pooh, he's drunk ! "

" *Drunk!* no, sir," yelled out Brandon ; " I'm mad, though, with the prudery of a little devil of fifteen, who has cost me

more trouble than it would take me to seduce every one of
your sisters—ha, ha! every one of the Miss Tufthunts, by Jove!
Miss Suky Tufthunt, Miss Dolly Tufthunt, Miss Anna-Maria
Tufthunt, and the whole bunch.   Come, sir, don't sit scowling
at *me*, or I'll brain you with the decanter." (Tufthunt was
down again on the sofa.)   " I've borne with the girl's mother,
and her father, and her sisters, and a cook in the house, and a
scoundrel of a painter, that I'm going to fight about her; and
for what?—why, for a letter, which says, ' George, I'll kill myself!   George, I'll kill myself!'—ha, ha! a little devil like that
killing herself—ha, ha! and I—I who—who adore her, who am
mad for——"

" Mad, I believe he is," said Tufthunt; and at this moment
Mr. Brandon was giving the most unequivocal signs of madness; he plunged his head into the corner of the sofa, and was
kicking his feet violently into the cushions.

" You don't understand him, Tufty, my boy," said Lord
Cinqbars, with a very superior air.   "You ain't up to these
things, I tell you; and I suspect, by Jove, that you never were
in love in your life.   *I* know what it is, sir.   And as for Brandon, heaven bless you!   I've often seen him in that way when
we were abroad.   When he has an intrigue, he's mad about it.
Let us see, there was the Countess Fritzch, at Baden-Baden;
there was the woman at Pau; and that girl at Paris, was it?—
no, at Vienna.   He went on just so about them all; but I'll tell
you what, when *we* do the thing, we do it easier, my boy, hay?"

And so saying, my lord cocked up his little sallow, beardless
face into a grin, and then fell to eyeing a glass of execrable
claret across a candle.   *An intrigue*, as he called it, was the
little creature's delight; and until the time should arrive when
he could have one himself, he loved to talk of those of his friends.

As for Tufthunt, we may fancy how that gentleman's
previous affection for Brandon was increased by the latter's
brutal addresses to him.   Brandon continued to drink and to
talk, though not always in the sentimental way in which he had
spoken about his loves and injuries.   Growing presently madly
jocose as he had before been madly melancholy, he narrated to
the two gentlemen the particulars of his quarrel with Fitch,
mimicking the little painter's manner in an excessively comic
way, and giving the most ludicrous account of his person, kept
his companions in a roar of laughter.   Cinqbars swore that
he would see the fun in the morning, and agreed that if the
painter wanted a second, either he or Tufthunt would act for
him.

Now my Lord Cinqbars had an excessively clever servant, a merry rogue, whom he had discovered in the humble capacity of scout's assistant at Christchurch, and raised to be his valet. The chief duties of the valet were to black his lord's beautiful boots, that we have admired so much, and put his lordship to bed when overtaken with liquor. He heard every word of the young men's talk (it being his habit, much encouraged by his master, to join occasionally in the conversation) ; and in the course of the night, when at supper with Monsieur Donnerwetter and Mdlle. Augustine, he related every word of the talk above stairs, mimicking Brandon quite as cleverly as the latter had mimicked Fitch. When then, after making his company laugh by describing Brandon's love-agonies, Mr. Tom informed them how that gentleman had a rival, with whom he was going to fight a duel the next morning—an artist-fellow with an immense beard, whose name was Fitch, to his surprize Mdlle. Augustine burst into a scream of laughter, and exclaimed, " *Feesh, Feesh ! c'est notre homme ;*—it is our man, sare ! Saladin, remember you Mr. Fish ? "

Saladin said gravely, " Missa Fis, Missa Fis ! know 'um quite well, Missa Fis ! Painter-man, big beard, gib Saladin bit injyrubby, Missus lub Missa Fis ! "

It was too true, the fat lady was the famous MRS. CARRICK-FERGUS, and she had come all the way from Rome in pursuit of her adored painter.

CHAPTER IX.

WHICH THREATENS DEATH, BUT CONTAINS A GREAT DEAL OF MARRYING.

As the morrow was to be an eventful day in the lives of all the heroes and heroines of this history, it will be as well to state how they passed the night previous. Brandon, like the English before the battle of Hastings, spent the evening in feasting and carousing ; and Lord Cinqbars, at twelve o'clock, his usual time after his usual quantity of drink, was carried up to bed by the servant kept by his lordship for that purpose. Mr. Tufthunt took this as a hint to wish Brandon good-night, at the same time promising that he and Cinqbars would not fail him in the morning about the duel.

Shall we confess that Mr. Brandon, whose excitement now began to wear off, and who had a dreadful headache, did not at all relish the idea of the morrow's combat.

"If," said he, "I shoot this crack-brained painter, all the world will cry out, 'Murder!' If he shoot me, all the world will laugh at me! And yet, confound him! he seems so bent upon blood, that there is no escaping a meeting."

"At any rate," Brandon thought, "there will be no harm in a letter to Caroline." So, on arriving at home, he sat down and wrote a very pathetic one; saying that he fought in her cause, and if he died, his last breath should be for her. So having written, he jumped into bed, and did not sleep one single wink all night.

As Brandon passed his night like the English, Fitch went through his like the Normans, in fasting, and mortification, and meditation. The poor fellow likewise indited a letter to Caroline : a very long and strong one, interspersed with pieces of poetry, and containing the words we have just heard him utter out of the window. Then he thought about making his will; but he recollected, and, indeed, it was a bitter thought to the young man, that there was not one single soul in the wide world cared for him—except, indeed, thought he, after a pause, that poor Mrs. Carrickfergus at Rome, who *did* like me, and was the only person who ever bought my drawings. So he made over all his sketches to her, regulated his little property, found that he had money enough to pay his washer-woman ; and so, having disposed of his worldly concerns, Mr. Fitch also jumped into bed, and speedily fell into a deep sleep. Brandon could hear him snoring all night, and did not feel a bit the more comfortable because his antagonist took matters so unconcernedly.

Indeed, our poor painter had no guilty thoughts in his breast, nor any particular revenge against Brandon, now that the first pangs of mortified vanity were over. But, with all his vagaries, he was a man of spirit ; and after what had passed in the morning, the treason that had been done him, and the insults heaped upon him, he felt that the duel was irrevocable. He had a misty notion, imbibed somewhere, that it was the part of a gentleman's duty to fight duels, and had long been seeking for an opportunity. "Suppose I do die," said he, "what's the odds? Caroline doesn't care for me. Dr. Wackerbart's boys won't have their drawing-lesson next Wednesday ; and no more will be said of poor Andrea."

And now for the garret. Caroline was wrapped up in her own woes, poor little soul ! and in the arms of the faithful

Becky cried herself to sleep. But the slow hours passed on and the tide, which had been out, now came in ; and the lamps waxed fainter and fainter ; and the watchman cried six o'clock ; and the sun arose and gilded the minarets of Margate ; and Becky got up and scoured the steps, and kitchen, and made ready the lodgers' breakfasts ; and at half-past eight there came a thundering rap at the door, and two gentlemen, one with a mahogany case under his arm, asked for Mr. Brandon, and were shown up to his room by the astonished Becky, who was bidden by Mr. Brandon to get breakfast for three.

The thundering rap awakened Mr. Fitch, who rose and dressed himself in his best clothes, gave a twist of the curling-tongs to his beard, and conducted himself throughout with perfect coolness. Nine o'clock struck, and he wrapped his cloak round him, and put under his cloak that pair of foils which we have said he possessed, and did not know in the least how to use. However, he had heard his *camarades d'atelier*, at Paris and Rome, say that they were the best weapons for duelling ; and so forth he issued.

Becky was in the passage as he passed down ; she was always scrubbing there. " Becky," said Fitch, in a hollow voice, " here is a letter ; if I should not return in half an hour, give it to Miss Gann, and promise on your honor that she shall not have it sooner." Becky promised. She thought the painter was at some of his mad tricks. He went out of the door sa luting her gravely.

But he went only a few steps and came back again. " Becky," said he, " you—you've always been a good girl to me, and here's something for you ; per'aps we sha'n't—we sha'n't see each other for some time." The tears were in his eyes as he spoke, and he handed her over seven shillings and four-pence halfpenny, being every farthing he possessed in the world.

" Well, I'm sure ! " said Becky ; and that was all she said, for she pocketed the money, and fell to scrubbing again.

Presently the three gentlemen up stairs came clattering down. " Lock bless you, don't be in such a 'urry ! " exclaimed Becky ; " it's full herly yet, and the water's not biling."

" We'll come back to breakfast, my dear," said one, a little gentleman in high-heeled boots ; " and, I thay, mind and have thum thoda-water." And he walked out, twirling his cane. His friend with the case followed him. Mr. Brandon came last.

He too turned back after he had gone a few paces. " Becky,"

said he, in a grave voice, "if I am not back in half-an-hour, give that to Miss Gann."

Becky was fairly flustered by this ; and after turning the letters round and round, and peeping into the sides, and looking at the seals very hard, she like a fool determined that she would not wait half-an-hour, but carry them up to Miss Caroline ; and so up she mounted, finding pretty Caroline in the act of lacing her stays.

And the consequences of Becky's conduct was that little Carry left off lacing her stays (a sweet little figure the poor thing looked in them ; but that is neither here nor there), took the letters, looked at one which she threw down directly ; at the other, which she eagerly opened, and having read a line or two, gave a loud scream, and fell down dead in a fainting fit !

    *   *   *   *   *

Waft us, O Muse ! to Mr. Wright's hotel, and quick narrate what chances there befel. Very early in the morning Mdlle. Augustine made her appearance in the apartment of Miss Runt, and with great glee informed the lady of the event which was about to take place. "Figurez-vous, mademoiselle, que notre homme va se battre—oh, but it will be droll to see him sword in hand ! "

"Don't plague me with your ojous servants' quarrels, Augustine ; that horrid courier is always quarrelling and tipsy."

"Mon Dieu, qu'elle est bête ! " exclaimed Augustine : "but I tell you it is not the courier ; it is he, l'objet, le peintre dont madame s'est amourachée, Monsieur Feesh."

"Mr. Fitch ! " cried Runt, jumping up in bed. "Mr. Fitch going to fight ! Augustine, my stockings—quick, my *robe-de-chambre*—tell me when, how, where ? "

And so Augustine told her that the combat was to take place at nine that morning, behind the Windmill, and that the gentleman with whom Mr. Fitch was to go out, had been dining at the hotel the night previous, in company with the little milor, who was to be his second.

Quick as lightning flew Runt to the chamber of her patroness. That lady was in a profound sleep ; and I leave you to imagine what were her sensations on awaking and hearing this dreadful tale.

Such is the force of love, that although, for many years, Mrs. Carrickfergus had never left her bed before noon, although in all her wild wanderings after the painter she, nevertheless, would have her tea and cutlet in bed, and her doze likewise, before she set forth on a journey—she now started up in an

instant, forgetting her nap, mutton-chops, everything, and began dressing with a promptitude which can only be equalled by
Harlequin when disguising himself in a pantomime. She would
have had an attack of nerves, only she knew there was no time
for it; and I do believe that twenty minutes were scarcely over
her head, as the saying is, when her bonnet and cloak were on,
and with her whole suite, and an inn-waiter or two whom she
pressed into her service, she was on full trot to the field of
action. For twenty years before, and from that to this, Marianne Carrickfergus never had or has walked so quickly.

  *   *   *   *   *

" Hullo, here'th a go !" exclaimed Lord Viscount Cinqbars,
as they arrived on the ground behind the Windmill; " cuth me
there'th only one man !"

This was indeed the case; Mr. Fitch, in his great cloak,
was pacing slowly up and down the grass, his shadow stretching far in the sunshine. Mr. Fitch was alone too; for the
fact is, he had never thought about a second. This he admitted
frankly, bowing with much majesty to the company as they
came up. " But that, gents," said he, " will make no difference,
I hope, nor prevent fair play from being done." And, flinging
off his cloak, he produced the foils, from which the buttons had
been taken off. He went up to Brandon, and was for offering
him one of the weapons, just as they do at the theatre. Brandon stepped back, rather abashed: Cinqbars looked posed;
Tufthunt delighted. " Ecod," said he, " I hope the bearded
fellow will give it him."

" Excuse me, sir," said Mr. Brandon ; " as the challenged
party, I demand pistols."

Mr. Fitch, with great presence of mind and gracefulness,
stuck the swords into the grass.

" Oh, pithtolth of courth," lisped my lord; and presently
called aside Tufthunt, to whom he whispered something in
great glee; to which Tufthunt objected at first, saying, " No,
d—— him, let him fight." " And your fellowship and living,
Tufty my boy?" interposed my lord; and then they walked
on. After a couple of minutes, during which Mr. Fitch was
employed in examining Mr. Brandon from the toe upwards to
the crown of his head, or hat, just as Mr. Widdicombe does
Mr. Cartlich, before those two gentlemen proceed to join in
combat on the boards of Astley's Amphitheatre (indeed poor
Fitch had no other standard of chivalry)—when Fitch had concluded this examination, of which Brandon did not know what

the deuce to make, Lord Cinqbars came back to the painter, and gave him a nod.

"Sir," said he, "as you have come unprovided with a second, I, with your leave, will act as one. My name is Cinqbars—Lord Cinqbars ; and though I had come to the ground to act as the friend of my friend here, Mr. Tufthunt will take that duty upon him ; and as it appears to me there can be no other end to this unhappy affair, we will proceed at once."

It is a marvel how Lord Cinqbars ever made such a gentlemanly speech. When Fitch heard that he was to have a lord for a second, he laid his hand on his chest, and vowed it was the greatest h-honor of his life, and was turning round to walk towards his ground, when my lord, gracefully thrusting his tongue into his cheek, and bringing his thumb up to his nose, twiddled about his fingers for a moment, and said to Brandon, "Gammon ! "

Mr. Brandon smiled, and heaved a great, deep, refreshing sigh. The truth was, a great load was taken off his mind, of which he was very glad to be rid ; for there was something in the coolness of that crazy painter that our fashionable gentleman did not at all approve of.

"I think, Mr. Tufthunt," said Lord Cinqbars, very loud, "that considering the gravity of the case—threatening horse-whipping, you know, lie on both sides, and lady in the case—I think we must have the barrier-duel."

"What's that ? " asked Fitch.

"The simplest thing in the world ; and," in a whisper, "let me add, the best for you. Look here. We shall put you at twenty paces, and a hat between you. You walk forward and fire when you like. When you fire, you stop ; and you both have the liberty of walking up to the hat. Nothing can be more fair than that."

"Very well," said Fitch ; and, with a great deal of preparation, the pistols were loaded.

"I tell you what," whispered Cinqbars to Fitch, "if I hadn't chosen this way you were a dead man. If he fires he hits you dead. You must not let him fire, but have him down first."

"I'll try," said Fitch, who was a little pale, and thanked his noble friend for his counsel. The hat was placed and the men took their places.

"Are you all ready ? "

"Ready," said Brandon.

"Advance when I drop my handkerchief. And presently down it fell. Lord Cinqbars crying, " Now ! "

The combatants both advanced, each covering his man.
When he had gone six paces, Fitch stopped, fired, and—missed.
He grasped his pistol tightly, for he was very near dropping it;
and then stood biting his lips, and looking at Brandon, who
grinned savagely, and walked up to the hat.

" Will you retract what you said of me yesterday, you
villain ? " said Brandon.

" I can't."

" Will you beg for life ? "

" No."

" Then take a minute, and make your peace with God, for
you are a dead man."

Fitch dropped his pistol to the ground, shut his eyes for a
moment, and flinging up his chest and clenching his fists, said,
" *Now I'm ready.*"

Brandon *fired*—and strange to say, Andrea Fitch, as he
gasped and staggered backwards, saw, or thought he saw, Mr.
Brandon's pistol flying up in the air, where it went off, and
heard that gentleman yell out an immense oath in a very
audible voice. When he came to himself, a thick stick was
lying at Brandon's feet ; Mr. Brandon was capering about the
ground, and cursing and shaking a maimed elbow, and a whole
posse of people were rushing upon them. The first was the
great German courier, who rushed upon that gentleman, and
shouted, " Schelm ! spitzbube ! blagard ! goward ! " in his ear.
" If I had not drown my stick and brogen his damt arm, he
wod have murdered dat boor young man."

The German's speech contained two unfounded assertions ;
in the first place Brandon would not have murdered Fitch ; and,
secondly, his arm was not broken—he had merely received a
blow on that part which anatomists call the funny-bone : a
severe blow, which sent the pistol spinning into the air, and
caused the gentleman to scream with pain. Two waiters seized
upon the murderer, too ; a baker, who had been brought from
his rounds, a bellman, several boys,—were yelling round him,
and shouting out, " Pole-e-eace ! "

Next to these came, panting and blowing, some women.
Could Fitch believe his eyes ?—that fat woman in red satin !—
yes—no—yes—he was, he was in the arms of Mrs. Carrickfergus !

* * * * * * *

The particulars of this meeting are too delicate to relate.
Suffice it that somehow matters were explained, Mr. Brandon was let loose, and a fly was presently seen to drive up

into which Mr. Fitch consented to enter with his new-found friend.

Brandon had some good movements in him. As Fitch was getting into the carriage, he walked up to him, and held out his left hand : " I can't offer you my right hand, Mr. Fitch, for that cursed courier's stick has maimed it ; but I hope you will allow me to apologize for my shameful conduct to you, and to say that I never in my life met a more gallant fellow than yourself."

" That he is, by Jove ! " said my Lord Cinqbars.

Fitch blushed as red as a peony, and trembled very much. " And yet," said he, " you would have murdered me just now, Mr. Brandon. I can't take your 'and, sir."

" Why, you great flat," said my lord wisely, " he couldn't have hurt you, nor you him. There wath no ballth in the pithtolth."

" What," said Fitch, starting back, " do you gents call that *a joke ?* Oh, my lord, my lord ! " And here poor Fitch actually burst into tears on the red satin bosom of Mrs. Carrickfergus : she and Miss Runt were crying as hard as they could. And so, amidst much shouting and huzzaing, the fly drove away.

" What a blubbering, abthurd donkey ! " said Cinqbars, with his usual judgment ; " ain't he, Tufthunt ? "

Tufthunt, of course, said yes ; but Brandon was in a virtuous mood. " By heavens ! I think his tears do the man honor. When I came out with him this morning, I intended to act fairly by him. And as for Mr. Tufthunt, who calls a man a coward because he cries—Mr. Tufthunt knows well what a pistol is, and that some men don't care to face it, brave as they are."

Mr. Tufthunt understood the hint, and bit his lips and walked on. And as for that worthy moralist, Mr. Brandon, I am happy to say that there was some good fortune in store for him, which, though similar in kind to that bestowed lately upon Mr. Fitch, was superior in degree.

It was no other than this, that forgetting all maidenly decency and decorum, before Lord Viscount Cinqbars and his friend, that silly little creature, Caroline Gann, rushed out from the parlor into the passage—she had been at the window ever since she was rid of her fainting fit ! and ah ! what agonies of fear had that little panting heart endured during the half-hour of her lover's absence !—Caroline Gann, I say, rushed into the passage, and leaped upon the neck of Brandon, and kissed him, and called him her dear, dear, dear, darling George, and sobbed, and laughed, until George, taking her round the waist gently, carried her into the little dingy parlor, and closed the door behind him."

" Egad," cried Cinqbars, " this is quite a *thene !* Hullo, Becky, Polly, what's your name ?—bring uth up the breakfatht ; and I hope you've remembered the thoda-water. Come along up thtairth, Tufty my boy."

* * * * * *

When Brandon came up stairs and joined them, which he did in a minute or two, consigning Caroline to Becky's care, his eyes were full of tears ; and when Cinqbars began to rally him in his usual delicate way, Brandon said gravely, " No laughing, sir, if you please ; for I swear that that lady before long shall be my wife."

" Your wife !—and what will your father say, and what will your duns say, and what will Miss Goldmore say, with her hundred thousand pounds ? " cried Cinqbars.

" Miss Goldmore be hanged," said Brandon, " and the duns too ; and my father may reconcile it to himself as he can." And here Brandon fell into a reverie.

" It's no use thinking," he cried, after a pause. " You see what a girl it is, Cinqbars. I love her—by heavens, I'm mad with love for her ! She shall be mine, let what will come of it. And besides," he added, in a lower tone of voice, " why need my father know anything about it ? "

" O flames and furies, what a lover it is ! " exclaimed his friend. " But, by Jove, I like your spirit ; and hang all Governors says I. Stop—a bright thought ! If you must marry, why here's Tom Tufthunt, the very man to do your business." Little Lord Cinqbars was delighted with the excitement of the affair, and thought to himself, " By Jove, this *is* an intrigue."

" What, is Tufthunt in orders ? " said Brandon.

" Yes," replied that reverend gentleman : " don't you see my coat ? I took orders six weeks ago, on my fellowship. Cinqbars' governor has promised me a living."

" And you shall marry George here, so you shall."

" What, without a licence ? "

" Hang the licence !—we won't peach, will we, George ? "

" Her family must know nothing of it," said George, " or *they* would."

" Why should they ? Why shouldn't Tom marry you in this very room, without any church or stuff at all ? "

Tom said : " You'll hold me out, my lord, if anything comes of it ; and, if Brandon likes, why, I *will*. He's done for if he does," muttered Tufthunt, " and I have had my revenge on him, the bullying, supercilious blackleg."

* * * * *

And so on that very day, in Brandon's room, without a license, and by that worthy clergyman the Rev. Thomas Tufthunt, with my Lord Cinqbars for the sole witness, poor Caroline Gann, who knew no better, who never heard of licences, and did not know what banns meant, was married in a manner to the person calling himself George Brandon; George Brandon not being his real name.

No writings at all were made, and the ceremony merely read through. Becky, Caroline's sole guardian, when the poor girl kissed her, and, blushing, showed her gold ring, thought all was in order: and the happy couple set off for Dover that day, with fifty pounds which Cinqbars lent the bridegroom.

Becky received a little letter from Caroline, which she promised to carry to her mamma at Swigby's: and it was agreed that she was to give warning, and come and live with her young lady. Next morning Lord Cinqbars and Tufthunt took the boat for London; the latter uneasy in mind, the former vowing that " he'd never spent such an exciting day in his life, and loved an intrigue of all things."

Next morning, too, the great travelling-chariot of Mrs. Carrickfergus rolled away with a bearded gentleman inside. Poor Fitch had been back to his lodgings to try one more chance with Caroline, and he arrived in time—to see her get into a post-chaise alone with Brandon.

Six weeks afterwards *Galignani's Messenger* contained the following announcement :—

" Married, at the British embassy, by Bishop Luscombe, Andrew Fitch, Esq., to Marianne Caroline Matilda, widow of the late Antony Carrickfergus, of Lombard Street and Gloucester Place, Esquire. The happy pair, after a magnificent *déjeûné*, set off for the south in their splendid carriage-and-four. Miss Runt officiated as bride's-maid ; and we remarked among the company Earl and Countess Crabs, General Sir Rice Curry, K.C.B., Colonel Wapshot, Sir Charles Swang, the Hon. Algernon Percy Deuceace and his lady, Count Punter, and others of the *élite* of the fashionables now in Paris. The bridegroom was attended by his friend Michael Angelo Titmarsh, Esquire ; and the lady was given away by the Right Hon. the Earl of Crabs. On the departure of the bride and bridegroom the festivities were resumed, and many a sparkling bumper of Meurice's champagne was quaffed to the health of the hospitable and interesting couple."

And with one more marriage this chapter shall conclude. About this time the British Auxiliary Legion came home from Spain ; and Lieut.-General Swabber, a knight of San Fernando, of the order of Isabella the Catholic, of the Tower and Sword, who, as plain Lieutenant Swabber, had loved Miss Isabella Macarty, as a general now actually married her. I leave you to suppose how glorious Mrs. Gann was, and how Gann got tipsy at the " Bag of Nails;" but as her daughters each insisted upon their 30*l.* a year income, and Mrs. Gann had so only 60*l.* left, she was obliged still to continue the lodging-house at Margate, in which have occurred the most interesting passages of this SHABBY GENTEEL STORY.

Becky never went to her young mistress, who was not heard of after she wrote the letter to her parent, saying that she was married to Mr. Brandon ; but, for *particular reasons,* her dear husband wished to keep his marriage secret, and for the present her beloved parents must be content to know she was happy. Gann missed his little Carry at first a good deal, but spent more and more of his time at the ale-house, as his house with only Mrs. Gann in it was too hot for him. Mrs. Gann talked unceasingly of her daughter the squire's lady, and her daughter the general's wife ; but never once mentioned Caroline after the first burst of wonder and wrath at her departure.

God bless thee, poor Caroline ! Thou art happy now, for some short space at least ; and here, therefore, let us leave thee.

7

THE ADVENTURES OF PHILIP

ON HIS WAY THROUGH THE WORLD;

SHOWING

WHO ROBBED HIM, WHO HELPED HIM, AND WHO
PASSED HIM BY.

TO

M. I. HIGGINS,

IN GRATEFUL REMEMBRANCE OF OLD FRIENDSHIP AND
KINDNESS.

Kensington, July, 1862.

THE
ADVENTURES OF PHILIP.

CHAPTER I.

DOCTOR FELL.

"NOT attend her own son when he is ill!" said my mother. "She does not deserve to have a son!" And Mrs. Pendennis looked towards her own only darling whilst uttering this indignant exclamation. As she looked, I know what passed through her mind. She nursed me, she dressed me in little caps and long-clothes, she attired me in my first jacket and trousers. She watched at my bedside through my infantile and juvenile ailments. She tended me through all my life, she held me to her heart with infinite prayers and blessings. She is no longer with us to bless and pray; but from heaven, where she is, I know her love pursues me; and often and often I think she is here, only invisible.

"Mrs. Firmin would be of no good," growled Dr. Goodenough. "She would have hysterics, and the nurse would have two patients to look after."

"Don't tell *me*," cries my mother, with a flush on her cheeks. "Do you suppose if that child" (meaning, of course, her paragon) "were ill, I would not go to him?"

"My dear, if that child were hungry, you would chop off your head to make him broth," says the doctor, sipping his tea.

"*Potage à la bonne femme*," says Mr. Pendennis. "Mother, we have it at the club. You would be done with milk, eggs, and a quantity of vegetables. You would be put to simmer for many hours in an earthen pan, and——"

"Don't be horrible, Arthur!" cries a young lady, who was my mother's companion of those happy days.

"And people when they knew you would like you very much."

My uncle looked as if he did not understand the allegory.

"What is this you are talking about? *potage à la*—what d'ye-call-'im?" says he. "I thought we were speaking of Mrs. Firmin, of Old Parr Street. Mrs. Firmin is a doosid delicate woman," interposed the Major. "All the females of that family are. Her mother died early. Her sister, Mrs. Twysden, is very delicate. She would be of no more use in a sick-room than a—than a bull in a china-shop, begad! and she might catch the fever, too."

"And so might you, Major!" cries the doctor. "Aren't you talking to me, who have just come from the boy? Keep your distance, or I shall bite you."

The old gentleman gave a little backward movement with his chair.

"Gad, it's no joking matter," says he; "I've known fellows catch fevers at—at ever so much past my age. At any rate, the boy is no boy of mine, begad! I dine at Firmin's house, who has married into a good family, though he is only a doctor and——"

"And pray what was my husband?" cried Mrs. Pendennis.

"Only a doctor, indeed!" calls out Goodenough. "My dear creature, I have a great mind to give him the scarlet fever this minute!"

"My father was a surgeon and apothecary, I have heard," says the widow's son.

"And what then? And I should like to know if a man of one of the most ancient families in the kingdom—in the empire, begad!—hasn't a right to pursoo a learned, a useful, an honorable profession. My brother John was——"

"A medical practitioner!" I say, with a sigh.

And my uncle arranges his hair, puts his handkerchief to his teeth, and says—

"Stuff! nonsense—no patience with these personalities, begad! Firmin is a doctor, certainly—so are you—so are others. But Firmin is a university man, and a gentleman. Firmin has travelled. Firmin is intimate with some of the best people in England, and has married into one of the first families. Gad, sir, do you suppose that a woman bred up in the lap of luxury—in the very lap, sir—at Ringwood and Whipham, and at Ringwood House in Walpole Street, where she was absolute mistress, begad—do you suppose such a woman is fit to be nurse tender in a sick-room? She never *was* fit for that, or for anything except—" (here the Major saw smiles on the countenances of some of his audience)—" except, I say, to preside at Ringwood House and—and adorn society, and that sort of thing. And if such a woman chooses to run away with her uncle's doctor, and marry below her rank—why, *I* don't think it's a laughing matter, hang me if I do."

"And so she stops at the Isle of Wight, whilst the poor boy remains at school," sighs my mother.

"Firmin can't come away. He is in attendance on the Grand Dook. The prince is never easy without Firmin. He has given him his Order of the Swan. They are moving heaven and earth in high quarters ; and I bet you even, Goodenough, that that boy whom you have been attending will be a baronet—if you don't kill him off with your confounded potions and pills, begad ! "

Dr. Goodenough only gave a humph and contracted his great eyebrows.

My uncle continued—

" I know what you mean. Firmin is a gentlemanly man—a handsome man. I remember his father, Brand Firmin, at Valenciennes with the Dook of York—one of the handsomest men in Europe. Firebrand Firmin they used to call him—a red-headed fellow—a tremendous duellist : shot an Irishman— became serious in after life, and that sort of thing—quarrelled with his son, who was doosid wild in early days. Gentlemanly man, certainly, Firmin. Black hair : his father had red. So much the better for the doctor ; but—but—we understand each other, I think, Goodenough ? and you and I have seen some queer fishes in our time."

And the old gentleman winked and took his snuff graciously, and, as it were, puffed the Firmin subject away.

" Was it to show me a queer fish that you took me to Dr. Firmin's house in Parr Street ? " asked Mr. Pendennis of his uncle. " The house was not very gay, nor the mistress very wise, but they were all as kind as might be ; and I am very fond of the boy."

" So did Lord Ringwood, his mother's uncle, like him," cried Major Pendennis. " That boy brought about a reconciliation between his mother and his uncle, after her runaway match. I suppose you know she ran away with Firmin, my dear ? "

My mother said " she had heard something of the story." And the major once more asserted that Dr. Firmin was a wild fellow twenty years ago. At the time of which I am writing he was Physician to the Plethoric Hospital, Physician to the Grand

Duke of Gröningen, and knight of his order of the Black Swan, member of many learned societies, the husband of a rich wife and a person of no small consideration.

As for his son, whose name figures at the head of these pages, you may suppose he did not die of the illness about which we had just been talking. A good nurse waited on him, though his mamma was in the country. Though his papa was absent, a very competent physician was found to take charge of the young patient, and preserve his life for the benefit of his family, and the purposes of this history.

We pursued our talk about Philip Firmin and his father, and his grand-uncle the Earl, whom Major Pendennis knew intimately well, untill Dr. Goodenough's carriage was announced, and our kind physican took leave of us, and drove back to London. Some who spoke on that summer evening are no longer here to speak or listen. Some who were young then have topped the hill and are descending towards the valley of the shadows. " Ah," says old Major Pendennis, shaking his brown curls, as the Doctor went away ; " did you see, my good soul, when I spoke about his *confrère*, how glum Goodenough looked ? They don't love each other, my dear. Two of a trade don't agree, and besides I have no doubt the other doctor-fellows are jealous of Firmin, because he lives in the best society. A man of good family, my dear. There has already been a great *rapprochement ;* and if Lord Ringwood is quite reconciled to him, there's no knowing what luck that boy of Firmin's may come to."

Although Dr. Goodenough might think but lightly of his *confrère*, a great portion of the public held him in much higher estimation : and especially in the little community of Grey Friars, of which the kind reader has heard in previous works of the present biographer, Dr. Brand Firmin was a very great favorite, and received with much respect and honor. Whenever the boys at school were afflicted with the common ailments of youth, Mr. Spratt, the school apothecary, provided for them ; and by the simple, though disgusting remedies which were in use in those times, generally succeeded in restoring his young patients to health. But if young Lord Egham (the Marquis of Ascot's son, as my respected reader very likely knows) happened to be unwell, as was frequently the case, from his lordship's great command of pocket-money and imprudent fondness for the contents of the pastrycook's shop ; or if any very grave case of illness occurred in the school, then, quick, the famous Dr. Firmin, of Old Parr Street, Burlington Gardens, was sent for ; and an illness must have been very severe, if *he* could not cure it. Dr. Firmin had been a school-fellow, and remained a special friend of the head-master. When young Lord Egham, before mentioned, (he was our only lord, and therefore we were a little proud and careful of our darling youth,) got the erysipelas, which swelled his head to the size of a pumpkin, the doctor triumphantly carried him through his illness, and was complimented by the head-boy in his Latin oration on the annual speech-day for his superhuman skill and godlike delight *salutem hominibus dando.* The head-master turned towards Dr. Firmin, and bowed : the governors and bigwigs buzzed to one another, and looked at him : the boys looked at him : the physician held his handsome head down towards his shirt-frill. His modest eyes would not look up from the spotless lining of the broad-brimmed hat on his knees. A murmur of applause hummed through the ancient hall, a scuffling of young feet, a rustling of new cassocks among the masters, and a refreshing blowing of noses ensued, as the orator polished off his period, and then passed to some other theme.

Amidst the general enthusiasm, there was one member of the auditory scornful and dissentient. This gentleman whispered to his comrade at the commencement of the phrase concerning the doctor the, I believe of Eastern derivation, monosyllable " Bosh ! " and he added sadly, looking towards the object of all his praise, " He can't construe the Latin—though it is all a parcel of humbug."

" Hush, Phil ! " said his friend ; and Phil's face flushed red, as Dr. Firmin, lifting up his eyes, looked at him for one moment ; for the recipient of all this laudation was no other than Phil's father.

The illness of which we spoke had long since passed away. Philip was a schoolboy no longer, but in his second year at the university, and one of half-a-dozen young men, ex-pupils of the school, who had come up for the annual dinner. The honors of this year's dinner were for Dr. Firmin, even more than for Lord Ascot in his star and ribbon, who walked with his arm in the doctor's into chapel. His lordship faltered when, in his after-dinner speech, he alluded to the inestimable services and skill of his tried old friend, whom he had known as a fellow-pupil in those walls—(loud cheers)—whose friendship had been the delight of his life—a friendship which he prayed might be the inheritance of their children. (Immense applause ; after which Dr. Firmin spoke.)

The Doctor's speech was perhaps a little commonplace ;

the Latin quotations which he used were not exactly novel; but Phil need not have been so angry or ill-behaved. He went on sipping sherry, glaring at his father, and muttering observations that were anything but complimentary to his parent. " Now look," says he, " he is going to be overcome by his feelings. He will put his handkerchief up to his mouth, and show his diamond ring. I told you so! It's too much. I can't swallow this * * * this sherry. I say, you fellows, let us come out of this, and have a smoke somewhere." And Phil rose up and quitted the dining-room, just as his father was declaring what a joy, and a pride, and a delight it was to him to think that the friendship which his noble friend honored him was likely to be transmitted to their children, and that when he had passed away from this earthly scene (cries of "No, no!" "May you live a thousand years!") it would be his joy to think that his son would always find a friend and protector in the noble, the princely house of Ascot.

We found the carriages waiting outside Grey Friars' Gate, and Philip Firman, pushing me into his father's, told the footman to drive home, and that the doctor would return in Lord Ascot's carriage. Home then to Old Parr Street we went, where many a time as a boy I had been welcome. And we retired to Phil's private den in the back buildings of the great house: and over our cigars we talked of the Founder's-day Feast, and the speeches delivered; and of the old Cistercians of our time, and how Thompson was married, and Johnson was in the army, and Jackson (not red-haired Jackson, pig-eyed Jackson,) was first in his year, and so forth; and in this twaddle were most happily engaged, when Phil's father flung open the tall door of the study.

" Here's the governor!" growled Phil; and in an undertone, " What does *he* want ?"

"The governor," as I looked up, was not a pleasant object to behold. Dr. Firmin had very white false teeth, which perhaps were a little too large for his mouth, and these grinned in the gas-light very fiercely. On his cheeks were black whiskers, and over his glaring eyes fierce black eyebrows, and his bald head glittered like a billiard-ball. You would hardly have known that he was the original of that melancholy philosophic portrait which all the patients admired in the doctor's waiting-room.

" I find, Philip, that you took my carriage," said the father; " and Lord Ascot and I had to walk ever so far for a cab !"

" Hadn't he got his own carriage ? I thought, of course, he

would have his carriage on a State-day, and that you would come home with the lord," said Philip.

"I had promised to bring *him* home, sir!" said the father.

"Well, sir, I'm very sorry," continued the son, curtly.

"Sorry!" screams the other.

"I can't say any more, sir, and I *am* very sorry," answers Phil; and he knocked the ash of his cigar into the stove.

The stranger within the house hardly knew how to look on its master or his son. There was evidently some dire quarrel between them. The old man glared at the young one, who calmly looked his father in the face. Wicked rage and hate seemed to flush from the doctor's eyes, and anon came a look of wild pitiful supplication towards the guest, which was most painful to bear. In the midst of what dark family mystery was I? What meant this cruel spectacle of the father's terrified anger, and the son's scorn?

"I—I appeal to you, Pendennis," says the doctor, with a choking utterance and a ghastly face.

"Shall we begin *ab ovo*, sir?" says Phil. Again the ghastly look of terror comes over the father's face.

"I—I promise to bring one of the first noblemen in England," gasps the doctor, "from a public dinner, in my carriage; and my son takes it, and leaves me and Lord Ascot to walk!— Is it fair, Pendennis? Is it the conduct of a gentleman to a gentleman; of a son to a father?"

"No, sir," I said, gravely, "nothing can excuse it." Indeed I was shocked at the young man's obduracy and undutifulness.

"I told you it was a mistake!" cries Phil, reddening. "I heard Lord Ascot order his own carriage; I made no doubt he would bring my father home. To ride in a chariot with a footman behind me, is no pleasure to me, and I would far rather have a Hansom and a cigar—there! It was a blunder, and I am sorry for it—there! And if I live to a hundred I can't say more."

"If you are sorry, Philip," groans the father, "it is enough."

"You remember, Pendennis, when—when my son and I were not on this—on this footing," and he looked up for a moment at a picture which was hanging over Phil's head—a portrait of Phil's mother; the lady of whom my own mother spoke, on that evening when we had talked of the boy's illness. Both the ladies had passed from the world now, and their images were but painted shadows on the wall.

The father had accepted an apology, though the son had made none. I looked at the elder Firmin's face, and the character written on it. I remembered such particulars of his early

history as had been told to me; and I perfectly recalled that
feeling of doubt and misliking which came over my mind when
I first saw the doctor's handsome face some few years previously, when my uncle first took me to the doctor's in Old Parr
Street; little Phil being then a flaxen-headed, pretty child, who
had just assumed his first trousers, and I a fifth-form boy at school.

My father and Dr. Firmin were members of the medical
profession. They had been bred up as boys at the same school,
whither families used to send their sons from generation to
generation, and long before people had ever learned that the
place was unwholesome. Grey Friars was smoky, certainly; I
think in the time of the Plague great numbers of people were
buried there. But had the school been situated in the most
picturesque swamp in England, the general health of the boys
could not have been better. We boys used to hear of epidem-
ics occurring in other schools, and were almost sorry that they
did not come to ours, so that we might shut up, and get longer
vacations. Even that illness which subsequently befell Phil
Firmin himself attacked no one else—the boys all luckily going
home for the holidays on the very day of poor Phil's seizure;
but of this illness more anon. When it was determined that
little Phil Firmin was to go to Grey Friars, Phil's father
bethought him that Major Pendennis, whom he met in the world
and society, had a nephew at the place, who might protect the
little fellow, and the Major took his nephew to see Dr. and Mrs.
Firmin one Sunday after church, and we had lunch at Old Parr
Street, and their little Phil was presented to me, whom I
promised to take under my protection. He was a simple little
man; an artless child, who had not the least idea of the dignity
of a fifth-form boy. He was quite unabashed in talking to me
and other persons, and has remained so ever since. He asked
my uncle how he came to have such odd hair. He partook freely
of the delicacies on the table. I remember he hit me with his
little fist once or twice, which liberty at first struck me with a
panic of astonishment, and then with a sense of the ridiculous
so exquisitely keen, that I burst out into a fit of laughter. It
was, you see, as if a stranger were to hit the Pope in the ribs,
and call him "Old boy;" as if Jack were to tweak one of the
giants by the nose; or Ensign Jones to ask the Duke of Wellington to take wine. I had a strong sense of humor, even in
those early days, and enjoyed this joke accordingly.

"Philip!" cries mamma, "you will hurt Mr. Pendennis.'

"I will knock him down!" shouts Phil. Fancy knocking
me down,—ME, a fifth-form boy!

" The child is a perfect Hercules," remarks the mother.

" He strangled two snakes in his cradle," says the doctor, looking at me. (It was then, as I remember, I felt *Dr. Fell* towards him.)

" La, Dr. Firmin ! " cries mamma, " I can't bear snakes. I remember there was one at Rome, when we were walking one day, a great, large snake, and I hated it, and I cried out, and I nearly fainted ; and my uncle Ringwood said I ought to like snakes, for one might be an agreeable rattle ; and I have read of them being charming in India, and I dare say you have, Mr. Pendennis, for I am told you are very clever ; and I am not in the least ; I wish I were ; but my husband is, very—and so Phil will be. Will you be a very clever boy, dear ? He was named after my dear Papa, who was killed at Busaco when I was quite, quite a little thing, and we wore mourning, and we went to live with my uncle Ringwood afterwards ; but Maria and I had both our own fortunes ; and I am sure I little thought I should marry a physician—la, one of uncle Ringwood's grooms, I should as soon have thought of marrying him !—but, you know, my husband is one of the cleverest men *in the world*. Don't tell me,—you are, dearest, and you know it ; and when a man is clever, I don't value his rank in life ; no, not if he was that fender ; and I always said to uncle Ringwood, ' Talent I will marry, for talent I adore ;' and I *did* marry you, Dr. Firmin, you know I did, and this child is your image. And you will be kind to him at school," says the poor lady, turning to me, her eyes filling with tears, "for talent is always kind, except uncle Ringwood, and he was very——"

" A little more wine, Mr. Pendennis ? " said the doctor— *Dr. Fell* still, though he was most kind to me. " I shall put my little man under your care, and I know you will keep him from harm. I hope you will do us the favor to come to Parr Street whenever you are free. In my father's time we used to come home of a Saturday from school, and enjoyed going to the play." And the Doctor shook me cordially by the hand, and, I must say, continued his kindness to me as long as ever I knew him. When we went away, my uncle Pendennis told me many stories about the great earl and family of Ringwood, and how Dr. Firmin had made a match—a match of the affec- tions—with this lady, daughter of Philip Ringwood, who was killed at Busaco ; and how she had been a great beauty, and was a perfect *grande dame* always ; and, if not the cleverest, certainly one of the kindest and most amiable women in the world.

In those days I was accustomed to receive the opinions of my informant with such respect that I at once accepted this statement as authentic. Mrs. Firmin's portrait, indeed, was beautiful : it was painted by young Mr. Harlowe, that year he was at Rome, and when in eighteen days he completed a copy of the " Transfiguration," to the admiration of all the Academy ; but I, for my part, only remember a lady weak, and thin, and faded, who never came out of her dressing-room until a late hour in the afternoon, and whose superannuated smiles and grimaces used to provoke my juvenile sense of humor. She used to kiss Phil's brow ! and, as she held the boy's hand in one of her lean ones, would say, " Who would suppose such a great boy as that could be my son ? " " Be kind to him when I am gone," she sighed to me, one Sunday evening, when I was taking leave of her, as her eyes filled with tears, and she placed the thin hand in mine for the last time. The doctor, reading by the fire, turned round and scowled at her from under his tall shining forehead. " You are nervous, Louisa, and had better go to your room, I told you you had," he said, abruptly. " Young gentlemen, it is time for you to be off to Grey Friars. Is the cab at the door, Brice ? " And he took out his watch— his great shining watch, by which he had felt the pulses of so many famous personages, whom his prodigious skill had rescued from disease. And at parting, Phil flung his arms round his poor mother, and kissed her under the glossy curls ; the borrowed curls ! and he looked his father resolutely in the face (whose own glance used to fall before that of the boy), and bade him a gruff good-night, ere we set forth for Grey Friars.

CHAPTER II.

AT SCHOOL AND AT HOME.

I DINED yesterday with three gentlemen, whose time of life may be guessed by their conversation, a great part of which consisted of Eton reminiscences and lively imitations of Dr. Keate. Each one, as he described how he had been flogged, mimicked to the best of his power the manner and the mode of operating of the famous doctor. His little parenthetical remarks during the ceremony were recalled with great facetiousness: the very *hwhish* of the rods were parodied with thrilling fidelity, and after a good hour's conversation, the subject was brought to a climax by a description of that awful night when the doctor called up squad after squad of boys from their beds in their respective boarding-houses, whipped through the whole night, and castigated I don't know how many hundred rebels. All these mature men laughed, prattled, rejoiced, and became young again, as they recounted their stories.; and each of them heartily and eagerly bade the stranger to understand how Keate was a thorough gentleman. Having talked about their floggings, I say, for an hour at least, they apologized to me for dwelling upon a subject which after all was strictly local: but, indeed, their talk greatly amused and diverted me, and I hope, and am quite ready, to hear all their jolly stories over again.

Be not angry, patient reader of former volumes by the author of the present history, if I am garrulous about Grey Friars, and go back to that ancient place of education to find the heroes of our tale. We are but young once. When we remember that time of youth, we are still young. He over whose head eight or nine lustres have passed, if he wishes to write of boys, must recall the time when he himself was a boy. Their habits change; their waists are longer or shorter; their shirt-collars stick up more or less; but the boy is the boy in King George's time as in that of his royal niece—once our maiden queen, now the anxious mother of many boys. And young fellows are honest, and merry, and idle, and mischievous, and timid, and brave, and studious, and selfish, and generous, and mean, and false, and truth-telling, and affectionate, and good, and bad, now as in former days. He with whom we have mainly to do is a gentleman of mature age now walking the street with boys of his own. He is not going to perish in the last chapter of these memoirs—to die of consumption with his love weeping by his bedside, or to blow his brains out in despair, because she has been married to his rival, or killed out of a gig, or otherwise done for in the last chapter but one. No, no; we will have no dismal endings. Philip Firmin is well and hearty at this minute, owes no man a shilling, and can enjoy his glass of port in perfect comfort. So, my dear miss, if you want a pulmonary romance, the present won't suit you. So, young gentleman. if you are for melancholy, despair, and sardonic satire, please to call at some other shop. That Philip shall have his trials is a matter of course—may they be interesting, though they do not end dismally! That he shall fall and trip in his course sometimes is pretty certain. Ah, who does not upon this life-journey of ours? Is not our want the occasion of our brother's charity, and thus does not good come out of that evil? When the traveller (of whom the Master spoke) fell among the thieves, his mishap was contrived to try many a heart beside his own—the Knave's who robbed him, the Levite's and Priest's who passed him by as he lay bleeding, the humble Samaritan's whose hand poured oil into his wound, and held out its pittance to relieve him.

So little Philip Firmin was brought to school by his mamma in her carriage, who entreated the housekeeper to have a special charge of that angelic child; and as soon as the poor lady's back was turned, Mrs. Bunce emptied the contents of the boy's trunk into one of sixty or seventy little cupboards, wherein reposed other boys' clothes and haberdashery: and then Mrs. Firmin requested to see the Rev. Mr. X., in whose house Philip was to board, and besought him, and explained many things to him, such as the exceeding delicacy of the child's constitution, &c., &c.; and Mr. X., who was very good-natured, patted the boy kindly on the head, and sent for the other boy, Philip Ringwood, Phil's cousin, who had arrived at Grey Friars an hour or two before; and Mr. X. told Ringwood to take care of the little fellow; and Mrs. Firmin, choking behind her pocket-handkerchief, gurgled out a blessing on the grinning youth, and at one time had an idea of giving Master Ringwood a sovereign, but paused, thinking he was too big a boy, and that she might not take such a liberty, and presently she was gone; and little Phil Firmin was introduced to the long-room and his schoolfellows of Mr. X.'s house; and having plenty of money, and naturally finding his way to the pastrycook's the next day, after school, he was met by his cousin Ringwood and robbed of half the tarts which he had purchased. A fortnight afterwards, the hospitable doctor and his wife asked their young kinsman to Old Parr Street, Burlington Gardens, and the two boys went; but Phil never mentioned anything to his parents regarding the robbery of tarts, being deterred, perhaps, from speaking by awful threats of punishment which his cousin promised to administer when they got back to school, in case of the little boy's confession. Subsequently, Master Ringwood was asked once in every term to Old Parr Street; but neither Mrs. Firmin, nor the doctor, nor Master Firmin liked the baronet's son, and Mrs. Firmin pronounced him a violent, rude boy.

I, for my part, left school suddenly and early, and my little *protégé* behind me. His poor mother, who had promised herself to come for him every Saturday, did not keep her promise. Smithfield is a long way from Piccadilly ; and an angry cow once scratched the panels of her carriage, causing her footman to spring from his board into a pig-pen, and herself to feel such a shock, that no wonder she was afraid of visiting the City afterwards. The circumstances of this accident she often narrated to us. Her anecdotes were not numerous, but she told them repeatedly. In imagination, sometimes, I can hear her ceaseless, simple cackle ; see her faint eyes, as she prattles on unconsciously, and watch the dark looks of her handsome, silent husband, scowling from under his eyebrows and smiling behind his teeth. I dare say he ground those teeth with suppressed rage sometimes. I dare say to bear with her endless volubility must have tasked his endurance. He may have treated her ill, but she tried him. She, on her part, may have been a not very wise woman, but she was kind to me. Did not her housekeeper make me the best of tarts, and keep goodies from the company dinners for the young gentlemen when they came home? Did not her husband give me of his fees ? I promise you, after I had seen Dr. Fell a few times, that first unpleasing impression produced by his darkling countenance and sinister good looks wore away. He was a gentleman. He had lived in the great world, of which he told anecdotes delightful to boys to hear ; and he passed the bottle to me as if I was a man.

I hope and think I remembered the injunction of poor Mrs. Firmin to be kind to her boy. As long as we stayed together at Grey Friars, I was Phil's champion whenever he needed my protection, though of course I could not always be present to guard the little scapegrace from all the blows which were aimed at his young face by pugilists of his own size. There were seven or eight years' difference between us (he says ten, which is absurd, and which I deny) ; but I was always remarkable for my affability, and, in spite of our disparity of age, would often graciously accept the general invitation I had from his father for any Saturday and Sunday when I would like to accompany Philip home.

Such an invitation is welcome to any schoolboy. To get away from Smithfield, and show our best clothes in Bond Street, was always a privilege. To strut in the Park on Sunday, and nod to the other fellows who were strutting there too, was better than remaining at school, " doing ' Diates aron,'" as the phrase used to be, having that endless roast-beef for dinner, and hear

ing two sermons in chapel. There may have been more lively
streets in London than Old Parr Street; but it was pleasanter
to be there than to look at Goswell Street over Grey Friars'
wall; and so the present biographer and reader's very humble
servant found Dr. Firmin's house an agreeable resort. Mamma
was often ailing, or if well, went out into the world with her
husband; in either case, we boys had a good dinner provided
for us, with the special dishes which Phil loved; and after dinner we adjourned to the play, not being by any means too proud
to sit in the pit with Mr. Brice, the doctor's confidential man.
On Sunday we went to church at Lady Whittlesea's, and back
to school in the evening; when the doctor almost always *gave
us a fee*. If he did not dine at home (and I own his absence
did not much damp our pleasure), Brice would lay a small en-
closure on the young gentleman's coats, which we transferred
to our pockets. I believe schoolboys disdain fees in the present
disinterested times.

Everything in Dr. Firmin's house was as handsome as might
be, and yet somehow the place was not cheerful. One's step
fell noiselessly on the faded Turkey carpet; the room was large,
and all save the dining-table in a dingy twilight. The picture
of Mrs. Firmin, looked at us from the wall, and followed us
about with wild violet eyes. Philip Firmin had the same violet
odd bright eyes, and the same colored hair of an auburn tinge;
in the picture it fell in long wild masses over the lady's back as
she leaned with bare arms on a harp. Over the sideboard was
the doctor, in a black velvet coat and a fur collar, his hand on
a skull, like Hamlet. Skulls of oxen, horned, with wreaths,
formed the cheerful ornaments of the cornice. On the side-
table glittered a pair of cups, given by grateful patients, looking
like receptacles rather for funereal ashes than for festive flowers
or wine. Brice, the butler, wore the gravity and costume of an
undertaker. The footman stealthily moved hither and thither,
bearing the dinner to us; we always spoke under our breath
whilst we were eating it. "The room don't look more cheerful
of a morning when the patients are sitting here, I can tell you,"
Phil would say; indeed, we could well fancy that it was dismal.
The drawing-room had a rhubarb-colored flock paper (on account
of the governor's attachment to the shop, Master Phil said), a
great piano, a harp smothered in a leather bag in a corner,
which the languid owner now never touched; and everybody's
face seemed scared and pale in the great looking-glasses, which
reflected you over and over again into the distance, so that you
seemed to twinkle off right through the Albany into Piccadilly.

Old Parr Street has been a habitation for generations of surgeons and physicians. I suppose the noblemen for whose use the street was intended in the time of the early Georges fled, finding the neighborhood too dismal, and the gentlemen in black coats came and took possession of the gilded, gloomy chambers which the sacred *mode* vacated. These mutations of fashion have always been matters of profound speculation to me. Why shall not one moralize over London, as over Rome, or Baalbec or Troy town? I like to walk among the Hebrews of Wardour Street, and fancy the place, as it once was, crowded with chairs and gilt chariots, and torches flashing in the hands of the running footmen. I have a grim pleasure in thinking that Golden Square was once the resort of the aristocracy, and Monmouth Street the delight of the genteel world. What shall prevent us Londoners from musing over the decline and fall of city sovereignties, and drawing our cockney morals? As the late Mr. Gibbon meditated his history leaning against a column in the Capitol, why should not I muse over mine, reclining under an arcade of the Pantheon? Not the Pantheon at Rome, in the Cabbage Market by the Piazza Navona, where the immortal Gods were worshipped,—the immortal gods who are now dead; but the Pantheon in Oxford Street, ladies, where you purchase feeble pomatums, music, glassware, and baby-linen; and which has its history too. Have not Selwyn, and Walpole, and March, and Carlisle figured there? Has not Prince Florizel flounced through the hall in his rustling domino, and danced there in powdered splendor? and when the ushers refused admission to lovely Sophy Baddeley, did not the young men, her adorers, draw their rapiers and vow to slay the doorkeepers; and crossing the glittering blades over the enchantress' head, make a warlike triumphal arch for her to pass under, all flushed, and smiling, and perfumed, and painted? The lives of streets are as the lives of men, and shall not the street-preacher if so minded, take for the text of his sermon the stones in the gutter? That you were once the resort of the fashion, O Monmouth Street! by the invocation of blessed St. Giles shall I not improve that sweet thought into a godly discourse, and make the ruin edifying? *O mes frères!* There were splendid thoroughfares, dazzling company, bright illuminations, in *our* streets when our hearts were young: we entertained in them a noble youthful company of chivalrous hopes and lofty ambitions; of blushing thoughts in snowy robes spotless and virginal. See in the embrasure of the window, where you sat looking to the stars. and nestling by the soft side of your first love, hang Mr. Moses' bargains of turned old clothes, very cheap ; of worn old boots, bedraggled in how much and how many people's mud ; a great bargain. See ! along the street, strewed with flowers once mayhap—a fight of beggars for the refuse of an apple-stall, or a tipsy basket-woman reeling shrieking to the station. O me ! O my beloved congregation ! I have preached this stale sermon to you for ever so many years. O my jolly companions, I have drunk many a bout with you, and always found *vanitas vanitatum* written on the bottom of the pot !

I choose to moralize now when I pass the place. The garden has run to seed, the walks are mildewed, the statues have broken noses, the gravel is dank with green moss, the roses are withered, and the nightingales have ceased to make love. It *is* a funereal street, Old Parr Street, certainly ; the carriages which drive there ought to have feathers on the roof, and the butlers who open the doors should wear weepers—so the scene strikes you now as you pass along the spacious empty pavement. You are bilious, my good man. Go and pay a guinea to one of the doctors in those houses ; there are still doctors there. He will prescribe taraxacum for you, or pil : hydrarg : Bless you ! in *my* time, to us gentlemen of the fifth form, the place was bearable. The yellow fogs didn't damp our spirits—and we never thought them too thick to keep us away from the play : from the chivalrous Charles Kemble, I tell you, my Mirabel, my Mercutio, my princely Falconbridge : from his adorable daughter (O my distracted heart !) : from the classic Young : from the glorious Long Tom Coffin : from the unearthly Vanderdecken—" Return, O my love, and we'll never, never part " (where art thou, sweet singer of that most thrilling ditty of my youth ?) : from the sweet, sweet *Victorine* and the *Bottle Imp*. Oh, to see that *Bottle Imp* again, and hear that song about the " Pilgrim of Love ! " Once, but—hush ;—this is a secret—we had private boxes, the doctor's grand friends often sending him these ; and finding the opera rather slow, we went to a concert in M–d–n Lane, near Covent Garden, and heard the most celestial glees, over a supper of fizzing sausages and mashed potatoes, such as the world has never seen since. We did no harm ; but I dare say it was very wrong. Brice, the butler, ought not to have taken us. We bullied him, and made him take us where we liked. We had rum-shrub in the housekeeper's room, where we used to be diverted by the society of *other* butlers of the neighboring nobility and gentry, who would step in. Perhaps it was wrong to leave us so to the company of servants. Dr. Firmin used to go to his grand parties, Mrs. Firmin to bed. " Did we enjoy the performance last night ? " our host would ask at breakfast. " Oh, yes, we enjoyed the performance ! " But my poor Mrs. Firmin fancied that we enjoyed *Semiramide* or the *Donna del Lago ;* whereas we had been to the pit at the Adelphi (out of our own money), and seen that jolly John Reeve, and laughed—laughed till we were fit to drop—and stayed till the curtain was down. And then we would come home, and, as aforesaid, pass a delightful hour over supper, and hear the anecdotes of Mr. Brice's friends, the other butlers. Ah, that was a time indeed ! There never was any liquor so good as rum-shrub, never ; and the sausages had a flavor of Elysium. • How hushed we were when Dr. Firmin, coming home from his parties, let himself in at the street door ! Shoeless, we crept up to our bedrooms. And we came down to breakfast with innocent young faces—and let Mrs. Firmin, at lunch, prattle about the opera ; and there stood Brice and the footman behind us, looking quite grave, the abominable hypocrites !

Then, sir, there was a certain way, out of the study window, or through the kitchen, and over the leads, to a building, gloomy indeed, but where I own to have spent delightful hours of the most flagitious and criminal enjoyment of some delicious little Havanas, ten to the shilling. In that building there were stables once, doubtless occupied by great Flemish horses and rumbling gold coaches of Walpole's time ; but a celebrated surgeon, when he took possession of the house, made a lecture-room of the premises,—" And this door," says Phil, pointing to one leading into the mews, " was very convenient for having *the bodies* in and out "—a cheerful reminiscence. Of this kind of furniture there was now very little in the apartment, except a dilapidated skeleton in a corner, a few dusty casts of heads, and bottles of preparations on the top of an old bureau, and some mildewed harness hanging on the walls. This apartment became Mr. Phil's smoking-room when, as he grew taller, he felt himself too dignified to sit in the kitchen regions : the honest butler and housekeeper themselves pointing out to their young master that his place was elsewhere than among the servants. So there, privately and with great delectation, we smoked many an abominable cigar in that dreary back room, the gaunt walls and twilight ceilings of which were by no means melancholy to us, who found forbidden pleasures the sweetest, after the absurd fashion of boys. Dr. Firmin was an enemy to smoking, and ever accustomed to speak of the practice with eloquent indignation. "It was a low practice—the habit of cabmen, pot-house frequenters, and Irish apple-women," the doctor would say, as Phil and his friend looked at each other with a stealthy joy. Phil's father was ever scented and neat, the pattern of handsome propriety. Perhaps he had a clearer perception regarding manners than respecting morals; perhaps his conversation was full of platitudes, his talk (concerning people of fashion chiefly) mean and uninstructive, his behavior to young Lord Egham rather fulsome and lacking of dignity. Perhaps, I say, the idea may have entered into young Mr. Pendennis's mind that his hospitable entertainer and friend, Dr. Firmin, of Old Parr Street, was what at the present day might be denominated an old humbug; but modest young men do not come quickly to such unpleasant conclusions regarding their seniors. Dr. Firmin's manners were so good, his forehead was so high, his frill so fresh, his hands so white and slim, that for some considerable time we ingenuously admired him; and it was not without a pang that we came to view him as he actually was—no, not as he actually was—no man whose early nurture was kindly can judge quite impartially the man who has been kind to him in boyhood.

I quitted school suddenly, leaving my little Phil behind me, a brave little handsome boy, endearing himself to old and young by his good looks, his gayety, his courage, and his gentlemanly bearing. Once in a way a letter would come from him, full of that artless affection and tenderness which fills boys' hearts, and is so touching in their letters. It was answered with proper dignity and condescension on the senior boy's part. Our modest little country home kept up a friendly intercourse with Dr. Firmin's grand London mansion, of which, in his visits to us, my uncle, Major Pendennis, did not fail to bring news. A correspondence took place between the ladies of each house. We supplied Mrs. Firmin with little country presents, tokens of my mother's good-will and gratitude towards the friends who had been kind to her son. I went my way to the university, having occasional glimpses of Phil at school. I took chambers in the Temple, which he found great delight in visiting; and he liked our homely dinner from Dick's, and a bed on the sofa, better than the splendid entertainments in Old Parr Street and his great gloomy chamber there. He had grown by this time to be ever so much taller than his senior, though he always persists in looking up to me unto the present day.

A very few weeks after my poor mother passed that judg-

ment on Mrs. Firmin, she saw reason to regret and revoke it
Phil's mother, who was afraid, or perhaps was forbidden, to
attend her son in his illness at school, was taken ill herself.

Phil returned to Grey Friars in a deep suit of black; the
servants on the carriage wore black too; and a certain tyrant
of the place, beginning to laugh and jeer because Firmin's eyes
filled with tears at some ribald remark, was gruffly rebuked by
Sampson Major, the cock of the whole school; and with the
question, "Don't you see the poor beggar's in mourning, you
great brute?" was kicked about his business.

When Philip Firmin and I met again, there was crape on
both our hats. I don't think either could see the other's face
very well. I went to see him in Parr Street, in the vacant, melancholy house, where the poor mother's picture was yet hanging
in her empty drawing-room.

"She was always fond of you, Pendennis," said Phil. "God
bless you for being so good to her. You know what it is to lose
—to lose what loves you best in the world. I didn't know how
—how I loved her, till I had lost her." And many a sob broke
his words as he spoke.

Her picture was removed from the drawing-room presently
into Phil's own little study—the room in which he sat and defied
his father. What had passed between them? The young man
was very much changed. The frank looks of old days were
gone, and Phil's face was haggard and bold. The doctor would
not let me have a word more with his son after he had found
us together, but with dubious appealing looks, followed me to
the door, and shut it upon me. I felt that it closed upon two
unhappy men.

CHAPTER III.

A CONSULTATION.

SHOULD I peer into Firmin's privacy, and find the key to
that secret? What skeleton was there in the closet? In the
Cornhill Magazine,[*] you may remember, there were some verses
about a portion of a skeleton. Did you remark how the poet
and present proprietor of the human skull at once settled the
sex of it, and determined off-hand that it must have belonged

[*] No. 12: December 1860.

to a woman? Such skulls are locked up in many gentlemen's hearts and memories. Bluebeard, you know, had a whole museum of them—as that imprudent little last wife of his found out to her cost. And, on the other hand, a lady, we suppose, would select hers of the sort which had carried beards when in the flesh. Given a neat locked skeleton cupboard, belonging to a man of a certain age, to ascertain the sex of the original owner of the bones, you have not much need of a picklock or a blacksmith. There is no use in forcing the hinge, or scratching the pretty panel. *We* know what is inside—we arch rogues and men of the world. Murders, I suppose, are not many—enemies and victims of our hate and anger, destroyed and trampled out of life by us, and locked out of sight : but corpses of our dead loves, my dear sir—my dear madam—have we not got them stowed away in cupboard after cupboard, in bottle after bottle? Oh, fie! And young people! What doctrine is this to preach to *them*, who spell your book by papa's and mamma's knees? Yes, and how wrong it is to let them go to church, and see and hear papa and mamma publicly on their knees, calling out, and confessing to the whole congregation, that they are sinners! So, though I had not the key, I could see through the panel and the glimmering of the skeleton inside.

Although the elder Firmin followed me to the door, and his eyes only left me as I turned the corner of the street, I felt sure that Phil ere long would open his mind to me, or give me some clue to that mystery. I should hear from him why his bright cheeks had become hollow, why his fresh voice, which I remember so honest and cheerful, was now harsh and sarcastic, with tones that often grated on the hearer, and laughter that gave pain. It was about Philip himself that my anxieties were. The young fellow had inherited from his poor mother a considerable fortune—some eight or nine hundred a year, we always understood. He was living in a costly, not to say extravagant manner. I thought Mr. Philip's juvenile remorses were locked up in the skeleton closet, and was grieved to think he had fallen in mischief's way. Hence, no doubt, might arise the anger between him and his father. The boy was extravagant and headstrong ; and the parent remonstrant and irritated.

I met my old friend Dr. Goodenough at the club one evening ; and as we dined together I discoursed with him about his former patient, and recalled to him that day, years back, when the boy was ill at school, and when my poor mother and Phil's own were yet alive.

Goodenough looked very grave.

"Yes," he said, "the boy was very ill; he was nearly gone at that time—at that time—when his mother was in the Isle of Wight, and his father dangling after a prince. We thought one day it was all over with him; but——"

"But a good doctor interposed between him and *pallida mors.*"

"A good doctor? a good nurse! The boy was delirious, and had a fancy to walk out of window, and would have done so, but for one of my nurses. You know her."

"What! the Little Sister?"

"Yes, the Little Sister."

"And it was she who nursed Phil through his fever, and saved his life? I drink her health. She is a good little soul."

"Good!" said the doctor, with his gruffest voice and frown. —(He was always most fierce when he was most tender-hearted.) "Good, indeed!" Will you have some more of this duck?— Do. You have had enough already, and it's very unwholesome. Good, sir? But for women, fire and brimstone ought to come down and consume this world. Your dear mother was one of the good ones. I was attending you when you were ill, at those horrible chambers you had in the Temple, at the same time when young Firmin was ill at Grey Friars. And I suppose I must be answerable for keeping two scrapegraces in the world."

"Why didn't Dr. Firmin come to see him?"

"Hm! his nerves were too delicate. Besides, he *did* come. Talk of the * * *"

The personage designated by asterisks was Phil's father, who was also a member of our club, and who entered the dining-room, tall, stately, and pale, with his stereotyped smile, and wave of his pretty hand. By the way, that smile of Firmin's was a very queer contortion of the handsome features. As you came up to him, he would draw his lips over his teeth, causing his jaws to wrinkle (or dimple if you will) on either side. Meanwhile his eyes looked out from his face, quite melancholy and independent of the little transaction in which the mouth engaged. Lips said, "I am a gentleman of fine manners and fascinating address, and I am supposed to be happy to see you. How do you do?" Dreary, sad, as into a great blank desert, looked the dark eyes. I *do* know one or two, but only one or two faces of men, when oppressed with care, which can yet smile *all over.*

Goodenough nods grimly to the smile of the other doctor, who blandly looks at our table, holding his chin in one of his pretty hands.

" How do ? " growls Goodenough.   " Young hopeful well ? "

" Young hopeful sits smoking cigars till morning with some friends of his," says Firmin, with the sad smile directed towards me this time.   " Boys will be boys."   And he pensively walks away from us with a friendly nod towards me ; examines the dinner-card in an attitude of melancholy grace ; points with the jewelled hand to the dishes which he will have served, and 's off, and simpering to another acquaintance at a distant table.

" I thought he would take that table," says Firmin's cynical *confrere.*

" In the draught of the door?   Don't you see how the candle flickers ?   It is the worst place in the room ! "

" Yes ; but don't you see who is sitting at the next table ? "

Now at the next table was a n–blem–n of vast wealth, who was growling at the quality of the mutton cutlets, and the half-pint of sherry which he had ordered for his dinner.   But as his lordship has nothing to do with the ensuing history, of course we shall not violate confidence by mentioning his name.   We could see Firmin smiling on his neighbor with his blandest melancholy, and the waiters presently bearing up the dishes which the doctor had ordered for his own refection.   *He* was no lover of mutton-chops and coarse sherry, as I knew, who had partaken of many a feast at his board.   I could see the diamond twinkle on his pretty hand, as it daintily poured out creaming wine from the ice-pail by his side—the liberal hand that had given me many a sovereign when I was a boy.

" I can't help liking him," said.I to my companion, whose scornful eyes were now and again directed towards his colleague.

" This port is very sweet.   Almost all port is sweet now," remarks the doctor.

" He was very kind to me in my school-days ; and Philip was a fine little fellow."

" Handsome a boy as ever I saw.   Does he keep his beauty ? Father was a handsome man—very.   Quite a lady-killer—I mean out of his practice ! " adds the grim doctor.   " What is the boy doing ? "

" He is at the university.   He has his mother's fortune. He is wild and unsettled, and I fear he is going to the bad a little."

" Is he ?   Shouldn't wonder ! " grumbles Goodenough.

We had talked very frankly and pleasantly until the appearance of the other doctor, but with Firmin's arrival Goodenough seemed to button up his conversation.   He quickly stumped away from the dining-room to the drawing-room, and sat over a novel there until time came when he was to retire to his patients or his home.

That there was no liking between the doctors, that there was a difference between Philip and his father, was clear enough to me : but the causes of these differences I had yet to learn. The story came to me piecemeal ; from confessions here, admissions there, deductions of my own. I could not, of course, be present at many of the scenes which I shall have to relate as though I had witnessed them ; and the posture, language, and inward thoughts of Philip and his friends, as here related, no doubt are the fancies of the narrator in many cases ; but the story is as authentic as many histories, and the reader need only give such an amount of credence to it as he may judge that its verisimilitude warrants.

Well, then, we must not only revert to that illness which befell when Philip Firmin was a boy at Grey Friars, but go back yet farther in time to a period which I cannot precisely ascertain.

The pupil's of old Gandish's painting academy may remember a ridiculous little man, with a great deal of wild talent, about the ultimate success of which his friends were divided. Whether Andrew was a genius, or whether he was a zany, was always a moot question among the frequenters of the Greek Street billiard-rooms, and the noble disciples of the Academy and St. Martin's Lane. He may have been crazy and absurd ; he may have had talent too : such characters are not unknown in art or in literature. He broke the Queen's English ; he was ignorant to a wonder ; he dressed his little person in the most fantastic raiment and queerest cheap finery ; he wore a beard, bless my soul ! twenty years before beards were known to wag in Britain. He was the most affected little creature, and, if you looked at him, would *pose* in attitudes of such ludicrous dirty dignity, that if you had had a dun waiting for money in the hall of your lodging-house, or your picture refused at the Academy—if you were suffering under ever so much calamity— you could not help laughing. He was the butt of all his acquaintances, the laughing-stock of high and low, and he had as loving, gentle, faithful, honorable a heart as ever beat in a little bosom. He is gone to his rest now ; his palette and easel are waste timber ; his genius, which made some little flicker of brightness, never shone much, and is extinct. In an old album that dates back for more than a score of years, I sometimes look at poor Andrew's strange wild sketches. He might have done something had he continued to remain poor; but a rich widow, whom he met at Rome, fell in love with the strange errant painter, pursued him to England, and married him in spite of himself.   His genius drooped under the servitude : he lived but a few short years, and died of consumption, of which the good Goodenough's skill could not cure him.

One day, as he was driving with his wife in her splendid barouche through the Haymarket, he suddenly bade the coachman stop, sprang over the side of the carriage before the steps could be let fall, and his astonished wife saw him shaking the hand of a shabbily dressed little woman who was passing,—shaking both her hands, and weeping, and gesticulating, and twisting his beard and mustaches, as his wont was when agitated.   Mrs. Montfitchet (the wealthy Mrs. Carrickfergus she had been, before she married the painter), the owner of a young husband, who had sprung from her side, and out of her carriage, in order to caress a young woman passing in the street, might well be disturbed by this demonstration ; but she was a kind-hearted woman, and when Montfitchet, on reascending into the family coach, told his wife the history of the person of whom he had just taken leave, she cried plentifully too. She bade the coachman drive straightway to her own house : she rushed up to her own apartment, whence she emerged, bearing an immense bag full of wearing apparel, and followed by a panting butler, carrying a bottle-basket and a pie : and she drove off, with her pleased Andrew by her side, to a court in St. Martin's Lane, where dwelt the poor woman with whom he had just been conversing.

It had pleased heaven, in the midst of dreadful calamity, to send her friends and succor.   She was suffering under misfortune, poverty, and cowardly desertion.   A man who had called himself Brandon when he took lodgings in her father's house, married her, brought her to London, tired of her, and left her. She had reason to think he had given a false name when he lodged with her father : he fled, after a few months, and his real name she never knew.   When he deserted her, she went back to her father, a weak man married to a domineering woman, who pretended to disbelieve the story of her marriage, and drove her from the door.   Desperate, and almost mad, she came back to London, where she still had some little relics of property that her fugitive husband left behind him.   He promised, when he left her, to remit her money ; but he sent none, or she refused it—or, in her wilderness, and despair, lost the dreadful paper which announced his desertion, and that he was married

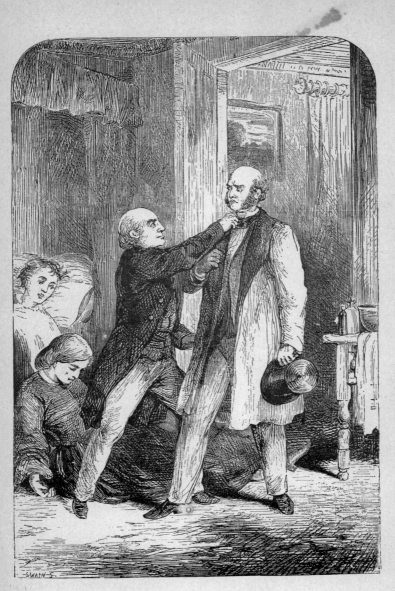

WHAT NATHAN SAID UNTO DAVID.

before, and that to pursue him would ruin him, and he knew she never would do *that*—no, however much he might have wronged her.

She was penniless then,—deserted by all,—having made away with the last trinket of her brief days of love, having sold the last little remnant of her poor little stock of clothing, alone in the great wilderness of London, when it pleased God to send her succor in the person of an old friend who had known her, and even loved her, in happier days. When the Samaritans came to this poor child, they found her sick and shuddering with fever. They brought their doctor to her, who is never so eager as when he runs up a poor man's stair. And, as he watched by the bed where her kind friends came to help her, he heard her sad little story of trust and desertion.

Her father was a humble person who had seen better days ; and poor little Mrs. Brandon had a sweetness and simplicity of manner which exceedingly touched the good doctor. She had little education, except that which silence, long-suffering, seclusion, will sometimes give. When cured of her illness, there was the great and constant evil of poverty to meet and overcome. How was she to live ? He got to be as fond of her as of a child of his own. She was tidy, thrifty, gay at times, with a little simple cheerfulness. The little flowers began to bloom as the sunshine touched them. Her whole life hitherto had been cowering under neglect, and tyranny, and gloom.

Mr. Montfitchet was for coming so often to look after the little outcast whom he had succored that I am bound to say Mrs. M. became hysterically jealous, and waited for him on the stairs as he came down swathed in his Spanish cloak, pounced on him, and called him a monster. Goodenough was also, I fancy, suspicious of Montfitchet, and Montfitchet of Goodenough. Howbeit, the doctor vowed that he never had other than the feeling of a father towards his poor little *protegée*, nor could any father be more tender. He did not try to take her out of her station in life. He found, or she found for herself, a work which she could do. "Papa used to say no one ever nursed him so nice as I did," she said. "I think I could do that better than anything, except my needle, but I like to be useful to poor sick people best. I don't think about myself then, sir." And for this business good Mr. Goodenough had her educated and employed.

The widow died in course of time whom Mrs. Brandon's father had married, and her daughters refused to keep him, speaking very disrespectfully of this old Mr. Gann, who was,

indeed, a weak old man. And now Caroline came to the rescue of her old father. She was a shrewd little Caroline. She
had saved a little money. Goodenough gave up a country-
house, which he did not care to use, and lent Mrs. Brandon
the furniture. She thought she could keep a lodging-house and
find lodgers. Montfitchet had painted her. There was a sort
of beauty about her which the artist admired. When Ridley
the Academician had the small-pox, she attended him, and
caught the malady. She did not mind ; not she. " It won't
spoil my beauty," she said. Nor did it. The disease dealt
very kindly with her little modest face. I don't know who gave
her the nick-name, but she had a good roomy house in Thornhaugh Street, an artist on the first and second floor ; and there
never was a word of scandal against the Little Sister, for
was not her father in permanence sipping gin-and-water in the
ground floor parlor ? As we called her " the Little Sister," her
father was called " the Captain "—a bragging, lazy, good-
natured old man—not a reputable Captain—and very cheerful,
though the conduct of his children, he said, had repeatedly
broken his heart.

I don't know how many years the Little Sister had been on
duty when Philip Firmin had his scarlet fever. It befell him
at the end of the term, just when all the boys were going home.
His tutor and his tutor's wife wanted their holidays, and sent
their own children out of the way. As Phil's father was absent,
Dr. Goodenough came, and sent his nurse in. The case grew
worse, so bad that Dr. Firmin was summoned from the Isle of
Wight, and arrived one evening at Grey Friars—Grey Friars so
silent now, so noisy at other times with the shouts and crowds
of the playground.

" Dr. Goodenough's carriage was at the door when Dr.
Firmin's carriage drove up.

" How was the boy ? "

" He had been very bad. He had been wrong in the head
all day, talking and laughing quite wild-like," the servant said.

The father ran up the stairs.

Phil was in a great room, in which were several empty beds
of boys gone home for the holidays. The windows were opened
into Grey Friars Square. Goodenough heard his colleague's
carriage drive up, and rightly divined that Phil's father had
arrived. He came out and met Firmin in the ante-room.

" Head has wandered a little. Better now, and quiet ; "
and the one doctor murmured to the other the treatment which
he had pursued.

Firmin stept in gently towards the patient, near whose side the Little Sister was standing.

"Who is it?" asked Phil.

"It is I, dear. Your father," said Dr. Firmin, with real tenderness in his voice.

The Little Sister turned round once, and fell down like a stone by the bedside.

"You infernal villain!" said Goodenough, with an oath, and a step forward. "You are the man!"

"Hush! The patient, if you please, Dr. Goodenough," said the other physician.

CHAPTER IV.

A GENTEEL FAMILY.

HAVE you made up your mind on the question of seeming and being in the world? I mean, suppose you *are* poor, is it right for you to *seem* to be well off? Have people an honest right to keep up appearances? Are you justified in starving your dinner-table in order to keep a carriage; to have such an expensive house that you can't by any possibility help a poor relation? to array your daughters in costly milliners' wares because they live with girls whose parents are twice as rich? Sometimes it is hard to say where honest pride ends and hypocrisy begins. To obtrude your poverty is mean and slavish; as it is odious for a beggar to ask compassion by showing his sores. But to simulate prosperity—to be wealthy and lavish thrice a year when you ask your friends, and for the rest of the time to munch a crust and sit by one candle—are the folks who practise this deceit worthy of applause or a whipping? Sometimes it is noble pride, sometimes shabby swindling. When I see Eugenia with her dear children exquisitely neat and cheerful; not showing the slightest semblance of poverty, or uttering the smallest complaint; persisting that Squanderfield, her husband, treats her well, and is good at heart; and denying that he leaves her and her young ones in want; I admire and reverence that noble falsehood—that beautiful constancy and endurance which disdains to ask compassion. When I sit at poor Jezebella's table, and am treated to her sham bounties and shabby splendor, I only feel angry for the hospitality, and that dinner, and guest, and host, are humbugs together.

Talbot Twysden's dinner-table is large, and the guests most respectable. There is always a bigwig or two present, and a dining dowager who frequents the greatest houses. There is a butler who offers you wine ; there's a *menu du dîner* before Mrs. Twysden ; and to read it you would fancy you were at a good dinner. It tastes of chopped straw. Oh, the dreary sparkle of that feeble champagne ; the audacity of that public-house sherry ; the swindle of that acrid claret ; the fiery twang of that clammy port! I have tried them all, I tell you ! It is sham wine, a sham dinner, a sham welcome, a sham cheerfulness among the guests assembled. I feel that that woman eyes and counts the cutlets as they are carried off the tables ; perhaps watches that one which you try to swallow. She has counted and grudged each candle by which the cook prepares the meal. Does her big coachman fatten himself on purloined oats and beans, and Thorley's food for cattle ? Of the rinsings of those wretched bottles the butler will have to give a reckoning in the morning. Unless you are of the very great *monde*, Twysden and his wife think themselves better than you are, and seriously patronize you. They consider it is a privilege to be invited to those horrible meals to which they gravely ask the greatest folks in the country. I actually met Winton there—the famous Winton—the best dinner-giver in the world (ah, what a position for man !) I watched him, and marked the sort of wonder which came over him as he tasted and sent away dish after dish, glass after glass. " Try that Château Margaux, Winton !" calls out our host. " It is some that Bottleby and I imported." Imported ! I see Winton's face as he tastes the wine, and puts it down. He does not like to talk about that dinner. He has lost a day. Twysden will continue to ask him every year ; will continue to expect to be asked in return, with Mrs. Twysden and one of his daughters ; and will express his surprise loudly at the club, saying, " Hang Winton ! Deuce take the fellow! He has sent me no game this year !" When foreign dukes and princes arrive, Twysden straightway collars them, and invites them to his house. And sometimes they go once—and then ask, " *Qui donc est ce Monsieur Tvisden, qui est ce drôle ?* " And he elbows his way up to them at the Minister's assemblies, and frankly gives them his hand. And calm Mrs. Twysden wriggles, and works, and slides, and pushes, and tramples if need be, her girls following behind her, until she too has come up under the eyes of the great man, and bestowed on him a

MR. FROG REQUESTS THE HONOR OF PRINCE OX'S COMPANY AT
DINNER.

smile and a curtsey. Twysden grasps prosperity cordially by
the hand. He says to success, "Bravo!" On the contrary, I
never saw a man more resolute in not knowing unfortunate
people, or more daringly forgetful of those whom he does not
care to remember. If this Levite met a wayfarer, going down
from Jerusalem, who had fallen among thieves, do you think he
would stop to rescue the fallen man? He would neither give
him wine, nor oil, nor money. He would pass on perfectly
satisfied with his own virtue, and leave the other to go, as best
he might, to Jericho.

What is this? Am I angry because Twysden has left off
asking me to his vinegar and chopped hay? No. I think not.
Am I hurt because Mrs. Twysden sometimes patronizes my
wife, and sometimes cuts her? Perhaps. Only women thoroughly know the insolence of women towards one another in the
world. That is a very stale remark. They receive and deliver
stabs, smiling politely. Tom Sayers could not take punishment
more gayly than they do. If you could but see *under* the skin,
you would find their little hearts scarred all over with little
lancet digs. I protest I have seen my own wife enduring the
impertinence of this woman, with a face as calm and placid as
she wears when old Twysden himself is talking to her, and
pouring out one of his maddening long stories. Oh, no! I am
not angry at all. I can see *that* by the way in which I am
writing of these folks. By the way, whilst I am giving this
candid opinion of the Twysdens, do I sometimes pause to
consider what they think of *me*? What do I care? Think what
you like. Meanwhile we bow to one another at parties. We
smile at each other in a sickly way. And as for the dinners in
Beaunash Street, I hope those who eat them enjoy their food.

Twysden is one of the chiefs now of the Powder and
Pomatum Office, (the Pigtail branch was finally abolished in
1833, after the Reform Bill, with a compensation to the retiring
under-secretary,) and his son is a clerk in the same office.
When they came out, the daughters were very pretty—even my
wife allows that. One of them used to ride in the Park with
her father or brother daily; and knowing what his salary and
wife's fortune were, and what the rent of his house in Beaunash
Street, everybody wondered how the Twysdens could make
both ends meet. They had horses, carriages, and a great
house fit for at least five thousand a year; they had not half
as much, as everybody knew; and it was supposed that old
Ringwood must make his niece an allowance. She certainly
worked hard to get it. I spoke of stabs anon, and poor little

breasts and sides scarred all over. No nuns, no monks, no fakeers take whippings more kindly than some devotees of the world ; and, as the punishment is one for edification, let us hope the world lays smartly on to back and shoulders, and uses the thong well.

When old Ringwood, at the close of his lifetime, used to come to visit his dear niece and her husband and children, he always brought a cat-o'-nine-tails in his pocket, and administered it to the whole household. He grinned at the poverty, the pretence, the meanness of the people, as they knelt before him and did him homage. The father and mother trembling brought the girls up for punishment, and piteously smiling, received their own boxes on the ear in presence of their children. "Ah !" the little French governess used to say, grinding her white teeth, "I like milor to come. All day you vip me. When milor come, he vip you, and you kneel down and kiss de rod."

They certainly knelt and took their whipping with the most exemplary fortitude. Sometimes the lash fell on papa's back, sometimes on mamma's : now it stung Agnes, and now it lighted on Blanche's pretty shoulders. But I think it was on the heir of the house, young Ringwood Twysden, that my lord loved best to operate. Ring's vanity was very thin-skinned, his selfishness easily wounded, and his contortions under punishment amused the old tormentor.

As my lord's brougham drives up—the modest little brown brougham, with the noble horse, the lord chancellor of a coachman, and the ineffable footman—the ladies, who know the whirr of the wheels, and may be quarrelling in the drawing-room, call a truce to the fight, and smooth down their ruffled tempers and raiment. Mamma is writing at her table, in that beautiful, clear hand which we all admire ; Blanche is at her book ; Agnes is rising from the piano quite naturally. A quarrel between those gentle, smiling, delicate creatures ! Impossible ! About your most common piece of hypocrisy how men will blush and bungle : how easily, how gracefully, how consummately, women will perform it !

"Well," growls my lord, "you are all in such pretty attitudes, I make no doubt you have been sparring. I suspect, Maria, the men must know what devilish bad tempers the girls have got. Who can have seen you fighting? You're quiet enough here, you little monkeys. I tell you what it is. Ladies'-maids get about and talk to the valets in the housekeeper's room. and the men tell their masters. Upon my word I believe

it was that business last year at Whipham which frightened
Greenwood off. Famous match. Good house in town and
country. No mother alive. Agnes might have had it her own
way, but for that——"

"We are not all angels in our family, uncle!" cries Miss
Agnes, reddening.

"And your mother is too sharp. The men are afraid of
you, Maria. I've heard several young men say so. At White's
they talk about it quite freely. Pity for the girls. Great pity.
Fellows come and tell me. Jack Hall, and fellows who go
about everywhere."

"I'm sure I don't care what Captain Hall says about me
—odious little wretch!" cries Blanche.

"There you go off in a tantrum! Hall never has any
opinion of his own. He only fetches and carries what other
people say. And he says, fellows say they are frightened of
your mother. La bless you! Hall has no opinion. A fellow
might commit murder, and Hall would wait at the door. Quite
a discreet man. But I told him to ask about you. And that's
what I hear. And he says that Agnes is making eyes at the
doctor's boy."

"It's a shame," cries Agnes, shedding tears under her
martyrdom.

"Older than he is ; but that's no obstacle. Good-looking
boy, I suppose you don't object to that ? Has his poor mother's
money, and his father's : must be well to do. A vulgar fellow,
but a clever fellow, and a determined fellow, the doctor—and a
fellow who, I suspect, is capable of anything. Shouldn't wonder
at that fellow marrying some rich dowager. Those doctors get
an immense influence over women ; and unless I'm mistaken
in my man, Maria, your poor sister got hold of a——"

"Uncle!" cries Mrs. Twysden, pointing to her daughters,
"before these——"

"Before those innocent lambs! Hem! Well, I think
Firmin is of the wolf sort :" and the old noble laughed, and
showed his own fierce fangs as he spoke.

"I grieve to say, my lord, I agree with you," remarks Mr.
Twysden. "I don't think Firmin a man of high principle. A
clever man ? Yes. An accomplished man ? Yes. A good
physician ? Yes. A prosperous man ? Yes. But what's a
man without principle ?"

"You ought to have been a parson, Twysden."

"Others have said so, my lord. My poor mother often
regretted that I didn't choose the Church. When I was at

Cambridge I used to speak constantly at the Union. I practised. I do not disguise from you that my aim was public life. I am free to confess I think the House of Commons would have been my sphere; and, had my means permitted, should certainly have come forward."

Lord Ringwood smiled, and winked to his niece—

"He means, my dear, that he would like to wag his jaws at my expense, and that I should put him in for Whipham."

"There are, I think, worse Members of Parliament," remarked Mr. Twysden.

"If there was a box of 'em like you, what a cage it would be!" roared my lord. "By George, I'm sick of jaw. And I would like to see a king of spirit in this country, who would shut up the talking-shops and gag the whole chattering crew!"

"I am a partisan of order—but a lover of freedom," continues Twysden. "I hold that the balance of our constitution——"

I think my lord would have indulged in a few of those oaths with which his old-fashioned conversation was liberally garnished; but the servant, entering at this moment, announces Mr. Philip Firmin; and ever so faint a blush flutters up in Agnes' cheek, who feels that the old lord's eye is upon her.

"So, sir, I saw you at the Opera last night," says Lord Ringwood.

"I saw you, too," says downright Phil.

The women looked terrified, and Twysden scared. The Twysdens had Lord Ringwood's box sometimes. But there were boxes in which the old man sat, and in which they never *could* see him.

"Why don't you look at the stage, sir, when you go to the Opera, and not at me? When you go to church you ought to look at the parson, oughtn't you?" growled the old man. "I'm about as good to look at as the fellow who dances first in the ballet—and very nearly as old. But if I were you, I should think looking at the Ellsler better fun."

And now you may fancy of what old, old times we are writing—times in which those horrible old male dancers yet existed —hideous old creatures, with low dresses and short sleeves, and wreaths of flowers, or hats and feathers round their absurd old wigs—who skipped at the head of the ballet. Let us be thankful that those old apes have almost vanished off the stage, and left it in possession of the beauteous bounders of the other sex. Ah, my dear young friends, time *will* be when these too will cease to appear more than mortally beautiful! To Philip, at his age, they yet looked as lovely as houris. As this time the simply young fellow, surveying the ballet from his stall at the Opera, mistook carmine for blushes, pearl-powder for native snows, and cotton-wool for natural symmetry ; and I dare say when he went into the world was not more clear-sighted about its rouged innocence, its padded pretensions, and its painted candor.

Old Lord Ringwood had a humorous pleasure in petting and coaxing Philip Firmin before Philip's relatives of Beaunash Street. Even the girls felt a little plaintive envy at the partiality which uncle Ringwood exhibited for Phil ; but the elder Twysdens and Ringwood Twysden, their son, writhed with agony at the preference which the old man sometimes showed for the doctor's boy. Phil was much taller, much handsomer, much stronger, much better tempered, and much richer, than young Twysden. He would be the sole inheritor of his father's fortune, and had his mother's thirty thousand pounds. Even when they told him his father would marry again, Phil laughed, and did not seem to care—" I wish him joy of his new wife," was all he could be got to say : " when he gets one, I suppose I shall go into chambers. Old Parr Street is not as gay as Pall Mall." I am not angry with Mrs. Twysden for having a little jealousy of her nephew. Her boy and girls were the fruit of a dutiful marriage ; and Phil was the son of a disobedient child. Her children were always on their best behavior before their great uncle ; and Phil cared for him no more than for any other man ; and he liked Phil the best. Her boy was as humble and eager to please as any of his lordship's humblest henchmen ; and Lord Ringwood snapped at him, browbeat him, and trampled on the poor darling's tenderest feelings, and treated him scarcely better than a lacquey. As for poor Mr. Twysden, my lord not only yawned unreservedly in his face—that could not be helped ; poor Talbot's talk set many of his acquaintance asleep—but laughed at him, interrupted him, and told him to hold his tongue. On this day, as the family sat together at the pleasant hour—the before-dinner hour—the fireside and tea-table hour—Lord Ringwood said to Phil—

" Dine with me to-day, sir ? "

" Why does he not ask me, with my powers of conversation ? " thought old Twysden to himself.

" Hang him, he always asks that beggar," writhed young Twysden, in his corner.

" Very sorry, sir, can't come. Have asked some fellows to dine at the ' Blue Posts,' " says Phil.

"Confound you, sir, why don't you put 'em off?" cries the old lord. " *You'd* put 'em off, Twysden, wouldn't you?"

"Oh, sir!" the heart of father and son both beat.

"You know you would; and you quarrel with this boy for not throwing his friends over. Good-night, Firmin, since you won't come."

And with this my lord was gone.

The two gentlemen of the house glumly looked from the window, and saw my lord's brougham driven swiftly away in the rain.

"I hate your dining at those horrid taverns," whispered a young lady to Phillip.

"It is better fun than dining at home," Philip remarks.

"You smoke and drink too much. You come home late, and you don't live in a proper *monde*, sir!" continues the young lady.

"What would you have me do?"

"Oh, nothing. You must dine with those horrible men," cries Agnes; "else you might have gone to Lady Pendleton's to-night."

"I can throw over the men easily enough, if you wish," answered the young man.

"I? I have no wish of the sort. Have you not already refused uncle Ringwood?"

" *You* are not Lord Ringwood," says Phil, with a tremor in his voice. "I don't know there is much I would refuse you."

"You silly boy! What do I ever ask you to do that you ought to refuse? I want you to live in our world, and not with your dreadful wild Oxford and Temple bachelors. I don't want you to smoke. I want you to go into the world of which you have the *entrée*—and you refuse your uncle on account of some horrid engagement at a tavern!"

"Shall I stop here? Aunt, will you give me some dinner—here?" asks the young man.

"We have dined: my husband and son dine out," said gentle Mrs. Twysden.

There was cold mutton and tea for the ladies; and Mrs. Twysden did not like to seat her nephew, who was accustomed to good fare and high living, to that meagre meal.

"You see I must console myself at the tavern," Philip said. "We shall have a pleasant party there."

"And pray who makes it?" asks the lady.

"There is Ridley the painter."

"My dear Philip! Do you know that his father was actu ally——"

" In the service of Lord Todmorden ? He often tells us so. He is a queer character, the old man."

" Mr. Ridley is a man of genius, certainly. His pictures are delicious, and he goes everywhere—but—but you provoke me, Philip, by your carelessness ; indeed you do. Why should you be dining with the sons of footmen, when the first houses in the country might be open to you ? You pain me, you foolish boy."

" For dining in company of a man of genius ? Come, Agnes ! " And the young man's brow grew dark. " Besides," he added, with a tone of sarcasm in his voice, which Miss Agnes did not like at all—"besides, my dear, you know he dines at Lord Pendleton's."

" What is that you are talking of Lady Pendleton, children ? " asked watchful mamma from her corner.

" Ridley dines there. He is going to dine with me at a tavern to-day. And Lord Halden is coming—and Mr. Winton is coming—having heard of the famous beefsteaks."

" Winton ! Lord Halden ! Beefsteaks ! Where ? By George ! I have a mind to go, too ! Where do you fellows dine ? *au cabaret ?* Hang me, I'll be one," shrieked little Twysden, to the terror of Philip, who knew his uncle's awful powers of conversation. But Twysden remembered himself in good time, and to the intense relief of young Firmin. " Hang me, I forgot ! Your aunt and I dine with the Bladeses. Stupid old fellow, the admiral, and bad wine—which is unpardonable ; but we must go—*on n'a que sa parole,* hey ? Tell Winton that I had meditated joining him, and that I have still some of that Château Margaux he liked. Halden's father I know well. Tell him so. Bring him here. Maria, send a Thursday card to Lord Halden ! You must bring him here to dinner, Philip. *That's* the best way to make acquaintance, my boy ! " And the little man swaggers off, waving a bed-candle, as if he was going to quaff a bumper of sparkling spermaceti.

The mention of such great personages as Lord Halden and Mr. Winton silenced the reproofs of the pensive Agnes.

" You won't care for our quiet fireside whilst you live with those fine people," she sighed. There was no talk now of his throwing himself away on bad company.

So Philip did not dine with his relatives : but Talbot Twysden took good care to let Lord Ringwood know how young Firmin had offered to dine with his aunt that day after refusing his lordship. And everything to Phil's discredit, and every act of extravagance or wildness which the young man committed, did Phil's uncle, and Phil's cousin Ringwood Twysden, convey to the old nobleman. Had not these been the informers, Lord Ringwood would have been angry : for he exacted obedience and servility from all round about him. But it was pleasanter to vex the Twysdens than to scold and browbeat Philip, and so his lordship chose to laugh and be amused at Phil's insubordination. He saw, too, other things of which he did not speak. He was a wily old man, who could afford to be blind upon occasion.

What do you judge from the fact that Philip was ready to make or break engagements at a young lady's instigation? When you were twenty years old, had no young ladies an influence over *you?* Were they not commonly older than yourself? Did your youthful passion lead to anything, and are you very sorry now that it did not? Suppose you had your soul's wish and married her, of what age would she be now? And now when you go into the world and see her, *do* you on your conscience very much regret that the little affair came to an end? Is it that (lean, or fat, or stumpy, or tall) woman with all those children whom you once chose to break your heart about ; and do you still envy Jones? Philip was in love with his cousin, no doubt, but at the university had he not been previously in love with the Tomkinsian professor's daughter Miss Budd ; and had he not already written verses to Miss Flower, his neighbor's daughter in Old Parr Street? And don't young men always begin by falling in love with ladies older than themselves? Agnes certainly was Philip's senior, as her sister constantly took care to inform him.

And Agnes might have told stories about Blanche, if she chose—as you may about me, and I about you. Not quite true stories, but stories with enough alloy of lies to make them serviceable coin ; stories such as we hear daily in the world ; stories such as we read in the most learned and conscientious history-books, which are told by the most respectable persons, and perfectly authentic until contradicted. It is only *our* histories that can't be contradicted (unless, to be sure, novelists contradict themselves, as sometimes they will). What *we* say about people's virtues, failings, characters, you may be sure is all true. And I defy any man to assert that my opinion of the Twysden family is malicious, or unkind or unfounded in any particular. Agnes wrote verses, and set her own and other writers' poems to music. Blanche was scientific, and attended the Albemarle Street lectures sedulously. They are both clever women as times go ; well educated and accomplished, and very well mannered when they choose to be pleasant. If you were a bachelor, say, with a good fortune, or a widower who wanted consolation, or a lady giving very good parties and belonging to the *monde*, you would find them agreeable people. If you were a little Treasury clerk, or a young barrister with no practice, or a lady, old or young, *not* quite of the *monde*, your opinion of them would not be so favorable. I have seen them cut, and scorn, and avoid, and caress, and kneel down and worship the same person. When Mrs. Lovel first gave parties, don't I remember the shocked countenances of the Twysden family? Were ever shoulders colder than yours, dear girls? Now they love her; they fondle her step-children; they praise her to her face and behind her handsome back; they take her hand in public; they call her by her Christian name; they fall into ecstasies over her toilettes, and would fetch coals for her dressing-room fire if she but gave them the word. *She* is not changed. She is the same lady who once was a governess, and no colder and no warmer since then. But you see her prosperity has brought virtues into evidence, which people did not perceive when she was poor. Could people see Cinderella's beauty when she was in rags by the fire, or untill she stepped out of her fairy coach in her diamonds? How *are* you to recognize a diamond in a dusthole? Only very clever eyes can do that. Whereas a lady in a fairy coach and eight naturally creates a sensation; and enraptured princes come and beg to have the honor of dancing with her.

In the character of infallible historian, then, I declare that if Miss Twysden at three-and-twenty feels ever so much or little attachment for her cousin who is not yet of age, there is no reason to be angry with her. A brave, handsome, blundering, downright young fellow, with broad shoulders, high spirits, (and quite fresh blushes on his face, with very good talents, (though he has been wofully idle, and requested to absent himself temporarily from his university,) the possessor of a competent fortune and the heir of another, may naturally make some impression on a lady's heart with whom kinsmanship and circumstance bring him into daily communion. When had any sound so hearty as Phil's laugh been heard in Beaunash Street? His jolly frankness touched his aunt, a clever woman. She would smile and say, " My dear Philip, it is not only what you say, but what you are going to say next, keeps me in such a perpetual tremor." There may have been a time once when she was frank and cordial herself: ever so long ago, when she and her sister were two blooming girls, lovingly clinging together, and just stepping forth into the world. But if you succeed in keeping a fine house on a small income ; in showing a cheerful face to the world though oppressed with ever so much care ; in bearing with dutiful reverence an intolerable old bore of a husband (and I vow it is this quality in Mrs. Twysden for which I most admire her) ; in submitting to defeats patiently ; to humiliations with smiles, so as to hold your own in your darling *monde ;* you may succeed, but you must give up being frank and cordial. The marriage of her sister to the doctor gave Maria Ringwood a great panic, for Lord Ringwood was furious when the news came. Then, perhaps, she sacrificed a little private passion of her own : then she set her cap at a noble young neighbor of my lord's, who jilted *her ;* then she took up with Talbot Twysden, Esquire, of the Powder and Pomatum Office, and made a very faithful wife to him, and was a very careful mother to his children. But as for frankness and cordiality, my good friend, accept from a lady what she can give you— good manners, pleasant talk, and decent attention. If you go to her breakfast-table, don't ask for a roc's egg, but eat that moderately fresh hen's egg which John brings you. When Mrs. Twysden is in her open carriage in the Park, how prosperous, handsome, and jolly she looks—the girls how smiling and young (that is, you know, considering all things) ; the horses look fat, the coachman and footman wealthy and sleek ; they exchange bows with the tenants of other carriages—well known aristocrats. Jones and Brown, leaning over the railings and seeing the Twysden equipage pass, have not the slightest doubt that it contains people of the highest wealth and fashion. " I say, Jones my boy, what noble family has the motto *Wel done Twys done ?* and what clipping girls there were in that barouche !" B. remarks to J. ; "and what a handsome young swell that is riding the bay mare, and leaning over and talking to the yellow-haired girl ! " And it is evident to one of those gentlemen, at least, that he has been looking at your regular first-rate tiptop people.

As for Phil Firmin on his bay mare, with his geranium in his button-hole, there is no doubt that Philippus looks as handsome, and as rich, and as brave as any lord. And I think Brown must have felt a little pang when his friend told him, " That a lord ! Bless you, it's only a swell doctor's son." But while J. and B. fancy all the little party very happy, they do not hear Phil whisper to his cousin, "I hope you liked *your partner* last night ? " and they do not see how anxious Mrs. Twysden is under her smiles, how she perceives Colonel

Shafto's cab coming up (the dancer in question), and how she would rather have Phil anywhere than by that particular wheel of her carriage ; how Lady Braglands has just passed them by without noticing them—Lady Braglands, who has a ball, and is determined *not* to ask that woman and her two endless girls ; and how, though Lady Braglands won't see Mrs. Twysden in her great staring equipage, and the three faces which have been beaming smiles at her, she instantly perceives Lady Lovel, who is passing ensconced in her little brougham, and kisses her fingers twenty times over. How should poor J. and B., who are not, *vous comprenez*, *du monde*, understand these mysteries ?

"That's young Firmin, is it, that handsome young fellow ? " says Brown to Jones.

"Doctor married the Earl of Ringwood's niece—ran away with her, you know."

"Good practice ? "

"Capital. First-rate. All the tiptop people. Great ladies' doctor. Can't do without him. Makes a fortune, besides what he had with his wife."

"We've seen his name—the old man's—on some very queer paper," says B., with a wink to J. By which I conclude they are city gentlemen. And they look very hard at friend Philip, as he comes to talk and shake hands with some pedestrians who are gazing over the railings at the busy and pleasant Park scene.

CHAPTER V.

THE NOBLE KINSMAN.

HAVING had occasion to mention a noble earl once or twice, I am sure no polite reader will consent that his lordship should push through this history along with the crowd of commoner characters, and without a special word regarding himself. If you are in the least familiar with Burke or Debrett, you know that the ancient family of Ringwood has long been famous for its great possessions, and its loyalty to the British crown.

In the troubles which unhappily agitated this kingdom after the deposition of the late reigning house, the Ringwoods were

implicated with many other families, but on the accession of
his Majesty George III. these differences happily ended, nor
had the monarch any subject more loyal and devoted than Sir
John Ringwood, Baronet, of Wingate and Whipham Market.
Sir John's influence sent three members to Parliament; and
during the dangerous and vexatious period of the American
war, this influence was exerted so cordially and consistently in
the cause of order and the crown, that his Majesty saw fit to
advance Sir John to the dignity of Baron Ringwood. Sir John's
brother, Sir Francis Ringwood, of Appleshaw, who followed the
profession of the law, also was promoted to be a Baron of his
Majesty's Court of Exchequer. The first Baron, dying A. D.
1786, was succeeded by the eldest of his two sons — John,
second Baron and first Earl of Ringwood. His lordship's
brother, the Honorable Colonel Philip Ringwood, died gloriously, at the head of his regiment and in the defence of his
country, in the battle of Busaco, 1810, leaving two daughters,
Louisa and Maria, who henceforth lived with the earl their
uncle.

The Earl of Ringwood had but one son, Charles Viscount
Cinqbars, who, unhappily, died of a decline in his twenty-second
year. And thus the descendants of Sir Francis Ringwood
became heirs to the earl's great estates of Wingate and Whipham Market, though not of the peerages which had been
conferred on the earl and his father.

Lord Ringwood had, living with him, two nieces, daughters
of his late brother, Colonel Philip Ringwood, who fell in the
Peninsular War. Of these ladies, the youngest, Louisa, was
his lordship's favorite; and though both the ladies had considerable fortunes of their own, it was supposed their uncle would
further provide for them, especially as he was on no very good
terms with his cousin, Sir John of the Shaw, who took the Whig
side in politics, whilst his lordship was a chief of the Tory
party.

Of these two nieces, the eldest, Maria, never any great
favorite with her uncle, married, 1824, Talbot Twysden, Esq., a
Commissioner of Powder and Pomatum Tax; but the youngest,
Louisa, incurred my lord's most serious anger by eloping with
George Brand Firmin, Esq., M.D., a young gentleman of Cam-
bridge University, who had been with Lord Cinqbars when he
died at Naples, and had brought home his body to Wingate
Castle.

The quarrel with the youngest niece, and the indifference
with which he generally regarded the elder (whom his lordship

was in the habit of calling an old schemer), occasioned at first a little *rapprochement* between Lord Ringwood and his heir, Sir John of Appleshaw ; but both gentlemen were very firm, not to to say obstinate, in their natures.   They had a quarrel with respect to the cutting off of a small entailed property, of which the earl wished to dispose ; and they parted with much rancor and bad language on his lordship's part, who was an especially free-spoken nobleman, and apt to call a spade a spade, as the saying is.

After this difference, and to spite his heir, it was supposed that the Earl of Ringwood would marry.   He was little more than seventy years of age, and had once been of a very robust constitution.   And though his temper was violent and his person not at all agreeable (for even in Sir Thomas Lawrence's picture his countenance is very ill-favored), there is little doubt he could have found a wife for the asking among the young beauties of his own county, or the fariest of May Fair.

But he was a cynical nobleman, and perhaps morbidly conscious of his own ungainly appearance.   "Of course I can buy a wife" (his lordship would say).   "Do you suppose people won't sell their daughters to a man of my rank and means ?   Now look at me, my good sir, and say whether any woman alive could fall in love with me ?   I have been married, and once was enough.   I hate ugly women, and your virtuous women, who tremble and cry in private, and preach at a man, bore me.   Sir John Ringwood of Appleshaw is an ass, and I hate him ; but I don't hate him enough to make myself miserable for the rest of my days, in order to spite him.   When I drop, I drop.   Do you suppose I care what comes after me ?"   And with much sardonical humor this old lord used to play off one good dowager after another who would bring her girl in his way.   He would send pearls to Emily, diamonds to Fanny, opera-boxes to lively Kate, books of devotion to pious Selinda and, at the season's end, drive back to his lonely great castle in the west.   They were all the same, such was his lordship's opinion.   I fear, a wicked and corrupt old gentleman, my dears. But ah, would not a woman submit to some sacrifices to reclaim that unhappy man ; to lead that gifted but lost being into the ways of right ; to convert to a belief in woman's purity that erring soul ?   They tried him with high-church altar-cloths for his chapel at Wingate ; they tried him with low-church tracts ; they danced before him ; they jumped fences on horseback : they wore bandeaux or ringlets, according as his taste dictated ; they were always at home when he called, and poor you and I were gruffly told they were engaged ; they gushed in gratitude over his bouquets ; they sang for him, and their mothers, concealing their sobs, murmured, " What an angel that Cecilia of mine is ? " Every variety of delicious chaff they flung to that old bird. But he was uncaught at the end of the season : he winged his way back to his western hills. And if you dared to say that Mrs. Netley had tried to take him, or Lady Trapboys had set a snare for him, you know you were a wicked, gross caluminator, and notorious everywhere for your dull and vulgar abuse of women.

Now, in the year 1830, it happened that this great nobleman was seized with a fit of the gout, which had very nearly consigned his estates to his kinsman the Baronet of Appleshaw. A revolution took place in a neighboring State. An illustrious reigning family was expelled from its country, and projects of reform (which would pretty certainly end in revolution) were rife in ours. The events in France, and those pending at home, so agitated Lord Ringwood's mind, that he was attacked by one of the severest fits of gout under which he ever suffered. His shrieks, as he was brought out of his yacht at Ryde to a house taken for him in the town, were dreadful ; his language to all persons about him was frightfully expressive, as Lady Quamley and her daughter, who sailed with him several times, can vouch. An ill return that rude old man made for all their kindness and attention to him. They had danced on board his yacht ; they had dined on board his yacht ; they had been out sailing with him, and cheerfully braved the inconveniences of the deep in his company. And when they ran to the side of his chair— as what would they not do to soothe an old gentleman in illness and distress ?—when they ran up to his chair as it was wheeled along the pier, he called mother and daughter by the most vulgar and opprobrious names, and roared out to them to go to a place which I certainly shall not more particularly mention.

Now it happened, at this period, that Dr. and Mrs. Firmin were at Ryde with their little boy, then some three years of age. The doctor was already taking his place as one of the most fashionable physicians then in London, and had begun to be celebrated for the treatment of this especial malady. (Firmin on " Gout and Rheumatism " was, you remember, dedicated to his Majesty George IV.) Lord Ringwood's valet bethought him of calling the doctor in, and mentioned how he was present in the town. Now Lord Ringwood was a nobleman who never would allow his angry feelings to stand in the way of his present comforts or ease. He instantly desired Mr. Firman's attendance, and submitted to his treatment: a part of which was a *hauteur* to the full as great as that which the sick man exhibited. Firmin's appearance was so tall and grand, that he looked vastly more noble than a great many noblemen. Six feet, a high manner, a polished forehead, a flashing eye, a snowy shirt-frill, a rolling velvet collar, a beautiful hand appearing under a velvet cuff—all these advantages he possessed and used. He did not make the slightest allusion to bygones, but treated his patient with a perfect courtesy and an impenetrable self-possession.

This defiant and darkling politeness did not always displease the old man. He was so accustomed to slavish compliance and eager obedience from all people round about him, that he sometimes wearied of their servility, and relished a little independence. Was it from calculation, or because he was a man of high spirit, that Firmin determined to maintain an independent course with his lordship? From the first day of their meeting he never departed from it, and had the satisfaction of meeting with only civil behavior from his noble relative and patient, who was notorious for his rudeness and brutality to almost every person who came in his way.

From hints which his lordship gave in conversation, he showed the doctor that he was acquainted with some particulars of the latter's early career. It had been wild and stormy. Firmin had incurred debts; had quarrelled with his father; had left the university and gone abroad; had lived in a wild society, which used dice and cards every night, and pistols sometimes in the morning; and had shown a fearful dexterity in the use of the latter instrument, which he employed against the person of a famous Italian adventurer, who fell under his hand at Naples. When this century was five-and-twenty years younger, the crack of the pistol-shot might still occasionally be heard in the suburbs of London in the very early morning; and the dice-box went round in many a haunt of pleasure. The knights of the Four Kings travelled from capital to capital, and engaged each other or made pray of the unwary. Now, the times are changed. The cards are confined in their boxes. Only *sous-officiers*, brawling in their provincial cafés over their dominos, fight duels. "Ah, dear me," I heard a veteran punter sigh the other day at Bays's, "isn't it a melancholy thing to think, that if I wanted to amuse myself with a fifty-pound note, I don't know the place in London where I could go and lose it?" And he fondly recounted the names of twenty places where he could have cheerfully staked and lost his money in his young time.

After a somewhat prolonged absence abroad, Mr. Firmin came back to this country, was permitted to return to the university, and left it with the degree of Bachelor of Medicine. We have told how he ran away with Lord Ringwood's niece, and incurred the anger of that nobleman. Beyond abuse and anger his lordship was powerless. The young lady was free to marry whom she liked, and her uncle to disown or receive him ; and accordingly she was, as we have seen, disowned by his lordship, until he found it convenient to forgive her. What were Lord Ringwood's intentions regarding his property, what were his accumulations, and who his heirs would be, no one knew. Meanwhile, of course, there were those who felt a very great interest on the point. Mrs. Twysden and her husband and children were hungry and poor. If uncle Ringwood had money to leave, it would be very welcome to those three darlings whose father had not a great income like Dr. Firmin. Philip was a dear, good, frank, amiable, wild fellow, and they all loved him. But he had his faults—that could not be concealed—and so poor Phil's faults were pretty constantly canvassed before uncle Ringwood, by dear relatives who knew them only too well. The dear relatives! How kind they are! I don't think Phil's aunt abused him to my lord. That quiet woman calmly and gently put forward the claims of her own darlings, and affectionately dilated on the young man's present prosperity, and magnificent future prospects. The interest of thirty thousand pounds now, and the inheritance of his father's great accumulations! What young man could want for more ? Perhaps he had too much already. Perhaps he was too rich to work. The sly old peer acquiesced in his niece's statements, and perfectly understood the point towards which they tended. "A thousand a year! What's a thousand a year ? " growled the old lord. "Not enough to make a gentleman, more than enough to make a fellow idle."

"Ah, indeed, it was but a small income," sighed Mrs. Twysden. "With a large house, a good establishment, and Mr. Twysden's salary from his office—it was but a pittance."

"Pittance! Starvation," growls my lord, with his usual frankness. "Don't I know what housekeeping costs ; and see how you screw ? Butlers and footmen, carriages and job-horses, rent and dinners—though yours, Maria, are not famous."

"Very bad—I know they are very bad," says the contrite lady, "I wish we could afford any better."

"Afford any better? Of course you can't. You are the crockery pots, and you swim down stream with the brass pots. I saw Twysden the other day walking down St. James's Street with Rhodes—that tall fellow." (Here my lord laughed, and showed many fangs, the exhibition of which gave a peculiarly fierce air to his lordship when in good-humor.) "If Twysden walks with a big fellow, he always tries to keep step with him. *You* know that." Poor Maria naturally knew her husband's peculiarities ; but she did not say that she had no need to be reminded of them.

"He was so blown he could hardly speak," continued uncle Ringwood ; "but he would stretch his little legs, and try and keep up. He has a little body, *le cher mari*, but a good pluck. Those little fellows often have. I've seen him half dead out shooting, and plunging over the ploughed fields after fellows with twice his stride. Why don't men sink in the world, I want to know ? Instead of a fine house, and a parcel of idle servants, why don't you have a maid and a leg of mutton, Maria ? You go half crazy in trying to make both ends meet. You know you do. It keeps you awake of nights ; *I* know that very well. You've got a house fit for people with four times your money. I lend you my cook and so forth ; but I can't come and dine with you unless I send the wine in. Why don't you have a pot of porter, and a joint, or some tripe?—tripe's a famous good thing. The miseries which people entail on themselves in trying to live beyond their means are perfectly ridiculous, by George ! Look at that fellow who opened the door to me ; he's as tall as one of my own men. Go and live in a quiet little street in Belgravia somewhere, and have a neat little maid. Nobody will think a penny the worse of you—and you will be just as well off as if you lived here with an extra couple of thousand a year. The advice I am giving you is worth half that, every shilling of it."

"It is very good advice ; but I think, sir, I should prefer the thousand pounds," said the lady.

"Of course you would. That is the consequence of your false position. One of the good points about that doctor is, that he is as proud as Lucifer, and so is his boy. They are not always hungering after money. They keep their independence ; though he'll have his own too, the fellow will. Why, when I first called him in, I thought, as he was a relation, he'd doctor me for nothing ; but he wouldn't. He would have his fee, by George ! and wouldn't come without it. Confounded independent fellow Firmin is. And so is the young one."

But when Twysden and his son (perhaps inspirited by Mrs. Twysden) tried once or twice to be independent in the presence of this lion, he roared, and he rushed at them, and he rent them, so that they fled from him howling. And this reminds me of an old story I have heard—quite an old, old story, such as kind old fellows at clubs love to remember—of my lord, when he was only Lord Cinqbars, insulting a half-pay lieutenant, in his own county, who horsewhipped his lordship in the most private and ferocious manner. It was said Lord Cinqbars had had a rencontre with poachers ; but it was my lord who was poaching and the lieutenant who was defending his own dove-cot. I do not say that this was a model nobleman ; but that, when his own passions or interests did not mislead him, he was a nobleman of very considerable acuteness, humor, and good sense ; and could give quite good advice on occasion. If men would kneel down and kiss his boots, well and good. There was the blacking, and you were welcome to embrace toe and heel. But those who would not, were free to leave the operation alone. The Pope himself does not demand the ceremony from Protestants ; and if they object to the slipper, no one thinks of forcing it into their mouths. Phil and his father probably declined to tremble before the old man, not because they knew he was a bully who might be put down, but because they were men of spirit, who cared not whether a man was bully or no.

I have told you I like Philip Firmin, though it must be confessed that the young fellow had many faults, and that his career, especially his early career, was by no means exemplary. Have I ever excused his conduct to his father, or said a word in apology of his brief and inglorious university career? I acknowledge his shortcomings with that candor which my friends exhibit in speaking of mine. Who does not see a friend's weaknesses, and is so blind that he cannot perceive that enormous beam in his neighbor's eye? Only a woman or two, from time to time. And even they are undeceived some day. A man of the world, I write about my friends as mundane fellow-creatures. Do you suppose there are many angels here? I say again, perhaps a woman or two. But as for you and me, my good sir, are there any signs of wings sprouting from *our* shoulder-blades? Be quiet. Don't pursue your snarling, cynical remarks, but go on with your story.

As you go through life, stumbling, and slipping, and staggering to your feet again, ruefully aware of your own wretched weakness, and praying, with a contrite heart, let us trust, that you may not be led into temptation, have you not often looked at other fellow-sinners, and speculated with an awful interest on their career? Some there are on whom, quite in their early lives, dark Ahrimanes has seemed to lay his dread mark: children, yet corrupt, and wicked of tongue; tender of age, yet cruel; who should be truth-telling and generous yet (they were at their mothers' bosoms yesterday), but are false and cold and greedy before their time. Infants almost, they practice the art and selfishness of old men. Behind their candid faces are wiles and wickedness, and a hideous precocity of artifice. I can recall such, and in the vista of far-off, unforgotten boyhood, can see marching that sad little procession of *enfans perdus*. May they be saved, pray heaven! Then there is the doubtful class, those who are still on trial; those who fall and rise again; those who are often worsted in life's battle; beaten down, wounded, imprisoned: but escape and conquer sometimes. And then there is the happy class about whom there seems no doubt at all: the spotless and white-robed ones, to whom virtue is easy; in whose pure bosoms faith nestles, and cold doubt finds no entrance; who are children, and good; young men, and good; husbands and fathers, and yet good. Why could the captain of our school write his Greek iambics without an effort, and without an error? Others of us blistered the page with unavailing tears and blots, and might toil ever so and come in lag last at the bottom of the form. Our friend Philip belongs to the middle class, in which you and I probably are, my dear sir—not yet, I hope, irredeemably consigned to that awful third class, whereof mention has been made.

But, being *homo*, and liable to err, there is no doubt Mr. Philip exercised his privilege, and there was even no little fear at one time that he should overdraw his account. He went from school to the university, and there distinguished himself certainly, but in a way in which very few parents would choose that their sons should excel. That he should hunt, that he should give parties, that he should pull a good oar in one of the best boats on the river, that he should speak at the Union —all these were very well. But why should he speak such awful radicalism and republicanism—he with noble blood in his veins, and the son of a parent whose interest at least it was to keep well with people of high station?

"Why, Pendennis," said Dr. Firmin to me with tears in his eyes, and much genuine grief exhibited on his handsome pale face—"why should it be said that Philip Firmin—both of whose grandfathers fought nobly for their king—should be forgetting the principles of his family, and—and, I haven't words to tell you how deeply he disappoints me. Why, I actually heard of him at that horrible Union advocating the death of Charles the First! I was wild enough myself when I was at the university, but I was a gentleman."

"Boys, sir, are boys," I urged. "They will advocate anything for an argument; and Philip would have taken the other side quite as readily."

"Lord Axminster and Lord St. Dennis told me of it at the club. I can tell you it has made a most painful impression," cried the father. "That my son should be a radical and a republican, is a cruel thought for a father; and I, who had hoped for Lord Ringwood's borough for him—who had hoped—who had hoped very much better things for him and from him. He is not a comfort to me. You saw how he treated me one night? A man might live on different terms, I think, with his only son!" And with a breaking voice, a pallid cheek, and a real grief at his heart, the unhappy physician moved away.

How had the doctor bred his son, that the young man should be thus unruly? Was the revolt the boy's fault, or the father's? Dr. Firmin's horror seemed to be because his noble friends were horrified by Phil's radical doctrine. At that time of my life, being young and very green, I had a little mischievous pleasure in infuriating Squaretoes, and causing him to pronounce that I was "a dangerous man." Now, I am ready to say that Nero was a monarch with many elegant accomplishments, and considerable natural amiability of disposition. I praise and admire success wherever I meet it. I make allowance for faults and shortcomings, especially in my superiors; and feel that, did we know all, we should judge them very differently. People don't believe me, perhaps, quite so much as formerly. But I don't offend: I trust I don't offend. Have I said anything painful? Plague on my blunders! I recall the expression. I regret it. I contradict it flat.

As I am ready to find excuses for everybody, let poor Philip come in for the benefit of this mild amnesty; and if he vexed his father, as he certainly did, let us trust—let us be thankfully sure—he was not so black as the old gentleman depicted him. Nay, if I have painted the Old Gentleman himself as rather black, who knows but that this was an error, not of his complexion, but of my vision? Phil was unruly because he was bold, and wild, and young. His father was hurt, naturally hurt, because of the boy's extravagances and follies. They will come together again, as father and son should. These little differences of temper will be smoothed and equalized anon. The boy *has* led a wild life. He has been obliged to leave college. He has given his father hours of anxiety and nights of painful watching. But stay, father, what of you? Have you shown to the boy the practice of confidence, the example of love and honor? Did you accustom him to virtue, and teach truth to the child at your knee? " Honor your father and mother." Amen. May his days be long who fulfils the command : but implied, though unwritten on the table, is there not the order, " Honor your son and daughter? " Pray heaven that we, whose days are already not few in the land, may keep this ordinance too.

What had made Philip wild, extravagant, and insubordinate? Cured of that illness in which we saw him, he rose up, and from school went his way to the university, and there entered on a life such as wild young men will lead. From that day of illness his manner towards his father changed, and regarding the change the elder Firmin seemed afraid to question his son. He used the house as if his own, came and absented himself at will, ruled the servants, and was spoiled by them ; spent the income which was settled on his mother and her children, and gave of it liberally to poor acquaintances. To the remonstrances of old friends he replied that he had a right to do as he chose with his own ; that other men who were poor might work, but that he had enough to live on, without grinding over classics and mathematics. He was implicated in more rows than one ; his tutors saw him not, but he and the proctors became a great deal too well acquainted. If I were to give a history of Mr. Philip Firmin at the university, it would be the story of an Idle Apprentice, of whom his pastors and masters were justified in prophesying evil. He was seen on lawless London excursions, when his father and tutor supposed him unwell in his rooms in college. He made acquaintance with jolly companions, with whom his father grieved that he should be intimate. He cut the astonished uncle Twysden in London Street, and blandly told him that he must be mistaken—he one Frenchman, he no speak English. He stared the master of his own college out of countenance, dashed back to college with a Turpin-like celerity, and was in rooms with a ready-proved alibi when inquiries were made. I am afraid there is no doubt that Phil screwed up his tutor's door ; Mr. Okes discovered him in the act. He had to go down, the young prodigal. I wish I could say he was repentant. But he appeared before his father with the utmost nonchalance ; said that he was doing no good at the

university, and should be much better away, and then went
abroad on a dashing tour to France and Italy, whither it is by
no means our business to follow him. Something had poisoned
the generous blood. The once kindly honest lad was wild and
reckless. He had money in sufficiency, his own horses and
equipage, and free quarters in his father's house. But father
and son scarce met, and seldom took a meal together. " I
know his haunts, but I don't know his friends, Pendennis," the
elder man said. " I don't think they are vicious, so much as
low. I do not charge him with vice, mind you ; but with idleness, and a fatal love of low company, and a frantic, suicidal
determination to fling his chances in life away. Ah, think
where he might be, and where he is ! "

Where he was ? Do not be alarmed. Philip was only
idling. Philip might have been much more industriously, more
profitably, and a great deal more wickedly employed. What is
now called Bohemia had no name in Philip's young days, though
many of us knew the country very well. A pleasant land, not
fenced with drab stucco, like Tyburnia or Belgravia ; not
guarded by a huge standing army of footmen ; not echoing with
noble chariots ; not replete with polite chintz drawing-rooms and
neat tea-tables ; a land over which hangs an endless fog, occasioned by much tobacco ; a land of chambers, billiard-rooms, supper-rooms, oysters ; a land of song ; a land where soda-water flows
freely in the morning : a land of tin-dish covers from taverns,
and frothing porter ; a land of lotos-eating (with lots of cayenne pepper), of pulls on the river, of delicious reading of
novels, magazines, and saunterings in many studios ; a land
where men call each other by their Christian names ; where
most are poor, where almost all are young, and where, if a few
oldsters do enter, it is because they have preserved more tenderly and carefully than other folks their youthful spirits, and
the delightful capacity to be idle. I have lost my way to Bohemia now, but it is certain that Prague is the most picturesque
city in the world.

Having long lived there, and indeed only lately quitted the
Bohemian land at the time whereof I am writing, I could not
quite participate in Dr. Firmin's indignation at his son persisting in his bad courses and wild associates. When Firmin had
been wild himself, he had fought, intrigued, and gambled in
good company. Phil chose his friends amongst a banditti
never heard of in fashionable quarters. Perhaps he liked to
play the prince in the midst of these associates, and was not
averse to the flattery which a full purse brought him among

men most of whose pockets had a meagre lining. He had not emigrated to Bohemia, and settled there altogether. At school and in his brief university career he had made some friends who lived in the world, and with whom he was still familiar. "These come and knock at my front door, my father's door," he would say, with one of his old laughs; "the Bandits, who have the signal, enter only by the dissecting-room. I know which are the most honest, and that it is not always the poor Freebooters who best deserve to be hanged."

Like many a young gentleman who has no intention of pursuing legal studies seriously, Philip entered at an inn of court, and kept his terms duly, though he vowed that his conscience would not allow him to practise (I am not defending the opinions of this squeamish moralist—only stating them). His acquaintance here lay amongst the Temple Bohemians. He had part of a set of chambers in Parchment Buildings, to be sure, and you might read on a door, "Mr. Cassidy, Mr. P. Firmin, Mr. Vanjohn;" but were these gentlemen likely to advance Philip in life? Cassidy was a newspaper reporter, and young Vanjohn a betting man who was always attending races. Dr. Firmin had a horror of newspaper-men, and considered they belonged to the dangerous classes, and treated them with a distant affability.

"Look at the governor, Pen," Philip would say to the present chronicler. "He always watches you with a secret suspicion, and has never got over his wonder at your being a gentleman. I like him when he does the Lord Chatham business, and condescends towards you, and give you his hand to kiss. He considers he is your better, don't you see? Oh, he is a paragon of a père noble, the governor is! and I ought to be a young Sir Charles Grandison." And the young scapegrace would imitate his father's smile, and the doctor's manner of laying his hand to his breast and putting out his neat right leg, all of which movements or postures were, I own, rather pompous and affected.

Whatever the paternal faults were, you will say that Philip was not the man to criticize them; nor in this matter shall I attempt to defend him. My wife has a little pensioner whom she found wandering in the street, and singing a little artless song. The child could not speak yet—only warble its little song; and had thus strayed away from home, and never once knew of her danger. We kept her for a while, until the police found her parents. Our servants bathed her, and dressed her, and sent her home in such neat clothes as the poor little wretch had never seen until fortune sent her in the way of those good-natured folks. She pays them frequent visits. When she goes away from us, she is always neat and clean ; when she comes to us, she is in rags and dirty : a wicked little slattern ! And pray, whose duty is it to keep her clean ? and has not the parent in this case forgotten to honor her daughter ? Suppose there is some reason which prevents Philip from loving his father—that the doctor has neglected to cleanse the boy's heart, and by carelessness and indifference has sent him erring into the world. If so, woe be to that doctor ! If I take my little son to the tavern to dinner, shall I not assuredly pay ? If I suffer him in tender youth to go astray, and harm comes to him, whose is the fault ?

Perhaps the very outrages and irregularities of which Phil's father complained, were in some degree occasioned by the elder's own faults. He was so laboriously obsequious to great men, that the son in a rage defied and avoided them. He was so grave, so polite, so complimentary, so artificial, that Phil, in revolt at such hypocrisy, chose to be frank, cynical, and familiar. The grave old bigwigs whom the doctor loved to assemble, bland and solemn men of the ancient school, who dined solemnly with each other at their solemn old houses—such men as old Lord Botley, Baron Bumpsher, Cricklade, (who published "Travels in Asia Minor," 4to, 1804,) the Bishop of St. Bees, and the like—wagged their old heads sadly when they col-logued in clubs, and talked of poor Firmin's scapegrace of a son. He would come to no good ; he was giving his good father much pain ; he had been in all sorts of rows and disturbances at the university, and the Master of Boniface reported most un-favorably of him. And at the solemn dinners in Old Parr Street—the admirable, costly, silent dinners—he treated these old gentlemen with a familiarity which caused the old heads to shake with surprise and choking indignation. Lord Botley and Baron Bumpsher had proposed and seconded Firmin's boy at the Megatherium club. The pallid old boys toddled away in alarm when he made his appearance there. He brought a smell of tobacco-smoke with him. He was capable of smoking in the drawing-room itself. They trembled before Philip, who, for his part, used to relish their senile anger ; and loved, as he called it, to tie all their pigtails together.

In no place was Philip seen or heard to so little advantage as in his father's house. " I feel like a humbug myself amongst those old humbugs," he would say to me. " Their old jokes, and their old compliments, and their virtuous old conversation sicken me. Are all old men humbugs, I wonder?" It is not pleasant to hear misanthropy from young lips, and to find eyes that are scarce twenty years old already looking out with distrust on the world.

In other houses than his own I am bound to say Philip was much more amiable, and he carried with him a splendor of gayety and cheerfulness which brought sunshine and welcome into many a room which he frequented. I have said that many of his companions were artists and journalists, and their clubs and haunts were his own. Ridley the Academician had Mrs. Brandon's rooms in Thornhaugh Street, and Philip was often in J. J.'s studio, or in the widow's little room below. He had a very great tenderness and affection for her; her presence seemed to purify him; and in her company the boisterous, reckless young man was invariably gentle and respectful. Her eyes used to fill with tears when she spoke about him; and when he was present, followed and watched him with sweet motherly devotion. It was pleasant to see him at her homely little fireside, and hear his jokes and prattle, with a fatuous old father, who was one of Mrs. Brandon's lodgers. Philip would play cribbage for hours with this old man, frisk about him with a hundred harmless jokes, and walk out by his invalid chair, when the old captain went to sun himself in the New Road. He was an idle fellow, Philip, that's the truth. He had an agreeable perseverance in doing nothing, and would pass half a day in perfect contentment over his pipe, watching Ridley at his easel. J. J. painted that charming head of Philip which hangs in Mrs. Brandon's little room—with the fair hair, the tawny beard and whiskers, and the bold blue eyes.

Phil had a certain after-supper song of "Garryowen na Gloria," which it did you good to hear, and which, when sung at his full pitch, you might hear for a mile round. One night I had been to dine in Russell Square, and was brought home in his carriage by Dr. Firmin, who was of the party. As we came through Soho, the windows of a certain club-room called the "Haunt" were open, and we could hear Philip's song booming through the night, and especially a certain wild-Irish war-whoop with which it concluded, amidst universal applause and enthusiastic battering of glasses.

The poor father sank back in the carriage as though a blow had struck him. "Do you hear his voice?" he groaned out. "Those are his haunts. My son, who might go anywhere, prefers to be captain in a pothouse, and sing songs in a tap-room!"

I tried to make the best of the case. I knew there was no harm in the place; that clever men of considerable note frequented it. But the wounded father was not to be consoled by such commonplaces; and a deep and natural grief oppressed him in consequence of the faults of his son.

What ensued by no means surprised me. Among Dr. Firmin's patients was a maiden lady of suitable age and large fortune, who looked upon the accomplished doctor with favorable eyes. That he should take a companion to cheer him in his solitude was natural enough, and all his friends concurred in thinking that he should marry. Every one had cognizance of the quiet little courtship, except the doctor's son, between whom and his father there were only too many secrets.

Some man in a club asked Philip whether he should condole with him or congratulate him on his father's approaching marriage? His what? The younger Firmin exhibited the greatest surprise and agitation on hearing of this match. He ran home: he awaited his father's return. When Dr. Firmin came home and betook himself to his study, Philip confronted him there. " This must be a lie, sir, which I have heard to-day," the young man said, fiercely.

" A lie! what lie, Philip?" asked the father. They were both very resolute and courageous men.

" That you are going to marry Miss Benson."

" Do you make my house so happy, that I don't need any other companion?" asked the father.

" That's not the question," said Philip, hotly. " You can't and mustn't marry that lady, sir."

" And why not, sir?"

" Because in the eyes of God and Heaven you are married already, sir. And I swear I will tell Miss Benson the story to-morrow, if you persist in your plan."

" So you know that story?" groaned the father.

" Yes. God forgive you," said the son.

" It was a fault of my youth that has been bitterly repented."

" A fault!—a crime!" said Philip.

" Enough, sir! Whatever my fault, it is not for you to charge me with it."

" If you won't guard your own honor, I must. I shall go to Miss Benson now."

" If you go out of this house you don't pretend to return to it."

" Be it so. Let us settle our accounts, and part, sir."

"Philip, Philip! you break my heart," cried the father.

"You don't suppose mine is very light, sir," said the son.

Philip never had Miss Benson for a mother-in-law. But father and son loved each other no better after their dispute.

CHAPTER VI.

BRANDON'S.

THORNHAUGH STREET is but a poor place now, and the houses look as if they had seen better days: but that house with the cut centre drawing-room window, which has the name of Brandon on the door, is as neat as any house in the quarter, and the brass plate always shines like burnished gold. About Easter time many fine carriages stop at that door, and splendid people walk in, introduced by a tidy little maid, or else by an athletic Italian, with a glossy black beard and gold earrings, who conducts them to the drawing-room floor, where Mr. Ridley, the painter, lives, and where his pictures are privately exhibited before they go to the Royal Academy.

As the carriages drive up, you will often see a red-faced man, in an olive-green wig, smiling blandly over the blinds of the parlor, on the ground-floor. That is Captain Gann, the father of the lady who keeps the house. I don't know how he came by the rank of captain, but he has borne it so long and gallantly that there is no use in any longer questioning the title. He does not claim it, neither does he deny it. But the wags who call upon Mrs. Brandon can always, as the phrase is, "draw" her father, by speaking of Prussia, France, Waterloo, or battles in general, until the Little Sister says, "Now, never mind about the battle of Waterloo, papa" (she says Pa—her *h*'s are irregular—I can't help it)—"Never mind about Waterloo, papa; you've told them all about it. And don't go on, Mr. Beans, don't, *please*, go on in that way."

Young Beans has already drawn "Captain Gann (assisted by Shaw, the Life-Guardsman) killing twenty-four French cuirassiers at Waterloo." "Captain Gann defending Hougoumont." "Captain Gann, called upon by Napoleon Bonaparte to lay down his arms, saying, 'A captain of militia dies, but never surrenders.'" "The Duke of Wellington pointing to the advancing Old Guard, and saying, 'Up, Gann, and at them.'"

And these sketches are so droll, that even the Little Sister, Gann's own daughter, can't help laughing at them. To be sure, she loves fun, the Little Sister ; laughs over droll books ; laughs to herself, in her little quiet corner at work ; laughs over pictures ; and, at the right place, laughs and sympathizes too. Ridley says, he knows few better critics of pictures than Mrs. Brandon. She has a sweet temper, a merry sense of humor, that makes the cheeks dimple and the eyes shine ; and a kind heart, that has been sorely tried and wounded, but is still soft and gentle. Fortunate are they whose hearts, so tried by suffering, yet recover their health. Some have illnesses from which there is no recovery, and drag through life afterwards, maimed and invalided.

But this Little Sister, having been subjected in youth to a dreadful trial and sorrow, was saved out of them by a kind Providence, and is now so thoroughly restored as to own that she is happy, and to thank God that she can be grateful and useful. When poor Montfitchet died, she nursed him through his illness as tenderly as his good wife herself. In the days of her own chief grief and misfortune, her father, who was under the domination of his wife, a cruel and blundering woman, thrust out poor little Caroline from his door, when she returned to it the broken-hearted victim of a scoundrel's seduction ; and when the old captain was himself in want and houseless, she had found him, sheltered and fed him. And it was from that day her wounds had begun to heal, and, from gratitude for this immense piece of good fortune vouchsafed to her, that her happiness and cheerfulness returned. Returned? There was an old servant of the family, who could not stay in the house because she was so abominably disrespectful to the captain, and this woman said she had never known Miss Caroline so cheerful, nor so happy, nor so good-looking, as she was now.

So Captain Gann came to live with his daughter, and patronized her with much dignity. He had a very few yearly pounds, which served to pay his club expenses, and a portion of his clothes. His club, I need not say, was at the " Admiral Byng," Tottenham Court Road, and here the captain met frequently a pleasant little society, and bragged unceasingly about his former prosperity.

I have heard that the country-house in Kent, of which he boasted, was a shabby little lodging-house at Margate, of which the furniture was sold in execution ; but if it had been a palace the captain would not have been out of place there, one or two people still rather fondly thought. His daughter, amongst

THE OLD FOGIES.

others, had tried to fancy all sorts of good of her father, and especially that he was a man of remarkably good manners. But she had seen one or two gentlemen since she knew the poor old father—gentlemen with rough coats and good hearts, like Dr. Goodenough ; gentlemen with superfine coats and superfine double-milled manners, like Dr. Firmin, and hearts—well, never mind about that point , gentlemen of no *h*'s, like the good, dear, faithful benefactor who had rescued her at the brink of despair ; men of genius, like Ridley ;—great hearty, generous, honest gentlemen, like Philip ;—and this illusion about Pa, I suppose, had vanished along with some other fancies of her poor little maiden youth. The truth is, she had an understanding with the " Admiral Byng : " the landlady was instructed as to the supplies to be furnished to the captain ; and as for his stories, poor Caroline knew them a great deal too well to believe in them any more.

I would not be understood to accuse the captain of habitual inebriety. He was a generous officer, and his delight was, when in cash, to order "glasses round" for the company at the club, to whom he narrated the history of his brilliant early days, when he lived in some of the tiptop society of this city, sir—a society in which, we need not say, the custom always is for gentlemen to treat other gentlemen to rum-and-water. Never mind—I wish we were all as happy as the captain. I see his jolly face now before me as it blooms through the window in Thornhaugh Street, and the wave of the somewhat dingy hand which sweeps me a gracious recognition.

The clergyman of the neighboring chapel was a very good friend of the Little Sister, and has taken tea in her parlor ; to which circumstance the captain frequently alluded, pointing out the very chair on which the divine sat. Mr. Gann attended his ministrations regularly every Sunday, and brought a rich, though somewhat worn, bass voice to bear upon the anthems and hymns at the chapel. His style was more florid than is general now among church singers, and, indeed, had been acquired in a former age and in the performance of rich Bacchanalian chants, such as delighted the contemporaries of our Incledons and Brahams. With a very little entreaty, the captain could be induced to sing at the club ; and I must own that Phil Firmin would draw the captain out, and extract from him a song of ancient days ; but this must be in the absence of his daughter, whose little face wore an air of such extreme terror and disturbance when her father sang, that he presently ceased from exercising his musical talents in her hearing. He hung up his lyre, whereof it must be owned that time had broken many of the once resounding chords.

With a sketch or two contributed by her lodgers—with a few gimcracks from the neighboring Wardour Street presented by others of her friends—with the chairs, tables, and bureaux as bright as bees'-wax and rubbing could make them—the Little Sister's room was a cheery little place, and received not a little company. She allowed Pa's pipe. "It's company to him," she said. "A man can't be doing much harm when he is smoking his pipe." And she allowed Phil's cigar. Anything was allowed to Phil, the other lodgers declared, who professed to be quite jealous of Philip Firmin. She had a very few books. "When I was a girl I used to be always reading novels," she said ; "but, la, they're mostly nonsense. There's Mr. Pendennis, who comes to see Mr. Ridley. I wonder how a married man can go on writing about love, and all that stuff!" And, indeed, it is rather absurd for elderly fingers to be still twanging Dan Cupid's toy bow and arrows. Yesterday is gone—yes, but very well remembered ; and we think of it the more now we know that To-morrow is not going to bring us much.

Into Mrs. Brandon's parlor Mr. Ridley's old father would sometimes enter of evenings, and share the bit of bread and cheese, or the modest supper of Mrs. Brandon and the captain. The homely little meal has almost vanquished out of our life now, but in former days it assembled many a family round its kindly board. A little modest supper-tray—a little quiet prattle—a little kindly glass that cheered and never inebriated. I can see friendly faces smiling round such a meal, at a period not far gone, but how distant! I wonder whether there are any old folks now, in old quarters of old country towns, who come to each other's houses in sedan-chairs, at six o'clock, and play at quadrille until supper-tray time? Of evenings Ridley and the captain, I say, would have a solemn game at cribbage, and the Little Sister would make make up a jug of something good for the two oldsters. She liked Mr. Ridley to come, for he always treated her father so respectful, and was quite the gentleman. And as for Mrs. Ridley, Mr. R.'s "good lady,"—was she not also grateful to the Little Sister for having nursed her son during his malady? Through their connection they were enabled to procure Mrs. Brandon many valuable friends ; and always were pleased to pass an evening with the captain, and were as civil to him as they could have been had he been at the very height of his prosperity and splendor. My private opinion of the old captain, you see, is that he was a worthless old captain, but most fortunate in his early ruin, after which he had lived very much admired and comfortable, sufficient whiskey being almost always provided for him.

Old Mr. Ridley's respect for her father afforded a most precious consolation to the Little Sister. Ridley liked to have the paper read to him. He was never quite easy with print, and to his last days, many words to be met with in newspapers and elsewhere used to occasion the good butler much intellectual trouble. The Little Sister made his lodger's bills out for him (Mr. R., as well as the captain's daughter, strove to increase a small income by the letting of furnished apartments), or the captain himself would take these documents in charge; he wrote a noble mercantile hand, rendered now somewhat shaky by time, but still very fine in flourishes and capitals, and very much at worthy Mr. Ridley's service. Time was, when his son was a boy, that J. J. himself had prepared these accounts, which neither his father nor his mother were very competent to arrange. "We were not, in our young time, Mr. Gann," Ridley remarked to his friend, "brought up to much scholarship; and very little book-learning was given to persons in *my* rank of life. It was necessary and proper for you gentlemen, of course, sir." "Of course, Mr. Ridley," winks the other veteran over his pipe. "But I can't go and ask my son John James to keep his old father's books now as he used to do—which to do so is, on the part of you and Mrs. Brandon, the part of true friendship, and I value it, sir, and so do my son John James reckonize and value it, sir." Mr. Ridley had served gentlemen of the *bonne école.* No nobleman could be more courtly and grave than he was. In Mr. Gann's manner there was more humorous playfulness, which in no way, however, diminished the captain's high breeding. As he continued to be intimate with Mr. Ridley, he became loftier and more majestic. I think each of these elders acted on the other, and for good; and I hope Ridley's opinion was correct, that Mr. Gann was ever the gentleman. To see these two good fogies together was a spectacle for edification. Their tumblers kissed each other on the table. Their elderly friendship brought comfort to themselves and their families. A little matter of money once created a coolness between the two old gentlemen. But the Little Sister paid the outstanding account between her father and Mr. Ridley: there never was any further talk of pecuniary loans between them; and when they went to the "Admiral Byng," each paid for himself.

Phil often heard of that nightly meeting at the "Admiral's Head," and longed to be of the company. But even when he saw the old gentlemen in the Little Sister's parlor, they felt dimly that he was making fun of them. The captain would not have been able to brag so at ease had Phil been continually watching him. "I have 'ad the honor of waiting on your worthy father at my Lord Todmorden's table. Our little club ain't no place for you, Mr. Philip, nor for my son, though he's a good son, and proud me and his mother is of him, which he have never gave us a moment's pain, except when he was ill, since he have came to man's estate, most thankful am I, and with my hand on my heart, for to be able to say so. But what is good for me and Mr. Gann, won't suit you young gentlemen. *You* ain't a tradesman, sir, else I'm mistaken in the family, which I thought the Ringwoods one of the best in England, and the Firmins, a good one likewise." Mr. Ridley loved the sound of his own voice. At the festive meetings of the club, seldom a night passed in which he did not compliment his brother Byngs and air his own oratory. Under this reproof Phil blused, and hung his conscious head with shame. "Mr. Ridley," says he, "you shall find I won't come where I am not welcome; and if I come to annoy you at the 'Admiral Byng,' may I be taken out on the quarterdeck and shot." On which Mr. Ridley pronounced Philip to be a "most sing'lar, astrornary, and ascentric young man. A good heart, sir. Most generous to relieve distress. Fine talent, sir; but I fear—I fear they won't come to much good, Mr. Gann—saving your presence, Mrs. Brandon, m'm, which, of course, you *always* stand up for him."

When Philip Firmin had had his pipe and his talk with the Little Sister in her parlor, he would ascend and smoke his second, third, tenth pipe in J. J. Ridley's studio. He would pass hours before J. J.'s easel, pouring out talk about politics, about religion, about poetry, about women, about the dreadful slavishness and meanness of the world ; unwearied in talk and idleness, as placid J. J. was in listening and labor. The painter had been too busy in life over his easel to read many books. His ignorance of literature smote him with a frequent shame. He admired book-writers, and young men of the university who quoted their Greek and their Horace glibly. He listened with deference to their talk on such matters ; no doubt-got good hints from some of them ; was always secretly pained and surprised when the university gentlemen were beaten in argument, or loud and coarse in conversation, as sometimes they would be. " J. J. is a very clever fellow of course," Mr. Jarman would say of him, " and the luckiest man in Europe. He loves painting, and he is at work all day. He loves toadying fine people, and he goes to a tea-party every night." You all knew Jarman of Charlotte Street, the miniature-painter? He was one of the kings of the "Haunt." His tongue spared no one. He envied all success, and the sight of prosperity made him furious : but to the unsuccessful he was kind ; to the poor eager with help and prodigal of compassion ; and that old talk about nature's noblemen and the glory of labor was very fiercely and eloquently waged by him. His friends admired him ; he was the soul of independence, and thought most men sneaks who wore clean linen and frequented gentlemen's society : but it must be owned his landlords had a bad opinion of him, and I have heard of one or two of his pecuniary transactions which certainly were not to Mr. Jarman's credit. Jarman was a man of remarkable humor. He was fond of the widow, and would speak of her goodness, usefulness, and honesty with tears in his eyes. She was poor and struggling yet. Had she been wealthy and prosperous, Mr. Jarman would not have been so alive to her merit.

We ascend to the room on the first floor, where the centre window has been heightened, so as to afford an upper light, and under that stream of radiance we behold the head of an old friend, Mr. J. J. Ridley, the R. Academician. Time has somewhat thinned his own copious locks, and prematurely streaked the head with silver. His face is rather wan ; the eager, sensitive hand which poises brush and palette, and quivers over the picture, is very thin : round his eyes are many lines of ill health and, perhaps, care, but the eyes are as bright as ever, and, when they look at the canvas or the model which he transfers to it, clear, and keen, and happy. He has a very sweet singing voice, and warbles at his work, or whistles at it, smiling. He sets his hand little feats of skill to perform, and smiles with a boyish pleasure at his own matchless dexterity. I have seen him, with an old pewter mustard-pot for a model, fashion a splendid silver flagon in one of his pictures ; paint the hair of an animal, the folds and flowers of a bit of brocade, and so forth, with a perfect delight in the work he was performing : a delight lasting from morning to sundown, during which time he was too busy to touch the biscuit and glass of water which was prepared for his frugal luncheon. He is greedy of the last minute of light. and never can be got from his darling pictures without a regret. To be a painter, and to have your hand in perfect command, I hold to be one of life's *summa bona*. The happy mixture of hand and head work must render the occupation supremely pleasant. In the day's work must occur endless delightful difficulties and occasions for skill. Over the details for that armor, that drapery, or what not, the sparkle of that eye, the downy blush of that cheek, the jewel on that neck, there are battles to be fought and victories to be won. Each day there must occur critical moments of supreme struggle and triumph, when struggle and victory must be both invigorating and exquisitely pleasing—as a burst across country is to a fine rider perfectly mounted, who knows that his courage and his horse will never fail him. There is the excitement of the game, and the gallant delight in winning it. Of this sort of admirable reward for their labor, no men, I think, have a greater share than painters (perhaps a violin-player perfectly and triumphantly performing his own beautiful composition may be equally happy). Here is occupation : here is excitement : here is struggle and victory : and here is profit. Can man ask more from fortune ? Dukes and Rothschilds may be envious of such a man.

Though Ridley has had his trials and troubles, as we shall presently learn, his art has mastered them all. Black care may have sat in crupper on that Pegasus, but has never unhorsed the rider. In certain minds, art is dominant and superior to all beside—stronger than love, stronger than hate, or care, or penury. As soon as the fever leaves the hand free, it is seizing and fondling the pencil. Love may frown and be false, but the other mistress never will. She is always true : always new : always the friend, companion, inestimable consoler. So John James Ridley sat at his easel from breakfast till sundown, and never left his work quite willingly. I wonder are men of other trades so enamored of theirs ; whether lawyers cling to the last to their darling reports ; or writers prefer their desks and inkstands to society, to friendship, to dear idleness ? I have seen no men in life loving their profession so much as painters, except, perhaps, actors, who, when not engaged themselves, always go to the play.

Before this busy easel Phil would sit for hours, and pour out endless talk and tobacco-smoke. His presence was a delight to Ridley's soul ; his face a sunshine ; his voice a cordial. Weakly himself, and almost infirm of body, with sensibilities tremulously keen, the painter most admired amongst men strength, health, good spirits, good breeding. Of these, in his youth, Philip had a wealth of endowment ; and I hope these

precious gifts of fortune have not left him in his maturer age.
I do not say that with all men Philip was so popular. There
are some who never can pardon good fortune, and in the company of gentlemen are on the watch for offence ; and, no doubt,
in his course through life, poor downright Phil trampled upon
corns enough of those who met him in his way. "Do you
know why Ridley is so fond of Firmin ?" asked Jarman.
" Because Firmin's father hangs on to the nobility by the pulse,
whilst Ridley, you know, is connected with them through the
side-board." So Jarman had the double horn for his adversary : he could despise a man for not being a gentleman, and
insult him for being one; I have met with people in the world
with whom the latter offence is an unpardonable crime—a cause
of ceaseless doubt, division, and suspicion. What more common or natural, Bufo, than to hate another for being what you
are not? The story is as old as frogs, bulls, and men.

Then, to be sure, besides your enviers in life, there are
your admirers. Beyond wit, which he understood—beyond
genius, which he had—Ridley admired good looks and manners, and always kept some simple hero whom he loved secretly
to cherish and worship. He loved to be amongst beautiful
women and aristocratical men. Philip Firmin, with his republican notions and downright bluntness of behavior to all men
of rank superior to him, had a grand high manner of his own ;
and if he had scarce twopence in his pocket, would have put
his hands in them with as much independence as the greatest
dandy who ever sauntered on Pall Mall pavement. What a
coolness the fellow had ! Some men may, not unreasonably,
have thought it impudence. It fascinated Ridley. To be such
a man ; to have such a figure and manner ; to be able to look
society in the face, slap it on the shoulder, if you were so
minded, and hold it by the button—what would not Ridley
give for such powers and accomplishments? You will please
to bear in mind, I am not saying that J. J. was right, only that
he was as he was. I hope we shall have nobody in this story
without his little faults and peculiarities. Jarman was quite
right when he said Ridley loved fine company. I believe his
pedigree gave him secret anguishes. He would rather have
been gentleman than genius ever so great ; but let you and me,
who have no weaknesses of our own, try and look charitably on
this confessed foible of my friend.

J. J. never thought of rebuking Philip for being idle. Phil
was as the lilies of the field, in the painter's opinion. He was
not called upon to toil or spin ; but to take his ease, and grow

and bask in sunshine, and be arrayed in glory. The little clique of painters knew what Firmin's means were. Thirty thousand pounds of his own. Thirty thousand pounds down, sir ; and the inheritance of his father's immense fortune ! A splendor emanated from this gifted young man. His opinions, his jokes, his laughter, his song, had the weight of thirty thousand down, sir ; and &c., &c. What call had *he* to work ? Would you set a young nobleman to be an apprentice ? Philip was free to be as idle as any lord, if he liked. He ought to wear fine clothes, ride fine horses, dine off plate, and drink champagne every day. J. J. would work quite cheerfully till sunset, and have an eightpenny plate of meat in Wardour Street and a glass of porter for his humble dinner. At the "Haunt," and similar places of Bohemian resort, a snug place near the fire was always found for Firmin. Fierce republican as he was, Jarman had a smile for his lordship, and used to adopt particularly dandified airs when he had been invited to Old Parr Street to dinner. I dare say Philip liked flattery. I own that he was a little weak in this respect, and that you and I, my dear sir, are, of course, far his superiors. J. J., who loved him, would have had him follow his aunt's and cousin's advice, and live in better company ; but I think the painter would not have liked his pet to soil his hands with too much work, and rather admired Mr. Phil for being idle.

The Little Sister gave him advice, to be sure, both as to the company he should keep and the occupation which was wholesome for him. But when others of his acquaintance hinted that his idleness would do him harm, she would not hear of their censure. "Why should he work if he don't choose?" she asked. "He has no call to be scribbling and scrabbling. You wouldn't have *him* sitting all day painting little dolls' heads on canvas, and working like a slave. A pretty idea, indeed ! His uncle will get him an appointment. That's the thing *he* should have. He should be secretary to an ambassador abroad, and he *will* be !" In fact Phil, at this period, used to announce his wish to enter the diplomatic service, and his hope that Lord Ringwood would further his views in that respect. Meanwhile he was the king of Thornhaugh Street. He might be as idle as he chose, and Mrs. Brandon had always a smile for him. He might smoke a great deal too much, but she worked dainty little cigar-cases for him. She hemmed his fine cambric pocket-handkerchiefs, and embroidered his crest at the corners. She worked him a waistcoat so splendid that he almost blushed to wear it, gorgeous as he was in apparel at this period, and sumptuous in chains, studs, and haberdashery. I fear Dr. Firmin, sighing out his disappointed hopes in respect of his son, has rather good cause for his dissatisfaction. But of these remonstrances the Little Sister would not hear. " Idle, why not? Why should he work? Boys will be boys. I dare say his grumbling old Pa was not better than Philip when *he* was young ! " And this she spoke with a heightened color in her little face, and a defiant toss of her head, of which I did not understand all the significance then ; but attributed her eager partisanship to that admirable injustice which belongs to all good women, and for which let us be daily thankful. I know, dear ladies, you are angry at this statement. But, even at the risk of displeasing *you*, we must tell the truth. You would wish to represent yourselves as equitable, logical, and strictly just. So, I dare say Dr. Johnson would have liked Mrs. Thrale to say to him, " Sir, your manners are graceful ; your person elegant, cleanly, and eminently pleasing ; your appetite small (especially for tea), and your dancing equal to the Violetta's ; " which, you perceive, is merely ironical. Women equitable, logical, and strictly just ! Mercy upon us ! If they were, population would cease, the world would be a howling wilderness. Well, in a word, this Little Sister petted and coaxed Philip Firmin in such an absurd way that every one remarked it—those who had no friends, no sweethearts, no mothers, no daughters, no wives, and those who were petted, and coaxed, and spoiled at home themselves ; as I trust, dearly beloved, is your case.

Now, again, let us admit that Philip's father had reason to be angry with the boy, and deplore his son's taste for low company ; but excuse the young man, on the other hand, somewhat for his fierce revolt and profound distaste at much in his home circle which annoyed him. " By heaven ! " he would roar out, pulling his hair and whiskers, and with many fierce ejaculations, according to his wont, " the solemnity of those humbugs sickens me so, that I should like to crown the old bishop with the soup-tureen, and box Baron Bumpsher's ears with the saddle of mutton. At my aunt's, the humbug is just the same. It's better done, perhaps ; but oh, Pendennis ! if you could but know the pangs which tore into my heart, sir, the vulture which gnawed at this confounded liver, when I saw women—women who ought to be pure—women who ought to be like angels—women who ought to know no art but that of coaxing our griefs away and soothing our sorrows—fawning, and cringeing, and scheming ; cold to this person, humble to that, flattering to the rich, and indifferent to the humble in station.   I tell you I have seen all this, Mrs. Pendennis !   I won't mention names, but I have met with those who have made me old before my time—a hundred years old !   The zest of life is passed from me " (here Mr. Phil would gulp a bumper from the nearest decanter at hand).   "But if I like what your husband is pleased to call low society, it is because I have seen the other.   I have dangled about at fine parties, and danced at fashionable balls.   I have seen mothers bring their virgin daughters up to battered old rakes, and ready to sacrifice their innocence for fortune or a title.   The atmosphere of those polite drawing-rooms stifles me.   I can't bow the knee to the horrible old Mammon.   I walk about in the crowds as lonely as if I was in a wilderness ; and don't begin to breathe freely until I get some honest tobacco to clear the air.   As for your husband " (meaning the writer of this memoir), "he cannot help himself ; he is a wordling, of the earth, earthy.   If a duke were to ask him to dinner to-morrow, the parasite owns that he would go.   Allow me, my friends, my freedom, my rough companions, in their work-day clothes.   I don't hear such lies and flatteries come from behind pipes, as used to pass from above white chokers when I was in the world."   And he would tear at his cravat, as though the mere thought of the world's conventionality wellnigh strangled him.

This, to be sure, was in a late state of his career, but I take up the biography here and there, so as to give the best idea I may of my friend's character.   At this time—he is out of the country just now, and besides, if he saw his own likeness staring him in the face, I am confident he would not know it—Mr. Philip, in some things, was as obstinate as a mule, and in others as weak as a woman.   He had a childish sensibility for what was tender, helpless, pretty or pathetic ; and a mighty scorn of imposture, wherever he found it.   He had many good purposes, which were often very vacillating, and were but seldom performed. He had a vast number of evil habits, whereof, you know, idleness is said to be the root.   Many of these evil propensities he coaxed and cuddled with much care ; and though he roared out *peccavi* most frankly when charged with his sins, this criminal would fall to peccation very soon after promising amendment. What he liked he would have.   What he disliked he could with the greatest difficulty be found to do.   He liked good dinners, good wine, good horses, good clothes, and late hours ; and in all these comforts of life (or any others which he fancied, or which were within his means) he indulged himself with perfect **freedom**.   He hated hypocrisy on his own part, and hypocrites in general. He said everything that came into his mind about things and people; and, of course, was often wrong and often prejudiced, and often occasioned howls of indignation or malignant whispers of hatred by his free speaking. He believed everything that was said to him until his informant had misled him once or twice, after which he would believe nothing. And here you will see that his impetuous credulity was as absurd as the subsequent obstinacy of his unbelief. My dear young friend, the profitable way in life is the middle way. Don't quite believe anybody, for he may mislead you; neither disbelieve him, for that is uncomplimentary to your friend. Black is not so very black; and as for white, *bon Dieu!* in our climate what paint will remain white long? If Philip was self-indulgent, I suppose other people are self-indulgent likewise: and besides you know, your faultless heroes have ever so long gone out of fashion. To be young, to be good-looking, to be healthy, to be hungry three times a day, to have plenty of money, a great alacrity of sleeping, and nothing to do—all these, I dare say, are very dangerous temptations to a man, but I think I know some who would like to undergo the dangers of the trial. Suppose there be holidays, is there not work-time too? Suppose to-day is feast-day; may not tears and repentance come to-morrow? Such times are in store for Master Phil, and so please to let him have rest and comfort for a chapter or two.

CHAPTER VII.

IMPLETUR VETERIS BACCHI.

THAT time, that merry time, of Brandon's, of Bohemia, of oysters, of idleness, of smoking, of song at night and profuse soda-water in the morning, of a pillow, lonely and bachelor it is true, but with few cares for bedfellows, of plenteous pocket-money, of ease for to-day and little heed for to-morrow, was often remembered by Philip in after days. Mr. Phil's views of life were not very exalted, were they? The fruits of this world, which he devoured with such gusto, I must own were of the common kitchen-garden sort; and the lazy rogue's ambition went no farther than to stroll along the sunshiny wall, eat his fill, and then repose comfortably in the arbor under the arched vine. Why did Phil's mother's parents leave her thirty thousand pounds? I dare say some misguided people would be glad to do as much for their sons; but, if I have ten, I am determined they shall either have a hundred thousand a piece, or else bare bread and cheese. "Man was made to labor, and to be lazy," Phil would affirm with his usual energy of expression. "When the Indian warrior goes on the hunting path, he is sober, active, indomitable. No dangers fright him, and no labors tire. He endures the cold of the winter; he couches on the forest leaves; he subsists on frugal roots or the casual spoil of his bow. When he returns to his village, he gorges to repletion; he sleeps, perhaps, to excess. When the game is devoured, and the fire-water exhausted, again he sallies forth into the wilderness; he outclimbs the 'possum and he throttles the bear. I am the Indian: and this 'Haunt' is my wigwam! Barbara my squaw, bring me oysters; bring me a jug of the frothing black beer of the pale-faces, or I will hang up thy scalp on my tent-pole?" And old Barbara, the good old attendant of this "Haunt" of Bandits, would say, "Law, Mr. Philip, how you do go on, to be sure!" Where is the "Haunt" now? and where are the merry men all who there assembled? The sign is down; the song is silent; the sand is swept from the floor; the pipes are broken, and the ashes are scattered.

A little more gossip about his merry days, and we have done. He, Philip, was called to the bar in due course, and at his call-supper we assembled a dozen of his elderly and youthful friends. The chambers in Parchment Buildings were given up to him for this day. Mr. Van John, I think, was away attending a steeple-chase; but Mr. Cassidy was with us, and several of Philip's acquaintances of school, college, and the world. There was Philip's father, and Philip's uncle Twysden, and I, Phil's revered and respectable school senior, and others of our ancient seminary. There was Burroughs, the second wrangler of his year, great in metaphysics, greater with the knife and fork. There was Stackpole, Eblana's favorite child—the glutton of all learning, the master of many languages, who stuttered and blushed when he spoke his own. There was Pinkerton, who, albeit an ignoramus at the university, was already winning prodigious triumphs at the Parliamentary bar, and investing in Consols to the admiration of all his contemporaries. There was Rosebury the beautiful, the May-Fair pet and delight of Almack's, the cards on whose mantel-piece made all men open the eyes of wonder, and some of us dart the scowl of envy. There was my Lord Egham, Lord Ascot's noble son. There was Tom Dale, who having carried on his university career too splendidly, had come to grief in the midst of it, and was now meekly earning his bread in the reporters' gallery, alongside of Cassidy. There was Macbride, who, having thrown up his fellowship and married his cousin, was now doing a brave battle with poverty, and making literature feed him until law should reward him more splendidly. There was Haythorn, the country gentleman, who ever remembered his old college chums, and kept the memory of that friendship up by constant reminders of pheasants and game in the season. There were Raby and Maynard from the Guards' Club (Maynard sleeps now under Crimean snows), who preferred arms to the toga ; but carried into their military life the love of their old books, the affection of their old friends. Most of these must be mute personages in our little drama. Could any chronicler remember the talk of all of them ?

Several of the guests present were members of the Inn of Court (the Upper Temple), which had conferred on Philip the degree of Barrister-at-Law. He had dined in his wig and gown (Blackmore's wig and gown) in the inn-hall that day, in company with other members of his inn ; and, dinner over, we adjourned to Phil's chambers in Parchment Buildings, where a dessert was served, to which Mr. Firmin's friends were convoked.

The wines came from Dr. Firmin's cellar. His servants were in attendance to wait upon the company. Father and son both loved splendid hospitalities, and, so far as creature comforts went, Philip's feast was richly provided. " A supper, I love a supper of all things ! And in order that I might enjoy yours, 'I only took a single mutton-chop for dinner ! " cried Mr. Twysden, as he greeted Philip. Indeed, we found him, as we arrived from Hall, already in the chambers, and eating the young barrister's dessert. " He's been here ever so long," says Mr. Brice, who officiated as butler, " pegging away at the olives and maccaroons. Shouldn't wonder if he has pocketed some." There was small respect on the part of Brice for Mr. Twysden, whom the worthy butler frankly pronounced to be a stingy 'umbug. Meanwhile, Talbot believed that the old man respected him, and always conversed with Brice, and treated him with a cheerful cordiality.

The outer Philistines quickly arrived, and but that the wine and men were older, one might have fancied oneself at a college wine-party. Mr. Twysden talked for the whole company. He was radiant. He felt himself in high spirits. He did the honors of Philip's table. Indeed, no man was more hospitable with other folks' wine. Philip himself was silent and nervous.

I asked him if the awful ceremony, which he had just undergone, was weighing on his mind?

He was looking rather anxiously towards the door; and, knowing somewhat of the state of affairs at home, I thought that probably he and his father had had one of the disputes which of late days had become so frequent between them.

The company were nearly all assembled and busy with their talk, and drinking the doctor's excellent claret, when Brice entering, announced Dr. Firmin and Mr. Tufton Hunt.

"Hang Mr. Tufton Hunt," Philip was going to say; but he started up, went forward to his father, and greeted him very respectfully. He then gave a bow to the gentlemen introduced as Mr. Hunt, and they found places at the table, the doctor taking his with his usual handsome grace.

The conversation, which had been pretty brisk until Dr. Firmin came, drooped a little after his appearance. "We had an awful row two days ago," Philip whispered to me. "We shook hands and are reconciled, as you see. He won't stay long. He will be sent for in half an hour or so. He will say he has been sent for by a duchess, and go and have tea at the club."

Dr. Firmin bowed, and smiled sadly at me, as Philip was speaking. I dare say I blushed somewhat, and felt as if the doctor knew what his son was saying to me. He presently engaged in conversation with Lord Egham; he hoped his good father was well?

"You keep him so, doctor. You don't give a fellow a chance," says the young lord.

"Pass the bottle, you young men! Hey! We intend to see you all out!" cries Talbot Twysden, on pleasure bent and of the frugal mind.

"Well said, sir," says the stranger introduced as Mr. Hunt; "and right good wine. Ha, Firmin! I think I know the tap!" and he smacked his lips over the claret. "It's your twenty-five, and no mistake."

"The red-nosed individual seems a connoisseur," whispered Rosebury at my side.

The stranger's nose, indeed, was somewhat rosy. And to this I may add that his clothes were black, his face pale, and not well shorn, his white neckcloth dingy, and his eyes bloodshot.

"He looks as if he had gone to bed in his clothes, and carries a plentiful flue about his person. Who *is* your father's esteemed friend?" continues the wag, in an under voice.

"You heard his name, Rosebury," says the young barrister, gloomily.

"I should suggest that your father is in difficulties, and attended by an officer of the sheriff of London, or perhaps subject to mental aberration, and placed under the control of a keeper."

"Leave me alone, do!" groaned Philip. And here Twysden, who was longing for an opportunity to make a speech, bounced up from his chair, and stopped the facetious barrister's further remarks by his own eloquence. His discourse was in praise of Philip, the new-made barrister. "What! if no one else will give that toast, your uncle will, and many a heartfelt blessing go with you too, my boy!" cried the little man. He was prodigal of benedictions. He dashed aside the tear-drop of emotion. He spoke with perfect fluency, and for a considerable period. He really made a good speech, and was greeted with deserved cheers when at length he sat down.

Phil stammered a few words in reply to his uncle's voluble compliments; and then Lord Ascot, a young nobleman of much familiar humor proposed Phil's father, his health, and song. The physician made a neat speech from behind his ruffled shirt. He was agitated by the tender feelings of a paternal heart, he said, glancing benignly at Phil, who was cracking filberts. To see his son happy; to see him surrounded by such friends; to know him embarked this day in a profession which gave the greatest scope for talents, the noblest reward for industry, was a proud and happy moment to him, Dr. Firmin. What had the poet observed? "*Ingenuas didicisse fideliter artes*" (hear hear!) "*emollit mores*,"—yes, "*emollit mores*." He drank a bumper to the young barrister (he waved his ring, with a thimbleful of wine in his glass). He pledged the young friends whom he saw assembled to cheer his son on his onward path. He thanked them with a father's heart! He passed his emerald ring across his eyes for a moment, and lifted them to the ceiling, from which quarter he requested a blessing on his boy. As though "spirits" approved of his invocation, immense thumps came from above, along with the plaudits which saluted the doctor's speech from the gentlemen round the table. But the upper thumps were derisory, and came from Mr. Buffers, of the third floor, who chose this method of mocking our harmless little festivities.

I think these cheers from the facetious Buffers, though meant in scorn of our party, served to enliven it and make us laugh. Spite of all the talking, we were dull; and I could not but allow the force of my neighbor's remark, that we were sat upon and smothered by the old men. One or two of the younger gentlemen chafed at the license for tobacco-smoking not being yet accorded. But Philip interdicted this amusement as yet.

"Don't," he said ; "my father don't like it. He has to see patients to-night ; and they can't bear the smell of tobacco by their bedsides."

The impatient youths waited with their cigar-cases by their sides. They longed for the withdrawal of the obstacle to their happiness.

"He won't go, I tell you. He'll be sent for," growled Philip to me.

The doctor was engaged in conversation to the right and left of him, and seemed not to think of a move. But, sure enough, at a few minutes after ten o'clock, Dr. Firmin's footman entered the room with a note, which Firmin opened and read, as Philip looked at me with a grim humor in his face. I think Phil's father knew that we knew he was acting. However, he went through the comedy quite gravely.

"A physician's time is not his own," he said, shaking his handsome, melancholy head. "Good-by, my dear lord ! Pray remember me at home ! Good-night, Philip, my boy, and good speed to you in your career ! Pray, pray don't move."

And he is gone, waving the fair hand and the broad-brimmed hat, with the beautiful white lining. Phil conducted him to the door, and heaved a sigh as it closed upon his father—a sigh of relief, I think, that he was gone.

"Exit Governor. What's the Latin for Governor ?" says Lord Egham, who possessed much native humor, but not very profound scholarship. "A most venerable old parent, Firmin. That hat and appearance would command any sum of money."

"Excuse me," lisps Rosebury, "But why didn't he take his elderly friend with him—the dilapidated clerical gentleman who is drinking claret so freely ? And also, why did he not remove your avuncular orator ? Mr. Twysden, your interesting young neophyte has provided us with an excellent specimen of the cheerful produce of the Gascon grape."

"Well, then, now the old gentleman is gone, let us pass the bottle and make a night of it. Hey, my lord ?" cries Twysden. "Philip, your claret is good ! I say, do you remember some Château Margaux I had, which Winton liked so ? It must be good if *he* praised it, I can tell you. I imported it myself, and gave him the address of the Bordeaux merchant ; and he said he had seldom tasted any like it. Those were his very words. I must get you fellows to come and taste it some day."

"Some day! What day? Name it, generous Amphitryon!" cries Rosebury.

"Some day at seven o'clock. With a plain, quiet dinner— a clear soup, a bit of fish, a couple of little entrées, and a nice little roast. That's my kind of dinner. And we'll taste that claret, young men. It is not a heavy wine. It is not a first-class wine. I don't mean even to say it is a dear wine, but it has a bouquet and a pureness. What, you *will* smoke, you fellows?"

"We *will* do it, Mr. Twysden. Better do as the rest of us do. Try one of these."

The little man accepts the proffered cigar from the young nobleman's box, lights it, hems and hawks, and lapses into silence.

"I thought that would do for him," murmurs the facetious Egham. "It is strong enough to blow his old head off, and I wish it would. That cigar," he continues, "was given to my father by the Duke of Medina Sidonia, who had it out of the Queen of Spain's own box. She smokes a good deal, but naturally likes 'em mild. I can give you a stronger one."

"Oh, no. I dare say this is very fine. Thank you!" says poor Talbot.

"Leave him alone, can't you!" says Philip. "Don't make a fool of him before the young men, Egham."

Phillip still looked very dismal in the midst of the festivity. He was thinking of his differences with his absent parent.

We might all have been easily consoled, if the doctor had taken away with him the elderly companion whom he had introduced to Phil's feast. He could not have been very welcome to our host, for Phil scowled at his guest, and whispered, "Hang Hunt!" to his neighbor.

"Hang Hunt"—the Reverend Tufton Hunt was his name— was in nowise disconcerted by the coolness of his reception. He drank his wine very freely; addressed himself to his neighbors affably; and called out a loud "Hear, hear!" to Twysden, when that gentleman announced his intention of making a night of it. As Mr. Hunt warmed with wine he spoke to the table. He talked a great deal about the Ringwood family, had been very intimate at Wingate, in old days, as he told Mr. Twysden, and an intimate friend of poor Cinqbars, Lord Ringwood's only son. Now the memory of the late Lord Cinqbars was not an agreeable recollection to the relatives of the house of Ringwood. He was in life a dissipated and disreputable young lord. His name was seldom mentioned in his family; never by his father, with whom he had had many quarrels.

"You know I introduced Cinqbars to your father, Philip?" calls out the dingy clergyman.

"I have heard you mention the fact," says Philip.

"They met at a wine in my room at Corpus. Brummell Firmin we used to call your father in those days. He was the greatest buck in the university—always a dressy man, kept hunters, gave the best dinners in Cambridge. We were a wild set. There was Cinqbars, Brand Firmin, Beryl, Toplady, about a dozen of us, almost all noblemen or fellow-commoners—fellows who all kept their horses and had their private servants."

This speech was addressed to the company, who yet did not seem much edified by the college recollections of the dingy elderly man.

"Almost all Trinity men, sir! We dined with each other week about. Many of them had their tandems. Desperate fellow across country your father was. And—but we don't tell tales out of school, hey?"

"No; please don't, sir," said Philip, clenching his fists, and biting his lips. The shabby, ill-bred, swaggering man was eating Philip's salt; Phil's lordly ideas of hospitality did not allow him to quarrel with the guest under his tent.

"When he went out in medicine, we were all of us astonished. Why, sir, Brand Firmin, at one time, was the greatest swell in the university," continued Mr. Hunt, "and such a plucky fellow! So was poor Cinqbars, though he had no stamina. He, I, and Firmin, fought for twenty minutes before Cains' Gate with about twenty bargemen, and you should have seen your father hit out! I was a handy one in those days, too, with my fingers. We learned the noble art of self-defence in my time, young gentlemen! We used to have Glover, the boxer, down from London who gave us lessons. Cinqbars was a pretty sparrer—but no stamina. Brandy killed him, sir—brandy killed him! Why, this is some of your governor's wine! He and I have been drinking it to-night in Parr Street, and talking over old times."

"I am glad, sir, you found the wine to your taste," says Philip, gravely.

"I did, Philip, my boy! And when your father said he was coming to your wine, I said I'd come too."

"I wish somebody would fling him out of the window," groaned Philip.

"A most potent, grave and, reverend senior," whispered Rosebury to me. "I read billiards, Boulogne, gambling-houses, in his noble lineaments. Has he long adorned your family circle, Firmin?"

"I found him at home about a month ago in my father's ante-room, in the same clothes, with a pair of mangy mustaches on his face; and he has been at our house every day since."

"*Echappc de Toulon,*" says Rosebury, blandly, looking towards the stranger. *Cela ce voit. Homme parfaitment distingue.* You are quite right, sir. I was speaking of you, and asking our friend Philip where it was I had the honor of meeting you abroad last year? This courtesy," he gently added, "will disarm tigers."

"I *was* abroad, sir, last year," said the other, nodding his head.

"Three to one he was in Boulogne jail, or perhaps officiating chaplain at a gambling house. Stop, I have it! Baden Baden, sir?"

"I was there, safe enough," says the clergyman. "It is a very pretty place; but the air of the *Apres* kills you. Ha! ha! Your father used to shake his elbow when he was a youngster, too, Philip! I can't help calling you Philip. I have known your father these thirty years. We were college chums, you know."

"Ah! what would I give," sighs Rosebury, "if that venerable being would but address me by my Christian name! Philip do something to make your party go. The old gentlemen are throttling it. Sing something, somebody! or let us drown our melancholy in wine. You expressed your approbation of this claret, sir, and claimed a previous acquaintance with it?"

"I've drunk two dozen of it in the last month," says Mr. Hunt, with a grin.

"Two dozen and four, sir," remarks Mr. Brice, putting a fresh bottle on the table.

"Well said, Brice! I make the Firmin Arms my headquarters; and honor the landlord with a good deal of my company," remarks Mr. Hunt.

"The Firmin Arms is honored by having such supporters!" says Phil, glaring, and with a heaving chest. At each moment he was growing more and more angry with that parson.

At a certain stage of conviviality Phil was fond of talking of his pedigree; and, though a professor of very liberal opinions, was not a little proud of some of his ancestors.

"Oh, come, I say! Sink the heraldry!" cries Lord Egham.

"I am very sorry! I would do anything to oblige you, but I can't help being a gentleman!" growls Philip.

"Oh, I say! if you intend to come King Richard III. over us—" breaks out my lord.

"Egham! your ancestors were sweeping counters when mine stood by King Richard in that righteous fight!" shouts Philip.

That monarch had conferred lands upon the Ringwood family. Richard III. was Philip's battle-horse; when he trotted it after dinner he was splendid in his chivalry.

"Oh, I say! If you are to saddle White Surrey, fight Bosworth Field, and murder the kids in the Tower!" continues Lord Egham.

"Serve the little brutes right!" roars Phil. "They were no more heirs of the blood royal of England than——"

"I dare say! Only I'd rather have a song now the old boy is gone. I say, you fellows, chant something, do now! Bar all this row about Bosworth Field and Richard the Third. Always does it when he's beer on board—always does it, give you my honor!" whispers the young nobleman to his neighbor.

"I am a fool! I am a fool!" cries Phil, smacking his forehead. "There are moments when the wrongs of my race *will* intervene. It's not your fault, Mr. What-d'ye-call-'im, that you alluded to my arms in a derisive manner. I bear you no malice! Nay, I ask your pardon! Nay! I pledge you in this claret, which is good, though it's my governor's. In our house everything isn't, hum——Bosh! its twenty-five claret, sir! Egham's father gave him a pipe of it for saving a life which which might be better spent; and I believe the apothecary would have pulled you through, Egham, just as well as my governor. But the wine's good! Good! Brice, some more claret! A song! Who spoke of a song? Warble us something, Tom Dale! A song, a song, a song!"

Whereupon the exquisite ditty of "Moonlight on the Tiles" was given by Tom Dale with all his accustomed humor. Then politeness demanded that our host should sing one of his songs, and as I have heard him perform it many times, I have the privilege of here reprinting it: premising that the tune and chorus were taken from a German song-book, which used to delight us melodious youth in bygone days. Philip accordingly lifted up his great voice and sang :—

DOCTOR LUTHER.

" For the souls' edification
  Of this decent congregation,
Worthy people! by your grant,
I will sing a holy chant,
  I will sing a holy chant.
If the ditty sound but oddly,
'Twas a father wise and godly,
Sang it so long ago.
    Then sing as Doctor Luther sang,
    As Doctor Luther sang,
    Who loves not wine, woman, and song,
    He is a fool his whole life long.

" He by custom patriarchal,
  Loved to see the beaker sparkle,
And he thought the wine improved,
Tasted by the wife he loved,
  By the kindly lips he loved.
Friends! I wish this custom pious
Duly were adopted by us,
To combine love, song, wine ;
    And sing as Doctor Luther sang,
    As Doctor Luther sang,
    Who loves not wine, woman, and song,
    He is a fool his whole life long.

" Who refuses this our credo,
  And demurs to drink as we do,
Were he holy as John Knox,
I'd pronounce him heterodox.
  I'd pronounce him heterodox,
And from out this congregation,
With a solemn commination,
Banish quick the heretic,
    Who would not sing as Luther sang,
    As Doctor Luther sang,
    Who loves not wine, woman, and song,
    He is a fool his whole life long."

The reader's humble servant was older than most of the party assembled at this symposium, which may have taken place some score of years back ; but as I listened to the noise, the fresh laughter, the songs remembered out of old university days, the talk and cant phrases of the old school of which most of us had been disciples, dear me, I felt quite young again, and when certain knocks came to the door about midnight, enjoyed quite a refreshing pang of anxious interest for a moment, deeming the proctors were rapping, having heard our shouts in the court below. The late comer, however, was only a tavern waiter, bearing a supper-tray; and we were free to speechify, shout, quarrel, and be as young as we liked, with nobody to find fault, except, perchance, the bencher below, who, I dare say, was kept awake with our noise.

When that supper arrived, poor Talbot Twysden, who had come so far to enjoy it, was not in a state to partake of it. Lord Egham's cigar had proved too much for him ; and the worthy gentleman had been lying on a sofa, in a neighboring room, for some time past, in a state of hopeless collapse. He had told us, whilst yet capable of speech, what a love and regard he had for Philip ; but between him and Philip's father there was but little love. They had had that worst and most irremediable of quarrels, a difference about twopence-halfpenny in the division of the property of their late father-in-law. Firmin still thought Twysden a shabby curmudgeon ; and Twysden considered Firmin an unprincipled man. When Mrs. Firmin was alive, the two poor sisters had had to regulate their affections by the marital orders, and to be warm, cool, moderate, freezing, according to their husbands' state for the time being. I wonder are there many real reconciliations? Dear Tomkins and I are reconciled, I know. We have met and dined at Jones's. And ah! how fond we are of each other! Oh, very! So with Firmin and Twysden. They met, and shook hands with perfect animosity. So did Twysden junior and Firmin junior. Young Twysden was the elder, and thrashed and bullied Phil as a boy, until the latter arose and pitched his cousin down stairs. Mentally, they were always kicking each other down stairs. Well, poor Talbot could not partake of the supper when it came, and lay in a piteous state on the neighboring sofa of the absent Mr. Van John.

Who would go home with him, where his wife must be anxious about him? I agreed to convoy him, and the parson said he was going our way, and would accompany us. We supported this senior through the Temple, and put him on the front seat of a cab. The cigar had disgracefully overcome him ; and any lecturer on the evils of smoking might have pointed his moral on the helpless person of this wretched gentleman.

The evening's feasting had only imparted animation to Mr. Hunt, and occasioned an agreeable *abandon* in his talk. I had seen the man before in Dr. Firmin's house, and own that his society was almost as odious to me as to the doctor's son Philip. On all subjects and persons, Phil was accustomed to speak his mind out a great deal too openly : and Mr. Hunt had been an object of special dislike to him ever since he had known Hunt. I tried to make the best of the matter. Few men of kindly feeling and good station are without a dependent or two. Men start together in the race of life ; and Jack wins, and Tom falls by his side. The successful man succors and reaches a friendly hand to the unfortunate competitor.

Remembrance of early times gives the latter a sort of right to call on his luckier comrade ; and a man finds himself pitying, then enduring, then embracing a companion for whom, in old days, perhaps, he never had had any regard or esteem. A prosperous man ought to have followers : if he has none, he has a hard heart.

This philosophizing was all very well. It was good for a man not to desert the friends of his boyhood. But to live with such a cad as that—with that creature, low, swaggering, besotted—" How could his father, who had fine tastes, and loved grand company, put up with such a fellow ? " asked Phil. " I don't know when the man is more odious : when he is familiar, or when he is respectful ; when he is paying compliments to my father's guests in Parr Street, or telling hideous old stale stories, as he did at my call-supper."

The wine of which Mr. Hunt freely partook on that occasion made him, as I have said, communicative. " Not a bad fellow, our host," he remarked, on his part, when we came away together. " Bumptious, good-looking, speaks his mind, hates me, and I don't care. He must be well to do in the world, Master Philip."

I said I hoped and thought so.

" Brummell Firmin must make four or five thousand a year. He was a wild fellow in my time, I can tell you—in the days of the wild Prince and Poins—stuck at nothing, spent his own money, ruined himself, fell on his legs somehow, and married a fortune. Some of us have not been so lucky. I had nobody to pay *my* debts. I missed my fellowship by idling and dissipating with those confounded hats and silver-laced gowns. I liked good company in those days—always did when I could get it. If you were to write my adventures, now, you would have to tell some queer stories. I've been everywhere ; I've seen high and low—'specially low. I've tried school-mastering, bear-leading, newspapering, America, West Indies. I've been in every city in Europe. I haven't been as lucky as Brummell Firmin. He rolls in his coach, he does, and I walk in my highlows. Guineas drop into his palm every day, and are uncommonly scarce in mine, I can tell you ; and poor old Tufton Hunt is not much better off at fifty odd than he was when he was an undergraduate at eighteen. How do you do, old gentleman ? Air do you good ? Here we are at Beaunash Street ; hope you've got the key, and missis won't see you." A large butler, too well bred to express astonishment at any event which occurred out of doors, opened Mr. Twysden's, and let in that lamentable gentleman. He was very pale and solemn. He gasped out a few words, intimating his intention to fix a day to ask us to come and dine soon, and taste that wine that Winton liked so. He waved an unsteady hand to us. If Mrs. Twysden was on the stairs to see the condition of her lord, I hope she took possession of the candle. Hunt grumbled as we came out ; " He might have offered us some refreshment after bringing him all that way home. It's only half-past one. There's no good in going to bed so soon as that. Let us go and have a drink somewhere. I know a very good crib close by. No, you won't? I say " (here he burst into a laugh which startled the sleeping street), " I know what you've been thinking all the time in the cab. You are a swell,—you are, too ! You have been thinking, ' This dreary old parson will try and borrow money from me.' But I won't, my boy. I've got a banker. Look here ! Fee, faw, fum. You understand. I can get the sovereigns out of my medical swell in Old Parr Street. I prescribe bleeding for him—I drew him to-night. He is a very kind fellow, Brummell Firmin is. He can't deny such a dear old friend anything. Bless him ! " And as he turned away to some midnight haunt of his own, he tossed up his hand in the air. I heard him laughing through the silent street, and Policeman X, tramping on his beat, turned round and suspiciously eyed him.

Then I thought of Dr. Firmin's dark melancholy face and eyes. Was a benevolent remembrance of old times the bond of union between these men ? All my house had long been asleep, when I opened and gently closed my house door. By the twinkling night-lamp I could dimly see child and mother softly breathing. Oh, blessed they on whose pillow no remorse sits ! Happy you who have escaped temptation !

I may have been encouraged in my suspicions of the dingy clergyman by Philip's own surmises regarding him, which were expressed with the speaker's usual candor. " The fellow calls for what he likes at the ' Firmin Arms,' " said poor Phil ; " and when my father's big wigs assemble, I hope the reverend gentleman dines with them. I should like to see him hobnobbing with old Bumpsher, or slapping the bishop on the back. He lives in Sligo Street, round the corner, so as to be close to our house and yet preserve his own elegant independence. Otherwise, I wonder he has not installed himself in Old Parr Street, where my poor mother's bedroom is vacant. The doctor does not care to use that room. I remember now how silent they were when together, and how terrified she always seemed before him. What has he done ? I know of one affair in his early life. Does this Hunt know of any more? They have been accomplices in some conspiracy, sir; I dare say with that young Cinqbars, of whom Hunt is for ever bragging : the worthy son of the worthy Ringwood. I say, does wickedness run in the blood? My grandfathers, I have heard, were honest men. Perhaps they were only not found out ; and the family taint will show in me some day. There are times when I feel the devil so strong within me, that I think some day he must have the mastery. I'm not quite bad yet : but I tremble lest I should go. Suppose I were to drown, and go down? It's not a jolly thing, Pendennis, to have such a father as mine. Don't humbug *me* with your charitable palliations and soothing surmises. You put me in mind of the world then, by Jove, you do! I laugh, and I drink, and I make merry, and sing, and smoke endless tobacco ; and I tell you, I always feel as if a little sword was dangling over my skull which will fall some day and split it. Old Parr Street is mined, sir,—mined ! And some morning we shall be blown into blazes—into blazes, sir ; mark my words ! That's why I'm so careless and so idle, for which you fellows are always bothering and scolding me. There's no use in settling down until the explosion is over, don't you see? *Incedo per ignes suppositos*, and, by George ! sir, I feel my bootsoles already scorching. Poor thing ! poor mother " (he apostrophized his mother's picture which hung in the room where we were talking), " were you aware of the secret, and was it the knowledge of that which made your poor eyes always look so frightened? She was always fond of you, Pen. Do you remember how pretty and graceful she used to look as she lay on her sofa up stairs, or smiled out of her carriage as she kissed her hand to us boys? I say, what if a woman marries, and is coaxed and wheedled by a soft tongue, and runs off, and afterwards finds her husband has a cloven foot ? "

" Ah, Philip ! "

" What is to be the lot of the son of such a man ? Is my hoof cloven, too ? " It was on the stove, as he talked, extended in American fashion. " Suppose there's no escape for me, and I inherit my doom, as another man does gout or consumption ? Knowing this fate, what is the use, then, of doing anything in particular ? I tell you, sir, the whole edifice of our present life will crumble in and smash." (Here he flings his pipe to the ground with an awful shatter.) "And until the catastrophe comes, what on earth is the use of setting to work, as you call it ? You might as well have told a fellow, at Pompeii, to select a profession the day before the eruption."

" If you know that Vesuvius is going to burst over Pompeii," I said, somewhat alarmed, " why not go to Naples, or farther if you will ? "

" Were there not men in the sentry-boxes at the city gates," asked Philip, " who might have run, and yet remained to be burned there ?   Suppose, after all, the doom isn't hanging over us,—and the fear of it is only a nervous terror of mine ?   Suppose it comes, and I survive it ?   The risk of the game gives a zest to it, old boy.   Besides, there is Honor : and some One Else is in the case, from whom a man *could* not part in an hour of danger."   And here he blushed a fine red, heaved a great sigh, and emptied a bumper of claret.

CHAPTER VIII.

WILL BE PRONOUNCED TO BE CYNICAL BY THE BENEVOLENT.

GENTLE readers will not, I trust, think the worst of their most obedient humble servant for the confession that I talked to my wife on my return home regarding Philip and his affairs. When I choose to be frank, I hope no man can be more open than myself : when I have a mind to be quiet, no fish can be more mute.   I have kept secrets so ineffably, that I have utterly forgotten them, until my memory was refreshed by people who also knew them.   But what was the use of hiding this one from the being to whom I open all, or almost all—say all, excepting just one or two of the closets of this heart ?   So I say to her, " My love ; it is as I suspected.   Philip and his cousin Agnes are carrying on together."

" Is Agnes the pale one, or the *very* pale one ? " asks the joy of my existence.

" No, the elder is Blanche.   They are both older than Mr. Firmin : but Blanche is the elder of the two."

" Well, I am not saying anything malicious, or contrary to the fact, am I, sir ? "

No.   Only I know by her looks, when another lady's name is mentioned, whether my wife likes her or not.   And I am bound to say, though this statement may meet with a denial, that her countenance does not vouchsafe smiles at the mention of all ladies' names.   " You don't go to the house ?   You and

Mrs. Twysden have called on each other, and there the matter
has stopped ? Oh, I know ! It is because poor Talbot brags
so about his wine, and gives such abominable stuff, that you
have such an un-Christian feeling for him !"

That is the reason, I dare say," says the lady.

" No. It is no such thing. Though you *do* know sherry
from port, I believe upon my conscience you do not avoid the
Twysdens because they give bad wine. Many others sin in that
way, and you forgive them. You like your fellow-creatures better
than wine—some fellow-creatures—and you dislike some fellow-
creatures worse than medicine. You swallow them, madam.
You say nothing, but your looks are dreadful. You make wry
faces : and when you have taken them, you want a piece of
sweetmeat to take the taste out of your mouth."

The lady, thus wittily addressed, shrugs her lovely shoulders.
My wife exasperates me in many things ; in getting up at insane
hours to go to early church, for instance ; in looking at me in a
particular way at dinner, when I am about to eat one of those
entrées which Dr. Goodenough declares disagree with me ; in
nothing more than in that obstinate silence, which she persists
in maintaining sometimes when I am abusing people, whom I
do not like, whom she does not like, and who abuse me. This
reticence makes me wild. What confidence can there be between
a man and his wife, if he can't say to her, " Confound So-and-
so, I hate him ; " or, " What a prig What-d'ye-call-'im is ! " or,
What a bloated aristocrat Thingamy has become since he got
his place ! " or what you will ?

" No," I continue, " I know why you hate the Twysdens,
Mrs. Pendennis. You hate them because they move in a world
which you can only occasionally visit. You envy them because
they are hand-in-glove with the great ; because they possess an
easy grace, and a frank and noble elegance with which common
country people and apothecaries' sons are not endowed."

" My dear Arthur, I do think you are ashamed of being an
apothecary's son ; you talk about it so often," says the lady.
Which was all very well : but you see she was not answering
my remarks about the Twysdens.

" You are right, my dear," I say then. " I ought not to be
censorious, being myself no more virtuous than my neighbor."

" I know people abuse you, Arthur ; but I think you are a
very good sort of man," says the lady, over her little tea-tray.

" And so are the Twysdens very good people—very nice,
artless, unselfish, simple, generous, well-bred people. Mr. Twysden is all heart : Twysden's conversational powers are remark-

able and pleasing : and Philip is eminently fortunate in getting one of those charming girls for a wife."

"I've no patience with them," cries my wife, losing that quality to my great satisfaction : for then I knew I had found the crack in Madam Pendennis's armor of steel, and had smitten her in a vulnerable little place.

"No patience with them ? Quiet, lady-like young women !" I cry.

"Ah," sighs my wife, "what have they got to give Philip in return for ——"

"In return for his thirty thousand ? They will have ten thousand pounds apiece when their mother dies."

"Oh ! I wouldn't have our boy marry a woman like one of those, not if she had a million. I wouldn't, my child and my blessing !" (This is addressed to a little darling who happens to be eating sweet cakes, in a high chair, off the little table by his mother's side, and who, though he certainly used to cry a good deal at that period, shall be a mute personage in this history.)

"You are alluding to Blanche's little affair with——"

"No, I am not, sir !"

"How do you know which one I meant, then ?——Or that notorious disappointment of Agnes, when Lord Farintosh became a widower ? If he wouldn't, she couldn't, you know, my dear. And I am sure she tried her best : at least, everybody said so."

"Ah ! I have no patience with the way in which you people of the world treat the most sacred of subjects—the most sacred, sir. Do you hear me ? Is a woman's love to be pledged, and withdrawn every day ? Is her faith and purity only to be a matter of barter, and rank, and social consideration ? I am sorry, because I don't wish to see Philip, who is good, and honest, and generous, and true as yet—however great his faults may be —because I don't wish to see him given up to——Oh ! its shocking, shocking !"

Given up to what ? to anything dreadful in this world, or the next ? Don't imagine that Philip's relations thought they were doing Phil any harm by condescending to marry him, or themselves any injury. A doctor's son, indeed ! Why, the Twysdens were far better placed in the world than their kinsmen of Old Parr Street ; and went to better houses. The year's levée and drawing-room would have been incomplete without Mr. and Mrs. Twysden. There might be families with higher titles, more wealth, higher positions ; but the world did not contain more respectable folks then the Twysdens: of this every one of the family was convinced, from Talbot himself down to his heir. If somebody or some Body of savans would write the history of the harm that has been done in the world by people who believe themselves to be virtuous, what a queer, edifying book it would be, and how poor oppressed rogues might look up! Who burn the Protestants?—the virtuous Catholics, to be sure. Who roast the Catholics?—the virtuous Reformers. Who thinks I am a dangerous character, and avoids me at the club?—the virtuous Squaretoes. Who scorns? who persecutes? who doesn't forgive?—the virtuous Mrs. Grundy. She remembers her neighbor's peccadilloes to the third and fourth generation; and if she finds a certain man fallen in her path, gathers up her affrighted garments with a shriek, for fear the muddy, bleeding wretch should contaminate her, and passes on.

I do not seek to create even surprises in this modest history, or condescend to keep candid readers in suspense about many matters which might possibly interest them. For instance, the matter of love has interested novel-readers for hundreds of years past, and doubtless will continue so to interest them. Almost all young people read love-books and histories with eagerness, as oldsters read books of medicine, and whatever it is—heart-complaint, gout, liver, palsy—cry, "Exactly so, precisely my case!" Phil's first love-affair, to which we are now coming, was false. I own it at once. And in this commencement of his career I believe he was not more or less fortunate than many and many a man and woman in this world. Suppose the course of true love always did run smooth, and everybody married his or her first love. Ah! what would marriage be?

A generous young fellow comes to market with a heart ready to leap out of his waistcoat, for ever thumping and throbbing, and so wild that he can't have any rest till he has disposed of it. What wonder if he falls upon a wily merchant in Vanity Fair, and barters his all for a stale bauble not worth sixpence? Phil chose to fall in love with his cousin; and I warn you that nothing will come of that passion, except the influence which it had upon the young man's character. Though my wife did not love the Twysdens, she loves sentiment, she loves love-affairs —all women do. Poor Phil used to bore *me* after dinner with endless rodomontades about his passion and his charmer; but my wife was never tired of listening. "You are a selfish, heartless, *blasé* man of the world, you are," he would say. "Your

own immense and undeserved good fortune in the matrimonial
lottery has rendered you hard, cold, crass, indifferent. You
have been asleep, sir, twice to-night, whilst I was talking. I
will go up and tell madam everything. *She* has a heart." And
presently, engaged with my book or my after-dinner doze, I
would hear Phil striding and creaking overhead, and plunging
energetic pokers in the drawing-room fire.

Thirty thousand pounds to begin with ; a third part of that
sum coming to the lady from her mother ; all the doctor's savings and property ;—here certainly was enough in possession
and expectation to satisfy many young couples ; and as Phil is
twenty-two, and Agnes (must I own it ?) twenty-five, and as
she has consented to listen to the warm outpourings of the
eloquent and passionate youth, and exchange for his fresh,
new-minted, golden sovereign heart, that used little threepenny-
piece, her own—why should they not marry at once, and so let
us have an end of them and this history ? They have plenty of
money to pay the parson and the post-chaise ; they may drive
off to the country, and live on their means, and lead an existence so humdrum and tolerably happy, that Phil may grow quite
too fat, lazy, and unfit for his present post of hero of a novel.
But stay—there are obstacles ; coy, reluctant, amorous delays.
After all, Philip is a dear, brave, handsome, wild, reckless,
blundering boy, treading upon everybody's dress-skirts, smashing the little Dresden ornaments, and the pretty little decorous
gimcracks of society, life, conversation ; but there is time yet.
Are you so very sure about that money of his mother's ? and
how is it that his father, the doctor, has not settled accounts
with him yet ? *C'est louche.* A family of high position and
principle must look to have the money matters in perfect order,
before they consign a darling accustomed to every luxury to the
guardianship of a confessedly wild and eccentric, though generous and amiable, young man. Besides — ah ! besides—
besides !

" * * * It's horrible, Arthur ! It's cruel, Arthur ! It's a
shame to judge a woman or Christian people so ! Oh ! my
loves ! my blessings ! would I sell *you ?* " says this young
mother, clutching a little belaced, befurbeloved being to her
heart, infantine, squalling, with blue shoulder-ribbons, a mottled
little arm that has just been vaccinated, and the sweetest red
shoes. " Would I sell *you ?* " says mamma. Little Arty, I say,
squalls ; and little Nelly looks up from her bricks with a wondering, whimpering expression.

Well, I am ashamed to say what the " besides " is ; but the

fact is, that young Woolcomb of the Life Guards Green, who has inherited immense West India property, and, we will say, just a teaspoonful of that dark blood which makes a man naturally partial to blonde beauties, has cast his opal eyes very warmly upon the golden-haired Agnes of late ; has danced with her not a little ; and when Mrs. Twysden's barouche appears by the Serpentine, you may not unfrequently see a pair of the neatest little yellow kid gloves just playing with the reins, a pair of the prettiest little boots just touching the stirrup, a magnificent horse dancing, and tittupping, and tossing, and performing the most graceful caracoles and gambadoes, and on the magnificent horse a neat little man with a blazing red flower in his bosom, and glancing opal eyes, and a dark complexion, and hair so *very* black and curly that I really almost think in some of the Southern States of America he would be likely to meet with rudeness in a railway car.

But in England we know better. In England Grenville Woolcomb is a man and a brother. Half of Arrowroot Island, they say, belongs to him ; besides Mangrove Hall, in Hertfordshire ; ever so much property in other counties, and that fine house in Berkeley Square. He is called the Black Prince behind the scenes of many theatres : ladies nod at him from those broughams which, you understand, need not be particularized. The idea of his immense riches is confirmed by the known fact that he is a stingy Black Prince, and most averse to parting with his money, except for his own adornment or amusement. When he receives at his country-house, his entertainments are, however, splendid. He has been flattered, followed, caressed all his life, and allowed by a fond mother to have his own way ; and as this has never led him to learning, it must be owned that his literary acquirements are small, and his writing defective. But in the management of his pecuniary affairs he is very keen and clever. His horses cost him less than any young man's in England who is so well mounted. No dealer has ever been known to get the better of him ; and, though he is certainly close about money, when his wishes have very keenly prompted him, no sum has been known to stand in his way.

Witness the purchase of the ——. But never mind scandal. Let bygones be bygones. A young doctor's son, with a thousand a year for a fortune, may be considered a catch in some circles, but not, *vous concevez*, in the upper regions of society. And dear woman—dear, angelic, highly accomplished, respectable woman—does she not know how to pardon many failings in our sex ? Age ? psha ! She will crown my bare old poll with the roses of her youth. Complexion ? What contrast is sweeter or more touching than Desdemona's golden ringlets on swart Othello's shoulder ? A past life of selfishness and bad company ? Come out from among the swine, my prodigal, and I will purify thee !

This is what is called cynicism, you know. Then I suppose my wife is a cynic, who clutches her children to her pure heart, and prays gracious heaven to guard them from selfishness, from worldliness, from heartlessness, from wicked greed.

CHAPTER IX.

CONTAINS ONE RIDDLE WHICH IS SOLVED, AND PERHAPS SOME MORE.

MINE is a modest muse, and as the period of the story arrives when a description of the love-making is justly due, my Mnemosyne turns away from the young couple, drops a little curtain over the embrasure where they are whispering, heaves a sigh from her elderly bosom, and lays a finger on her lip. Ah, Mnemosyne dear ! we will not be spies on the young people. We will not scold them. We won't talk about their doings much. When we were young, we too, perhaps, were taken in under Love's tent ; we have eaten of his salt : and partaken of his bitter, his delicious bread. Now we are padding the hoof lonely in the wilderness, we will not abuse our host, will we ? We will couch under the stars, and think fondly of old times, and to-morrow resume the staff and the journey.

And yet, if a novelist may chronicle any passion, its flames, its raptures, its whispers, its assignations, its sonnets, its quarrels, sulks, reconciliations, and so on, the history of such a love as this first of Phil's may be excusable in print, because I don't believe it was a real love at all, only a little brief delusion of the senses, from which I give you warning that our hero will recover before many chapters are over. What ! my brave boy, shall we give your heart away for good and all, for better or for worse, till death do you part ? What ! my Corydon and sighing swain, shall we irrevocably bestow you upon Phyllis, who, all the time you are piping and paying court to her, has Melibœus in the cupboard, and ready to be produced should

LAURA'S FIRESIDE.

he prove to be a more eligible shepherd than t'other? I am not such a savage towards my readers or hero, as to make them undergo the misery of such a marriage.

Philip was very little of a club or society man. He seldom or ever entered the "Megatherium," or when there stared and scowled round him savagely, and laughed strangely at the ways of the inhabitants. He made but a clumsy figure in the world, though in person, handsome, active, and proper enough; but he would for ever put his great foot through the World's flounced skirts, and she would stare, and cry out, and hate him. He was the last man who was aware of the Woolcomb flirtation, when hundreds of people, I dare say, were simpering over it.

"Who is that little man who comes to your house, and whom I sometimes see in the Park, aunt—that little man with the very white gloves and the very tawny complexion?" asks Philip.

"That is Mr. Woolcomb, of the Life Guards Green," aunt remembers.

"An officer is he?" says Philip, turning round to the girls. "I should have thought he would have done better for the turban and cymbals." And he laughs and thinks he has said a very clever thing. Oh, those good things about people and against people! Never, my dear young friend, say them to anybody—not to a stranger, for he will go away and tell; not to the mistress of your affections, for you may quarrel with her, and then *she* will tell; not to your son, for the artless child will return to his schoolfellows and say: "Papa says Mr. Blenkinsop is a muff." My child, or what not, praise everybody; and everybody will smile on you in return, a sham smile, and hold you out a sham hand; and, in a word, esteem you as you deserve. No. I think you and I will take the ups and the downs, the roughs and the smooths of this daily existence and conversation. We will praise those whom we like, though nobody repeat our kind sayings; and say our say about those whom we dislike, though we are pretty sure our words will be carried by tale-bearers, and increased and multiplied, and remembered long after we have forgotten them. We drop a little stone—a little stone that is swallowed up and disappears, but the whole pond is set in commotion, and ripples in continually widening circles long after the original little stone has popped down and is out of sight. Don't your speeches of ten years ago—maimed, distorted, bloated it may be out of all recognition—come strangely back to their author?

Phil, five minutes after he had made the joke, so entirely

forgot his saying about the black Prince and the cymbals, that, when Captain Woolcomb scowled at him with his fiercest eyes, young Firmin thought that this was the natural expression of the Captain's swarthy countenance, and gave himself no further trouble regarding it. " By George ! sir," said Phil afterwards, speaking of this officer, " I remarked that he grinned, and chatted and showed his teeth ; and remembering it was the nature of such baboons to chatter and grin, had no idea that this chimpanzee was more angry with me than with any other gentleman. You see, Pen, I am a white-skinned man ; I am pronounced even red-whiskered by the ill-natured. It is not the prettiest color. But I had no idea that I was to have a mulatto for a rival. I am not so rich, certainly, but I have enough. I can read and spell correctly, and write with tolerable fluency. I could not, you know, could I, reasonably suppose that I need fear competition, and that the black horse would beat the bay one ? Shall I tell you what she used to say to me ? There is no kissing and telling, mind you. No, by George. Virtue and prudence were for ever on her lips ! She warbled little sermons to me ; hinted gently that I should see to safe investments of my property, and that no man, not even a father, should be the sole and uncontrolled guardian of it. She asked me, sir, scores and scores of little sweet, timid, innocent questions about the doctor's property, and how much did I think it was, and how had he laid it out ? What virtuous parents that angel had ! How they brought her up, and educated her dear blue eyes to the main chance ! She knows the price of housekeeping, and the value of railway shares ; she invests capital for herself in this world and the next. She mayn't do right always, but wrong ? O fie, never ! I say, Pen, an undeveloped angel with wings folded under her dress ; not perhaps your mighty, snow-white, flashing pinions that spread out and soar up to the highest stars, but a pair of good serviceable drab dove-colored wings, that will support her gently and equably just over our heads, and help to drop her softly when she condescends upon us. When I think, sir, that I might have been married to a genteel angel and am single still,—oh ! it's despair, its despair ! "

But Philip's little story of disappointed hopes and bootless passion must be told in terms less acrimonious and unfair than the gentleman would use, naturally of a sanguine, swaggering talk, prone to exaggerate his own disappointments, and call out, roar—I dare say swear—if his own corn was trodden upon, as loudly as some men who may have a leg taken off.

This I can vouch for Miss Twysden, Mrs. Twysden and all the rest of the family :—that if they, what you call, jilted Philip, they did so without the slightest hesitation or notion that they were doing a dirty action. Their actions never *were* dirty or mean ; they were necessary, I tell you, and calmly proper. They ate cheese parings with graceful silence; they cribbed from board-wages ; they turned hungry servants out of doors ; they remitted no chance in their own favor ; they slept gracefully under scanty coverlids ; they lighted niggard fires ; they locked the caddy with the closest lock, and served the teapot with the smallest and least frequent spoon. But you don't suppose they thought they were mean, or that they did wrong ? Ah ! it is admirable to think of many, many, ever so many respectable families of your acquaintance and mine, my dear friend, and how they meet together and humbug each other ! " My dear, I have cribbed half an inch of plush out of James's small-clothes." " My love, I have saved a halfpenny out of Mary's beer. Isn't it time to dress for the duchess's ; and don't you think John might wear that livery of Thomas's, who only had it a year, and died of the small-pox ? It's a little tight for him, to be sure, but," &c. What is this ? I profess to be an impartial chroni-cler of poor Phil's fortunes, misfortunes, friendships, and what-nots, and am getting almost as angry with these Twysdens as Philip ever was himself.

Well, I am not mortally angry with poor Traviata tramping the pavement, with the gas-lamp flaring on her poor painted smile, else my indignant virtue and squeamish modesty would never walk Piccadilly or get the air. But Laïs, quite moral, and very neatly, primly, and straitly laced ;—Phryne, not the least dishevelled, but with a fixature for her hair, and the best stays, fastened by mamma ; — your High Church or Evangelical Aspasia, the model of all proprieties, and owner of all virgin-purity blooms, ready to sell her cheek to the oldest old fogy who has money and a title ;—*these* are the Unfortunates, my dear brother and sister sinners, whom I should like to see repentant and specially trounced first. Why, some of these are put into reformatories in Grosvenor Square. They wear a prison dress of diamonds and Chantilly lace. Their parents cry, and thank heaven as they sell them ; and all sorts of re-vered bishops, clergy, relations, dowagers, sign the book, and ratify the ceremony. Come ! let us call a midnight meeting of those who have been sold in marriage, I say, and what a re-spectable, what a genteel, what a fashionable, what a brilliant, what an imposing, what a multitudinous assembly we will have ; and where's the room in all Babylon big enough to hold them ?

Look into that grave, solemn, dingy, somewhat naked, but
elegant drawing-room, in Beaunash Street, and with a little
fanciful opera-glass you may see a pretty little group or two
engaged at different periods of the day. It is after lunch, and
before Rotten Row ride time (this story, you know, relates to a
period ever so remote, and long before folks thought of riding
in the Park in the forenoon). After lunch, and before Rotten
Row time, saunters into the drawing-room a fair-haired young
fellow with large feet and chest, careless of gloves, with auburn
whiskers blowing over a loose collar, and—must I confess it?
—a most undeniable odor of cigars about his person. He
breaks out regarding the debate of the previous night, or the
pamphlet of yesterday, or the poem of the day previous, or the
scandal of the week before, or upon the street-sweeper at the
corner, or the Italian and monkey before the Park—upon whatever, in a word, moves his mind for the moment. If Philip has
had a bad dinner yesterday (and happens to remember it), he
growls, grumbles, nay, I dare say, uses the most blasphemous
language against the cook, against the waiters, against the
steward, against the committee, against the whole society of the
club where he has been dining. If Philip has met an organ-girl
with pretty eyes and a monkey in the street, he has grinned and
wondered over the monkey; he has wagged his head, and sung all
the organ's tunes; he has discovered that the little girl is the
most ravishing beauty eyes ever looked on, and that her scoundrelly Savoyard father is most likely an Alpine miscreant who
has bartered away his child to a pedlar of the beggarly cheesy
valleys, who has sold her to a friend *qui fait la traite des hurdi-
gurdies*, and has disposed of her in England. If he has to
discourse on the poem, pamphlet, magazine article—it is written
by the greatest genius, or the greatest numskull, that the world
now exhibits. *He* write! A man who makes fire rhyme
with Marire! This vale of tears and world which we inhabit
does not contain such an idiot. Or have you seen Dobbins's
poem? Agnes, mark my words for it, there is a genius in
Dobbins which some day will show what I have always surmised,
what I have always imagined possible, what I have always felt
to be more than probable, what, by George! I feel to be perfectly certain, and any man is a humbug who contradicts it, and
a malignant miscreant, and the world is full of fellows who
will never give another man credit; and I swear that to recognize and feel merit in poetry, painting, music, rope-dancing,
anything, is the greatest delight and joy of my existence. I say
—what was I saying?

"You were saying, Philip, that you love to recognize the merits of all men whom you see," says gentle Agnes, "and I believe you do."

"Yes!" cries Phil, tossing about the fair locks. "I think I do. Thank heaven, I do. I know fellows who can do many things better than I do—everything better than I do."

"Oh, Philip!" sighs the lady.

"But I don't hate 'em for it."

"You never hated any one, sir. You are too brave! Can you fancy Philip hating any one, mamma?"

"Mamma is writing: "Mr. and Mrs. TALBOT TWYSDEN request the honor of Admiral and Mrs. DAVIS LOCKER'S company at dinner on Thursday the so-and-so." "Philip what?" says mamma, looking up from her card. "Philip hating any one! Philip eating any one! Philip! we have a little dinner on the 24th. We shall ask your father to dine. We must not have too many of the family. Come in afterwards, please."

"Yes, aunt," says downright Phil, "I'll come, if you and the girls wish. You know tea is not my line; and I don't care about dinners, except in my own way, and with——"

"And with your own horrid set, sir!"

"Well," says Sultan Philip, flinging himself out on the sofa, and lording on the ottoman, "I like mine ease and mine inn."

"Ah, Philip! you grow more selfish every day. I mean men do," sighed Agnes.

You will suppose mamma leaves the room at this juncture. She has that confidence in dear Philip and the dear girls, that she sometimes *does* leave the room when Agnes and Phil are together. She will leave REUBEN, the eldest born, with her daughters: but my poor dear little younger son of a Joseph, if you suppose she will leave the room and *you* alone in it—O my dear Joseph, you may just jump down the well at once! Mamma, I say, has left the room at last, bowing with a perfect sweetness and calm grace and gravity; and she has slipped down the stairs, scarce more noisy than the shadow that slants over the faded carpet (oh! the faded shadow, the faded sunshine!)—mamma is gone, I say, to the lower regions, and with perfect good breeding is torturing the butler on his bottle-rack —is squeezing the housekeeper in her jam-closet—is watching the three cold cutlets shuddering in the larder behind the wires —is blandly glancing at the kitchen-maid until the poor wench fancies the piece of bacon is discovered which she gave to the crossing-sweeper—and calmly penetrating John until he feels sure his inmost heart is revealed to her, as it throbs within his worsted-laced waistcoat, and she knows about that pawning of master's old boots, (beastly old highlows!) and—and, in fact, all the most intimate circumstances of his existence. A wretched maid, who has been ironing collars, or what not, gives her mistress a shuddering curtsey, and slinks away with her laces; and meanwhile our girl and boy are prattling in the drawing-room.

About what? About everything on which Philip chooses to talk. There is nobody to contradict him but himself, and then his pretty hearer vows and declares he has not been so very contradictory. He spouts his favorite poems. "Delightful! Do, Philip, read us some Walter Scott! He is, as you say, the most fresh, the most manly, the most kindly of poetic writers—not of the first class, certainly. In fact, he has written most dreadful bosh, as you call it so drolly; and so has Wordsworth, though he is one of the greatest of men, and has reached sometimes to the very greatest height and sublimity of poetry; but now you put it, I must confess he is often an old bore, and I certainly should have gone to sleep during the 'Excursion,' only you read it so nicely. You don't think the new composers as good as the old ones, and love mamma's old-fashioned playing? Well, Philip, it is delightful, so lady-like, so feminine!" Or, perhaps, Philip has just come from Hyde Park, and says, "As I passed by Apsley House, I saw the Duke come out, with his old blue frock and white trousers and clear face. I have seen a picture of him in an old *European Magazine*, which I think I like better than all—gives me the idea of one of the brightest men in the world. The brave eyes gleam at you out of the picture; and there's a smile on the resolute lips, which seems to ensure triumph. Agnes, Assaye must have been glorious!"

"Glorious, Philip!" says Agnes, who had never heard of Assaye before in her life. Arbela, perhaps; Salamis, Marathon, Agincourt, Blenheim, Busaco — where dear grandpapa was killed—Waterloo, Armageddon; but Assaye? Quevoulez vous?

"Think of that ordinarily prudent man, and how greatly he knew how to dare when occasion came! I should like to have died after winning such a game. He has never done anything so exciting since."

"A game? I thought it was a battle just now," murmurs Agnes in her mind; but there may be some misunderstanding. "Ah, Philip," she says, "I fear excitement is too much the life of all young men now. When will you be quiet and steady, sir?"

"And go to an office every day, like my uncle and cousin;

and read the newspaper for three hours, and trot back and see you."

"Well, sir! that ought not to be such very bad amusement," says one of the ladies.

"What a clumsy wretch I am! my foot is always trampling on something or somebody!" groans Philip.

"You must come to us, and we will teach you to dance, Bruin!" says gentle Agnes, smiling on him. I think when very much agitated, her pulse must have gone up to forty. Her blood must have been a light pink. The heart that beat under that pretty white chest, which she exposed so liberally, may have throbbed pretty quickly once or twice with waltzing, but otherwise never rose or fell beyond its natural gentle undulation. It may have had throbs of grief at a disappointment occasioned by the milliner not bringing a dress home ; or have felt some little fluttering impulse of youthful passion when it was in short frocks, and Master Grimsby at the dancing-school showed some preference for another young pupil out of the nursery. But feelings, and hopes, and blushes, and passions now? Psha! They pass away like nursery dreams. Now there are only proprieties. What is love, young heart? It is two thousand a year, at the very lowest computation ; and, with the present rise in wages and house-rent, that calculation can't last very long. Love? Attachment? Look at Frank Maythorn, with his vernal blushes, his leafy whiskers, his sun-shiny, laughing face, and all the birds of spring carolling in his jolly voice ; and old General Pinwood hobbling in on his cork leg, with his stars and orders, and leering round the room from under his painted eyebrows. Will my modest nymph go to Maythorn, or to yonder leering Satyr, who totters towards her in his white and rouge? Nonsense. She gives her garland to the old man, to be sure. He is ten times as rich as the young one. And so they went on in Arcadia itself, *really*. Not in that namby-pamby ballet and idyll world, where they tripped up to each other in rhythm, and talked hexameters ; but in the real downright, no-mistake country—Arcadia—where Tityrus, fluting to Amaryllis in the shade, had his pipe very soon put out when Melibœus (the great grazier) performed on his melodious, exquisite, irresistible cowhorn ; and where Daphne's mother dressed her up with ribbons and drove her to market, and sold her, and swapped her, and bartered her like any other lamb in the fair. This one has been trotted to the market so long now that she knows the way herself. Her baa has been heard for—do not let us count how many seasons. She has

nibbled out of countless hands; frisked in many thousand
dances; come quite harmless away from goodness knows how
many wolves. Ah! ye lambs and raddled innocents of our
Arcadia! Ah, old *Ewe!* Is it of your ladyship this fable is
narrated? I say it is as old as Cadmus, and man- and mutton-
kind.

"So, when Philip comes to Beaunash Street, Agnes listens
to him most kindly, sweetly, gently, and affectionately. Her
pulse goes up very nearly half a beat when the echo of his
horse's heels is heard in the quiet street. It undergoes a cor-
responding depression when the daily grief of parting is encountered and overcome. Blanche and Agnes don't love each other
very passionately. If I may say as much regarding those two
lambkins, they butt at each other—they quarrel with each other
—but they have secret understandings. During Phil's visits
the girls remain together, you understand, or mamma is with
the young people. Female friends may come in to call on Mrs.
Twysden, and the matrons whisper together, and glance at the
cousins, and look knowing. "Poor orphan boy!" mamma
says to a sister matron. "I am like a mother to him since my
dear sister died. His own home is so blank, and ours so
merry, so affectionate! There may be intimacy, tender regard,
the utmost confidence between cousins—there may be future
and even closer ties between them—but you understand, dear
Mrs. Matcham, no engagement between them. He is eager,
hot-headed, impetuous, and imprudent, as we all know. She
has not seen the world enough—is not sure of herself, poor
dear child! Therefore every circumspection, every caution is
necessary. There must be no engagement, no letters between
them. My darling Agnes does not write to ask him to dinner
without showing the note to me or her father. My dearest girls
respect themselves." "Of course, my dear Mrs. Twysden,
they are admirable, both of them. Bless you, darlings! Agnes,
you look radiant! Ah, Rosa, my child, I wish you had dear
Blanche's complexion!"

"And isn't it monstrous keeping that poor boy hanging on
until Mr. Woolcomb has made up his mind about coming forward?" says dear Mrs. Matcham to her own daughter, as her
brougham door closes on the pair. "Here he comes! Here
is his cab. Maria Twysden is one of the smartest women in
England—that she is."

"How odd it is, mamma, that the *beau cousin* and Captain
Woolcomb are always calling, and never call together!" remarks the *ingénue.*

"They might quarrel if they met. They say young Mr. Firmin is very quarrelsome and impetuous!" says mamma.

"But how are they kept apart?"

"Chance, my dear! mere chance!" says mamma. And they agree to say it is chance—and they agree to pretend to believe one another. And the girl and the mother know everything about Woolcomb's property, everything about Philip's property and expectations, everything about all the young men in London, and those coming on. And Mrs. Matcham's girl fished for Captain Woolcomb last year in Scotland, at Loch-hookey; and stalked him to Paris; and they went down on their knees to Lady Banbury when they heard of the theatricals at the Cross; and pursued that man about until he is forced to say, "Confound me! hang me! it's too bad of that woman and her daughter, it is now, I give you my honor it is! And all the fellows chaff me! And she took a house in Regent's Park, opposite our barracks, and asked for her daughter to learn to ride in our school—I'm blest if she didn't, Mrs. Twysden! and I thought my black mare would have kicked her off one day— I mean the daughter—but she stuck on like grim death; and the fellows call them Mrs. Grim Death and her daughter. Our surgeon called them so, and a doosid rum fellow—and they chaff me about it, you know—ever so many of the fellows do— and *I'm* not going to be had in that way by Mrs. Grim Death and her daughter! No, not as I knows, if you please!"

"You are a dreadful man, and you gave her a dreadful name, Captain Woolcomb!" says mamma.

"It wasn't me. It was the surgeon, you know, Miss Agnes: a doosid funny and witty fellow, Nixon is—and sent a thing once to *Punch*, Nixon did. I heard him make the riddle in Albany Barracks and it riled Foker so! You've no idea how it riled Foker, for he's in it!"

"In it?" asks Agnes, with the gentle smile, the candid blue eyes—the same eyes, expression, lips, that smile and sparkle at Philip.

"Here it is! Capital! Took it down. Wrote it into my pocket-book at once as Nixon made it. '*All doctors like my first, that's clear!*' Doctor Firmin does that. Old Parr Street party! Don't you see, Miss Agnes? FEE! Don't you see?"

"Fee! Oh, you droll thing!" cries Agnes, smiling, radiant, very much puzzled.

"'My second,'" goes on the young officer—"'*My second gives us Foker's beer!*'"

"'*My whole's the shortest month in all the year!*' Don't

you see, Mrs. Twysden? FEE-BREWERY, DON'T YOU SEE? February! A doosid good one, isn't it now? and I wonder *Punch* never put it in. And upon my word, I used to spell it Febuary before, I did ; and I dare say ever so many fellows do still. And I know the right way now, and all from that riddle which Nixon made."

The ladies declare he is a droll man, and full of fun. He rattles on, artlessly telling his little stories of sport, drink, adventure, in which the dusky little man himself is a prominent figure. Not honey-mouthed Plato would be listened to more kindly by those three ladies. A blank, frank smile shines over Talbot Twysden's noble face, as he comes in from his office, and finds the creole prattling. "What! *you* here, Woolcomb? Hay! Glad to see you!" And the gallant hand goes out and meets and grasps Woolcomb's tiny kid glove.

"He has been so amusing, papa! He has been making us die with laughing! Tell papa that riddle you made, Captain Woolcomb?"

"That riddle I made? That riddle Nixon, our surgeon, made. 'All doctors like my first, that's clear,'" &c.

And *da capo*. And the family, as he expounds this admirable rebus, gather round the young officer in a group, and the curtain drops.

As in a theatre booth at a fair there are two or three performances in a day, so in Beaunash Street a little genteel comedy is played twice :—at four o'clock with Mr. Firmin, at five o'clock with Mr. Woolcomb ; and for both young gentlemen, same smiles, same eyes, same voice, same welcome. Ah, bravo ! ah, encore !

CHAPTER X.

IN WHICH WE VISIT "ADMIRAL BYNG.

FROM long residence in Bohemia, and fatal love of bachelor ease and habits, Master Philip's pure tastes were so destroyed, and his manners so perverted that, you will hardly believe it, he was actually indifferent to the pleasures of the refined home we have just been describing ; and, when Agnes was away, sometimes even when she was at home, was quite relieved to get out of Beaunash Street. He is hardly twenty yards from the door, when out of his pocket there comes a case ; out of the case there jumps an aromatic cigar, which is scattering fragrance around as he is marching briskly northwards to his next house of call. The pace is even more lively now than when he is hastening on what you call the wings of love to Beaunash Street. At the house whither he is now going, he and the cigar are always welcome. There is no need of munching orange chips, or chewing scented pills, or flinging your weed away half a mile before you reach Thornhaugh Street—the low, vulgar place. I promise you Phil may smoke at Brandon's, and find others doing the same. He may set the house on fire, if so minded, such a favorite is he there ; and the Little Sister, with her kind, beaming smile, will be there to bid him welcome. How that woman loved Phil, and how he loved her, is quite a curiosity ; and both of them used to be twitted with this attachment by their mutual friends, and blush as they acknowledged it. Ever since the little nurse had saved his life as a schoolboy, it was *à la vie à la mort* between them. Phil's father's chariot used to come to Thornhaugh Street sometimes —at rare times—and the doctor descend thence and have colloquies with the Little Sister. She attended a patient or two of his. She was certainly very much better off in her money matters in these late years, since she had known Dr. Firmin. Do you think she took money from him ?" As a novelist, who knows everything about his people, I am con- strained to say, Yes. She took enough to pay some little bills of her weak-minded old father, and send the bailiff's hand from his old collar. But no more. " I think you owe him as much as that," she said to the doctor. But as for compliments between them—" Dr. Firmin, I would die rather than be beholden to you for anything," she said, with her little limbs all in a tremor, and her eyes flashing anger. " How dare you, sir, after old days, be a coward and pay compliments to me ; I will tell your son of you, sir ! " and the little woman looked as if she could have stabbed the elderly libertine there as he stood. And he shrugged his handsome shoulders : blushed a little too, perhaps : gave her one of his darkling looks, and departed. She had believed him once. She had married him, as she fancied. He had tired of her ; forsaken her ; left her—left her even without a name. She had not known his for long years after her trust and his deceit. " No, sir, I wouldn't have your name now, not if it were a lord's, I wouldn't, and a coronet on your carriage. You are beneath me now, Mr. Brand Firmin ! " she had said.

How came she to love the boy so ?   Years back, in her own horrible extremity of misery, she could remember a week or two cf a brief, strange, exquisite happiness, which came to her in the midst of her degradation and desertion, and for a few days a baby in her arms, with eyes like Philip's.   It was taken from her, after a few days—only sixteen days.   Insanity came upon her, as her dead infant was carried away :—insanity, and fever, and struggle—ah ! who knows how dreadful ?   She never does.   There is a gap in her life which she never can recall quite.   But George Brand Firmin, Esq., M.D., knows how very frequent are such cases of mania, and that women who don't speak about them often will cherish them for years after they appear to have passed away.   The Little Sister says, quite gravely, sometimes, " They are allowed to come back.   They do come back.   Else what's the good of little cherubs bein' born, and smilin', and happy, and beautiful—say, for sixteen days, and then an end ?   I've talked about it to many ladies in grief sim'lar to mine was, and it comforts them. ˉAnd when I saw that child on his sick-bed, and he lifted his eyes, *I knew him*, I tell you, Mrs. Ridley.   I don't speak about it ; but I knew him, ma'am ; my angel came back again.   I know him by the eyes.   Look at 'em.   Did you ever see such eyes ? They look as if they had seen heaven.   His father's don't." Mrs. Ridley believes this theory solemnly, and I think I know a lady, nearly connected with myself, who can't be got quite to disown it.   And this secret opinion to women in grief and sorrow over their new-born lost infants Mrs. Brandon persists in imparting.   " *I* know a case," the nurse murmurs, " of a poor mother who lost her child at sixteen days old ; and sixteen years after, on the very day, she saw him again."

Philip knows so far of the Little Sister's story, that he is the object of this delusion, and, indeed, it very strangely and tenderly affects him.   He remembers fitfully the illness through which the Little Sister tended him, the wild paroxysms of his fever, his head throbbing on her shoulders—cool tamarind drinks which she applied to his lips—great gusty night shadows flickering through the bare school dormitory—the little figure of the nurse gliding in and out of the dark.   He must be aware of the recognition, which we know of, and which took place at his bedside, though he has never mentioned it—not to his father, not to Caroline.   But he clings to the woman, and shrinks from the man.   Is it instinctive love and antipathy ? The special reason for his quarrel with his father the junior Firmin has never explicitly told me then or since.   I have known sons much more confidential, and who, when their fathers tripped and stumbled, would bring their acquaintances to jeer at the patriarch in his fall.

One day, as Philip enters Thornhaugh Street, and the Sister's little parlor there, fancy his astonishment on finding his father's dingy friend, the Rev. Tufton Hunt, at his ease by the fireside. "Surprised to see *me* here, eh?" says the dingy gentleman, with a sneer at Philip's lordly face of wonder and disgust. "Mrs. Brandon and I turn out to be very old friends."

"Yes, sir, old acquaintances," says the Little Sister, very gravely.

"The Captain brought me home from the club at the 'Byng.' Jolly fellows the Byngs. My service to you, Mr. Gann and Mrs. Brandon." And the two persons addressed by the gentleman, who is "taking some refreshment," as the phrase is, made a bow in acknowledgment of this salutation.

"You should have been at Mr. Philip's call-supper, Captain Gann," the divine resumes. "That *was* a night! Tiptop swells—noblemen—first-rate claret. That claret of your father's, Philip, is pretty nearly drunk down. And your song was famous. Did you ever hear him sing, Mrs. Brandon?"

"Who do you mean by *him*?" says Philip, who always boiled with rage before this man.

Caroline divines the antipathy. She lays a little hand on Philip's arm. "Mr. Hunt has been having too much, I think," she says. "I *did* know him ever so long ago, Philip!"

"What does he mean by Him?" again says Philip, snorting at Tufton Hunt.

"Him?—Dr. Luther's Hymn! 'Wein, Weber, und Gesang,' to be sure!" cries the clergyman, humming the tune. "I learned it in Germany myself—passed a good deal of time in Germany, Captain Gann—six months in a specially shady place—*Quod* Strasse, in Frankfort-on-the-Maine—being persecuted by some wicked Jews there. And there was another poor English chap in the place, too, who used to chirp that song behind the bars, and died there, and disappointed the Philistines. I've seen a deal of life, I have; and met with a precious deal of misfortune; and borne it pretty stoutly, too, since your father and I were at college together, Philip. You don't do anything in this way? Not so early, eh? It's good rum, Gann, and no mistake." And again the chaplain drinks to the Captain, who waves the dingy hand of hospitality towards his dark guest.

For several months past Hunt had now been a resident in

London, and a pretty constant visitor at Dr. Firmin's house. He came and went at his will. He made the place his house of call; and in the doctor's trim, silent, orderly mansion, was perfectly free, talkative, dirty, and familiar. Philip's loathing for the man increased till it reached a pitch of frantic hatred. Mr. Phil, theoretically a Radical, and almost a Republican (in opposition, perhaps, to his father, who, of course, held the highly respectable line of politics)—Mr. Sansculotte Phil was personally one of the most aristocratic and overbearing of young gentlemen ; and had a contempt and hatred for mean people, for base people, for servile people, and especially for too familiar people, which was not a little amusing sometimes, which was provoking often, but which he never was at the least pains of disguising. His uncle and cousin Twysden, for ex-ample, he treated not half so civilly as their footmen. Little Talbot humbled himself before Phil, and felt not always easy in his company. Young Twysden hated him, and did not dis-guise his sentiments at the club, or to their mutual acquaint-ance behind Phil's broad back. And Phil, for his part, adopted towards his cousin a kick-me-down-stairs manner, which I own must have been provoking to that gentleman, who was Phil's senior by three years, a clerk in a public office, a member of several good clubs, and altogether a genteel member of society. Phil would often forget Ringwood Twysden's presence, and pursue his own conversation entirely regardless of Ringwood's observations. He *was* very rude, I own. *Que voulez-vous ?* We have all of us our little failings, and one of Philip's was an ignorant impatience of bores, parasites, and pretenders.

So no wonder my young gentleman was not very fond of his father's friend, the dingy jail chaplain. I, who am the most tolerant man in the world, as all my friends know, liked Hunt little better than Phil did. The man's presence made me un-easy. His dress, his complexion, his teeth, his leer at women— *Que sçais-je ?*—everything was unpleasant about this Mr. Hunt, and his gayety and familiarity more specially disgusting than even his hostility. The wonder was that battle had not taken place between Philip and the jail clergyman, who, I suppose,-was accustomed to be disliked, and laughed with cynical good humor at the other's disgust.

Hunt was a visitor of many tavern parlors ; and one day, strolling out of the "Admiral Byng," he saw his friend Dr. Firmin's well-known equipage stopping at a door in Thornhaugh Street, out of which the doctor presently came ; "Brandon" was on the door. Brandon, Brandon ? Hunt remembered a

dark transaction of more than twenty years ago—of a woman
deceived by this Firmin, who then chose to go by the name of
Brandon. " He lives with her still, the old hypocrite, or he
has gone back to her," thought the parson. Oh, you old sinner! And the next time he called in Old Parr Street on his
dear old college friend, Mr. Hunt was specially jocular, and
frightfully unpleasant and familiar.

"Saw your trap Tottenham Court Road way," says the
slang parson, nodding to the physician.

"Have some patients there. People are ill in Tottenham
Court Road," remarks the doctor.

" *Pallida mors æquo pede*—hay, doctor? What used Flaccus
to say, when we were undergrads ? "

" *Æquo pede*," sighs the doctor, casting up his fine eyes to
the ceiling.

"Sly old fox! Not a word will he say about her!" thinks
the clergyman. "Yes, yes, I remember. And, by Jove! Gann
was the name."

Gann was also the name of that queer old man who frequented the " Admiral Byng," where the ale was so good—
the old boy whom they called the Captain. Yes ; it was clear
now. That ugly business was patched up. The astute Hunt
saw it all. The doctor still kept up a connection with the—
the party. And that is her old father, sure enough. "The
old fox, the old fox ! I've earthed him, have I ? This is a good
game. I wanted a little something to do, and this will excite
me," thinks the clergyman.

I am describing what I never could have seen or heard,
and can guarantee only verisimilitude, not truth, in my report
of the private conversation of these worthies. The end of
scores and scores of Hunt's conversations with his friend was
the same—an application for money. If it rained when Hunt
parted from his college chum, it was, " I say, doctor, I shall
spoil my new hat, and I'm blest if I have any money to take a
cab. Thank you, old boy. Au revoir." If the day was fine,
it was, " My old blacks show the white seams so, that you
must out of your charity rig me out with a new pair. Not your
tailor. He is too expensive. Thank you—a couple of sovereigns will do." And the doctor takes two from the mantel-
piece, and the divine retires, jingling the gold in his greasy
pocket.

The doctor is going after the few words about *pallida mors*,
and has taken up that well-brushed broad hat, with that ever-
fresh lining, which we all admire in him—" Oh, I say, Firmin ! "

breaks out the clergyman. "Before you go out, you must lend me a few sovs, please. They've cleaned me out in Air Street. That confounded roulette! It's a madness with me.

"By George!" cries the other, with a strong execration, "you are too bad, Hunt. Every week of my life you come to me for money. You have had plenty. Go elsewhere. I won't give it you."

"Yes, you will, old boy," says the other, looking at him a terrible look; "for——"

"For what?" says the doctor, the veins of his tall forehead growing very full.

"For old times' sake," says the clergyman. "There's seven of 'em on the table in bits of paper—that'll do nicely. And he sweeps the fees with a dirty hand into a dirty pouch. "Halloa! Swearin' and cursin' before a clergyman. Don't cut up rough, old fellow! Go and take the air. It'll cool you."

"I don't think I would like that fellow to attend me, if I was sick," says Hunt, shuffling away, rolling the plunder in his greasy hand. "I don't think I'd like to meet him by moonlight alone, in a *very* quiet lane. He's a determined chap. And his eyes mean *miching malecho*, his eyes do. Phew!" And he laughs, and makes a rude observation about Dr. Firmin's eyes.

That afternoon, the gents who used the "Admiral Byng" remarked the reappearance of the party who looked in last evening, and who now stood glasses round, and made himself uncommon agreeable to be sure. Old Mr. Ridley says he is quite the gentleman. "Hevident have been in foring parts a great deal, and speaks the languages. Probbly have 'ad misfortunes, which many 'ave 'ad them. Drinks rum-and-water tremenjous. 'Ave scarce no heppytite. Many get into this way from misfortunes. A plesn man, most well informed on almost every subjeck. Think he's a clergyman. He and Mr. Gann have made quite a friendship together, he and Mr. Gann 'ave. Which they talked of Watloo, and Gann is very fond of that, Gann is, most certny." I imagine Ridley delivering these sentences, and alternate little volleys of smoke, as he sits behind his sober calumet and prattles in the tavern parlor.

After Dr. Firmin has careered through the town, standing by sick-beds with his sweet sad smile, fondled and blessed by tender mothers who hail him as the saviour of their children, touching ladies' pulses with a hand as delicate as their own, patting little fresh cheeks with courtly kindness—little cheeks that owe their roses to his marvellous skill; after he has soothed and comforted my lady, shaken hands with my lord, looked in at the clubs, and exchanged courtly salutations with brother bigwigs, and driven away in the handsome carriage with the noble horses—admired, respecting, respectful, saluted, saluting—so that every man says, " Excellent man, Firmin. Excellent doctor, excellent man. Safe man. Sound man. Man of good family. Married a rich wife. Lucky man." And so on. After the day's triumphant career, I fancy I see the doctor driving homeward, with those sad eyes, that haggard smile.

He comes whirling up Old Parr Street just as Phil saunters in from Regent Street, as usual, cigar in mouth. He flings away the cigar as he sees his father, and they enter the house together.

" Do you dine at home, Philip ? " the father asks.

" Do you, sir ? I will if you do," says the son, " and if you are alone."

" Alone. Yes. That is, there'll be Hunt, I suppose, whom you don't like. But the poor fellow has few places to dine at. What? D—— Hunt? That's a strong expression about a poor fellow in misfortune, and your father's old friend."

I am afraid Philip had used that wicked monosyllable whilst his father was speaking, and at the mention of the clergyman's detested name. " I beg your pardon, father. It slipped out in spite of me. I can't help it. I hate the fellow."

" You don't disguise your likes or dislikes, Philip," says, or rather groans, the safe man, the sound man, the prosperous man, the lucky man, the miserable man. For years and years he has known that his boy's heart has revolted from him, and detected him, and gone from him; and with shame and remorse, and sickening feeling, he lies awake in the night-watches, and thinks how he is alone—alone in the world. Ah! Love your parents, young ones! Oh Father Beneficent! strengthen our hearts; strengthen and purify them so that we may not have to blush before our children!

" You don't disguise your likes and dislikes, Philip," says the father then, with a tone that smites strangely and keenly on the young man.

There is a great tremor in Philip's voice, as he says, " No, father, I can't bear that man, and I can't disguise my feelings. I have just parted from the man. I have just met him."

" Where?"

" At—at Mrs. Brandon's, father." He blushes like a girl as he speaks.

At the next moment he is scared by the execration which hisses from his father's lips, and the awful look of hate which the elder's face assumes—the fatal, forlorn, fallen, lost look which, man and boy, has oftened frightened poor Phil. Philip did not like that look, nor indeed that other one, which his father cast at Hunt, who presently swaggered in.

"What! *you* dine here? We rarely do papa the honor of dining with him," says the parson, with his knowing leer. "I suppose, doctor, it is to be fatted-calf day now the prodigal has come home. There's worse things than a good fillet of veal; eh?"

Whatever the meal might be, the greasy chaplain leered and winked over it as he gave it his sinister blessing. The two elder guests tried to be lively and gay, as Philip thought, who took such little trouble to disguise his own moods of gloom or merriment. Nothing was said regarding the occurrences of the morning when my young gentleman had been rather rude to Mr. Hunt; and Philip did not need his father's caution to make no mention of his previous meeting with their guest. Hunt, as usual, talked to the butler, made sidelong remarks to the footman, and garnished his conversation with slippery double-entendre and dirty old-world slang. Betting-houses, gambling-houses, Tattersall's fights, and their frequenters, were his cheerful themes, and on these he descanted as usual. The doctor swallowed this dose, which his friend poured out, without the least expression of disgust. On the contrary, he was cheerful: he was for an extra bottle of claret—it never could be in better order than it was now.

The bottle was scarce put on the table, and tasted and pronounced perfect, when—oh! disappointment!—the butler reappears with a note for the doctor. One of his patients. He must go. She has little the matter with her. She lives hard by, in May Fair. "You and Hunt finish this bottle, unless I am back before it is done; and if it is done, we'll have another," says Dr. Firmin, jovially. "Don't stir, Hunt"—and Dr. Firmin is gone, leaving Philip alone with the guest to whom he had certainly been rude in the morning.

"The doctor's patients often grow very unwell about claret time," growls Mr. Hunt, some few minutes after. "Never mind. The drink's good—good! as somebody said at your famous call-supper, *Mr.* Philip—won't call you Philip, as you don't like it. You were uncommon crusty to me this morning, to be sure. In my time there would have been bottles broke, or worse, for that sort of treatment."

" I have asked your pardon," Philip said.   " I was annoyed about—no matter what—and had no right to be rude to Mrs. Brandon's guest."

" I say, did you tell the governor that you saw me in Thornhaugh Street ? " asks Hunt.

" I was very rude and ill-tempered, and again I confess I was wrong," said Phil, boggling and stuttering, and turning very red.   He remembered his father's injunction.

" I say again, sir, did you tell your father of our meeting this morning ? " demands the clergyman.

" And pray, sir, what right have you to ask me about my private conversation with my father ? " asks Philip, with towering dignity.

" You won't tell me ? "   Then you *have* told him.   He's a nice man, your father is, for a moral man."

" I am not anxious for your opinion about my father's morality, Mr. Hunt," says Philip, gasping in a bewildered manner, and drumming the table.   " I am here to replace him in his absence, and treat his guest with civility."

" Civility !   Pretty civility ! " says the other, glaring at him.

" Such as it is, sir, it is my best, and—I—I have no other," groans the young man.

" Old friend of your father's, a university man, a Master of Arts, a gentleman born, by Jove ! a clergyman—though I sink that——"

" Yes, sir, you do sink that,"·says Philip.

" Am I a dog," shrieks out the clergyman, " to be treated by you in this way ?   Who are you ?   Do you know who you are ? "

" Sir, I am striving with all my strength to remember," says Philip.

" Come ! I say ! don't try any of your confounded airs on *me !* " shrieks Hunt, with a profusion of oaths, and swallowing glass after glass from the various decanters before him.   " Hang me, when I was a young man, I would have sent one—two at your nob, though you were twice as tall !   Who are you, to patronize your senior, your father's old pal—a university man : you confounded, supercilious——"

" I am here to pay every attention to my father's guest," says Phil ; " but, if you have finished your wine, I shall be happy to break up the meeting, as early as you please."

" You shall pay me ; I swear you shall," said Hunt.

" Oh, Mr. Hunt ! " cried Philip, jumping up, and clenching his great fists, " I should desire nothing better."

The man shrank back, thinking Philip was going to strike him (as Philip told me in describing the scene), and made for the bell. But when the butler came, Philip only asked for coffee ; and Hunt, uttering a mad oath or two, staggered out of the room after the servant. Brice said he had been drinking before he came. He was often so. And Phil blessed his stars that he had not assaulted his father's guest then and there, under his own roof-tree.

He went out into the air. He gasped and cooled himself under the stars. He soothed his feelings by his customary consolation of tobacco. He remembered that Ridley in Thornhaugh Street held a divan that night ; and jumped into a cab, and drove to his old friend.

The maid of the house, who came to the door as the cab was driving away, stopped it ; and as Phil entered the passage, he found the Little Sister and his father talking together in the hall. The doctor's broad hat shaded his face from the hall-lamp, which was burning with an extra brightness, but Mrs. Brandon's was very pale, and she had been crying.

She gave a little scream when she saw Phil. "Ah ! is it you, dear?" she said. She ran up to him : seized both his hands : clung to him, and sobbed a thousand hot tears on his hand. "I never will. Oh, never, never, never !" she murmured.

The doctor's broad chest heaved as with a great sigh of relief. He looked at the woman and at his son with a strange smile ;—not a sweet smile.

"God bless you, Caroline," he said, in his pompous, rather theatrical way.

"Good-night, sir," said Mrs. Brandon, still clinging to Philip's hand, and making the doctor a little humble curtsey. And when he was gone, again she kissed Philip's hand, and dropped her tears on it, and said, "Never, my dear ; no, never, never !"

CHAPTER XI.

IN WHICH PHILIP IS VERY ILL-TEMPERED.

PHILIP had long divined a part of his dear little friend's history. An educated young girl had been found, cajoled, deserted by a gentleman of the world. And poor Caroline was the victim, and Philip's own father the seducer. He easily guessed as much as this of the sad little story. Dr. Firmin's part in it was enough to shock his son with a thrill of disgust, and to increase the mistrust, doubt, alienation, with which the father had long inspired the son. What would Philip feel, when all the pages of that black book were opened to him, and he came to hear of a false marriage, and a ruined and outcast woman, deserted for years by the man to whom he himself was most bound ? In a word, Philip had considered this as a mere case of early libertinism, and no more ; and it was as such, in the very few words which he may have uttered to me respecting this matter, that he had chosen to regard it. I knew no more than my friend had told me of the story as yet ; it was only by degrees that I learned it, and as events, now subsequent, served to develop and explain it.

The elder Firmin, when questioned by his old acquaintance, and, as it appeared, accomplice of former days, regarding the end of a certain intrigue at Margate, which had occurred some four or five and twenty years back, and when Firmin, having reason to avoid his college creditors, chose to live away and bear a false name, had told the clergyman a number of false-hoods which appeared to satisfy him. What had become of that poor little thing about whom he had made such a fool of himself ? Oh, she was dead, dead ever so many years before. He had pensioned her off. She had married, and died in Can-ada—yes, in Canada. Poor little thing ! Yes, she was a good little thing, and, at one time, he had been very soft about her. I am sorry to have to state of a respectable gentleman that he told lies, and told lies habitually and easily. But, you see, if you commit a crime, and break a seventh commandment let us say, or an eighth, or choose any number you will—you will prob-ably have to back the lie of action by the lie of the tongue, and so you are fairly warned, and I have no help for you. If I murder a man, and the policeman inquires, " Pray, sir, did you cut this here gentleman's throat ? " I must bear false wit-ness, you see, out of self-defence, though I may be naturally a most reliable, truth-telling man. And so with regard to many crimes which gentlemen commit—it is painful to have to say respecting gentlemen, but they become neither more nor less than habitual liars, and have to go lying on through life to you, to me, to the servants, to their wives, to their children, to—— oh, awful name ! I bow and humble myself. May we kneel, may we kneel, nor strive to speak our falsehoods before Thee !

And so, my dear sir, seeing that after committing any infraction of the moral laws, you must tell lies in order to back yourself out of your scrape, let me ask you, as a man of honor and a gentleman, whether you had not better forego the crime, so as to avoid the unavoidable, and unpleasant, and daily recurring necessity of the subsequent perjury? A poor young girl of the lower orders, cajoled, or ruined, more or less, is of course no great matter. The little baggage is turned out of doors—worse luck for her!—or she gets a place, or she marries one of her own class, who has not the exquisite delicacy belonging to "gentle blood"—and there is an end of her. But if you marry her privately and irregularly yourself, and then throw her off, and then marry somebody else, you are brought to book in all sorts of unpleasant ways. I am writing of quite an old story, be pleased to remember. The first part of the history I myself printed some twenty years ago; and if you fancy I allude to any more modern period, madam, you are entirely out in your conjecture.

It must have been a most unpleasant duty for a man of fashion, honor, and good family, to lie to a poor tipsy, disreputable bankrupt merchant's daughter, such as Caroline Gann, but George Brand Firmin, Esq., M.D., had no other choice, and when he lied—as in severe cases, when he administered calomel—he thought it best to give the drug freely. Thus he lied to Hunt, saying that Mrs. Brandon was long since dead in Canada; and he lied to Caroline, prescribing for her the very same pill, as it were, and saying that Hunt was long since dead in Canada too. And I can fancy few more painful and humiliating positions for a man of rank and fashion and reputation, than to have to demean himself so far as to tell lies to a little low-bred person, who gets her bread as a nurse of the sick, and has not the proper use of her *h*'s.

"Oh, yes, Hunt!" Firmin had said to the Little Sister, in one of those sad little colloquies which sometimes took place between him and his victim, his wife of old days. "A wild, bad man, Hunt was—in days when I own I was little better! I have deeply repented since, Caroline; of nothing more than of my conduct to you; for you were worthy of a better fate, and you loved me truly—madly."

"Yes," says Caroline.

"I was wild then! I was desperate! I had ruined my fortunes, estranged my father from me, was hiding from my creditors under an assumed name—that under which I saw you. Ah, why did I ever come to your house, my poor child? The mark of the demon was upon me. I did not dare to speak of marriage before my father. You have yours, and tend him with your ever constant goodness. Do you know that my father would not see me when he died? Oh, it's a cruel thing to think of!" And the suffering creature slaps his tall forehead with his trembling hand; and some of his grief about his own father, I dare say, is sincere, for he feels the shame and remorse of being alienated from his own son.

As for the marriage—that it was a most wicked and unjustifiable deceit, he owned; but he was wild when it took place, wild with debt and with despair at his father's estrangement from him—but the fact was, it was no marriage.

"I am glad of that!" sighed the poor Little Sister.

"Why?" asked the other eagerly. His love was dead, but his vanity was still hale and well. "Did you care for somebody else, Caroline? Did you forget your George, whom you used to——"

"No!" said the little woman, bravely. "But I couldn't live with a man who behaved to any woman so dishonest as you behaved to me. I liked you because I thought you was a gentleman. My poor painter was whom you used to despise and trample to hearth—and my dear dear Philip is, Mr. Firmin. But gentlemen tell the truth! Gentlemen don't deceive poor innocent girls, and desert 'em without a penny!"

"Caroline! I was driven by my creditors. I——"

"Never mind. It's over now. I bear you no malice, Mr. Firmin, but I would not marry you, no, not to be doctor's wife to the Queen!"

This had been the Little Sister's language when there was no thought of the existence of Hunt, the clergyman who had celebrated their marriage; and I don't know whether Firmin was most piqued or pleased at the divorce which the little woman pronounced of her own decree. But when the ill-omened Hunt made his appearance, doubts and terrors filled the physician's mind. Hunt was needy, greedy, treacherous, unscrupulous, desperate. He could hold this marriage over the doctor. He could threaten, extort, expose, perhaps invalidate Philip's legitimacy. The first marriage, almost certainly, was null, but the scandal would be fatal to Firmin's reputation and practice. And the quarrel with his son entailed consequences not pleasant to think of. You see George Firmin, Esq., M.D., was a man with a great development of the back head; when he willed a thing, he willed so fiercely that he *must* have it, never mind the consequences. And so he had willed to make himself master of poor little Caroline : and so he had willed, as a young man, to have horses, splendid entertainments, roulette and écarté, and so forth ; and the bill came at its natural season, and George Firmin, Esq., did not always like to pay. But for a grand, prosperous, highly bred gentleman in the best society—with a polished forehead and manners, and universally looked up to—to have to tell lies to a poor, little, timid, uncomplaining, sick-room nurse, it *was* humiliating, wasn't it ? And I can feel for Firmin.

To have to lie to Hunt was disgusting : but somehow not so exquisitely mean and degrading as to have to cheat a little trusting, humble, houseless creature, over the bloom of whose gentle young life his accursed foot had already trampled. But then this Hunt was such a cad and ruffian that there need be no scruple about humbugging *him ;* and if Firmin had had any humor he might have had a grim sort of pleasure in leading the dirty clergyman a dance thro' bush thro' briar. So, perhaps (of course I have no means of ascertaining the fact), the doctor did not altogether dislike the duty which now devolved on him of hoodwinking his old acquaintance and accomplice. I don't like to use such a vulgar phrase regarding a man in Doctor Firmin's high social position, as to say of him and the jail-chaplain that it was "thief catch thief ;" but at any rate Hunt is such a low, graceless, friendless vagabond, that if he comes in for a few kicks, or is mystified, we need not be very sorry. When Mr. Thurtell is hung we don't put on mourning. His is a painful position for the moment ; but, after all, he has murdered Mr. William Weare.

Firmin was a bold and courageous man, hot in pursuit, fierce in desire, but cool in danger, and rapid in action. Some of his great successes as a physician arose from his daring and successful practice in sudden emergency. While Hunt was only lurching about the town an aimless miscreant, living from dirty hand to dirty mouth, and as long as he could get drink, cards, and shelter, tolerably content, or at least pretty easily appeased by a guinea-dose or two — Firmin could adopt the palliative system ; soothe his patient with an occasional bounty ; set him to sleep with a composing draught of claret or brandy ; and let the day take care of itself. He might die ; he might have a fancy to go abroad again ; he might be transported for forgery or some other rascaldom, Dr. Firmin would console himself ; and he trusted to the chapter of accidents to get rid of his friend. But Hunt, aware that the woman was alive whom he had actually, though unlawfully married to Firmin, became an enemy whom it was necessary to subdue, to cajole, or to bribe, and the sooner the doctor put himself on his defence the better. What should the defence be? Perhaps the most effectual was a fierce attack on the enemy; perhaps it would be better to bribe him. The course to be taken would be best ascertained after a little previous reconnoitring.

" He will try and inflame Caroline," the doctor thought, "by representing her wrongs and her rights to her. He will show her that, as my wife, she has a right to my name and a share of my income. A less mercenary woman never lived than this poor little creature. She disdains money, and, except for her father's sake, would have taken none of mine. But to punish me for certainly rather shabby behavior; to claim and take her own right and position in the world as an honest woman, may she not be induced to declare war against me, and stand by her marriage? After she left home, her two Irish half-sisters deserted her and spat upon her; and when she would have returned, the heartless women drove her from the door. Oh, the vixens! And now to drive by them in her carriage, to claim a maintenance from me, and to have a right to my honorable name, would she not have her dearest revenge over her sisters by so declaring her marriage?"

Firmin's noble mind misgave him very considerably on this point. He knew women, and how those had treated their little sister. Was it in human nature not to be revenged? These thoughts rose straightway in Firmin's mind, when he heard that the much dreaded meeting between Caroline and the chaplain had come to pass.

As he ate his dinner with his guest, his enemy, opposite to him, he was determining on his plan of action. The screen was up, and he was laying his guns behind it, so to speak. Of course he was as civil to Hunt as the tenant to his landlord when he comes with no rent. So the doctor laughed, joked, bragged, talked his best, and was thinking the while what was to be done against the danger.

He had a plan which might succeed. He must see Caroline immediately. He knew the weak point of her heart, and where she was most likely to be vulnerable. And he would act against her as barbarians of old acted against their enemies, when they brought the captive wives and children in front of the battle, and bade the foe strike through them. He knew how Caroline loved his boy. It was through that love he would work upon her. As he washes his pretty hands for dinner, and bathes his noble brow, he arranges his little plan. He orders himself to be sent for soon after the second bottle of claret—and it appears the doctor's servants were accustomed to the delivery of these messages from their master to himself. The plan arranged, now let us take our dinner and our wine, and make ourselves comfortable until the moment of action. In his wild-oats days, when travelling abroad with wild and noble companions, Firmin had fought a duel or two, and was always remarkable for his gayety of conversation and the fine appetite which he showed at breakfast before going on to the field. So, perhaps, Hunt, had he not been stupefied by previous drink, might have taken the alarm by remarking Firmin's extra courtesy and gayety, as they dined together. It was *nunc vinum, cras æquor*.

When the second bottle of claret was engaged, Dr. Firmin starts. He has an advance of half-an-hour at least on his adversary, or on the man who may be his adversary. If the Little Sister is at home, he will see her—he will lay bare his candid heart to her, and make a clean breast of it. The Little Sister was at home.

"I want to speak to you very particularly about that case of poor Lady Humandhaw," says he, dropping his voice.

"I will step out, my dear, and take a little fresh air," says Captain Gann; meaning that he will be off to the "Admiral Byng;" and the two are together.

"I have had something on my conscience. I have deceived you, Caroline," says the doctor, with the beautiful shining fore-head and hat.

"Ah, Mr. Firmin," says she, bending over her work; "you've used me to that."

"A man whom you knew once, and who tempted me for his own selfish ends to do a very wrong thing by you—a man whom I thought dead is alive:—Tufton Hunt, who performed that—that illegal ceremony at Margate, of which so often and often on my knees I have repented, Caroline!"

The beautiful hands are clasped, the beautiful deep voice thrills lowly through the room; and if a tear or two can be squeezed out of the beautiful eyes, I dare say the doctor will not be sorry.

"He has been here to-day. Him and Mr. Philip was here and quarrelled. Philip has told you, I suppose, sir?"

"Before heaven, 'on the word of a gentleman,' when I said he was dead, Caroline, I thought he was dead! Yes, I declare, at our college, Maxwell—Dr. Maxwell—who had been at Cambridge with us, told me that our old friend Hunt had died in Canada." (This, my beloved friends and readers, may not

NURSE AND DOCTOR.

have been the precise long bow which George Firmin, Esq.'
M.D., pulled; but that he twanged a famous lie out, whenever
there was occasion for the weapon, I assure you is an undoubted fact.) "Yes, Dr. Maxwell told me our old friend was dead
—our old friend? My worst enemy and yours! But let that
pass. It was he, Caroline, who led me into crimes which I
have never ceased to deplore."

"Ah, Mr. Firmin," sighs the Little Sister, "since I've known
you, you was big enough to take care of yourself in that way."

"I have not come to excuse myself, Caroline," says the deep
sweet voice. "I have done you enough wrong, and I feel it
here—at this heart. I have not come to speak about myself,
but of some one I love the best of all the world—the only being
I *do* love—some one you love, you good and generous soul—
—about Philip."

"What is it about Philip?" asks Mrs. Brandon, very
quickly.

"Do you want harm to happen to him?"

"Oh, my darling boy, no!" cries the Little Sister, clasping
her little hands.

"Would you keep him from harm?"

"Ah, sir, you know I would. When he had the scarlet
fever, didn't I pour the drink down his poor throat, and nurse
him, and tend him, as if, as if—as a mother would her own child?"

"You did, you did, you noble, noble woman; and heaven
bless you for it! A father does. I am not all heartless, Caroline, as you deem me, perhaps."

"I don't think it's much merit, your loving *him*," says Caroline, resuming her sewing. And, perhaps, she thinks within
herself, "What is he a-coming to?" You see she was a shrewd
little person, when her passions and partialities did not overcome her reason; and she had come to the conclusion that this
elegant Dr. Firmin, whom she had admired so once, was a—not
altogether veracious gentleman. In fact, I heard her myself
say afterwards, "La! he used to talk so fine, and slap his hand
on his heart, you know; but I usedn't to believe him, no more
than a man in a play." "It's not much merit your loving that
boy," says Caroline, then. "But what about him, sir?"

Then Firmin explained. This man Hunt was capable of
any crime for money or revenge. Seeing Caroline was alive * *

"I s'pose you told him I was dead too, sir," says she, looking up from the work.

"Spare me, spare me! Years ago, perhaps, when I had
lost sight of you. I may, perhaps have thought * * *"

"And it's not to you, George Brandon—it's not to you," cries Caroline, starting up, and speaking with her sweet, innocent, ringing voice ; "it's to kind, dear friends,—it's to my good God that I owe my life, which you had flung it away. And I paid you back by guarding your boy's dear life, I did, under—under Him who giveth and taketh. And bless His name ! "

"You are a good woman, and I am a bad, sinful man, Caroline," says the other. "You saved my Philip's—our Philip's life, at the risk of your own. Now I tell you that another immense danger menaces him, and may come upon him any day as long as yonder scoundrel is alive. Suppose his character is assailed ; suppose, thinking you dead, I married another ? "

"Ah, George, you never thought me dead ; though, perhaps, you wished it, sir. Many would have died," added the poor Little Sister.

"Look, Caroline ! If I was married to you, my wife— Philip's mother—was not my wife, and he is her natural son. The property he inherits does not belong to him. The children of his grandfather's other daughter claim it, and Philip is a beggar. Philip, bred as he has been—Philip, the heir to a mother's large fortune."

"And—and his father's, too ? " asks Caroline, anxiously.

"I daren't tell you—though, no, by heaven ! I can trust you with everything. My own great gains have been swallowed up in speculations which have been almost all fatal. There has been a fate hanging over me, Caroline—a righteous punishment for having deserted you. I sleep with a sword hanging over my head, which may fall and destroy me. I walk with a volcano under my feet, which may burst any day and annihilate me. And people speak of the famous Dr. Firmin, the rich Dr. Firmin, the prosperous Dr. Firmin ! I shall have a title soon, I believe. I am believed to be happy, and I am alone ; and the wretchedest man alive."

"Alone, are you ? " said Caroline. "There was a womnn once who would have kept by you, only you—you flung her away. Look here, George Brandon. It's over with us. Years and years ago it lies where a cherub was buried. But I love my Philip ; and I won't hurt him, no, never, never, never ! "

And as the doctor turned to go away, Caroline followed him wistfully into the hall, and it was there that Philip found them.

Caroline's tender "never," "never," rang in Philip's memory as he sat at Ridley's party, amidst the artists and authors there assembled. Phil was thoughtful and silent. He did not laugh very loud. He did not praise or abuse anybody outrageously, as was the wont of that most emphatic young gentleman. He scarcely contradicted a single person ; and perhaps, when Larkins and Scumble's last picture was beautiful, or Bunch, the critic of the *Connoisseur*, praised Bowman's last novel, contented himself with a scornful "Ho !" and a pull at his whiskers, by way of protest and denial. Had he been in his usual fine spirits, and enjoying his ordinary flow of talk, he would have informed Larkins and the assembled company not only that Scumble was an impostor, but that he, Larkins, was an idiot for admiring him. He would have informed Bunch that he was infatuated about that jackass Bowman, that cockney, that wretched ignoramus, who didn't know his own or any other language. He would have taken down one of Bowman's stories from the shelf, and proved the folly, the imbecility, and crass ignorance of that author. (Ridley has a simple little stock of novels and poems in an old cabinet in his studio, and reads them still with much artless wonder and respect.) Or, to be sure, Phil would have asserted propositions the exact contrary of those here maintained, and declared that Bowman was a genius, and Scumble a most accomplished artist. But then, you know, somebody else must have commenced by taking the other side. Certainly a more paradoxical, and provoking, and obstinate, and contradictory disputant than Mr. Phil I never knew. I never met Dr. Johnson, who died before I came up to town ; but I do believe Phil Firmin would have stood up and argued even with *him*.

At these Thursday divans the host provided the modest and kindly refreshment, and Betsy the maid, or Virgilio the model, travelled to and fro with glasses and water. Each guest brought his own smoke, and I promise you there were such liberal contributions of the article, that the studio was full of it ; and new-comers used to be saluted by a roar of laughter as you heard, rather than saw, them entering, and choking in the fog. It was, " Hilloa, Prodgers ! is that you, old boy ? " and the beard of Prodgers (that famous sculptor) would presently loom through the cloud. It was, "Newcome, how goes ? " and Mr. Clive Newcome (a mediocre artist, I must own, but a famous good fellow, with an uncommonly pretty villa and pretty and rich wife at Wimbledon) would make his appearance, and be warmly greeted by our little host. "It was, "Is that you, F. B. ? would you like a link, old boy, to see you through the fog ? " And the deep voice of Frederick Bayham, Esquire (the eminent critic on Art), would boom out of the tobacco-mist, and would exclaim, "A link? I would like a drink." Ah, ghosts of youth, again ye draw near! Old figures glimmer through the cloud. Old songs echo out of the distance. What were you saying anon about Dr. Johnson, boys? I am sure some of us must remember him. As for me, I am so old, that I might have been at Edial school—the other pupil along with little Davy Garrick and his brother.

We had a bachelor's supper in the Temple so lately that I think that we must pay but a very brief visit to a smoking party in Thornhaugh Street, or the ladies will say that we are too fond of bachelor habits, and keep our friends away from their charming and amiable society. A novel must not smell of cigars much, nor should its refined and genteel page be stained with too frequent brandy-and-water. Please to imagine, then, the prattle of the artists, authors, and amateurs assembled at Ridley's divan. Fancy Jarman, the minature painter, drinking more liquor than any man present, asking his neighbor (*sub voce*) why Ridley does not give his father (the old butler) five shillings to wait; suggesting that perhaps the old man is gone out, and is getting seven-and-sixpence elsewhere; praising Ridley's picture aloud, and sneering at it in an undertone; and when a man of rank happens to enter the room, shambling up to him and fawning on him, and cringing to him with fulsome praise and flattery. When the gentleman's back is turned, Jarman can spit epigrams at it. I hope he will never forgive Ridley, and always continue to hate him: for hate him Jarman will, as long as he is prosperous, and curse him as long as the world esteems him. Look at Pym, the incumbent of St. Bronze hard by, coming in to join the literary and artistic assembly, and choking in his white neckcloth to the diversion of all the company who can see him! Sixteen, eighteen, twenty men are assembled. Open the windows, or sure they will all be stifled with the smoke! Why, it fills the whole house so, that the Little Sister has to open the parlor window on the ground-floor, and gasp for fresh air.

Phil's head and cigar are thrust out from a window above, and he lolls there, musing about his own affairs, as his smoke ascends to the skies. Young Mr. Philip Firmin is known to be wealthy, and his father gives very good parties in Old Parr Street, so Jarman sidles up to Phil and wants a little fresh air too. He enters into conversation by abusing Ridley's picture that is on the easel.

Everybody is praising it; what do *you* think of it, Mr. Firmin? Very queer drawing about those eyes, isn't there?

"Is there?" growls Phil.

"Very loud color."

"Oh!" says Phil.

"The composition is so clearly prigged from Raphael."

"Indeed!"

"I beg your pardon. I don't think you know who I am," continues the other, with a simper.

"Yes, I do," says Phil, glaring at him. "You're a painter, and your name is Mr. Envy."

"Sir!" shrieks the painter; but he is addressing himself to the tails of Phil's coat, the superior half of Mr. Firmin's body is stretching out of the window. Now, you may speak of a man behind his back, but not to him. So Mr. Jarman withdraws, and addresses himself, face to face, to somebody else in the company. I daresay he abuses that upstart, impudent, bumptious young doctor's son. Have I not owned that Philip was often very rude? and to-night he is in a specially bad humor.

As he continues to stare into the street, who is that who has just reeled up to the railings below, and is talking in at Mrs. Brandon's window? Whose blackguard voice and laugh are those which Phil recognizes with a shudder? It is the voice and laugh of our friend Mr. Hunt, whom Philip left not very long since, near his father's house in Old Parr Street, and both of those familiar sounds are more vinous, more odious, more impudent than they were even two hours ago.

"Hilloa! I say!" he calls out with a laugh and a curse. "Pst! Mrs. What-d'you-call-em! Hang it! don't shut the window. Let a fellow in!" and he looks towards the upper window, where Philip's head and bust appear dark before the light, Hunt cries out, "Holloa! what game's up now, I wonder? Supper and ball. Shouldn't be surprised." And he hiccups a waltz tune, and clatters time to it with his dirty boots.

"Mrs. What-d'you-call-em! Mrs. B—!" the sot then recommences to shriek out. "Must see you—most particular business. Private and confidential. Hear of something to your advantage." And rap, rap, rap, he is now thundering at the door. In the clatter of twenty voices, few hear Hunt's noise except Philip; or, if they do, only imagine that another of Ridley's guests is arriving.

At the halldoor there is talk and altercation, and the high shriek of a well-known odious voice. Philip moves quickly from his window, shoulders friend Jarman at the studio door, and hustling past him obtains, no doubt, more good wishes from that ingenious artist.   Philip is so rude and overbearing that I really have a mind to depose him from his place of hero —only, you see, we are committed.   His name is on the page overhead, and we can't take it down and put up another.   The Little Sister is standing in her hall by the just opened door, and remonstrating with Mr. Hunt, who appears to wish to force his way in.

"Pooh! shtuff, my dear!   If he's here I musht see him— particular business—get out of that!" and he reels forward and against little Caroline's shoulder.

"Get away, you brute, you!" cries the little lady.   "Go home, Mr. Hunt; you are worse than you were this morning." She is a resolute little woman, and puts out a firm little arm against this odious invader.   She has seen patients in hospital raging in fever: she is not frightened by a tipsy man.   "La! is it you, Mr. Philip?   Who ever will take this horrid man?   He ain't fit to go up stairs among the gentlemen; indeed he ain't."

"You said Firmin was here—and it isn't the father.   It's the cub!   I want the doctor.   Where's the doctor?" hiccups the chaplain, lurching against the wall; and then he looks at Philip with bloodshot eyes, that twinkle hate.   "Who wantsh you, I shlike to know?   Had enough of you already to-day. Conceited brute.   Don't look at *me* in that sortaway!   I ain't afraid of you—ain't afraid anybody.   Time was when I was a young man fight you as soon as look at you.   I say, Philip!"

"Go home, now.   Do go home, there's a good man," says the landlady.

"I say!   Look here—hic—hi!   Philip!   On your word as a gentleman, your father's not here?   He's a sly old boots, Brummell Firmin is—Trinity man—I'm not a Trinity man— Corpus man.   I say, Philip, give us your hand.   Bear no malice. Look here—something very particular.   After dinner—went into Air Street—you know—*rouge gagne, et couleur*—cleaned out.   Cleaned out, on the honor of a gentleman and master of arts of the University of Cambridge.   So was your father—no, he went out in medicine.   I say, Philip, hand us out five sovereigns, and let's try the luck again!   What, you won't!   It's mean, I say.   Don't be mean."

"Oh, here's five shillings!   Go and have a cab.   Fetch a cab for him, Virgilio, do!" cries the mistress of the house.

"That's not enough, my dear!" cries the chaplain, advancing towards Mrs. Brandon, with such a leer and air, that Philip half choked with passion, runs forward, grips Hunt by the collar, and crying out, "You filthy scoundrel! as this is not my house, I may kick you out of it!"—in another instant has run Hunt through the passage, hurled him down the steps, and sent him sprawling into the kennel.

"Row down below," says Rosebury, placidly, looking from above. "Personal conflict. Intoxicated individual—in gutter. Our impetuous friend has floored him."

Hunt, after a moment, sits up and glares at Philip. He is not hurt. Perhaps the shock has sobered him. He thinks, perhaps, Philip is going to strike again. "Hands off, BASTARD!" shrieks out the prostrate wretch.

"O Philip, Philip! He's mad, he's tipsy!" cries out the Little Sister, running into the street. She puts her arms round Philip. "Don't mind him, dear—he's mad! Policeman! The gentleman has had too much. Come in, Philip; come in!"

She took him into her little room. She was pleased with the gallantry of the boy. She liked to see him just now, standing over her enemy, courageous, victorious, her champion. "La! how savage he did look; and how brave and strong you are! But the little wretch ain't fit to stand before such as you!" And she passed her little hand down his arm, of which the muscles were all in a quiver from the recent skirmish.

"What did the scoundrel mean by calling me bastard?" said Philip, the wild blue eyes glaring round about with more than ordinary fierceness.

"Nonsense, dear! Who minds anything he says, that beast? His language is always horrid; he's not a gentleman. He had had too much this morning when he was here. What matters what he says? He won't know anything about it to-morrow. But it was kind of my Philip to rescue his poor little nurse, wasn't it? Like a novel. Come in, and let me make you some tea. Don't go to no more smoking: you have had enough. Come in and talk to me."

And, as a mother, with sweet pious face, yearns to her little children from her seat, she fondles him, she watches him; she fills her teapot from her singing kettle. She talks—talks in her homely way, and on this subject and that. It is a wonder how she prattles on, who is generally rather silent. She won't see Phil's eyes, which are following her about very strangely and fiercely. And when again he mutters, "What did he mean by * * *" "La, my dear, how cross you are!" she breaks out. "It's always so; you won't be happy without your cigar. Here's a cheroot, a beauty! Pa brought it home from the club.

A China captain gave him some. You must light it at the little end. There!" And if I could draw the picture which my mind sees of her lighting Phil's cheroot for him, and smiling the while, the little innocent Delilah coaxing and wheedling this young Samson, I know it would be a pretty picture. I wish Ridley would sketch it for me.

CHAPTER XII.

DAMOCLES.

ON the next morning, at an hour so early that Old Parr Street was scarce awake, and even the maids who wash the broad steps of the houses of the tailors and medical gentlemen who inhabit that region had not yet gone down on their knees before their respective doors, a ring was heard at Dr. Firmin's night-bell, and when the door was opened by the yawning attendant, a little person in a gray gown and a black bonnet made her appearance, handed a note to the servant, and said the case was most urgent and the doctor must come at once. Was not Lady Humandhaw the noble person whom we last mentioned, as the invalid about whom the doctor and the nurse had spoken a few words on the previous evening? The Little Sister, for it was she, used the very same name to the servant, who retired grumbling to waken up his master and deliver the note.

Nurse Brandon sat awhile in the great gaunt dining-room where hung the portrait of the doctor in his splendid black collar and cuffs, and contemplated this masterpiece until an invasion of housemaids drove her from the apartment, when she took refuge in that other little room to which Mrs. Firmin's portrait had been consigned.

"That's like him ever so many years and years ago," she thinks. "It is a little handsomer ; but it has his wicked look that I used to think so killing, and so did my sisters, both of them—they were ready to tear out each other's eyes for jealousy. And that's Mrs. Firmin! Well, I suppose the painter haven't flattered her. If he have she could have been no great things, Mrs. F. couldn't." And the doctor, entering softly by the opened door and over the thick Turkey carpet, comes up to her noiselessly, and finds the Little Sister gazing at the portrait of the departed lady.

"Oh, it's you, is it. I wonder whether you treated her no better than you treated me, Dr. F. I've a notion she's not the only one. She don't look happy, poor thing," says the little lady.

"What is it, Caroline? asked the deep-voiced doctor; "and what brings you so early?"

The Little Sister then explains to him. "Last night after he went away Hunt came, sure enough. He had been drinking. He was very rude, and Philip wouldn't bear it. Philip had a good courage of his own and a hot blood. And Philip thought Hunt was insulting her, the Little Sister. So he up with his hand and down goes Mr. Hunt on the pavement. Well, when he was down he was in a dreadful way, and he called Philip a dreadful name."

"A name? what name?" Then Caroline told the doctor the name Mr. Hunt had used; and if Firmin's face usually looked wicked, I dare say it did not seem very angelical when he heard how this odious name had been applied to his son. "Can he do Philip a mischief?" Caroline continued. "I thought I was bound to tell his father. Look here Dr. F., I don't want to do my dear boy a harm. But suppose what you told me last night isn't true—as I don't think you much mind! —mind—saying things that are incorrect you know, when us women are in the case. But suppose when you played the villain, thinking only to take in a poor innocent girl of sixteen, it was you who were took in, and that I was your real wife after all? There would be a punishment!"

"I should have an honest and good wife, Caroline," said the doctor, with a groan.

"This would be a punishment, not for you, but for my poor Philip," the woman goes on. "What has he done, that his honest name should be took from him—and his fortune perhaps? I have been lying broad awake all night thinking of him. Ah, George Brandon! Why, why did you come to my poor old father's house, and bring this misery down on me, and on your child unborn?"

"On myself, the worst of all," says the doctor.

"You deserve it. But it's an innocent that has had, or will have, to suffer most. O George Brandon! Think of a poor child, flung away, and left to starve and die, without even so much as knowing your real name! Think of your boy, perhaps brought to shame and poverty through your fault!"

"Do you suppose I don't often think of my wrong?" says the doctor. "That it does not cause me sleepless nights, and

hours of anguish? Ah! Caroline!" and he looks in the glass;
" I am not shaved, and it's very unbecoming," he thinks; that
is, if I may dare to read his thoughts, as I do to report his
unheard words.

"You think of your wrong now it may be found out, I dare
say!" says Caroline. "Suppose this Hunt turns against you?
He is desperate; mad for drink and money; has been in jail
—as he said this very night to me and my papa. He'll do or
say anything. If you treat him hard, and Philip *have* treated
him hard—not harder than served him right though—he'll pull
the house down and himself under it; but he'll be revenged.
Perhaps he drank so much last night that he may have forgot.
But I fear he means mischief, and I came here to say so, and
hoping that you might be kep' on your guard, Doctor F., and if
you have to quarrel with him, I don't know what you ever will
do, I am sure—no more than if you had to fight a chimney-
sweep in the street. I have been awake all night thinking, and
as soon as ever I saw the daylight, I determined I would run
and tell you."

"When he called Philip that name, did the boy seem much
disturbed?" asked the doctor.

"Yes; he referred to it again and again—though I tried to
coax him out of it. But it was on his mind last night, and I
am sure he will think of it the first thing this morning. Ah,
yes, doctor! conscience will sometimes let a gentleman doze;
but after discovery has come, and opened your curtains, and
said, 'You desired to be called early!' there's little use in trying to sleep much. You look very much frightened, Doctor F.,"
the nurse continues. "You haven't such a courage as Philip
has; or as you had when you were a young man, and came a
leading poor girls astray. You used to be afraid of nothing
then. Do you remember that fellow on board the steamboat in
Scotland in our wedding-trip, and, la! I thought you was going
to kill him. That poor little Lord Cinqbars told me ever so
many stories then about your courage and shooting people. It
wasn't very courageous, leaving a poor girl without even a name,
and scarce a guinea, was it? But I ain't come to call up old
stories—only to warn you. Even in old times, when he married us, and I thought he was doing a kindness, I never could
abide this horrible man. In Scotland, when you was away
shooting with your poor little lord, the things Hunt used to say
and *look* was dreadful. I wonder how ever you, who were
gentlemen, could put up with such a fellow! Ah, that was a
sad honeymoon of ours! I wonder why I'm a thinking of it

now? I suppose it's from having seen the picture of the other one—poor lady!"

"I have told you, Caroline, that I was so wild and desperate at that unhappy time, I was scarcely accountable for my actions. If I left you, it was because I had no other resource but flight. I was a ruined, penniless man, but for my marriage with Ellen Ringwood. You don't suppose the marriage was happy? Happy! when have I ever been happy? My lot is to be wretched, and bring wretchedness down on those I love! On you, on my father, on my wife, on my boy—I am a doomed man. Ah, that the innocent should suffer for me!" And our friend looks askance in the glass, at the blue chin, and hollow eyes which make his guilt look the more haggard.

"I never had my lines," the Little Sister continued, "I never knew there were papers, or writings, or anything but a ring and a clergyman, when you married me. But I've heard tell that people in Scotland don't want a clergyman at all; and if they call themselves man and wife, they are man and wife. Now, sir, Mr. and Mrs. Brandon certainly did travel together in Scotland—witness that man whom you were going to throw into the lake for being rude to your wife—and * * * La! Don't fly out so! It wasn't me, a poor girl of sixteen, who did wrong. It was you, a man of the world, who was years and years older."

When Brandon carried off his poor little victim and wife, there had been a journey to Scotland, where Lord Cinqbars, then alive, had sporting quarters. His lordship's chaplain, Mr. Hunt, had been of the party, which fate very soon afterwards separated. Death seized on Cinqbars at Naples. Debt caused Firmin—Brandon, as he called himself then—to fly the country. The chaplain wandered from jail to jail. And as for poor little Caroline Brandon, I suppose the husband who had married her under a false name thought that to escape her, leave her, and disown her altogether was an easier and less dangerous plan than to continue relations with her. So one day, four months after their marriage, the young couple being then at Dover, Caroline's husband happened to go out for a walk. But he sent away a portmanteau by the back door when he went out for the walk, and as Caroline was waiting for her little dinner some hours after, the porter who carried the luggage came with a little note from her dearest G. B.: and it was full of little fond expressions of regard and affection, such as gentlemen put into little notes; but dearest G. B. said the bailiffs were upon him, and one of them had arrived that morning, and he must fly : and he took half the money he had, and left half for his little Carry. And he would be back soon, and arrange matters ; or tell her where to write and follow him. And she was to take care of her little health, and to write a great deal to her Georgy. And she did not know how to write very well then ; but she did her best, and improved a great deal ; for, indeed, she wrote a great deal, poor thing. Sheets and sheets of paper she blotted with ink and tears. And then the money was spent ; and the next money ; and no more came, and no more letters. And she was alone at sea, sinking, sinking, when it pleased heaven to send that friend who rescued her. It is such a sad, sad little story, that in fact I don't like dwelling on it ; not caring to look upon poor innocent, trusting creatures in pain.

* * Well, then, when Caroline exclaimed, " La ! don't fly out so, Dr. Firmin ! " I suppose the doctor had been crying out, and swearing fiercely, at the recollections of his friend Mr. Brandon, and at the danger which possibly hung over that gentleman. Marriage ceremonies are dangerous risks in jest or in earnest. You can't pretend to marry even a poor old bankrupt lodging-house-keeper's daughter without some risk of being brought subsequently to book. If you have a vulgar wife alive, and afterwards choose to leave her and marry an earl's niece, you will come to trouble, however well connected you are and highly placed in society. If you have had thirty thousand pounds with wife No. 2, and have to pay it back on a sudden, the payment may be inconvenient. You may be tried for bigamy, and sentenced, goodness knows to what punishment. At any rate, if the matter is made public, and you are a most respectable man, moving in the highest scientific and social circles, those circles may be disposed to request you to walk out of their circumference. A novelist, I know, ought to have no likes, dislikes, pity, partiality for his characters ; but I declare I cannot help feeling a respectful compassion for a gentleman who, in consequence of a youthful, and, I am sure, sincerely regretted folly, may be liable to lose his fortune, his place in society, and his considerable practice. Punishment hasn't a right to come with such a *pede claudo*. There ought to be limitations ; and it is shabby and revengeful of Justice to present her little bill when it has been more than twenty years owing. * * * Having had his talk out with the Little Sister, having a long-past crime suddenly taken down from the shelf ; having a remorse long since supposed to be dead and buried, suddenly starting up in the most blustering, boisterous, inconvenient manner ; having a rage and terror tearing him within ; I can fancy this most respectable physician going about his day's work, and most sincerely sympathize with him. Who is to heal the physician ? Is he not more sick at heart than most of his patients that day ? He has to listen to Lady Megrim cackling for half an hour at least, and describing her little ailments. He has to listen, and never once to dare to say, " Confound you, old chatterbox ! What are you prating about your ailments to me, who am suffering real torture whilst I am smirking in your face ? " He has to wear the inspiriting smile, to breathe the gentle joke, to console, to whisper hope, to administer remedy ; and all day, perhaps, he sees no one so utterly sick, so sad, so despairing, as himself.

The first person on whom he had to practise hypocrisy that day was his own son, who chose to come to breakfast—a meal of which son and father seldom now partook in company. " What does he know, and what does he suspect ? " are the father's thoughts ; but a louring gloom is on Philip's face, and the father's eyes look into the son's, but cannot penetrate their darkness.

" Did you stay late last night, Philip ? " says papa.

" Yes, sir, rather late," answers the son.

" Pleasant party ? "

" No, sir, stupid. Your friend Mr. Hunt wanted to come in. He was drunk, and rude to Mrs. Brandon, and I was obliged to put him out of the door. He was dreadfully violent and abusive."

" Swore a good deal, I suppose ? "

" Fiercely, sir, and called names."

I dare say Philip's heart beat so when he said these last words, that they were inaudible ; at all events, Philip's father did not appear to pay much attention to the words, for he was busy reading the *Morning Post*, and behind that sheet of fashionable news hid whatever expression of agony there might be on his face. Philip afterwards told his present biographer of this breakfast meeting and dreary *tete-à-tete*. " I burned to ask what was the meaning of that scoundrel's words of the past night," Philip said to his biographer ; " but I did not dare, somehow. You see, Pendennis, it is not pleasant to say point-blank to your father, ' Sir, are you a confirmed scoundrel, or are you not ? Is it possible that you have made a double marriage, as yonder other rascal hinted ; and that my own legitimacy and my mother's fair fame, as well as poor, harmless Caroline's honor and happiness, have been destroyed by your crime?' But I had lain awake all night thinking about **that** scoundrel Hunt's words, and whether there was any meaning beyond drunken malice in what he said." So we find that three people had passed a bad night in consequence of Mr. Firmin's evil behavior of five-and-twenty years back, which surely was a most unreasonable punishment for a sin of such old date. I wish, dearly beloved brother sinners, we could take all the punishment for our individual crimes on our individual shoulders : but we drag them all down with us—that is the fact ; and when Macheath is condemned to hang, it is Polly and Lucy who have to weep and suffer and wear piteous mourning in their hearts long after the dare-devil rogue has jumped off the Tyburn ladder.

"Well, sir, he did not say a word," said Philip, recounting the meeting to his friend ; "not a word, at least, regarding the matter both of us had on our hearts. But about fashion, parties, politics, he discoursed much more freely than was usual with him. He said I might have had Lord Ringwood's seat for Whipham, but for my unfortunate politics. What made a Radical of me, he asked, who was naturally one of the most haughty of men ? " ("and that, I think, perhaps I am," says Phil, "and a good many liberal fellows are.") I should calm down, he was sure—I should calm down, and be of the politics *des hommes du monde.*"

Philip could not say to his father, "Sir, it is seeing you cringe before great ones that has set my own back up." There were countless points about which both father and son could not speak ; and an invisible, unexpressed, perfectly unintelligible mistrust, always was present when those two were *tête-à-tête.*

Their meal was scarce ended when entered to them Mr. Hunt, with his hat on. I was not present at the time, and cannot speak as a certainty ; but I should think at his ominous appearance Philip may have turned red and his father pale. "Now is the time," both, I daresay, thought ; and the doctor remembered his stormy young days of foreign gambling, intrigue and duel, when he was put on his ground before his adversary, and bidden, at a given signal, to fire. One, two, three ! Each man's hand was armed with malice and murder. Philip had plenty of pluck for his part, but I should think on such an occasion might be a little nervous and fluttered, whereas his father's eye was keen, and his aim rapid and steady.

"You and Philip had a difference last night, Philip tells me," said the doctor.

"Yes, and I promised he should pay me," said the clergyman.

" And I said I should desire no better," says Mr. Phil.

" He struck his senior, his father's friend—a sick man, a clergyman," gasped Hunt.

" Were you to repeat what you did last night, I should repeat what I did," said Phil. " You insulted a good woman."

" It's a lie, sir," cries the other.

" You insulted a good woman, a lady in her own house, and I turned you out of it," said Phil.

" I say again, it is a lie, sir ! " screams Hunt, with a stamp on the table.

" That you should give me the lie, or otherwise, is perfectly immaterial to me. But whenever you insult Mrs. Brandon, or any harmless woman in my presence, I shall do my best to chastise you," cries Philip of the red mustaches, curling them with much dignity.

" You hear him, Firmin ? " says the parson.

" Faith, I do, Hunt ! " says the physician ; " and I think he means what he says, too."

" Oh ! *you* take that line, do you ? " cries Hunt of the dirty hands, the dirty teeth, the dirty neckcloth.

" I take what you call that line ; and whenever a rudeness is offered to that admirable woman in my son's hearing, I shall be astonished if he does not resent it," says the doctor. " Thank you, Philip ! "

The father's resolute speech and behavior gave Philip great momentary comfort. Hunt's words of the night before had been occupying the young man's thoughts. Had Firmin been criminal, he could not be so bold.

" You talk this way in presence of your son ? You have been talking over the matter together before ? " asks Hunt.

" We have been talking over the matter before—yes. We were engaged on it when you came into breakfast," says the doctor. " Shall we go on with the conversation where we left it off ? "

" Well, do—that is, if you dare," said the clergyman, somewhat astonished.

" Philip, my dear, it is ill for a man to hide his head before his own son ; but if I am to speak—and speak I must one day or the other—why not now ? "

" Why at all, Firmin ? " asks the clergyman, astonished at the other's rather sudden resolve.

" Why ? Because I am sick and tired of you, Mr. Tufton Hunt," cries the physician, in his most lofty manner, " of you and your presence in my house ; your blackguard behavior and your rascal extortions—because you will force me to speak one day or the other—and now, Philip, if you like, shall be the day."

"Hang it, I say! Stop a bit!" cries the clergyman.

"I understand you want some more money from me."

"I did promise Jacobs I would pay him to-day, and that was what made me so sulky last night; and, perhaps, I took a little too much. You see my mind was out of order; and what's the use of telling a story that is no good to any one, Firmin—least of all to you," cries the parson, darkly.

"Because, you ruffian, I'll bear with you no more," cries the doctor, the veins of his forehead swelling as he looks fiercely at his dirty adversary. "In the last nine months, Philip, this man has had nine hundred pounds from me."

"The luck has been so very bad, so bad, upon my honor, now," grumbles the parson.

"To-morrow he will want more; and the next day more; and the next day more; and, in fine, I won't live with this accursed man of the sea round my neck. You shall have the story; and Mr. Hunt shall sit by and witness against his own crime and mine. I had been very wild at Cambridge, when I was a young man. I had quarrelled with my father, lived with a dissipated set, and beyond my means; and had had my debts paid so often by your grandfather, that I was afraid to ask for more. He was stern to me; I was not dutiful to him. I own my fault. Mr. Hunt can bear witness to what I say.

"I was in hiding at Margate, under a false name. You know the name."

"Yes, sir, I think I know the name," Philip said, thinking he liked his father better now than he had ever liked him in his life, and sighing, "Ah, if he had always been frank and true with me!"

"I took humble lodgings with an obscure family." [If Dr. Firmin had a prodigious idea of his own grandeur and importance, you see I cannot help it—and he was long held to be such a respectable man.] "And there I found a young girl—one of the most innocent beings that ever a man played with and betrayed. Betrayed, I own it, heaven forgive me! The crime has been the shame of my life, and darkened my whole career with misery. I got a man worse than myself, if that could be. I got Hunt for a few pounds, which he owed me, to make a sham marriage between me and poor Caroline. My money was soon gone. My creditors were after me. I fled the country, and I left her."

"A sham marriage! a sham marriage!" cries the clergy-

man. " Didn't you make me perform it by holding a pistol to
my throat ? A fellow won't risk transportation for nothing.
But I owed him money for cards, and he had my bill, and he
said he would let me off, and that's why I helped him. Never
mind. I am out of the business now, Mr. Brummell Firmin
and you are in it. I have read the Act, sir. The clergyman
who performs the marriage is liable to punishment, if informed
against within three years, and it's twenty years or more. But
you, Mr. Brummell Firmin,—your case is different ; and you,
my young gentleman, with the fiery whiskers, who strike down
old men of a night,—you may find some of us know how to revenge ourselves, though we are down." And with this, Hunt
rushed to his greasy hat, and quitted the house, discharging
imprecations at his hosts as he passed through the hall.

Son and father sat awhile silent, after the departure of their
common enemy. At last the father spoke.

" This is the sword that has always been hanging over my
head, and it is now falling, Philip."

" What can the man do ? Is the first marriage a good marriage ? " asked Philip, with alarmed face.

" It is no marriage. It is void to all intents and purposes.
You may suppose I have taken care to learn the law about that.
Your legitimacy is safe, sure enough. But that man can ruin
me, or nearly so. He will try to-morrow, if not to-day. As
long as you or I can give him a guinea, he will take it to the
gambling-house. I had the mania on me myself once. My
poor father quarrelled with me in consequence, and died without seeing me. I married your mother—heaven help her, poor
soul ! and forgive me for being but a harsh husband to her—
with a view of mending my shattered fortunes. I wished she
had been more happy, poor thing. But do not blame me utterly,
Philip. I was desperate, and she wished for the marriage so
much ! I had good looks and high spirits in those days. People said so." [And here he glances obliquely at his own handsome portrait.] " Now I am a wreck, a wreck ! "

" I conceive, sir, that this will annoy you ; but how can it
ruin you ? " asked Philip.

" What becomes of my practice as a family physician ? The
practice is not now what it was, between ourselves, Philip, and
the expenses greater than you imagine. I have made unlucky
speculations. If you count upon much increase of wealth from
me, my boy, you will be disappointed ; though you were never
mercenary, no, never. But the story bruited about by this rascal, of a physician of eminence engaged in two marriages, do

you suppose my rivals won't hear it, and take advantage of it —my patients hear it, and avoid me ?"

" Make terms with the man at once, then, sir, and silence him."

" To make terms with a gambler is impossible. My purse is always there open for him to thrust his hand into when he loses. No man can withstand such a temptation. I am glad you have never fallen into it. I have quarrelled with you sometimes for living with people below your rank : perhaps you were right, and I was wrong. I have liked, always did, I don't disguise it, to live with persons of station. And these, when I was at the University, taught me play and extravagance ; and in the world haven't helped me much. Who would ? Who would ?" and the doctor relapsed into meditation.

A little catastrophe presently occurred, after which Mr. Philip Firmin told me the substance of this story. He described his father's long acquiescence in Hunt's demands, and sudden resistance to them, and was at a loss to account for the change. I did not tell my friend in express terms, but I fancied I could account for the change of behavior. Dr. Firmin, in his interviews with Caroline, had had his mind set at rest about one part of his danger. The doctor need no longer fear the charge of a double marriage. The Little Sister resigned her claims past, present, future.

If a gentleman is sentenced to be hung, I wonder is it a matter of comfort to him or not to know beforehand the day of the operation ? Hunt would take his revenge. When and how ? Dr. Firmin asked himself. Nay, possibly, you will have to learn that this eminent practitioner walked about with more than danger hanging imminent over him. Perhaps it was a rope : perhaps it was a sword : some weapon of execution, at any rate, as we frequently may see. A day passes : no assassin darts at the doctor as he threads the dim opera-colonnade passage on his way to his club. A week goes by : no stiletto is plunged into his well-wadded breast as he steps from his carriage at some noble patient's door. Philip says he never knew his father more pleasant, easy, good-humored, and affable than during this period, when he must have felt that a danger was hanging over him of which his son at this time had no idea. I dined in Old Parr Street once in this memorable period (memorable it seemed to me from immediately subsequent events). Never was the dinner better served : the wine more excellent : the guests and conversation more gravely respectable than at this entertainment ; and my neighbor remarked with pleasure how the father and son seemed to be on much better terms than ordinary. The doctor addressed Philip pointedly once or twice; alluded to his foreign travels, spoke of his mother's family—it was most gratifying to see the pair together. Day after day passes so. The enemy has disappeared. At least, the lining of his dirty hat is no longer visible on the broad marble table of Dr. Firmin's hall.

But one day—it may be ten days after the quarrel—a little messenger comes to Philip, and says, " Philip dear, I am sure there is something wrong; that horrible Hunt has been here with a very quiet, soft-spoken old gentleman, and they have been going on with my poor pa about my wrongs and his—his, indeed! —and they have worked him up to believe that somebody has cheated his daughter out of a great fortune; and who can that somebody be but your father? And whenever they see me coming, papa and that horrid Hunt go off to the ' Admiral Byng:' and one night when pa came home he said, ' Bless you, bless you, my poor, innocent, injured child; and blessed you *will* be, mark a fond father's words!' They are scheming something against Philip and Philip's father. Mr. Bond the soft-spoken old gentleman's name is: and twice there has been a Mr. Walls to inquire if Mr. Hunt was at our house."

" Mr. Bond?—Mr. Walls?—A gentleman of the name of Bond was uncle Twysden's attorney. An old gentleman, with a bald head, and one eye bigger than the other? "

" Well, this old man has one smaller than the other, I do think," said Caroline. " First man who came was Mr. Walls— a rattling young fashionable chap, always laughing, talking about theatres, operas, every thing—came home from the ' Byng' along with pa and his new friend—oh! I do hate him, that man, that Hunt!—then he brought the old man, this Mr. Bond. What are they scheming against you, Philip? I tell you this matter is all about you and your father."

Years and years ago, in the poor mother's lifetime, Philip remembered an outbreak of wrath on his father's part, who called uncle Twysden a swindling miser, and this very Mr. Bond a scoundrel who deserved to be hung, for interfering in some way in the management of a part of the property which Mrs. Twysden and her sister inherited from their own mother. That quarrel had been made up, as such quarrels are. The brothers-in-law had continued to mistrust each other; but there was no reason why the feud should descend to the children; and Philip and his aunt, and one of her daughters at least, were on good terms together. Philip's uncle's lawyers engaged with father's debtor and enemy against Dr. Firmin : the alliance boded no good.

"I won't tell you what I think, Philip," said the father. "You are fond of your cousin ? "

"Oh ! for ev——"

"For ever, of course ! At least until we change our mind, or one of us grows tried, or finds a better mate."

"Ah, sir ! " cries Philip, but suddenly stops in his remonstrance.

"What were you going to say, Philip, and why do you pause ? "

"I was going to say, father, if I might without offending, that I think you judge hardly of women. I know two who have been very faithful to you."

"And I a traitor to both of them. Yes ; and my remorse, Philip, my remorse ! " says his father in his deepest tragedy voice, clutching his hand over a heart that I believe beat very coolly. But, psha ! why am I, Philip's biographer, going out of the way to abuse Philip's papa ? Is not the threat of bigamy and exposure enough to disturb any man's equanimity ? I say again, suppose there is another sword—a rope, if you will so call it—hanging over the head of our Damocles of Old Parr Street ? * * * * Howbeit, the father and the son met and parted in these days with unusual gentleness and cordiality. And these were the last days in which they were to meet together. Nor could Philip recall without satisfaction, afterwards, that the hand which he took was pressed and given with a real kindness and cordiality.

Why were these the last days son and father were to pass together? Dr. Firmin is still alive. Philip is a very tolerably prosperous gentleman. He and his father parted good friends, and it is the biographer's business to narrate how and wherefore. When Philip told his father that Messrs. Bond and Selby, his uncle Twysden's attorneys, were suddenly interested about Mr. Brandon and his affairs, the father instantly guessed, though the son was too simple as yet to understand, how it was that these gentlemen interfered. If Mr. Brandon-Firmin's marriage with Miss Ringwood was null, her son was illegitimate, and her fortune went to her sister. Painful as such a duty might be to such tender-hearted people as our Twysden acquaintances to deprive a dear nephew of his fortune, yet, after all, duty is duty, and a parent must sacrifice everything for justice and his own children. "Had I been in such a case," Talbot Twysden subsequently and repeatedly declared, "I should never have been easy a moment if I thought I possessed wrongfully a beloved nephew's property. I could not have slept in peace; I could not have shown my face at my own club, or to my own conscience, had I the weight of such an injustice on my mind." In a word, when he found that there was a chance of annexing Philip's share of the property to his own, Twysden saw clearly that his duty was to stand by his own wife and children.

The information upon which Talbot Twysden, Esq., acted, was brought to him at his office by a gentleman in dingy black, who, after a long interview with him, accompanied him to his lawyer, Mr. Bond, before mentioned. Here, in South Square, Gray's Inn, the three gentlemen held a consultation, of which the results began quickly to show themselves. Messrs. Bond and Selby had an exceedingly lively, cheerful, jovial, and intelligent confidential clerk, who combined business and pleasure with the utmost affability, and was acquainted with a thousand queer things, and queer histories about queer people in this town; who lent money; who wanted money; who was in debt: and who was outrunning the constable; whose diamonds were in pawn; whose estates were over-mortgaged; who was over-building himself; who was casting eyes of longing at what pretty opera dancer—about races, fights, bill brokers, *quicquid agunt homines.* This Tom Walls had a deal of information, and imparted it so as to make you die of laughing.

The Reverend Tufton Hunt brought this jolly fellow first to the "Admiral Byng," where his amiability won all hearts at the club. At the "Byng" it was not very difficult to gain Captain Gann's easy confidence. And this old man was, in the course of a very trifling consumption of rum-and-water, brought to see that his daughter had been the object of a wicked conspiracy, and was the rightful and most injured wife of a man who ought to declare her fair fame before the world, and put her in possession of a portion of his great fortune.

A great fortune? How great a fortune? Was it three hundred thousand, say? Those doctors, many of them, had fifteen thousand a-year. Mr. Walls (who perhaps knew better) was not at liberty to say what the fortune was: but it was a shame that Mrs. Brandon was kept out of her rights, that was clear.

Old Gann's excitement, when this matter was first broached to him (under vows of profound secrecy) was so intense that his old reason tottered on its rickety old throne. He wellnigh burst with longing to speak upon this mystery. Mr. and Mrs. Oves, the esteemed landlord and lady of the "Byng," never

saw him so excited. He had a great opinion of the judgment
of his friend, Mr. Ridley ; in fact, he must have gone to Bedlam,
unless he had talked to somebody on this most nefarious transaction, which might make the blood of every Briton curdle with
horror—as he was free to say.

Old Mr. Ridley was of a much cooler temperament, and altogether a more cautious person. The doctor rich? He
wished to tell no secrets, nor to meddle in no gentleman's affairs : but he have heard very different statements regarding
Dr. Firmin's affairs.

When dark hints about treason, wicked desertion, rights
denied, "and a great fortune which you are kep' out of, my
poor Caroline, by a rascally wolf in sheep's clothing, you are ;
and I always mistrusted him, from the moment I saw him, and
said to your mother, ' Emily, that Brandon is a bad fellow,
Brandon is ;' and bitterly, bitterly I've rued ever receiving him
under my roof." When speeches of this nature were made to
Mrs. Caroline, strange to say, the little lady made light of them.
" Oh, nonsense, Pa ! Don't be bringing that sad old story up
again. I have suffered enough from it already. If Mr. F. left
me, he wasn't the only one who flung me away ; and I have
been able to live, thank mercy, through it all."

This was a hard hit, and not to be parried. The truth is,
that when poor Caroline, deserted by her husband, had come
back, in wretchedness, to her father's door, the man, and the
wife who then ruled him, had thought fit to thrust her away.
And she had forgiven them : and had been enabled to heap a
rare quantity of coals on that old gentleman's head.

When the Captain remarked his daughter's indifference and
unwillingness to reopen this painful question of her sham
marriage with Firmin, his wrath was moved, and his suspicion
excited. "Ha !" says he, "have this man been a tampering
with you again ? "

" Nonsense, Pa !" once more says Caroline. " I tell you,
it is this fine-talking lawyers' clerk has been tampering with
you. You're made a tool of, Pa ! and you've been made a tool
of all your life ! "

" Well, now, upon my honor, my good madam," interposes
Mr. Walls.

" Don't talk to me, sir ! I don't want any lawyers' clerks
to meddle in my business ! " cries Mrs. Brandon, very briskly.
"I don't know what you're come about. I don't want to know,
and I'm most certain it is for no good."

I suppose it was the ill success of his ambassador that

brought Mr. Bond himself to Thornhaugh Street; and a more kind, fatherly, little man never looked than Mr. Bond, although he may have had one eye smaller than the other. "What is this, my dear madam, I hear from my confidential clerk, Mr. Walls?" he asked of the Little Sister. "You refuse to give him your confidence because he is only a clerk? I wonder whether you will accord it to me as a principal?"

"She may, sir, she may—every confidence!" says the Captain, laying his hand on that snuffy satin waistcoat which all his friends so long admired on him. "She *might* have spoken to Mr. Walls."

"Mr. Walls is not a family man. I am. I have children at home, Mrs. Brandon, as old as you are," says the benevolent Bond. "I would have justice done them, and for you too."

"You're very good to take so much trouble about me all of a sudden, to be sure," says Mrs. Brandon, demurely. "I suppose you don't do it for nothing."

"I should not require much fee to help a good woman to her rights; and a lady I don't think needs much persuasion to be helped to her advantage," remarks Mr. Bond.

"That depends who the helper is."

"Well, if I can do you no harm, and help you possibly to a name, to a fortune, to a high place in the world, I don't think you need be frightened. I don't look very wicked or very artful, do I!"

"Many is that don't look so. I've learned as much as that about you gentlemen," remarks Mrs. Brandon.

"You have been wronged by one man, and doubt all."

"Not all. Some, sir!"

"Doubt about me if I can by any possibility injure you. But how and why should I? Your good father knows what has brought me here. I have no secret from him. Have I, Mr. Gann, or Captain Gann, as I have heard you addressed?"

"Mr., sir—plain Mr.—No, sir; your conduct have been most open, honorable, and like a gentleman. Neither would you, sir, do aught to disparage Mrs. Brandon; neither would I, her father. No ways, I think, would a parent do harm to his own child. May I offer you any refreshment, sir?" and a shaky, a dingy, but a hospitable hand, is laid upon the glossy cupboard, in which Mrs. Brandon keeps her modest little store of strong waters.

"Not one drop, thank you! You trust me, I think, more than Mrs. Firm—I beg your pardon—Mrs. Brandon, is disposed to do"

At the utterance of that monosyllable *Firm* Caroline became so white, and trembled so, that her interlocutor stopped, rather alarmed at the effect of his word—his word!—his syllable of a word.

The old lawyer recovered himself with much grace.

"Pardon me, madam," he said; "I know your wrongs; I know your most melancholy history; I know your name, and was going to use it, but it seemed to renew painful recollections to you, which I would not needlessly recall."

Captain Gann took out a snuffy pocket-handkerchief, wiped two red eyes and a shirt-front, and winked at the attorney, and gasped in a pathetic manner.

"You know my story and name, sir, who are a stranger to me. Have you told this old gentleman all about me and my affairs, pa?" asks Caroline, with some asperity. "Have you told him that my ma never gave me a word of kindness—that I toiled for you and her like a servant—and when I came back to you, after being deceived and deserted, that you and ma shut the door in my face? You did! you did! I forgive you; but a hundred thousand billion years can't mend that injury, father, while you broke a poor child's heart with it that day! My pa has told you all this, Mr. What's-your-name? I'm s'prized he didn't find something pleasanter to talk about, I'm sure!"

"My love!" interposed the captain.

"Pretty love! to go and tell a stranger in a public-house, and ever so many there besides, I suppose, your daughter's misfortunes, pa. Pretty love! That's what I've had from you!"

"Not a soul, on the honor of a gentleman, except me and Mr. Walls."

"Then what do you come to talk about me at all for? and what scheme on *hearth* are you driving at? and what brings this old man here?" cries the landlady of Thornhaugh Street, stamping her foot.

"Shall I tell you frankly, my good lady? I called you Mrs. Firmin now, because, on my honor and word, I believe such to be your rightful name—because you are the lawful wife of George Brand Firmin. If such be your lawful name, others bear it who have no right to bear it—and inherit property to which they can lay no just claim. In the year 1827, you, Caroline Gann, a child of sixteen, were married by a clergyman whom you know, to George Brand Firmin, calling himself George Brandon. He was guilty of deceiving you; but you were guity of no deceit. He was a hardened and wily man; but you were an innocent child out of a schoolroom. And though he thought the marriage was not binding upon him, binding it is by Act of Parliament and judges' decision; and you are as assuredly George Firmin's wife, madam, as Mrs. Bond is mine!"

"You have been cruelly injured, Caroline," says the Captain, wagging his old nose over his handkerchief.

Caroline seemed to be very well versed in the law of the transaction. "You mean, sir," she said slowly, "that if me and Mr. Brandon was married to each other, he knowing that he was only playing at marriage, and me believing that it was all for good, we are really married."

"Undoubtedly you are, madam—my client has—that is, I have had advice on the point."

"But if we both knew that it was—was only a sort of a marriage—an irregular marriage, you know?"

"Then the Act says that to all intents and purposes the marriage is null and void."

"But you didn't know, my poor innocent child!" cries Mr. Gann. "How should you? How old was you? She was a child in the nursery, Mr. Bond, when the villain inveigled her away from her poor old father. *She* knew nothing of irregular marriages."

"Of course she didn't, the poor creature," cries the old gentlemen, rubbing his hands together with perfect good-humor. "Poor young thing, poor young thing!"

As he was speaking, Caroline, very very pale and still, was sitting looking at Ridley's sketch of Philip, which hung in her little room. Presently she turned round on the attorney, folding her little hands over her work.

"Mr. Bond," she said, "girls, though they may be ever so young, know more than some folks fancy. I was more than sixteen when that—that business happened. I wasn't happy at home, and eager to get away. I knew that a gentleman of his rank wouldn't be likely really to marry a poor Cinderella out of a lodging-house, like me. If the truth must be told, I—I knew it was no marriage—never thought it was a marriage—not for good, you know."

And she folds her little hands together as she utters the words, and I dare say once more looks at Philip's portrait.

"Gracious goodness, madam, you must be under some error!" cries the attorney. "How should a child like you know that the marriage was irregular?"

"Because I had no lines!" cries Claroline quickly. "Never asked for none! And our maid we had then said to me, 'Miss

Carry, where's your lines? And it's no good without.' And I knew it wasn't! And I'm ready to go before the Lord Chancellor to-morrow and say so!" cries Caroline, to the bewilderment of her father and her cross-examinant.

"Pause, pause! my good madam!" exclaims the meek old gentleman, rising from his chair.

"Go and tell this to them as sent you, sir!" cries Caroline, very imperiously, leaving the lawyer amazed, and her father's face in a bewilderment, over which we will fling his snuffy old pocket-handkerchief.

"If such is unfortunately the case—if you actually mean to abide by this astonishing confession—which deprives you of a high place in society—and—and casts down the hope we had formed of redressing your injured reputation—I have nothing for it! I take my leave, madam! Good morning, Mr. Hum! —Mr. Gann!" And the old lawyer walks out of the Little Sister's room.

"She won't own to the marriage! She is fond of some one else—the little suicide!" thinks the old lawyer, as he clatters down the street to a neighboring house, where his anxious principal was in waiting. "She's fond of some one else!"

Yes. But the some one else whom Caroline loved was Brand Firmin's son: and it was to save Philip from ruin that the poor Little Sister chose to forget her marriage to his father.

CHAPTER XIII.

LOVE ME LOVE MY DOG.

WHILST the battle is raging, the old folks and ladies peep over the battlements, to watch the turns of the combat, and the behavior of the knights. To princesses in old days, whose lovely hands were to be bestowed upon the conqueror, it must have been a matter of no small interest to know whether the slim young champion with the lovely eyes on the milk white steed should vanquish, or the dumpy, elderly, square-shouldered, squinting, carroty whiskerando of a warrior who was laying about him so savagely; and so in this battle, on the issue of which depended the keeping or losing of poor Philip's inheritance, there were several non-combatants deeply interested.

Or suppose we withdraw the chivalrous simile (as in fact the conduct and views of certain parties engaged in the matter were anything but what we call chivalrous), and imagine a wily old monkey who engages a cat to take certain chestnuts out of the fire, and pussy putting her paw through the bars, seizing the nut and then dropping it? Jacko is disappointed and angry, shows his sharp teeth, and bites if he dares. When the attorney went down to do battle for Philip's patrimony, some of those who wanted it were spectators of the fight, and lurking up a tree hard by. When Mr. Bond came forward to try and seize Phil's chestnuts, there was a wily old monkey who thrust the cat's paw out, and proposed to gobble up the smoking prize.

If you have ever been at the "Admiral Byng," you know, my dear madam, that the parlor where the club meets is just behind Mrs. Oves's bar, so that by lifting up the sash of the window which communicates between the two apartments, that good-natured woman may put her face into the club-room, and actually be one of the society. Sometimes for company, old Mr. Ridley goes and sits with Mrs. O—— in her bar, and reads the paper there. He is slow at his reading. The long words puzzle the worthy gentleman. As he has plenty of time to spare, he does not grudge it to the study of his paper.

On the day when Mr. Bond went to persuade Mrs. Brandon in Thornhaugh Street to claim Dr. Firmin for her husband, and to disinherit poor Philip, a little gentleman wrapt most solemnly and mysteriously in a great cloak appeared at the bar of the "Admiral Byng," and said in an aristocratic manner, "You have a parlor, show me to it." And being introduced to the parlor, (where there are fine pictures of Oves, Mrs. O——, and "Spotty-nose," their favorite defunct bull-dog,) sat down and called for a glass of sherry and a newspaper.

The civil and intelligent potboy of the "Byng" took the party *The Advertiser* of yesterday (which to-day's paper was in 'and) and when the gentleman began to swear over the old paper, Frederic gave it as his opinion to his mistress that the new comer was a harbitrary gent,—as, indeed, he was, with the comission, perhaps, of a single letter; a man who bullied everybody who would submit to be bullied. In fact, it was our friend Talbot Twysden, Esq., Commissioner of the Powder and Pomatum Office; and I leave those who know him to say whether *he* is arbitrary or not.

To him presently came that bland old gentleman, Mr. Bond, who also asked for a parlor and some sherry-and-water; and this is how Philip and his veracious and astute biographer came to know for a certainty that dear uncle Talbot was the person who wished to—to have Philip's chestnuts.

Mr. Bond and Mr. Twysden had been scarcely a minute together, when such a storm of imprecations came clattering through the glass window which communicates with Mrs. Oves's bar, that I dare say they made the jugs and tumblers clatter on the shelves, and Mr. Ridley, a very modest-spoken man, reading his paper, lay it down with a scared face, and say—"Well, I never." Nor did he often, I dare to say.

This volley was fired by Talbot Twysden, in consequence of his rage at the news which Mr. Bond brought him.

"Well, Mr. Bond; well, Mr. Bond! What does she say?" he asked of his emissary.

"She will have nothing to do with the business, Mr. Twysden. We can't touch it; and I don't see how we can move her. She denies the marriage as much as Firmin does; says she knew it was a mere sham when the ceremony was performed."

"Sir, you didn't bribe her enough," shrieked Mr. Twysden. "You have bungled this business; by George you have, sir."

"Go and do it yourself, sir, if you are not ashamed to appear in it," says the lawyer. "You don't suppose I did it because I liked it; or want to take that poor young fellow's inheritance from him, as you do."

"I wish justice and the law, sir. If I were wrongfully detaining his property I would give it up. I would be the first to give it up. I desire justice and law, and employ you because you are a law agent. Are you not?"

"And I have been on your errand, and shall send in my bill in due time; and there will be an end of my connection with you as your law agent, Mr. Twysden," cried the old lawyer.

"You know, sir, how badly Firmin acted to me in the last matter."

"Faith, sir, if you ask my opinion as a law agent, I don't think there was much to choose between you. How much is the sherry-and-water?—keep the change. Sorry I'd no better news to bring you, Mr. T., and as you are dissatisfied, again recommend you to employ another law agent."

"My good sir, I——"

"My good sir, I have had other dealings with your family, and am no more going to put up with your highti-tightiness than I would with Lord Ringwood's when I was one of *his* law agents. I am not going to tell Mr. Philip Firmin that his uncle and aunt propose to ease him of his property; but if anybody

else does—that good little Mrs. Brandon—or that old goose
Mr. What-d'ye-call-um, her father—I don't suppose he will be
over well pleased. I am speaking as a gentleman now, not as
a law agent. You and your nephew had each a half share of
Mr. Philip Firmin's grandfather's property, and you wanted it
all, that's the truth, and set a law agent to get it for you; and
swore at him because he could not get it from its right owner.
And so, sir, I wish you a good-morning, and recommend you to
take your papers to some other agent, Mr. Twysden." And
with this, *exit* Mr. Bond. And now, I ask you, if that secret
could be kept which was known through a trembling glass door
to Mrs. Oves of the "Admiral Byng," and to Mr. Ridley the
father of J. J., and the obsequious husband of Mrs. Ridley?
On that very afternoon, at tea-time, Mrs. Ridley was made
acquainted by her husband (in his noble and circumlocutory
manner) with the conversation which he had overheard. It
was agreed that an embassy should be sent to J. J. on the
business, and his advice taken regarding it; and J. J.'s opinion
was that the conversation certainly should be reported to Mr.
Philip Firmin, who might afterwards act upon it as he should
think best.

What? His own aunt, cousins, and uncle agreed in a
scheme to overthrow his legitimacy, and deprive him of his
grandfather's inheritance? It seemed impossible. Big with
the tremendous news, Philip came to his adviser, Mr. Pendennis, of the Temple, and told him what had occurred on the
part of father, uncle, and Little Sister. Her abnegation had
been so noble, that you may be sure Philip appreciated it; and
a tie of friendship was formed between the young man and the
little lady even more close and tender than that which had
bound them previously. But the Twysdens, his kinsfolk, to
employ a lawyer in order to rob him of his inheritance!—Oh,
it was dastardly! Philip bawled, and stamped, and thumped
his sense of the wrong in his usual energetic manner. As for
his cousin Ringwood Twysden, Phil had often entertained a
strong desire to wring his neck and pitch him down stairs.
"As for Uncle Talbot: that he is an old pump, that he is a
pompous old humbug, and the queerest old sycophant, I grant
you; but I couldn't have believed him guilty of this. And as
for the girls—oh, Mrs. Pendennis, you who are good, you who
are kind, although you hate them, I know you do—you can't
say, you won't say, that they were in the conspiracy?"

"But suppose Twysden was asking only for what he con-
ceives to be his rights?" asked Mr. Pendennis. "Had your

father been married to Mrs. Brandon, you would not have been Dr. Firmin's legitimate son. Had you not been his legitimate son, you had no right to a half-share of your grandfather's property. Uncle Talbot acts only the part of honor and justice in the transaction. He is Brutus, and he orders you off to death, with a bleeding heart."

"And he orders his family out of the way," roars Phil, "so that they mayn't be pained by seeing the execution! I see it all now. I wish somebody would send a knife through me at once, and put an end to me. I see it all now. Do you know that for the last week I have been to Beaunash Street, and found nobody? Agnes had the bronchitis, and her mother was attending to her; Blanche came for a minute or two, and was as cool—as cool as I have seen Lady Iceberg be cool to her. Then they must go away for change of air. They have been gone these three days; whilst Uncle Talbot and that viper of a Ringwood have been closeted with their nice new friend, Mr. Hunt. Oh, conf——! I beg your pardon, ma'am; but I know you always allow for the energy of my language."

"I should like to see that Little Sister, Mr. Firmin. She has not been selfish, or had any scheme but for your good," remarks my wife.

"A little angel who drops her h's—a little heart, so good and tender that I melt as I think of it," says Philip, drawing his big hand over his eyes. What have men done to get the love of some women? We don't earn it; we don't deserve it, perhaps. We don't return it. They bestow it on us. I have given nothing back for all this love and kindness, but I look a little like my father of old days, for whom—for whom she had an attachment. And see now how she would die to serve me! You are wonderful, women are! your fidelities and your fickle-nesses alike marvellous. What can any woman have found to adore in the doctor? Do you think my father could ever have been adorable, Mrs. Pendennis? And yet I have heard my poor mother say she was obliged to marry him. She knew it was a bad match, but she couldn't resist it. In what was my father so irresistible? He is not to *my* taste. Between ourselves, I think he is a——well, never mind what."

"I think we had best not mind what?" says my wife with a smile.

"Quite right—quite right; only I blurt out everything that is on my mind. Can't keep it in," cries Phil, gnawing his mustachios. "If my fortune depended on my silence I should be a beggar, that's the fact. And, you see, if you had such a father as mine, you yourself would find it rather difficult to hold your tongue about him. But now, tell me: this ordering away of the girls and Aunt Twysden, whilst the little attack upon my property is being carried on—isn't it queer?"

"The question is at an end," said Mr. Pendennis. "You are restored to your *atavis regibus* and ancestral honors. Now that Uncle Twysden can't get the property without you; have courage, my boy—he may take it, along with the encumbrance."

Poor Phil had not known—but some of us, who are pretty clearsighted when our noble selves are not concerned, had perceived that Philip's dear aunt was playing fast and loose with the lad, and when his back was turned was encouraging a richer suitor for her daughter.

Hand on heart I can say of my wife, that she meddles with her neighbors as little as any person I ever knew; but when treacheries in love affairs are in question, she fires up at once, and would persecute to death almost the heartless male or female criminal who would break love's sacred laws. The idea of a man or woman trifling with that holy compact awakens in her a flame of indignation. In curtain confidences (of which let me not vulgarize the arcana) she had given me her mind about some of Miss Twysden's behavior with that odious blackamoor, as she chose to call Captain Woolcomb, who, I own, had a very slight tinge of complexion; and when, quoting the words of Hamlet regarding his father and mother, I asked, "Could she on this fair mountain leave to feed, and batten on this Moor?" Mrs. Pendennis cried out that this matter was all too serious for jest, and wondered how her husband could make word plays about it. Perhaps she has not the exquisite sense of humor possessed by some folks; or is it that she has more reverence? In her creed, if not in her church, marriage is a sacrament, and the fond believer never speaks of it without awe.

Now, as she expects both parties to the marriage engagement to keep that compact holy, she no more understands trifling with it than she could comprehend laughing and joking in a church. She has no patience with flirtations as they are called. "Don't tell me, sir," says the enthusiast, "a light word between a man and a married woman ought not to be permitted." And this is why she is harder on the woman than the man, in cases where such dismal matters happen to fall under discussion. A look, a word from a woman, she says, will check a libertine thought or word in a man; and these cases might be stopped at once if the woman but showed the slightest resolution. She is thus more angry (I am only mentioning the peculiarities, not defending the ethics of this individual moralist)—she is, I say, more angrily disposed towards the woman than the man in such delicate cases ; and, I am afraid, considers that women are for the most part only victims because they choose to be so.

Now, we had happened during this season to be at several entertainments, routs, and so forth, where poor Phil, owing to his unhappy Bohemian preferences and love of tobacco, &c., was not present—and where we saw Miss Agnes Twysden carrying on such a game with the tawny Woolcomb as set Mrs. Laura in a tremor of indignation. What though Agne's blue-eyed mamma sat near her blue-eyed daughter and kept her keen clear orbs perfectly wide open and cognizant of all that happened? So much the worse for her, the worse for both. It was a shame and a sin that a Christian English mother should suffer her daughter to deal lightly with the most holy, the most awful of human contracts ; should be preparing her child who knows for what after misery of mind and soul. Three months ago, you saw how she encouraged poor Philip, and now see her with this mulatto !

"Is he not a man, and a brother, my dear?" perhaps at this Mr. Pendennis interposes.

"Oh, for shame, Pen, no levity on this—no sneers and laughter on this the most sacred subject of all." And here, I dare say the woman falls to caressing her own children and hugging them to her heart as her manner was when moved. *Que voulez vous ?* There are some women in the world to whom love and truth are all in all here below. Other ladies there are who see the benefit of a good jointure, a town and country house, and so forth, and who are not so very particular as to the character, intellect, or complexion of gentlemen who are in a position to offer their dear girls these benefits. In fine, I say, that regarding this blue-eyed mother and daughter, Mrs. Laura Pendennis was in such a state of mind that she was ready to tear their blue eyes out.

Nay, it was with no little difficulty that Mrs. Laura could be induced to hold her tongue upon the matter and not give Philip her opinion. "What ?" she would ask, "the poor young man is to be deceived and cajoled ; to be taken or left as it suits these people ; to be made miserable for life certainly if she married him ; and his friends are not to dare to warn him ? The cowards ! The cowardice of you men, Pen, upon matters of opinion, of you masters and lords of creation, is really despicable, sir ! You dare not have opinions, or holding them you dare not declare them and act by them. You compromise with crime every day because you think it would be officious to declare yourself and interfere. You are not afraid of outraging morals, but of inflicting *ennui* upon society, and losing your popularity. You are as cynical as—as, what was the name of the horrid old man who lived in the tub—Demosthenes ?—well, Diogenes, then, and the name does not matter a pin, sir. You are as cynical, only you wear fine ruffled shirts and wristbands, and you carry your lantern dark. It is not right to ' put your oar in ' as you say in your jargon (and even your slang is a sort of cowardice, sir, for you are afraid to speak the feelings of your heart :—) it is not right to meddle and speak the truth, not right to rescue a poor soul who is drowning—of course not. What call have you fine gentlemen of the world to put your oar in ? Let him perish ! What did he in that galley ? That is the language of the world, baby, darling. And, my poor, poor child, when you are sinking, nobody is to stretch out a hand to save you ! " As for that wife of mine, when she sets forth the maternal plea, and appeals to the exuberant school of philosophers, I know there is no reasoning with her. I retire to my books, and leave her to kiss out the rest of the argument over the children.

Philip did not know the extent of the obligation which he owed to his little friend and guardian, Caroline ; but he was aware that he had no better friend than herself in the world ; and I dare say, returned to her, as the wont is in such bargains between man and woman—woman and man, at least—a sixpence for that pure gold treasure, her sovereign affection. I suppose Caroline thought her sacrifice gave her a little authority to counsel Philip ; for she it was who, I believe, first bid him to inquire whether that engagement which he had virtually contracted with his cousin was likely to lead to good, and was to be binding upon him but not on her ? She brought Ridley to add his doubts to her remonstrances. She showed Philip that not only his uncle's conduct, but his cousin's, was interested, and set him to inquire into it further.

That peculiar form of bronchitis under which poor dear Agnes was suffering was relieved by absence from London. The smoke, the crowded parties and assemblies, the late hours, and perhaps, the gloom of the house in Beaunash Street, distressed the poor dear child ; and her cough was very much soothed by that fine, cutting east wind, which blows so liberally along the Brighton cliffs, and which is so good for coughs as we all know. But there was one fault in Brighton which could not be helped in her bad case : it is too near London. The air, that chartered libertine, can blow down from London quite easily ; or people can come from London to Brighton, bringing I dare say, the insidious London fog along with them. At any rate, Agnes, if she wished for quiet, poor thing, might have gone farther and fared better. Why, if you owe a tailor a bill, he can run down and present it in a few hours. Vulgar, inconvenient acquaintances thrust themselves upon you at every moment and corner. Was ever such a *tohubohu* of people as there assembles? You can't be tranquil, if you will. Organs pipe and scream without cease at your windows. Your name is put down in the papers when you arrive ; and everybody meets everybody ever so many times a day.

On finding that his uncle had set lawyers to work, with the charitable purpose of ascertaining whether Philip's property was legitimately his own, Philip was a good deal disturbed in mind. He could not appreciate that high sense of moral obligation by which Mr. Twysden was actuated. At least, he though that these inquiries should not have been secretly set a-foot ; and as he himself was perfectly open—a great deal too open, perhaps—in his words and his actions, he was hard with those who attempted to hoodwink or deceive him.

It could not be ; ah ! no, it never could be, that Agnes the pure and gentle was privy to this conspiracy. But then, how very—very often of late she had been from home ; how very, very cold Aunt Twysden's shoulder had somehow become. Once, when he reached the door, a fishmonger's boy was leaving a fine salmon at the kitchen,—a salmon and a tub of ice. Once, twice, at five o'clock, when he called, a smell of cooking pervaded the hall,—that hall which culinary odors very seldom visited. Some of those noble Twysden dinners were on the *tapis*, and Philip was not asked. Not to be asked was no great deprivation ; but who were the guests ? To be sure, these were trifles light as air ; but Philip smelt mischief in the steam of those Twysden dinners. He chewed that salmon with a bitter sauce as he saw it sink down the area steps and disappear with its attendant lobster in the dark kitchen region.

Yes ; eyes were somehow averted that used to look into his very frankly ; a glove somehow had grown over a little hand which once used to lie very comfortably in his broad palm. Was anybody else going to seize it, and it was going to paddle in that blackamoor's unblest fingers ? Ah ! fiends and tortures ! a gentleman may cease to love, but does he like a woman to cease to love him ? People carry on ever so long for fear of that de-

HAND AND GLOVE.

claration that all is over. No confession is more dismal to make. The sun of love has set. We sit in the dark. I mean you, dear madam, and Corydon, or I and Amaryllis; uncomfortably, with nothing more to say to one another; with the night dew falling, and a risk of catching cold, drearily contemplating the fading west, with "the cold remains of lustre gone, of fire long past away." Sink, fire of love! Rise, gentle moon, and mists of chilly evening. And my good Madam Amaryllis, let us go home to some tea and a fire.

So Philip determined to go and seek his cousin. Arrived at his hotel (and if it were the * * I can't conceive Philip in much better quarters), he had the opportunity of inspecting those delightful newspaper arrivals, a perusal of which has so often edified us at Brighton. Mr. and Mrs. Penfold, he was informed, continued their residence, No. 96, Horizontal Place; and it was with those guardians he knew his Agnes was staying. He speeds to Horizontal Place. Miss Twysden is out. He heaves a sigh, and leaves a card. Has it ever happened to you to leave a card at *that* house—that house which was once THE house—almost your own; where you were ever welcome; where the kindest hand was ready to grasp yours, the brightest eye to greet you? And now your friendship has dwindled away to a little bit of pasteboard, shed once a year, and poor dear Mrs. Jones (it is with J. you have quarrelled) still calls on the ladies of your family and slips her husband's ticket upon the hall table. Oh, life and time, that it should have come to this! Oh, gracious powers! Do you recall the time when Arabella Thompson was Arabella Briggs? You call and talk *fadaises* to her (at first she is rather nervous, and has the children in); you talk rain and fine weather; the last novel; the next party; Thompson in the City? Yes, Mr. Thompson is in the City. He's pretty well, thank you. Ah! Daggers, ropes, and poisons, has it come to this? You are talking about the weather, and another's man's health, and another man's children, of which she is mother, to *her*? Time was the weather was all a burning sunshine, in which you and she basked; or if clouds gathered, and a storm fell, such a glorious rainbow haloed round you, such delicious tears fell and refreshed you, that the storm was more ravishing than the calm. And now another man's children are sitting on her knee—their mother's knee; and once a year Mr. and Mrs. John Thompson request the honor of Mr. Brown's company at dinner; and once a year you read in *The Times*, "In Nursery Street, the wife of J. Thompson, Esq., of a Son." To come to the once-beloved one's door, and find the knocker tied up with a white kid glove, is humiliating—say what you will, it is humiliating.

Philip leaves his card, and walks on to the Cliff, and of course, in three minutes, meets Clinker. Indeed who ever went to Brighton for half an hour without meeting Clinker?

"Father pretty well? His old patient, Lady Geminy, is down here with the children; what a number of them there are, to be sure? Come to make any stay? See your cousin, Miss Twysden, is here with the Penfolds. Little party at the Grigsons' last night; she looked uncommonly well; danced ever so many times with the Black Prince, Woolcomb of the Greens. Suppose I may congratulate you. Six thousand five hundred a year now, and thirteen thousand when his grandmother dies; but those negresses live for ever. I suppose the thing is settled. I saw them on the pier just now, and Mrs. Penfold was reading a book in the arbor. Book of sermons it was—pious woman, Mrs. Penfold. I dare say they are on the pier still." Striding with hurried steps Philip Firmin makes for the pier. The breathless Clinker cannot keep alongside of his face. I should like to have seen it when Clinker said that "the thing" was settled between Mrs. Twysden and the cavalry gentleman.

There were a few nursery governesses, maids, and children, paddling about at the end of the pier; and there was a fat woman reading a book in one of the arbors—but no Agnes, no Woolcomb. Where can they be? Can they be weighing each other? or buying those mad pebbles, which people are known to purchase? or having their *silhouettes* done in black? Ha! ha! Woolcomb would hardly have *his* face done in black? The idea would provoke odious comparisons. I see Philip is in a dreadfully bad sarcastic humor.

Up there comes from one of those trap doors which lead down from the pier-head to the green sea-waves ever restlessly jumping below—up there comes a little Skye-terrier dog with a red collar, who as soon as she sees Philip, sings, squeaks, whines, runs, jumps, *flumps* up on him, if I may use the expression, kisses his hands, and with eyes, tongue, paws, and tail shows him a thousand marks of welcome and affection. "What, Brownie, Brownie!" Philip is glad to see the dog, an old friend who has many a time licked his hand and bounced upon his knee.

The greeting over, Brownie, wagging her tail with prodigious activity, trots before Philip — trots down an opening, down the steps under which the waves shimmer greenly, and into quite a quiet remote corner just over the water, whence you may command a most beautiful view of the sea, the shore, the Marine Parade, and the "Albion Hotel," and where, were I five-and-twenty say, with nothing else to do, I would gladly pass a quarter of an hour talking about "Glaucus, or the Wonders of the Deep" with the object of my affections.

Here, amongst the labyrinth of piles, Brownie goes flouncing along till she comes to a young couple who are looking at the view just described. In order to view it better, the young man has laid his hand, a pretty little hand most delicately gloved, on the lady's hand; and Brownie comes up and muzzles against her, and whines and talks as much as to say, "Here's somebody," and the lady says, "Down Brownie, miss."

"It's no good, Agnes, that dog," says the gentleman (he has very curly, not to say woolly hair, under his natty little hat). "I'll give you a pug with a nose you can hang your hat on. I do know of one now. My man Rummins knows of one. Do you like pugs?"

"I adore them," says the lady.

"I'll give you one, if I have to pay fifty pounds for it. And they fetch a good figure, the real pugs do, I can tell you. Once in London there was an exhibition of 'em, and——"

"Brownie, Brownie, down!" cries Agnes. The dog was jumping at a gentleman, a tall gentleman with a red mustache and beard, who advances through the chequered shade, under the ponderous beams, over the translucent sea.

"Pray don't mind, Brownie won't hurt me," says a perfectly well-known voice, the sound of which sends all the color shuddering out of Miss Agnes' pink cheeks.

"You see I gave my cousin this dog, Captain Woolcomb," says the gentleman; "and the little slut remembers me. Perhaps Miss Twysden prefers the pug better."

"Sir!"

"If it has a nose you can hang your hat on, it must be a very pretty dog, and I suppose you intend to hang your hat on it a good deal."

"Oh, Philip!" says the lady; but an attack of that dreadful coughing stops further utterance.

CHAPTER XIV.

CONTAINS TWO OF PHILIP'S MISHAPS.

You know that, in some parts of India, infanticide is the common custom. It is part of the religion of the land, as, in other districts, widow-burning used to be. I can't imagine that ladies like to destroy either themselves or their children, though they submit with bravery, and even cheerfulness, to the decrees of that religion which orders them to make away with their own or their young ones' lives. Now, suppose you and I, as Europeans, happened to drive up where a young creature was just about to roast herself, under the advice of her family and the highest dignitaries of her church : what could we do ? Rescue her ? No such thing. We know better than to inter-fere with her, and the laws and usages of her country. We turn away with a sigh from the mournful scene ; we pull out our pocket-handkerchiefs, tell coachman to drive on, and leave her to her sad fate.

Now about poor Agnes Twysden : how, in the name of goodness, can we help her ? You see she is a well-brought-up and religious young woman of the Brahminical sect. If she is to be sacrificed, that old Brahmin, her father, that good and devout mother, that most special Brahmin her brother, and that admirable girl her straitlaced sister, all insist upon her under-going the ceremony, and deck her with flowers ere they lead her to that dismal altar flame. Suppose, I say, she has made up her mind to throw over poor Philip, and take on with some one else ? What sentiment ought our virtuous bosoms to enter-tain towards her ? Anger ? I have just been holding a con-versation with a young fellow in rags and without shoes, whose bed is commonly a dry arch, who has been repeatedly in prison, whose father and mother were thieves, and whose grandfathers were thieves ;—are we to be angry with him for following the paternal profession ? With one eye brimming with pity, the other steadily keeping watch over the family spoons, I listen to his artless tale. I have no anger against that child ; nor towards thee, Agnes, daughter of Talbot the Brahmin.

For though duty is duty, when it comes to the pinch, it is often hard to do. Though dear papa and mamma say that here is a gentleman with ever so many thousands a year, an undoubted part in So-and-So-shire, and whole islands in the western main, who is wildly in love with your fair skin and blue eyes, and is ready to fling all his treasures at your feet ; yet, after all, when you consider that he is very ignorant, though very cunning : very stingy, though very rich ; very ill-tempered, probably, if faces and eyes and mouths can tell truth : and as for Philip Firmin—though actually his legitimacy is dubious, as we have lately heard, in which case his maternal fortune is ours —and as for his paternal inheritance, we don't know whether the doctor is worth thirty thousand pounds or a shilling ;—yet, after all—as for Philip—he is man ; he is a gentleman ; he has brains in his head, and a great honest heart of which he has offered to give the best feelings to his cousin :—I say, when a poor girl has to be off with that old love, that honest and fair love, and be on with the new one, the dark one, I feel for her ; and though the Brahmins are, as we know, the most genteel sect in Hindostan, I rather wish the poor child could have belonged to some lower and less rigid sect. Poor Agnes ! to think that he has sat for hours, with mamma and Blanche or the governess, of course, in the room (for, you know, when she and Philip were quite wee wee things dear mamma had little amiable plans in view) ; has sat for hours by Miss Twysden's side pouring out his heart to her ; has had, mayhap, little precious moments of confidential talk—little hasty whispers in corridors, on stairs, behind window-curtains, and—and so forth in fact. She must remember all this past ; and can't, without some pang, listen on the same sofa, behind the same window-curtains, to her dark suitor pouring out his artless tales of barracks, boxing, horseflesh, and the tender passion. He is dull, he is mean, he is ill-tempered, he is ignorant, and the other was * * * * ; but she will do her duty : oh, yes ! she will do her duty ! Poor Agnes ! *C'est à fendre le cœur.* I declare I quite feel for her.

When Philip's temper was roused, I have been compelled, as his biographer, to own how very rude and disagreeable he could be ; and you must acknowledge that a young man has some reason to be displeased, when he finds the girl of his heart hand-in-hand with another young gentleman in an occult and shady recess of the woodwork of Brighton Pier. The green waves are softly murmuring : so is the officer of the Life-Guards Green. The waves are kissing the beach. Ah, agonizing thought ! I will not pursue the simile, which may be but a jealous man's mad fantasy. Of this I am sure, no pebble on that beach is cooler than polished Agnes. But, then, Philip drunk with jealousy is not a reasonable being like Philip sober. "He had a dreadful temper," Philip's dear aunt said of him afterwards,—" I trembled for my dear gentle child, united for ever to a man of that violence. Never, in my secret mind, could I think that their union could be a happy one. Besides, you know, the nearness of their relationship. My scruples on that score, dear Mrs. Candour, never, never could be quite got over." And these scruples came to weigh whole tons, when Mangrove Hall, the House in Berkeley Square, and Mr. Woolcomb's West India island were put into the scale along with them.

Of course there was no good in remaining amongst those damp, reeking timbers, now that the pretty little *tete-à-tete* was over. Little Brownie hung fondling and whining round Philip's ankles, as the party ascended to the upper air. " My child, how pale you look !" cries Mrs. Penfold, putting down her volume. Out of the Captain's open eyeballs shot lurid flames, and hot blood burned behind his yellow cheeks. In a quarrel, Mr. Philip Firmin could be particularly cool and self-possessed. When Miss Agnes rather piteously introduced him to Mrs. Penfold, he made a bow as polite and gracious as any performed by his royal father. " My little dog knew me," he said, caressing the animal. " She is a faithful little thing, and she led me down to my cousin ; and—Captain Woolcomb, I think, is your name, sir ? "

As Philip curls his mustache and smiles blandly, Captain Woolcomb pulls his and scowls fiercely. " Yes, sir," he mutters, " my name is Woolcomb." Another bow and a touch of the hat from Mr. Firmin. A touch ?—a gracious wave of the hat ; acknowledged by no means so gracefully by Captain Woolcomb.

To these remarks Mrs. Penfold says, " Oh !" In fact, " Oh !" is about the best thing that could be said under the circumstances.

" My cousin, Miss Twysden, looks so pale because she was out very late dancing last night. I hear it was a very pretty ball. But ought she to keep such late hours, Mrs. Penfold, with her delicate health ? Indeed, you ought not, Agnes ! Ought she to keep late hours, Brownie ? There—don t, you little foolish thing ! I gave my cousin the dog : and she's very fond of me—the dog is—still. You were saying, Captain Woolcomb, when I came up, that you would give Miss Twysden a dog on whose nose you could hang your * * * * I beg pardon ? "

Mr. Woolcomb, as Philip made this second allusion to the peculiar nasal formation of the pug, ground his little white teeth together, and let slip a most improper monosyllable. More acute bronchial suffering was manifested on the part of Miss Twysden. Mrs. Penfold said, " The day is clouding over. I think, Agnes, I will have my chair, and go home."

" May I be allowed to walk with you as far as your house ? " says Philip, twiddling a little locket which he wore at his watch-chain. It was a little gold locket, with a little pale hair inside. Whose hair could it have been that was so pale and fine? As for the pretty, hieroglyphical A. T. at the back, those letters might indicate Alfred Tennyson, or Anthony Trollope, who might have given a lock of *their* golden hair to Philip, for I know he is an admirer of their works.

Agnes looked guiltily at the little locket. Captain Woolcomb pulled his mustache so, that you would have thought he would have pulled it off ; and his opal eyes glared with fearful confusion and wrath.

" Will you please to fall back and let me speak to you, Agnes ? Pardon me, Captain Woolcomb, I have a private message for my cousin ; and I came from London expressly to deliver it."

" If Miss Twysden desires me to withdraw, I fall back in one moment," says the Captain, clenching the little lemon-colored gloves.

" My cousin and I have lived together all our lives, and I bring her a family message. Have you any particular claim to hear it, Captain Woolcomb ? "

" Not if Miss Twysden don't want me to hear it. * * * D— the little brute."

" Don't kick poor little harmless Brownie ! He sha'n't kick you, shall he, Brownie ? "

" If the brute comes between my shins, I'll kick her ! " shrieks the Captain. " Hang her, I'll throw her into the sea ! "

" Whatever you do to my dog, I swear I will do to you ! " whispers Philip to the Captain.

" Where are you staying ? " shrieks the Captain. " Hang you, you shall hear from me.

" Quiet—' Bedford Hotel.' Easy, or I shall think you want the ladies to overhear."

" Your conduct is horrible, sir," says Agnes, rapidly, in the French language. " Mr. does not comprehend it."

" —— it ! If you have any secrets to talk, I'll withdraw fast enough, Miss Agnes," says Othello.

"Oh, Grenville? can I have any secrets from you? **Mr.** Firmin is my first-cousin. We have lived together all our lives' Philip, I—I don't know whether mamma announced to you— my—my engagement with Captain Grenville Woolcomb." The agitation has brought on another severe bronchial attack. Poor, poor little Agnes! What it is to have a delicate throat!

The pier tosses up to the skies, as though it had left its moorings—the houses on the cliff dance and reel, as though an earthquake was driving them—the sea walks up into the lodg- ing-houses—and Philip's legs are falling from under him: it is only for a moment. When you have a large, tough double tooth out, doesn't the chair go up to the ceiling, and your head come off, too? But, in the next instant, there is a grave gentle- man before you, making you a bow, and concealing something in his right sleeve. The crash is over. You are a man again. Philip clutches hold of the chain pier for a minute: it does not sink under him. The houses, after reeling for a second or two, reassume the perpendicular, and bulge their bow-windows towards the main. He can see the people looking from the windows, the carriages passing, Professor Spurrier riding on the cliff with eighteen young ladies, his pupils. In long after- days he remembers those absurd little incidents with a curious tenacity.

"This news," Philip says, "was not—not altogether unex- pected. I congratulate my cousin, I am sure. Captain Wool- comb, had I known this for certain, I am sure I should not have interrupted you. You were going, perhaps, to ask me to your hospitable house, Mrs. Penfold?"

"Was she though?" cries the Captain.

"I have asked a friend to dine with me at the 'Bedford,' and shall go to town, I hope, in the morning. Can I take anything for you, Agnes? Good-by:" and he kisses his hand in quite a *dégagé* manner, as Mrs. Penfold's chair turns east- ward, and he goes to the west. Silently the tall Agnes sweeps along, a fair hand laid upon her friend's chair.

It's over! it's over! She has done it. He was bound, and kept his honor, but she did not: it was she who forsook him. And I fear very much Mr. Philip's heart leaps with pleasure and an immense sensation of relief at thinking he is free. He meets half-a-dozen acquaintances on the cliff. He laughs, jokes, shakes hands, invites two or three to dinner in the gayest manner. He sits down on that green, not very far from his inn, and is laughing to himself, when he suddenly feels something nestling at his knees, — rubbing, and nestling, and whining plaintively. "What, is that you?" It is little Brownie, who has followed him. Poor little rogue!

Then Philip bent down his head over the dog, and as it jumped on him, with little bleats, and whines, and innocent caresses, he broke out into a sob, and a great refreshing rain of tears fell from his eyes. Such a little illness! Such a mild fever! Such a speedy cure! Some people have the complaint so mildly that they are scarcely ever kept to their beds. Some bear its scars for ever.

Philip sat resolutely at the hotel all night, having given special orders to the porter to say that he was at home, in case any gentleman should call. He had a faint hope, he afterwards owned, that some friend of Captain Woolcomb might wait on him on that officer's part. He had a faint hope that a letter might come explaining that treason,—as people will have a sick, gnawing, yearning, foolish desire for letters—letters which contain nothing—which never did contain anything—letters which, nevertheless, you——. You know, in fact, about those letters, and there is no earthly use in asking to read Philip's. Have we not all read those love letters which, after love-quarrels, come into court sometimes? We have all read them; and how many have written them? Nine o'clock. Ten o'clock. Eleven o'clock. No challenge from the Captain; no explanation from Agnes. Philip declares he slept perfectly well. But poor little Brownie the dog made a piteous howling all night in the stables. She was not a well-bred dog. You could not have hung the least hat on her nose.

We compared anon our dear Agnes to a Brahmin lady, meekly offering herself up to sacrifice according to the practice used in her her highly respectable caste. Did we speak in anger or in sorrow?—surely in terms of respectful grief and sympathy. And if we pity her, ought we not likewise to pity her highly respectable parents? When the notorious Brutus ordered his sons to execution, you can't suppose he was such a brute as to be pleased? All three parties suffered by the transaction: the sons, probably, even more than their austere father; but it stands to reason that the whole trio were very melancholy. At least, were I a poet or musical composer, I certainly should make them so. The sons, piping in a very minor key indeed; the father's manly basso, accompanied by deep wind instruments, and interrupted by appropriate sobs. Though pretty fair Agnes is being led to execution, I don't suppose she likes it, or that her parents are happy, who are compelled to order the tragedy.

17

That the rich young proprietor of Mangrove Hall should be fond of her was merely a coincidence, Mrs. Twysden afterwards always averred. Not for mere wealth—ah, no! not for mines of gold—would they sacrifice their darling child. But when that sad Firmin affair happened, you see it also happened that Captain Woolcomb was much struck by dear Agnes, whom he met everywhere. Her scapegrace of a cousin would go nowhere. He preferred his bachelor associates, and horrible smoking and drinking habits, to the amusements and pleasures of more refined society. He neglected Agnes. There is not the slightest doubt he neglected and mortified her, and his wilful and frequent absence showed how little he cared for her. Would you blame the dear girl for coldness to a man who himself showed such indifference to her? " No, my good Mrs. Candour. Had Mr. Firmin been ten times as rich as Mr. Woolcomb, I should have counselled my child to refuse him. *I* take the responsibility of the measure entirely on myself—I, and her father, and her brother." So Mrs. Twysden afterwards spoke, in circles where an absurd and odious rumor ran, that the Twysdens had forced their daughter to jilt young Mr. Firmin in order to marry a wealthy quadroon. People will talk, you know, *de me, de te.* If Woolcomb's dinners had not gone off so after his marriage, I have little doubt the scandal would have died away, and he and his wife might have been pretty generally respected and visited.

Nor must you suppose, as we have said, that dear Agnes gave up her first love without a pang. That bronchitis showed how acutely the poor thing felt her position. It broke out very soon after Mr. Woolcomb's attentions became a little particular; and she actually left London in consequence. It is true that he could follow her without difficulty, but so, for the matter of that, could Philip, as we have seen when he came down and behaved so rudely to Captain Woolcomb. And before Philip came, poor Agnes could plead, " My father pressed me sair," as in the case of the notorious Mrs. Robin Gray.

Father and mother both pressed her sair. Mrs. Twysden, I think I have mentioned, wrote an admirable letter, and was aware of her accomplishment. She used to write reams of gossip regularly every week to dear uncle Ringwood when he was in the country : and when her daughter Blanche married, she is said to have written several of her new son's sermons. As a Christian mother, was she not to give her daughter her advice at this momentous period of her life ? That advice went

against poor Philip's chances with his cousin, who was kept
acquainted with all the circumstances of the controversy of
which we have just seen the issue. I do not mean to say that
Mrs. Twysden gave an impartial statement of the case. What
parties in a lawsuit do speak impartially on their own side or
their adversaries'? Mrs. Twysden's view, as I have learned
subsequently, and as imparted to her daughter, was this :—
That most unprincipled man, Dr. Firmin, who had already
attempted, and unjustly, to deprive the Twysdens of a part of
their property, had commenced in quite early life his career of
outrage and wickedness against the Ringwood family. He had
led dear Lord Ringwood's son, poor dear Lord Cinqbars, into
a career of vice and extravagance which caused the premature
death of that unfortunate young nobleman. Mr. Firmin had
then made a marriage, in spite of the tears and entreaties of
Mrs. Twysden, with her late unhappy sister, whose whole life
had been made wretched by the doctor's conduct. But the
climax of outrage and wickedness was, that when he—he, a low,
penniless adventurer—married Colonel Ringwood's daughter,
he was married already, as could be sworn by the repentant
clergyman who had been forced, by threats of punishment
which Dr. Firmin held over him, to perform the rite ! " The
mind "—Mrs. Talbot Twysden's fine mind—" shuddered at the
thought of such wickedness." But most of all (for to think ill
of any one whom she had once loved gave her pain) there was
reason to believe that the unhappy Philip Firmin was his
father's accomplice, and that he knew of his *own illegitimacy*,
which he was determined to set aside by any *fraud or artifice*—
(she trembled, she wept to have to say this : O heaven ! that
there should be such perversity in thy creatures !) And so
little store did Philip set by *his mother's honor*, that he actually
visited the abandoned woman who acquiesced in her own
infamy, and had brought such unspeakable disgrace on the
Ringwood family ! The thought of this crime had caused Mrs.
Twysden and her dear husband nights of sleepless anguish—
had made them *years and years* older—had stricken their hearts
with a grief which must endure to the *end of their days*. With
people so unscrupulous, so grasping, so artful as Dr. Firmin
and (must she say ?) his son, they were bound to be *on their
guard;* and though they had *avoided* Philip, she had deemed it
right, on the rare occasions when she and the young man whom
she must now call her *illegitimate* nephew met, to behave as
though she knew nothing of this most dreadful controversy.

"And now, dearest child " * * * Surely the moral is obvious? The dearest child "must see at once that any foolish plans which were formed in childish days and under *former delusions* must be cast aside for ever as impossible, as unworthy of a Twysden—of a Ringwood. Be not concerned for the young man himself," wrote Mrs. Twysden—"I blush that he should bear that dear father's name who was slain in honor on Busaco's glorious field. P. F. has *associates* amongst whom he has ever been much more at home than in our refined circle, and habits which will cause him to forget you only too easily. And if near you is one whose ardor shows itself in his every word and action, whose wealth and property may raise you to a place worthy of my child, need I say, a mother's, a father's blessing go with you." This letter was brought to Miss Twysden, at Brighton, by a special messenger; and the superscription announced that it was "honored by Captain Grenville Woolcomb."

Now when Miss Agnes has had a letter to this effect (I may at some time tell you how I came to be acquainted with its contents); when she remembers all the abuse her brother lavishes against Philip as, heaven bless some of them! dear relatives can best do; when she thinks how cold he has of late been— how he *will* come smelling of cigars—how he won't conform to the usages *du monde,* and has neglected all the decencies of society—how she often can't understand his strange rhapsodies about poetry, painting, and the like, nor how he can live with such associates as those who seem to delight him—and now how he is showing himself actually *unprincipled* and abetting his horrid father; when we consider mither pressing sair, and all these points in mither's favor, I don't think we can order Agnes to instant execution for the resolution to which she is coming. She will give him up—she will give him up. Good-by, Philip. Good-by the past. Be forgotten, be forgotten, fond words spoken in not unwilling ears! Be still and breathe not, eager lips, that have trembled so near to one another! Unlock, hands, and part for ever, that seemed to be formed for life's long journey! Ah, to part for ever is hard; but harder and more humiliating still to part without regret!

That papa and mamma had influenced Miss Twysden in her behavior my wife and I could easily imagine, when Philip, in his wrath and grief, came to us and poured out the feelings of his heart. My wife is a repository of men's secrets, an untiring consoler and comforter; and she knows many a sad story which we are not at liberty to tell, like this one of which this person, Mr. Firmin, has given us possession.

"Father and mother's orders," shouts Philip, "I dare say,

Mrs. Pendennis ; but the wish was father to the thought of parting, and it was for the blackamoor's parks and acres that the girl jilted me. Look here. I told you just now that I slept perfectly well on that infernal night after I had said farewell to her. Well, I didn't. It was a lie. I walked ever so many times the whole length of the cliff, from Hove to Rottingdean almost, and then went to bed afterwards, and slept a little out of sheer fatigue. And as I was passing by Horizontal Terrace (—I happened to pass by there two or three times in the moonlight, like a great jackass—) you know those verses of mine which I have hummed here sometimes ? " (hummed ! he used to *roar* them !) " ' When the locks of burnished gold, lady, shall to silver turn ! ' Never mind the rest. You know the verses about fidelity and old age ? She was singing them on that night to that negro. And I heard the beggar's voice say, ' Bravo ! ' through the open windows."

"Ah, Philip ! it was cruel," says my wife, heartily pitying our friend's anguish and misfortune. " It was cruel indeed. I am sure we can feel for you. But think what certain misery a marriage with such a person would have been ! Think of your warm heart given away for ever to that heartless creature."

" Laura, Laura, have you not often warned me not to speak ill of people ? " says Laura's husband.

" I can't help it sometimes," cries Laura in a transport. " I try and do my best not to speak ill of my neighbors ; but the worldliness of those people shocks me so that I can't bear to be near them. They are so utterly tied and bound by conventionalities, so perfectly convinced of their own excessive high-breeding, that they seem to me more odious and more vulgar than quite low people ; and I'm sure Mr. Philip's friend, the Little Sister, is infinitely more ladylike than this dreary aunt or either of his supercilious cousins ! " Upon my word, when this lady did speak her mind, there was no mistaking her meaning.

I believe Mr. Firmin took a considerable number of people into his confidence regarding this love affair. He is one of those individuals who can't keep their secrets ; and when hurt he roars so loudly that all his friends can hear. It has been remarked that the sorrows of such persons do not endure very long ; nor surely was there any great need in this instance that Philip's heart should wear a lengthened mourning. Ere long he smoked his pipes, he played his billiards, he shouted his songs ; he rode in the Park for the pleasure of severely cutting his aunt and cousins when their open carriage passed, or of riding down Captain Woolcomb or his cousin Ringwood, should either of those worthies come in his way.

One day, when the old Lord Ringwood came to town for his accustomed spring visit, Philip condescended to wait upon him, and was announced to his lordship just as Talbot Twysden and Ringwood his son were taking leave of their noble kinsman. Philip looked at them with a flashing eye and a distended nostril, according to his swaggering wont. I dare say they on their part bore a very mean and hangdog appearance; for my lord laughed at their discomfiture, and seemed immensely amused as they slunk out of the door when Philip came hectoring in.

"So, sir, there has been a family row. Heard all about it: at least, their side. Your father did me the favor to marry my niece, having another wife already?"

"Having no other wife already, sir—though my dear relations were anxious to show that he had."

"Wanted your money; thirty thousand pound is not a trifle. Ten thousand apiece for those children. And no more need of any confounded pinching and scraping, as they have to do at Beaunash Street. Affair off between you and Agnes? Absurd affair. So much the better."

"Yes, sir, so much the better."

"Have ten thousand apiece. Would have twenty thousand if they got yours. Quite natural to want it."

"Quite."

"Woolcomb a sort of negro, I understand. Fine property here: besides the West India rubbish. Violent man—so people tell me. Luckily Agnes seems a cool, easy-going woman, and must put up with the rough as well as the smooth in marrying a property like that. Very lucky for you that the woman persists there was no marriage with your father. Twysden says the doctor bribed her. Take it he's not got much money to bribe, unless you gave some of yours."

"I don't bribe people to bear false witness, my lord—and if——"

"Don't be in a huff; I didn't say so. Twysden says so—perhaps thinks so. When people are at law they believe anything of one another."

"I don't know what other people may do, sir. If I had another man's money, I should not be easy until I had paid him back. Had my share of my grandfather's property not been lawfully mine—and for a few hours I thought it was not

—please God, I would have given it up to its rightful owners—at least, my father would."

"Why, hang it all, man, you don't mean to say your father has not settled with you?"

Philip blushed a little. He had been rather surprised that there had been no settlement between him and his father.

"I am only of age a few months, sir. I am not under any apprehension. I get my dividends regularly enough. One of my grandfather's trustees, General Baynes, is in India. He is to return almost immediately, or we should have sent a power of attorney out to him. There's no hurry about the business."

Philip's maternal grandfather, and Lord Ringwood's brother, the late Colonel Philip Ringwood, had died possessed of but trifling property of his own; but his wife had brought him a fortune of sixty thousand pounds, which was settled on their children, and in the names of trustees—Mr. Briggs, a lawyer, and Colonel Baynes, an East India officer, and friend of Mrs. Philip Ringwood's family. Colonel Baynes had been in England some eight years before; and Philip remembered a kind old gentleman coming to see him at school, and leaving tokens of his bounty behind. The other trustee, Mr. Briggs, a lawyer of considerable county reputation, was dead long since, having left his affairs in an involved condition. During the trustee's absence and the son's minority, Philip's father received the dividends on his son's property, and liberally spent them on the boy. Indeed, I believe that for some little time at college, and during his first journeys abroad, Mr. Philip spent rather more than the income of his maternal inheritance, being freely supplied by his father, who told him not to stint himself. He was a sumptuous man, Dr. Firmin—open-handed—subscribing to many charities—a lover of solemn good cheer. The doctor's dinners and the doctor's equipages were models in their way; and I remember the sincere respect with which my uncle the Major (the family guide in such matters) used to speak of Dr. Firmin's taste. "No duchess in London, sir," he would say, " drove better horses than Mrs. Firmin. Sir George Warrender, sir, could not give a better dinner, sir, than that to which we sat down yesterday." And for the exercise of these civic virtues the doctor had the hearty respect of the good Major.

"Don't tell me, sir," on the other hand, Lord Ringwood would say; "I dined with the fellow once—a swaggering fellow, sir; but a servile fellow. The way he bowed and flattered was perfectly absurd. Those fellows think we like it—and we

may. Even at my age, I like flattery—any quantity of it; and
not what you call delicate, but strong, sir. I like a man to
kneel down and kiss my shoe-strings. I have my own opinion
of him afterwards, but that is what I like—what all men like;
and that is what Firmin gave in quantities. But you could see
that his house was monstrously expensive. His dinner was
excellent, and you saw it was good every day—not like your
dinners, my good Maria; not like your wines, Twysden, which,
hang it, I can't swallow, unless I send 'em in myself. Even at
my own house, I don't give that kind of wine on common occasions which Firmin used to give. I drink the best myself, of
course, and give it to some who know; but I don't give it to
common fellows, who come to hunting dinners, or to girls and
boys who are dancing at my balls."

"Yes; Mr. Firmin's dinners were very handsome—and a
pretty end came of the handsome dinners!" sighed Mrs.
Twysden.

"That's not the question; I am only speaking about the
fellow's meat and drink, and they were both good. And it's
my opinion, that fellow will have a good dinner wherever he
goes."

I had the fortune to be present at one of these feasts, which
Lord Ringwood attended, and at which I met Philip's trustee,
General Baynes, who had just arrived from India. I remember
now the smallest details of the little dinner,—the brightness of
the old plate, on which the doctor prided himself, and the quiet
comfort, not to say splendor, of the entertainment. The
General seemed to take a great liking to Philip, whose grandfather had been his special friend and comrade in arms. He
thought he saw something of Philip Ringwood in Philip Firmin's face.

"Ah, indeed!" growls Lord Ringwood.

"You ain't a bit like him," says the downright General.
"Never saw a handsomer or more open-looking fellow than
Philip Ringwood."

"Oh! I daresay I looked pretty open myself forty years
ago," said my lord; "now I'm shut, I suppose. I don't see
the least likeness in this young man to my brother."

"That is some sherry as old as the century," whispers the
host; "it is the same the Prince Regent liked so at a Mansion
House dinner, five-and-twenty years ago."

"Never knew anything about wine; was always tippling
liqueurs and punch. What do you give for this sherry,
doctor?"

The doctor sighed, and looked up to the chandelier. "Drink it while it lasts, my good lord ; but don't ask me the price. The fact is, I don't like to say what I gave for it."

"You need not stint yourself in the price of sherry, doctor," cries the General gayly ; "you have but one son, and he has a fortune of his own, as I happen to know. You haven't dipped it, Master Philip ? "

"I fear, sir, I may have exceeded my income sometimes, in the last three years ; but my father has helped me."

"Exceeded nine hundred a year ! Upon my word ! When I was a sub, my friends gave me fifty pounds a year, and I never was a shilling in debt ! What are men coming to now ? "

"If doctor's drink Prince Regent's sherry at ten guineas a dozen, what can you expect of their sons, General Baynes ? " grumbles my lord.

"My father gives you his best, my lord," says Philip gayly ; "if you know of any better, he will get it for you. *Si non his utere mecum !* Please to pass me that decanter, Pen ! "

I thought the old lord did not seem ill pleased at the young man's freedom ; and now, as I recall it, think I can remember that a peculiar silence and anxiety seemed to weigh upon our host—upon him whose face was commonly so anxious and sad.

The famous sherry, which had made many voyages to Indian climes before it acquired its exquisite flavor, had travelled some three or four times round the doctor's polished table, when Brice, his man, entered with a letter on a silver tray. Perhaps Philip's eyes and mine exchanged glances in which ever so small a scintilla of mischief might sparkle. The doctor often had letters when he was entertaining his friends ; and his patients had a knack of falling ill at awkward times.

"Gracious heavens ! " cries the doctor, when he read the despatch—it was a telegraphic message. "The poor Grand Duke ! "

"What Grand Duke ? " asks the surly lord of Ringwood.

"My earliest patron and friend — the Grand Duke of Gröningen ! Seized this morning at eleven at Potzendorff ! Has sent for me. I promised to go to him if ever he had need of me. I must go ! I can save the night train yet. General ! our visit to the City must be deferred till my return. Get a portmanteau, Brice ; and call a cab at once. Philip will entertain my friends for the evening. My dear lord, you won't mind an old doctor leaving you to attend an old patient ? I will write from Gröningen. I shall be there on Friday morning.

Farewell, gentlemen!   Brice, another bottle of that sherry !   I pray, don't let anybody stir !   God bless you, Philip my boy!" And with this the doctor went up, took his son by the hand, and laid the other very kindly on the young man's shoulder. Then he made a bow round the table to his guests—one of his graceful bows, for which he was famous.   I can see the sad smile on his face now, and the light from the chandelier over the dining-table glancing from his shining forehead, and casting deep shadows on to his cheek from his heavy brows.

The departure was a little abrupt, and of course cast somewhat of a gloom upon the company.

" My carriage ain't ordered till ten—must go on sitting here, I suppose. Confounded life doctor's must be ! Called up any hour in the night ! Get their fees ! Must go !" growled the great man of the party.

" People are glad enough to have them when they are ill, my lord.   I think I have heard that once when you were at Ryde * * *"

The great man started back as if a little shock of cold water had fallen on him ; and then looked at Philip with not unfriendly glances.   " Treated for gout—so he did.   Very well, too !" said my lord ; and whispered, not inaudibly, " Cool hand, that boy !"   And then his lordship fell to talk with General Baynes about his campaigning, and his early acquaintance with his own brother, Philip's grandfather.

The general did not care to brag about his own feats of arms, but was loud in praises of his old comrade.   Philip was pleased to hear his grandsire so well spoken of.   The General had known Dr. Firmin's father also, who likewise had been a colonel in the famous old Peninsular army.   " A Tartar that fellow was, and no mistake !" said the good officer.   " Your father has a strong look of him ; and you have a glance of him at times.   But you remind me of Philip Ringwood not a little ; and you could not belong to a better man."

" Ha !" says my lord.   There had been differences between him and his brother.   He may have been thinking of days when they were friends.   Lord Ringwood now graciously asked if General Baynes was staying in London?   But the General had only come to do this piece of business, which must now be delayed.   He was too poor to live in London.   He must look out for a country place, where he and his six children could live cheaply.   " Three boys at school, and one at college, Mr. Philip—you know what that must cost ; though, thank my stars, my college boy does not spend nine hundred a year

Nine hundred! Where should we be if he did?" In fact, the days of nabobs are long over, and the General had come back to his native country with only very small means for the support of a great family.

When my lord's carriage came, he departed, and the other guests presently took their leave. The General, who was a bachelor for the nonce, remained awhile, and we three prattled over cheroots in Philip's smoking-room. It was a night like a hundred I have spent there, and yet how well I remember it! We talked about Philip's future prospects, and he communicated his intentions to us in his lordly way. As for practising at the bar: "No, sir," he said, in reply to General Baynes' queries; he should not make much hand of that; shouldn't if he were ever so poor. He had his own money, and his father's;" and he condescended to say that "he might, perhaps, try for Parliament should an eligible opportunity offer." "Here's a fellow born with a silver spoon in his mouth," says the General, as we walked away together. "A fortune to begin with; a fortune to inherit. My fortune was two thousand pounds, and the price of my two first commissions; and when I die my children will not be quite so well off as their father was when he began!"

Having parted with the old officer at his modest sleeping quarters near his club, I walked to my own home, little thinking that yonder cigar, of which I had shaken some of the ashes in Philip's smoking-room, was to be the last tobacco I ever should smoke there. The pipe was smoked out. The wine was drunk. When that door closed on me, it closed for the last time—at least was never more to admit me as Philip's, as Dr. Firmin's, guest and friend. I pass the place often now. My youth comes back to me as I gaze at those blank, shining windows. I see myself a boy and Philip a child; and his fair mother; and his father, the hospitable, the melancholy, the magnificent. I wish I could have helped him. I wish somehow he had borrowed money. He never did. He gave me his often. I have never seen him since that night when his own door closed upon him.

On the second day after the doctor's departure, as I was at breakfast with my family, I received the following letter:—

"MY DEAR PENDENNIS,—Could I have seen you in private on Tuesday night, I might have warned you of the calamity which was hanging over my house. But to what good end? That you should know a few weeks, hours, before what all the world will ring with to-morrow? Neither you nor I, nor one whom we both love, would have been the happier for knowing my misfortunes a few hours sooner. In four-and-twenty hours every club in London will be busy with talk of the departure of the celebrated Dr. Firmin—the wealthy

Dr. Firmin; a few months more and (I have strict and *confidential* reason to believe) hereditary rank would have been mine, but Sir George Firmin would have been an insolvent man, and his son Sir Philip a beggar. Perhaps the thought of this honor has been one of the reasons which has determined me on expatriating myself sooner than I otherwise needed to have done.

"George Firmin, the honored, the wealthy physician, and his son a beggar? I see you are startled at the news! You wonder how, with a great practice, and no great ostensible expenses, such ruin should come upon me—upon him. It has seemed as if for years past Fate has been determined to make war upon George Brand Firmin; and who can battle against Fate? A man universally admitted to be of good judgment, I have embarked in mercantile speculations the most promising. Everything upon which I laid my hand has crumbled to ruin; but I can say with the Roman bard, '*Impavidum ferient ruinæ.*' And, almost penniless, almost aged, an exile driven from my country, I seek another where I do not despair—*I even have a firm belief* that I shall be enabled to repair my shattered fortunes! My race has never been deficient in courage, and Philip and *Philip's father* must use all theirs, so as to be enabled to face the dark times which menace them. *Si celeres quatit pennas Fortuna*, we must resign what she gave us, and bear our calamity with unshaken hearts!

"There is a man, I own to you, whom I cannot, I must not face. General Baynes has just come from India, with but very small savings, I fear; and these are jeopardized by his imprudence and my most cruel and unexpected misfortune. I need not tell you that *my all* would have been my boy's. My will, made long since, will be found in the tortoiseshell secretaire standing in my consulting-room under the picture of Abraham offering up Isaac. In it you will see that everything, except annuities to old and deserving servants and a legacy to one excellent and faithful woman whom I own I have wronged—my all, which once was considerable, *is left to my boy*.

"I am now worth less than nothing, and have compromised Philip's property along with my own. As a man of business, General Baynes, Colonel Ringwood's old companion in arms, was culpably careless, and I—alas! that I must own it—deceived him. Being the only surviving trustee (Mrs. Philip Ringwood's other trustee was an unprincipled attorney who has been long dead), General B. signed a paper authorizing, as he imagined, my bankers to receive Philip's dividends; but, in fact, giving me the power to dispose of the capital sum. On my honor, as a man, as a gentleman, as a father, Pendennis, I hoped to replace it! I took it; I embarked it in speculations in which it sank down with ten times the amount of my own private property. Half-year after half-year, with straitened means and with the *greatest difficulty to myself*, my poor boy has had his dividend; and *he* at least has never known what was want or anxiety until now. Want? Anxiety? Pray Heaven he never may suffer the sleepless anguish, the racking care which has pursued me! '*Post equitem sedet atra cura*,' our favorite poet says. Ah! how truly, too, does he remark, '*Patriæ quis exul se quoque fugit?*' Think you where I go grief and remorse will not follow me? They will never leave me until I shall return to this country—for that I *shall* return, my heart tells me—until I can reimburse General Baynes, who stands indebted to Philip through his incautiousness and my overpowering necessity; and my heart—an erring but fond *father's* heart—tells me that my boy will not eventually lose a penny by my misfortune.

"I own, between ourselves, that this illness of the Grand Duke of Gröningen was a pretext which I put forward. You will hear of me ere long from the place whither for some time past I have determined on bending my steps. I placed 100*l.* on Saturday, to Philip's credit, at his banker's. I take little more than that sum with me; depressed, yet *full of hope*; having done wrong, yet *determined* to retrieve it, and *vowing* that ere I die my poor boy shall not have to blush at bearing the name of

> "GEORGE BRAND FIRMIN.

"Good-by, dear Philip! Your old friend will tell you of my misfortunes. When I write again, it will be to tell you where to address me; and wherever I am, or whatever misfortunes oppress me, think of me always as your fond

> "FATHER."

I had scarce read this awful letter when Philip Firmin himself came into our breakfast-room looking very much disturbed.

CHAPTER XV.

SAMARITANS.

THE children trotted up to their friend with outstretched hands and their usual smiles of welcome. Philip patted their heads, and sat down with very woe-begone aspect at the family table. "Ah, friends," said he, "do you know all?"

"Yes, we do," said Laura, sadly, who has ever compassion for other's misfortunes.

"What! is it all over the town already?" asked poor Philip.

"We have a letter from your father this morning." And we brought the letter to him, and showed him the affectionate special message for himself.

"His last thought was for you, Philip!" cries Laura. "See here, those last kind words!"

Philip shook his head. "It is not untrue, what is written here: but it is not all the truth." And Philip Firmin dismayed us by the intelligence which he proceeded to give. There was an execution in the house in Old Parr Street. A hundred clamorous creditors had appeared there. Before going away, the doctor had taken considerable sums from those dangerous financiers to whom he had been of late resorting. They were in possession of numberless lately signed bills, upon which the desperate man had raised money. He had professed to share with Philip, but he had taken the great share, and left Philip two hundred pounds of his own money. All the rest was gone. All Philip's stock had been sold out. The father's fraud had made him master of the trustee's signature: and Philip Firmin, reputed to be so wealthy, was a beggar, in my room. Luckily he had few, or very trifling, debts. Mr. Philip had a lordly impatience of indebtedness, and, with a good bachelor-income, had paid for all his pleasures as he enjoyed them.

Well! He must work. A young man ruined at two-and-twenty, with a couple of hundred pounds yet in his pocket, hardly knows that he is ruined. He will sell his horses—live in chambers—has enough to go on for a year. "When I am very hard put to it," says Philip, "I will come and dine with the children at one. I dare say you haven't dined much at Williams's in the Old Bailey? You can get a famous dinner there for a shilling—beef, bread, potatoes, beer, and a penny for the waiter." Yes, Philip seemed actually to enjoy his discomfiture. It was long since we had seen him in such spirits. "The weight is off my mind now. It has been throttling me for some time past. Without understanding why or wherefore, I have always been looking out for this. My poor father had ruin written in his face; and when those bailiffs made their appearance in Old Parr Street yesterday, I felt as if I had known them before. I had seen their hooked beaks in my dreams."

"That unlucky General Baynes, when he accepted your mother's trust, took it with its consequences. If the sentry falls asleep on his post, he must pay the penalty," says Mr. Pendennis, very severely.

"Great powers, you would not have me come down on an old man with a large family, and ruin them all?" cries Philip.

"No: I don't think Philip will do that," says my wife, looking exceedingly pleased.

"If men accept trusts they must fulfil them, my dear," cries the master of the house.

"And I must make that old gentleman suffer for my father's wrong? If I do, may I starve! there!" cries Philip.

"And so that poor Little Sister has made her sacrifice in vain!" sighed my wife. "As for the father—oh, Arthur! I can't tell you how odious that man was to me. There was something dreadful about him. And in his manner to women —oh!—— "

"If he had been a black draught, my dear, you could not have shuddered more naturally."

"Well, he was horrible; and I know Philip will be better now he is gone."

Women often make light of ruin. Give them but the beloved objects, and poverty is a trifling sorrow to bear. As for Philip, he, as we have said, is gayer than he has been for years past. The doctor's flight occasions not a little club talk: but, now he is gone, many people see quite well that they were aware of his insolvency, and always knew it must end so. The case is told, is canvassed, is exaggerated as such cases will be. I dare say it forms a week's talk. But people know that poor Philip is his father's largest creditor, and eye the young man with no unfriendly looks when he comes to his club after his mishap,— with burning cheeks, and a tingling sense of shame, imagining that all the world will point at and avoid him as the guilty fugitive's son.

"No: the world takes very little heed of his misfortune. One or two old acquaintances are kinder to him than before. A few say his ruin, and his obligation to work, will do him good. Only a very, very few avoid him, and look unconscious as he passes them by. Amongst these cold countenances, you, of course, will recognize the faces of the whole Twysden family. Three statues, with marble eyes, could not look more stony-calm than Aunt Twysden and her two daughters, as they pass in the stately barouche. The gentlemen turn red when they see Philip. It is rather late times for Uncle Twysden to begin blushing, to be sure. "Hang the fellow! he will, of course, be coming for money. Dawkins, I am not at home, mind, when young Mr. Firmin calls." So says Lord Ringwood, regarding Philip fallen among thieves. Ah, thanks to Heaven, travellers find Samaritans as well as Levites on life's hard way! Philip told us with much humor of a rencontre which he had had with his cousin, Ringwood Twysden, in a public place. Twysden was enjoying himself with some young clerks of his office; but as Philip advanced upon him, assuming his fiercest scowl and most hectoring manner, the other lost heart, and fled. And no wonder. "Do you suppose," says Twysden, "I will willingly sit in the same room with that cad, after the manner in which he has treated my family! No, sir!" And so the tall door in Beaunash Street is to open for Philip Firmin no more.

The tall door in Beaunash Street flies open readily enough for another gentleman. A splendid cab-horse reins up before it every day. A pair of varnished boots leap out of the cab, and spring up the broad stairs, where somebody is waiting with a smile of genteel welcome—the same smile—on the same sofa —the same mamma at her table writing her letters. And beautiful bouquets from Covent Garden decorate the room. And after half an hour mamma goes out to speak to the house-keeper, *vous comprenez*. And there is nothing particularly new under the sun. It will shine to-morrow upon pretty much the same flowers, sports, pastimes, &c., which it illuminated yesterday. And when your love-making days are over, miss, and you are married, and advantageously established, shall not your little sisters, now in the nursery, trot down and play their little games? Would you, on your conscience, now—you who are rather inclined to consider Miss Agnes Twysden's conduct as heartless—would you, I say, have her cry her pretty eyes out about a young man who does not care much for her, for whom

she never did care much herself, and who is now, moreover, a beggar, with a ruined and disgraced father and a doubtful legitimacy? Absurd! That dear girl is like a beautiful fragrant
bower-room at the "Star and Garter" at Richmond, with
honeysuckles mayhap trailing round the windows, from which
you behold one of the most lovely and pleasant of wood and
river scenes. The tables are decorated with flowers, rich wine-
cups sparkle on the board, and Captain Jones's party have
everything they can desire. Their dinner over, and that company gone, the same waiters, the same flowers, the same cups
and crystals, array themselves for Mr. Brown and *his* party.
Or, if you won't have Agnes Twysden compared to the "Star
and Garter Tavern," which must admit mixed company, liken
her to the chaste moon who shines on shepherds of all complexions, swarthy or fair.

When oppressed by superior odds, a commander is forced
to retreat, we like him to show his skill by carrying off his guns,
treasure, and camp equipages. Doctor Firmin, beaten by fortune and compelled to fly, showed quite a splendid skill and
coolness in his manner of decamping, and left the very smallest
amount of spoils in the hands of the victorious enemy. His
wines had been famous amongst the grave epicures with whom
he dined : he used to boast, like a worthy *bon-vivant* who knows
the value of wine-conversation after dinner, of the quantities
which he possessed, and the rare bins which he had in store ;
but when the executioners came to arrange his sale, there was
found only a beggarly account of empty bottles, and I fear some
of the unprincipled creditors put in a great quantity of bad
liquor which they endeavored to foist off on the public as the
genuine and carefully selected stock of a well-known connoisseur. News of this dishonest proceeding reached Dr. Firmin
presently in his retreat ; and he showed by his letter a generous
and manly indignation at the manner in which his creditors had
tampered with his honest name and reputation as a *bon-vivant*.
He have bad wine ! For shame ! He had the best from the
best wine-merchant, and paid, or rather owed, the best prices
for it ; for of late years the doctor had paid no bills at all :
and the wine-merchant appeared in quite a handsome group of
figures in his schedule. In like manner his books were pawned
to a book auctioneer ; and Brice, the butler, had a bill of sale
for the furniture. Firmin retreated, we will not say with the
honors of war, but as little harmed as possible by defeat. Did
the enemy want the plunder of his city? He had smuggled
almost all his valuable goods over the wall. Did they desire

his ships? He had sunk them: and when at length the con-
querors poured into his stronghold, he was far beyond the reach
of their shot. Don't we often hear still that Nana Sahib is
alive and exceedingly comfortable? We do not love him; but
we can't help having a kind of admiration for that slippery
fugitive who has escaped from the dreadful jaws of the lion. In
a word, when Firmin's furniture came to be sold, it was a marvel how little his creditors benefited by the sale. Contemptuous
brokers declared there never was such a shabby lot of goods.
A friend of the house and poor Philip bought in his mother's
picture for a few guineas; and as for the doctor's own state
portrait, I am afraid it went for a few shillings only, and in the
midst of a roar of Hebrew laughter. I saw in Wardour Street,
not long after, the doctor's sideboard, and what dealers cheerfully call the sarcophagus cellaret. Poor doctor! his wine was
all drunken; his meat was eaten up; but his own body had
slipped out of the reach of the hook-beaked birds of prey.

We had spoken rapidly in undertones, innocently believing
that the young people round about us were taking no heed of
our talk. But in a lull of the conversation, Mr. Pendennis
junior, who had always been a friend to Philip, broke out with
—" Philip! if you are so *very* poor, you'll be hungry, you know,
and you may have my piece of bread and jam. And I don't
want it, mamma," he added; "and you know Philip has often
and often given me things."

Philip stooped down and kissed this good little Samaritan.
" I'm not hungry, Arty, my boy," he said; "and I'm not so poor
but I have got—look here—a fine new shilling for Arty!"

" Oh, Philip, Philip!" cried mamma.

" Don't take the money, Arthur," cried papa.

And the boy, with a rueful face but a manly heart, prepared
to give back the coin. "It's quite a new one; and it's a very
pretty one: but I won't have it, Philip, thank you," he said,
turning very red.

" If he won't, I vow I will give it to the cabman," said Philip.

" Keeping a cab all this while? Oh, Philip, Philip!" again
cries mamma the economist.

" Loss of time is loss of money, my dear lady," says Philip,
very gravely. " I have ever so many places to go to. When I
am set in for being ruined, you shall see what a screw I will become! I must go to Mrs. Brandon, who will be very uneasy,
poor dear, until she knows the worst."

" Oh, Philip, I should like so to go with you!" cries Laura.
" Pray, give her our very best regards and respects."

" *Merci !* " said the young man, and squeezed Mrs. Pendennis's hand in his own big one. " I will take your message to her, Laura. *J'aime qu'on l'aime, savez-vous ?* "

" That means, I love those who love her," cries little Laura ; "but, I don't know," remarked this little person afterwards to her paternal confidant, " that I like *all* people to love my mamma. That is, I don't like *her* to like them, papa—only you may, papa, and Ethel may, and Arthur, may, and, I think, Philip may, now he is poor and quite, quite alone—and we will take care of him, won't we ? ·And, I think, I'll buy him something with my money which Aunt Ethel gave me."

" And I'll give him my money," cries a boy.

" And I'll div him my—my——" Psha ! what matters what the little sweet lips prattle in their artless kindness ? But the soft words of love and pity smote the mother's heart with an exquisite pang of gratitude and joy ; and I know where her thanks were paid for those tender words and thoughts of her little ones.

Mrs. Pendennis made Philip promise to come to dinner, and also to remember not to take a cab—which promise Mr. Firmin had not much difficulty in executing, for he had but a few hundred yards to walk across the Park from his club ; and I must say that my wife took a special care of our dinner that day, preparing for Philip certain dishes which she knew he liked, and enjoining the butler of the establishment (who also happened to be the owner of the house) to fetch from his cellar the very choicest wine in his possession.

I have previously described our friend and his boisterous, impetuous, generous nature. When Philip was moved, he called to all the world to witness his emotion. When he was angry, his enemies were all the rogues and scoundrels in the world. He vowed he would have no mercy on them, and desired all his acquaintances to participate in his anger. How could such an open-mouthed son have such a close-spoken father ? I dare say you have seen very well-bred young people, the children of vulgar and ill-bred parents ; the swaggering father have a silent son ; the loud mother a modest daughter. Our friend is not Amadis or Sir Charles Grandison ; and I don't set him up for a moment as a person to be revered or imitated ; but try to draw him faithfully, and as nature made him. As nature made him, so he was. I don't think he tried to improve himself much. Perhaps few people do. They suppose they do : and you read, in apologetic memoirs, and fond biographies, how this man cured his bad temper, and t'other worked and strove until he grew to be almost faultless. Very well and good, my good people. You can learn a language ; you can master a science ; I have heard of an old square-toes of sixty who learned, by study and intense application, very satisfactorily to dance ; but can you, by taking thought, add to your moral stature ? Ah me ! the doctor who preaches is only taller than most of us by the height of the pulpit : and when he steps down, I dare say he cringes to the duchess, growls at his children, scolds his wife about the dinner. All is vanity, look you : and so the preacher is vanity, too.

Well, then, I must again say that Philip roared his griefs : he shouted his laughter : he bellowed his applause : he was extravagant in his humility as in his pride, in his admiration of his friends and contempt for his enemies · I dare say not a just man, but I have met juster men not half so honest ; and certainly not a faultless man, though I know better men not near so good. So, I believe, my wife thinks : else why should she be so fond of him ? Did we not know boys who never went out of bounds, and never were late for school, and never made a false concord or quantity, and never came under the ferule ; and others who were always playing truant, and blundering, and being whipped ; and yet, somehow, was not Master Naughtyboy better liked than Master Goodchild ? When Master Naughtyboy came to dine with us on the first day of his ruin, he bore a face of radiant happiness—he laughed, he bounced about, he caressed the children ; now he took a couple on his knees ; now he tossed the baby to the ceiling ; now he sprawled over a sofa, and now he rode upon a chair ; never was a penniless gentleman more cheerful. As for his dinner, Phil's appetite was always fine, but on this day an ogre could scarcely play a more terrible knife and fork. He asked for more and more, until his entertainers wondered to behold him. " Dine for to-day and to-morrow too ; can't expect such fare as this every day, you know. This claret, how good it is ! May I pack some up in paper, and take it home with me ? " The children roared with laughter at this admirable idea of carrying home wine in a sheet of paper. I don't know that it is always at the best jokes that children laugh :—children and wise men too.

When we three were by ourselves, and freed from the company of servants and children, our friend told us the cause of his gayety. " By George ! " he swore, " it is worth being ruined to find such good people in the world. My dear, kind Laura "— here the gentleman brushes his eyes with his fist—" it was as much as I could do this morning to prevent myself from hugging you in my arms, you were so generous, and—and so kind, and so tender, and so good, by George.   And after leaving you, where do you think I went ? ”

“ I think I can guess, Philip,” says Laura.

“ Well,” says Philip, winking his eyes again, and tossing off a great bumper of wine, “ I went to her, of course.   I think she is the best friend I have in the world.   The old man was out, and I told her about everything that had happened.   And what do you think she has done ?   She says she has been expecting me—she has ; and she has gone and fitted up a room with a nice little bed at the top of the house, with everything as neat and trim as possible ; and she begged and prayed I would go and stay with her—and I said I would, to please her.   And then she takes me down to her room ; and she jumps up to a cupboard, which she unlocks ; and she opens and takes three-and-twenty pounds out of a—out of a tea—out of a tea-caddy— confound me !—and she says, ‘ Here, Philip,” she says, and— Boo ! what a fool I am ! ” and here the orator fairly broke down in his speech.

CHAPTER XVI.

IN WHICH PHILIP SHOWS HIS METTLE.

WHEN the poor Little Sister proffered her mite, her all, to Philip, I dare say some sentimental passages occurred between them which are much too trivial to be narrated.   No doubt her pleasure would have been at that moment to give him not only that gold which she had been saving up against rent-day, but the spoons, the furniture, and all the valuables of the house, including, perhaps, J. J.’s bric-à-brac, cabinets, china, and so forth.   To perform a kindness, an act of self-sacrifice ;— are not these the most delicious privileges of female tenderness ? Philip checked his little friend’s enthusiasm.   He showed her a purse full of money, at which sight the poor little soul was rather disappointed.   He magnified the value of his horses, which, according to Philip’s calculation, were to bring him at least two hundred pounds more than the stock which he had already in hand ; and the master of such a sum as this, she was forced to confess, had no need to despair.   Indeed, she had never in her life possessed the half of it.   Her kind dear little offer of a home in her house he would accept sometimes, and with gratitude. Well, there was a little consolation in that. In a moment that active little housekeeper saw the room ready; flowers on the mantel-piece; his looking-glass, which her father could do quite well with the little one, as he was always shaved by the barber now; the quilted counterpane, which she had herself made :—I know not what more improvements she devised; and I fear that at the idea of having Philip with her, this little thing was as extravagantly and unreasonably happy as we have just now seen Philip to be. What was that last dish which Pætus and Arria shared in common? I have lost my Lempriere's dictionary (that treasury of my youth), and forget whether it was a cold dagger *au naturel*, or a dish of hot coals *à la Romaine* of which they partook; but, whatever it was, she smiled, and delightedly received it, happy to share the beloved one's fortune.

Yes: Philip would come home to his Little Sister sometimes: sometimes of a Saturday, and they would go to church on Sunday, as he used to do when he was a boy at school. "But then, you know," says Phil, "law is law; study is study. I must devote my whole energies to my work—get up very early."

"Don't tire your eyes, my dear," interposes Mr. Philip's soft, judicious friend.

"There must be no trifling with work," says Philip, with awful gravity. "There's Benton the Judge: Benton and Burbage, you know."

"Oh, Benton and Burbage!" whispers the Little Sister, not a little bewildered.

"How do you suppose he became a judge before forty?"

"Before forty who? law, bless me!"

"Before *he* was forty, Mrs. Carry. When he came to work, he had his own way to make: just like me. He had a small allowance from his father: that's not like me. He took chambers in the Temple. He went to a pleader's office. He read fourteen, fifteen hours every day. He dined on a cup of tea and a mutton-chop."

"La, bless me, child! I wouldn't have you to do that, not to be Lord Chamberlain—Chancellor what's his name? Destroy your youth with reading, and your eyes, and go without your dinner? You're not used to that sort of thing, dear; and it would kill you!"

Philip smoothed his fair hair off his ample forehead, and nodded his head, smiling sweetly. I think his inward monitor hinted to him that there was not much danger of his killing himself by over work. "To succeed at the law, as in all other professions," he continued, with much gravity, "requires the greatest perseverance, and industry, and talent ; and then, perhaps, you don't succeed. Many have failed who have had all these qualities."

"But they haven't talents like my Philip, I know they haven't. And I had to stand up in a court once, and was cross-examined by a vulgar man before a horrid deaf old judge ; and I'm sure if your lawyers are like them I don't wish you to succeed at all. And now, look ! there's a nice loin of pork coming up. Pa loves roast pork ; and you must come and have some with us ; and every day and all days, my dear, I should like to see you seated there." And the Little Sister frisked about here, and bustled there, and brought a cunning bottle of wine from some corner, and made the boy welcome. So that, you see, far from starving, he actually had two dinners on that first day of his ruin.

Caroline consented to a compromise regarding the money, on Philip's solemn vow and promise that she should be his banker whenever necessity called. She rather desired his poverty for the sake of its precious reward. She hid away a little bag of gold for her darling's use whenever he should need it. I dare say she pinched and had shabby dinners at home, so as to save yet more, and so caused the Captain to grumble. Why, for that boy's sake, I believe she would have been capable of shaving her lodgers' legs of mutton, and levying a tax on their tea-caddies and baker's stuff. If you don't like unprincipled attachments of this sort, and only desire that your womankind should love you for yourself, and according to your deserts, I am your very humble servant. Hereditary bondswomen ! you know, that were you free, and did you strike the blow, my dears, you were unhappy for your pain, and eagerly would claim your bonds again. What poet has uttered that sentiment ? It is perfectly true, and I know will receive the cordial approbation of the dear ladies.

Philip has decreed in his own mind that he will go and live in those chambers in the Temple where we have met him. Van John, the sporting gentleman, had determined for special reasons to withdraw from law and sport in this country, and Mr. Firmin took possession of his vacant sleeping-chamber. To furnish a bachelor's bedroom need not be a matter of much cost ; but Mr. Philip was too good-natured a fellow to haggle about the valuation of Van John's bedsteads and chests of drawers, and generously took them at twice their value. He and Mr. Cassidy now divided the rooms in equal reign. Ah, happy rooms, bright rooms, rooms near the sky, to remember you is to be young again! for I would have you to know that when Philip went to take possession of his share of the fourth floor in the Temple, his biographer was still comparatively juvenile, and in one or two very old-fashioned families was called "young Pendennis."

So Philip Firmin dwelt in a garret; and the fourth part of a laundress and the half of a boy now formed the domestic establishment of him who had been attended by housekeepers, butlers, and obsequious liveried menials. To be freed from that ceremonial and etiquette of plush and worsted lace was an immense relief to Firmin. His pipe need not lurk in crypts or back closets now: its fragrance breathed over the whole chambers, and rose up to the sky, their near neighbor.

The first month or two after being ruined, Philip vowed, was an uncommonly pleasant time. He had still plenty of money in his pocket; and the sense that, perhaps, it was imprudent to take a cab or drink a bottle of wine, added a zest to those enjoyments which they by no means possessed when they were easy and of daily occurrence. I am not certain that a dinner of beef and porter did not amuse our young man almost as well as banquets much more costly to which he had been accustomed. He laughed at the pretensions of his boyish days, when he and other solemn young epicures used to sit down to elaborate tavern banquets, and pretend to criticize vintages, and sauces, and turtle. As yet there was not only content with his dinner, but plenty therewith; and I do not wish to alarm you by supposing that Philip will ever have to encounter any dreadful extremities of poverty or hunger in the course of his history. The wine in the jug was very low at times, but it never was quite empty. This lamb was shorn, but the wind was tempered to him.

So Philip took possession of his rooms in the Temple, and began actually to reside there just as the long vacation commenced, which he intended to devote to a course of serious study of the law and private preparation, before he should venture on the great business of circuit and the bar. Nothing is more necessary for desk-men than exercise, so Philip took a good deal; especially on the water, where he pulled a famous oar. Nothing is more natural after exercise than refreshment; and Mr. Firmin, now he was too poor for claret, showed a great capacity for beer. After beer and bodily labor, rest, of course, is necessary; and Firmin slept nine hours, and looked as rosy as a girl in her first season. Then such a man, with such a frame and health, must have a good appetite for breakfast. And then every man who wishes to succeed at the bar, in the senate, on the bench, in the House of Peers, on the Woolsack, must know the quotidian history of his country; so, of course, Philip read the newspaper. Thus, you see, his hours of study were perforce curtailed by the necessary duties which distracted him from his labors.

It has been said that Mr. Firmin's companion in chambers, Mr. Cassidy, was a native of the neighboring kingdom of Ireland, and engaged in literary pursuits in this country. A merry, shrewd, silent, observant little man, he, unlike some of his compatriots, always knew how to make both ends meet; feared no man alive in the character of a dun; and out of small earnings managed to transmit no small comforts and subsidies to old parents living somewhere in Munster. Of Cassidy's friends was Finucane, now editor of the *Pall Mall Gazette*; he married the widow of the late eccentric and gifted Captain Shandon, and Cass himself was the fashionable correspondent of the *Gazette*, chronicling the marriages, deaths, births, dinner-parties of the nobility. These Irish gentlemen knew other Irish gentlemen, connected with other newspapers, who formed a little literary society. They assembled at each other's rooms, and at haunts where social pleasure was to be purchased at no dear rate. Philip Firmin was known to many of them before his misfortunes occurred, and when there was gold in plenty in his pocket, and never-failing applause for his songs.

When Pendennis and his friends wrote in this newspaper, it was impertinent enough, and many men must have heard the writers laugh at the airs which they occasionally thought proper to assume. The tone which they took amused, annoyed, tickled, was popular. It was continued, and, of course, caricatured by their successors. They worked for very moderate fees: but paid themselves by impertinence, and the satisfaction of assailing their betters. Three or four persons were reserved from their abuse; but somebody was sure every week to be tied up at their post, and the public made sport of the victim's contortions. The writers were obscure barristers, ushers, and college men, but they had omniscience at their pens' end, and were ready to lay down the law on any given subject—to teach any man his business, were it a bishop in his pulpit, a Minister in his place in the House, a captain on his quarter-deck, a tailor on his shop-board, or a jockey in his saddle.

Since those early days of the *Pall Mall Gazette*, when

old Shandon wielded his truculent tomahawk, and Messrs.
W--rr--ngt--n and P--nd--nn--s followed him in the war path, the
Gazette had passed through several hands ; and the victims
who were immolated by the editors of to-day were very likely
the objects of the best puffery of the last dynasty. To be
flogged in what was your own schoolroom—that, surely, is a
queer sensation ; and when my Report was published on the
decay of the sealing-wax trade in the three kingdoms (owing to
the prevalence of gummed envelopes,—as you may see in that
masterly document) I was horsed up and smartly whipped in
the *Gazette* by some of the rods which had come out of pickle
since my time. Was not good Dr. Guillotin executed by his
own neat invention ? I don't know who was the Monsieur
Sanson who operated on me ; but have always had my idea
that Digges, of Corpus, was the man to whom my flagellation
was entrusted. His father keeps a ladies' school at Hackney ;
but there is an air of fashion in everything which Digges writes,
and a chivalrous conservatism which makes me pretty certain
that D. was my scarifier. All this, however, is naught. Let us
turn away from the author's private griefs and egotisms to
those of the hero of the story.

Does any one remember the appearance some twenty years
ago of a little book called " Trumpet Calls "—a book of songs
and poetry, dedicated to his brother officers by Cornet Canterton ? His trumpet was very tolerably melodious, and the cornet played some small airs on it with some little grace and
skill. But this poor Canterton belonged to the Life-Guards
Green, and Philip Firmin would have liked to have the lives
of one or two troops at least of that corps. Entering into Mr.
Cassidy's room, Philip found the little volume. He set to
work to exterminate Canterton. He rode him down, trampled
over his face and carcase, knocked the "Trumpet Calls" and
all the teeth down the trumpeter's throat. Never was such a
smashing article as he wrote. And Mugford, Mr. Cassidy's
chief and owner, who likes always to have at least one man
served up and hashed small in the *Pall Mall Gazette,* happened
at this very juncture to have no other victim ready in his larder. Philip's review appeared there in print. He rushed off
with immense glee to Westminster, to show us his performance.
Nothing must content him but to give a dinner at Greenwich
on his success. Oh, Philip ! We wished that this had not
been his first fee ; and that sober law had given it to him, and
not the graceless and fickle muse with whom he had been
flirting. For, truth to say, certain wise old heads which wag-

ged over his performance could see but little merit in it. His style was coarse, his wit clumsy and savage. Never mind characterizing either now. He has seen the error of his ways, and divorced with the muse whom he never ought to have wooed.

The shrewd Cassidy not only could not write himself, but knew he could not—or, at least, pen more than a plain paragraph, or a brief sentence to the point, but said he would carry this paper to his chief. "His Excellency" was the nickname by which this chief was called by his familiars. Mugford— Frederick Mugford was his real name—and putting out of sight that little defect in his character, that he committed a systematic literary murder once a week, a more worthy good-natured little murderer did not live. He came of the old school of the press. Like French marshals, he had risen from the ranks, and retained some of the manners and oddities of the private soldier. A new race of writers had grown up since he enlisted as a printer's boy—men of the world, with the manners of other gentlemen. Mugford never professed the least gentility. He knew that his young men laughed at his peculiarities, and did not care a fig for their scorn. As the knife with which he conveyed his victuals to his mouth went down his throat at the plenteous banquets which he gave, he saw his young friends wince and wonder, and rather relish their surprise. Those lips never cared in the least about placing his *h's* in right places. They used bad language with great freedom—(to hear him bullying a printing office was a wonder of eloquence)— but they betrayed no secrets, and the words which they uttered you might trust. He had belonged to two or three parties, and had respected them all. When he went to the Under-Secretary's office he was never kept waiting; and once or twice Mrs. Mugford, who governed him, ordered him to attend the Saturday reception of the Ministers' ladies, where he might be seen, with dirty hands, it is true, but a richly embroidered waistcoat and fancy satin tie. His heart, however, was not in these entertainments. I have heard him say that he only came because Mrs. M. would have it ; and he frankly owned that he "would rather 'ave a pipe, and a drop of something 'ot, than all your ices and rubbish."

Mugford had a curious knowledge of what was going on in the world, and of the affairs of countless people. When Cass brought Philip's article to his Excellency, and mentioned the author's name, Mugford showed himself to be perfectly familiar with the histories of Philip and his father. "The old chap has nobbled the young fellow's money, almost every shilling of it, I hear. Knew he never would carry on. His discounts would have killed any man. Seen his paper about this ten year. Young one is a gentleman—passionate fellow, hawhaw fellow, but kind to the poor. Father never was a gentleman, with all his fine airs and fine waistcoats. I don't set up in that line myself, Cass, but I tell you I know 'em when I see 'em."

Philip had friends and private patrons whose influence was great with the Mugford family, and of whom he little knew. Every year Mrs. M. was in the habit of contributing a Mugford to the world. She was one of Mrs. Brandon's most regular clients ; and year after year, almost from his first arrival in London, Ridley, the painter, had been engaged as portrait-painter to this worthy family. Philip and his illness ; Philip and his horses, splendors, and entertainments ; Philip and his lamentable downfall and ruin, had formed the subject of many an interesting talk between Mrs. Mugford and her friend the Little Sister ; and as we know Caroline's infatuation about the young fellow, we may suppose that his good qualities lost nothing in the description. When that article in the *Pall Mall Gazette* appeared, Nurse Brandon took the omnibus to Haverstock Hill, where, as you know, Mugford had his villa ;—arrived at Mrs. Mugford's, *Gazette* in hand, and had a long and delightful conversation with that lady. Mrs. Brandon bought I don't know how many copies of that *Pall Mall Gazette*. She now asked for it repeatedly in her walks at sundry ginger-beer shops, and of all sorts of news-vendors. I have heard that when the Mugfords first purchased the *Gazette*, Mrs. M. used to drop bills from her pony-chaise, and distribute placards setting forth the excellence of the journal. "We keep our carriage, but we ain't above our business, Brandon," that good lady would say. And the business prospered under the management of these worthy folks ; and the pony-chaise unfolded into a noble barouche ; and the pony increased and multiplied, and became a pair of horses ; and there was not a richer piece of gold-lace round any coachman's hat in London than now decorated John, who had grown with the growth of his master's fortunes, and drove the chariot in which his worthy employers rode on the way to Hampstead, honor, and prosperity.

"All this pitching into the poet is very well, you know, Cassidy," says Mugford to his subordinate. "It's like shooting a butterfly with a blunderbuss ; but if Firmin likes that kind of sport, I don't mind. There won't be any difficulty about taking his copy at our place. The duchess knows another old woman who is a friend of his " (" the duchess " was the title which Mr. Mugford was in the playful habit of conferring upon his wife). " It's my belief young F. had better stick to the law, and leave the writing rubbish alone. But he knows his own affairs best, and, mind you, the duchess is determined we shall give him a helping hand."

Once, in the days of his prosperity, and in J. J.'s company, Philip had visited Mrs. Mugford and her family—a circumstance which the gentleman had almost forgotten. The painter and his friend were taking a Sunday walk, and came upon Mugford's pretty cottage and garden, and were hospitably entertained there by the owners of the place. It has disappeared, and the old garden has long since been covered by terraces and villas, and Mugford, and Mrs. M., good souls, where are they? But the lady thought she had never seen such a fine-looking young fellow as Philip; cast about in her mind which of her little female Mugfords should marry him; and insisted upon offering her guest champagne. Poor Phil! So, you see, whilst, perhaps, he was rather pluming himself upon his literary talent, and imagining that he was a clever fellow, he was only the object of a job on the part of two or three good folks, who knew his history, and compassionated his misfortunes.

Mugford recalled himself to Philip's recollection, when they met after the appearance of Mr. Phil's first performance in the *Gazette*. If he still took a sundry walk, Hampstead way, Mr. M. requested him to remember that there was a slice of beef and a glass of wine at the old shop. Philip remembered it well enough now : the ugly room, the ugly family, the kind worthy people. Ere long he learned what had been Mrs. Brandon's connection with them, and the young man's heart was softened and grateful as he thought how this kind, gentle creature had been able to befriend him. She, we may be sure, was not a little proud of her protégé. I believe she grew to fancy that the whole newspaper was written by Philip. She made her fond parent read it aloud as she worked. Mr. Ridley, senior, pronounced it was remarkably fine, really now ; without, I think, entirely comprehending the meaning of the sentiments which Mr. Gann gave forth in his rich loud voice, and often dropping asleep in his chair during this sermon.

In the autumn, Mr. Firmin's friends, Mr. and Mrs. Pendennis, selected the romantic seaport town of Boulogne for their holiday residence ; and having roomy quarters in the old town, we gave Mr. Philip an invitation to pay us a visit whenever he could tear himself away from literature and law. He came in high spirits. He amused us by imitations and descriptions of his new proprietor and master, Mr. Mugford—his blunders, his bad language, his good heart. One day, Mugford expected a celebrated literary character to dinner, and Philip and Cassidy were invited to meet him. The great man was ill, and was unable to come. "Don't dish up the side-dishes," called out Mugford to his cook, in the hearing of his other guests. "Mr. Lyon ain't a coming." They dined quite sufficiently without the side-dishes, and were perfectly cheerful in the absence of the lion. Mugford patronized his young men with amusing good-nature. "Firmin, cut the goose for the duchess, will you? Cass can't say Bo! to one, he can't. Ridley, a little of the stuffing. It'll make your hair curl." And Philip was going to imitate a frightful act with the cold steel (with which I have said Philip's master used to convey food to his mouth), but our dear innocent third daughter uttered a shriek of terror, which caused him to drop the dreadful weapon. Our darling little Florence is a nervous child, and the sight of an edged tool causes her anguish, ever since our darling little Tom nearly cut his thumb off with his father's razor.

Our main amusement in this delightful place was to look at the sea-sick landing from the steamers; and one day, as we witnessed this phenomenon, Philip sprang to the ropes which divided us from the arriving passengers, and with a cry of "How do you do, General?" greeted a yellow-faced gentleman, who started back, and, to my thinking, seemed but ill inclined to reciprocate Philip's friendly greeting. The General was fluttered, no doubt, by the bustle and interruptions incidental to the landing. A pallid lady, the partner of his existence probably, was calling out, "Noof et doo domestiques, Doo!" to the sentries who kept the line, and who seemed little interested by this family news. A governess, a tall young lady, and several more-male and female children, followed the pale lady, who, as I thought, looked strangely frightened when the gentleman addressed as General communicated to her Philip's name. "Is that him?" said the lady in questionable grammar; and the tall young lady turned a pair of large eyes upon the individual designated as "him," and showed a pair of dank ringlets, out of which the envious sea-nymphs had shaken all the curl.

The general turned out to be General Baynes; the pale lady was Mrs. General B.; the tall young lady was Miss Charlotte Baynes, the General's eldest child; and the other six, forming nine, or "noof," in all, as Mrs. General B. said, were the other members of the Baynes family. And here I may as well say why the General looked alarmed on seeing Philip, and why the General's lady frowned at him. In action, one of the bravest of men, in common life General Baynes was timorous and weak. Specially he was afraid of Mrs. General Baynes, who ruled him with a vigorous authority. As Philip's trustee, he had allowed Philip's father to make away with the boy's money. He learned with a ghastly terror that he was answerable for his own remissness and want of care. For a long while he did not dare to tell his commander-in-chief of this dreadful penalty which was hanging over him. When at last he ventured upon this confession, I do not envy him the scene which must have ensued between him and his commanding officer. The morning after the fatal confession, when the children assembled for breakfast and prayers, Mrs. Baynes gave their young ones their porridge : she and Charlotte poured out the tea and coffee for the elders, and then addressing her eldest son Ochterlony, she said, " Ocky, my boy, the General has announced a charming piece of news this morning."

" Bought that pony, sir ? " says Ocky.

" Oh, what jolly fun ! " says Moira, the second son.

" Dear, dear papa ! what's the matter, and why do you look so ? " cries Charlotte, looking behind her father's paper.

That guilty man would fain have made a shroud of his *Morning Herald*. He would have flung the sheet over his whole body, and lain hidden there from all eyes.

" The fun, my dears, is that your father is ruined : that's the fun. Eat your porridge now, little ones. Charlotte, pop a bit of butter in Carrick's porridge ; for you mayn't have any to-morrow."

" Oh, gammon," cries Moira.

" You'll soon see whether it is gammon or not, sir, when you'll be starving, sir. Your father has ruined us—and a very pleasant morning's work, I am sure."

And she calmly rubs the nose of her youngest child who is near her, and too young, and innocent, and careless, perhaps, of the world's censure as yet to keep in a strict cleanliness her own dear little snub nose and dappled cheeks.

" We are only ruined, and shall be starving soon, my dears, and if the General has bought a pony—as I dare say he has ; he is quite capable of buying a pony when we are starving— the best thing we can do is to eat the pony. M'Grigor, don't laugh. Starvation is no laughing matter. When we were at Dumdum, in '36, we ate some colt. Don't you remember Jubber's colt—Jubber of the Horse Artillery, General ? Never tasted anything more tender in all my life. Charlotte, take Jany's hands out of the marmalade! We are all ruined, my dears, as sure as our name is Baynes." Thus did the mother of the family prattle on in the midst of her little ones, and announce to them the dreadful news of impending starvation. "General Baynes, by his carelessness, had allowed Dr. Firmin to make away with the money over which the General had been set as sentinel. Philip might recover from the trustee, and no doubt would. Perhaps he would not press his claim? My dear, what can you expect from the son of such a father? Depend on it, Charlotte, no good fruit can come from a stock like that. The son is a bad one, the father is a bad one, and your father, poor dear soul, is not fit to be trusted to walk the street without some one to keep him from tumbling. Why did I allow him to go to town without me? We were quartered at Colchester then : and I could not move on account of your brother M'Grigor. 'Baynes,' I said to your father, 'as sure as I let you go away to town without me, you will come to mischief.' And go he did, and come to mischief he did. And through his folly I and my poor children must go and beg our bread in the streets—I and my seven poor, robbed, penniless little ones. Oh, it's cruel, cruel ! "

Indeed, one cannot fancy a more dismal prospect for this worthy mother and wife than to see her children without provision at the commencement of their lives and her luckless husband robbed of his life's earnings, and ruined just when he was too old to work.

What was to become of them ? Now poor Charlotte thought, with pangs of a keen remorse, how idle she had been, and how she had snubbed her governesses, and how little she knew, and how badly she played the piano. Oh, neglected opportunities! Oh, remorse, now the time was past and irrecoverable! Does any young lady read this who, perchance, ought to be doing her lessons ? My dear, lay down the story-book at once. Go up your schoolroom, and practise your piano for two hours this moment ; so that you may be prepared to support your family, should ruin in any case fall upon *you*. A great girl of sixteen, I pity Charlotte Baynes's feelings of anguish. She can't write a very good hand ; she can scarcely answer any question to speak of in any educational books ; her pianoforte playing is very very so-so indeed. If she is to go out and get a living for the family, how, in the name of goodness, is she to set about it ? What are they to do with the boys, and the money that has been put away for Ochterlony when he goes to college, and for Moira's commission? "Why, we can't afford to keep them at Dr. Pybus's, where they were doing so well; and they were ever so much better and more gentlemanlike than Colonel Chandler's boys; and to lose the army will break Moira's heart, it will. And the little ones, my little blue-eyed Carrick, and my darling Jany, and my Mary, that I nursed almost miraculously out of her scarlet fever. God help them! God help us all!" thinks the poor mother. No wonder that her nights are wakeful, and her heart in a tumult of alarm at the idea of the impending danger.

And the father of the family?—the stout old General whose battles and campaigns are over, who has come home to rest his war-worn limbs, and make his peace with heaven ere it calls him away—what must be his feelings when he thinks that he has been entrapped by a villain into committing an imprudence which makes his children penniless and himself dishonored and a beggar? When he found what Dr. Firmin had done, and how he had been cheated, he went away, aghast, to his lawyer, who could give him no help. Philip's mother's trustee was answerable to Philip for his property. It had been stolen through Baynes's own carelessness, and the law bound him to replace it. General Baynes's man of business could not help him out of his perplexity at all; and I hope my worthy reader is not going to be too angry with the General for what he did. *You* never would, my dear sir, I know. No power on earth would induce *you* to depart one inch from the path of rectitude; or, having done an act of imprudence, to shrink from bearing the consequence. The long and short of the matter is, that poor Baynes and his wife, after holding agitated, stealthy councils together—after believing that every strange face they saw was a bailiff's coming to arrest them on Philip's account—after horrible days of remorse, misery, guilt—I say the long and the short of the matter was that these poor people determined to run away. They would go and hide themselves anywhere—in an impenetrable pine forest in Norway—up an inaccessible mountain in Switzerland. They would change their names; dye their mustaches and honest old white hair; fly with their little ones away, away, away, out of the reach of law and Philip; and the first flight lands them on Boulogne Pier, and there is Mr. Philip holding out his hand and actually eyeing them as they get out of the steamer! Eyeing them? It is the eye of heaven that is on those criminals. Holding out his hand to them? It is the hand of fate that is on their wretched shoulders. No wonder they shuddered and turned pale. That which I took for sea-sickness, I am sorry to say was a guilty conscience : and where is the steward, my dear friends, who can relieve us of that?

As this party came staggering out of the Custom-house, poor Baynes still found Philip's hand stretched out to catch hold of him, and saluted him with a ghastly cordiality. "These are your children, General, and this is Mrs. Baynes?" says Philip, smiling, and taking off his hat.

"Oh, yes! I'm Mrs. General Baynes!" says the poor woman ; "and these are the children—yes, yes. Charlotte, this is Mr. Firmin, of whom you have heard us speak; and these are my boys, Moira and Ochterlony."

"I have had the honor of meeting General Baynes at Old Parr Street. Don't you remember, sir?" says Mr. Pendennis, with great affability to the General.

"What, *another* who knows me?" I dare say the poor wretch thinks ; and glances of a dreadful meaning pass between the guilty wife and the guilty husband.

"You are going to stay at any hotel?"

"'Hôtel des Bains!'" "'Hôtel du Nord!'" "'Hôtel d'Angleterre!'" here cry twenty commissioners in a breath.

"Hotel? Oh, yes! That is, we have not made up our minds whether we shall go on to-night or whether we shall stay," say those guilty ones, looking at one another, and then down to the ground ; on which one of the children, with a roar, says—

"Oh, ma, what a story! You said you'd stay to-night ; and I was so sick in the beastly boat and I *won't* travel any more!" And tears choke his artless utterance. "And you said Bang to the man who took your keys, you know you did," resumes the innocent, as soon as he can gasp a further remark.

"Who told *you* to speak?" cried mamma, giving the boy a shake.

"This is the way to the 'Hôtel des Bains,'" says Philip, making Miss Baynes another of his best bows. And Miss Baynes makes a curtsey, and her eyes look up at the handsome young man—large brown honest eyes in a comely round face, on each side of which depend two straight wisps of brown hair that were ringlets when they left Folkestone a few hours since.

"Oh, I say, look at those women with the short petticoats! and wooden shoes, by George! Oh! it's jolly, ain't it?" cries one young gentleman.

"By George, there's a man with earrings on! There is, Ocky, upon my word!" calls out another. And the elder boy, turning round to his father, points to some soldiers. " Did you ever see such little beggars ? " he says, tossing his head up. " They wouldn't take such fellows into our line."

" I am not at all tired, thank you," says Charlotte. " I am accustomed to carry him." I forgot to say that the young lady had one of the children asleep on her shoulder ; and another was toddling at her side, holding by his sister's dress, and admiring Mr. Firmin's whiskers, that flamed and curled very luminously and gloriously, like to the rays of the setting sun.

" I am very glad we met, sir," says Philip, in the most friendly manner, taking leave of the General at the gate of his hotel. " I hope you won't go away to-morrow, and that I may come and pay my respects to Mrs. Baynes." Again he salutes that lady with a *coup de chapeau.* Again he bows to Miss Baynes. She makes a pretty curtsey enough, considering that she has a baby asleep on her shoulder. And they enter the hotel, the excellent Marie marshalling them to fitting apartments, where some of them, I have no doubt, will sleep very soundly. How much more comfortably might poor Baynes and his wife have slept had they known what were Philip's feelings regarding them !

We both admired Charlotte, the tall girl who carried her little brother, and around whom the others clung. And we spoke loudly in Miss Charlotte's praises to Mrs. Pendennis, when we joined that lady at dinner. In the praise of Mrs. Baynes we had not a great deal to say, further than that she seemed to take command of the whole expedition, including the general officer, her husband.

Though Marie's beds at the " Hôtel des Bains " are as comfortable as any beds in Europe, you see that admirable chambermaid cannot lay out a clean, easy conscience upon the clean, fragrant pillow-case ; and General and Mrs. Baynes owned, in after days, that one of the most dreadful nights they ever passed was that of their first landing in France. What refugee from his country can fly from himself ? Railways were not as yet in that part of France. The General was too poor to fly with a couple of private carriages, which he must have had for his family of "noof," his governess, and two servants. Encumbered with such a train, his enemy would speedily have pursued and overtaken him. It is a fact that immediately after landing at his hotel, he and his commanding officer went off to see when they could get places for—never mind the name of the place where they really thought of taking refuge. They never told, but Mrs. General Baynes had a sister, Mrs. Major

MacWhirter (married to MacW. of the Bengal Cavalry), and the sisters loved each other very affectionately, especially by letter, for it must be owned that they quarrelled frightfully when together ; and Mrs. MacWhirter never could bear that her younger sister should be taken out to dinner before her, because she was married to a superior officer. Well, their little differences were forgotten when the two ladies were apart. The sisters wrote to each other prodigious long letters, in which household affairs, the children's puerile diseases, the relative prices of veal, eggs, chickens, the rent of lodging and houses in various places, were fully discussed. And as Mrs. Baynes showed a surprising knowledge of Tours, the markets, rents, clergymen, society there, and as Major and Mrs. Mac. were staying there, I have little doubt, for my part, from this and another not unimportant circumstance, that it was to that fair city our fugitives were wending their way, when events occurred which must now be narrated, and which caused General Baynes at the head of his domestic regiment to do what the King of France with twenty thousand men is said to have done in old times.

Philip was greatly interested about the family. The truth is, we were all very much bored at Boulogne. We read the feeblest London papers at the reading-room with frantic assiduity. We saw all the boats come in : and the day was lost when we missed the Folkestone boat or the London boat. We consumed much time and absinthe at cafés ; and tramped leagues upon that old pier every day. Well, Philip was at the " Hôtel des Bains " at a very early hour next morning, and there he saw the General, with a woe-worn face, leaning on his stick, and looking at his luggage, as it lay piled in the porte-cochère of the hotel. There they lay, thirty-seven packages in all, including washing-tubs, and a child's India sleeping-cot ; and all these packages were ticketed M. LE GENERAL BAYNES, OFFICIER ANGLAIS, TOURS, TOURAINE, FRANCE. I say, putting two and two together ; calling to mind Mrs. General's singular knowledge of Tours and familiarity with the place and its prices ; remembering that her sister Emily—Mrs. Major Mac-Whirter, in fact—was there ; and seeing thirty-seven trunks, bags, and portmanteaus, all directed " M. le Général Baynes, Officier Anglais, Tours, Touraine," am I wrong in supposing that Tours was the General's destination ? On the other hand, we have the old officer's declaration to Philip that he did not know where he was going. Oh, you sly old man ! Oh, you gray old fox, beginning to double and to turn at sixty-seven

years of age! Well? The General was in retreat, and he did
not wish the enemy to know upon what lines he was retreating.
What is the harm of that, pray? Besides, he was under the
orders of his commanding officer, and when Mrs. General gave
her orders, I should have liked to see any officer of hers
disobey.

"What a pyramid of portmanteaus! You are not thinking
of moving to-day, General?" says Philip.

"It is Sunday, sir," says the General; which you will perceive was not answering the question; but, in truth, except for
a very great emergency, the good General would not travel on
that day.

"I hope the ladies slept well after their windy voyage."

"Thank you. My wife is an old sailor, and has made two
voyages out and home to India." Here, you understand, the
old man is again eluding his interlocutor's artless queries.

"I should like to have some talk with you, sir, when you
are free," continues Philip, not having leisure as yet to be
surprised at the other's demeanor.

"There are other days beside Sunday for talk on business,"
says that piteous sly-boots of an old officer. Ah, conscience!
conscience! Twenty-four Sikhs, sword in hand, two dozen
Pindarries, Mahrattas, Ghoorkas, what you please—that old
man felt that he would rather have met them than Philip's
unsuspecting blue eyes. These, however, now lighted up with
rather an angry, "Well, sir, as you don't talk business on Sunday, may I call on you to-morrow morning."

And what advantage had the poor old fellow got by all this
doubling and hesitating and artfulness?—a respite until to-
morrow morning! Another night of horrible wakefulness and
hopeless guilt, and Philip waiting ready the next morning with
his little bill, and, "Please pay me the thirty thousand which
my father spent and you owe me. Please turn out into the
streets with your wife and family, and beg and starve. Have
the goodness to hand me out your last rupee. Be kind enough
to sell your children's clothes and your wife's jewels, and hand
over the proceeds to me. I'll call to-morrow. Bye, bye."

Here there came tripping over the marble pavement of the
hall of the hotel a tall young lady in a brown silk dress and
rich curling ringlets falling upon her fair young neck—beautiful
brown curling ringlets, *vous comprenez*, not wisps of moistened
hair, and a broad clear forehead, and two honest eyes shining
below it, and cheeks not pale as they were yesterday; and lips
redder still; and she says, "Papa, papa, won't you come to

breakfast ? The tea is——" What the precise state of the tea is I don't know—none of us ever shall—for here she says, " Oh, Mr. Firmin ! " and makes a curtsey.

To which remark Philip replied, " Miss Baynes, I hope you are very well this morning and not the worse for yesterday's rough weather.

" I am quite well, thank you," was Miss Baynes's instant reply. The answer was not witty to be sure ; but I don't know that under the circumstances she could have said anything more appropriate. Indeed, never was a pleasanter picture of health and good-humor than the young lady presented ; a difference more pleasant to note than Miss Charlotte's pale face from the steamboat on Saturday, and shining, rosy, happy, and innocent, in the cloudless Sabbath morn.

" A Madame,
" Madame le Major MacWhirter,
" à Tours,
" Touraine,
" France.

" *Tintelleries, Boulogne sur•Mer,*
" *Wednesday, August 24, 18—.*

" DEAREST EMILY,—After suffering *more dreadfully* in the *two hours'* passage from Folkestone to this place than I have in four passages out and home from India, except in that terrible storm off the Cape, in September, 1824, when I certainly did suffer most cruelly on board that horrible troopship, we reached this place last Saturday evening, having a *full determination* to proceed immediately on our route. *Now*, you will perceive that our minds are changed. We found this place pleasant, and the lodgings besides most neat, comfortable, and well found in everything, *more reasonable* than you proposed to get for us at Tours, which I am told also is damp, and might bring on the general's *jungle fever again.* Owing to the hooping-cough having just been in the house, which, praised be mercy, all my dear ones have had it, including dear baby, who is quite well through it, and recommended sea air, we got this house *more reasonable* than prices you mention at Tours. A whole house : little room for two boys ; nursery ; nice little room for Charlotte, and a *den for the General.* I don't know how *ever* we should have brought our party safe all the way to Tours. *Thirty-seven* articles of luggage, and Miss Flixby, who announced herself as perfect French governess, acquired at Paris—perfect, *but perfectly useless.* She can't understand the French people when they speak to her, and goes about the house *in a most bewildering way. I am the interpreter ;* poor Charlotte is much too timid to speak when I am by. I have rubbed up the old French which we learned at Chiswick at Miss Pinkerton's ; and I find *my Hindostanee* of great help : which I use it when we are at a loss for a word, and it answers *extremely well.* We pay for lodgings, the whole house —— francs per month. Butchers' meat and poultry plentiful but dear. A grocer in the Grande Rue sells excellent wine at fifteenpence per bottle ; and groceries pretty much at English prices. Mr. Blowman at the English chapel of the Tintelleries has a fine voice, and appears to be *a most excellent clergyman.* I have heard him only once, however, on Sunday evening, when I was so agitated and *so unhappy in my mind* that I own I took little note of his sermon.

" The cause of that agitation *you know*, having imparted it to you in my letters of July, June, and 24th of May, ult. My poor simple, guileless Baynes, was trustee to Mrs. Dr. Firmin, before she married that most unprincipled man. When we were at home last, and exchanged to the 120th from the 99th, my poor husband was inveigled by the horrid man into signing a paper which put the doctor in possession of *all his wife's property ;* whereas Charles thought he was only signing a power of attorney, enabling him to receive his son's dividends. Dr. F., *after the most atrocious deceit, forgery, and criminality of every kind*, fled the country ; and Hunt and Pegler, our solicitors, informed us that the General was answerable *for the wickedness of this miscreant.* He is *so weak* that he has been *many and many* times on the point of going to young Mr. F. and giving *up everything.*

It was only by my prayers, by my *commands*, that I have been enabled to keep him quiet ; and, indeed, Emily, the effort has *almost killed him*. Brandy repeatedly I was obliged to administer on *the dreadful night* of our arrival here.

"For *the first person* we met on landing was Mr. Philip Firmin, *with a pert friend of his*, Mr. Pendennis, whom I don't at all like, though his wife is an amiable person like Emma Fletcher of the Horse Artillery: not with Emma's *style*, however, but still amiable, and disposed to be most civil. Charlotte has taken a great fancy to her, as she always does to every new person. Well, fancy our state on landing, when a young gentleman calls out, 'How do you do, General?' and turns out to be Mr. Firmin! I thought I should have lost Charles in the night. I have seen him before going into action as calm, and sleep and smile as sweet, as *any babe*. It was all I could do to keep up his courage: and, but for me, but for my prayers, but for *my agonies*, I think he would have jumped out of bed, and gone to Mr. F. *that night*, and said, 'Take everything I have.'

"The young man I own has behaved in *the most honorable way*. He came to see us *before breakfast* on Sunday, when the poor General was so ill that I thought he would have *fainted over his tea*. He was too ill to go to church, where I went alone, with my dear ones, having, as I own, but very small comfort in the sermon: but oh, Emily, fancy, on our return, when I went into our room, I found my General on his knees with his Church service before him, crying, crying like a baby! You know I am hasty in my temper sometimes, and his is *indeed an angel's*—and I said to him, 'Charles Baynes, be a man, and don't cry like a child!' 'Ah,' says he, 'Eliza, do *you* kneel, and thank God too ;' on which I said that I thought I did not require instruction *in my religion* from him or any man, except a clergyman, and many of these are *but poor instructors, as you know*.

"'He has been here,' says Charles ; when I said, 'Who has been here?' 'That noble young fellow,' says my General ; 'that noble, noble Philip Firmin.' Which noble his conduct I own it has been. 'Whilst you were at church he came again—here into this very room, where I was sitting, doubting and despairing, with the Holy Book before my eyes, and no comfort out of it. And he said to me, "General, I want to talk to you about my grandfather's will. You don't suppose that because my father has deceived you and ruined me, I will carry the ruin farther, and visit his wrong upon children and innocent people?" Those were the young man's words,' my General said ; and, 'oh, Eliza!' says he, 'what pangs of remorse I felt when I remembered we had used hard words about him,' which I own we had, for his manners are rough and haughty, and I *have heard things* of him which I do believe now can't be true.

"All Monday my poor man was obliged to keep his bed with a smart attack of his fever. But yesterday he was quite bright *and well again*, and the Pendennis party took Charlotte for a drive, and showed themselves *most polite*. She reminds me of Mrs. Tom Fletcher of the Horse Artillery, but that I think I have mentioned before. My paper is full ; and with our best to MacWhirter and the children, I am always my dearest Emily's affectionate sister,   "ELIZA BAYNES."

CHAPTER XVII.

BREVIS ESSE LABORO.

NEVER, General Baynes afterwards declared, did fever come and go so pleasantly as that attack to which we have seen the Mrs. General advert in her letter to her sister, Mrs. Major MacWhirter. The cold fit was merely a lively, pleasant chatter and rattle of the teeth ; the hot fit an agreeable warmth ; and though the ensuing sleep, with which I believe such aguish attacks are usually concluded, was enlivened by several dreams of death, demons, and torture, how felicitous it was to wake and find that dreadful thought of ruin removed which had always, for the last few months, ever since Dr. Firmin's flight and the knowledge of his own imprudence, pursued the good-natured gentleman! What! this boy might go to college, and that get his commission; and their meals need be embittered by no more dreadful thoughts of the morrow, and their walks no longer were dogged by imaginary bailiffs, and presented a jail in the vista! It was too much bliss; and again and again the old soldier said his thankful prayers, and blessed his bene-factor.

Philip thought no more of his act of kindness, except to be very grateful, and very happy that he had rendered other people so. He could no more have taken the old man's all, and plunged that innocent family into poverty, than he could have stolen the forks off my table. But other folks were disposed to rate his virtue much more highly; and amongst these was my wife, who chose positively to worship this young gentleman, and I believe would have let him smoke in her drawing-room if he had been so minded, and though her genteelest acquaint-ances were in the room. Goodness knows what a noise and what piteous looks are produced if ever the master of the house chooses to indulge in a cigar after dinner; but then, you under-stand, *I* have never declined to claim mine and my children's right because an old gentleman would be inconvenienced: and this is what I tell Mrs. Pen. If I order a coat from my tailor, must I refuse to pay him because a rogue steals it, and ought I to expect to be let off? Women won't see matters of fact in a matter-of-fact point of view, and justice, unless it is tinged with a little romance, gets no respect from them.

So, forsooth, because Philip has performed this certainly most generous, most dashing, most reckless piece of extrava-gance, he is to be held up as a perfect *preux chevalier*. The most riotous dinners are ordered for him. We are to wait until he comes to breakfast, and he is pretty nearly always late. The children are to be sent round to kiss Uncle Philip, as he is now called. The children? I wonder the mother did not jump up and kiss him too. *Elle en était capable.* As for the osculations which took place between Mrs. Pendennis and her new-found young friend, Miss Charlotte Baynes, they were perfectly ridic-ulous; two school children could not have behaved more ab-surdly; and I don't know which seemed to be the younger of these two. There were colloquies, assignations, meetings on the ramparts, on the pier, where know I?—and the servants and little children of the two establishments were perpetually trotting to and fro with letters from dearest Laura to dearest Charlotte, and dearest Charlotte to her dearest Mrs. Pendennis.

Why, my wife absolutely went the length of saying that dearest Charlotte's mother, Mrs. Baynes, was a worthy, clever woman, and a good mother—a woman whose tongue never ceased clacking about the regiment, and all the officers, and all the officers' wives; of whom, by the way, she had very little good to tell.

" A worthy mother, is she, my dear ? " I say. "But, oh, mercy ! Mrs. Baynes would be an awful mother-in-law ! "

I shuddered at the thought of having such a commonplace, hard, ill-bred woman in a state of quasi authority over me.

On this Mrs. Laura must break out in quite a petulant tone—" Oh, how *stale* this kind of thing is, Arthur, from a man *qui veut passer pour un homme d'esprit !* You are always attacking mothers-in-law ! "

"Witness Mrs. Mackenzie, my love — Clive Newcome's mother-in-law. That's a nice creature ; not selfish, not wicked, not——"

" Not nonsense, Arthur ! "

" Mrs. Baynes knew Mrs. Mackenzie in the West Indies, as she knew all the female army. She considers Mrs. Mackenzie was a most elegant, handsome, dashing woman—only a little too fond of the admiration of our sex. There was, I own, a fascination about Captain Goby. Do you remember, my love, that man with the stays and dyed hair, who——"

" Oh, Arthur ! When our girls marry, I suppose you will teach their husbands to abuse, and scorn, and mistrust *their* mother-in-law. Will he, my darlings ? will he, my blessings ? " (This apart to the children, if you please.) " Go ! I have no patience with such talk ! "

" Well, my love, Mrs. Baynes is a most agreeable woman ; and, when I have heard that story about the Highlanders at the Cape of Good Hope a few times more " (I do not tell it here, for it has nothing to do with the present history), " I dare say I shall begin to be amused by it."

" Ah ! here comes Charlotte, I'm glad to say. How pretty she is ! What a color ! What a dear creature ! "

To all which of course I could not say a contradictory word, for a prettier, fresher lass than Miss Baynes, with a sweeter voice, face, laughter, it was difficult to see.

" Why does mamma like Charlotte better than she likes us ? " says our dear and justly indignant eldest girl.

" I could not love her better if I were her *mother-in-law*," says Laura, running to her young friend, casting a glance at me over her shoulder ; and that kissing nonsense begins between the two ladies. To be sure the girl looks uncommonly bright and pretty with her pink cheeks, her bright eyes, her slim form, and that charming white India shawl which her father brought home for her.

To this osculatory party enters presently Mr. Philip Firmin, who has been dawdling about the ramparts ever since breakfast. He says he has been reading law there. He has found a jolly quiet place to read law, has he? And much good may it do him! Why has he not gone back to his law and his reviewing?

"You must—you *must* stay on a little longer. You have only been here five days. Do, Charlotte, ask Philip to stay a little."

All the children sing in a chorus, "Oh, do, Uncle Philip, stay a little longer!" Miss Baynes says, "I hope you will stay, Mr. Firmin," and looks at him.

"Five days has he been here? Five years. Five lives. Five hundred years. What do you mean? In that little time of—let me see, a hundred and twenty hours, and, at least, a half of them for sleep and dinner (for Philip's appetite was very fine)—do you mean that in that little time, his heart, cruelly stabbed by a previous monster in female shape, has healed, got quite well, and actually begun to be wounded again? Have two walks on the pier, as many visits to the Tintelleries (where he hears the story of the Highlanders at the Cape of Good Hope with respectful interest), a word or two about the weather, a look or two, a squeezekin, perhaps, of a little handykin—I say, do you mean that this absurd young idiot, and that little round-faced girl, pretty, certainly, but only just out of the schoolroom —do you mean to say that they have—— Upon my word, Laura, this is too bad. Why, Philip has not a penny piece in the world."

"Yes, he has a hundred pounds, and expects to sell his mare for ninety at least. He has excellent talents. He can easily write three articles a week in the *Pall Mall Gazette*. I am sure no one writes so well, and it is much better done and more amusing than it used to be. That is three hundred a year. Lord Ringwood must be applied to, and must and shall get him something. Don't you know that Captain Baynes stood by Colonel Ringwood's side at Busaco, and that they were the closest friends? And pray how did *we* get on, I should like to know? How did *we* get on, baby?"

"How did we det on?" says the baby.

"Oh, woman! woman!" yells the father of the family.

" Why, Philip Firmin has all the habits of a rich man with the pay of a mechanic. Do you suppose he ever sat in a second-class carriage in his life, or denied himself any pleasure to which he had a mind ? He gave five francs to a beggar-girl yesterday."

" He had always a noble heart," says my wife. " He gave a fortune to a whole family a week ago ; and " (out comes the pocket-handkerchief—oh, of course, the pocket-handkerchief)— " and—' God loves a cheerful giver ! ' "

" He is careless ; he is extravagant ; he is lazy ;—I don't know that he is remarkably clever——"

" Oh, yes ! he is your friend, of course. Now, abuse him— *do*, Arthur ! "

" And, pray, when did you become acquainted with this astounding piece of news ? " I inquire.

" When ? From the very first moment when I saw Char-lotte looking at him, to be sure. The poor child said to me only yesterday, ' Oh, Laura ! he is our preserver ! ' And their preserver he has been, under Heaven."

" Yes. But he has not got a five-pound note ! " I cry.

" Arthur, I am surprised at you. Oh, men are awfully worldly ! Do you suppose Heaven will not send him help at its good time, and be kind to him who has rescued so many from ruin ? Do you suppose the prayers, the blessings of that father, of those little ones, of that dear child will not avail him ? Suppose he has to wait a year, ten years, have they not time, and will not the good day come ? "

Yes. This was actually the talk of a woman of good sense and discernment, when her prejudices and romance were not in the way, and she looked forward to the marriage of those folks some ten years hence, as confidently as if they were both rich, and going to St. George's to-morrow.

As for making a romantic story of it, or spinning out love conversations between Jenny and Jessamy, or describing moonlight raptures and passionate outpourings of two young hearts and so forth—excuse me, *s'il vous plait*. I am a man of the world, and of a certain age. Let the young people fill in this outline, and color it as they please. Let the old folks who read lay down the book a minute, and remember. It is well remembered, isn't it, that time ? Yes, good John Anderson, and Mrs. John. Yes, good Darby and Joan. The lips won't tell now what they did once. To-day is for the happy, and to-morrow for the young, and yesterday, is not that dear and here too ?

I was in the company of an elderly gentleman, not very long since, who was perfectly sober, who is not particularly handsome, or healthy, or wealthy, or witty ; and who, speaking of his past life, volunteered to declare that he would gladly live every minute of it over again. Is a man who can say that a hardened sinner, not aware how miserable he ought to be by rights, and therefore really in a most desperate and deplorable condition ; or is he *fortunatus nimium,* and ought his statue to be put up in the most splendid and crowded thoroughfares of the town ? Would you, who are reading this, for example, like to live *your* life over again ? What has been its chief joy ? What are to-day's pleasures ? Are they so exquisite that you would prolong them for ever ? Would you like to have the roast beef on which you have dined brought back again to the table, and have more beef, and more, and more ? Would you like to hear yesterday's sermon over and over again—eternally voluble ? Would you like to get on the Edinburgh mail, and travel outside for fifty hours as you did in your youth ? You might as well say you would like to go into the flogging-room, and take a turn under the rods : you would like to be thrashed over again by your bully at school : you would like to go to the dentist's, where your dear parents were in the habit of taking you : you would like to be taking hot Epsom salts, with a piece of dry bread to take away the taste : you would like to be jilted by your first love : you would like to be going in to your father to tell him you had contracted debts to the amount of $x + y + z$, whilst you were at the university. As I consider the passionate griefs of childhood, the weariness and sameness of shaving, the agony of corns, and the thousand other ills to which flesh is heir, I cheerfully say it for one, I am not anxious to wear it for ever. No. I do not want to go to school again. I do not want to hear Trotman's sermon over again. Take me out and finish me. Give me the cup of hemlock at once. Here's a health to you, my lads. Don't weep, my Simmias. Be cheerful, my Phædon. Ha ! I feel the co-o-old stealing, stealing upwards. Now it is in my ankles—no more gout in my foot : now my knees are numb. What is—is that poor executioner crying too ? Good-by. Sacrifice a cock to Æscu —to Æscula— * * * Have you ever read the chapter in "Grote's History?" Ah ! When the Sacred Ship returns from Delos, and is telegraphed as entering into port, may we be at peace and ready !

What is this funeral chant, when the pipes should be playing gayly as Love, and Youth, and Spring, and Joy are dancing under the windows? Look you. Men not so wise as Socrates have their demons, who will be heard to whisper in the queerest times and places. Perhaps I shall have to tell of a funeral presently, and shall be outrageously cheerful ; or of an execution, and shall split my sides with laughing. Arrived at my time of life, when I see a penniless young friend falling in love and thinking of course of committing matrimony, what can I do but be melancholy? How is a man to marry who has not enough to keep ever so miniature a brougham— ever so small a house—not enough to keep himself, let alone a wife and family? Gracious powers ! is it not blasphemy to marry without fifteen hundred a year? Poverty, debt, pro-tested bills, duns, crime, fall assuredly on the wretch who has not fifteen—say at once two thousand a year ; for you can't live decently in London for less. And a wife whom you have met a score of times at balls or breakfasts, and with her best dresses and behavior at a country house ;—how do you know how she will turn out ; what her temper is ; what her relations are likely to be? Suppose she has poor relations, or loud coarse brothers who are always dropping in to dinner? What is her mother like? and can you bear to have that woman meddling and domineering over your establishment? Old General Baynes was very well ; a weak, quiet and presentable old man : but Mrs. General Baynes, and that awful Mrs. Major MacWhirter,—and those hobbledehoys of boys in creaking shoes, hectoring about the premises? As a man of the world I saw all these dreadful liabilities impending over the husband of Miss Charlotte Baynes, and could not view them without horror. Gracefully and slightly, but wittily and in my sarcastic way, I thought it my duty to show up the oddities of the Baynes family to Philip. I mimicked the boys, and their clumping blucher-boots. I touched off the dreadful military ladies, very smartly and cleverly as I thought, and as if I never supposed that Philip had any idea of Miss Baynes. To do him justice, he laughed once or twice ; then he grew very red. His sense of humor is very limited ; that even Laura allows. Then he came out with a strong expression, and said it was a confounded shame, and strode off with his cigar. And when I remarked to my wife how susceptible he was in some things, and how little in the matter of joking, she shrugged her shoul-ders and said, " Philip not only understood perfectly well what I said, but would tell it all to Mrs. General and Mrs. Major on the first opportunity." And this was the fact, as Mrs. Baynes took care to tell me *afterwards*. She was aware who was her *enemy*.

She was aware who spoke ill of her, and her blessed darling *behind our backs*. And " do you think it was to see *you* or any one belonging to your *stuck-up house,* sir, that we came to you so often, which we certainly did, day and night, breakfast and supper, and no thanks to you ? No, sir ! ha, ha ! '' I can see her flaunting out of my sitting-room as she speaks, with a strident laugh, and snapping her dingily gloved fingers at the door. Oh, Philip, Philip ! To think that you were such a coward as to go and tell her ! But I pardon him. From my heart I pity and pardon him.

For the step which he is meditating you may be sure that the young man himself does not feel the smallest need of pardon or pity. He is in a state of happiness so crazy that it is useless to reason with him. Not being at all of a poetical turn originally, the wretch is actually perpetrating verse in secret, and my servants found fragments of his manuscript on the dressing-table in his bedroom. *Heart* and *art, sever* and *for ever,* and so on ; what stale rhymes are these ? I do not feel at liberty to give in entire the poem which our maid found in Mr. Philip's room, and brought sniggering to my wife, who only said, " Poor thing ! " The fact is, it was too pitiable. Such maundering rubbish ! such stale rhymes, and such old thoughts ! But then, says Laura, " I dare say all people's love-making is not amusing to their neighbors ; and I know who wrote not very wise love-verses when he was young." No, I won't publish Philip's verses, until some day he shall mortally offend me. I can recall some of my own written under similar circumstances with twinges of shame ; and shall drop a veil of decent friendship over my friend's folly.

Under that veil, meanwhile, the young man is perfectly contented, nay, uproariously happy. All earth and nature smiles round about him. " When Jove meets his Juno, in Homer, sir," says Philip, in his hectoring way, " don't immortal flowers of beauty spring up around them, and rainbows of celestial hues bend over their heads ? Love, sir, flings a halo round the loved one. Where she moves rise roses, hyacinths, and ambrosial odors. Don't talk to me about poverty, sir ! He either fears his fate too much or his desert is small, who dares not put it to the touch and win or lose it all ! Haven't I endured poverty ? Am I not as poor now as a man can be— and what is there in it ? Do I want for anything ? Haven't I got a guinea in my pocket ? Do I owe any man anything ? Isn't there manna in the wilderness for those who have faith to walk in it ? That's where you fail, Pen. By all that is sacred, you have no faith; your heart is cowardly, sir; and if you are to escape, as perhaps you may, I suspect it is by your wife that you will be saved. Laura has a trust in heaven, but Arthur's morals are a genteel atheism. Just reach me that claret— the wine's not bad. I say your morals are a genteel atheism, and I shudder when I think of your condition. Talk to *me* about a brougham being necessary for the comfort of a woman! A broomstick to ride to the moon! And I don't say that a brougham is not a comfort, mind you; but that, when it is a necessity, mark you, heaven will provide it! Why, sir, hang it, look at me! Ain't I suffering in the most abject poverty? I ask you is there a man in London so poor as I am? And since my father's ruin do I want for anything? I want for shelter for a day or two. Good. There's my dear Little Sister ready to give it me. I want for money. Does not that sainted widow's cruse pour its oil out for me? Heaven bless and reward her. Boo!'" (Here, for reasons which need not be named, the orator squeezes his fists into his eyes.) "I want shelter; ain't I in good quarters? I want work; haven't I got work, and did you not get it for me? You should just see, sir, how I polished off that book of travels this morning. I read some of the article to Char——, to Miss ——, to some friends, in fact. I don't mean to say that they are very intellectual people, but your common humdrum average audience is the public to try. Recollect Molière and his housekeeper, you know."

"By the housekeeper, do you mean Mrs. Baynes?" I ask, in my *amontillado* manner. (By the way, who ever heard of *amontillado* in the early days of which I write?) "In manner she would do, and I dare say in accomplishments; but I doubt about her temper."

"You're almost as worldly as the Twysdens, by George, you are! Unless persons are of a certain *monde*, you don't value them. A little adversity would do you good, Pen; and I heartily wish you might get it, except for the dear wife and children. You measure your morality by May Fair standards; and if an angel unawares came to you in pattens and a cotton umbrella, you would turn away from her. *You* would never have found out the Little Sister. A duchess—God bless her! A creature of an imperial generosity, and delicacy, and intrepidity, and the finest sense of humor; but she drops her *h*'s often, and how could you pardon such a crime? Sir, you are my better in wit and a dexterous application of your powers; but I think, sir," says Phil, curling the flaming mustache, "I am your superior in a certain magnanimity; though, by Jove, old fellow, man and boy, you have always been one of the best fellows in the world to P. F.; one of the best fellows, and the most generous, and the most cordial,—that you have: only you *do* rile me when you sing in that confounded May Fair twang."

Here one of the children summoned us to tea—and "Papa was laughing, and uncle Philip was flinging his hands about and pulling his beard off," said the little messenger.

"I shall keep a fine lock of it for you, Nelly, my dear," says uncle Philip. On which the child said, "Oh, no! I know whom you'll give it to, don't I, mamma?" and she goes up to her mamma, and whispers.

Miss Nelly knows? At what age do those little match-makers begin to know, and how soon do they practise the use of their young eyes, their little smiles, wiles, and ogles? This young woman, I believe, coquetted while she was yet a baby in arms, over her nurse's shoulder. Before she could speak, she could be proud of her new vermilion shoes, and would point out the charms of her blue sash. She was jealous in the nursery, and her little heart had beat for years and years before she left off pinafores.

For whom will Philip keep a lock of that red, red gold which curls round his face? Can you guess? Of what color is the hair in that little locket which the gentleman himself occultly wears? A few months ago, I believe, a pale straw-colored wisp of hair occupied that place of honor; now it is a chestnut-brown, as far as I can see, of precisely the same color as that which waves round Charlotte Baynes' pretty face, and tumbles in clusters on her neck, very nearly the color of Mrs. Paynter's this last season. So, you see, we chop and we change: straw gives place to chestnut, and chestnut is succeeded by ebony; and, for our own parts, we defy time; and if you want a lock of my hair, Belinda, take this pair of scissors, and look in that cupboard, in the bandbox marked No. 3, and cut off a thick glossy piece, darling, and wear it, dear, and my blessings go with thee! What is this? Am I sneering because Corydon and Phyllis are wooing and happy? You see I pledged myself not to have any sentimental nonsense. To describe love-making is immoral and immodest; you know it is. To describe it as it really is, or would appear to you and me as lookers-on, would be to describe the most dreary farce, to chronicle the most tautological twaddle. To take a note of sighs, hand-squeezes, looks at the moon, and so forth—does this business become our dignity as historians? Come away from those foolish young people—they don't want us ; and dreary as their farce is, and tautological as their twaddle, you may be sure that it amuses them, and that they are happy enough without us. Happy? Is there any happiness like it, pray? Was it not rapture to watch the messenger, to seize the note, and fee the bearer?—to retire out of sight of all prying eyes, and read :— " Dearest! Mamma's cold is better this morning. The Joneses came to tea, and Julia sang. I did not enjoy it, as my dear was at his *horrid dinner*, where I hope he amused himself. Send me a word by Buttles, who brings this, if only to say you are your Louisa's own, own," &c., &c., &c. That used to be the kind of thing. In such coy lines artless Innocence used to whisper its little vows. So she used to smile ; so she used to warble ; so she used to prattle. Young people, at present engaged in the pretty sport, be assured your middle-aged parents have played the game, and remember the rules of it. Yes, under papa's bow-window of a waiscoat is a heart which took very violent exercise when that waist was slim. Now he sits tranquilly in his tent, and watches the lads going in for their innings. Why, look at grandmamma in her spectacles reading that sermon. In *her* old heart there is a corner as romantic still as when she used to read the " Wild Irish Girl " or the " Scottish Chiefs " in the days of her misshood. And as for your grandfather, my dears, to see him now you would little suppose that that calm, polished, dear old gentleman was once as wild—as wild as Orson. * * * * Under my windows, as I write, there passes an itinerant flower merchant. He has his roses and geraniums on a cart, drawn by a quadruped—a little long-eared quadruped, which lifts up its voice, and sings after its manner. When I was young, donkeys used to bray precisely the same way ; and others will heehaw so, when we are silent and our ears hear no more.

CHAPTER XVIII.

DRUM IST'S SO WOHL MIR IN DER WELT.

OUR new friends lived for a while contentedly enough at Boulogne, where they found comrades and acquaintances gathered together from those many regions which they had visited in the course of their military career. Mrs. Baynes, out of the field, was the commanding officer over the General. She ordered his clothes for him, tied his neckcloth into a neat bow, and, on tea-party nights, pinned his brooch into his shirt-frill. She gave him to understand when he had had enough to eat or drink at dinner, and explained, with great frankness, how this or that dish did not agree with him. If he was disposed to exceed, she would call out, in a loud voice : " Remember, General, what you took this morning ! " Knowing his constitution, as she said, she knew the remedies which were necessary for her husband, and administered them to him with great liberality. Resistance was impossible, as the veteran officer acknowledged. " The boys have fought about the medicine since we came home," he confessed, " but she has me under her thumb, by George. She really is a magnificent physician, now. She has got some invaluable prescriptions, and in India she used to doctor the whole station." She would have taken the present writer's little household under her care, and proposed several remedies for my children, until their alarmed mother was obliged to keep them out of her sight. I am not saying this was an agreeable woman. Her voice was loud and harsh. The anecdotes which she was for ever narrating related to military personages in foreign countries, with whom I was unacquainted, and whose history failed to interest me. She took her wine with much spirit, whilst engaged in this prattle. I have heard talk not less foolish in much finer company, and known people delighted to listen to anecdotes of the duchess and the marchioness who would yawn over the history of Captain Jones's quarrels with his lady, or Mrs. Major Wolfe's monstrous flirtations with young Ensign Kyd. My wife, with the mischievousness of her sex, would mimic the Baynes' conversation very drolly, but always insisted that she was not more really vulgar than many much greater persons.

For all this, Mrs. General Baynes did not hesitate to declare that we were " stuck up " people ; and from the very first setting eyes on us she declared that she viewed us with a constant darkling suspicion. Mrs. P. was a harmless, washed-out creature, with nothing in her. As for that high and mighty Mr. P. and *his* airs, she would be glad to know if the wife of a British general officer who had seen service in *every part of the globe*, and met the *most distinguished* governors, generals, and their ladies, several of whom *were noblemen*—she would be glad to know whether such people were not good enough for, &c., &c. Who has not met with these difficulties in life, and who can escape them ? " Hang it, sir," Phil would say, twirling the red mustache, " I like to be hated by some fellows ;" and it must be owned that Mr. Philip got what he liked. I suppose Mr. Philip's friend and biographer had something of the same feeling. At any rate, in regard of this lady the hypocrisy of politeness was very hard to keep up ; wanting us for reasons of her own, she covered the dagger with which she would have stabbed us : but we knew it was there clenched in her skinny hand in her meagre pocket. She would pay us the most fulsome compliments with anger raging out of her eyes—a little hate-bearing woman, envious, malicious, but loving her cubs, and nursing them, and clutching them in her lean arms with a jealous strain. It was "Good-by, darling ! I shall leave you here with your friends. Oh, how kind you are to her, Mrs. Pendennis ! How can I ever thank you, and Mr. P., I am sure ;" and she looked as if she could poison both of us, as she went away, curtseying and darting dreary parting smiles.

This lady had an intimate friend and companion in arms, Mrs. Colonel Bunch, in fact, of the —th Bengal Cavalry, who was now in Europe with Bunch and their children, who were residing at Paris for the young folks' education. At first, as we have heard, Mrs. Baynes' predilections had been all for Tours, where her sister was living, and lodgings were cheap and food reasonable in proportion. But Bunch happening to pass through Bolougne on his way to his wife at Paris, and meeting his old comrade, gave General Baynes such an account of the cheapness and the pleasures of the French capital as to induce the General to think of bending his steps thither. Mrs. Baynes would not hear of such a plan. She was all for her dear sister and Tours ; but when, in the course of conversation, Colonel Bunch described a ball at the Tuileries, where he and Mrs. B. had been received with the most flattering politeness, by the royal family, it was remarked that Mrs. Baynes' mind underwent a change. When Bunch went on to aver that the balls at Government House at Calcutta were nothing compared to those at the Tuileries or the Prefecture of the Seine ; that the English were invited and respected everywhere ; that the ambassador was most hospitable ; that the clergymen were admirable ; and that at their boarding-house, kept by Madame le Générale Baronne de Smolensk, at the " Petit Château d'Espange," Avenue de Valmy, Champs Elysées, they had balls twice a month, the most comfortable apartments, the most choice society, and every comfort and luxury at so many francs per month, with an allowance for children—I say Mrs. Baynes was very greatly moved. " It is not," she said, " in consequence of the balls at the Ambassador's or the Tuileries, for I am an old woman; and in spite of what you say, Colonel, I can't fancy, after Government House, anything more magnificent in any French palace. It is not for *me*, goodness knows, I speak: but the children should have education, and my Charlotte an entrée into the world; and what you say of the invaluable clergyman, Mr. X——, I have been thinking of it all night; but above all, above all, of the chances of education for my darlings. Nothing should give way to that—nothing!" On this a long and delightful conversation and calculation took place. Bunch produced his bills at the Baroness de Smolensk's. The two gentlemen jotted up accounts, and made calculations all through the evening. It was hard even for Mrs. Baynes to force the figures into such a shape as to make them accord with the General's income; but, driven away by one calculation after another, she returned again and again to the charge, until she overcame the stubborn arithmetical difficulties, and the pounds, shillings, and pence lay prostrate before her. They could save upon this point; they could screw upon that; they *must* must make a sacrifice to educate the children. "Sarah Bunch and her girls go to Court, indeed! Why shouldn't mine go?" she asked. On which her General said, "By George, Eliza, that's the point you are thinking of." On which Eliza said "No," and repeated "No" a score of times, growing more angry as she uttered each denial. And she declared before heaven she did *not* want to go to any Court. Had she not refused to be presented at home, though Mrs. Colonel Flack went, because she did not choose to go to the wicked expense of a train? And it was base of the General, *base* and *mean* of him to say so. And there was a fine scene, as I am given to understand; not that I was present at this family fight: but my informant was Mr. Firmin; and Mr. Firmin had his information from a little person who, about this time, had got to prattle out all the secrets of her young heart to him; who would have jumped off the pier-head with her hand in his if he had said "Come," without his hand if he had said "Go:" a little person whose whole life had been changed—changed for a month past—changed in one minute, that minute when she saw Philip's fiery whiskers and heard his great big voice saluting her father amongst the commissioners on the *quai* before the custom-house.

Tours was, at any rate, a hundred and fifty miles farther off than Paris from——from a city where a young gentleman lived in whom Miss Charlotte Baynes felt an interest; hence, I suppose, arose her delight that her parents had determined upon taking up their residence in the larger and nearer city. Besides, she owned, in the course of her artless confidences to my wife, that, when together, mamma and aunt MacWhirter quarrelled unceasingly; and had once caused the old boys, the Major and the General, to call each other out. She preferred, then, to live away from aunt Mac. She had never had such a friend as Laura, never. She had never been so happy as at Boulogne, never. She should always love everybody in our house, that she should, for ever and ever—and so forth, and so forth. The ladies meet; cling together; osculations are carried round the whole family circle, from our wandering eldest boy, who cries, " I say, hullo! what are you kissing me so about?" to darling baby, crowing and sputtering unconscious in the rapturous young girl's embraces. I tell you, these two women were making fools of themselves, and they were burning with enthusiasm for the "preserver" of the Baynes family, as they called that big fellow yonder, whose biographer I have aspired to be. The lazy rogue lay basking in the glorious warmth and sunshine of early love. He would stretch his big limbs out in our garden; pour out his feelings with endless volubility; call upon *hominum divumque voluptas, alma Venus;* vow that he had never lived or been happy until now; declared that he laughed poverty to scorn and all her ills; and fume against his masters of the *Pall Mall Gazette,* because they declined to insert certain love verses which Mr. Philip now composed almost every day. Poor little Charlotte! And didst thou receive those treasures of song; and wonder over them, not perhaps comprehending them altogether; and lock them up in thy heart's inmost casket as well as in thy little desk; and take them out in quiet hours, and kiss them, and bless heaven for giving thee such jewels? I dare say. I can fancy all this, without seeing it. I can read the little letters in the little desk, without picking lock or breaking seal. Poor little letters! Sometimes they are not spelt right, quite; but I don't know that the style is worse for that. Poor little letters! You are flung to the winds sometimes and forgotten with all your sweet secrets and loving artless confessions; but not always—no, not always. As for Philip, who was the most careless creature alive, and left all his clothes and haberdashery sprawling on his bedroom floor, he had at this time a breast-pocket stuffed out with papers which crackled in the most ridiculous way. He was always looking down at this precious pocket, and putting one of his great hands over it as though he would guard it. The pocket did not contain bank-notes, you may be sure of that. It contained documents stating that mamma's cold is better ; the Joneses came to tea, and Julia sang, &c. Ah, friend, however old you are now, however cold you are now, however tough, I hope you, too, remember how Julia sang, and the Joneses came to tea.

Mr. Philip stayed on week after week, declaring to my wife that she was a perfect angel for keeping him so long. Bunch wrote from his boarding-house more and more enthusiastic reports about the comforts of the establishment. For his sake, Madame la Baronne de Smolensk would make unheard-of sacrifices, in order to accommodate the General and his distinguished party. The balls were going to be perfectly splendid that winter. There were several old Indians living near ; in fact they could form a regular little club. It was agreed that Baynes should go and reconnoitre the ground. He did go. Madame de Smolensk, a most elegant woman, had a magnificent dinner for him—quite splendid, I give you my word, but only what thèy have every day. Soup, of course, my love ; fish, capital wine, and, I should say, some five or six and thirty made dishes. The General was quite enraptured. Bunch had put his boys to a famous school, where they might " whop " the French boys, and learn all the modern languages. The little ones would dine early ; the baroness would take the whole family at an astonishingly cheap rate. In a word, the Baynes' column got the route for Paris shortly before our family-party was crossing the seas to return to London fogs and duty.

You have, no doubt, remarked how, under certain tender circumstances, women will help one another. They help where they ought not to help. When Mr. Darby ought to be separated from Miss Joan, and the best thing that could happen for both would be a *lettre de cachet* to whip off Mons. Darby to the Bastile for five years, and an order from her parents to lock up Mademoiselle Jeanne in a convent, some aunt, some relative, some pitying female friend is sure to be found, who will give the pair a chance of meeting, and turn her head away whilst those unhappy lovers are warbling endless good-byes close up to each other's ears. My wife, I have said, chose to feel this absurd sympathy for the young people about whom we have been just talking. As the days for Charlotte's departure drew near, this wretched, misguiding matron would take the girl out walking into I know not what unfrequented bye-lanes, quiet streets, rampart-nooks, and the like ; and la ! by the most singular coincidence, Mr. Philip's hulking boots would assuredly come tramping after the women's little feet. What will you say, when I tell you, that I myself, the father of the family, the renter of the old-fashioned house, Rue Roucoule, Haute Ville, Boulogne-sur-Mer—as I am going into my own study— am met at the threshold by Helen, my eldest daughter, who puts her little arms before the glass door at which I was about to enter, and says, " You must not go in there, papa ! Mamma says we none of us are to go in there."

" And why, pray ? " I ask.

" Because Uncle Philip and Charlotte are talking secrets there ; and nobody is to disturb them—*nobody !* "

Upon my word, wasn't this too monstrous ? Am I Sir Pandarus of Troy become ? Am I going to allow a penniless young man to steal away the heart of a young girl who has not twopence halfpenny to her fortune ? Shall I, I say, lend myself to this most unjustifiable intrigue ?

" Sir," says my wife (we happened to have been bred up from childhood together, and I own to have had one or two foolish initiatory flirtations before I settled down to matrimonial fidelity)—" Sir," says she, " when you were so wild—so spoony, I think is your elegant word—about Blanche, and used to put letters into a hollow tree for her at home, I used to see the letters, and I never disturbed them. These two people have much warmer hearts, and are a great deal fonder of each other, than you and Blanche used to be. I should not like to separate Charlotte from Philip now. It is too late, sir. She can never like anybody else as she likes him. If she lives to be a hundred, she will never forget him. Why should not the poor thing be happy a little, while she may ? "

An old house, with a green old courtyard and an ancient mossy wall, through breaks of which I can see the roofs and gables of the quaint old town, the city below, the shining sea, and the white English cliffs beyond ; a green old courtyard, and a tall old stone house rising up in it, grown over with many a creeper on which the sun casts flickering shadows ; and under the shadows, and through the glass of a tall gray window, I can just peep into a brown twilight parlor, and there I see two hazy figures by a table. One slim figure has brown hair, and one has flame-colored whiskers. Look, a ray of sunshine has just peered into the room, and is lighting the whiskers up !

" Poor little thing," whispers my wife, very gently. " They are going away to-morrow. Let them have their talk out. She is crying her little eyes out, I am sure. Poor little Charlotte ! "

Whilst my wife was pitying Miss Charlotte in this pathetic

way, and was going, I dare say, to have recourse to her own
pocket-handkerchief, as I live there came a burst of laughter
from the darkling chamber where the two lovers were billing
and cooing. First came Mr. Philip's great boom (such a roar
—such a haw-haw, or hee-haw, I never heard any other *two*-
legged animal perform). Then follows Miss Charlotte's tinkling
peal; and presently that young person comes out into the
garden, with her round face not bedewed with tears at all, but
perfectly rosy, fresh, dimpled, and good-humored. Charlotte
gives me a little curtsey, and my wife a hand and a kind glance.
They retreat through the open casement, twining round each
other, as the vine does round the window; though which is the
vine and which is the window in this simile, I pretend not to
say—I can't see through either of them, that is the truth.
They pass through the parlor, and into the street beyond,
doubtless: and as for Mr. Philip, I presently see *his* head
popped out of his window in the upper floor with his great pipe
in his mouth. He can't "work" without his pipe, he says;
and my wife believes him. Work indeed!

Miss Charlotte paid us another little visit that evening,
when we happened to be alone. The children were gone to
bed. The darlings! Charlotte must go up and kiss them.
Mr. Philip Firmin was out. She did not seem to miss him in
the least, nor did she make a single inquiry for him. We had
been so good to her—so kind. How could she ever forget our
great kindness? She had been so happy—oh! so happy!
She had never been so happy before. She would write often
and often, and Laura would write constantly—wouldn't she?
"Yes, dear child!" says my wife. And now a little more
kissing, and it is time to go home to the Tintilleries. What a
lovely night! Indeed the moon was blazing in full round in
the purple heavens, and the stars were twinkling by myriads.

"Good-by, dear Charlotte; happiness go with you!" I
seize her hand. I feel a paternal desire to kiss her fair, round
face. Her sweetness, her happiness, her artless good-humor,
and gentleness has endeared her to us all. As for me, I love
her with a fatherly affection. "Stay, my dear!" I cry, with a
happy gallantry, "I'll go home with you to the Tintilleries."

You should have seen the fair round face *then!* Such a
piteous expression came over it! She looked at my wife; and
as for that Mrs. Laura she pulled the tail of my coat.

"What do you mean, my dear?" I ask.

"Don't go out on such a dreadful night. You'll catch
cold!" says Laura.

"Cold, my love!" I say. "Why, it's as fine a night as ever——"

"Oh! you—you *stoopid!*" says Laura, and begins to laugh. And there goes Miss Charlotte tripping away from us without a word more.

Philip came in about half an hour afterwards. And do you know I very strongly suspect that he had been waiting round the corner. Few things escape *me*, you see, when I have a mind to be observant. And, certainly, if I had thought of that possibility and that I might be spoiling sport, I should not have proposed to Miss Charlotte to walk home with her.

At a very early hour on the next morning my wife arose, and spent, in my opinion, a great deal of unprofitable time, in compiling a heap of sandwiches, which were tied up in a copy of the *Pall Mall Gazette*. That persistence in making sandwiches, in providing cakes and other refreshments for a journey, is a strange infatuation in women ; as if there was not always enough to eat to be had at road inns and railway stations ! What a good dinner we used to have at Montreuil in the old days, before railways were, and when the diligence spent four or six and twenty cheerful hours on its way to Paris ! I think the finest dishes are not to be compared to that well-remembered frican-deau of youth, nor do wines of the most dainty vintage surpass the rough, honest, blue ordinaire which was served at the plenteous inn-table. I took our bale of sandwiches down to the office of the Messageries, whence our friends were to start. We saw six of the Baynes family packed into the interior of the diligence ; and the boys climb cheerily into the rotonde. Charlotte's pretty lips and hands wafted kisses to us from her corner. Mrs. General Baynes commanded the column, pushed the little ones into their places in the ark, ordered the General and young ones hither and thither with her parasol, declined to give the grumbling porters any but the smallest gratuity, and talked a shrieking jargon of French and Hindostanee to the people assembled round the carriage. My wife has that com-mand over me that she actually made me demean myself so far as to deliver the sandwich parcel to one of the Baynes boys. I said, "Take this," and the poor wretch held out his hand eagerly, evidently expecting that I was about to tip him with a five-franc piece or some such coin. *Fouette, cocher !* The horses squeal. The huge machine jingles over the road, and rattles down the street. Farewell, pretty Charlotte, with your sweet face and sweet voice and kind eyes ! But why, pray, is Mr. Philip Firmin not here to say farewell too?

CHARLOTTE'S CONVOY.

Before the diligence had got under way, the Baynes boys had fought, and quarrelled, and wanted to mount on the imperial or cabriolet of the carriage, where there was only one passenger as yet. But the conductor called the lads off, saying that the remaining place was engaged by a gentleman who they were to take up on the road. And who should this turn out to be? Just outside the town a man springs up to the imperial; his light luggage, it appears, was on the coach already, and that luggage belonged to Philip Firmin. Ah, monsieur! and that was the reason, was it, why they were so merry yesterday —the parting day? Because they were not going to part just then. Because, when the time of execution drew near, they had managed to smuggle a little reprieve! Upon my conscience, I never heard of such imprudence in the whole course of my life! Why, it is starvation—certain misery to one and the other. " I don't like to meddle in other people's affairs," I say to my wife; " but I have no patience with such folly, or with myself for not speaking to General Baynes on the subject. I shall write to the General."

" My dear, the General knows all about it," says Charlotte's, Philip's (in my opinion) most injudicious friend. " We have talked about it, and, like a man of sense, the General makes light of it. ' Young folks will be young folks,' he says; ' and, by George! ma'am, when I married—I should say, when Mrs. B. ordered me to marry her—she had nothing, and I but my captain's pay. People get on, somehow. Better for a young man to marry, and keep out of idleness and mischief; and I promise you, the chap who marries my girl gets a treasure. I like the boy for the sake of my old friend Phil Ringwood. I don't see that the fellows with the rich wives are much the happier, or that men should wait to marry until they are gouty old rakes.' " And, it appears, the General instanced several officers of his own acquaintance; some of whom had married when they were young and poor; some who had married when they were old and sulky; some who had never married at all. And he mentioned his comrade, my own uncle, the late Major Pendennis, whom he called a selfish old creature, and hinted that the Major had jilted some lady in early life, whom he would have done much better to marry.

And so Philip is actually gone after his charmer, and is pursuing her *summa diligentia?* The Baynes family has allowed this penniless young law student to make love to their daughter, or accompany them to Paris, to appear as the almost recognized son of the house. " Other people, when they were young, wanted to make imprudent marriages," says my wife (as if that wretched *tu quoque* were any answer to my remark!) "This penniless law student might have had a good sum of money if he chose to press the Baynes family to pay him what, after all, they owe him." And so poor little Charlotte was to be her father's ransom! To be sure little Charlotte did not object to offer herself up in payment of her papa's debt! And though I objected as a moral man and a prudent man, and a father of a family, I could not be very seriously angry. I am secretly of the disposition of the time-honored *père de famille* in the comedies, the irascible old gentleman in the crop wig and George-the-Second coat, who is always menacing "Tom the young Dog" with his cane. When the deed is done, and Miranda (the little sly-boots!) falls before my square-toes and shoe-buckles and Tom, the young dog, kneels before me in his white ducks, and they cry out in a pretty chorus, "Forgive, us grandpapa!" I say, "Well, you rogue, boys will be boys. Take her, sirrah! Be happy with her; and, hark ye! in this pocket-book you will find ten thousand," &c., &c. You all know the story: I cannot help liking it, however old it may be. In love, somehow, one is pleased that young people should dare a little. Was not Bessy Eldon famous as an economist, and Lord Eldon celebrated for wisdom and caution? and did not John Scott marry Elizabeth Surtees when they had scarcely twopence a year between them? "Of course, my dear," I say to the partner of my existence, "now this madcap fellow is utterly ruined, now is the very time he ought to marry. The accepted doctrine is that a man should spend his own fortune, then his wife's fortune, and then he may begin to get on at the bar. Philip has a hundred pounds, let us say; Charlotte has nothing; so that in about six weeks we may look to hear of Philip being in successful practice——"

"Successful nonsense!" cries the lady. "Don't go on like a cold-blooded calculating machine! You don't believe a word of what you say, and a more imprudent person never lived than you yourself were as a young man." This was departing from the question, which women will do. "Nonsense!" again says my romantic being of a partner-of-existence. "Don't tell ME, sir. They WILL be provided for! Are we to be for ever taking care of the morrow, and not trusting that we shall be cared for? *You* may call your way of thinking prudence. I call it *sinful worldliness*, sir." When my life-partner speaks in a certain strain, I know that remonstrance is useless, and argument unavailing, and I generally resort to cowardly subterfuges, and sneak out of the conversation by a pun, a side joke, or some other flippancy. Besides, in this case, though I argue against my wife, my sympathy is on her side. I know Mr. Philip is imprudent and headstrong, but I should like him to succeed, and be happy. I own he is a scapegrace, but I wish him well.

So, just as the diligence of Lafitte and Caillard is clearing out of Boulogne town, the conductor causes the carriage to stop, and a young fellow has mounted up on the roof in a twinkling ; and the postilion says " Hi !" to his horses, and away those squealing grays go clattering. And a young lady, happening to look out of one of the windows of the intérieur, has perfectly recognized the young gentleman who leaped up to the roof so nimbly : and the two boys who were in the rotonde would have recognized the gentleman, but that they were already eating the sandwiches which my wife had provided. And so the diligence goes on, until it reaches that hill, where the girls used to come and offer to sell you apples ; and some of the passengers descend and walk, and the tall young man on the roof jumps down, and approaches the party in the interior, and a young lady cries out " La !" and her mamma looks impenetrably grave, and not in the least surprised ; and her father gives a wink of one eye, and says, " It's him, is it, by George !" and the two boys coming out of the rotonde, their mouths full of sandwich, cry out, " Hullo ! It's Mr. Firmin."

" How do you, do ladies ? " he says, blushing as red as an apple, and his heart thumping—but that may be from walking up hill. And he puts a hand towards the carriage window, and a little hand comes out and lights on his. And Mrs. General Baynes, who is reading a religious work, looks up and says, " Oh ! how do you do, Mr. Firmin ? " And this is the remarkable dialogue that takes place. It is not very witty ; but Philip's tones send a rapture into one young heart : and when he is absent, and has climbed up to his place in the cabriolet, the kick of his boots on the roof gives the said young heart inexpressible comfort and consolation. Shine stars and moon. Shriek gray horses through the calm night. Snore sweetly, papa and mamma, in your corners, with your pocket-handkerchiefs tied round your old fronts ! I suppose, under all the stars of heaven, there is nobody more happy than that child in that carriage—that wakeful girl, in sweet maiden meditation— who has given her heart to the keeping of the champion who is so near her. Has he not been always their champion and preserver ? Don't they owe to his generosity everything in life? One of the little sisters wakes wildly, and cries in the night,

and Charlotte takes the child into her arms and soothes her.
"Hush, dear! He's there—he's there," she whispers, as she
bends over the child. Nothing wrong can happen with *him*
there, she feels. If the robbers were to spring out from yonder
dark pines, why, he would jump down, and they would all fly
before him! The carriage rolls on through sleeping villages,
and as the old team retires all in a halo of smoke, and the
fresh horses come clattering up to their pole, Charlotte sees a
well-known white face in the gleam of the carriage lanterns.
Through the long avenues the great vehicle rolls on its course.
The dawn peers over the poplars: the stars quiver out of sight:
the sun is up in the sky, and the heaven is all in a flame. The
night is over—the night of nights. In all the round world,
whether lighted by stars or sunshine, there were not two people
more happy than these had been.

A very short time afterwards, at the end of October, our
own little sea-side sojourn came to an end. That astounding
bill for broken glass, chairs, crockery, was paid. The London
steamer takes us all on board on a beautiful, sunny autumn
evening, and lands us at the Custom-house Quay in the midst
of a deep, dun fog, through which our cabs have to work their
way over greasy pavements, and bearing two loads of silent
and terrified children. Ah, that return, if but after a fortnight's
absence and holiday! Oh, that heap of letters lying in a
ghastly pile, and yet so clearly visible in the dim twilight of
master's study! We cheerfully breakfast by candlelight for the
first two days after my arrival at home, and I have the pleasure
of cutting a part of my chin off because it is too dark to shave
at nine o'clock in the morning.

My wife can't be so unfeeling as to laugh and be merry
because I have met with an accident which temporarily dis-
figures me. If the dun fog makes her jocular, she has a very
queer sense of humor. She has a letter before her, over which
she is perfectly radiant. When she is especially pleased I can
see by her face and a particular animation and affectionateness
towards the rest of the family. On this present morning her
face beams out of the fog-clouds. The room is illuminated
by it, and perhaps by the two candles which are placed one
on either side of the urn. The fire crackles, and flames, and
spits most cheerfully; and the sky without, which is of the hue
of brown paper, seems to set off the brightness of the little
interior scene.

"A letter from Charlotte, papa," cries one little girl, with
an air of consequence. "And a letter from Uncle Philip,

papa!" cries another, "and they like Paris so much," continues the little reporter.

" And there, sir, didn't I tell you ? " cries the lady, handing me over a letter.

" Mamma always told you so," echoes the child, with an important nod of the head; " and I shouldn't be surprised if he were to be *very rich*, should you, mamma ? " continues this arithmetician.

I would not put Miss Charlotte's letter into print if I could, for do you know that little person's grammar was frequently incorrect; there were three or four words spelt wrongly; and the letter was so *scored* and *marked* with *dashes* under *every* other *word*, that it is clear to me her education had been neglected; and as I am very fond of her, I do not wish to make fun of her. And I can't print Mr. Philip's letter, for I haven't kept it. Of what use keeping letters? I say, Burn, burn, burn. No heart-pangs. No reproaches. No yesterday. Was it happy, or miserable? To thinks of it is always melancholy. Go to! I dare say it is the thought of that fog, which is making this sentence so dismal. Meanwhile there is Madame Laura's face smiling out of the darkness, as pleased as may be; and no wonder, she is always happy when her friends are so.

Charlotte's letter contained a full account of the settlement of the Baynes family at Madame Smolensk's boarding-house, where they appear to have been really very comfortable, and to have lived at a very cheap rate. As for Mr. Philip, he made his way to a crib, to which his artist friends had recommended him, on the Faubourg St. Germain side of the water — the " Hotel Poussin," in the street of that name, which lies, you know, between the Mazarin Library and the Musée des Beaux Arts. In former days, my gentleman had lived in state and bounty in the English hotels and quarter. Now he found himself very handsomely lodged for thirty francs per month, and with five or six pounds, he has repeatedly said since, he could carry through the month very comfortably. I don't say, my young traveller, that *you* can be so lucky now-a-days. Are we not telling a story of twenty years ago? Aye, marry. Ere steam-coaches had begun to scream on French rails; and when Louis Philippe was king.

As soon as Mr. Philip Firmin is ruined he must needs fall in love. In order to be near the beloved object, he must needs follow her to Paris, and give up his promised studies for the bar at home; where, to do him justice, I believe the fellow would never have done any good. And he has not been in Paris a

fortnight when that fantastic jade Fortune, who had seemed to
fly away from him, gives him a smiling look of recognition, as
if to say, "Young gentleman, I have not quite done with you."

The good fortune was not much. Do not suppose that
Philip suddenly drew a twenty-thousand pound prize in a lottery.
But, being in much want of money, he suddenly found himself
enabled to earn some in a way pretty easy to himself.

In the first place, Philip found his friends Mr. and Mrs.
Mugford in a bewildered state in the midst of Paris, in which
city Mugford would never consent to have a *laquais de place*,
being firmly convinced to the day of his death that he knew the
French language quite sufficiently for all purposes of conversation. Philip, who had often visited Paris before, came to
the aid of his friends in a two-franc dining-house, which he frequented for economy's sake ; and they, because they thought
the banquet there provided not only cheap, but most magnificent and satisfactory. He interpreted for them, and rescued
them from their perplexity, whatever it was. He treated them
handsomely to caffy on the bullyvard, as Mugford said on returning home and in recounting the adventure to me. " He
can't forget that he has been a swell : and he does do things
like a gentleman, that Firmin does. He came back with us to
our hotel—Meurice's," said Mr. Mugford, " and who should
drive into the yard and step out of his carriage but Lord Ringwood—you know Lord Ringwood ? everybody knows him. As
he gets out of his carriage—'What ! is that you, Philip ? ' says
his lordship, giving the young fellow his hand. ' Come and
breakfast with me to-morrow morning.' And away he goes
most friendly."

How came it to pass that Lord Ringwood, whose instinct
of self-preservation was strong—who, I fear, was rather a selfish nobleman—and who, of late, as we have heard, had given
orders to refuse Mr. Philip entrance at his door—should all
of a sudden turn round and greet the young man with
cordiality ? In the first place, Philip had never troubled his
lordship's knocker at all ; and second, as luck would have it,
on this very day of their meeting his lordship had been
to dine with that well-known Parisan resident and *bon-vivant*,
my Lord Viscount Trim, who had been governor of the Sago
Islands when Colonel Baynes was there with his regiment, the
gallant 100th. And the General and his old West India governor meeting at church, my Lord Trim straightway asked
General Baynes to dinner, where Lord Ringwood was present,
along with other distinguished company, whom at present we

need not particularize. Now it has been said that Philip Ringwood, my lord's brother, and Captain Baynes in early youth
had been close friends, and that the Colonel had died in the
Captain's arms. Lord Ringwood, who had an excellent memory
when he chose to use it, was pleased on this occasion to remember General Baynes and his intimacy with his brother in
old days. And of those old times they talked ; the General
waxing more eloquent, I suppose, than his wont over Lord
Trim's excellent wine. And in the course of conversation
Philip was named, and the General, warm with drink, poured
out a most enthusiastic eulogium on his young friend, and mentioned how noble and self-denying Philip's conduct had been in
his own case. And perhaps Lord Ringwood was pleased at
hearing the praises of his brother's grandson ; and perhaps he
thought of old times, when he had a heart, and he and his
brother loved each other. And though he might think Philip
Firmin an absurd young blockhead for giving up any claims
which he might have on General Baynes, at any rate I have no
doubt his lordship thought, "This boy is not likely to come
begging money from me !" Hence, when he drove back to his
hotel on the very night after this dinner, and in the courtyard
saw that Philip Firmin, his brother's grandson, the heart of the
old nobleman was smitten with a kindly sentiment, and he bade
Philip to come and see him.

I have described some of Philip's oddities, and amongst
these was a very remarkable change in his appearance, which
ensued very speedily after his ruin. I know that the greater
number of story readers are young, and those who are ever so
old remember that their own young days occurred but a very,
very short while ago. Don't you remember, most potent, grave,
and reverend senior, when you were a junior, and actually
rather pleased with new clothes ? Does a new coat or a waistcoat cause you any pleasure now ? To a well-constituted middle-aged gentleman, I rather trust a smart new suit causes a
sensation of uneasiness—not from the tightness of the fit, which
may be a reason—but from the gloss and splendor. When my
late kind friend, Mrs. ——, gave me the emerald tabinet waistcoat, with the gold shamrocks, I wore it once to go to Richmond to dine with her ; but I buttoned myself so closely in an
upper coat, that I am sure nobody in the omnibus saw what a
painted vest I had on. Gold sprigs and emerald tabinet, what
a gorgeous raiment ! It has formed for ten years the chief
ornament of my wardrobe ; and though I have never dared to
wear it since, I always think with a secret pleasure of possess-

ing that treasure. Do women, when they are sixty, like hand-some and fashionable attire, and a youthful appearance? Look at Lady Jezebel's blushing cheek, her raven hair, her splendid garments! But this disquisition may be carried to too great a length. I want to note a fact which has occurred not seldom in my experience—that men who have been great dandies will often and suddenly give up their long accustomed splendor of dress, and walk about, most happy and contented, with the shabbiest of coats and hats. No. The majority of men are not vain about their dress. For instance, within a very few years, men used to have pretty feet. See in what a resolute way they have kicked their pretty boots off almost to a man, and wear great, thick, formless, comfortable walking boots, of shape scarcely more graceful than a tub!

When Philip Firmin first came on the town, there were dandies still; there were dazzling waistcoats of velvet and brocade, and tall stocks and cataracts of satin; there were pins, studs, neck-chains, I know not what fantastic splendors of youth. His varnished boots grew upon forests of trees. He had a most resplendent silver-gilt dressing-case, presented to him by his father (for which, it is true, the doctor neglected to pay, leaving that duty to his son). "It is a mere ceremony," said the worthy doctor, "a cumbrous thing you may fancy at first; but take it about with you. It looks well on a man's dressing-table at a country-house. It *poses* a man, you under-stand. I have known women come in and peep at it. A trifle you may say, my boy; but what is the use of flinging any chance in life away?" Now, when misfortune came, young Philip flung away all these magnificent follies. He wrapped himself *virtute sua;* and I am bound to say a more queer-looking fellow than friend Philip seldom walked the pavement of London or Paris. He could not wear the nap off all his coats, or rub his elbows into rags in six months; but as he would say of himself with much simplicity, "I do think I run to seed more quickly than any fellow I ever knew. All my socks in holes, Mrs. Pendennis; all my shirt-buttons gone, I give you my word. I don't know how the things hold together, and why they don't tumble to pieces. I suspect I must have a bad laundress." Suspect! My children used to laugh and crow as they sowed buttons on to him. As for the Little Sister, she broke into his apartments in his absence, and said that it turned her hair gray to see the state of his poor wardrobe. I believe that Mrs. Brandon put surreptitious linen into his drawers. He did not know. He wore the shirts in a contented spirit. The glossy boots began to crack and then to burst, and Philip wore them with perfect equanimity. Where were the beautiful lavender and lemon gloves of last year? His great naked hands (with which he gesticulates so grandly) were as brown as an Indian's now. We had liked him heartily in his days of splendor; we loved him now in his threadbare suit.

I can fancy the young man striding into the room where his lordship's guests were assembled. In the presence of great or small, Philip has always been entirely unconcerned, and he is one of the half-dozen men I have seen in my life upon whom rank made no impression. It appears that, on occasion of this breakfast, there were one or two dandies present who were aghast at Philip's freedom of behavior. He engaged in conversation with a famous French statesman; contradicted him with much energy in his own language; and when the statesman asked whether monsieur was membre du Parlement? Philip burst into one of his roars of laughter, which almost breaks the glasses on a table, and said, "Je suis journaliste, monsieur, à vos ordres!" Young Timbury of the embassy was aghast at Philip's insolence; and Dr. Botts, his lordship's travelling physician, looked at him with a terrified face. A bottle of claret was brought, which almost all the gentlemen present began to swallow, until Philip, tasting his glass, called out, "Faugh! It's corked!" "So it is, and very badly corked," growls my lord, with one of his usual oaths. "Why didn't some of you fellows speak? Do you like corked wine?" There were gallant fellows round that table who would have drunk corked black dose, had his lordship professed to like senna. The old host was tickled and amused. Your mother was a quiet soul, and your father used to bow like a dancing-master. You ain't much like him. I dine at home most days. Leave word in the morning with my people, and come when you like, Philip," he growled. A part of this news Philip narrated to us in his letter, and other part was given verbally by Mr. and Mrs. Mugford on their return to London. "I tell you, sir," says Mugford, "he has been taken by the hand by some of the tiptop people, and I have booked him at three guineas a week for a letter to the *Pall Mall Gazette.*"

And this was the cause of my wife's exultation and triumphant "Didn't I tell you!" Philip's foot was on the ladder; and who so capable of mounting to the top? When happiness and a fond and lovely girl were waiting for him there, would he lose heart, spare exertion, or be afraid to climb? He had no truer well-wisher than myself, and no friend who liked him better, though, I dare say, many admired him much more than I did. But these were women for the most part; and women become so absurdly unjust and partial to persons whom they love, when these latter are in misfortune, that I am surprised Mr. Philip did not quite lose his head in his poverty, with such fond flatterers and sycophants round about him. Would you grudge him the consolation to be had from these sweet uses of adversity! Many a heart would be hardened but for the memory of past griefs; when eyes, now averted, perhaps, were full of sympathy, and hands, now cold, were eager to soothe and succor.

CHAPTER XIX.

QU'ON EST BIEN A VINGT ANS.

A FAIR correspondent—and I would parenthetically hint that all correspondents are *not* fair—points out the discrepancy existing between the text and the illustrations of our story; and justly remarks that the story dated more than twenty years back, while the costumes of the actors of our little comedy are of the fashion of to-day.

My dear madam, these anachronisms must be, or you would scarcely be able to keep any interest for our characters. What would be a woman without a crinoline petticoat, for example? an object ridiculous, hateful, I suppose hardly proper. What would you think of a hero who wore a large high black-satin stock cascading over a figured silk waistcoat; and a blue dress-coat, with brass buttons, mayhap? If a person so attired came up to ask you to dance, could you refrain from laughing? Time was when young men so decorated found favor in the eyes of damsels who had never beheld hooped petticoats, except in their grandmother's portraits. Persons who flourished in the first part of the century never thought to see the hoops of our ancestor's age rolled downwards to our contemporaries and children. Did we ever imagine that a period would arrive when our young men would part their hair down the middle, and wear a piece of tape for a neckcloth? As soon should we have thought of their dyeing their bodies with woad, and arraying themselves like ancient Britons. So the ages have their dress and undress; and the gentlemen and ladies of Victoria's time

are satisfied with their manner of raiment; as no doubt in
Boadicea's court they looked charming tattooed and painted
blue.

The times of which we write, the times of Louis Philippe
the king, are so altered from the present, that when Philip
Firmin went to Paris it was absolutely a cheap place to live in;
and he has often bragged in subsequent days of having lived
well during a month for five pounds, and bought a neat waistcoat with a part of the money. "A capital bedroom, *au
premier*, for a franc a day, sir," he would call all persons to
remark, "a bedroom as good as yours, my lord, at Meurice's.
Very good tea or coffee breakfast, twenty francs a month, with
lots of bread and butter. Twenty francs a month for washing,
and fifty for dinner and pocket-money—that's about the figure.
The dinner, I own, is shy, unless I come and dine with my
friends; and then I make up for banyan days." And so saying
Philip would call out for more truffled patridges, or affably filled
his goblet with my Lord Ringwood's best Sillery. "At those
shops," he would observe, "where I dine, I have beer: I can't
stand the wine. And you see, I can't go to the cheap English
ordinaries, of which there are many, because English gentlemen's
servants are there, you know, and it's not pleasant to sit with a
fellow who waits on you the day after."

"Oh! the English servants go to the cheap ordinaries, do
they?" asks my lord, greatly amused, "and you drink *biere
de Mars* at the shop where you dine?"

"And dine very badly, too, I can tell you. Always come
away hungry. Give me some champagne—the dry, if you
please. They mix very well together—sweet and dry. Did
you ever dine at Flicoteau's, Mr. Pecker?"

"*I* dine at one of your horrible two-franc houses?" cries
Mr. Pecker, with a look of terror. "Do you know, my lord,
there are actually houses where people dine for two francs?"

"Two francs! Seventeen sous!" bawls out Mr. Firmin.
"The soup, the beef, the rôti, the salad, the dessert, and the
whitey-brown bread at discretion. It's not a good dinner,
certainly—in fact, it is a dreadful bad one. But to dine so
would do some fellows a great deal of good."

"What do you say, Pecker? Flicoteau's; seventeen sous.
We'll make a little party and try, and Firmin shall do the
honors of his restaurant," says my lord, with a grin.

"Mercy!" gasps Mr. Pecker.

"I had rather dine here, if you please, my lord," says the
young man. "This is cheaper, and certainly better."

My lord's doctor, and many of the guests at his table, my lord's henchmen, flatterers, and led captains, looked aghast at the freedom of the young fellow in the shabby coat. If *they* dared to be familiar with their host, there came a scowl over that noble countenance which was awful to face. They drank his corked wine in meekness of spirit. They laughed at his jokes trembling. One after another, they were the objects of his satire ; and each grinned piteously, as he took his turn of punishment. Some dinners are dear, though they cost nothing. At some great tables are not toads served along with the *entrées* ? Yes, and many amateurs are exceedingly fond of the dish.

How do Parisians live at all ? is a question which has often set me wondering. How do men in public offices, with fifteen thousand francs, let us say, for a salary—and this, for a French official, is a high salary—live in handsome apartments ; give genteel entertainments ; clothe themselves and their families with much more sumptuous raiment than English people of the same station can afford ; take their country holiday, a six weeks' sojourn, *aux eaux ;* and appear cheerful and to want for nothing ? Paterfamilias, with six hundred a year in London, knows what a straitened life his is, with rent high, and beef at a shilling a pound. Well, in Paris, rent is higher, and meat is dearer ; and yet madame is richly dressed when you see her ; monsieur has always a little money in his pocket for his club or his café ; and something is pretty surely put away every year for the marriage portion of the young folks. " Sir," Philip used to say, describing this period of his life, on which and on most subjects regarding himself, by the way, he was wont to be very eloquent, " when my income was raised to five thousand francs a year, I give you my word I was considered to be rich by my French acquaintance. I gave four sous to the waiter at our dining-place :—in that respect I was always ostentatious :—and I believe they called me Milor. I should have been poor in the Rue de la Paix : but I was wealthy in the Luxembourg quarter. Don't tell me about poverty, sir ! Poverty is a bully if you are afraid of her, or truckle to her. Poverty is good-natured enough if you meet her like a man. You saw how my poor old father was afraid of her, and thought the world would come to an end if Dr. Firmin did not keep his butler, and his footman, and his fine house, and fine chariot and horses ? He was a poor man, if you please. He must have suffered agonies in his struggle to make both ends meet. Everything he bought must have cost him twice the honest price ; and when I think of nights that must have been passed without sleep—of that proud man having to smirk and cringe before creditors—to coax butchers, by George, and wheedle tailors—I pity him ; I can't be angry any more. That man has suffered enough. As for me, haven't you remarked that since I have not got a guinea in the world, I swagger, and am a much greater swell than before ? " And the truth is that a Prince Royal could not have called for his *gens* with a more magnificent air than Mr. Philip when he summoned the waiter, and paid for his *petit verre.*

Talk of poverty, indeed ! That period, Philip vows, was the happiest of his life. He liked to tell in after days of the choice acquaintance of Bohemians which he had formed. Their jug, he said, though it contained but small beer, was always full. Their tobacco, though it bore no higher rank than that of caporal, was plentiful and fragrant. He knew some admirable medical students ; some artists who only wanted talent and industry to be at the height of their profession : and one or two of the magnates of his own calling, the newspaper correspondents, whose houses and tables were open to him. It was wonderful what secrets of politics he learned and transmitted to his own paper. He pursued French statesmen of those days with prodigious eloquence and vigor. At the expense of that old king he was wonderfully witty and sarcastical. He reviewed the affairs of Europe, settled the destinies of Russia, denounced the Spanish marriages, disposed of the Pope, and advocated the Liberal cause in France with an untiring eloquence. " Absinthe used to be my drink, sir," so he was good enough to tell his friends. " It makes the ink run, and imparts a fine eloquence to the style. Mercy upon us, how I would belabor that poor King of the French under the influence of absinthe, in that café opposite the Bourse where I used to make my letter ! Who knows, sir, perhaps the influence of those letters precipitated the fall of the Bourbon dynasty ! Before I had an office, Gilligan, of the *Century,* and I, used to do our letters at that café ; we compared notes and pitched into each other amicably."

Gilligan of the *Century,* and Firmin of the *Pall Mall Gazette,* were, however, very minor personages amongst the London newspaper correspondents. Their seniors of the daily press had handsome apartments, gave sumptuous dinners, were closeted with ministers' secretaries, and entertained members of the Chamber of Deputies. Philip, on perfectly easy terms with himself and the world, swaggering about the embassy balls —Philip, the friend and relative of Lord Ringwood—was viewed by his professional seniors and superiors with an eye of favor, which was not certainly turned on all gentlemen following his calling. Certainly poor Gilligan was never asked to those dinners, which some of the newspaper ambassadors gave, whereas Philip was received not inhospitably. Gilligan received but a cold shoulder at Mrs. Morning Messenger's Thursdays ; and as for being asked to dinner, " Bedad, that fellow, Firmin, has an air with him which will carry him through anywhere ! " Phil's brother correspondent owned. " He seems to patronize an ambassador when he goes up and speaks to him ; and he says to a secretary, 'My good fellow, tell your master that Mr. Firmin, of the *Pall Mall Gazette*, wants to see him, and will thank him to step over to the Café de la Bourse.' " I don't think Philip, for his part, would have seen much matter of surprise in a Minister stepping over to speak to him. To him all folk were alike, great and small ; and it is recorded of him that when, on one occasion, Lord Ringwood paid him a visit at his lodgings in the Faubourg St. Germain, Philip affably offered his lordship a *cornet* of fried potatoes, with which, and plentiful tobacco of course, Philip and one or two of his friends were regaling themselves when Lord Ringwood chanced to call on his kinsman.

A crust and a carafon of small beer, a correspondence with a weekly paper, and a remuneration such as that we have mentioned,—was Philip Firmin to look for no more than this pittance, and not to seek for more permanent and lucrative employment ? Some of his friends at home were rather vexed at what Philip chose to consider his good fortune ; namely, his connection with the newspaper, and the small stipend it gave him. He might quarrel with his employer any day. Indeed no man was more likely to fling his bread and butter out of window than Mr. Philip. He was losing precious time at the bar ; where he, as hundreds of other poor gentlemen had done before him, might make a career for himself. For what are colonies made ? Why do bankruptcies occur ? Why do people break the peace and quarrel with policemen, but that barristers may be employed as judges, commissioners, magistrates ? A reporter to a newspaper remains all his life a newspaper reporter. Philip, if he would but help himself, had friends in the world who might aid effectually to advance him. So it was we pleaded with him, in the language of moderation, urging the dictates of common sense. As if moderation and common sense could be got to move that mule of a Philip Firmin ; as if any persuasion of ours could induce him to do anything but what he liked to do best himself !

"That *you* should be worldly, my poor fellow" (so Philip wrote to his present biographer)—"that you should be thinking of money and the main chance, is no matter of surprise to me. You have suffered under that curse of manhood, that destroyer of generosity in the mind, that parent of selfishness —a little fortune. You have your wretched hundreds" (my candid correspondent stated the sum correctly enough ; and I wish it were double or treble ; but that is not here the point :) "paid quarterly. The miserable pittance numbs your whole existence. It prevents freedom of thought and action. It makes a screw of a man who is certainly not without generous impulses, as I know, my poor old Harpagon ; for hast thou not offered to open thy purse to me ? I tell you I am sick of the way in which people in London, especially good people, think about money. You live up to your income's edge. You are miserably poor. You brag and flatter yourselves that you owe no man anything ; but your estate has creditors upon it as insatiable as any usurer, and as hard as any bailiff. You call me reckless, and prodigal, and idle, and all sorts of names, because I live in a single room, do as little work as I can, and go about with holes in my boots : and you flatter yourself you are prudent, because you have a genteel house, a grave flunkey out of livery, and two greengrocers to wait when you give your half-dozen dreary dinner-parties. Wretched man ! You are a slave : not a man. You are a pauper, with a good house and good clothes. You are so miserably prudent, that all your money is spent for you, except the few wretched shillings which you allow yourself for pocket-money. You tremble at the expense of a cab. I believe you actually look at half-a-crown before you spend it. The landlord is your master. The livery-stablekeeper is your master. A train of ruthless, useless servants are your pitiless creditors, to whom you have to pay exorbitant dividends every day. I, with a hole in my elbow, who live upon a shilling dinner, and walk on cracked boot soles, am called extravagant, idle, reckless, I don't know what ; while you, forsooth, consider yourself prudent. Miserable delusion ! You are flinging away heaps of money on useless flunkeys, on useless maid-servants, on useless lodgings, on useless finery—and you say, 'Poor Phil! what a sad idler he is ! how he flings himself away ! in what a wretched, disreputable manner he lives !' Poor Phil is as rich as you are, for he has enough, and is content. Poor Phil can afford to be idle, and you can't. You must work in order to keep that great hulking footman, that great rawboned cook, that army of babbling nursery-maids, and I don't know what more.

And if you choose to submit to the slavery and degradation inseparable from your condition;—the wretched inspection of candle ends, which you call order;—the mean self-denials, which you must daily practice—I pity you, and don't quarrel with you. But I wish you would not be so insufferably virtuous, and ready with your blame and pity for *me*. If I am happy, pray need you be disquieted? Suppose I prefer independence, and shabby boots? Are not these better than to be pinched by our abominable varnished conventionalism, and to be denied the liberty of free action? My poor fellow, I pity you from my heart; and it grieves me to think how those fine honest children—honest, and hearty, and frank, and open as yet—are to lose their natural good qualities, and to be swathed, and swaddled, and stifled out of health and honesty by that obstinate worldling their father. Don't tell *me* about the world; I know it. People sacrifice the next world to it, and are all the while proud of their prudence. Look at my miserable relations, steeped in respectability. Look at my father. There is a chance for him, now he is down and in poverty. I have had a letter from him, containing more of that dreadful worldly advice which you Pharisees give. If it weren't for Laura and the children, sir, I heartily wish you were ruined like your affectionate—P. F.

"N.B., P. S.—Oh, pen! I am so happy! She is such a little darling! I bathe in her innocence, sir! I strengthen myself in her purity. I kneel before her sweet goodness and unconsciousness of guile. I walk from my room, and see her every morning before seven o'clock. I see her every afternoon. She loves you and Laura. And you love her, don't you? And to think that six months ago I was going to marry a woman without a heart! Why, sir, blessings be on the poor old father for spending our money, and rescuing me from that horrible fate! I might have been like that fellow in the 'Arabian Nights,' who married Amina—the respectable woman, who dined upon grains of rice, but supped upon cold dead body. Was it not worth all the money I ever was heir to to have escaped from that ghoul? Lord Ringwood says he thinks I was well out of that. He calls people by Anglo-Saxon names, and uses very expressive monosyllables; and of Aunt Twysden, of Uncle Twysden, of the girls, and their brother, he speaks in a way which makes me see he has come to just conclusions about them.

"P. S. No. 2.— Ah, Pen! She is such a darling. I think I am the happiest man in the world."

And this was what came of being ruined! A scapegrace,

who, when he had plenty of money in his pocket, was ill-tempered, imperious, and discontented ; now that he is not worth twopence, declares himself the happiest fellow in the world! Do you remember, my dear, how he used to grumble at our claret, and what wry faces he made when there was only cold meat for dinner ? The wretch is absolutely contented with bread and cheese and small beer, even that bad beer which they have in Paris !

Now and again, at this time, and as our mutual avocations permitted, I saw Philip's friend, the Little Sister. He wrote to her dutifully from time to time. He told her of his love affair with Miss Charlotte ; and my wife and I could console Caroline, by assuring her that this time the young man's heart was given to a worthy mistress. I say console, for the news, after all, was sad for her. In the little chamber which she always kept ready for him, he would lie awake, and think of some one dearer to him than a hundred poor Carolines. She would devise something that should be agreeable to the young lady. At Christmas time there came to Miss Baynes a wonderfully worked cambric pocket-handkerchief, with "Charlotte" most beautifully embroidered in the corner. It was this poor widow's mite of love and tenderness which she meekly laid down in the place where she worshipped. "And I have six for him, too, ma'am," Mrs. Brandon told my wife. "Poor fellow! his shirts was in a dreadful way when he went away from here, and that you know, ma'am." So you see this wayfarer, having fallen among undoubted thieves, yet found many kind souls to relieve him, and many a good Samaritan ready with his twopence, if need were.

The reason why Philip was the happiest man in the world of course you understand. French people are very early risers ; and at the little hotel where Mr. Philip lived, the whole crew of the house were up hours before lazy English masters and servants think of stirring. At ever so early an hour Phil had a fine bowl of coffee and milk and bread for his breakfast ; and he was striding down to the Invalides, and across the bridge to the Champs Elysées, and the fumes of his pipe preceded him with a pleasant odor. And a short time after passing the Rond Point in the Elysian fields, where an active fountain was flinging up showers of diamonds to the sky,—after, I say, leaving the Rond Point on his right, and passing under umbrageous groves in the direction of the present Castle of Flowers, Mr. Phillip would see a little person. Sometimes a young sister or brother came with the little person. Sometimes only a

blush fluttered on her cheek, and a sweet smile beamed in her
face as she came forward to greet him. For the angels were
scarce purer than this young maid; and Una was no more
afraid of the lion, than Charlotte of her companion with the
loud voice and the tawny mane. I would not have envied that
reprobate's lot who should have dared to say a doubtful word
to this Una: but the truth is, she never thought of danger, or
met with any. The workmen were going to their labor; the dandies were asleep; and considering their age, and the relationship in which they stood to one another, I am not surprised at
Philip for announcing that this was the happiest time of his
life. In later days, when two gentlemen of mature age happened to be in Paris together, what must Mr. Philip Firmin
do but insist upon walking me sentimentally to the Champs
Elysées, and looking at an old house there, a rather shabby old
house in a garden. "That was the place," sighs he. "That
was Madame de Smolensk's. That was the window, the third
one, with the green jalousie. By Jove, sir, how happy and how
miserable I have been behind that green blind!" And my
friend shakes his large fist at the somewhat dilapidated mansion, whence Madame de Smolensk and her boarders have
long since departed.

I fear that baroness had engaged in her enterprise with in-
sufficient capital, or conducted it with such liberality that her
profits were eaten up by her boarders. I could tell dreadful
stories impugning the baroness's moral character. People said
she had no right to the title of baroness at all, or to the noble
foreign name of Smolensk. People are still alive who knew
her under a different name. The baroness herself was what
some amateurs call a fine woman, especially at dinner-time,
when she appeared in black satin and with cheeks that blushed
up as far as the eyelids. In her *peignoir* in the morning, she
was perhaps the reverse of fine. Contours which were round at
night, in the forenoon appeared lean and angular. Her roses
only bloomed half an hour before dinner-time on a cheek which
was quite yellow until five o'clock. I am sure it is very kind of
elderly and ill-complexioned people to supply the ravages of
time or jaundice, and present to our view a figure blooming
and agreeable, in place of an object faded and withered. Do
you quarrel with your opposite neighbor for painting his house
front or putting roses in his balcony? You are rather thankful for the adornment. Madame de Smolensk's front was so
decorated of afternoons. Geraniums were set pleasantly under
those first-floor windows, her eyes. Carcel lamps beamed

from those windows: lamps which she had trimmed with her
own scissors, and into which that poor widow poured the oil
which she got somehow and anyhow. When the dingy breakfast *papillotes* were cast of an afternoon, what beautiful black
curls appeared round her brow! The dingy *papillotes* were put
away in the drawer: the *peignoir* retired to its hook behind the
door: the satin raiment came forth, the shining, the ancient,
the well-kept, the well-wadded: and at the same moment the
worthy woman took that smile out of some cunning box on her
scanty toilet-table—that smile which she wore all the evening
along with the rest of her toilette, and took out of her mouth
when she went to bed and to think—to think how both ends
were to be made to meet.

Philip said he respected and admired that woman: and
worthy of respect she was in her way. She painted her face
and grinned at poverty. She laughed and rattled with care
gnawing at her side. She had to coax the milkman out of his
human kindness: to pour oil—his own oil—upon the stormy
épicier's soul: to melt the butterman: to tap the wine-merchant: to mollify the butcher: to invent new pretexts for the
landlord: to reconcile the lady boarders, Mrs. General Baynes,
let us say, and the Honorable Mrs. Boldero, who were always
quarrelling: to see that the dinner, when procured, was cooked
properly; that François, to whom she owed ever so many months'
wages, was not too rebellious or intoxicated; that Auguste, also
her creditor, had his glass clean and his lamps in order. And
this work done and the hour of six o'clock arriving, she had to
carve and be agreeable to her table; not to hear the growls of
the discontented (and at what table-d'hôte are there not grum-
blers?); to have a word for everybody present; a smile and
a laugh for Mrs. Bunch (with whom there had been very likely
a dreadful row in the morning); a remark for the Colonel; a
polite phrase for the General's lady; and even a good word
and compliment for sulky Auguste, who just before dinner-time
had unfolded the napkin of mutiny about his wages.

Was not this enough work for a woman to do? To conduct
a great house without sufficient money, and make soup, fish,
roasts, and half a dozen entrées out of wind as it were? to con-
jure up wine in piece and by the dozen? to laugh and joke
without the least gayety? to receive scorn, abuse, rebuffs, insolence, with gay good-humor? and then to go to bed wearied
at night, and have to think about figures and that dreadful,
dreadful sum in arithmetic—given 5*l.* to pay 6*l.*? Lady Macbeth is supposed to have been a resolute woman: and great.

tall, loud, hectoring females are set to represent the character.
I say No. She was a weak woman. She began to walk in her
sleep, and blab after one disagreeable little incident had occurred in her house. She broke down, and got all the people
away from her own table in the most abrupt and clumsy manner, because that drivelling, epileptic husband of hers fancied he
saw a ghost. In Lady Smolensk's place Madame de Macbeth
would have broken down in a week, and Smolensk lasted for
years. If twenty gibbering ghosts had come to the boarding-
house dinner, madame would have gone on carving her dishes,
and smiling and helping the live guests, the paying guests ;
leaving the dead guests to gibber away and help themselves.
" My poor father had to keep up appearances," Phil would say,
recounting these things in after days ; " but how ? You know
he always looked as if he was going to be hung." Smolensk
was the gayest of the gay always. That widow would have
tripped up to her funeral pile and kissed her hands to her friends
with a smiling " Bon jour ! "

"Pray, who was Monsieur de Smolensk ? " asks a simple
lady who may be listening to our friend's narrative.

" Ah, my dear lady ! there was a pretty disturbance in the
house when *that* question came to be mooted, I promise you,"
says our friend, laughing, as he recounts his adventures. And,
after all, what does it matter to you and me and this story who
Smolensk was ? I am sure this poor lady had hardships enough
in her life campaign, and that Ney himself could not have faced
fortune with a constancy more heroical.

Well. When the Bayneses first came to her house, I tell
you Smolensk and all round her smiled, and our friends thought
they were landed in a real rosy Elysium in the Champs of that
name. Madame had a *Charrick à l' Indienne* prepared in compliment to her guests. She had had many Indians in her establishment. She adored Indians. *N'était ce la polygamie*—they
were most estimable people the Hindus. Surtout, she adored
Indian shawls. That of Madame la Générale was ravishing.
The company at Madame's was pleasant. The Honorable Mrs.
Boldero was a dashing woman of fashion and respectability,
who had lived in the best world—it was easy to see that. The
young ladies' duets were very striking. The Honorable Mr.
Boldero was away shooting in Scotland at his brother, Lord
Strongitharm's, and would take Gaberlunzie Castle and the
duke's on his way south. Mrs. Baynes did not know Lady
Estridge, the ambassadress ? When the Estridges returned
from Chantilly, the Honorable Mrs. B. would be delighted to

MORNING GREETINGS.

introduce her. "Your pretty girl's name is Charlotte? So is Lady Estridge's—and very nearly as tall;—fine girls the Estridges; fine long necks—large feet—but your girl, Lady Baynes, has beautiful feet. Lady Baynes, I said? Well, you must be Lady Baynes soon. The General *must* be a K.C.B. after his services. What, you know Lord Trim? He will, and must, do it for you. If not, my brother Strongitharm shall." I have no doubt Mrs. Baynes was greatly elated by the attentions of Lord Strongitharm's sister; and looked him out in the *Peerage*, where his Lordship's arms, pedigree, and residence of Gaberlunzie Castle are duly recorded. The Honorable Mrs. Boldero's daughters, the Misses Minna and Brenda Boldero, played some rattling sonatas on a piano which was a good deal fatigued by their exertions, for the young ladies' hands were very powerful. And madame said, "Thank you," with her sweetest smile; and Auguste handed about on a silver tray—I say silver, so that the convenances may not be wounded—well, say silver that was blushing to find itself copper—handed up on a tray a white drink which make the Baynes boys cry out, "I say, mother, what's this beastly thing?" On which madame, with the sweetest smile, appealed to the company, and said, "They love orgeat, these dear infants!" and resumed her picquet with old M. Bidois—that odd old gentleman in the long brown coat, with the red ribbon, who took so much snuff and blew his nose so often and so loudly. One, two, three rattling sonatas Minna and Brenda played; Mr. Clancy, of Trinity College, Dublin (M. de Clanci, madame called him), turning over the leaves, and presently being persuaded to sing some Irish melodies for the ladies. I don't think Miss Charlotte Baynes listened to the music much. She was listening to another music, which she and Mr. Firmin were performing together. Oh, how pleasant that music used to be! There was a sameness in it, I dare say, but still it was pleasant to hear the air over again. The pretty little duet *à quatre mains*, where the hands cross over, and hop up and down the keys, and the heads get so close, so close. Oh, duets, oh, regrets! Psha! no more of this. Go down stairs, old dotard. Take your hat and umbrella and go walk by the sea-shore, and whistle a toothless old solo. "These are our quiet nights," whispers M. de Clanci to the Baynes ladies, when the evening draws to an end. "Madame's Thursdays are, I promise ye, much more fully attended." Good-night, good-night. A squeeze of a little hand, a hearty hand-shake from papa and mamma, and Philip is striding through the dark Elysian fields and over the Place of

Concord to his lodgings in the Faubourg St. Germain. Or, stay! What is that glowworm beaming by the wall opposite Madame de Smolensk's house?—a glowworm that wafts an aromatic incense and odor? I do believe it is Mr. Philip's cigar. And he is watching, watching a window by which a slim figure flits now and again. Then darkness falls on the little window. The sweet eyes are closed. Oh, blessings, blessings be upon them! The stars shine overhead. And homeward stalks Mr. Firmin, talking to himself, and brandishing a great stick.

I wish that poor Madame Smolensk could sleep as well as the people in her house. But care, with the cold feet, gets under the coverlid, and says, "Here I am; you know that bill is coming due to-morrow." Ah, atra cura! can't you leave the poor thing a little quiet? Hasn't she had work enough all day?

CHAPTER XX.

COURSE OF TRUE LOVE.

WE beg the gracious reader to remember that Mr. Philip's business at Paris was only with a weekly London paper as yet; and hence that he had on his hands a great deal of leisure. He could glance over the state of Europe; give the latest news from the salons, imparted to him, I do believe, for the most part, by some brother hireling scribes; be present at all the theatres by deputy; and smash Louis Philippe or Messieurs Guizot and Thiers in a few easily turned paragraphs, which cost but a very few hours' labor to that bold and rapid pen. A wholesome though humiliating thought it must be to great and learned public writers, that their eloquent sermons are but for the day; and that, having read what the philosophers say on Tuesday or Wednesday, we think about their yesterday's sermons or essays no more. A score of years hence, men will read the papers of 1861 for the occurrences narrated —births, marriages, bankruptcies, elections, murders, deaths, and so forth; and not for the leading articles. "Though there was some of my letters," Mr. Philip would say, in after times, "that I fondly fancied the world would not willingly let die. I wanted to have them or see them reprinted in a volume, but I could find no publisher willing to undertake the risk. A fond being, who fancies there is genius in everything I say or write, would have had me reprint my letters to the *Pall Mall Gazette;* but I was too timid, or she, perhaps, was too confident. The letters never were republished. Let them pass." They *have* passed. And he sighs, in mentioning this circumstance ; and I think tries to persuade himself, rather than others, that he is an unrecognized genius.

" And then, you know," he pleads, " I was in love, sir, and spending all my days at Omphale's knees. I didn't do justice to my powers. If I had had a daily paper, I still think I might have made a good public writer ; and that I had the stuff in me—the stuff in me, sir ! "

The truth is that, if he had had a daily paper, and ten times as much work as fell to his lot, Mr. Philip would have found means of pursuing his inclination, as he ever through life has done. The being whom a young man wishes to see, he sees. What business is superior to that of seeing her ? 'Tis a little Hellespontine matter keeps Leander from his Hero ? He would die rather than not see her. Had he swum out of that difficulty on that stormy night, and carried on a few months later, it might have been, " Beloved ! my cold and rheumatism are so severe that the doctor says I must not *think* of cold bathing at night ;" or, " Dearest ! we have a party at tea, and you mustn't expect your ever fond Lambda to-night," and so forth, and so forth. But in the heat of his passion water could not stay him ; tempests could not frighten him ; and in one of them he went down, while poor Hero's lamp was twinkling and spending its best flame in vain. So Philip came from Sestos to Abydos daily—across one of the bridges, and paying a halfpenny toll very likely—and, late or early, poor little Charlotte's virgin lamps were lighted in her eyes, and watching for him.

Philip made many sacrifices, mind you : sacrifices which all men are not in the habit of making. When Lord Ringwood was in Paris, twice, thrice he refused to dine with his lordship, until that nobleman smelt a rat, as the saying is—and said, " Well, youngster, I suppose you are going where there is metal more attractive. When you come to twelve lustres, my boy, you'll find vanity and vexation in that sort of thing, and a good dinner better, and cheaper, too, than the best of them." And when some of Philip's rich college friends met him in his exile, and asked him to the " Rocher " or the " Trois Frères," he would break away from those banquets ; and as for meeting at those feasts doubtful companions, whom young men will sometimes invite to their entertainments, Philip turned from such with scorn and anger. His virtue was loud, and he proclaimed it loudly. He expected little Charlotte to give him credit for it, and told her of his self-denial. And she believed anything he said ; and delighted in everything he wrote ; and copied out his articles for the *Pall Mall Gazette;* and treasured his poems in her desk of desks : and there never was in all Sestos, in all Abydos, in all Europe, in all Asia Minor or Asia Major, such a noble creature as Leander, Hero thought ; never, never ! I hope, young ladies, you may all have a Leander on his way to the tower where the light of your love is burning steadfastly. I hope, young gentlemen, you have each of you a beacon in sight, and may meet with no mishap in swimming to it.

From my previous remarks regarding Mrs. Baynes, the reader has been made aware that the General's wife was no more faultless than the rest of her fellow-creatures ; and having already candidly informed the public that the writer and his family were no favorites of this lady, I have now the pleasing duty of recording my own opinions regarding *her*. Mrs. General B. was an early riser. She was a frugal woman ; fond of her young, or, let us say, anxious to provide for their maintenance ; and here, with my best compliments, I think the catalogue of her good qualities is ended. She had a bad, violent temper ; a disagreeable person, attired in very bad taste ; a shrieking voice ; and two manners, the respectful and the patronizing, which were both alike odious. When she ordered Baynes to marry her, gracious powers ! why did he not run away ? Who dared first to say that marriages are made in heaven ? We know that there are not only blunders, but roguery in the marriage office. Do not mistakes occur every day, and are not the wrong people coupled ? Had heaven anything to do with the bargain by which young Miss Blushrose was sold to old Mr. Hoarfrost ? Did heaven order Miss Tripper to throw over poor Tom Spooner, and marry the wealthy Mr. Bung ? You may as well say that horses are sold in heaven, as you know, are groomed, are doctored, are chanted on to the market, and warranted by dexterous horse-vendors as possessing every quality of blood, pace, temper, age. Against these Mr. Greenhorn has his remedy sometimes ; but against a mother who sells you a warranted daughter, what remedy is there ? You have been jockeyed by false representations into bidding for the Cecilia, and the animal is yours for life. She shies, kicks, stumbles, has an infernal temper, is a crib-biter—and she was warranted to you by her mother as the most perfect, good-tempered creature, whom the most timid might manage! You have bought her. She is yours. Heaven bless you! Take her home, and be miserable for the rest of your days. You have no redress. You have done the deed. Marriages were made in heaven, you know; and in yours you were as much sold as Moses Primrose was when he bought the gross of green spectacles.

I don't think poor General Baynes ever had a proper sense of his situation, or knew how miserable he ought by rights to have been. He was not uncheerful at times: a silent man, liking his rubber and his glass of wine; a very weak person in the common affairs of life, as his best friends must own; but, as I have heard, a very tiger in action. "I know your opinion of the General," Philip used to say to me, in his grandiloquent way. "You despise men who don't bully their wives; you do, sir! You think the General weak, I know, I know. Other brave men were so about women, as I dare say you have heard. This man, so weak at home, was mighty on the war-path; and in his wigwam are the scalps of countless warriors."

"In his wig *what?*" say I. The truth is, on his meek head the General wore a little curling chestnut top-knot, which looked very queer and out of place over that wrinkled and war-worn face.

"If you choose to laugh at your joke, pray do," says Phil, majestically. "I make a noble image of a warrior. You prefer a barber's pole. *Bon!* Pass me the wine. The veteran whom I hope to salute as father ere long—the soldier of twenty battles;—who saw my own brave grandfather die at his side—die at Busaco, by George; you laugh at on account of his wig. It's a capital joke." And here Phil scowled and slapped the table, and passed his hand across his eyes, as though the death of his grandfather, which occurred long before Philip was born, caused him a very serious pang of grief. Philip's newspaper business brought him to London on occasions. I think it was on one of these visits that we had our talk about General Baynes. And it was at the same time Philip described the boarding-house to us, and its inmates, and the landlady, and the doings there.

For that struggling landlady, as for all women in distress, our friend had a great sympathy and liking; and she returned Philip's kindness by being very good to Mademoiselle Charlotte, and very forbearing with the General's wife and his other

children. The appetites of those little ones were frightful, the
temper of Madame la Générale was almost intolerable, but
Charlotte was an angel, and the General was a mutton—a true
mutton. Her own father had been so. The brave are often
muttons at home. I suspect that, though Madame could have
made but little profit by the General's family, his monthly pay-
ments were very welcome to her meagre little exchequer.
"Ah! if all my locataires were like him!" sighed the poor
lady. "That Madame Boldero, whom the Generaless treats
always as Honorable, I wish I was as sure of her! And others
again!"

I never kept a boarding-house, but I am sure there must be
many painful duties attendant on that profession. What can
you do if a lady or gentleman doesn't pay his bill? Turn him
or her out? Perhaps the very thing that lady or gentleman
would desire. They go. Those trunks which you have insanely
detained, and about which you have made a fight and a scandal,
do not contain a hundred francs' worth of goods, and your debt-
ors never come back again. You do not like to have a row in
a boarding-house any more than you would like to have a party
with scarlet fever in your best bedroom. The scarlet-fever
party stays, and the other boarders go away. What, you ask,
do I mean by this mystery? I am sorry to have to give up
names, and titled names. I am sorry to say the Honorable
Mrs. Boldero did not pay her bills. She was waiting for remittances, which the Honorable Boldero was dreadfully remiss in
sending. A dreadful man! He was still at his Lordship's at
Gaberlunzie Castle, shooting the wild deer and hunting the roe.
And though the Honorable Mrs. B.'s heart was in the Highlands, of course how could she join her Highland chief without
the money to pay Madame? The Highlands, indeed! One
dull day it came out that the Honorable Boldero was amusing
himself in the Highlands of Hesse Homburg; and engaged in
the dangerous sport which is to be had in the green plains
about Loch Badenbadenoch!

"Did you ever hear of such depravity? The woman is a
desperate and unprincipled adventuress! I wonder Madame
dares to put me and my children and my General down at table
with such people as those, Philip!" cries Madame la Générale.
"I mean those opposite—that woman and her two daughters
who haven't paid madame a shilling for three months—who
owes me five hundred francs, which she borrowed until next
Tuesday, expecting a remittance—a pretty remittance indeed—
from Lord Strongitharm. Lord Strongitharm, I dare say! And

she pretends to be most intimate at the embassy ; and that she would introduce us there, and at the Tuileries : and she told me Lady Garterton had the small-pox in the house ; and when I said all ours had been vaccinated, and I didn't mind, she fobbed me off with some other excuse ; and it's my belief that the woman's a *humbug*. Overhear me ! I don't care if she *does* overhear me. No. You may look as much as you like, my *Honorable* Mrs. Boldero ; and I don't care if you do overhear me. Ogoost ! Pomdytare pour le Générale ! How tough madame's boof is, and it's boof, boof, boof every day, till I'm sick of boof. Ogoost ! why don't you attend to my children ? " And so forth.

By this report of the worthy woman's conversation, you will see that the friendship which had sprung up between the two ladies had come to an end, in consequence of painful pecuniary disputes between them ; that to keep a boarding-house can't be a very pleasant occupation ; and that even to dine in a boarding-house must be only bad fun when the company is frightened and dull, and when there are two old women at table ready to fling the dishes at each other's fronts. At the period of which I now write, I promise you, there was very little of the piano-duet business going on after dinner. In the first place, everybody knew the girls' pieces ; and when they began, Mrs. General Baynes would lift up a voice louder than the jingling old instrument, thumped Minna and Brenda ever so loudly. " Perfect strangers to me, Mr. Clancy, I assure you. Had I known her, you don't suppose I would have lent her the money. Honorable Mrs. Boldero, indeed ! Five weeks she has owed me five hundred frongs. Bong swor, Monseiur Bidois ! Sang song frong pas payy encor ! Prommy pas payy ! " Fancy, I say, what a dreary life that must have been at the select boarding-house, where these two parties were doing battle daily after dinner ! Fancy, at the select soriées, the General's lady seizing upon one guest after another, and calling out her wrongs, and pointing to the wrong-doer ; and poor Madame Smolensk, smirking and smiling, and flying from one end of the salon to the other, and thanking M. Pivoine for his charming romance, and M. Brumm for his admirable performance on the violoncello, and even asking those poor Miss Bolderos to perform their duet—for her heart melted towards them. Not ignorant of evil, she had learned to succor the miserable. She knew what poverty was, and had to coax scowling duns, and wheedle vulgar creditors. " Tenez, Monsieur Philippe," she said, " the Générale is too cruel. There are others here who might complain, and are silent." Philip felt all this ; the conduct of his future mother-in-law filled him with dismay and horror. And sometime after these remarkable circumstances, he told me, blushing as he spoke, a humiliating secret. "Do you know, sir," says he, "that that autumn I made a pretty good thing out of it with one thing or another. I did my work for the *Pall Mall Gazette :* and Smith of the *Daily Intelligencer,* wanting a month's holiday, gave me his letter and ten francs a day. And at that very time I met Redman, who had owed me twenty pounds ever since we were at college, and who was just coming back flush from Homburg, and paid me. Well, now. Swear you won't tell. Swear on your faith as a Christian man! With this money I went, sir, privily to Mrs. Baldero. I said if she would pay the dragon—I mean Mrs. Baynes—I would lend her the money. And I *did* lend her the money, and the Baldero never paid back Mrs. Baynes. Don't mention it. Promise me you won't tell Mrs. Baynes. I never expected to get Redman's money, you know, and am no worse off than before. One day of the Grandes Eaux we went to Versailles, I think, and the Honorable Mrs. Baldero gave us the slip. She left the poor girls behind her in pledge, who, to do them justice, cried and were in a dreadful way ; and when Mrs. Baynes, on her return, began shrieking about her ' sang song frong,' Madame Smolensk fairly lost patience for once, and said, ' Mais, Madame, vous nous fatiguez, avec vos cinq cent francs ;' on which the other muttered something about ' Ansolong,' but was briskly taken up by her husband, who said, ' By George, Eliza, madame is quite right. And I wish the five hundred francs were in the sea.' "

Thus, you understand, if Mrs. General Baynes thought some people were "stuck-up people," some people can—and hereby do by these presents—pay off Mrs. Baynes, by furnishing the public with a candid opinion of that lady's morals, manners, and character. How could such a shrewd woman be dazzled so repeatedly by ranks and titles ? There used to dine at Madame Smolensk's boarding-house a certain German baron, with a large finger ring, upon a dingy finger, towards whom the lady was pleased to cast the eye of favor, and who chose to fall in love with her pretty daughter ; young Mr. Clancy, the Irish poet, was also smitten with the charms of the fair young lady ; and this intrepid mother encouraged both suitors, to the unspeakable agonies of Philip Firmin, who felt often that whilst he was away at his work these inmates of Madame Smolensk's house were near his charmer—at her side at lunch, ever handing her the cup at breakfast, on the watch for her when she walked forth in the garden ; and I take the pangs of jealousy to have formed a part of those unspeakable sufferings which Philip said he endured in the house whither he came courting.

Little Charlotte, in one or two of her letters to her friends in Queen Square, London, meekly complained of Philip's tendency to jealousy. " Does he think, after knowing him, I can think of these horrid men ?" she asked. " I don't understand what Mr. Clancy is talking about, when he comes to me with his ' pomes and potry ; ' and who can read poetry like Philip himself ? Then the German baron—who does not call even himself baron : it is mamma who will insist upon calling him so —has such very dirty things, and smells so of cigars, that I don't like to come near him. Philip smokes too, but his cigars are quite pleasant. Ah, dear friend, how *could* he ever think such men as these were to be put in comparaison with him ! And he scolds so ; and scowls at the poor men in the evening when he comes ! and his temper is so high ! Do say a *word* to him —quite cautiously and gently, you know—in behalf of your fondly attached and most happy—only he will make me unhappy sometimes ; but you'll prevent him, won't you ?—CHARLOTTE B."

I could fancy Philip hectoring through the part of Othello, and his poor young Desdemona not a little frightened at his black humors. Such sentiments as Mr. Philip felt strongly, he expressed with an uproar. Charlotte's correspondent, as usual, made light of these little domestic confidences and grievances. " Women don't dislike a jealous scolding," she said. " It may be rather tiresome, but it is always a compliment. Some husbands think so well of themselves, that they can't condescend to be jealous." " Yes," I say, " women prefer to have tyrants over them. A scolding you think is a mark of attention. Hadn't you better adopt the Russian system at once, and go out and buy me a whip, and present it to me with a curtsey, and your compliments ; and a meek prayer that I should use it." " Present you a whip ! present you a goose !" says the lady, who encourages scolding in other husbands, it seems, but won't suffer a word from her own.

Both disputants had set their sentimental hearts on the marriage of this young man and this young woman. Little Charlotte's heart was so bent on the match, that it would break, we fancied, if she were disappointed ; and in her mother's behavior we felt, from the knowledge we had of the woman's disposition, there was a serious cause for alarm. Should a better

offer present itself, Mrs. Baynes, we feared, would fling over
poor Philip : or it was in reason and nature, that he would come
to a quarrel with her, and in the course of the pitched battle
which must ensue between them, he would fire off expressions
mortally injurious.   Are there not many people, in every one's
acquaintance, who as soon as they have made a bargain, repent
of it ?   Philip, as "preserver" of General Baynes, in the first
fervor of family gratitude for that act of self-sacrifice on the
young man's part, was very well.   But gratitude wears out ; or
suppose a woman says, "It is my duty to my child to recall my
word ; and not allow her to fling herself away on a beggar."
Suppose that you and I, strongly incline to do a mean action,
get a good, available, and moral motive for it ?   I trembled for
poor Philip's course of true love, and little Charlotte's chances,
when these surmises crossed my mind.   There was a hope still
in the honor and gratitude of General Baynes.   *He* would not
desert his young friend and benefactor.   Now General Baynes
was a brave man of war, and so was John of Marlborough a
brave man of war ; but it is certain that both were afraid of
their wives.

We have said by whose invitation and encouragement General Baynes was induced to bring his family to the boarding-
house at Paris ; the instigation, namely, of his friend and companion in arms, the gallant Colonel Bunch.   When the Baynes
family arrived, the Bunches were on the steps of madame's
house, waving a welcome to the new-comers.   It was, " Here
we are, Bunch, my boy."   " Glad to see you, Baynes.   Right
well you're looking, and so's Mrs. B."   And the General replies,
"And so are you, Bunch ; and so do *you*, Mrs. B."   " How do,
boys ?   How d'you do, Miss Charlotte ?   Come to show the
Paris fellows what a pretty girl is, hey ?   Blooming like a rose,
Baynes ! "   " I'm telling the General," cries the Colonel to the
General's lady, " the girl's the very image of her mother."   In
this case poor Charlotte must have looked like a yellow rose,
for Mrs. Baynes was of a bilious temperament and complexion,
whereas Miss Charlotte was as fresh pink and white as—what
shall we say ?—as the very freshest strawberries mingled with
the very nicest cream.

The two old soldiers were of very great comfort to one
another.   They toddled down to Galignani's together daily,
and read the papers there.   They went and looked at the
reviews in the Carrousel, and once or twice to the Champ de
Mars :—recognizing here and there the numbers of the Regiments against which they had been engaged in the famous an-

cient wars. They did not brag in the least about their achievements, they winked and understood each other. They got their old uniforms out of their old boxes, and took a *voiture de remise*, by Jove! and went to be presented to Louis Philippe. They bought a catalogue, and went to the Louvre, and wagged their honest old heads before the pictures; and, I dare say, winked and nudged each other's brave old sides at some of the nymphs in the statue gallery. They went out to Versailles with their families; loyally stood treat to the ladies at the restaurateur's. (Bunch had taken down a memorandum in his pocket-book from Benyon, who had been the duke's aide-de-camp in the last campaign, to "go to Beauvillier's," only Beauvillier's had been shut up for twenty years.) They took their families and Charlotte to the Théâtre Français, to a tragedy; and they had books: and they said it was the most confounded nonsense they ever saw in their lives; and I am bound to say that Bunch, in the back of the box, snored so, that, though in retirement, he created quite a sensation. "Corneal," he owns, was too much for him : give him Shakespeare : give him John Kemble : give him Mrs. Siddons : give him Mrs. Jordan. But as for this sort of thing? "I think our play days are over, Baynes,—hey?" And I also believe that Miss Charlotte Baynes, whose knowledge of the language was imperfect as yet, was very much bewildered during the tragedy, and could give but an imperfect account of it. But then Philip Firmin was in the orchestra stalls; and had he not sent three bouquets for the three ladies, regretting that he could not come to see somebody in the Champs Elysées, because it was his post day, and he must write his letter for the *Pall Mall Gazette?* There he was, *her* Cid; her peerless champion : and to give up father and mother for *him?* our little Chimène thought such a sacrifice not too difficult. After that dismal attempt at the theatre, the experiment was not repeated. The old gentlemen preferred their whist to those pompous Alexandrines sung through the nose, which Colonel Bunch, a facetious little Colonel, used to imitate, and, I am given to understand, very badly.

The good gentlemen's ordinary amusement was a game at cards after dinner; and they compared Madame's to an East Indian ship, quarrels and all. Sarah went on just in that way on board the "Burrumpooter." Always rows about precedence, and the services, and the deuce knows what. Women always will. Sarah Bunch went on in that way : and Eliza Baynes also went on in that way; but I should think, from the most trustworthy information, that Eliza was worse than Sarah.

"About any person with a title, that woman will make a fool of herself to the end of the chapter," remarked Sarah of her friend. "You remember how she used to go on at Barrackpore about that little shrimp, Stony Battersby, because he was an Irish viscount's son? See how she flings herself at the head of this Mrs. Boldero,—with her airs, and her paint, and her black front! I can't bear the woman! I know she has not paid madame. I know she is no better than she should be—and to see Eliza Baynes coaxing her, and sidling up to her, and flattering her;—it's too bad, that it is! A woman who owes ever so much to madame! a woman who doesn't pay her washerwoman!"

"Just like the 'Burrumpooter' over again, my dear," cries Colonel Bunch. "You and Eliza Baynes were always quarrelling, that's the fact. Why did you ask her to come here? I knew you would begin again, as soon as you met." And the truth was that these ladies were always fighting and making up again.

"So you and Mrs. Bunch were old acquaintances?" asked Mrs. Boldero of her new friend. "My dear Mrs. Baynes! I should hardly have thought it : your manners are so different! Your friend, if I may be so free as to speak, has the camp manner. You have not the camp manner at all. I should have thought you—excuse me the phrase, but I'm so open, and always speak my mind out—you haven't the camp manner at all. You seem as if you were one of us. Minna! doesn't Mrs. Baynes put you in mind of Lady Hm——?" (The name is inaudible, in consequence of Mrs. Boldero's exceeding shyness in mentioning names—but the girls see the likeness to dear Lady Hm—— at once.) "And when you bring your dear girl to London you'll know the lady I mean, and judge for your self. I assure you I am not disparaging you, my dear Mrs. Baynes, in comparing you to her!"

And so the conversation goes on. If Mrs. Major MacWhirter at Tours chose to betray secrets, she could give extracts from her sister's letters to show how profound was the impression created in Mrs. General Baynes's mind by the professions and conversations of the Scotch lady.

"Didn't the General shoot and love deer-stalking? The dear General must come to Gaberlunzie Castle, where she would promise him a Highland welcome. Her brother Strongitharm was the most amiable of men ; *adored* her and her girls : there was talk even of marrying Minna to the Captain, but she, for her part, could not *endure* the marriage of first-cousins. There was a tradition against such marriages in their family. Of three Bolderos and Strongitharms who married their first-cousins, one was drowned in Gaberlunzie lake three weeks after the marriage; one lost his wife by a galloping consumption, and died a monk at Rome; and the third married a fortnight before the battle of Culloden, where he was slain at the head of the Strongitharms. Mrs. Baynes had *no idea* of the splendor of Gaberlunzie Castle; seventy bedrooms and thirteen company-rooms, besides the picture-gallery! In Edinburgh, the Strongitharm had the right to wear his bonnet in the presence of his sovereign." "A bonnet! how very odd, my dear! But with ostrich plumes, I dare say it may look well, especially as the Highlanders wear frocks, too." "Lord Strongitharm had no house in London, having almost ruined himself in building his princely castle in the North. Mrs. Baynes *must* come there and meet their noble relatives and all the Scottish nobility." "Nor do *I* care about these vanities, my dear, but to bring my sweet Charlotte into the world: is it not a mother's duty?"

Nor only to her sister, but likewise to Charlotte's friends of Queen Square, did Mrs. Baynes impart this delightful news. But this is in the first ardor of the friendship which arises between Mrs. Baynes and Mrs. Boldero, and before those unpleasant money disputes of which we have spoken.

Afterwards, when the two ladies have quarrelled regarding the memorable "sang song frong," I think Mrs. Bunch came round to Mrs. Boldero's side. "Eliza Baynes is too hard on her. It is too cruel to insult her before those two unhappy daughters. The woman is an odious woman, and a vulgar woman, and a schemer, and I always said so. But to box her ears before her daughters—her honorable friend of last week! it's a shame of Eliza!"

"My dear, you'd better tell her so!" says Bunch, drily. "But if you do, tell her when I'm out of the way, please!" And accordingly, one day when the two old officers return from their stroll, Mrs. Bunch informs the Colonel that she has had it out with Eliza; and Mrs. Baynes, with a heated face, tells the General that she and Mrs. Colonel Bunch have quarrelled; and she is determined it shall be for the last time. So that poor Madame de Smolensk has to interpose between Mrs. Baynes and Mrs. Boldero; between Mrs. Baynes and Mrs. Bunch, and to sit surrounded by glaring eyes, and hissing inuendoes, and in the midst of feuds unhealable. Of course, from the women the quarrelling will spread to the gentlemen. That always happens. Poor madame trembles. Again Bunch gives his neighbor his word that it is like the "Burrumpooter" East Indiaman—the "Burrumpooter" in very bad weather, too.

"At any rate, *we* won't be lugged into it, Baynes, my boy!" says the Colonel, who is of a sanguine temperament, to his friend.

"Hey, hey! don't be too sure, Bunch; don't be too sure," sighs the other veteran, who, it may be, is of a more despond-ing turn, as, after a battle at luncheon, in which the Amazons were fiercely engaged, the two old warriors take their walk to Galignani's.

Towards his Charlotte's relatives poor Philip was respectful by duty and a sense of interest, perhaps. Before marriage, especially, men are very kind to the relatives of the beloved object. They pay compliments to mamma; they listen to papa's old stories, and laugh appositely; they bring presents for the innocent young ones, and let the little brothers kick their shins. Philip endured the juvenile Bayneses very kindly; he took the boys to Franconi's, and made his conversation as suitable as he could to the old people. He was fond of the old General, a simple and worthy old man; and had, as we have said, a hearty sympathy and respect for Madame Smolensk, admiring her constancy and good-humor under her many trials. But those who have pursued his memoirs are aware that Mr. Firmin could make himself, on occasions, not a little disagreeable. When sprawling on a sofa, engaged in conversation with his charmer, he would not budge when other ladies entered the room. He scowled at them, if he did not like them. He was not at the least trouble to conceal his likes or dislikes. He had a manner of fixing his glass in his eye, putting his thumbs into the arm-holes of his waistcoat, and talking and laughing very loudly at his own jokes or conceits, which was not pleasant or respectful to ladies.

"Your loud young friend, with the cracked boots, is very *mauvais ton*, my dear Mrs. Baynes," Mrs. Boldero remarked to her new friend, in the first ardor of their friendship. "A rela-ative of Lord Ringwood's, is he? Lord Ringwood is a very queer person. A son of that dreadful Dr. Firmin, who ran away after cheating everybody? Poor young man! He can't help having such a father, as you say, and most good, and kind, and generous of you to say so. And the General and the Honorable Philip Ringwood were early companions together, I dare say. But having such an unfortunate father as Dr. Firmin, I think Mr. Firmin might be a little less *prononcé*;

don't you? And to see him in cracked boots, sprawling over the sofas, and hear him, when my loves are playing their duets, laughing and talking so very loud,—I confess isn't pleasant to me. I am not used to that kind of *monde*, nor are my dear loves. You are under great obligations to him, and he has behaved nobly, you say? Of course. To get into your society an unfortunate young man will be on his best behavior, though he certainly does not condescend to be civil to us. But * * * * What! that young man engaged to that lovely, innocent, charming child, your daughter? My dear creature, you frighten me! A man, with such a father; and, excuse me, with such a manner; and without a penny in the world, engaged to Miss Baynes! Goodness, powers! It must never be. It shall not be, my dear Mrs. Baynes. Why, I have written to my nephew Lenox to come over, Strongitharm's favorite son and my favorite nephew. I have told him that there is a sweet young creature here, whom he must and ought to see. How well that dear child would look presiding at Strongitharm Castle? And you are going to give her to that dreadful young man with the loud voice and cracked boots—that smoky young man—oh, impossible!"

Madame had, no doubt, given a very favorable report of her new lodgers to the other inmates of her house; and she and Mrs. Boldero had concluded that all general officers returning from India were immensely rich. To think that her daughter might be the Honorable Mrs. Strongitharm, Baroness Strongitharm, and walk in a coronation in robes, with a coronet in her hand! Mrs. Baynes yielded in loyalty to no woman, but I fear her wicked desires compassed a speedy royal demise, as this thought passed through her mind of the Honorable Lenox Strongitharm. She looked him out in the *Peerage*, and found that young nobleman designated as the Captain of Strongitharm. Charlotte might be the Honorable Mrs. Captain of Strongitharm! When poor Phil stalked in after dinner that evening in his shabby boots and smoky paletot, Mrs. Baynes gave him but a grim welcome. He went and prattled unconsciously by the side of his little Charlotte, whose tender eyes dwelt upon his, and whose fair cheeks flung out their blushes of welcome. He prattled away. He laughed out loud whilst Minna and Brenda were thumping their duet. "Taisez-vous donc, Monsieur Philippe," cries madame, putting her finger to her lip. The Honorable Mrs. Boldero looked at dear Mrs. Baynes, and shrugged her shoulders. Poor Philip! would he have laughed so loudly (and so rudely, too, as I own), had he known what was passing in the minds of those women? Treason was passing there: and before that glance of knowing scorn, shot from the Honorable Mrs. Boldero's eyes, dear Mrs. General Baynes faltered. How very curt and dry she was with Philip! how testy with Charlotte! Poor Philip, knowing that his charmer was in the power of her mother, was pretty humble to this dragon; and attempted, by uncouth flatteries, to soothe and propitiate her. She had a queer, dry humor, and loved a joke; but Phil's fell very flat this night. Mrs. Baynes received his pleasantries with an "Oh, indeed! She was sure she heard one of the children crying in their nursery. Do, pray, go and see, Charlotte, what that child is crying about." And away goes poor Charlotte, having but dim presentiment of misfortune as yet. Was not mamma often in an ill humor; and were they not all used to her scoldings?

As for Mrs. Colonel Bunch, I am sorry to say that, up to this time, Philip was not only no favorite with her, but was heartily disliked by that lady. I have told you our friend's faults. He was loud: he was abrupt: he was rude often: and often gave just cause of annoyance by his laughter, his disrespect, and his swaggering manner. To those whom he liked he was as gentle as a woman; and treated them with an extreme tenderness and touching rough respect. But those persons about whom he was indifferent, he never took the least trouble to conciliate or please. If they told long stories, for example, he would turn on his heel, or interrupt them by observations of his own on some quite different subject. Mrs. Colonel Bunch, then, positively disliked that young man, and I think had very good reasons for her dislike. As for Bunch, Bunch said to Baynes, "Cool hand, that young fellow!" and winked. And Baynes said to Bunch, "Queer chap. Fine fellow, as I have reason to know pretty well. I play a club. No club? I mark honors and two tricks." And the game went on. Clancy hated Philip: a meek man whom yet Firmin had managed to offend. "That man," the poet Clancy remarked, "has a manner of treading on me corrans which is intolerable to me!"

The truth is, Philip was always putting his foot on some other foot, and trampling it. And as for the Boldero clan, Mr. Firmin treated them with the most amusing insolence, and ignored them as if they were out of existence altogether. So you see the poor fellow had not with his poverty learned the least lesson of humility, or acquired the very earliest rudiments of the art of making friends. I think his best friend in the house was its mistress, Madame Smolensk. Mr. Philip treated

her as an equal : which mark of affability he was not in the habit of bestowing on all persons. Some great people, some rich people, some would-be-fine people, he would patronize with an insufferable audacity. Rank or wealth do not seem somehow to influence this man, as they do common mortals. He would tap a bishop on the waistcoat, and contradict a duke at their first meeting. I have seen him walk out of church during a stupid sermon, with an audible remark perhaps to that effect, and as if it were a matter of course that he should go. If the company bored him at dinner, he would go to sleep in the most unaffected manner. At home we were always kept in a pleasant state of anxiety, not only by what he did and said, but by the idea of what he might do or say next. He did not go to sleep at madame's boarding-house, preferring to keep his eyes open to look at pretty Charlotte's. And were there ever such sapphires as his ? she thought. And hers ? Ah ! if they have tears to shed, I hope a kind fate will dry them quickly !

CHAPTER XXI.

TREATS OF DANCING, DINING, DYING.

OLD schoolboys remember how, when pious Æneas was compelled by painful circumstances to quit his country, he and his select band of Trojans founded a new Troy, where they landed ; raising temples to the Trojan gods ; building streets with Trojan names ; and endeavoring, to the utmost of their power, to recall their beloved native place. In like manner, British Trojans and French Trojans take their Troy everywhere. Algiers I have only seen from the sea ; but New Orleans and Leicester Square I have visited ; and have seen a quaint old France still lingering on the banks of the Mississippi ; a dingy modern France round that great Globe of Mr. Wyld's, which they say is coming to an end. There are French cafés, billiards estaminets, waiters, markers, poor Frenchmen, and rich Frenchmen, in a new Paris—shabby and dirty, it is true—but offering the emigrant the dominos, the chopine, the petit-verre of the patrie. And do not British Trojans, who emigrate to the continent of Europe, take their Troy with them ? You all know the quarters of Paris which swarm with us Trojans. From Peace Street to the Arch of the Star are collected thousands of refugees from our Ilium. Under the arcades of the Rue de Rivoli you meet, at certain hours, as many of our Trojans as of the natives. In the Trojan inns of " Meurice," the " Louvre," &c., we swarm. We have numerous Anglo-Trojan doctors and apothecaries, who give us the dear pills and doses of Pergamus. We go to Mrs. Guerre or kind Mrs. Colombin, and can purchase the sandwiches of Troy, the pale ale and sherry of Troy, and the dear, dear muffins of home. We live for years, never speaking any language but our native Trojan ; except to our servants, whom we instruct in the Trojan way of preparing toast for breakfast ; Trojan bread-sauce for fowls and patridges ; Trojan corned beef, &c. We have temples where we worship according to the Trojan rites. A kindly sight is that which one beholds of a Sunday in the Elysian fields and the St. Honoré quarter, of processions of English grown people and children, stalwart, red-cheeked, marching to their churches, their gilded prayer-books in hand, to sing in a stranger's land the sacred songs of their Zion. I am sure there are many English in Paris who never speak to any native above the rank of a waiter or shopman. Not long since I was listening to a Frenchman at Folkestone, speaking English to the waiters and acting as interpreter for his party. He spoke pretty well and very quickly. He was irresistibly comical. I wonder how we maintained our gravity. And you and I, my dear friend, when *we* speak French, I dare say we are just as absurd. As absurd ! And why not ? Don't you be discouraged, young fellow. *Courage, mon jeune ami!* Remember, Trojans have a conquering way with them. When Æneas landed at Carthage, I dare say he spoke Carthaginian with a ridiculous Trojan accent ; but, for all that, poor Dido fell desperately in love with him. Take example by the son of Anchises, my boy. Never mind the grammar or the pronunciation, but tackle the lady, and speak your mind to her as best you can.

This is the plan which the Vicomte de Loisy used to adopt. He was following a *course* of English according to the celebrated *méthode Jobson*. The *cours* assembled twice a week : and the Vicomte, with laudable assiduity, went to all English parties to which he could gain an introduction, for the purpose of acquiring the English language, and marrying *une Anglaise.* This industrious young man even went *au Temple* on Sundays for the purpose of familiarizing himself with the English language ; and as he sat under Doctor Murrogh Macmanus of T. C. D., a very eloquent preacher at Paris in those days, the Vicomte acquired a very fine pronunciation. Attached to the cause of unfortunate monarchy all over the world, the Vicomte had fought in the

Spanish-Carlist armies. He waltzed well : and madame thought
his cross looked nice at her parties. Will it be believed that
Mrs. General Baynes took this gentleman into special favor;
talked with him at *soirée* after *soirée ;* never laughed at his English ; encouraged her girl to waltz with him (which he did to
perfection, whereas poor Philip was but a hulking and clumsy
performer) ; and showed him the very greatest favor, until one
day, on going into Mr. Bonus's, the house-agent (who lets lodgings, and sells British pickles, tea, sherry, and the like), she
found the Vicomte occupying a stool as clerk in Mr. Bonus's
establishment, where for twelve hundred francs a year he gave
his invaluable services during the day! Mrs. Baynes took poor
madame severely to task for admitting such a man to her assemblies. Madame was astonished. Monsieur was a gentleman
of ancient family who had met with misfortunes. He was earning his maintenance. To sit in a bureau was not a dishonor.
Knowing that *boutique* meant shop and *garçon* meant boy, Mrs.
Baynes made use of the words *boutique garçon* the next time
she saw the Vicomte. The little man wept tears of rage and
mortification. There was a very painful scene, at which, thank
mercy, poor Charlotte thought, Philip was not present. Were
it not for the General's *cheveux blancs* (by which phrase the
Vicomte very kindly designated General Baynes's chestnut top-
knot), the Vicomte would have had reason from him. "Charming miss," he said to Charlotte, "your respectable papa is safe
from my sword ! Madame your mamma has addressed me
words which I qualify not. But you—you are too 'andsome, too
good, to despise a poor soldier, a poor gentleman !" I have
heard the Vicomte still dances at boarding-houses and is still in
pursuit of an *Anglaise*. He must be a wooer now almost as
elderly as the good General whose scalp he respected.

Mrs. Baynes was, to be sure, a heavy weight to bear for
poor madame, but her lean shoulders were accustomed to many
a burden ; and if the General's wife was quarrelsome and
odious, he, as madame said, was as soft as a mutton ; and
Charlotte's pretty face and manners were the admiration of all.
The yellow Miss Bolderos, those hapless elderly orphans left in
pawn, might bite their lips with envy, but they never could
make them as red as Miss Charlotte's smiling mouth. To the
honor of Madame Smolensk be it said that, never by word or
hint, did she cause those unhappy young ladies any needless
pain. She never stinted them of any meal. No full-priced
pensioner of madame's could have breakfast, luncheon, dinners
served more regularly. The day after their mother's flight,

that good Madame Smolensk took early cups of tea to the girls'
rooms, with her own hands ; and I believe helped to do the
hair of one of them, and otherwise to sooth them in their misfortune. They could not keep their secret. It must be owned
that Mrs. Baynes never lost an opportunity of deploring their
situation and acquainting all new-comers with their mother's
flight and transgression. But she was good-natured to the cap-
tives in her grim way : and admired madame's forbearance
regarding them. The two old officers were now especially
polite to the poor things : and the General rapped one of his
boys over the knuckles for saying to Miss Brenda, " If your
uncle is a lord, why doesn't he give you any money ? " "And
these girls used to hold their heads above mine, and their
mother used to give herself such airs ! " cried Mrs. Baynes.
" And Eliza Baynes used to flatter those poor girls and their
mother, and fancy they were going to make a woman of fashion
of her ! " said Mrs. Bunch. " We all have our weaknesses.
Lords are not yours, my dear. Faith, I don't think you know
one," says stout little Colonel Bunch. " I wouldn't pay a
duchess such court as Eliza paid that woman ! " cried Sarah ;
and she made sarcastic inquiries of the General, whether Eliza
had heard from her friend the Honorable Mrs. Boldero ? But
for all this Mrs. Bunch pitied the young ladies, and I believe
gave them a little supply of coin from her private purse. A
word as to their private history. Their mamma became the
terror of boarding-house keepers : and the poor girls practised
their duets all over Europe. Mrs. Boldero's noble nephew, the
present Strongitharm (as a friend who knows the fashionable
world informs me) was victimized by his own uncle, and a most
painful affair occurred between them at a game at " blind
hookey." The Honorable Mrs. Boldero is living in the precincts of Holyrood ; one of her daughters is happily married to
a minister ; and the other to an apothecary who was called in
to attend her in quinsy. So I am inclined to think that phrase
about " select " boarding-houses is a mere complimentary term ;
and as for the strictest references being given and required, I
certainly should not lay out extra money for printing *that* expression in my advertisement, were I going to set up an establishment myself.

Old college friends of Philip's visited Paris from time to
time ; and rejoiced in carrying him off to " Borel's " or the
" Trois Frères," and hospitably treating him who had been so
hospitable in his time. Yes, thanks be to heaven, there are
good Samaritans in pretty large numbers in this world, and

hands ready enough to succor a man in misfortune. I could name two of three gentlemen who drive about in chariots and look at people's tongues and write queer figures and queer Latin on note-paper, who occultly made a purse containing some seven or ten score fees, and sent them out to Dr. Firmin in his banishment. The poor wretch had behaved as ill as might be, but he was without a penny or a friend. I dare say Dr. Good-enough, amongst other philanthropists, put his hands into his pocket. Having heartily disliked and mistrusted Firmin in prosperity, in adversity he melted towards the poor fugitive wretch: he even could believe that Firmin had some skill in his profession, and in his practice was not quite a quack.

Philip's old college and school cronies laughed at hearing that, now his ruin was complete, he was thinking about mar-riage. Such a plan was of a piece with Mr. Firmin's known prudence and foresight. But they made an objection to his proposed union, which had struck us at home previously. Papa-in-law was well enough, or at least inoffensive: but ah, ye powers! what a mother-in-law was poor Phil laying up for his future days! Two or three of our mutual companions made this remark on returning to work and chambers after their autumn holiday. We never had too much charity for Mrs. Baynes; and what Philip told us about her did not serve to in-crease our regard.

About Christmas Mr. Firmin's own affairs brought him on a brief visit to London. We were not jealous that he took up quarters with his little friend, of Thornhaugh Street, who was contented that he should dine with us, provided she could have the pleasure of housing him under her kind shelter. High and mighty people as we were—for under what humble roofs does not Vanity hold her sway?—we, who knew Mrs. Brandon's vir-tues, and were aware of her early story, would have conde-scended to receive her into our society; but it was the little lady herself who had her pride, and held aloof. "My parents did not give me the education you have had, ma'am," Caroline said to my wife. "My place is not here, I know very well; unless you should be took ill, and *then*, ma'am, you'll see that I will be glad enough to come. Philip can come and see *me;* and a blessing it is to me to set eyes on him. But I shouldn't be happy in your drawing-room, nor you in having me. The dear children look surprised at my way of talking; and no wonder: and they laugh sometimes to one another, God bless 'em! I don't mind. My education was not cared for. I scarce had any schooling but what I taught myself. My Pa hadn't the

means of learning me much : and it is too late to go to school
at forty odd. I've got all his stockings and things darned ;
and his linen, poor fellow !—beautiful : I wish they kep' it as
nice in France, where he is ! You'll give my love to the young
lady, won't you, ma'am ? and oh ! it's a blessing to me to hear
how good and gentle she is ! He has a high temper, Philip
have : but them he likes can easy manage him. You have been
his best kind friends ; and so will she be, I trust ; and they
may be happy though they're poor. But they've time to get
rich, haven't they ? And it's not the richest that's the happiest,
that I can see in many a fine house where Nurse Brandon goes
and has her eyes open, though she don't say much, you know."
In this way Nurse Brandon would prattle on to us when she
came to see us. She would share our meal, always thanking
by name the servant who helped her. She insisted on calling our children " Miss " and " Master," and I think those
young satirists did not laugh often or unkindly at her peculiarities. I know they were told that Nurse Brandon was very
good ; and that she took care of her father in his old age ; and
that she had passed through very great griefs and trials ; and
that she had nursed Uncle Philip when he had been very ill
indeed, and when many people would have been afraid to come
near him ; and that her life was spent in tending the sick, and
in doing good to her neighbor.

One day during Philip's stay with us we happen to read in
the paper Lord Ringwood's arrival in London. My lord had a
grand town-house of his own which he did not always inhabit.
He liked the cheerfulness of a hotel better. Ringwood House
was too large and too dismal. He did not care to eat a solitary
mutton-chop in a great dining-room surrounded by ghostly
images of dead Ringwoods—his dead son, a boy who had died
in his boyhood ; his dead brother attired in the uniform of his
day (in which picture there was no little resemblance to Philip
Firmin, the Colonel's grandson) ; Lord Ringwood's dead self,
finally, as he appeared still a young man, when Lawrence
painted him, and when he was the companion of the Regent
and his friends. " Ah ! that's the fellow I least like to look
at," the old man would say, scowling at the picture, and
breaking out into the old-fashioned oaths which garnished
many conversations in his young days. " That fellow could
ride all day ; and sleep all night, or go without sleep as he
chose ; and drink his four bottles and never have a headache ;
and break his collar-bone, and see the fox killed three hours
after. That was once a man, as old Marlborough said, looking

at his own picture. Now my doctor's my master ; my doctor
and the infernal gout over him. I live upon pap and puddens,
like a baby ; only I've shed all my teeth, hang 'em. If I drink
three glasses of sherry, my butler threatens me. You young
fellow, who haven't twopence in your pocket, by George, I
would like to change with you. Only you wouldn't, hang you,
you wouldn't. Why, I don't believe Todhunter would change with
me : would you, Todhunter?—and you're about as fond of a
great man as any fellow I ever knew. Don't tell me. You *are*,
sir. Why, when I walked with you on Ryde sands one day, I
said to that fellow, ' Todhunter, don't you think I could order
the sea to stand still ? ' I did. And you had never heard of
King Canute, hanged if you had, and never read any book
except the Stud-book and Mrs. Glasse's Cookery, hanged if
you did." Such remarks and conversations of his relative has
Philip reported to me. Two or three men about town had very
good imitations of this toothless, growling, blasphemous old
cynic. He was splendid and penurious ; violent and easily led ;
surrounded by flatterers and utterly lonely. He had old-world
notions, which I believe have passed out of the manners of
great folks now. He thought it beneath him to travel by
railway, and his post-chaise was one of the last on the road.
The tide rolled on in spite of this old Canute, and has long
since rolled over him and his post-chaise. Why, almost all his
imitators are actually dead ; and only this year, when old
Jack Mummers gave an imitation of him at " Bays's " (where
Jack's mimicry used to be received with shouts of laughter but
a few years since), there was a dismal silence in the coffee-
room, except from two or three young men at a near table, who
said, " What is the old fool mumbling and swearing at now ?
An imitation of Lord Ringwood, and who was he ? " So our
names pass away, and are forgotten : and the tallest statues,
do not the sands of time accumulate and overwhelm *them ? I*
have not forgotten my lord ; any more than I have forgotten
the cock of my school, about whom, perhaps, you don't care to
hear. I see my lord's bald head, and hooked beak, and bushy
eyebrows, and tall velvet collar, and brass buttons, and great
black mouth, and trembling hand, and trembling parasites
around him, and I can hear his voice, and great oaths, and
laughter. You parasites of to-day are bowing to other great
people ; and this great one, who was alive only yesterday, is as
dead as George IV. or Nebuchadnezzar.

Well, we happen to read that Philip's noble relative Lord
Ringwood has arrived at —— Hotel, whilst Philip is staying

with us; and I own that I counsel my friend to go and wait upon his lordship. He had been very kind at Paris: he had evidently taken a liking to Philip. Firmin ought to go and see him. Who knows? Lord Ringwood might be inclined to do something for his brother's grandson.

This was just the point which any one who knew Philip should have hesitated to urge upon him. To try and make him bow and smile on a great man with a view to future favors, was to demand the impossible from Firmin. The king's men may lead the king's horses to the water, but the king himself can't make them drink. I own that I came back to the subject, and urged it repeatedly on my friend. "I *have* been," said Philip, sulkily. "I have left a card upon him. If he wants me, he can send to No. 120, Queen Square, Westminster, my present hotel. But if you think he will give me anything beyond a dinner, I tell you you are mistaken."

We dined that day with Philip's employer, worthy Mr. Mugford, of the *Pall Mall Gazette*, who was profuse in his hospitalities, and especially gracious to Philip. Mugford was pleased with Firmin's letters; and you may be sure that severer critics did not contradict their friend's good-natured patron. We drove to the suburban villa at Hampstead, and steaming odors of soup, mutton, onions, rushed out into the hall to give us welcome, and to warn us of the good cheer in store for the party. *This* was not one of Mr. Mugford's days for countermanding side dishes, I promise you. Men in black with noble white cotton gloves were in waiting to receive us; and Mrs. Mugford, in a rich blue satin and feathers, a profusion of flounces, laces, marabouts, jewels, and eau-de-Cologne, rose to welcome us from a stately sofa, where she sat surrounded by her children. These, too, were in brilliant dresses, with shining new-combed hair. The ladies, of course, instantly began to talk about their children, and my wife's unfeigned admiration for Mrs. Mugford's last baby I think won that worthy lady's good-will at once. I made some remark regarding one of the boys as being the picture of his father, which was not lucky. I don't know why, but I have it from her husband's own admission, that Mrs. Mugford always thinks I am "chaffing" her. One of the boys frankly informed me there was goose for dinner; and when a cheerful cloop was heard from a neighboring room, told me that was Pa drawing the corks. Why should Mrs. Mugford reprove the outspoken child and say, "James, hold your tongue, do now?" Better wine than was poured forth, when those corks were drawn, never flowed from bottle.—I say, I never saw better wine nor more bottles. If ever a table may be said to have groaned, that expression might with justice be applied to Mugford's mahogany. Talbot Twysden would have feasted forty people with the meal here provided for eight by our most hospitable entertainer. Though Mugford's editor was present, who thinks himself a very fine fellow, I assure you, but whose name I am not at liberty to divulge, all the honors of the entertainment were for the *Paris Correspondent*, who was specially requested to take Mrs. M. to dinner. As an earl's grand-nephew, and a lord's great-grandson, of course we felt that this place of honor was Firmin's rights. How Mrs. Mugford pressed him to eat ! She carved—I am very glad she would not let Philip carve for her, for he might have sent the goose into her lap—she carved, I say, and I really think she gave him more stuffing than to any of us, but that may have been mere envy on my part. Allusions to Lord Ringwood were repeatedly made during dinner. " Lord R. has come to town, Mr. F., I perceive," says Mugford, winking. "You've been to see him, of course ? " Mr. Firmin glared at me very fiercely, he had to own he *had* been to call on Lord Ringwood. Mugford led the conversation to the noble lord so frequently that Philip madly kicked my shins under the table. I don't know how many times I had to suffer from that foot which in its time has trampled on so many persons : a kick for each time Lord Ringwood's name, houses, parks, properties, were mentioned, was a frightful allowance. Mrs. Mugford would say, " May I assist you to a little pheasant, Mr. Firmin ? I dare say they are not as good as Lord Ringwood's " (a kick from Philip) ; or Mugford would exclaim, " Mr. F., try that 'ock ! Lord Ringwood hasn't better wine than that." (Dreadful punishment upon my tibia under the table.) " John ! Two 'ocks, me and Mr. Firmin. Join us, Mr. P.," and so forth And after dinner, to the ladies—as my wife, who betrayed their mysteries, informed me—Mrs. Mugford's conversation was incessant regarding the Ringwood family and Firmin's relationship to that noble house. The meeting of the old lord and Firmin in Paris was discussed with immense interest. " His lordship called him Philip most affable ! he was very fond of Mr Firmin." A little bird had told Mrs. Mugford that somebody else was very fond of Mr. Firmin. She hoped it would be a match, and that his lordship would do the handsome thing by his *nephew*. What ? My wife wondered that Mrs. Mugford should know about Philip's affairs ? (and wonder indeed she did). A little bird had told Mrs. M—, a friend of both ladies,

that dear, good little nurse Brandon, who was engaged——and
here the conversation went off into mysteries which I certainly
shall not reveal. Suffice it that Mrs. Mugford was one of Mrs.
Brandon's best, kindest, and most constant patrons—or might
I be permitted to say matrons?—and had received a most
favorable report of us from the little nurse. And here Mrs.
Pendennis gave a verbatim report not only of our hostess's
speech, but of her manner and accent. "Yes, ma'am," says
Mrs. Mugford to Mrs. Pendennis, "our friend Mrs. B. has told
me of *a certain gentleman* whose name shall be nameless. His
manner is cold, not to say 'aughty. He seems to be laughing
at people sometimes—don't say No; I saw him once or twice
at dinner, both him and Mr. Firmin. But he is a true friend,
Mrs. Brandon says he is. And when you know him, his heart
is good." Is it? Amen. A distinguished writer has composed, in not very late days, a comedy of which the cheerful
moral is, that we are "not so bad as we seem." Aren't we?
Amen, again. Give us thy hearty hand, Iago! Tartuffe, how
the world has been mistaken in you! Macbeth! put that little
affair of the murder out of your mind. It was a momentary
weakness; and who is not weak at times? Blifil, a more
maligned man than you does not exist! O humanity! how we
have been mistaken in you! Let us expunge the vulgar expression "miserable sinners" out of all prayer-books; open the
port-holes of all hulks; break the chains of all convicts; and
unlock the boxes of all spoons.

As we discussed Mr. Mugford's entertainment on our return
home, I improved the occasion with Philip; I pointed out the
reasonableness of the hopes which he might entertain of help
from his wealthy kinsman, and actually forced him to promise
to wait upon my lord the next day. Now, when Philip Firmin
did a thing against his will, he did it with a bad grace. When
he is not pleased, he does not pretend to be happy; and when
he is sulky, Mr. Firmin is a very disagreeable companion.
Though he never once reproached me afterwards with what happened, I own that I have had cruel twinges of conscience since.
If I had not sent him on that dutiful visit to his grand-uncle,
what occurred might never, perhaps, have occurred at all. I
acted for the best, and that I aver; however I may grieve for
the consequences which ensued when the poor fellow followed
my advice.

If Philip held aloof from Lord Ringwood in London, you
may be sure Philip's dear cousins were in waiting on his lordship, and never lost an opportunity of showing their respectful

sympathy. Was Lord Ringwood ailing? Mr. Twysden, or Mrs. Twysden, or the dear girls, or Ringwood their brother, were daily in his lordship's ante-chamber, asking for news of his health. They bent down respectfully before Lord Ringwood's major-domo. They would have given him money, as they always averred, only what sum could they give to such a man as Rudge? They actually offered to bribe Mr. Rudge with their wine, over which he made horrible faces. They fawned and smiled before him always. I should like to have seen that calm Mrs. Twysden, that serene, high-bred woman, who would cut her dearest friend if misfortune befell her, or the world turned its back;—I should like to have seen, and *can* see her in my mind's eye, simpering and coaxing, and wheedling this footman. She made cheap presents to Mr. Rudge : she smiled on him and asked after his health. And of course Talbot Twysden flattered him too in Talbot's jolly way. It was a wink, and nod, and a hearty " How do you do?"—and (after due inquiries made and answered about his lordship) it would be, " Rudge! I think my housekeeper has a good glass of port-wine in her room, if you happen to be passing that way, and my lord don't want you!" And with a grave courtesy, I can fancy Mr. Rudge bowing to Mr. and Mrs. Twysden, and thanking them and descending to Mrs. Blenkinsop's skinny room where the port-wine is ready—and if Mr. Rudge and Mrs. Blenkinsop are confidential, I can fancy their talking over the characters and peculiarities of the folks up stairs. Servants sometimes actually do ; and if master and mistress are humbugs, these wretched menials sometimes find them out.

Now, no duke could be more lordly and condescending in his bearing than Mr. Philip Firmin toward the menial throng. In those days when he had money in his pockets, he gave Mr. Rudge out of his plenty ; and the man remembered his generosity when he was poor ; and declared—in a select society, and in the company of the relative of a person from whom I have the information—declared in the presence of Captain Gann at the " Admiral B—ng Club " in fact, that Mr. Heff was always a swell ; but since he was done, he, Rudge, " was blest if that young chap warn't a greater swell than hever." And Rudge actually liked this poor young fellow better than the family in Beaunash Street, whom Mr. R. pronounced to be " a shabby lot." And in fact it was Rudge as well as myself, who advised that Philip should see his lordship.

When at length Philip paid his second visit, Mr. Rudge said " My lord will see you, sir, I think. He has been speaking of you. He's very unwell. He's going to have a fit of the gout, I think. I'll tell him you are here." And coming back to Philip, after a brief disappearance, and with rather a scared face, he repeated the permission to enter, and again cautioned him, saying, that "my lord was very queer."

In fact, as we learned afterwards, through the channel previously indicated, my lord, when he heard that Philip had called, cried, "He *has*, has he? Hang him, send him in;" using, I am constrained to say, in place of the monosyllable "hang," a much stronger expression.

"Oh, it's you, is it?" says my lord. "You have been in London ever so long. Twysden told me of you yesterday.'

"I have called before, sir," said Philip very quietly.

"I wonder you have the face to call at all, sir!" cries the old man, glaring at Philip. His lordship's countenance was of a gamboge color: his noble eyes were blood-shot and starting; his voice, always very harsh and strident, was now specially unpleasant; and from the crater of his mouth, shot loud exploding oaths.

"Face, my lord?" says Philip, still very meek.

"Yes, if you call that a face which is covered over with hair like a baboon!" growled my lord, showing his tusks. "Twysden was here last night, and tells me some pretty news about you."

Philip blushed; he knew what the news most likely would be.

"Twysden says that now you are a pauper, by George, and living by breaking stones in the street,—you have been such an infernal, drivelling, hanged fool, as to engage yourself to another pauper!"

Poor Philip turned white from red; and spoke slowly: "I beg your pardon, my lord, you said——"

"I said you were a hanged fool, sir!" roared the old man; "can't you hear?"

"I believe I am a member of your family, my lord," says Philip, rising up. In a quarrel, he would sometimes lose his temper, and speak out his mind; or sometimes, and then he was most dangerous, he would be especially calm and Grandisonian.

"Some hanged adventurer, thinking you were to get money from me, has hooked you for his daughter, has he?"

"I have engaged myself to a young lady, and I am the poorer of the two," says Philip.

"She thinks you will get money from me," continues his lordship.

"Does she? I never did!" replied Philip.

"By heaven, you sha'n't, unless you give up this rubbish."

"I sha'n't give her up, sir, and I shall do without the money," said Mr. Firmin very boldly.

"Go to Tartarus!" screamed the old man.

On which Philip told us, "I said, 'Seniores priores, my lord,' and turned on my heel. So you see if he was going to leave me something, and he nearly said he was, that chance is passed now, and I have made a pretty morning's work." And a pretty morning's work it was: and it was I who had set him upon it! My brave Philip not only did not rebuke me for having sent him on this errand, but took the blame of the business on himself. "Since I have been engaged," he said, "I am growing dreadfully avaricious, and am almost as sordid about money as those Twysdens. I cringed to that old man: I crawled before his gouty feet. Well, I could crawl from here to Saint James's Palace to get some money for my little Charlotte." Philip cringe and crawl! If there were no posture-masters more supple than Philip Firmin, kotowing would be a lost art, like the *Menuet de la Cour*. But fear not, ye great! Men's backs were made to bend, and the race of parasites is still in good repute.

When our friend told us how his brief interview with Lord Ringwood had begun and ended, I think those who counselled Philip to wait upon his grand-uncle felt rather ashamed of their worldly wisdom and the advice which they had given. We ought to have known our Huron sufficiently to be aware that it was a dangerous experiment to set him bowing in lord's ante-chambers. Were not his elbows sure to break some courtly china, his feet to trample and tear some lace train? So all the good we had done was to occasion a quarrel between him and his patron. Lord Ringwood avowed that he had intended to leave Philip money; and by trusting the poor fellow into the old nobleman's sick-chamber, we had occasioned a quarrel between the relatives, who parted with mutual threats and anger. "Oh, dear me!" I groaned in connubial colloquies. "Let us get him away. He will be boxing Mugford's ears next, and telling Mrs. Mugford that she is vulgar, and a bore." He was eager to get back to his work, or rather to his lady-love at Paris. We did not try to detain him. For fear of further accidents we were rather anxious that he should be gone. Crestfallen and sad, I accompanied him to the Boulogne boat. He paid for his place in the second cabin, and stoutly bade us adieu. A rough night: a wet, slippery deck: a crowd of frowzy fellow-passengers: and poor Philip in the midst of them in a thin cloak, his yellow hair and beard blowing about: I see the steamer now, and left her with I know not what feelings of contrition and shame. Why had I sent Philip to call upon that savage, over-bearing old patron of his? Why compelled him to that boot-less act of submission? Lord Ringwood's brutalities were matters of common notoriety. A wicked, dissolute, cynical old man: and we must try to make friends with this mammon of unrighteousness, and set poor Philip to bow before him and flatter him! Ah, *mea culpa, mea culpa!* The wind blew hard that winter night, and many tiles and chimney-pots blew down: and as I thought of poor Philip tossing in the frowzy second cabin, I rolled about my own bed very uneasily.

"I looked into "Bay's Club" the day after, and there fell on both the Twysdens. The parasite of a father was clinging to the button of a great man when I entered: the little reptile of a son came to the club in Captain Woolcomb's brougham, and in that distinguished mullatto officer's company. They looked at me in a peculiar way. I was sure they did. Talbot Twysden, pouring his loud braggart talk in the ear of poor Lord Lepel, eyed me with a glance of triumph, and talked and swag-gered so that I should hear. Ringwood Twysden and Wool-comb, drinking absinthe to whet their noble appetites, ex-changed glances and grins. Woolcomb's eyes were of the color of the absinthe he swallowed. I did not see that Twysden tore off one of Lord Lepel's buttons, but that nobleman, with a scared countenance, moved away rapidly from his little persecutor. "Hang him, throw him over, and come to me!" I heard the generous Twysden say. "I expect Ringwood and one or two more." At this proposition, Lord Lepel, in a trem-ulous way, muttered that he could not break his engagement, and fled out of the club.

Twysden's dinners, the polite reader has been previously informed, were notorious; and he constantly bragged of having the company of Lord Ringwood. Now it so happened that on this very evening, Lord Ringwood, with three of his followers, henchmen, or led captains, dined at Bays's Club, being deter-mined to see a pantomime in which a very pretty young Colum-bine figured: and some one in the house joked with his lordship, and said, "Why, you are going to dine with Talbot Twysden. He said, just now, that he expected you."

"Did he?" said his lordship. "Then Talbot Twysden told a hanged lie!" And little Tom Eaves, my informant, remem-bered these remarkable words, because of a circumstance which now almost immediately followed.

A very few days after Philip's departure, our friend, the Little Sister, came to us at our breakfast-table, wearing an expression of much trouble and sadness on her kind little face ; the causes of which sorrow she explained to us, as soon as our children had gone away to their schoolroom. Amongst Mrs. Brandon's friends, and one of her father's constant companions, was the worthy Mr. Ridley, father of the celebrated painter of that name, who was himself of much too honorable and noble a nature to be ashamed of his humble paternal origin. Companionship between father and son could not be very close or intimate ; especially as in the younger Ridley's boyhood, his father, who knew nothing of the fine arts, had looked upon the child as a sickly, half-witted creature, who would be to his parents but a grief and a burden. But when J. J. Ridley, Esq., began to attain eminence in his profession, his father's eyes were opened ; in place of neglect and contempt, he looked up to his boy with a sincere, *naïve* admiration, and often, with tears, has narrated the pride and pleasure which he felt on the day when he waited on John James at his master Lord Todmorden's table. Ridley senior now felt that he had been unkind and unjust to his boy in the latter's early days, and with a very touching humility the old man acknowledged his previous injustice, and tried to atone for it by present respect and affection.

Though fondness for his son, and delight in the company of Captain Gann, often drew Mr. Ridley to Thornhaugh Street, and to the "Admiral Byng" Club, of which both were leading members, Ridley senior belonged to other clubs at the West End, where Lord Todmorden's butler consorted with the confidential butlers of others of the nobility : and I am informed that in those clubs Ridley continued to be called "Todmorden" long after his connection with that venerable nobleman had ceased. He continued to be called Lord Todmorden, in fact, just as Lord Popinjoy is still called by his old friends Popinjoy, though his father is dead, and Popinjoy, as everybody knows, is at present Earl of Pintado.

At one of these clubs of their order, Lord Todmorden's man was in the constant habit of meeting Lord Ringwood's man, when their lordships (master and man) were in town. These gentlemen had a regard for each other ; and, when they met, communicated to each other their views of society, and their opinions of the characters of the various noble lords and influential commoners whom they served. Mr. Rudge knew everything about Philip Firmin's affairs, about the Doctor's flight, about Philip's generous behavior. "Generous ! *I* call it ad-

miral!" old Ridley remarked, while narrating this trait of
our friend's—and his present position. And Rudge contrasted
Philip's manly behavior with the conduct of some *sneaks* which
he would not name them, but which they were always speaking
ill of the poor young fellow behind his back, and sneaking up
to my lord, and greater skinflints and meaner humbugs never
were: and there was no accounting for tastes, but he, Rudge,
would not marry *his* daughter to a black man.

Now: that day when Mr. Firmin went to see my Lord Ringwood was one of my lord's very worst days, when it was almost
as dangerous to go near him as to approach a Bengal tiger.
When he is going to have a fit of gout, his lordship (Mr. Rudge
remarked) " was hawful." He curse and swear, he do, at every
body; even the clergy or the ladies—all's one. On that very
day when Mr. Firmin called he had said to Mr. Twysden, 'Get
out, and don't come slandering, and backbiting, and bullying
that poor devil of a boy any more. It's blackguardly, by
George, sir—it's blackguardly.' And Twysden came out with
his tail between his legs, and he says to me—'Rudge,' says he,
'my lord's uncommon bad to-day.' Well, he hadn't been gone
an hour when pore Philip comes, bad luck to him, and my lord,
who had just heard from Twysden all about that young woman
—that party at Paris, Mr. Ridley—and it *is* about as great a
piece of folly as ever I heard tell of—my lord turns upon the
pore young fellar and call him names worse than Twysden.
But Mr. Firmin ain't that sort of man, he isn't. He won't suffer
any man to call *him* names; and I suppose he gave my lord his
own back again, for I heard my lord swear at him tremendous,
I did, with my own ears. When my lord has the gout flying
about I told you he is awful. When he takes his colchicum
he's worse. Now, we have got a party at Whipham at Christmas, and at Whipham we must be. And he took his colchicum
night before last, and to-day he was in such a tremendous rage
of swearing, cursing, and blowing up everybody, that it was as
if he was *red hot*. And when Twysden and Mrs. Twysden
called that day—(if you kick that fellar out at the hall door,
I'm blest if he won't come smirking down the chimney)—he
wouldn't see any of them. And he bawled out after me, 'If
Firmin comes, kick him down stairs—do you hear?' with ever
so many oaths and curses against the poor fellow, while he
vowed he would never see his hanged impudent face again.
But this wasn't all, Ridley. He sent for Bradgate, his lawyer,
that very day. He had back his will, which I signed myself as
one of the witnesses—me and Wilcox, the master of the hotel—

and I know he had left Firmin something in it. Take my word for it. To that poor young fellow he means mischief." A full report of this conversation Mr. Ridley gave to his little friend Mrs. Brandon, knowing the interest which Mrs. Brandon took in the young gentleman ; and with these unpleasant news Mrs. Brandon came off to advise with those who—the good nurse was pleased to say—were Philip's best friends in the world. We wished we could give the Little Sister comfort : but all the world knew what a man Lord Ringwood was—how arbitrary, how revengeful, how cruel !

I knew Mr. Bradgate the lawyer, with whom I had business, and called upon him, more anxious to speak about Philip's affairs than my own. I suppose I was too eager in coming to my point, for Bradgate saw the meaning of my questions, and declined to answer them. " My client and I are not the dearest friends in the world," Bradgate said, " but I must keep his counsel, and must not tell you whether Mr. Firmin's name is down in his lordship's will or not. How should I know ? He may have altered his will. He may have left Firmin money ; he may have left him none. I hope young Firmin does not count on a legacy. That's all. He may be disappointed if he does. Why, *you* may hope for a legacy from Lord Ringwood, and you may be disappointed. I know scores of people who do hope for something, and who won't get a penny." And this was all the reply I could get at that time from the oracular little lawyer.

I told my wife, as of course every dutiful man tells everything to every dutiful wife :—but, though Bradgate discouraged us, there was somehow a lurking hope still that the old nobleman would provide for our friend. Then Philip would marry Charlotte. Then he would earn ever so much more money by his newspaper. Then he would be happy ever after. My wife counts eggs not only before they are hatched, but before they are laid. Never was such an obstinate hopefulness of character. I, on the other hand, take a rational and despondent view of things ; and if they turn out better than I expect, as sometimes they will, I affably own that I have been mistaken.

But an early day came when Mr. Bradgate was no longer needful, or when he thought himself released from the obligations of silence with regard to his noble client. It was two days before Christmas, and I took my accustomed afternoon saunter to " Bays's," where other *habitués* of the club were assembled. There was no little buzzing and excitement among the frequenters of the place. Talbot Twysden always arrived

at "Bays's" at ten minutes past four, and scuffled for the
evening paper, as if its contents were matter of great importance
to Talbot. He would hold men's buttons, and discourse to
them the leading article out of that paper with an astounding
emphasis and gravity. On this day, some ten minutes after his
accustomed hour, he reached the club. Other gentlemen were
engaged in perusing the evening journal. The lamps on the
tables lighted up the bald heads, the gray heads, dyed heads,
and the wigs of many assembled fogies—murmurs went about
the room : " Very sudden." " Gout in the stomach." " Dined
here only four days ago." " Looked very well." " Very well ?
No ! Never saw a fellow look worse in my life." " Yellow as
a guinea." " Couldn't eat." " Swore dreadfully at the waiters,
and at Tom Eaves who dined with him." " Seventy-six, I see.
—Born in the same year with the Duke of York." " Forty
thousand a year." " Forty ? fifty-eight thousand three hundred,
I tell you. Always been a saving man." " Estate goes to his
cousin, sir John Ringwood : not a member here—member of
' Boodle's.' " " Hated each other furiously. Very violent
temper, the old fellow was. Never got over the Reform Bill,
they used to say." " Wonder whether he'll leave anything to
old bow-wow Twys—" Here enters Talbot Twysden, Esq.—
" Ha, Colonel ! How are you ? What's the news to-night ?
Kept late at my office, making up accounts. Going down to
Whipham to-morrow to pass Christmas with my wife's uncle—
Ringwood, you know. Always go down to Whipham at Christmas. Keeps the pheasants for us. No longer a hunting man
myself. Lost my nerve, by George."

Whilst the braggart little creature indulged in this pompous
talk, he did not see the significant looks which were fixed upon
him, or if he remarked them, was perhaps pleased by the
attention which he excited. " Bays's " had long echoed with
Twysden's account of Ringwood, the pheasants, his own loss
of nerve in hunting, and the sum which their family would inherit at the death of their noble relative.

" I think I have heard you say Sir John Ringwood inherits
after your relatives ? " asked Mr. Hookham.

" Yes ; the estate, not the title. The earldom goes to my
lord and his heirs—Hookham. Why shouldn't he marry again ?
I often say to him, ' Ringwood, why don't you marry, if it's
only to disappoint that Whig fellow, Sir John ? You are fresh
and hale, Ringwood. You may live twenty years, five-and-twenty
years. If you leave your niece and my children anything, we're
not in a hurry to inherit,' I say ; ' why don't you marry ? ' "

" Ah ! Twysden, he's past marrying," groans Mr. Hookham.

" Not at all. Sober man, now. Stout man. Immense powerful man. Healthy man, but for gout. I often say to him, ' Ringwood ! I say——' "

" Oh, for mercy's sake, stop this ! " groans old Mr. Tremlett, who always begins to shudder at the sound of poor Twysden's voice. "Tell him, somebody."

" Haven't you heard, Twysden ? Haven't you seen ? Don't you know ? " asks Mr. Hookham, solemnly.

" Heard, seen, known—what ? " cries the other.

" An accident has happened to Lord Ringwood. Look at the paper. Here it is." And Twysden pulls out his great gold eyeglasses, holds the paper as far as his little arm will reach, and —— and merciful Powers ! —— but I will not venture to depict the agony on that noble face. Like Timanthes the painter, I hide this Agamemnon with a veil. I cast the *Globe* newspaper over him. *Illabatur orbis :* and let imagination depict our Twysden under the ruins.

What Twysden read in the *Globe* was a mere curt paragraph ; but in next morning's *Times* there was one of those obituary notices to which noblemen of eminence must submit from the mysterious necrographer engaged by that paper.

CHAPTER XXII.

PULVIS ET UMBRA SUMUS.

THE first and only Earl of Ringwood has submitted to the fate which peers and commoners are alike destined to undergo. Hastening to his magnificent seat of Whipham Market, where he proposed to entertain an illustrious Christmas party, his lordship left London scarcely recovered from an attack of gout to which he has been for many years a martyr. The disease must have flown to his stomach, and suddenly mastered him. At Turreys Regum, thirty miles from his own princely habitation, where he had been accustomed to dine on his almost royal progresses to his home, he was already in a state of dreadful suffering, to which his attendants did not pay the attention which his condition ought to have excited ; for when laboring under this most painful malady his outcries were loud, and his language and demeanor exceedingly violent. He angrily refused to send for medical aid at Turreys, and insisted on continuing his journey homewards. He was one of the old school, who would never enter a railway (though his fortune was greatly increased by the passage of the railway through his property) ; and his own horses always met him at " Popper's Tavern," an obscure hamlet, seventeen miles from his princely seat. He made no sign on arriving at " Poppers," and spoke no word, to the now serious alarm of his servants. When they came to light his carriage-lamps, and look into his post-chaise, the lord of many thousand acres, and according to report, of immense wealth, was dead. The journey from Turreys had been the last stage of a long prosperous, and, if not a famous, at least a notorious and magnificent career.

"The late John George, Earl and Baron Ringwood and Viscount Cinqbars, entered into public life at the dangerous period before the French Revolution ; and commenced his career as the friend and companion of the Prince of Wales. When his Royal Highness seceded from the Whig party, Lord Ringwood also joined the Tory side of politicians, and an earldom was the price of his fidelity. But on the elevation of Lord Steyne to a marquisate, Lord Ringwood quarrelled for a while with his royal patron and friend, deeming his own services unjustly slighted, as a like dignity was not conferred on himself. On several occasions he gave his vote against Government, and caused his nominees in the House of Commons to vote with the Whigs. He never was reconciled to his late Majesty George IV., of whom he was in the habit of speaking with characteristic bluntness. The approach of the Reform Bill, however, threw this nobleman definitively on the Tory side, of which he has ever since remained, if not an eloquent, at least a violent supporter. He was said to be a liberal landlord, so long as his tenants did not thwart him in his views. His only son died early ; and his lordship, according to report, has long been on ill terms with his kinsman and successor, Sir John Ringwood, of Appleshaw, Baronet. The Barony has been in this ancient family since the reign of George I., when Sir John Ringwood was ennobled, and Sir Francis, his brother, a Baron of the Exchequer, was advanced to the dignity of Baronet by the first of our Hanoverian sovereigns."

This was the article which my wife and I read on the morning of Christmas eve, as our children were decking lamps and looking-glasses with holly and red berries for the approaching festival. I had despatched a hurried note, containing the news, to Philip on the night previous. We were painfully anxious about his fate now, when a few days would decide it. Again my business or curiosity took me to see Mr. Bradgate, the lawyer. He was in possession of the news of course. He was not averse to talk about it. The death of his client unsealed the lawyer's lips partially: and I must say Bradgate spoke in a manner not flattering to his noble deceased client. The brutalities of the late nobleman had been very hard to bear. On occasion of their last meeting his oaths and disrespectful behavior had been specially odious. He had abused almost every one of his relatives. His heir, he said, was a prating, republican humbug. He had a relative (whom Bradgate said he would not name) who was a scheming, swaggering, swindling lick-spittle parasite, always cringing at his heels and longing for his death. And he had another relative, the impudent son of a swindling doctor, who had insulted him two hours before in his own room ;—a fellow who was a pauper, and going to propagate a breed for the workhouse ; for, after his behavior of that day, he would be condemned to the lowest pit of Acheron, before he, Lord Ringwood, would give that scoundrel a penny of his money. " And his lordship desired me to send him back his will," said Mr. Bradgate. And he destroyed that will before he went away : it was not the first he had burned. " And I may tell you, now all is over, that he had left his brother's grandson a handsome legacy in that will, which your poor friend might have had, but that he went to see my lord in his unlucky fit of gout." Ah, mea culpa ! mea culpa ! And who sent Philip to see his relative in that unlucky fit of gout ? Who was so worldly-wise—so Twysden-like, as to counsel Philip to flattery and submission ? But for that advice he might be wealthy now ; he might be happy ; he might be ready to marry his young sweetheart. Our Christmas turkey choked me as I ate of it. The lights burned dimly, and the kisses and laughter under the mistletoe were but melancholy sport. But for my advice, how happy might my friend have been ! I looked askance at the honest faces of my children. What would they say if they knew their father had advised a friend to cringe, and bow, and humble himself before a rich, wicked old man ? I sat as mute at the pantomime as at a burial ; the laughter of the little ones smote me as with a reproof. A burial ? With plumes and lights, an upholsterers' pageantry, and mourning by the yard measure, they were burying my Lord Ringwood, who might have made Philip Firmin rich but for me.

All lingering hopes regarding our friend were quickly put to an end. A will was found at Whipham, dated a year back in

24

which no mention was made of poor Philip Firmin. Small legacies—disgracefully shabby, and small, Twysden said—were left
to the Twysden family, with the full-length portrait of the late earl
in his coronation robes, which, I should think, must have given
but small satisfaction to his surviving relatives ; for his lordship
was but an ill-favored nobleman, and the price of the carriage
of the large picture from Whipham was a tax which poor Talbot made very wry faces at paying. Had the picture been accompanied by thirty or forty thousand pounds, or fifty thousand
—why should he not have left them fifty thousand ?—how different Talbot's grief would have been ! Whereas when Talbot
counted up the dinners he had given to Lord Ringwood, all of
which he could easily calculate by his cunning ledgers and
journals in which was noted down every feast at which his lordship attended, every guest assembled, and every bottle of wine
drunk, Twysden found that he had absolutely spent more money
upon my lord than the old man had paid back in his will. But
all the family went into mourning, and the Twysden coachman
and footman turned out in black worsted epaulettes in honor of
the illustrious deceased. It is not every day that a man gets a
chance of publicly bewailing the loss of an earl his relative. I
suppose Twysden took many hundred people into his confidence
on this matter, and bewailed his uncle's death and his own
wrongs whilst clinging to many scores of button-holes.

And how did poor Philip bear the disappointment ? He
must have felt it, for I fear we ourselves had encouraged him
in the hope that his grand-uncle would do something to relieve
his necessity. Philip put a bit of crape round his hat, wrapped
himself in his shabby old mantle, and declined any outward
show of grief at all. If the old man had left him money, it had
been well. As he did not,—a puff of cigar, perhaps, ends the
sentence, and our philosopher gives no further thought to his
disappointment. Was not Philip the poor as lordly and independent as Philip the rich ? A struggle with poverty is a wholesome wrestling-match at three or five and twenty. The sinews
are young, and are braced by the contest. It is upon the aged
that the battle falls hardly, who are weakened by failing health,
and perhaps enervated by long years of prosperity.

Firmin's broad back could carry a heavy burden, and he was
glad to take all the work which fell in his way. Phipps, of the
Daily Intelligencer, wanting an assistant, Philip gladly sold four
hours of his day to Mr. Phipps : translated page after page of
newspapers, French and German ; took an occasional turn at
the Chamber of Deputies, and gave an account of a sitting of

importance, and made himself quite an active lieutenant. He began positively to save money. He wore dreadfully shabby clothes, to be sure: for Charlotte could not go to his chamber and mend his rags as the Little Sister had done: but when Mrs. Baynes abused him for his shabby appearance—and indeed it must have been mortifying sometimes to see the fellow in his old clothes swaggering about in Madame Smolensk's apartments, talking loud, contradicting, and laying down the law—Charlotte defended her maligned Philip. "Do you know why Monsieur Philip has those shabby clothes?" she asked of Madame de Smolensk. "Because he has been sending money to his father in America." And Smolensk said that Monsieur Philip was a brave young man, and that he might come dressed like an Iroquois to her soirée, and he should be welcome. And Mrs. Baynes was rude to Philip when he was present, and scornful in her remarks when he was absent. And Philip trembled before Mrs. Baynes; and he took her boxes on the ear with much meekness; for was not his Charlotte a hostage in her mother's hands, and might not Mrs. General B. make that poor little creature suffer?

One or two Indian ladies of Mrs. Baynes' acquaintance happened to pass this winter in Paris, and these persons, who had furnished lodgings in the Faubourg St. Honoré, or the Champs Elysées, and rode in their carriages with very likely, a footman on the box, rather looked down upon Mrs. Baynes for living in a boarding-house, and keeping no equipage. No woman likes to be looked down upon by any other woman, especially by such a creature as Mrs. Batters, the lawyer's wife, from Calcutta, who was not in society, and did not go to Government House, and here was driving about in the Champs Elysées, and giving herself such airs, indeed! So was Mrs. Doctor Macoon, with her *lady's-maid*, and her *man-cook*, and her *open carriage*, and her *close carriage*. (Pray read these words with the most withering emphasis which you can lay upon them.) And who was Mrs. Macoon, pray? Madame Béret, the French milliner's daughter, neither more nor less. And this creature must scatter her mud over her betters who went on foot. "I am telling my poor girls, madame," she would say to Madame Smolensk, "that if I had been a milliner's girl, or their father had been a pettifogging attorney, and not a soldier, who has served his sovereign in every quarter of the world, they would be *better dressed* than they are now, poor chicks!—we might have a fine apartment in the Faubourg St. Honoré—we need not live at a boarding-house."

"And if *I* had been a milliner, Madame la Générale," cried Smolensk, with spirit, "perhaps I should not have had need to keep a boarding-house. My father was a general officer, and served his emperor too. But what will you? We have all to do disagreeable things, and to live with disagreeable people, madame!" And with this Smolensk makes Mrs. General Baynes a fine curtsey, and goes off to other affairs or guests. She was of the opinion of many of Philip's friends. "Ah, Monsieur Philip," she said to him, "when you are married, you will live far from that woman; is it not?"

Hearing that Mrs. Batters was going to the Tuileries, I am sorry to say a violent emulation inspired Mrs. Baynes, and she never was easy until she persuaded her General to take her to the ambassador's and to the entertainments of the citizen king who governed France in those days. It would cost little or nothing. Charlotte must be brought out. Her aunt, MacWhirter, from Tours, had sent Charlotte a present of money for a dress. To do Mrs. Baynes justice, she spent very little money upon her own raiment, and extracted from one of her trunks a costume which had done duty at Barrackpore and Calcutta. "After hearing that Mrs. Batters went, I knew she never would be easy," General Baynes said, with a sigh. His wife denied the accustion as an outrage; said that men always imputed the worst motives to women, whereas her wish, heaven knows, was only to see her darling child properly presented, and her husband in his proper rank in the world. And Charlotte looked lovely, upon the evening of the ball; and Madame Smolensk dressed Charlotte's hair very prettily, and offered to lend Auguste to accompany the General's carriage; but Ogoost revolted, and said, "Non, merci! he would do anything for the General and Miss Charlotte—but for the Générale, no, no, no!" and he made signs of violent abnegation. And though Charlotte looked as sweet as a rosebud, she had little pleasure in her ball, Philip not being present. And how could he be present, who had but one old coat, and holes in his boots?

So you see, after a sunny autumn, a cold winter comes, when the wind is bad for delicate chests and muddy for little shoes. How could Charlotte come out at eight o'clock through mud or snow of a winter's morning, if she had been out at an evening party late over-night? Mrs. General Baynes began to go out a good deal to the Paris evening parties—I mean to the parties of us Trojans—parties where there are forty English people, three Frenchmen, and a German who plays the piano. Charlotte was very much admired. The fame of her good looks spread abroad. I promise you that there were persons of much more importance than the poor Vicomte de *Garcon-boutique*, who were charmed by her bright eyes, her bright smiles, her artless, rosy beauty. Why, little Hely, of the Embassy, actually invited himself to Mrs. Doctor Macoon's, in order to see this young beauty, and danced with her without ceasing : Mr. Hely, who was the pink of fashion, you know ; who danced with royal princesses ; and was at all the grand parties of the Faubourg St. Germain. He saw her to her carriage (a very shabby fly, it must be confessed ; but Mrs Baynes told him they had been accustomed to a very different kind of equipage in India). He actually called at the boarding-house, and left his card, *M. Walsingham Hely, attaché à l'Ambassade de S. M. Britannique*, for General Baynes and his lady. To what balls would Mrs. Baynes like to go ? to the Tuileries ? to the Embassy ? to the Faubourg St. Germain ? to the Faubourg St. Honoré ? I could name many more persons of distinction who were fascinated by pretty Miss Charlotte. Her mother felt more and more ashamed of the shabby fly, in which our young lady was conveyed to and from her parties ;—of the shabby fly, and of that shabby cavalier who was waiting sometimes to put Miss Charlotte into her carriage. Charlotte's mother's ears were only too acute when disparaging remarks were made about that cavalier. What ? engaged to that queer red-bearded fellow, with the ragged shirt-collars, who trod upon everybody in the polka ? A newspaper writer, was he ? The son of that doctor who ran away after cheating everybody ? What a very odd thing of General Baynes to think of engaging his daughter to such a person !

So Mr. Firmin was not asked to many distinguished houses, where his Charlotte was made welcome ; where there was dancing in the salon, very mild negus and cakes in the *salle-à-manger*, and cards in the lady's bedroom. And he did not care to be asked ; and he made himself very arrogant and disagreeable when he was asked ; and he would upset tea-trays, and burst out into roars of laughter at all times, and swagger about the drawing-room as if he were a man of importance—he indeed—giving himself such airs, because his grandfather's brother was an earl ! And what had the earl done for him, pray ? And what right had he to burst out laughing when Miss Crackley sang a little out of tune ? What could General Baynes mean by selecting such a husband for that nice, modest young girl ?

The old General sitting in the best bedroom, placidly playing at whist with the other British fogies, does not hear these remarks, perhaps, but little Mrs. Baynes with her eager eyes and ears sees and knows everything. Many people have told *her* that Philip is a bad match for her daughter. She has heard him contradict calmly quite wealthy people. Mr. Hobday, who has a house in Carlton Terrace, London, and goes to the first houses in Paris, Philip has contradicted him point blank, until Mr. Hobday turned quite red, and Mrs. Hobday didn't know where to look. Mr. Peplow, a clergyman and a baronet's eldest son, who will be one day the Rev. Sir Charles Peplow of Peplow Manor, was praising Tomlinson's poems, and offered to read them out at Mr. Badger's—he reads very finely, though a little perhaps through his nose—and when he was going to begin, Mr. Firmin said, "My dear Peplow, for heaven's sake don't give us any of that rot. I would as soon hear one of your own prize poems." Rot, indeed! What an expression! Of course Mr. Peplow was very much annoyed. And this from a mere newspaper writer. Never heard of such rudeness! Mrs. Tuffin said she took her line at once after seeing this Mr. Firmin. "He may be an earl's grand-nephew, for what I care. He may have been at college, he has not learned good manners there. He may be clever, I don't profess to be a judge. But he is most overbearing, clumsy, and disagreeable. I shall not ask him to my Tuesdays; and Emma, if he asks you to dance, I beg you will do no such thing!" A bull, you understand, in a meadow, or on a prairie with a herd of other buffaloes, is a noble animal: but a bull in a china-shop is out of place; and even so was Philip amongst the crockery of those little simple tea-parties, where his mane, and hoofs, and roar, caused endless disturbance.

These remarks concerning the accepted son-in-law Mrs. Baynes heard and, at proper moments, repeated. She ruled Baynes; but was very cautious, and secretly afraid of him. Once or twice she had gone too far in her dealings with the quiet old man, and he had revolted, put her down and never forgiven her. Beyond a certain point, she dared not provoke her husband. She would say, "Well, Baynes, marriage is a lottery: and I am afraid our poor Charlotte has not pulled a prize:" on which the General would reply, "No more have others, my dear!" and so drop the subject for the time being. On another occasion it would be, "You heard how rude Philip Firmin was to Mr. Hobday?" and the General would answer, "I was at cards, my dear." Again she might say, "Mrs. Tuffin says she will not have Philip Firmin to her Tuesdays, my dear;" and the General's rejoinder would be, "Begad, so much the better for him!" "Ah," she groans, "he's always offending some one!" "I don't think he seems to please *you* much, Eliza!" responds the General : and she answers, "No, he don't, and that I confess; and I don't like to think, Baynes, of my sweet child given up to certain poverty, and such a man!" At which the General with some of his garrison phrases would break out with a "Hang it, Eliza, do you suppose I think it is a very good match?" and turn to the wall, and, I hope, to sleep.

As for poor little Charlotte, her mother is not afraid of little Charlotte : and when the two are alone the poor child knows she is to be made wretched by her mother's assaults upon Philip. Was there ever anything so bad as his behavior, to burst our laughing when Miss Crackley was singing? Was he called upon to contradict Sir Charles Peplow in that abrupt way, and as good as tell him he was a fool? It was very wrong certainly, and poor Charlotte thinks, with a blush perhaps, how she was just at the point of admiring Sir Charles Peplow's reading very much, and had been prepared to think Tomlinson's poems delightful, until Philip ordered her to adopt a contemptuous opinion of the poet. "And did you see how he was dressed? a button wanting on his waistcoat, and a hole in his boot?"

"Mamma," cries Charlotte, turning very red. "He might have been better dressed—if—if——"

"That is, you would like your own father to be in prison, your mother to beg her bread, your sisters to go in rags, and your brothers to starve, Charlotte, in order that we should pay Philip Firmin back the money of which his father robbed him! Yes. That's your meaning. You needn't explain yourself. I can understand quite well, thank you. Good-night. I hope *you'll* sleep well; *I* sha'n't after this conversation. Good-night, Charlotte!" Ah, me. O course of true love, didst thou ever run smooth? As we peep into that boarding-house; whereof I have already described the mistress as wakeful with racking care regarding the morrow; wherein lie the Miss Bolderos, who must naturally be very uncomfortable, being on sufferance and as it were in pain, as they lie on their beds;—what sorrows do we not perceive brooding over the nightcaps? There is poor Charlotte who has said her prayer for her Philip; and as she lays her young eyes on the pillow, they wet it with their tears. Why does her mother for ever and for ever speak against him? Why is her father so cold when Philip's name is mentioned?

Could Charlotte ever think of any but him? Oh, never, never! And so the wet eyes are veiled at last; and close in doubt and fear and care. And in the next room to Charlotte's, a little yellow old woman lies stark awake; and in the bed by her side an old gentleman can't close his eyes for thinking—my poor girl is promised to a beggar. All the fine hopes which we had of his getting a legacy from that lord are over. Poor child, poor child, what will become of her?

Now, Two Sticks, let us fly over the river Seine to Mr. Philip Firmin's quarters: to Philip's house, who has not got a penny; to Philip's bed, who has made himself so rude and disagreeable at that tea-party. He has no idea that he has offended anybody. He has gone home perfectly well pleased. He has kicked off the tattered boot. He has found a little fire lingering in his stove by which he has smoked the pipe of thought. Ere he has jumped into his bed he has knelt a moment beside it; and with all his heart—oh! with all his heart and soul—has committed the dearest one to heaven's loving protection! And now he sleeps like a child.

CHAPTER XXIII.

IN WHICH WE STILL HOVER ABOUT THE ELYSIAN FIELDS.

THE describer and biographer of my friend Mr. Philip Firmin has tried to extenuate nothing; and, I hope, has set down naught in malice. If Philip's boots had holes in them, I have written that he had holes in his boots. If he had a red beard, there it is red in this story. I might have oiled it with a tinge of brown, and painted it a rich auburn. Towards modest people he was very gentle and tender; but I must own that in general society he was not always an agreeable companion. He was often haughty and arrogant: he was impatient of old stories: he was intolerant of commonplaces. Mrs. Baynes' anecdotes of her garrison experiences in India and Europe got a very impatient hearing from Mr. Philip; and though little Charlotte gently remonstrated with him, saying, "Do, do let mamma tell her story out; and don't turn away and talk about something else in the midst of it; and don't tell her you have heard the story before, you rude man! If she is not pleased with you, she is angry with me, and I have to suffer when you are gone away." Miss Charlotte did not say how much she had to suffer when Philip was absent; how constantly her mother found fault with him; what a sad life, in consequence of her attachment to him, the young maiden had to lead; and I fear that clumsy Philip, in his selfish thoughtlessness, did not take enough count of the sufferings which his behavior brought on the girl. You see I am acknowledging that there were many faults on his side, which, perhaps, may in some degree excuse or account for those which Mrs. General Baynes certainly committed towards him. She did not love Philip naturally; and do you suppose she loved him because she was under great obligations to him? Do you love your creditor because you owe him more than you can ever pay? If I never paid my tailor, should I be on good terms with him? I might go on ordering suits of clothes from now to the year nineteen hundred; but I should hate him worse year after year. I should find fault with his cut and his cloth: I dare say I should end by thinking his bills extortionate, though I never paid them. Kindness is very indigestible. It disagrees with very proud stomachs. I wonder was that traveller who fell among the thieves grateful afterwards to the Samaritan who rescued him? He gave money certainly; but he did not miss it. The religious opinions of Samaritans are lamentably heterodox. O brother! may we help the fallen still though they never pay us, and may we lend without exacting the usury of gratitude!

Of this I am determined, that whenever I go courting again, I will not pay my addresses to my dear creature—day after day, and from year's end to year's end, very likely, with the dear girl's mother, father, and half-a-dozen young brothers and sisters in the room. I shall begin by being civil to the old lady, of course. She is flattered at first by having a young fellow coming courting to her daughter. She calls me "dear Edward;" works me a pair of braces; writes to mamma and sisters, and so forth. Old gentleman says, "Brown, my boy" (I am here fondly imagining myself to be a young fellow named Edward Brown, attached, let us say, to Miss Kate Thompson) —Thompson, I say, says, "Brown, my boy, come to dinner at seven. Cover laid for you always." And of course, delicious thought! that cover is by dearest Kate's side. But the dinner is bad sometimes. Sometimes I come late. Sometimes things are going badly in the City. Sometimes Mrs. Thompson is out of humor;—she always thought Kate might have done better. And in the midst of these doubts and delays, suppose JONES appears, who is older, but of a better temper, a better family, and—plague on him!—twice as rich? What are engagements? What are promises? It is sometimes an affectionate mother's DUTY to break her promise, and that duty the resolute matron will do.

Then Edward is Edward no more, but Mr. Brown; or, worse still, nameless in the house. Then the knife and fork are removed from poor Kate's side, and she swallows her own sad meal in tears. Then if one of the little Thompsons says, artlessly, " Papa, I met Teddy Brown in Regent Street; he looked so ——" " Hold your tongue, unfeeling wretch!" cries mamma. " Look at that dear child!" Kate is swooning. She has sal-volatile. The medical man is sent for. And presently —Charles Jones is taking Kate Thompson to dinner. Long voyages are dangerous; so are long courtships. In long voyages passengers perpetually quarrel (for that Mrs. General could vouch); in long courtships the same danger exists; and how much the more when in that latter ship you have a mother who is for ever putting in her oar! And then to think of the annoyance of that love voyage when you and the beloved and beloved's papa, mamma, half-a-dozen brothers and sisters, are all in one cabin! For economy's sake the Bayneses had no sitting-room at Madame's—for you could not call that room on the second floor a sitting-room which had two beds in it, and in which the young ones practised the piano, with poor Charlotte as their mistress. Philip's courting had to take place for the most part before the whole family; and to make love under such difficulties would have been horrible and maddening and impossible almost, only we have admitted that our young friends had little walks in the Champs Elysées; and then you must own that it must have been delightful for them to write each other perpetual little notes, which were delivered occultly under the very nose of papa and mamma, and in the actual presence of the other boarders at Madame's, who, of course, never saw anything that was going on. Yes, those sly monkeys actually made little post-offices about the room. There was, for instance, the clock on the mantel-piece in the salon on which was carved the old French allegory, " *Le temps fait passer l'amour.*" One of those artful young people would pop a note into Time's boat, where you may be sure no one saw it. The trictrac board was another post-office. So was the drawer of the music-stand. So was the Sèvres china flower-pot, &c., &c.; to each of which repositories in its turn the lovers confided the delicious secrets of their wooing.

Have you ever looked at your love-letters to Darby, when

you were courting, dear Joan ? They are sacred pages to read.
You have his tied up somewhere in a faded ribbon. You scarce
need spectacles as you look at them. The hair grows black ;
the eyes moisten and brighten ; the cheeks fill and blush again.
I protest there is nothing so beautiful as Darby and Joan in the
world. I hope Philip and his wife will be Darby and Joan to
the end. I tell you they are married ; and don't want to make
any mysteries about the business. I disdain that sort of artifice.
In the days of the old three-volume novels, didn't you always
look at the end, to see that Louisa and the earl (or young
clergyman as the case might be) were happy. If they died, or
met with other grief, for my part I put the book away. This
pair, then, are well ; are married ; are, I trust, happy ; but
before they married, and afterwards, they had great griefs and
troubles, as no doubt you have had, dear sir or madam, since
you underwent that ceremony. Married ? Of course they are.
Do you suppose I would have allowed little Charlotte to meet
Philip in the Champs Elysées with only a giddy little boy of a
brother for a companion, who would turn away to see Punch,
Guignol, the soldiers marching by, the old woman's gingerbread
and toffy stall and so forth ? Do you, I say, suppose I would
have allowed those two to go out together, unless they were to
be married afterwards ? Out walking together they did go ;
and once, as they were arm-in-arm in the Champs Elysées,
whom should they see in a fine open carriage but young Twysden and Captain and Mrs. Woolcomb, to whom, as they passed,
Philip doffed his hat with a profound bow, and whom he
further saluted with a roar of immense laughter. Woolcomb
must have heard the peal. I dare say it brought a little blush
into Mrs. Woolcomb's cheek ; and—so, no doubt, added to the
many attractions of that elegant lady. I have no secrets about
my characters, and speak my mind about them quite freely.
They said that Woolcomb was the most jealous, stingy, ostentatious, cruel little brute ; that he led his wife a dismal life.
Well, if he *did ?* I'm sure I don't care. "There is that
swaggering bankrupt beggar Firmin !" cries the tawny bridegroom, biting his mustache. "Impudent ragged blackguard,"
says Twysden minor, "I saw him."

"Hadn't you better stop the carriage, and abuse him to
himself, and not to me ?" says Mrs. Woolcomb, languidly,
flinging herself back on her cushions.

"Go on, hang you ! Ally ! Vite !" cry the gentlemen in
the carriage to the *laquais de place* on the box.

"I can fancy you don't care about seeing him," resumes

Mrs. Woolcomb. " He has a violent temper, and I would not have you quarrel for the world." So I suppose Woolcomb again swears at the *laquais de place :* and the happy couple, as the saying is, roll away to the Bois de Boulogne.

"What makes you laugh so ? " says little Charlotte, fondly, as she trips along by her lover's side.

"Because I am so happy, my dearest ! " says the other, squeezing to his heart the little hand that lies on his arm. As he thinks on yonder woman, and then looks into the pure eager face of the sweet girl beside him, the scornful laughter occasioned by the sudden meeting which is just over hushes ; and an immense feeling of thankfulness fills the breast of the young man :—thankfulness for the danger from which he has escaped, and for the blessed prize which has fallen to him.

But Mr. Philip's walks were not to be all as pleasant as this walk ; and we are now coming to a history of wet, slippery roads, bad times, and winter weather. All I can promise about this gloomy part is, that it shall not be a long story. You will acknowledge we made very short work with the love-making, which I give you my word I consider to be the very easiest part of the novel-writer's business. As those rapturous scenes between the captain and the heroine are going on, a writer who knows his business may be thinking about anything else—about the ensuing chapter, or about what he is going to having for dinner, or what you will ; therefore, as we passed over the raptures and joys of the courting so very curtly, you must please to gratify me by taking the grief in a very short measure. If our young people are going to suffer, let the pain be soon over. " Sit down in the chair, Miss Baynes, if you please, and you, Mr. Firmin, in this. Allow me to examine you ; just open your mouth, if you please ; and—oh, oh, my dear miss—there it is out ! A little eau-de-Cologne and water, my dear. And now, Mr. Firmin, if you please, we will—what fangs ! what a big one ! Two guineas. Thank you. Good-morning. Come to me once a year. John, show in the next party." About the ensuing painful business, then, I protest I don't intend to be much longer occupied than the humane and dexterous operator to whom I have made so bold as to liken myself. If my pretty Charlotte is to have a tooth out, it shall be removed as gently as possible, poor dear. As for Philip, and his great red-bearded jaw, I don't care so much if the tug makes *him* roar a little. And yet they remain, they remain and throb in after life, those wounds of early days. Have I not said how, as I chanced to walk with Mr. Firmin in Paris, many years after the domestic circumstances here recorded, he paused before the window of that house near the Champs Elysées where Madame Smolensk once held her *pension*, shook his fist at a *jalousie* of the now dingy and dilapidated mansion, and intimated to me that he had undergone severe sufferings in the chamber lighted by yonder window? So have we all suffered; so, very likely, my dear young miss or master who peruses this modest page, will you have to suffer in your time. You will not die of the operation, most probably: but it is painful: it makes a gap in the mouth, *voyez-vous?* and years and years, maybe, after, as you think of it, the smart is renewed, and the dismal tragedy enacts itself over again.

Philip liked his little maiden to go out, to dance, to laugh, to be admired, to be happy. In her artless way she told him of her balls, her tea-parties, her pleasures, her partners. In a girl's first little season nothing escapes her. Have you not wondered to hear them tell about the events of the evening, about the dresses of the dowagers, about the compliments of the young men, about the behavior of the girls, and what not?

Little Charlotte used to enact the over-night's comedy for Philip, pouring out her young heart in her prattle as her little feet skipped by his side. And to hear Philip roar with laughter! It would have done you good. You might have heard him from the Obelisk to the Etoile. People turned round to look at him, and shrugged their shoulders wonderingly, as good-natured French folks will do. How could a man who had been lately ruined, a man who had just been disappointed of a great legacy from the Earl his great-uncle, a man whose boots were in that lamentable condition, laugh so, and have such high spirits? To think of such an impudent ragged blackguard, as Ringwood Twysden called his cousin, daring to be happy! The fact is, that clap of laughter smote those three Twysden people like three boxes on the ear, and made all their cheeks tingle and blush at once. At Philip's merriment clouds which had come over Charlotte's sweet face would be chased away. As she clung to him doubts which throbbed at the girl's heart would vanish. When she was acting those scenes of the past night's entertainment, she was not always happy. As she talked and prattled, her own spirits would rise; and hope and natural joy would spring in her heart again, and come flushing up to her cheek. Charlotte was being a hypocrite, as, thank heaven, all good women sometimes are. She had griefs: she hid them from him. She had doubts and fears: they fled when he came in view, and she clung to his strong arm, and looked in his honest blue eyes. She did not tell him of those painful nights when *her* eyes were wakeful and tearful. A yellow old woman in a white jacket, with a nightcap and a night-light, would come, night after night, to the side of her little bed ; and there stand, and with her grim voice bark against Philip. That old woman's lean finger would point to all the rents in poor Philip's threadbare paletot of a character—point to the holes and tear them wider open. She would stamp on those muddy boots. She would throw up her peaked nose at the idea of the poor fellow's pipe,—his pipe, his great companion and comforter when his dear little mistress was away. She would discourse on the partners of the night ; the evident attentions of this gentleman, the politeness and high breeding of that.

And when that dreary nightly torture was over, and Charlotte's mother had left the poor child to herself, sometimes Madame Smolensk, sitting up over her ledgers and bills, and wakeful with her own cares, would steal up and console poor Charlotte ; and bring her some tisane, excellent for the nerves ; and talk to her about—about the subject of which Charlotte best liked to hear. And though Smolensk was civil to Mrs. Baynes in the morning, as her professional duty obliged her to be, she has owned that she often felt a desire to strangle Madame la Générale for her conduct to her little angel of a daughter ; and all because Monsieur Philippe smells the pipe, parbleu ! " What ? a family that owes you the bread which they eat ; and they draw back for a pipe ! The cowards, the cowards ! A soldier's daughter is not afraid of it. Merci ! Tenez, M. Philippe," she said to our friend when matters came to an extremity. " Do you know what in your place I would do ? To a Frenchman I would not say so ; that understands itself. But these things make themselves otherwise in England. I have no money, but I have a cachemire. Take him ; and if I were you, I would make a little voyage to Gretna Grin."

And now, if you please, we will quit the Champs Elysées. We will cross the road from Madame's boarding-house. We will make our way into the Faubourg St. Honoré, and actually enter a gate over which the L–on, the Un–c–rn, and the R–y–l Cr–wn and A--ms of the Three K–ngd–ms are sculptured, and going under the porte-cochère, and turning to the right, ascend a little stair, and ask of the attendant on the landing who is in the chancellerie ? The attendant says, that several of those *messieurs y sont*. In fact, on entering the room, you find Mr. Montcomb,—let us say—Mr. Lawndes, Mr. Halkin, and our young friend Mr. Walsingham Hely, seated at their respective tables in the midst of considerable smoke. Smoking in the midst of these gentlemen, and bestriding his chair, as though it were his horse, sits that gallant young Irish chieftian, The O'Rourke. Some of the gentlemen are copying, in a large handwriting, despatches on foolscap paper. I would rather be torn to pieces by O'Rourke's wildest horses, than be understood to hint at what those despatches, at what those despatch-boxes contain. Perhaps they contain some news from the Court of Spain, where some intrigues are carried on, a knowledge of which would make your hair start off your head ; perhaps that box, for which a messenger is waiting in a neighboring apartment, has locked up twenty-four yards of Chantilly lace for Lady Belweather, and six new French farces for Tom Tiddler of the Foreign Office, who is mad about the theatre. It is years and years ago ; how should I know what there is in those despatch-boxes ?

But the work, whatever it may be, is not very pressing—for there is only Mr. Chesham—did I say Chesham before, by the way ? You may call him Mr. Sloanestreet if you like. There is only Chesham (and he always takes things to the grand serious) who seems to be much engaged in writing ; and the conversation goes on.

"Who gave it ? " asks Montcomb.

"The black man, of course, gave it. We would not pretend to compete with such a long purse as his. You should have seen what faces he made at the bill ! Thirty francs a bottle for Rhine wine. He grinned with the most horrible agony when he read the addition. He almost turned yellow. He sent away his wife early. How long that girl was hanging about London ; and think of her hooking a millionaire at last ! Othello is a frightful screw, and diabolically jealous of his wife."

"What is the name of the little man who got so dismally drunk, and began to cry about old Ringwood ? "

"Twysden—the woman's brother. Don't you know Humbug Twysden, the father ? The youth is more offensive than the parent."

"A most disgusting little beast. Would come to the Variétés, because we said we were going : would go to Lamoignon's, where the Russians gave a dance and a lansquenet. Why didn't you come, Hely ? "

Mr. Hely.—I tell you I hate the whole thing. Those painted old actresses give me the horrors. What do I want with winning Montcomb's money who hasn't got any ? Do you think it gives me any pleasure to dance with old Caradol ? She puts me in mind of my grandmother—only she is older. Do you think I want to go and see that insane old Boutzoff leering at Corinne and Palmyrine, and making a group of three old women together! I wonder how you fellows can go on. Aren't you tired of truffles and écrevisses à la Bordelaise; and those old opera people, whose withered old carcases are stuffed with them?

The O'R.—There was Cérisette, I give ye me honor. Ye never saw. She fell asleep in her cheer——

Mr. Lowndes.—in her *hwhat*, O'R.?

The O'R.—Well, in her CHAIR then! And Figaroff smayred her feece all over with the craym out of a Charlotte Roose. She's a regular bird and mustache, you know, Cérisette has.

Mr. Hely.—Charlotte, Charlotte! Oh! (*He clutches his hair madly. His elbows are on the table.*)

Mr. Lowndes.—It's that girl he meets at the tea-parties, where he goes to be admired.

Mr. Hely.—It is better to drink tea than, like you fellows, to muddle what brains you have with bad champagne. It is better to look, and to hear, and to see, and to dance with a modest girl, than, like you fellows, to be capering about in taverns with painted old hags like that old Cérisette, who has got a face like a *pomme cuite*, and who danced before Lord Malmesbury at the Peace of Amiens. She did, I tell you; and before Napoleon.

Mr. Chesham.—(*Looks up from his writing.*)—There was no Napoleon then. It is of no consequence, but——

Lowndes.—Thank you, I owe you one. You're a most valuable man, Chesham, and a credit to your father and mother.

Mr. Chesham.—Well, the First Consul was Bonaparte.

Lowndes.—I am obliged to you. I say I am obliged to you, Chesham, and if you would like any refreshment order it *meis sumptibus*, old boy—at my expense.

Chesham.—These fellows will never be serious. (*He resumes his writing.*)

Hely.—(*Iterum, but very low.*)—Oh, Charlotte, Char——

Mr. Lowndes.—Hely is raving about that girl—that girl with the horrible old mother in yellow, don't you remember? and old father—good old military party, in a shabby old coat—who was at the last ball. What was the name? O'Rourke, what is the rhyme for Baynes?

The O'R.—Pays, and be hanged to you. You're always makin' fun on me, you little cockney!

Mr. Montcomb.—Hely was just as bad about the Danish

girl. You know, Walse, you composed ever so many verses to
her, and wrote home to your mother to ask leave to marry her!

The O'R.—I'd think him big enough to marry without anybody's leave—only they wouldn't have him because he's so ugly.

Mr. Hely.—Very good, O'Rourke. Very neat and good.
You were diverting the company with an anecdote. Will you
proceed?

The O'R.—Well, then, the Cérisette had been dancing both
on and off the stage till she was dead tired, I suppose, and so
she fell dead asleep, and Figaroff, taking the what-d'ye-call-'im
out of the Charlotte Roose, smayred her face all——

Voice without.—Deet Mosho RINGWOOD TWYSDEN, sivoplay,
poor l'honorable Moshoo Lownds!

Servant.—Monsieur TWYSDEN!

Mr. Twysden.—Mr. Lowndes, how are you?

Mr. Lowndes.—Very well, thank you; how are you?

Mr. Hely.—Lowndes is uncommonly brilliant to-day.

Mr. Twysden.—Not the worse for last night? Some of us
were a little elevated, I think!

Mr. Lowndes.—Some of us quite the reverse. (Little cad,
what does he want? Elevated! he couldn't keep his little legs!)

Mr. Twysden.—Eh! Smoking, I see. Thank you. I very
seldom do—but as you are so kind—puff. Eh—uncommonly
handsome person that, eh—Madame Cérisette.

The O'R.—Thank ye for telling us.

Mr. Lowndes.—If she meets with *your* applause, Mr. Twysden, I should think Mademoiselle Cérisette is all right.

The O'R.—Maybe they'd raise her salary if ye told her.

Mr. Twysden.—Heh—I see you're chaffing me. We have
a good deal of that kind of thing in Somerset—in our—in—
hem! This tobacco is a little strong. I *am* a little shaky this
morning. Who, by the way, is that Prince Boutzoff who played
lansquenet with us? Is he one of the Livonian Boutzoffs, or
one of the Hessian Boutzoffs? I remember at my poor uncle's,
Lord Ringwood, meeting a Prince Blucher de Boutzoff, something like this man, by the way. You knew my poor uncle?

Mr. Lowndes.—Dined with him here three months ago at
the "Trois Frères."

Mr. Twysden.—Been at Whipham, I dare say? I was bred
up there. It was said once that I was to have been his heir.
He was very fond of me. He was my godfather.

The O'R.—Then he gave you a mug, and it wasn't a beauty
(*sotto voce*).

Mr. Twysden.—You said somethin'? I was speaking of

Whipham, Mr. Lowndes—one of the finest places in England, I should say, except Chatsworth, you know, and *that* sort of thing. My grandfather built it—I mean my *great* grandfather, for I'm of the Ringwood family.

Mr. Lowndes.—Then was Lord Ringwood your grandfather, or your grand godfather?

Mr. Twysden.—He! he! My mother was his own niece. My grandfather was his own brother, and I am——

Mr. Lowndes.—Thank you. I see now.

Mr. Halkin. — Das ist sehr interessant   Ich versichere ihnen das ist SEHR interessant.

Mr. Twysden.—Said somethin'? (This cigar is really—I'll throw it away, please.) I was saying that at Whipham, where I was bred up, we would be forty at dinner, and as many more in the upper servants' hall.

Mr. Lowndes.—And you dined in the—you had pretty good dinners?

Mr. Twysden.—A French chef. Two aids, besides turtle from town. Two or three regular cooks on the establishment, besides kitchen-maids, roasters, and that kind of thing, you understand. How many have you here now? In Lord Estridge's kitchen you can't do, I should say, at least without,—let me see—why, in *our* small way—and if you come to London my father will be dev'lish glad to see you—we——

Mr. Lowndes.—How is Mrs. Woolcomb this morning? That was a fair dinner Woolcomb gave us yesterday.

Mr. Twysden—He has plenty of money, plenty of money. I hope, Lowndes, when you come to town—the first time you come, mind—to give you a hearty welcome and some of my father's old por——

Mr. Hely.—Will nobody kick this little beast out?

Servant.—Monsieur Chesham peut-il voir M. Firmin?

Mr. Chesham.—Certainly. Come in, Firmin!

Mr. Twysden.—Mr. Fearmang—Mr. Fir—Mr. *who?* You don't mean to say you receive *that* fellow, Mr. Chesham?

Mr. Chesham.—What fellow? and what do you mean, Mr. What-d'ye-call-'im?

Mr. Twysden. — *That* blackg——oh—that is, I—I beg your——

Mr. Firmin (entering and going up to Mr. Chesham).—I say, give me a bit of news of to-day. What were you saying about that—hum and hum and haw—mayn't I have it? (*He is talking confidentially with Mr. Chesham, when he sees Mr. Twysden.*) What! you have got *that* little cad here?

Mr. Lowndes.—You know Mr. Twysden, Mr. Firmin. He was just speaking about you.

Mr. Firmin—Was he? So much the worse for me.

Mr. Twysden.—Sir! We don't speak. You've no right to speak to me in this manner! Don't speak to me: and I won't speak to you, sir—there! Good-morning, Mr. Lowndes! Remember your promise to come and dine with us when you come to town. And—one word—(*he holds Mr. Lowndes by the button. By the way, he has very curious resemblances to Twysden senior*) —we shall be here for ten days certainly. I think Lady Estridge has something next week. I have left our cards, and——

Mr. Lowndes.—Take care. *He* will be there (*pointing to Mr. Firmin*).

Mr. Twysden.—What? *That* beggar? You don't mean to say Lord Estridge will receive such a fellow as——Good-by, good-by! (*Exit Mr. Twysden.*)

Mr. Firmin.—I caught that little fellow's eye. He's my cousin, you know. We have had a quarrel. I am sure he was speaking about me.

Mr. Lowndes.—Well, now you mention it, he *was* speaking about you.

Mr. Firmin.—Was he? Then *don't believe him*, Mr. Lowndes. That is my advice.

Mr. Hely (*at his desk composing*).—" Maiden of the blushing cheek, maiden of the—oh, Charlotte, Char——" he bites his pen and dashes off rapid rhymes on Government paper.

Mr. Firmin.—What does he say? He said Charlotte.

Mr. Lowndes.—He is always in love and breaking his heart, and he puts it into poems; he wraps it up in paper, and falls in love with somebody else. Sit down and smoke a cigar, won't you?

Mr. Firmin.—Can't stay. Must make up my letter. We print to-morrow.

Mr. Lowndes.—Who wrote that article pitching into Peel?

Mr. Firmin.—Family secret—can't say—good-by. (*Exit Mr. Firmin.*)

Mr. Chesham.—In my opinion a most ill-advised and intemperate article. That journal, the *Pall Mall Gazette*, indulges in a very needless acrimony, I think.

Mr. Lowndes.—Chesham does not like to call a spade a spade. He calls it a horticultural utensil. You have a great career before you, Chesham. You have a wisdom and gravity beyond your years. You bore us slightly, but we all respect you—we do indeed. What was the text at church last Sunday? Oh, by the way, Hely, you little miscreant, *you* were at church!

Mr. Chesham.—You need not blush, Hely. I am not a joking man; but this kind of jesting does not strike me as being particularly amusing, Lowndes.

Mr. Lowndes.—You go to church because you are good, because your aunt was a bishop or something. But Hely goes because he is a little miscreant. You hypocritical little beggar, you got yourself up as if you were going to a *déjeûné*, and you had your hair curled, and you were seen singing out of the same hymn-book with that pretty Miss Baynes, you little wheedling sinner; and you walked home with the family—my sisters saw you—to a boarding-house where they live—by Jove! you did. And I'll tell your mother!

Mr. Chesham.—I wish you would not make such a noise, and let me do my work, Lowndes. You——

Here Asmodeus whisks us out of the room, and we lose the rest of the young men's conversation. But enough has been overheard, I think, to show what direction young Mr. Hely's thoughts had taken. Since he was seventeen years of age (at the time when we behold him he may be twenty-three), this romantic youth has been repeatedly in love: with his elderly tutor's daughter, of course; with a young haberdasher at the university; with his sister's confidential friend; with the blooming young Danish beauty last year; and now, I very much fear, a young acquaintance of ours has attracted the attention of this imaginative Don Juan. Whenever Hely is in love, he fancies his passion will last for ever, makes a confidant of the first person at hand, weeps plenteously, and writes reams of verses. Do you remember how in a previous chapter we told you that Mrs. Tuffin was determined she would *not* ask Philip to her *soirées*, and declared him to be a forward and disagreeable young man? She was glad enough to receive young Walsingham Hely, with his languid air, his drooping head, his fair curls, and his flower in his button-hole; and Hely, being then in hot pursuit of one of the tall Miss Blacklocks, went to Mrs. Tuffin's, was welcomed there with all the honors; and there, fluttering away from Miss Blacklock, our butterfly lighted on Miss Baynes. Now Miss Baynes would have danced with a mop-stick, she was so fond of dancing: and Hely, who had practised in a thousand Chaumières, Mabilles (or whatever was the public dance-room then in vogue), was a most amiable, agile, and excellent partner. And she told Philip next day what a nice little partner she had found—poor Philip, who was not asked to that paradise of a party. And Philip said that he knew the little man ; that he believed he was rich ; that he wrote pretty little verses :—in a word, Philip, in his leonine ways, regarded little Hely as a lion regards a lapdog.

Now this little Slyboots had a thousand artful little ways. He had a very keen sensibility and a fine taste, which was most readily touched by innocence and beauty. He had tears, I won't say at command ; for they were under no command, and gushed from his fine eyes in spite of himself. Charlotte's innocence and freshness smote him with a keen pleasure. Bon Dieu ! What was that great, tall Miss Blacklock who had tramped through a thousand ball-rooms, compared to this artless, happy creature ? He danced away from Miss Blacklock and after Charlotte the moment he saw our young friend ; and the Blacklocks, who knew all about him, and his money, and his mother, and his expectations—who had his verses in their poor album, by whose carriage he had capered day after day in the Bois de Boulogne—stood scowling and deserted, as this young fellow danced off with that Miss Baynes, who lived in a boarding-house, and came to parties in a cab with her horrid old mother ! The Blacklocks were as though they were not henceforth for Mr. Hely. They asked him to dinner. Bless my soul, he utterly forgot all about it ! He never came to their box on their night at the opera. Not one twinge of remorse had he. Not one pang of remembrance. If he *did* remember them, it was when they bored him, like those tall tragic women in black who are always coming in their great long trains to sing sermons to Don Juan. Ladies, your name is down in his lordship's catalogue ; his servant has it ; and you, Miss Anna, are number one thousand and three.

But as for Miss Charlotte, that is a different affair. What innocence ! What a *fraîcheur !* What a merry good-humor ! Don Slyboots is touched, he is tenderly interested : her artless voice thrills through his frame ; he trembles as he waltzes with her ; as his fine eyes look at her, psha ! what is that film coming over them ? O Slyboots, Slyboots ! And as she has nothing to conceal, she has told him all he wants to know before long. This is her first winter in Paris : her first season of coming out. She has only been to two balls before, and two plays and an opera. And her father met Mr. Hely at Lord Trim's. That was her father playing at whist. And they lived at Madame Smolensk's boarding-house in the Champs Elysées. And they had been to Mr. Dash's, and to Mrs. Blank's, and she believed they were going to Mrs. Star's on Friday. And did they go

to Church? Of course they went to church, to the Rue
d'Aguesseau, or wherever it might be. And Slyboots went to
church next Sunday. You may perhaps guess to what church.
And he went the Sunday after. And he sang his own
songs, accompanying himself on the guitar, at his lodgings.
And he sang elsewhere. And he had a very pretty little voice,
Slyboots had. I believe those poems under the common title
of "Gretchen" in our Walsingham's charming volume were all
inspired by Miss Baynes. He began to write about her and
himself the very first night after seeing her. He smoked cigar-
ettes and drank green tea. He looked so pale—so pale and
sad that he quite pitied himself in the looking-glass in his apartments in the Rue Miroménil. And he compared himself to a
wrecked mariner, and to a grave, and to a man entranced and
brought to life. And he cried quite freely and satisfactorily by
himself. And he went to see his mother and sister next day
at the "Hotel de la Terrasse," and cried to them and said he
was in love this time for ever and ever. And his sister called
him a goose. And after crying he ate an uncommonly good
dinner. And he took every one into his confidence, as he always did whenever he was in love : always telling, always making verses, and always crying. As for Miss Blacklock, he
buried the dead body of that love deep in the ocean of his soul.
The waves engulphed Miss B. The ship rolled on. The
storm went down. And the stars rose, and the dawn was in
his soul, &c. Well, well! The mother was a vulgar woman,
and I am glad you are out of it. And what sort of people are
General Baynes and Mrs. Baynes.

"Oh, delightful people! Most distinguished officer, the
father ; modest—doesn't say a word. The mother, a most
lively, brisk, agreeable woman. You must go and see her,
ma'am. I desire you'll go immediately."

"And leave cards with P. P. C. for the Miss Blacklocks!"
says Miss Hely, who was a plain lively person. And both
mother and sister spoiled this young Hely ; as women ought
always to spoil a son, a brother, a father, husband, grandfather
—any male relative, in a word.

To see this spoiled son married was the good-natured
mother's fond prayer. An eldest son had died a rake ; a victim
to too much money, pleasure, idleness. The widowed mother
would give anything to save this one from the career through
which the elder had passed. The young man would be one
day so wealthy, that she knew many and many a schemer
would try and entrap him. Perhaps, she had been made to

marry his father because he was rich ; and she remembered the gloom and wretchedness of her own union. Oh, that she could see her son out of temptation, and the husband of an honest girl ! It was the young lady's first season ? So much the more likely that she should be unworldly. "The General —don't you remember a nice old gentleman—in a—well, in a wig—that day we dined at Lord Trim's, when that horrible old Lord Ringwood was there ? That was General Baynes ; and he broke out so enthusiastically in defence of a poor young man—Dr. Firmin's son—who was a bad man, I believe ; but I shall never have confidence in another doctor again, that I sha'n't. And we'll call on these people, Fanny. Yes, in a brown wig—the General, I perfectly well remember him, and Lord Trim said he was a most distinguished officer. And I have no doubt his wife will be a most agreeable person. Those Generals' wives who have travelled over the world must have acquired a quantity of delightful information. At a boarding-house, are they ? I dare say very pleasant and amusing. And we'll drive there and call on them immediately."

On that day, as Macgrigor and Moira Baynes were disporting in the little front garden of Madame Smolensk's, I think Moira was just about to lick Macgrigor, when his fratricidal hand was stopped by the sight of a large yellow carriage—a large London dowager family carriage—from which descended a large London family footman, with side-locks begrimed with powder, with calves such as only belong to large London family footmen, and with cards in his hand. "Ceci Madame Smolensk ? " says the large menial. "Oui," says the boy, nodding his head ; on which the footman was puzzled, for he thought from his readiness in the use of the French language that the boy was a Frenchman.

" Ici demure General Bang ? " continued the man.

" Hand us over the cards, John. Not at home," said Moira.

" *Who* ain't at 'ome ? " inquired the menial.

" General Baynes, my father, ain't at home. He shall have the pasteboard when he comes in. ' Mrs. Hely ? ' Oh, Mac, it's the same name as that young swell who called the other day ! Ain't at home, John. Gone out to pay some visits. Had a fly on purpose. Gone out with my sister. 'Pon my word, they have John." And from this accurate report of the boy's behavior, I fear that the young Baynes must have been brought up at a classical and commercial academy, where economy was more studied then politeness.

Philip comes trudging up to dinner, and as this is not his

post day, arrives early ; he hopes, perhaps, for a walk with Miss Charlotte, or a coze in Madame Smolensk's little private room. He finds the two boys in the forecourt; and they have Mrs. Hely's cards in their hands ; and they narrate to him the advent and departure of the lady in the swell carriage, the mother of the young swell with the flower in his button-hole, who came the other day on such a jolly horse. " Yes. And he was at church last Sunday, Philip, and he gave Charlotte a hymn-book. And he sang : he sang like the piper who played before Moses, Pa said. And Ma said it was wicked, but it wasn't : only Pa's fun, you know. And Ma said *you* never came to church. Why don't you ? "

Philip had no taint of jealousy in his magnanimous composition, and would as soon have accused Charlotte of flirting with other men as of stealing Madame's silver spoons. " So you have had some fine visitors," he says, as the fly drives up. " I remember that rich Mrs. Hely, a patient of my father's. My poor mother used to drive to her house."

" Oh, we have seen a great deal of Mr. Hely, Philip ! " cries Miss Charlotte, not heeding the scowls of her mother, who is nodding and beckoning angrily to the girl.

" You never once mentioned him. He is one of the greatest dandies about Paris : quite a lion," remarks Philip.

" Is he ? What a funny little lion ! I never thought about him," says Miss Charlotte, quite simply. O ingratitude ! ingratitude ! And we have told how Mr. Walsingham was crying his eyes out for her.

" She never thought about him ? " cries Mrs. Baynes, quite eagerly.

" The piper, is it, you're talking about ? " asks papa. " I called him piper, you see, because he piped so sweetly at ch— Well, my love ? "

Mrs. Baynes was nudging her General at this moment. She did not wish that the piper should form the subject of conversation, I suppose.

" The piper's mother is very rich, and the piper will inherit after her. She has a fine house in London. She gives very fine parties. She drives in a great carriage, and she has come to call upon you, and ask you to her balls, I suppose."

Mrs. Baynes was delighted at this call. And when she said " I'm sure *I* don't value fine people, or their fine parties, or their fine carriages, but I wish that my dear child should see the world,"—I don't believe a word which Mrs. Baynes said. She was much more pleased than Charlotte at the idea of visiting this fine lady ; or else, why should she have coaxed, and wheedled, and been so particularly gracious to the General all the evening ? She wanted a new gown. The truth is, her yellow *was* very shabby ; whereas Charlotte, in plain white muslin, looked pretty enough to be able to dispense with the aid of any French milliner. I fancy a consultation with Madame and Mrs. Bunch. I fancy a fly ordered, and a visit to the milliner's the next day. And when the pattern of the gown is settled with the milliner, I fancy the terror on Mrs. Baynes's weazened face when she ascertains the amount of the bill. To do her justice, the General's wife had spent little upon her own homely person. She chose her gowns ugly, but cheap. There were so many backs to clothe in that family that the thrifty mother did not heed the decoration of her own.

CHAPTER XXIV.

NEC DULCES AMORES SPERNE, PUER, NEQUE TU CHOREAS.

" My dear," Mrs. Baynes said to her daughter, " You are going out a great deal in the world now. You will go to a great number of places where poor Philip cannot hope to be admitted."

" Not admit Philip, mamma ! then I'm sure I don't want to go," cries the girl.

" Time enough to leave off going to parties when you can't afford it and marry him. When I was a lieutenant's wife, I didn't go to any parties out of the regiment, my dear ! "

" Oh, then, I am sure I shall *never* want to go out ! " Charlotte declares.

" You fancy he will always stop at home, I dare say. Men are not all so domestic as your papa. Very few love to stop at home like him. Indeed, I may say I have made his home comfortable. But one thing is clear, my child. Philip can't always expect to go where we go. He is not in the position in life. Recollect, your father is a general officer, C.B., and may be K.C.B. soon, and your mother is a general officer's lady. *We* may go anywhere. I might have gone to the drawing-room at home if I chose. Lady Biggs would have been delighted to present me. Your aunt has been to the drawing-

room, and she is only Mrs. Major MacWhirter ; and most
absurd it was of Mac to let her go. But she rules him in
everything, and they have no children. I have, goodness
knows ! I sacrifice myself for my children. You little know
what I deny myself for my children. I said to Lady Biggs,
' No, Lady Biggs ; my husband may go. He should go. He
has his uniform, and it will cost him nothing except a fly and a
bouquet for the man who drives ; but *I* will not spend money on
myself for the hire of diamonds and feathers, and, though I
yield in loyalty to *no* person, I dare say my Sovereign *won't
miss* me.' And I don't think her Majesty did. She has other
things to think of besides Mrs. General Baynes, I suppose.
She is a mother, and can appreciate a mother's sacrifices for
her children."

If I have not hitherto given you detailed reports of Mrs.
General Baynes' conversation, I don't think, my esteemed
reader, you will be very angry.

"Now, child," the General's lady continued, "let me warn
you not to talk much to Philip about those places to which you
go without him, and to which his position in life does not
allow of his coming. Hide anything from him ? Oh, dear, no !
Only for his own good, you understand. I don't tell everything to your papa. I should only worrit him and vex him.
When anything will please him, and make him happy, *then* I
tell him. And about Philip ? Philip, I must say it, my dear—
I must as a mother say it—has his faults. He is an *envious*
man. Don't look shocked. He thinks very well of himself ;
and having been a great deal spoiled, and made too much of
in his unhappy father's time, he is so proud and haughty that
he *forgets his position*, and thinks he ought to live with the
highest society. Had Lord Ringwood left him a fortune, as
Philip *led us to expect* when we gave our consent to this most
unlucky match—for that my dear child should marry a beggar
is most unlucky and most deplorable ; I can't help saying so,
Charlotte,—if I were on my deathbed I couldn't help saying
so ; and I wish with all my heart we had never seen or heard
of him.—There ? Don't go off in one of your tantrums !
What was I saying, pray ? I say that Philip is in no position,
or rather in a very humble one, which—a mere newspaper-
writer and a subaltern too—everybody acknowledges it to be.
And if he hears us talking about our parties to which we have
a right to go—to which you have a right to go with your
mother, a general officer's lady—why he'll be offended. He
won't like to hear about them and think he can't be invited ;

and you had better not talk about them at all, or about the people you meet and dance with. At Mrs. Hely's you may dance with Lord Headbury, the ambassador's son. And if you tell Philip he will be offended. He will say that you boast about it. When I was only a lieutenant's wife at Barrackpore, Mrs. Captain Capers used to go to Calcutta to the Government House balls. I didn't go. But I was offended, and I used to say that Flora Capers gave herself airs, and was always boasting of her intimacy with the Marchioness of Hastings. We don't like our equals to be better off than ourselves. Mark my words. And if you talk to Philip about the people whom you meet in society, and whom he can't from his unfortunate station expect to know, you will offend him. That was why I nudged you to-day when you were going on about Mr. Hely. Anything so absurd! I saw Philip getting angry at once, and biting his mustaches, as he always does when he is angry— and swears quite out loud—so vulgar! There! you are going to be angry again, my love; I never saw anything like you! Is this my Charly who never was angry? I know the world, dear, and you don't. Look at me, how I manage your papa, and I tell you don't talk to Philip about things which offend him! Now, dearest, kiss your poor old mother who loves you. Go up stairs and bathe your eyes, and come down happy to dinner." And at dinner Mrs. General Baynes was uncommonly gracious to Philip: and when gracious she was especially odious to Philip, whose magnanimous nature accommodated itself ill to the wheedling artifices of an ill-bred old woman.

Following this wretched mother's advice, my poor Charlotte spoke scarcely at all to Philip of the parties to which she went, and the amusements which she enjoyed without him. I dare say Mrs. Baynes was quite happy in thinking that she was "guiding" her child rightly. As if a coarse woman, because she is mean, and greedy, and hypocritical, and fifty years old, has a right to lead a guileless nature into wrong! Ah! if some of us old folks were to go to school to our children, I am sure, madam, it would do us a great deal of good. There is a fund of good sense and honorable feeling about my great-grandson Tommy, which is more valuable than all his grandpapa's experience and knowledge of the world. Knowledge of the world forsooth! Compromise, selfishness modified, and double dealing. Tom disdains a lie: when he wants a peach, he roars for it. If his mother wishes to go to a party, she coaxes, and wheedles, and manages, and smirks, and curtseys for months, in order to get her end; takes twenty rebuffs and comes up to the scratch again smiling ;—and this woman is for ever lecturing her daughters, and preaching to her sons upon virtue, honesty, and moral behavior !

Mrs. Hely's little party at the "Hôtel de la Terrasse" was very pleasant and bright ; and Miss Charlotte enjoyed it, although her swain was not present. But Philip was pleased that his little Charlotte should be happy. She beheld with wonderment Parisian duchesses, American millionaires, dandies from the embassies, deputies and peers of France with large stars and wigs like papa. She gayly described her party to Philip ; described, that is to say, everything but her own success, which was undoubted. There were many beauties at Mrs. Hely's, but nobody fresher or prettier. The Miss Blacklocks retired very early and in the worst possible temper. Prince Slyboots did not in the least heed their going away. His thoughts were all fixed upon little Charlotte. Charlotte's mamma saw the impression which the girl made, and was filled with a hungry joy. Good-natured Mrs. Hely complimented her on her daughter. " Thank God, she is as good as she is pretty," says her mother, I am sure speaking seriously this time regarding her daughter. Prince Slyboots danced with scarce anybody else. He raised a perfect whirlwind of compliments round about Charlotte. She was quite a simple person, and did not understand one-tenth part of what he said to her. He strewed her path with roses of poesy : he scattered garlands of sentiment before her all the way from the ante-chamber down stairs, and so to the fly which was in waiting to take her and parents home to the boarding-house. " By George, Charlotte, I think you have smitten that fellow," cries the General, who was infinitely amused by young Hely—his raptures, his affectations, his long hair, and what Baynes called his low dress. A slight white tape and a ruby button confined Hely's neck. His hair waved over his shoulders. Baynes had never seen such a specimen. At the mess of the stout 120th, the lads talked of their dogs, horses, and sport. A young civilian, smattering in poetry, chattering in a dozen languages, scented, smiling, perfectly at ease with himself and the world, was a novelty to the old officer.

And now the Queen's birthday arrived—and that it may arrive for many scores of years yet to come is, I am sure, the prayer of all of us—and with the birthday his Excellency Lord Estridge's grand annual fête in honor of his sovereign. A card for their ball was left at Madam Smolensk's, for General, Mrs. and Miss Baynes ; and no doubt Monsieur Slyboots Walsing-

MISS CHARLOTTE AND HER PARTNERS.

ham Hely was the artful agent by whom the invitation was forwarded. Once more the General's veteran uniform came out from the tin-box, with its dingy epaulets and little cross and ribbon. His wife urged upon him strongly the necessity of having a new wig, wigs being very cheap and good at Paris— but Baynes said a new wig would make his old coat look very shabby, and a new uniform would cost more money than he would like to afford. So shabby he went *de cap à pied*, with a moulting feather, a threadbare suit, a tarnished wig, and a worn-out lace, *sibi constans*. Boots, trousers, sash, coat, were all old and worse for wear, and "faith," says he, "my face follows suit." A brave, silent man was Baynes; with a twinkle of humor in his lean, wrinkled face.

And if General Baynes was shabbily attired at the Embassy ball, I think I know a friend of mine who was shabby too. In the days of his prosperity, Mr. Philip was *parcus cultor et infrequens* of balls, routs, and ladies' company. Perhaps because his father was angered at Philip's neglect of his social advantages and indifference as to success in the world, Philip was the more neglectful and indifferent. The elder's comedy-smiles, and solemn, hypocritical politeness caused scorn and revolt on the part of the younger man. Philip despised the humbug, and the world to which such humbug could be welcome. He kept aloof from tea-parties then: his evening-dress clothes served him for a long time. I cannot say how old his dress-coat was at the time of which we are writing. But he had been in the habit of respecting that garment and considering it new and handsome for many years past. Meanwhile the coat had shrunk, or its wearer had grown stouter; and his grand embroidered, embossed, illuminated, carved and gilt velvet dress waistcoat, too, had narrowed, had become absurdly tight and short, and I dare say was the laughing-stock of many of Philip's acquaintances, whilst he himself, poor simple fellow, was fancying that it was a most splendid article of apparel. You know in the Palais Royal they hang out the most splendid reach-me-down dressing-gowns, waistcoats, and so forth. "No," thought Philip, coming out of his cheap dining-house, and swaggering along the arcades, and looking at the tailors' shops, with his hands in his pockets. "My brown velvet dress waistcoat with the gold sprigs, which I had made at college, is a much more tasty thing than these gaudy ready-made articles. And my coat is old certainly, but the brass buttons are still very bright and handsome, and, in fact, it is a most becoming and gentlemanlike thing." And under this delusion the honest fellow dressed himself in his old clothes, lighted a pair of candles, and looked at himself with satisfaction in the looking-glass, drew on a pair of cheap gloves which he had bought, walked by the Quays, and over the Deputies' Bridge, across the Place Louis XV., and strutted up the Faubourg St. Honoré to the Hotel of the British Embassy. A half-mile *queue* of carriages was formed along the street, and of course the entrance to the hotel was magnificently illuminated.

A plague on those cheap gloves! Why had not Philip paid three francs for a pair of gloves, intead of twenty-nine sous? Mrs. Baynes had found a capital cheap glove shop, whither poor Phil had gone in the simplicity of his heart; and now as he went in under the grand illuminated *porte-cochère*, Philip saw that the gloves had given way at the thumbs, and that his hands appeared through the rents, as red as raw beef-steaks. It is wonderful how red hands will look through holes in white gloves. "And there's that hole in my boot, too," thought Phil; but he had put a little ink over the seam, and so the rent was imperceptible. The coat and waistcoat were tight, and of a past age. Never mind. The chest was broad, the arms were muscular and long, and Phil's face, in the midst of a halo of fair hair and flaming whiskers, looked brave, honest, and handsome. For awhile his eyes wandered fiercely and restlessly all about the room from group to group; but now—ah! now—they were settled. They had met another pair of eyes, which lighted up with glad welcome when they beheld him. Two young cheeks mantled with a sweet blush. These were Charlotte's cheeks: and hard by them were mamma's, of a very different color. But Mrs. General Baynes had a knowing turban on, and a set of garnets round her old neck, like gooseberries set in gold.

They admired the rooms: they heard the names of the great folks who arrived, and beheld many famous personages. They made their curtseys to the ambassadress. Confusion! With a great rip, the thumb of one of those cheap gloves of Philip's parts company from the rest of the glove, and he is obliged to wear it crumpled up in his hand: a dreadful mishap —for he is going to dance with Charlotte, and he will have to give his hand to the *vis-à-vis*.

Who comes up smiling, with a low neck, with waving curls and whiskers, pretty little hands exquisitely gloved, and tiny feet? 'Tis Hely Walsingham, lightest in the dance. Most affably does Mrs. General Baynes greet the young fellow. Very brightly and happily do Charlotte's eyes glance towards her favorite partner. It is certain that poor Phil can't hope at all to dance like Hely. "And see what nice neat feet and hands he has got," says Mrs. Baynes. "Comme il est bien ganté! A gentleman ought to be always well gloved."

"Why did you send me to the twenty-nine-sous-shop?" says poor Phil, looking at his tattered hand-shoes and red obtrusive thumb.

"Oh, you!"—(here Mrs. Baynes shrugs her yellow old shoulders.) "*Your* hand would burst through any gloves! How do you do, Mr. Hely? Is your mamma here? Of course she is! What a delightful party she gave us! The dear ambassadress looks quite unwell—most pleasing manners, I am sure; Lord Estridge, what a perfect gentleman!"

The Bayneses were just come. For what dance was Miss Baynes disengaged? "As many as ever you like!" cries Charlotte, who, in fact, called Hely her little dancing-master, and never thought of him except as a partner. "Oh, too much happiness! Oh, that this could last for ever!" sighed Hely, after a waltz, polka, mazurka, I know not what, and fixing on Charlotte the full blaze of his beauteous blue eyes. "For ever?" cries Charlotte, laughing. "I'm very fond of dancing, indeed; and you dance beautifully; but I don't know that I should like to dance for ever." Ere the words are over, he is whirling her round the room again. His little feet fly with surprising agility. His hair floats behind him. He scatters odors as he spins. The handkerchief with which he fans his pale brow is like a cloudy film of muslin—and poor old Philip sees with terror that *his* pocket-handkerchief has got three great holes in it. His nose and one eye appeared through one of the holes while Phil was wiping his forehead. It was very hot. He was very hot. He was hotter, though standing still, than young Hely who was dancing. "He! he! I compliment you on your gloves, and your handkerchief, I'm sure," sniggers Mrs. Baynes, with a toss of her turban. Has it not been said that a bull is a strong, courageous, and noble animal, but a bull in a china-shop is not in his place? "There you go. Thank you! I wish you'd go somewhere else," cries Mrs. Baynes, in a fury. Poor Philip's foot has just gone through her flounce. How red is he! how much hotter than ever! There go Hely and Charlotte, whirling round like two opera-dancers! Philip grinds his teeth, he buttons his coat across his chest. How very tight it feels! How savagely his eyes glare! Do young men still look savage and solemn at balls? An ingenuous young Englishman ought to do that duty of

dancing, of course. Society calls upon him. But I doubt
whether he ought to look cheerful during the performance, or
flippantly engage in so grave a matter.

As Charlotte's sweet round face beamed smiles upon Philip
over Hely's shoulders, it looked so happy that he never thought
of grudging her her pleasure : and happy he might have remained in this contemplation, regarding not the circle of dancers
who were galloping and whirling on at their usual swift rate,
but her, who was the centre of all joy and pleasure for him ;—
when suddenly a shrill voice was heard behind him, crying,
"Get out of the way, hang you ! " and suddenly there bounced
against him Ringwood Twysden, pulling Miss Flora Trotter
round the room, one of the most powerful and intrepid dancers
of the season at Paris. They hurtled past Philip ; they shot
him forward against a pillar. He heard a screech, an oath, and
another loud laugh from Twysden, and beheld the scowls of
Miss Trotter as that rapid creature bumped at length into a
place of safety.

I told you about Philip's coat. It was very tight. The
daylight had long been struggling to make an entry at the
seams. As he staggered up against the wall, crack ! went a
great hole at his back ; and crack ! one of his gold buttons
came off, leaving a rent in his chest. It was in those days
when gold buttons still lingered on the breasts of some brave
men, and we have said simple Philip still thought his coat a
fine one.

There was not only a rent of the seam, there was not only
a burst button, but there was also a rip in Philip's rich cut-
velvet waistcoat, with the gold sprigs, which he thought so
handsome — a great, heart-rending scar. What was to be
done ? Retreat was necessary. He told Miss Charlotte of the
hurt he had received, whose face wore a very comical look of
pity at his misadventure—he covered part of his wound with
his gibus hat—and he thought he would try and make his way
out by the garden of the hotel, which, of course, was illuminated,
and bright, and crowded, but not so very bright and crowded
as the salons, galleries, supper-rooms, and halls of gilded
light in which the company, for the most part, assembled.

So our poor wounded friend wandered into the garden, over
which the moon was shining with the most blank indifference
at the fiddling, feasting, and parti-colored lamps. He says that
his mind was soothed by the aspect of yonder placid moon and
twinkling stars, and he had altogether forgotten his trumpery
little accident and torn coat and waistcoat : but I doubt about

the entire truth of this statement, for there have been some occasions when he, Mr. Philip, has mentioned the subject, and owned that he was mortified and in a rage.

Well. He went into the garden: and was calming himself by contemplating the stars, when, just by that fountain where there is Pradier's little statue of—Moses in the Bulrushes, let us say—round which there was a beautiful row of illuminated lamps, lighting up a great coronal of flowers, which my dear readers are at liberty to select and arrange according to their own exquisite taste;—near this little fountain he found three gentlemen talking together.

The high voice of one Philip could hear, and knew from old days. Ringwood Twysden, Esquire, always liked to talk and to excite himself with other persons' liquor He had been drinking the Sovereign's health with great assiduity, I suppose, and was exceedingly loud and happy. With Ringwood was Mr. Woolcomb, whose countenance the lamps lit up in a fine lurid manner, and whose eyeballs gleamed in the twilight: and the third of the group was our young friend Mr. Lowndes.

"I owed him one, you see, Lowndes," said Mr. Ringwood Twysden. "I hate the fellow! Hang him, always did! I saw the great hulkin' brute standin' there. Couldn't help myself. Give you my honor, couldn't help myself. I just drove Miss Trotter at him—sent her elbow well into him, and spun him up against the wall. The buttons cracked off the beggar's coat, begad! What business had he there, hang him? Gad, sir, he made a cannon off an old woman in blue, and went into * * * *"

Here Mr. Ringwood's speech came to an end: for his cousin stood before him, grim and biting his mustache.

"Hullo!" piped the other. "Who wants you to overhear my conversation? Dammy, I say! I * * * *"

Philip put out that hand with the torn glove. The glove was in a dreadful state of disruption now. He worked the hand well into his kinsman's neck, and twisting Ringwood round into a proper position, brought that poor old broken boot so to bear upon the proper quarter, that Ringwood was discharged into the little font, and lighted amidst the flowers, and the water, and the oil-lamps, and made a dreadful mess and splutter amongst them. And as for Philip's coat, it was torn worse than ever.

I don't know how many of the brass buttons had revolted and parted company from the poor old cloth, which cracked and split, and tore under the agitation of that beating angry bosom. I blush as I think of Mr. Firmin in this ragged state, a great rent all across his back, and his prostrate enemy lying howling in the water, amidst the sputtering, crashing oil-lamps at his feet. When Cinderella quitted her first ball, just after the clock struck twelve, we all know how shabby she looked. Philip was a still more disreputable object when he slunk away. I don't know by what side door Mr. Lowndes eliminated him. He also benevolently took charge of Philip's kinsman and antagonist, Mr. Ringwood Twysden. Mr. Twysden's hands, coat-tails, &c., were very much singed and scalded by the oil, and cut by the broken glass, which was all extracted at the Beaujon Hospital, but not without much suffering on the part of the patient. But though young Lowndes spoke up for Philip, in describing the scene (I fear not without laughter), his Excellency caused Mr. Firmin's name to be erased from his party lists : and I am sure no sensible man will defend Philip's conduct for a moment.

Of this lamentable fracas which occurred in the Hotel Garden, Miss Baynes and her parents had no knowledge for awhile. Charlotte was too much occupied with her dancing, which she pursued with all her might ; papa was at cards with some sober male and female veterans, and mamma was looking with delight at her daughter, whom the young gentlemen of many embassies were charmed to choose for a partner. When Lord Headbury, Lord Estridge's son, was presented to Miss Baynes, her mother was so elated that she was ready to dance too. I do not envy Mrs. Major MacWhirter, at Tours, the perusal of that immense manuscript in which her sister recorded the events of the ball. Here was Charlotte, beautiful, elegant, accomplished, *admired everywhere*, with young men, young *noblemen* of immense property and expectations, *wild about her ;* and engaged by a promise to a rude, ragged, *presumptuous*, ill-bred young man, *without a penny in the world*—wasn't it provoking ? Ah, poor Philip ! How that little sour, yellow mother-in-law elect did scowl at him when he came with rather a shamefaced look to pay his duty to his sweetheart on the day after the ball ! Mrs. Baynes caused her daughter to dress with extra smartness, had forbidden the poor child to go out, and coaxed her, and wheedled her, and dressed her with I know not what ornaments of her own, with a fond expectation that Lord Headbury, that the yellow young Spanish *attaché*, that the sprightly Prussian secretary, and Walsingham Hely, Charlotte's partners at the ball, would certainly call ; and the only equipage that appeared at Madame Smolensk's gate was a hack cab, which drove up at evening, and out of which poor Philip's well-known tattered boots came striding. Such a fond mother as Mrs. Baynes may well have been out of humor.

As for Philip, he was unusually shy and modest. He had been sitting at home all the morning in state, and in company with a Polish colonel, who lived in his hotel, and whom Philip had selected to be his second in case the battle of the previous night should have any suite. He had left that colonel in company with a bag of tobacco and an order for unlimited beer, whilst he himself ran up to catch a glimpse of his beloved. The Bayneses had not heard of the battle of the previous night. They were full of the ball, of Lord Estridge's affability, of the Golconda ambassador's diamonds, of the appearance of the royal princes who honored the fête, of the most fashionable Paris talk in a word. Philip was scolded, snubbed, and coldly received by mamma ; but he was used to that sort of treatment, and greatly relieved by finding that she was unacquainted with his own disorderly behavior. He did not tell Charlotte about the quarrel : a knowledge of it might alarm the little maiden ; and so for once our friend was discreet, and held his tongue.

But if he had any influence with the editor of *Galignani's Messenger*, why did he not entreat the conductors of that admirable journal to forego all mention of the fracas at the Embassy ball? Two days after the fête, I am sorry to say, there appeared a paragraph in the paper narrating the circumstances of the fight. And the guilty Philip found a copy of that paper on the table before Mrs. Baynes and the General when he came to the Champs Elysées according to his wont. Behind that paper sat Major-General Baynes, C.B., looking confused, and beside him his lady frowning like Rhadamanthus. But no Charlotte was in the room.

CHAPTER XXV.

INFANDI DOLORES.

PHILIP's heart beat very quickly at seeing this grim pair, and the guilty newspaper before them, on which Mrs. Baynes' lean right hand was laid. "So, sir," she cried, "you still honor us with your company: after distinguishing yourself as

you did the night before last. Fighting and boxing like a
porter at his Excellency's ball. It's disgusting! I have no
other word for it: disgusting!" And here I suppose she
nudged the General, or gave him some look or signal by which
he knew he was to come into action; for Baynes straightway
advanced and delivered his fire.

"Faith, sir, more bub-ub-blackguard conduct I never heard
of in my life! That's the only word for it: the only word for
it," cries Baynes.

"The General knows what blackguard conduct is, and
yours is that conduct, Mr. Firmin! It is all over the town: is
talked of everywhere: will be in all the newspapers. When his
lordship heard of it, he was furious. Never, never, will you be
admitted into the Embassy again, after disgracing yourself as
you have done," cries the lady.

"Disgracing yourself, that's the word.—And disgraceful
your conduct was, begad!" cries the officer second in command.

"You don't know my provocation," pleaded poor Philip.
"As I came up to him Twysden was boasting that he had
struck me—and—and laughing at me."

"And a pretty figure you were to come to a ball. Who
could help laughing, sir?"

"He bragged of having insulted me, and I lost my temper,
and struck him in return. The thing is done and can't be
helped," growled Philip.

"Strike a little man before ladies! Very brave indeed!"
cries the lady.

"Mrs. Baynes!"

"I call it cowardly. In the army we consider it cowardly
to quarrel before ladies," continues Mrs. General B.

"I have waited at home for two days to see if he wanted
any more," groaned Philip.

"Oh, yes! After insulting and knocking a little man down,
you want to murder him! And you call that the conduct of a
Christian—the conduct of a gentleman!"

"The conduct of a ruffian, by George!" says General Baynes.

"It was prudent of you to choose a very little man, and to
have the ladies within hearing!" continues Mrs. Baynes. "Why,
I wonder you haven't beaten my dear children next. Don't
you, General, wonder he has not knocked down our poor boys?
They are quite small. And it is evident that ladies being present is no hindrance to Mr. Firmin's *boxing-matches*."

"The conduct is gross and unworthy of a gentleman,"
reiterates the General.

" You hear what that man says—that old man, who never says an unkind word ? That veteran, who has been in twenty battles, and never struck a man before women yet ? Did you, Charles ? *He* has given you his opinion. He has called you a name which I won't soil my lips with repeating, but which you deserve. And do you suppose, sir, that I will give my blessed child to a man who has acted as you have acted, and been called a —— ? Charles ! General ! I will go to my grave rather than see my daughter given up to a such a man ! "

" Good heavens ! " said Philip, his knees trembling under him. " You don't mean to say that you intend to go from your word, and——"

" Oh ! you threaten about money do you ? Because your father was a cheat, you intend to try and make us suffer, do you ? " shrieks the lady. " A man who strikes a little man be-fore ladies will commit any act of cowardice, I dare say. And if you wish to beggar my family, because your father was a rogue——"

" My dear ! " interposes the General.

" Wasn't he a rogue, Baynes ? Is there any denying it ? Haven't you said so a hundred and a hundred times ? A nice family to marry into ! No, Mr. Firmin ! You may insult me as you please. You may strike little men before ladies. You may lift your great wicked hand against that poor old man, in one of your tipsy fits : but I know a mother's love, a mother's duty—and I desire that we see you no more."

" Great Powers ! " cries Philip, aghast. " You don't mean to—to separate me from Charlotte, General ? I have your word. You encouraged me. I shall break my heart. I'll go down on my knees to that fellow. I'll—oh !—you don't mean what you say ! " And, scared and sobbing, the poor fellow clasped his strong hands together, and appealed to the General.

Baynes was under his wife's eye. " I think," he said, "your conduct has been confoundedly bad, disorderly, and ungentle-manlike. You can't support my child, if you marry her. And if you have the least spark of honor in you, as you say you have, it is you, Mr. Firmin, who will break off the match, and release the poor child from certain misery. By George, sir, how is a man who fights and quarrels in a nobleman's ball-room to get on in the world ? How is a man, who can't afford a de-cent coat to his back, to keep a wife ? The more I have known you, the more I have felt that the engagement would bring misery upon my child ! Is that what you want ? A man of honor——" (" *Honor !* " in italics, from Mrs. Baynes.) " Hush, my dear!—A man of spirit would give her up, sir. What have you to offer but beggary, by George? Do you want my girl to come home to your lodgings, and mend your clothes?"——" I think I put that point pretty well, Bunch, my boy," said the General, talking of the matter afterwards. " I hit him there, sir."

The old soldier did indeed strike his adversary there with a vital stab. Philip's coat, no doubt, was ragged, and his purse but light. He had sent money to his father out of his small stock. There were one or two servants in the old house in Parr Street, who had been left without their wages, and a part of these debts Philip had paid. He knew his own violence of temper, and his unruly independence. He thought very humbly of his talents, and often doubted of his capacity to get on in the world. In his less hopeful moods, he trembled to think that he might be bringing poverty and unhappiness upon his dearest little maiden, for whom he would joyfully have sacrificed his blood, his life. Poor Philip sank back sickening and faint-ing almost under Baynes's words.

" You'll let me—you'll let me see her ? " he gasped out.

" She's unwell. She is in her bed. She can't appear to-day ! " cried the mother.

" Oh, Mrs. Baynes ! I must—I must see her," Philip said ; and fairly broke out in a sob of pain.

" This is the man that strikes men before women ! " said Mrs. Baynes. " Very courageous, certainly ! "

" By George, Eliza ! " the General cried out, starting up, " its too bad——"

" Infirm of purpose, give me the daggers ! " Philip yelled out, whilst describing the scene to his biographer in after days. " Macbeth would never have done the murders but for that lit-tle quiet woman at his side. When the Indian prisoners are killed, the squaws always invent the worst tortures. You should have seen that fiend and her livid smile, as she was drilling her gimlets into my heart. I don't know how I of-fended her. I tried to like her, sir. I had humbled myself before her. I went on her errands. I played cards with her. I sat and listened to her dreadful stories about Barrackpore and the Governor-General. I wallowed in the dust before her, and she hated me. I can see her face now : her cruel yellow face, and her sharp teeth, and her gray eyes. It was the end of August, and pouring a storm that day. I suppose my poor child was cold and suffering up stairs, for I heard the poking of a fire in her little room. When I hear a fire poked overhead now—twenty years after—the whole thing comes back to me ;

and I suffer over again that infernal agony. Were I to live a thousand years, I could not forgive her. I never did her a wrong, but I can't forgive her. Ah, my heaven, how that woman tortured me!"

"I think I know one or two similar instances," said Mr. Firmin's biographer.

"You are always speaking ill of women," said Mr. Firmin's biographer's wife.

"No, thank heaven!" said the gentleman. "I think I know some of whom I never thought or spoke a word of evil. My dear, will you give Philip some more tea?" and with this the gentleman's narrative is resumed.

The rain was beating down the avenue as Philip went into the street. He looked up at Charlotte's window: but there was no sign. There was a flicker of a fire there. The poor girl had the fever, and was shuddering in her little room, weeping and sobbing on Madame Smolensk's shoulder. "Que c'était pitié à voir," Madame said. Her mother had told her she must break from Philip; had invented and spoken a hundred calumnies against him; declared that he never cared for her; that he had loose principles, and was for ever haunting theatres and bad company. "It's not true, dear mother, it's not true!" the little girl had cried, flaming up in revolt for a moment: but she soon subsided in tears and misery, utterly broken by the thought of her calamity. Then her father had been brought to her, who had been made to believe some of the stories against poor Philip, and who was commanded by his wife to impress them upon the girl. And Baynes tried to obey orders; but he was scared and cruelly pained by the sight of his little maiden's grief and suffering. He attempted a weak expostulation, and began a speech or two. But his heart failed him. He retreated behind his wife. *She* never hesitated in speech or resolution, and her language became more bitter as her ally faltered. Philip was a drunkard; Philip was a prodigal; Philip was a frequenter of dissolute haunts and loose companions. She had the best authority for what she said. Was not a mother anxious for the welfare of her own child? ("Begad, you don't suppose your own mother would do anything that was not for your welfare, now?" broke in the General, feebly.) "Do you think if he had not been drunk he would have ventured to commit such an atrocious outrage as that at the Embassy? And do you suppose I want a drunkard and a beggar to marry my daughter? Your ingratitude, Charlotte, is horrible!" cries mamma. And poor Philip, charged with

drunkenness, had dined for seventeen sous, with a carafon of
beer, and had counted on a supper that night by little Charlotte's side : so, while the child lay sobbing on her bed, the
mother stood over her, and lashed her. For General Baynes,
—a brave man, a kind-hearted man,—to have to look on whilst
this torture was inflicted, must have been a hard duty. He
could not eat the boarding-house dinner, though he took his
place at the table at the sound of the dismal bell. Madame
herself was not present at the meal ; and you know poor Charlotte's place was vacant. Her father went up stairs, and paused
by her bedroom door, and listened. He heard murmurs within,
and madame's voice, as he stumbled at the door, cried harshly,
" Qui est là ? " He entered. Madame was sitting on the bed,
with Charlotte's head on her lap. The thick brown tresses
were falling over the child's white night-dress, and she lay
almost motionless, and sobbing feebly. " Ah, it is you, General ! " said madame. " You have done a pretty work, sir ! "
" Mamma says, won't you take something, Charlotte dear ? "
faltered the old man. " Will you leave her tranquil ! " said
madam, with her deep voice. The father retreated. When
madame went out presently to get that panacea, *une tasse de
thé*, for her poor little friend, she found the old gentleman
seated on a portmanteau at his door. " Is she—is she a little
better now ? " he sobbed out. Madame shrugged her shoulders,
and looked down on the veteran with superb scorn. " Vous
n'êtes qu'un poltron, Général ! " she said, and swept down stairs.
Baynes was beaten indeed. He was suffering horrible pain.
He was quite unmanned, and tears were trickling down his old
cheeks as he sat wretchedly there in the dark. His wife did
not leave the table as long as dinner and dessert lasted. She
read *Galignani* resolutely afterwards. She told the children
not to make a noise, as their sister was up stairs with a bad
headache. But she revoked that statement as it were (as she
revoked at cards presently), by asking the Miss Bolderos to
play one of their duets.

I wonder whether Philip walked up and down before the
house that night ? Ah ! it was a dismal night for all of them ·
a racking pain, a cruel sense of shame, throbbed under Baynes's
cotton tassel ; and as for Mrs. Baynes, I hope there was not
much rest or comfort under *her* old nightcap. Madame passed
the greater part of the night in a great chair in Charlotte's bedroom, where the poor child heard the hours toll one after the
other, and found no comfort in the dreary rising of the dawn.

At a very early hour of the dismal rainy morning, what made

poor little Charlotte fling her arms round madame, and cry out, "Ah, que je vous aime ! ah, que vous êtes bonne, madame !" and smile almost happily through her tears ? In the first place, madame went to Charlotte's dressing-table, whence she took a pair of scissors. Then the little maid sat up on her bed, with her brown hair clustering over her shoulders ; and madame took a lock of it, and cut a thick curl ; and kissed poor little Charlotte's red eyes ; and laid her pale cheek on the pillow, and carefully covered her ; and bade her, with many tender words, to go to sleep. "If you are very good, and will go to sleep, he shall have it in half an hour," madame said. "And as I go down stairs, I will tell Françoise to have some tea ready for you when you ring." And this promise, and the thought of what madame was going to do, comforted Charlotte in her misery. And with many fond, fond prayers for Philip, and consoled by thinking, "Now she must have gone the greater part of the way ; now she must be with him ; now he knows I will never, never love any but him," she fell asleep at last on her moistened pillow : and was smiling in her sleep, and I dare say dreaming of Philip, when the noise of the fall of a piece of furniture roused her, and she awoke out of her dream to see the grim old mother, in her white nightcap and white dressing-gown, standing by her side.

Never mind. "She has seen him now. She has told him now," was the child's very first thought as her eyes fairly opened. "He knows that I never, never will think of any but him." She felt as if she was actually there in Philip's room, speaking herself to him ; murmuring vows which her fond lips had whispered many and many a time to her lover. And now he knew she would never break them, she was consoled and felt more courage.

"You have had some sleep, Charlotte ?" asks Mrs. Baynes.

"Yes, I have been asleep, mamma." As she speaks, she feels under the pillow a little locket containing—what ? I suppose a scrap of Mr. Philip's lank hair.

"I hope you are in a less wicked frame of mind than when I left you last night," continues the matron.

"Was I wicked for loving Philip ? Then I am wicked still, mamma !" cries the child, sitting up in her bed. And she clutches that little lock of hair which nestles under her pillow.

"What nonsense, child ! This is what you get out of your stupid novels. I tell you he does not think about you. He is quite a reckless, careless libertine."

"Yes, so reckless and careless that we owe him the bread

we eat. He doesn't think of me! Doesn't he? Ah—" Here
she paused as a clock in a neighboring chamber began to strike.
"Now," she thought, "he has got my message!" A smile
dawned over her face. She sank back on her pillow, turning
her head from her mother. She kissed the locket, and murmured : "Not think of me! Don't you, don't you, my dear!"
She did not heed the woman by her side, hear her voice, or for
a moment seem aware of her presence. Charlotte was away in
Philip's room ; she saw him talking with her messenger ; heard
his voice so deep and so sweet ; knew that the promises he had
spoken he never would break. With gleaming eyes and flushing cheeks she looked at her mother, her enemy. She held
her talisman locket and pressed it to her heart. No, she would
never be untrue to him! No, he would never, never desert her!
And as Mrs. Baynes looked at the honest indignation beaming
in the child's face, she read Charlotte's revolt, defiance, perhaps victory. The meek child who never before had questioned
an order, or formed a wish which she would not sacrifice at her
mother's order, was now in arms asserting independence. But
I should think mamma is not going to give up the command
after a single act of revolt ; and that she will try more attempts
than one to cajole or coerce her rebel.

Meanwhile let Fancy leave the talisman locket nestling on
Charlotte's little heart (in which soft shelter methinks it were
pleasant to linger). Let her wrap a shawl round her, and affix
to her feet a pair of stout goloshes ; let her walk rapidly
through the muddy Champs Elysées, where, in this inclement
season, only a few policemen and artisans are to be found
moving. Let her pay a halfpenny at the Pont des Invalides,
and so march stoutly along the quays, by the Chamber of Deputies, where as yet deputies assemble : and trudge along the
river side, until she reaches Seine Street, into which, as you all
know, the Rue Poussin debouches. This was the road brave
Madame Smolensk took on a gusty, rainy autumn morning,
and on foot, for five-franc pieces were scarce with the good
woman. Before the " Hôtel Poussin " (*ah, qu'on y était bien à
vingt ans !*) is a little painted wicket which opens, ringing, and
then there is the passage, you know, with the stair leading to
the upper regions, to Monsieur Philippe's room, which is on
the first floor, as is that of Bouchard, the painter, who has his
atelier over the way. A bad painter is Bouchard, but a worthy
friend, a cheery companion, a modest, amiable gentleman.
And a rare good fellow is Laberge of the second floor, the poet
from Carcassonne, who pretends to be studying law, but whose

heart is with the Muses, and whose talk is of Victor Hugo and
Alfred de Musset, whose verses he will repeat to all comers.
Near Laberge (I think I have heard Philip say) lived Escasse,
a Southern man too—a capitalist—a clerk in a bank, *quoi!*—
whose apartment was decorated sumptuously with his own furniture, who had Spanish wine and sausages in cupboards, and
a bag of dollars for a friend in need. Is Escasse alive still?
Philip Firmin wonders, and that old Colonel, who lived on the
same floor, and who had been a prisoner in England? What
wonderful descriptions that Colonel Dujarret had of *les Meess
Anglaises* and their singularities of dress and behavior! Though
conquered and a prisoner, what a conqueror and enslaver he
was, when in our country! You see, in his rough way, Philip
used to imitate these people to his friends, and we almost fancied
we could see the hotel before us. It was very clean; it was
very cheap; it was very dark; it was very cheerful;—capital
coffee and bread-and-butter for breakfast for fifteen sous; capital bedroom *au premier* for thirty francs a month—dinner if
you would for I forget how little, and a merry talk round the
pipes and the grog afterwards—the grog, or the modest *eau
sucrée.* Here Colonel Dujarret recorded his victories over both
sexes. Here Colonel Tymowski sighed over his enslaved Po-
land. Tymowski was the second who was to act for Philip, in
case the Ringwood Twysden affair should have come to any
violent conclusion. Here Laberge bawled poetry to Philip,
who no doubt in his turn confided to the young Frenchman his
own hopes and passion. Deep into the night he would sit
talking of his love, of her goodness, of her beauty, of her innocence, of her dreadful mother, of her good old father. *Que
sçais-je?* Have we not said that when this man had anything
on his mind, straightway he bellowed forth his opinions to the
universe? Philip, away from his love, would roar out her
praises for hours and hours to Laberge, until the candles burned
down, until the hour for rest was come and could be delayed
no longer. Then he would hie to bed with a prayer for her;
and the very instant he awoke begin to think of her, and bless
her, and thank God for her love. Poor as Mr. Philip was, yet
as the possessor of health, content, honor, and that priceless
pure jewel the girl's love, I think we will not pity him much;
though, on the night when he received his dismissal from Mrs.
Baynes, he must have passed an awful time, to be sure. Toss,
Philip, on your bed of pain, and doubt, and fear. Toll, heavy
hours, from night till dawn. Ah! 'twas a weary night through
which two sad young hearts heard you tolling.

At a pretty early hour the various occupants of the crib at the Rue Poussin used to appear in the dingy little salle-à-manger, and partake of the breakfast there provided. Monsieur Menou, in his shirt-sleeves, shared and distributed the meal. Madame Menou, with a Madras handkerchief round her grizzling head, laid down the smoking coffee on the shining oilcloth, whilst each guest helped himself out of a little museum of napkins to his own particular towel. The room was small: the breakfast was not fine: the guests who partook of it were certainly not remarkable for the luxury of clean linen; but Philip —who is many years older now than when he dwelt in this hotel, and is not pinched for money at all you will be pleased to hear, (and between ourselves has become rather a gourmand),—declares he was a very happy youth at this humble " Hôtel Poussin," and sighs for the days when he was sighing for Miss Charlotte.

Well, he has passed a dreadful night of gloom and terror. I doubt that he has bored Laberge very much with his tears and despondency. And now morning has come, and, as he is having his breakfast with one or more of the before-named worthies, the little boy-of-all-work enters, grinning, his *plumet* under his arm, and cries " Une dame pour M. Philippe ! "

" Une dame ! " says the French colonel, looking up from his paper. " Allez, mauvais sujet ! "

" Grand Dieu ! what has happened ? " cries Philip, running forward, as he recognizes Madame's tall figure in the passage. They go up to his room, I suppose, regardless of the grins and sneers of the little boy with the *plumet*, who aids the maidservant to make the beds; and who thinks Monsieur Philippe has a very elderly acquaintance.

Philip closes the door upon his visitor, who looks at him with so much hope, kindness, confidence in her eyes, that the poor fellow is encouraged almost ere she begins to speak. " Yes, you have reason; I come from the little person," Madame Smolensk said. " The means of resisting that poor dear angel ! She has passed a sad night ! What ? You, too, have not been to bed, poor young man ! " Indeed Philip had only thrown himself on his bed, and had kicked there, and had groaned there, and had tossed there; and had tried to read, and, I dare say, remembered afterwards, with a strange interest, the book he read, and that other thought which was throbbing in his brain all the time whilst he was reading, and whilst the wakeful hours went wearily tolling by.

" No, in effect," says poor Philip, rolling a dismal cigar-

ette; "the night has not been too fine. And she has suffered too? Heaven bless her!" And then Madame Smolensk told how the little dear angel had cried all the night long, and how the Smolensk had not succeeded in comforting her, until she promised she would go to Philip, and tell him that his Charlotte would be his for ever and ever; that she never could think of any man but him; that he was the best, and the dearest, and the bravest, and the truest Philip, and that she did not believe one word of those wicked stories told against him by——
"Hold, Monsieur Philippe, I suppose Madame la Générale has been talking about you, and loves you no more," cried Madame Smolensk. "We other women are assassins—assassins, see you! But Madame la Générale went too far with the little maid. She is an obedient little maid, the dear Miss!—trembling before her mother, and always ready to yield—only now her spirit is roused; and she is yours only. The little dear, gentle child! Ah, how pretty she was, leaning on my shoulder. I held her there—yes, there, my poor garçon, and I cut this from her neck, and brought it to thee. Come, embrace me. Weep; that does good, Philip. I love thee well. Go—and thy little—it is an angel!" And so, in the hour of their pain, myriads of manly hearts have found woman's love ready to soothe their anguish.

Leaving to Philip that thick curling lock of brown hair, (from a head where now, mayhap, there is a line or two of matron silver,) this Samaritan plods her way back to her own house, where her own cares await her. But though the way is long, madame's step is lighter now, as she thinks how Charlotte at the journey's end is waiting for news of Philip; and I suppose there are more kisses and embraces, when the good soul meets with the little suffering girl, and tells her how Philip will remain for ever true and faithful; and how true love must come to a happy ending; and how she, Smolensk, will do all in her power to aid, comfort, and console her young friends. As for the writer of Mr. Philip's memoirs, you see I never try to make any concealments. I have told you, all along, that Charlotte and Philip are married, and I believe they are happy. But it is certain that they suffered dreadfully at this time of their lives; and my wife says that Charlotte, if she alludes to the period and the trial, speaks as though they had both undergone some hideous operation, the remembrance of which for ever causes a pang to the memory. So, my young lady, will you have your trial one day, to be borne, pray heaven, with a meek spirit. Ah, how surely the turn comes to all of us!

Look at Madame Smolensk at her luncheon-table, this day
after her visit to Philip at his lodging, after comforting little
Charlotte in her pain. How brisk she is! How good-natured!
How she smiles! How she speaks to all her company, and
carves for her guests! You do not suppose she has no griefs
and cares of her own? You know better. I dare say she is
thinking of her creditors; of her poverty; of that accepted
bill which will come due next week, and so forth. The Samaritan who rescues you, most likely, has been robbed and has
bled in his day, and it is a wounded arm that bandages yours
when bleeding.

If Anatole, the boy who scoured the plain at the "Hôtel
Poussin," with his *plumet* in his jacket-pocket, and his slippers
soled with scrubbing brushes, saw the embrace between Philip
and his good friend, I believe, in his experience at that hotel,
he never witnessed a transaction more honorable, generous, and
blameless. Put what construction you will on the business,
Anatole, you little imp of mischief! your mother never gave
you a kiss more tender than that which Madame Smolensk
bestowed on Philip—than that which she gave Philip—than
that which she carried back from him and faithfully placed on
poor little Charlotte's pale round cheek. The world is full of
love and pity, I say. Had there been less suffering, there
would have been less kindness. I, for one, almost wish to be
ill again, so that the friends who succored me might once more
come to my rescue.

To poor little wounded Charlotte in her bed, our friend the
mistress of the boarding-house brought back inexpressible
comfort. Whatever might betide, Philip would never desert
her! "Think you I would ever have gone on such an embassy
for a French girl, or interfered between her and her parents?"
madame asked. "Never, never! But you and Monsieur
Philippe are already betrothed before heaven; and I should
despise you, Charlotte, I should despise him, were either to
draw back." This little point being settled in Miss Charlotte's
mind, I can fancy she is immensely soothed and comforted;
that hope and courage settle in her heart; that the color comes
back to her young cheeks; that she can come and join her
family as she did yesterday. "I told you she never cared
about him," says Mrs. Baynes to her husband. "Faith, no:
she can't have cared for him much," says Baynes, with something of a sorrow that his girl should be so light-minded. But
you and I, who have been behind the scenes, who have peeped
into Philip's bedroom and behind poor Charlotte's modest cur-

tains, know that the girl had revolted from her parents ; and
so children will if the authority exercised over them is too
tyrannical or unjust. Gentle Charlotte, who scarce ever resisted, was aroused and in rebellion : honest Charlotte, who
used to speak all her thoughts, now hid them, and deceived
father and mother ; —yes, deceived : — what a confession to
make regarding a young lady, the *prima donna* of our opera !
Mrs. Baynes is, as usual, writing her lengthy scrawls to sister
MacWhirter at Tours, and informs the Major's lady that she
has very great satisfaction in at last being able to announce
"that that most imprudent and in all respects ineligible engagement between her Charlotte and *a certain young man*, son of a
bankrupt London physician, is come to an end. Mr. F's conduct has been so wild, so *gross*, so *disorderly* and *ungentleman-
like*, that the General (and you know, Maria, how soft and
sweet a tempered man Baynes is) has told Mr. Firmin his opinion
in unmistakable words, and forbidden him to continue his visits.
After seeing him every day for six months, during which time
she has accustomed herself to his peculiarities, and his often
coarse and odious expressions and conduct, no wonder the
separation has been a shock to dear Char, though I believe the
young man feels nothing who has been *the cause of all this grief*.
That he cares but little for *her*, has been my opinion *all along,*
though she, artless child, gave him her whole affection. He
has been accustomed to throw over women ; and the brother
of a young lady whom Mr. F. *had courted and left* (and who has
made a most excellent match since), showed his indignation at
Mr. F.'s conduct at the Embassy ball the other night, on which
the young man took advantage of his greatly superior size and
strength to begin a *vulgar boxing-match*, in which both parties
were severely wounded. Of course you saw the paragraph in
Galignani about the whole affair. I sent our dresses, but it did
not print them, though our names appeared as amongst the
company. Anything more singular than the appearance of
Mr. F. you cannot well imagine. I wore my garnets ; Charlotte (who attracted universal admiration) was in &c., &c. Of
course the separation has occasioned her a good deal of pain ;
for Mr. F. certainly behaved with much kindness and forbearance on a previous occasion. But the General will *not hear*
of the continuance of the connection. He says the young
man's conduct has been too gross and shameful ; and when
once roused, you know, I might as well attempt to chain a tiger
as Baynes. Our poor Char will suffer no doubt in consequence
of the behavior of this brute, but she has ever been an obedient

child, who knows how to honor her father and mother. *She bears up wonderfully*, though, of course, the dear child suffers at the parting. I think if *she were to go to you and MacWhirter at Tours for a month or two*, she would be all the better for *change of air*, too, dear Mac. Come and fetch her, and we will pay the *dawk*. She would go to certain poverty and wretchedness did she marry this most violent and disreputable young man. The General sends regards to Mac, and I am," &c.

That these were the actual words of Mrs. Baynes's letter I cannot, as a veracious biographer, take upon myself to say. I never saw the document, though I have had the good fortune to peruse others from the same hand. Charlotte saw the letter some time after, upon one of those not unfrequent occasions, when a quarrel occurred between the two sisters—Mrs. Major and Mrs. General—and Charlotte mentioned the contents of the letter to a friend of mine who has talked to me about his affairs, and especially his love affairs, for many and many a long hour. And shrewd old woman as Mrs. Baynes may be, you may see how utterly she was mistaken in fancying that her daughter's obedience was still secure. The little maid had left father and mother, at first with their eager sanction ; her love had been given to Firmin ; and an inmate—a prisoner if you will—under her father's roof, her heart remained with Philip, however time or distance might separate them.

And now, as we have the command of Philip's desk, and are free to open and read the private letters which relate to his history, I take leave to put in a document which was penned in his place of exile by his worthy father, upon receiving the news of the quarrel described in the last chapter of these memoirs :—

Astor House, New York, September 27.

" DEAR PHILIP,—I received the news in your last kind and affectionate letter with not unmingled pleasure : but ah, what pleasure in life does not carry its *amari aliquid* along with it ! That you are hearty, cheerful, and industrious, earning a small competence, I am pleased indeed to think : that you talk about being married to a penniless girl I can't say gives me a very sincere pleasure. With your good looks, good manners, attainments, you might have hoped for a better match than a half-pay officer's daughter. But 'tis useless speculating on what might have been. We are puppets in the hands of fate, most of us. We are carried along by a power stronger than ourselves. It has driven me, at sixty years of age, from competence, general respect, high position, to poverty and exile. So be it ! *laudo manentem*, as my delightful old friend and philosopher teaches me—*si celeres quatit pennas*—you know the rest. Whatever our fortune may be, I hope that my Philip and his father will bear it with the courage of gentlemen.

" Our papers have announced the death of your poor mother's uncle, Lord Ringwood, and I had a fond lingering hope that he might have left some token of remembrance to his brother's grandson. He has not. You have *probam pauperiem sine dote*. You have courage, health, strength, and talent. I was in greater straits than you are at your age. *My* father was not as indulgent as yours, I hope and trust, has been. From debt and dependence I worked myself up to a proud position by my own efforts. That the storm overtook me and engulphed me afterwards, is true. But I am like the merchant of my favorit: poet: I still hope—ay, at 63!—to mend my shattered ships, *indocilis pauperiem pati.* I still hope to pay back to my dear boy that fortune which ought to have been his, and which went down in my own shipwreck. Something tells me I must—I will!

"I agree with you that your escape from Agnes Twysden has been a *piece of good fortune for you,* and am much diverted by your account of her *dusky inamorato!* Between ourselves, the fondness of the Twysdens for money amounted to meanness. And though I always received Twysden in dear old Parr Street, as I trust a gentleman should, his company was insufferably tedious to me, and his vulgar loquacity odious. His son also was little to my taste. Indeed I was *heartily relieved* when I found your connection with that family was over, knowing their rapacity about money, and that it was your fortune, not you, they were anxious to secure for Agnes.

"You will be glad to hear that I am in not inconsiderable practice already. My reputation as a physician had preceded me to this country. My work on Gout was favorably noticed here, and in Philadelphia, and in Boston, by the scientific journals of those great cities. People are more generous and compassionate towards misfortune here than in our cold-hearted island. I could mention several gentlemen of New York who have suffered shipwreck like myself, and are now prosperous and respected. I had the good fortune to be of considerable professional service to Colonel J. B. Fogle, of New York, on our voyage out; and the Colonel, who is a leading personage here, has shown himself not at all ungrateful. Those who fancy that at New York people cannot appreciate and understand the manners of a gentleman, are *not a little mistaken;* and a man who, like myself, has lived with the best society in London, has, I flatter myself, not lived in that society *quite in vain.* The Colonel is proprietor and editor of one of the most brilliant and influential journals of the city. You know that arms and the toga are often worn here by the same individual, and——

"I had actually written thus far when I read in the Colonel's paper—*New York Emerald*—an account of your battle with your cousin at the Embassy ball. Oh, you pugnacious Philip! Well, young Twysden was very vulgar, very rude and overbearing, and, I have no doubt, deserved the chastisement you gave him. By the way, the correspondent of the *Emerald* makes some droll blunders regarding you in his letter. We are all fair game for publicity in this country, where the press is free *with a vengeance;* and your private affairs, or mine, or the President's, or our gracious Queen's, for the matter of that, are discussed with a freedom which certainly *amounts to licence.* The Colonel's lady is passing the winter in Paris, where I should wish you to pay your respects to her. Her husband has been most kind to me. I am told that Mrs. F. lives in the very choicest French society, and the friendship of this family may be useful to you as to your affectionate father,

"G. B. F.

"Address as usual, until you hear further from me, as Dr. Brandon, New York. I wonder whether Lord Estridge has asked you after his old college friend? When he was Headbury and at Trinity, he and a certain pensioner whom men used to nickname Brummell Firmin were said to be the best dressed men in the university. Estridge has advanced to rank, to honors! You may rely on it, that he will have one of the *very next* vacant garters. What a different, what an unfortunate career, has been his quondam friend's!— an exile, an inhabitant of a small room in a great hotel, where I sit at a scrambling public table with all sorts of coarse people! The way in which they bolt their dinner, often *with a knife,* shocks me. Your remittance was most welcome, small as it was. It shows my Philip has *a kind heart.* Ah! why, why are you thinking of marriage, who are so poor? By the way, your encouraging account of your circumstances has induced me to draw upon you for 100 dollars. The bill will go to Europe by the packet which carries this letter, and has kindly been cashed for me by my friends, Messrs. Plaster and Shinman, of Wall Street, respected bankers of this city. Leave your card with Mrs. Fogle. Her husband himself may be useful to you and your ever attached

"FATHER."

We take the *New York Emerald* at "Bays's," and in it I had read a very amusing account of our friend Philip, in an ingenious correspondence entitled "Letters from an Attaché," which appeared in that journal. I even copied the paragraph to show to my wife, and perhaps to forward to our friend.

"I promise you," wrote the attaché, "the new country did not disgrace the old at the British Embassy ball on Queen Vic's birthday. Colonel Z. B. Hoggins's lady, of Albany, and the peerless bride of Elijah J. Dibbs, of Twenty-ninth Street in your city, were the observed of all observers for splendor, for elegance, for refined native beauty. The Royal Dukes danced with nobody else ; and at the attention of one of the Princes to the lovely Miss Dibbs, I observed his Royal Duchess looked as black as thunder. Supper handsome. Back Delmonico to beat it. Champagne so-so. By the way, the young fellow who writes here for the *Pall Mall Gazette* got too much of the champagne on board—as usual, I am told. The Honorable R. Twysden, of London, was rude to my young chap's partner, or winked at him offensively, or trod on his toe, or I don't know what—but young F. followed him into the garden ; hit out at him ; sent him flying like a spread eagle into the midst of an illumination, and left him there sprawling. Wild, rampageous fellow this young F. ; has already spent his own fortune, and ruined his poor old father, who has been forced to cross the water. Old Louis Philippe went away early. He talked long with our Minister about his travels in our country. I was standing by, but in course ain't so ill-bred as to say what passed between them."

In this way history is written. I dare say about others besides Philip, in English papers as well as American, have fables been narrated.

CHAPTER XXVI.

CONTAINS A TUG OF WAR.

WHO was the first to spread the report that Philip was a prodigal and had ruined his poor confiding father ? I thought I knew a person who might be interested in getting under any shelter, and sacrificing even his own son for his own advantage. I thought I knew a man who had done as much already, and surely might do so again ; but my wife flew into one of her tempests of indignation, when I hinted something of this, clutched her own children to her heart, according to her maternal wont, asked me was there any power would cause me to belie *them ?* and sternly rebuked me for daring to be so wicked, heartless, and cynical. My dear creature, wrath is no answer. You call me heartless and cynic, for saying men are false and wicked. Have you never heard to what lengths some bank-rupts will go? To appease the wolves who chase them in the winter forest, have you not read how some travellers will cast all their provisions out of the sledge? then, when all the provis-ions are gone, don't you know that they will fling out perhaps the sister, perhaps the mother, perhaps the baby, the little dear tender innocent? Don't you see him tumbling among the howl-ing pack, and the wolves gnashing, gnawing, crashing, gobbling him up in the snow? O horror—horror! My wife draws all the young ones to her breast as I utter these fiendish remarks. She hugs them in her embrace, and says, " For shame ! " and that I am a monster, and so on. Go to! Go down on your knees, woman, and acknowledge the sinfulness of our human-kind. How long had our race existed ere murder and vio-lence began? and how old was the world ere brother slew brother?

Well, my wife and I came to a compromise. I might have my opinion, but was there any need to communicate it to poor Philip? No, surely. So I never sent him the extract from the *New York Emerald;* though, of course, some other good-natured friend did, and I don't think my magnanimous friend cared much. As for supposing that his own father, to cover his own character, would lie away his son's—such a piece of artifice was quite beyond Philip's comprehension, who has been all his life slow in appreciating roguery, or recognizing that there is meanness and double-dealing in the world. When he once comes to understand the fact ; when he once comprehends that Tartuffe is a humbug and swelling Bufo is a toady ; then my friend becomes as absurdly indignant and mistrustful as before he was admiring and confiding. Ah, Philip! Tartuffe has a number of good, respectable qualities ; and Bufo, though an underground odious animal, may have a precious jewel in his head. 'Tis you are cynical. *I* see the good qualities in these rascals whom you spurn. I see. I shrug my shoulders. I smile : and you call me cynic.

It was long before Philip could comprehend why Charlotte's mother turned upon him, and tried to force her daughter to forsake him. " I have offended the old woman in a hundred ways," he would say. " My tobacco annoys her; my old clothes offend her ; the very English I speak is often Greek to her, and she can no more construe my sentences than I can the Hindostanee jargon she talks to her husband at dinner." " My dear fellow, if you had ten thousand a year she would try and construe your sentences, or accept them even if not understood,"

I would reply. And some men, whom you and I know to be mean, and to be false, and to be flatterers and parasites, and to be inexorably hard and cruel in their own private circles, will surely pull a long face to-morrow, and say, "Oh! the man's so cynical."

I acquit Baynes of what ensued. I hold Mrs. B. to have been the criminal — the stupid criminal. The husband, like many other men extremely brave in active life, was at home timid and irresolute. Of two heads that lie side by side on the same pillow for thirty years, one must contain the stronger power, the more enduring resolution. Baynes, away from his wife, was shrewd, courageous, gay at times: when with her he was fascinated, torpid under the power of this baleful superior creature. "Ah, when we were subs together in camp in 1803, what a lively fellow Charley Baynes was!" his comrade, Colonel Bunch, would say. "That was before he ever saw his wife's yellow face; and what a slave she has made of him!"

After that fatal conversation which ensued on the day succeeding the ball, Philip did not come to dinner at Madame's according to his custom. Mrs. Baynes told no family stories, and Colonel Bunch, who had no special liking for the young gentleman, did not trouble himself to make any inquiries about him. One, two, three days passed, and no Philip. At last the Colonel says to the General, with a sly look at Charlotte, "Baynes, where is our young friend with the mustache? We have not seen him these three days." And he gives an arch look at poor Charlotte. A burning blush flamed up in little Charlotte's pale face, as she looked at her parents and then at their old friend. "Mr. Firmin does not come, because papa and mamma have forbidden him," says Charlotte. "I suppose he only comes where he is welcome." And, having made this audacious speech, I suppose the little maid tossed her little head up; and wondered, in the silence which ensued, whether all the company could hear her heart thumping.

Madame, from her central place, where she is carving, sees, from the looks of her guests, the indignant flushes on Charlotte's face, the confusion on her father's, the wrath on Mrs. Baynes's, that some dreadful words are passing; and in vain endeavors to turn the angry current of talk. "Un petit canard délicieux, goûtez-en, madame!" she cries. Honest Colonel Bunch sees the little maid with eyes flashing with anger, and trembling in every limb. The offered duck having failed to create a diversion, he, too, tries a feeble commonplace. "A little difference, my dear," he says, in an under voice. "There will be such in the best-regulated families. Canard sauvage très bong, madame, avec——" but he is allowed to speak no more, for——

"What would you do, Colonel Bunch," little Charlotte breaks out with her poor little ringing, trembling voice—"that is, if you were a young man, if another young man struck you, and insulted you?" I say she utters this in such a clear voice, that Françoise, the *femme-de-chambre*, that Auguste, the footman, that all the guests hear, that all the knives and forks stop their clatter.

"Faith, my dear, I'd knock him down if I could," says Bunch; and he catches hold of the little maid's sleeve, and would stop her speaking if he could.

"And that is what Philip did," cries Charlotte aloud; "and mamma has turned him out of the house—yes, out of the house, for acting like a man of honor!"

"Go to your room this instant, Miss!" shrieks mamma. As for old Baynes, his stained old uniform is not more dingy-red than his wrinkled face and his throbbing temples. He blushes under his wig, no doubt, could we see beneath that ancient artifice.

"What is it? madame your mother dismisses you of my table? I will come with you, my dear Miss Charlotte!" says madame, with much dignity. "Serve the sugared plate, Auguste! My ladies, you will excuse me! I go to attend the dear miss, who seems to me ill." And she rises up, and she follows poor little blushing, burning, weeping Charlotte: and again, I have no doubt, takes her in her arms, and kisses, and cheers, and caresses her—at the threshold of the door—there by the staircase, among the cold dishes of the dinner, where Moira and Macgrigor had one moment before been marauding.

"Courage, ma fille, courage, mon enfant! Tenez! Behold something to console thee!" and madame takes out of her pocket a little letter, and gives it to the girl, who at sight of it kisses the superscription, and then, in an anguish of love, and joy, and grief, falls on the neck of the kind woman, who consoles her in her misery. Whose writing is it Charlotte kisses? Can you guess by any means? Upon my word, Madame Smolensk, I never recommend ladies to take daughters to *your* boarding-house. And I like you so much, I would not tell of you, but you know the house is shut up this many a long day. Oh! the years slip away fugacious; and the grass has grown over graves; and many and many joys and sorrows have been born and have died since then for Charlotte and Philip: but that grief aches still in their bosoms at times; and that sorrow throbs at Charlotte's heart again whenever she looks at a little yellow letter in her trinket-box : and she says to her children, " Papa wrote that to me before we were married, my dears." There are scarcely half-a-dozen words in the little letter, I believe ; and two of them are "for ever."

I could draw a ground-plan of Madame's house in the Champs Elysées if I liked, for has not Philip shown me the place and described it to me many times ?   In front, and facing the road and garden, were Madame's room and the salon ; to the back was the salle-à-manger ; and a stair ran up the house (where the dishes used to be laid during dinner-time, and where Moira and Macgrigor fingered the meats and puddings).   Mrs. General Baynes's rooms were on the first floor, looking on the Champs Elysées, and into the garden-court of the house below. And on this day, as the dinner was necessarily short (owing to unhappy circumstances), and the gentlemen were left alone glumly drinking their wine or grog, and Mrs. Baynes had gone up stairs to her own apartment, had slapped her boys and was looking out of window—was it not provoking that of all days in the world young Hely should ride up to the house on his capering mare, with his flower in his button-hole, with his little varnished toe-tips just touching his stirrups, and after performing various caracolades and gambadoes in the garden, kiss his yellow-kidded hand to Mrs. General Baynes at the window, hope Miss Baynes was quite well, and ask if he might come in and take a cup of tea ?   Charlotte, lying on madame's bed in the ground-floor room, heard Mr. Hely's sweet voice asking after her health, and the crunching of his horse's hoofs on the gravel, and she could even catch glimpses of that little form as the horse capered about in the court, though of course he could not see her where she was lying on the bed with her letter in her hand.   Mrs. Baynes at her window had to wag her withered head from the casement, to groan out, " My daughter is lying down, and has a bad headache, I am sorry to say," and then she must have had the mortification to see Hely caper off, after waving her a genteel adieu.   The ladies in the front salon, who assembled after dinner witnessed the transaction, and Mrs. Bunch, I dare say, had a grim pleasure at seeing Eliza Baynes's young sprig of fashion, of whom Eliza was for ever bragging, come at last, and obliged to ride away, not bootless, certainly, for where were feet more beautifully *chaussés* ? but after a boot-less errand.

Meanwhile the gentlemen sat awhile in the dining-room, after the British custom which such veterans liked too well to

give up.   Other two gentlemen boarders went away, rather
alarmed by that storm and outbreak in which Charlotte had
quitted the dinner-table, and left the old soldiers together, to
enjoy, according to their after-dinner custom, a sober glass of
"something hot," as the saying is.   In truth, Madame's wine
was of the poorest ; but what better could you expect for the
money ?

Baynes was not eager to be alone with Bunch, and I have
no doubt began to blush again when he found himself *tête-à-tête*
with his old friend.   But what was to be done ?   The General
did not dare to go up stairs to his own quarters, where poor
Charlotte was probably crying, and her mother in one of her
tantrums.   Then in the salon there were the ladies of the
boarding-house party, and there Mrs. Bunch would be sure to
be at him.   Indeed, since the Bayneses were launched in the
great world, Mrs. Bunch was untiringly sarcastic in her remarks
about lords, ladies, attachés, ambassadors, and fine people in
general.   So Baynes sat with his friend, in the falling evening,
in much silence, dipping his old nose in the brandy-and-water.

Little square-faced, red-faced, whisker-dyed Colonel Bunch
sat opposite his old companion, regarding him not without
scorn.   Bunch had a wife.   Bunch had feelings.   Do you suppose those feelings had not been worked upon by that wife in
private colloquies ?   Do you suppose—when two old women
have lived together in pretty much the same rank of life—if
one suddenly gets promotion, is carried off to higher spheres,
and talks of her new friends, the countesses, duchesses, am-
bassadresses, as of course she will—do you suppose, I say, that
the unsuccessful woman will be pleased at the successful
woman's success ?   Your knowledge of your own heart, my
dear lady, must tell you the truth in this matter.   I don't want
you to acknowledge that you are angry because your sister has
been staying with the Duchess of Fitzbattleaxe, but you are,
you know.   You have made sneering remarks to your husband
on the subject, and such remarks, I have no doubt, were made
by Mrs. Colonel Bunch to *her* husband, regarding her poor
friend Mrs. General Baynes.

During this parenthesis we have left the General dipping
his nose in the brandy-and-water.   He can't keep it there for
ever.   He must come up for air presently.   His face must come
out of the drink, and sigh over the table.

"What's this business, Baynes ?" says the Colonel.
"What's the matter with poor Charley ?"

"Family affairs—differences will happen," says the General.

" I do hope and trust nothing has gone wrong with her and young Firmin, Baynes ? "

The General does not like those fixed eyes staring at him under those bushy eyebrows, between those bushy, blackened whiskers.

" Well, then, yes, Bunch, something *has* gone wrong ; and given me and—and Mrs. Baynes—a deuced deal of pain too. The young fellow has acted like a blackguard, brawling and fighting at an ambassador's ball, bringing us all to ridicule. He's not a gentleman ; that's the long and short of it, Bunch ; and so let's change the subject."

" Why, consider the provocation he had ! " cries the other, disregarding entirely his friend's prayer. " I heard them talking about the business at *Galignani's* this very day. A fellow swears at Firmin ; runs at him ; brags that he has pitched him over ; and is knocked down for his pains. By George ! I think Firmin was quite right. Were any man to do as much to me or you, what should we do, even at our age ? "

" We are military men. I said I didn't wish to talk about the subject, Bunch," says the General in rather a lofty manner.

" You mean that Tom Bunch has no need to put his oar in ? "

" Precisely so," says the other, curtly.

" Mum's the word ! Let us talk about the dukes and duchesses at the ball. *That's* more in your line, now," says the Colonel, with rather a sneer.

" What do you mean by duchesses and dukes ? What do you know about them, or what the deuce do I care ? " asks the General.

" Oh, they are tabooed too ! Hang it, there's no satisfying you," growls the Colonel.

" Look here, Bunch," the General broke out ; " I must speak, since you won't leave me alone. I am unhappy. You can see that well enough. For two or three nights past I have had no rest. This engagement of my child and Mr. Firmin can't come to any good. You see what he is—an overbearing, ill-conditioned, quarrelsome fellow. What chance has Charley of being happy with such a fellow ? "

" I hold my tongue, Baynes. You told me not to put my oar in," growls the Colonel.

" Oh, if that's the way you take it, Bunch, of course there's no need for me to go on any more," cries General Baynes. " If an old friend won't give an old friend advice, by George, or help him in a strait, or say a kind word when he's unhappy,

I have done. I have known you for forty years, and I am mistaken in you—that's all."

"There's no contenting you. You say, ' Hold your tongue,' and I shut my mouth. I hold my tongue, and you say, ' Why don't you speak ?' Why don't I? Because you won't like what I say, Charles Baynes : and so what's the good of more talking ?"

"Confound it !" cries Baynes, with a thump of his glass on the table, "but what *do* you say ?"

"I say, then, as you will have it," cries the other, clenching his fists in his pockets,—" I say you are wanting a pretext for breaking off this match, Baynes. I don't say it is a good one, mind ; but your word is passed, and your honor engaged to a young fellow to whom you are under deep obligation."

"What obligation ? Who has talked to you about my private affairs ?" cries the General, reddening. "Has Philip Firmin been bragging about his—— ?"

"You have yourself, Baynes. When you arrived here, you told me over and over again what the young fellow had done : and you certainly thought he acted like a gentlemen *then*. If you choose to break your word to him now——"

"Break my word ! Great powers, do you know what you are saying, Bunch ? "

"Yes, and what you are doing, Baynes."

"Doing ? and what ? "

"A damned shabby action ; that's what you are doing, if you want to know. Don't tell *me*. Why, do you suppose Sarah—do you suppose everybody doesn't see what you are at ? You think you can get a better match for the girl, and you and Eliza are going to throw the young fellow over : and the fellow who held his hand, and might have ruined you, if he liked. I say it is a cowardly action ! "

"Colonel Bunch, do you dare to use such a word to me ? " calls out the General, starting to his feet.

"Dare be hanged ! I say it's a shabby action !" roars the other, rising too.

"Hush ! unless you wish to disturb the ladies ! Of course you know what your expression means, Colonel Bunch ? " and the General drops his voice and sinks back to his chair.

"I know what my words mean, and I stick to 'em, Baynes," growls the other ; "which is more than you can say of yours."

"I am dee'd if any man alive shall use this language to me," says the General, in the softest whisper, " without accounting to me for it."

"Did you ever find me backward, Baynes, at that kind of thing?" growls the Colonel, with a face like a lobster and eyes starting from his head.

"Very good, sir. To-morrow, at your earliest convenience. I shall be at *Galignani's* from eleven till one. With a friend, if possible.—What is it, my love? A game at whist? Well, no, thank you; I think I won't play cards to-night."

It was Mrs. Baynes who entered the room when the two gentlemen were quarrelling; and the bloodthirsty hypocrites instantly smoothed their ruffled brows and smiled on her with perfect courtesy.

"Whist—no! I was thinking should we send out to meet him? He has never been in Paris."

"Never been in Paris?" said the General, puzzled."

"He will be here to-night, you know. Madame has a room ready for him."

"The very thing, the very thing!" cries General Baynes, with great glee. And Mrs. Baynes, all unsuspicious of the quarrel between the old friends, proceeds to inform Colonel Bunch that Major MacWhirter was expected that evening. And then that tough old Colonel Bunch knew the cause of Baynes's delight. A second was provided for the General— the very thing Baynes wanted.

We have seen how Mrs. Baynes, after taking counsel with her General, had privately sent for MacWhirter. Her plan was that Charlotte's uncle should take her for awhile to Tours, and make her hear reason. Then Charley's foolish passion for Philip would pass away. Then, if he dared to follow her so far, her aunt and uncle, two dragons of virtue and circumspection, would watch and guard her. Then, if Mrs. Hely was still of the same mind, she and her son might easily take the post to Tours, where, Philip being absent, young Walsingham might plead his passion. The best part of the plan, perhaps, was the separation of our young couple. Charlotte would recover. Mrs. Baynes was sure of that. The little girl had made no outbreak until that sudden insurrection at dinner which we have witnessed; and her mother, who had domineered over the child all her life, thought she was still in her power. She did not know that she had passed the bounds of authority, and that with her behavior to Philip her child's allegiance had revolted.

Bunch then, from Baynes's look and expression, perfectly understood what his adversary meant, and that the General's second was found. His own he had in his eye—a tough little

old army surgeon of Peninsular and Indian times, who lived
hard by, who would aid as second and doctor too, if need were
—and so kill two birds with one stone, as they say. The Colonel
would go forth that very instant and seek for Dr. Martin, and
be hanged to Baynes, and a plague on the whole transaction
and the folly of two old friends burning powder in such a
quarrel. But he knew what a bloodthirsty little fellow that
henpecked, silent Baynes was when roused ; and as for himself
—a fellow use that kind of language to *me ?* By George, Tom
Bunch was not going to baulk him !

Whose was that tall figure prowling about Madame's house
in the Champs Elysées when Colonel Bunch issued forth in
quest of his friend ; who had been watched by the police and
mistaken for a suspicious character ; who had been looking up
at Madame's windows now that the evening shades had fallen?
Oh, you goose of a Philip ! (for of course, my dears, you guess
that the spy was P. F., Esq.) you look up at the *premier*, and
there is the Beloved in Madame's room on the ground floor ;
—in yonder room, where a lamp is burning and casting a faint
light across the bars of the *jalousie*. If Philip knew she was
there he would be transformed into a clematis, and climb up
the bars of the window, and twine round them all night. But
you see he thinks she is on the first floor ; and the glances of
his passionate eyes are taking aim at the wrong windows. And
now Colonel Bunch comes forth in his stout strutting way, in
his little military cape—quick march—and Philip is startled
like a guilty thing surprised, and dodges behind a tree in the
avenue.

The Colonel departed on his murderous errand. Philip
still continues to ogle the window of his heart (the wrong window), defiant of the policeman, who tells him to *circuler*. He
has not watched here many minutes more, ere a hackney-coach
drives up with portmanteaus on the roof and a lady and gentleman within.

You see Mrs. MacWhirter thought she, as well as her husband, might have a peep at Paris. As Mac's coach-hire was
paid, Mrs. Mac could afford a little outlay of money. And if
they were to bring Charlotte back—Charlotte in grief and agitation, poor child—a matron, an aunt, would be a much fitter
companion for her than a major, however gentle. So the pair
of MacWhirters journeyed from Tours—a long journey it was
before railways were invented—and after four-and-twenty hours
of squeeze in the diligence, presented themselves at nightfall
at Madame Smolensk's.

The Baynes' boys dashed into the garden at the sound of wheels. "Mamma—mamma! it's uncle Mac!" these innocents cried: as they ran to the railings. "Uncle Mac! what could bring him? Oh! they are going to send me to him! they are going to send me to him!" thought Charlotte, starting on her bed. And on this I dare say, a certain locket was kissed more vehemently than ever.

"I say, Ma!" cries the ingenuous Moira, jumping back to the house; "it's uncle Mac, and aunt Mac, too!"

"*What?*" cries mamma, with anything but pleasure in her voice; and then turning to the dining-room, where her husband still sat, she called out, "General! here's MacWhirter and Emily!"

Mrs. Baynes gave her sister a very grim kiss.

"Dearest Eliza, I thought it was such a good opportunity of coming, and that I might be so useful, you know!" pleads Emily.

"Thank you. How do you do, MacWhirter?" says the grim Général.

"Glad to see you, Baynes my boy!"

"How d'ye do, Emily? Boys, bring your uncle's traps. Didn't know Emily was coming Mac. Hope there's room for her!" sighs the General, coming forth from his parlor.

The Major was struck by the sad looks and pallor of his brother-in-law. "By George, Baynes, you look as yellow as a guinea. How's Tom Bunch?"

"Come into this room along with me. Have some brandy-and-water, Mac. Auguste! Odevie O sho!" calls the General; and Auguste, who out of the new comers' six packages has daintily taken one very small mackintosh cushion, says "Comment? encore du grog, Général?" and, shrugging his shoulders, disappears to procure the refreshment at his leisure.

The sisters disappear to their embraces; the brothers-in-law retreat to the salle-*à*-manger, where General Baynes has been sitting, gloomy and lonely, for half an hour past, thinking of his quarrel with his old comrade, Bunch. He and Bunch have been chums for more than forty years. They have been in action together, and honorably mentioned in the same report. They have had a great regard for each other; and each knows the other is an obstinate old mule, and, in a quarrel, will die rather than give way. They have had a dispute out of which there is only one issue. Words have passed which no man, however old, by George! can brook from any friend, however intimate, by Jove! No wonder Baynes is grave. His family is large ; his means are small. To-morrow he may be under fire of an old friend's pistol. In such an extremity he knows how each will behave. No wonder, I say, the General is solemn.

"What's in the wind now, Baynes?" asks the Major, after a little drink and a long silence. "How is poor little Char?"

"Infernally ill—I mean behaved infernally ill," says the General, biting his lips.

"Bad business! Bad business! Poor little child!" cries the Major.

"Insubordinate little devil!" says the pale General, grinding his teeth. "We'll see which shall be master!"

"What! you have had words?"

"At this table, this very day. She sat here and defied her mother and me, by George! and flung out of the room like a tragedy queen. She must be tamed, Mac, or my name's not Baynes."

MacWhirter knew his relative of old, and that this quiet, submissive man, when angry, worked up to a white heat as it were. "Sad affair; hope you'll both come round, Baynes," sighs the Major, trying bootless commonplaces ; and seeing this last remark had no effect, he bethought him of recurring to their mutual friend. "How's Tom Bunch?" the Major asked, cheerily.

At this question Baynes grinned in such a ghastly way that MacWhirter eyed him with wonder. "Colonel Bunch is very well," the General said, in a dismal voice ; "at least, he was half an hour ago. He was sitting there ;" and he pointed to an empty spoon lying in an empty beaker, whence the spirit and water had departed.

"What has been the matter, Baynes?" asked the Major. "Has anything happened between you and Tom?"

"I mean that, half an hour ago, Colonel Bunch used words to me which I'll bear from no man alive : and you have arrived just in the nick of time, MacWhirter, to take my message to him. Hush! here's the drink."

"Voici, Messieurs!" Auguste at length has brought up a second supply of brandy-and-water. The veterans mingled their jorums ; and whilst his brother-in-law spoke, the alarmed MacWhirter sipped occasionally *intentusque ora tenebat*.

CHAPTER XXVII.

I CHARGE YOU, DROP YOUR DAGGERS!

GENERAL BAYNES began the story which you and I have heard at length. He told it in his own way. He grew very angry with himself whilst defending himself. He had to abuse Philip very fiercely, in order to excuse his own act of treason. He had to show that his act was not his act; that, after all, he never had promised; and that, if he had promised, Philip's atrocious conduct ought to absolve him from any previous promise. I do not wonder that the General was abusive, and out of temper. Such a crime as he was committing can't be performed cheerfully by a man who is habitually gentle, generous, and honest. I do not say that men cannot cheat, cannot lie, cannot inflict torture, cannot commit rascally actions, without in the least losing their equanimity; but these are men habitually false, knavish, and cruel. They are accustomed to break their promises, to cheat their neighbors in bargains, and what not. A roguish word or action more or less is of little matter to them: their remorse only awakens after detection, and they don't begin to repent till they come sentenced out of the dock. But here was an ordinarily just man withdrawing from his promise, turning his back on his benefactor, and justifying himself to himself by maligning the man whom he injured. It is not an uncommon event, my dearly beloved brethren and esteemed miserable sister sinners; but you like to say a preacher is "cynical" who admits this sad truth—and, perhaps, don't care to hear about the subject on more than one day in the week.

So, in order to make out some sort of case for himself, our poor good old General Baynes chose to think and declare that Philip was so violent, ill-conditioned, and abandoned a fellow, that no faith ought to be kept with him; and that Colonel Bunch had behaved with such brutal insolence that Baynes must call him to account. As for the fact that there was another, a richer, and a much more eligible suitor, who was likely to offer for his daughter, Baynes did not happen to touch on this point at all; preferring to speak of Philip's homeless poverty, disreputable conduct, and gross and careless behavior.

Now MacWhirter, having, I suppose, little to do at Tours, had read Mrs. Baynes's letters to her sister Emily, and remembered them. Indeed, it was but very few months since

Eliza Baynes's letters had been full of praise of Philip, of his love for Charlotte, and of his noble generosity in foregoing the great claim which he had upon the General, his mother's careless trustee. Philip was the first suitor Charlotte had had : in her first glow of pleasure, Charlotte's mother had covered yards of paper with compliments, interjections, and those *scratches* or *dashes* under her words, by which some ladies are accustomed to point their satire or emphasize their delight. He was an admirable young man—wild, but generous, handsome, noble ! He had forgiven his father thousands and thousands of pounds which the doctor owed him—all his mother's fortune ; and he had acted *most nobly* by her trustees—that she must say, though poor dear weak Baynes was one of them ! Baynes who was as simple as a child. Major Mac and his wife had agreed that Philip's forbearance was very generous and kind, but after all that there was no special cause for rapture at the notion of their niece marrying a struggling young fellow without a penny in the world ; and they had been not a little amused with the change of tone in Eliza's later letters, when she began to go out in the great world, and to look coldly upon poor, penniless Firmin, her hero of a few months since. Then Emily remembered how Eliza had always been fond of great people ; how her head was turned by going to a few parties at Government House ; how absurdly she went on with that little creature Fitzrickets (because he was an Honorable, forsooth,) at Dumdum. Eliza was a good wife to Baynes ; a good mother to the children ; and made both ends of a narrow income meet with surprising dexterity ; but Emily was bound to say of her sister Eliza, that a more, &c., &c., &c. And when the news came at length that Philip was to be thrown overboard, Emily clapped her hands together and said to her husband, " Now, Mac, didn't I always tell you so ? If she could get a fashionable husband for Charlotte, I *knew* my sister would put the doctor's son to the door ! " That the poor child would suffer considerably, her aunt was assured. Indeed, before her own union with Mac, Emily had undergone heart-breakings and pangs of separation on her account. The poor child would want comfort and companionship. *She* would go to fetch her niece. And though the Major said, " My dear, you want to go to Paris, and buy a new bonnet," Mrs. MacWhirter spurned the insinuation, and came to Paris from a mere sense of duty.

So Baynes poured out his history of wrongs to his brother-in-law, who marvelled to hear a man, ordinarily chary of words and cool of demeanor, so angry and so voluble. If he had

done a bad action, at least, after doing it, Baynes had the grace
to be very much out of humor. If I ever, for my part, do anything wrong in my family, or to them, I accompany that action
with a furious rage and blustering passion. I won't have wife
or children question it. No querulous Nathan of a family
friend (or an incommodious conscience, maybe,) shall come
and lecture *me* about my ill-doings. No—no. Out of the
house with him! Away, you preaching bugbear, don't try to
frighten *me!* Baynes, I suspect, to browbeat, bully, and outtalk
the Nathan pleading in his heart—Baynes will outbawl that
prating monitor, and thrust that inconvenient preacher out of
sight, out of hearing, drive him with angry words from the gate.
Ah! in vain we expel him; and bid John say, not at home!
There he is when we wake, sitting at our bedfoot. We throw
him overboard for daring to put an oar in our boat. Whose
ghastly head is that looking up from the water and swimming
alongside us, row we never so swiftly? Fire at him. Brain
him with an oar, one of you, and pull on! Flash goes the
pistol. Surely that oar has stove the old skull in? See! there
comes the awful companion popping up out of water again, and
crying, "Remember, remember, I am here, I am here!"
Baynes had thought to bully away one monitor by the threat
of a pistol, and here was another swimming alongside of his
boat. And would you have it otherwise, my dear reader, for
you, for me? That you and I shall commit sins, in this, and
ensuing years, is certain; but I hope—I hope they won't be
past praying for. Here is Baynes, having just done a bad action, in a dreadfully wicked, murderous, and dissatisfied state
of mind. His chafing, bleeding temper is one raw; his whole
soul one rage, and wrath, and fever. Charles Baynes, thou old
sinner, I pray that heaven may turn thee to a better state of
mind. I will kneel down by thy side, scatter ashes on my own
bald pate, and we will quaver out *Peccavimus* together.

"In one word, the young man's conduct has been so outrageous and disreputable that I can't, Mac, as a father of a
family, consent to my girl's marrying him. Out of a regard for
her happiness, it is my duty to break off the engagement," cries
the General, finishing the story.

"Has he formally released you from that trust business?"
asked the Major.

"Good heavens, Mac!" cries the General, turning very red.
"You know I am as innocent of all wrong towards him as you
are!"

"Innocent—only you did not look to your trust——"

"I think ill of him, sir. I think he is a wild, reckless, over-bearing young fellow," calls out the General, very quickly, "who would make my child miserable ; but I don't think he is such a blackguard as to come down on a retired elderly man with a poor family—a numerous family ; a man who has bled and fought for his sovereign in the Peninsula, and in India, as the 'Army List' will show you, by George! I don't think Firmin will be such a scoundrel as to come down on me, I say ; and I must say, MacWhirter, I think it most unhandsome of you to allude to it—most unhandsome, by George!"

"Why, you are going to break off your bargain with him ; why should he keep his compact with you?" asks the gruff Major.

"Because," shouted the General, "it would be a sin and a shame that an old man with seven children, and broken health, who has served in every place—yes, in the West and East Indies, by George!—in Canada—in the Peninsula, and at New Orleans ;—because he has been deceived and humbugged by a miserable scoundrel of a doctor into signing a sham paper, by George! should be ruined, and his poor children and wife driven to beggary, by Jove! as you seem to recommend young Firmin to do, Jack MacWhirter ; and I'll tell you what, Major Mac-Whirter, I take it dee'd unfriendly of you ; and I'll trouble you not to put your oar into *my boat*, and meddle with *my affairs*, that's all, and I'll know who's at the bottom of it, by Jove! It's the gray mare, Mac—it's your *better half*, MacWhirter—it's that confounded, meddling, sneaking, backbiting, domineer-ing——"

"What next?" roared the Major. "Ha, ha, ha! Do you think I don't know, Baynes, who has put you on doing what I have no hesitation in calling a most sneaking and rascally action—yes, a rascally action, by George! I am not going to mince matters! Don't come your Major-General or your Mrs. Major-General over me! It's Eliza that has set you on. And if Tom Bunch has been telling you that you have been breaking from your word, and are acting shabbily, Tom is right ; and you may get somebody else to go out with you, General Baynes, for, by George, I won't!"

"Have you come all the way from Tours, Mac, in order to insult me?" asks the General.

"I came to do you a friendly turn ; to take charge of your poor girl, upon whom you are being very hard, Baynes. And this is the reward I get! Thank you. No more grog! What I have had is rather *too strong* for me already." And the Major

28

looks down with an expression of scorn at the emptied beaker, the idle spoon before him.

As the warriors were quarrelling over their cups, there came to them a noise as of brawling and of female voices without. "Mais, madame !" pleads Madame Smolensk, in her grave way. "Taisez-vous, madame, laissez-moi tranquille, s'il vous plait !" exclaims the well-known voice of Mrs. General Baynes, which I own was never very pleasant to me, either in anger or good-humor. "And your Little,—who tries to sleep in my chamber !" again pleads the mistress of the boarding-house. "Vous n'avez pas droit d'appeler Mademoiselle Baynes petite !" calls out the General's lady. And Baynes, who was fighting and quarrelling himself just now, trembled when he heard her. His angry face assumed an alarmed expression. He looked for means of escape. He appealed for protection to MacWhirter, whose nose he had been ready to pull anon. Samson was a mighty man, but he was a fool in the hands of a woman. Hercules was a brave man and a strong, but Omphale twisted him round her spindle. Even so Baynes, who had fought in India, Spain, America, trembled before the partner of his bed and name.

It was an unlucky afternoon. Whilst the husbands had been quarrelling in the dining-room over brandy-and-water, the wives, the sisters, had been fighting over their tea in the salon. I don't know what the other boarders were about. Philip never told me. Perhaps they had left the room to give the sisters a free opportunity for embraces and confidential communication. Perhaps there were no lady boarders left. Howbeit, Emily and Eliza had tea ; and before that refreshing meal was concluded, those dear women were fighting as hard as their husbands in the adjacent chamber.

Eliza, in the first place, was very angry at Emily's coming without invitation. Emily, on her part, was angry with Eliza for being angry. "I am sure, Eliza," said the spirited and injured MacWhirter, "that is the third time you have alluded to it since we have been here. Had you and all your family come to Tours, Mac and I would have made them welcome— children and all ; and I am sure yours make trouble enough in a house."

"A private house is not like a boarding-house, Emily. Here Madame makes us pay frightfully for extras," remarks Mrs. Baynes.

"I am sorry I came, Eliza. Let us say no more about it. I can't go away to-night," says the other.

" And most unkind it is that speech to make, Emily. Any more tea ? "

" Most unpleasant to have to make that speech, Eliza. To travel a whole day and night—and I never able to sleep in a diligence—to hasten to my sister because I thought she was in trouble, because I thought a sister might comfort her ; and to be received as you re—as you—oh, oh, oh—boh ! How stoopid I am ! " A handkerchief dries the tears : a smelling-bottle restores a little composure. " When you came to us at Dumdum, with two—o—o children in the whooping-cough, I am sure Mac and I gave you a very different welcome. "

The other was smitten with remorse. She remembered her sister's kindness in former days. " I did not mean, sister, to give you pain," she said. " But I am very unhappy myself, Emily. My child's conduct is making me most unhappy. "

"And very good reason you have to be unhappy, Eliza, if woman ever had," says the other.

" Oh, indeed, yes ! " gasps the General's lady.

" If any woman ought to feel remorse, Eliza Baynes, I am sure it's you. Sleepless nights ! What was mine in the diligence, compared to the nights you must have ? I said so to myself. ' I am wretched, ' I said, ' but what must *she* be ? ' "

"Of course, as a feeling mother, I feel that poor Charlotte is unhappy, my dear."

" But what makes her so, my dear ? " cries Mrs. MacWhirter, who presently showed that she was mistress of the whole controversy. " No wonder Charlotte is unhappy, dear love ! Can a girl be engaged to a young man, a most interesting young man, a clever, accomplished, highly educated young man—— "

"*What ?* " cries Mrs. Baynes.

"Haven't I your letters ? I have them all in my desk. They are in that hall now. Didn't you tell me so over and over again ; and rave about him, till I thought you were in love with him yourself almost ? " cries Mrs. Mac.

" A most indecent observation ! " cries out Eliza Baynes, in her deep, awful voice. " No woman, no sister, shall say that to me ! "

" Shall I go and get the letters ? It used to be, ' Dear Philip has just left us. Dear Philip has been more than a son to me. He is our preserver ! ' Didn't you write all that to me over and over again ? And because you have found a richer husband for Charlotte, you are going to turn your preserver out of doors ! "

" Emily MacWhirter, am I to sit here and be accused of

crimes, *uninvited*, mind—*uninvited*, mind, by my sister? Is a general officer's lady to be treated in this way by a brevet-major's wife? Though you are my senior in age, Emily, I am yours in rank. Out of any room in England, but this, I go before you! And if you have come *uninvited* all the way from Tours to insult me in my own house——"

"House, indeed! pretty house! Everybody else's house as well as yours!"

"Such as it is, I never asked you to come into it, Emily!"

"Oh, yes! You wish me to go out in the night. MAC! I say!"

"Emily!" cries the Generaless.

"MAC, I say!" screams the Majoress, flinging open the door of the salon, "my sister wishes me to go. Do you hear me?"

"Au nom de Dieu, madame, pensez à cette pauvre petite, qui souffre à côté," cries the mistress of the house, pointing to her own adjoining chamber, in which, we have said, our poor little Charlotte was lying.

"Nappley pas Madamaselle Baynes petite, sivoplay!" booms out Mrs. Baynes' contralto.

"MacWhirter, I say, Major MacWhirter!" cries Emily, flinging open the door of the dining-room where the two gentlemen were knocking their own heads together. "MacWhirter! My sister chooses to insult me, and say that a brevet-major's wife——"

"By George! are you fighting, too?" asks the General.

"Baynes, Emily MacWhirter has insulted me!" cries Mrs. Baynes.

"It seems to have been a settled thing beforehand," yells the General. "Major MacWhirter has done the same thing by me! He has forgotten that he is a gentleman, and that I am."

"He only insults you because he thinks you are his relative, and must bear everything from him," says the General's wife.

"By George! I will NOT bear everything from him!" shouts the General. The two gentlemen and their two wives are squabbling in the hall. Madame and the servants are peering up from the kitchen-regions. I dare say the boys from the topmost banisters are saying to each other, "Row between Ma and Aunt Mac!" I dare say scared little Charlotte, in her temporary apartment, is, for awhile, almost forgetful of her own grief; and wondering what quarrel is agitating her aunt and mother, her father and uncle? Place the remaining male and female boarders about the corridors and on the landings, in various attitudes expressive of interest, of satiric commentary, wrath at being disturbed by unseemly domestic quarrel: —in what posture you will. As for Mrs. Colonel Bunch, she, poor thing, does not know that the General and her own Colonel have entered on a mortal quarrel. She imagines the dispute is only between Mrs. Baynes and her sister as yet ; and she has known this pair quarrelling for a score of years past. "Toujours comme ça, fighting vous savez, et puis make it up again. Oui," she explains to a French friend on the landing.

In the very midst of this storm Colonel Bunch returns, his friend and second, Dr. Martin, on his arm. He does not know that two battles have been fought since his own combat. His, we will say, was Ligny. Then came Quatre-Bras, in which Baynes and MacWhirter were engaged. Then came the general action of Waterloo. And here enters Colonel Bunch, quite unconscious of the great engagements which have taken place since his temporary retreat in search of reinforcements.

"How are you, MacWhirter?" cries the Colonel of the purple whiskers. " My friend, Dr. Martin!" And as he addresses himself to the General, his eyes almost start out of his head, as if they would shoot themselves into the breast of that officer.

"My dear, hush! Emily MacWhirter, had we not better defer this most painful dispute ? The whole house is listening to us !" whispers the General, in a rapid low voice. "Doctor —Colonel Bunch—Major MacWhirter, had we not better go into the dining-room ? "

The General and the Doctor go first, Major MacWhirter and Colonel Bunch pause at the door. Says Bunch to MacWhirter : " Major, you act as the General's friend in this affair ? It's most awkward, but, by George! Baynes has said things to me that I won't bear, were he my own flesh and blood, by George ! And I know him a deuced deal too well to think he will ever apologize ! "

" He has said things to ME, Bunch, that I won't bear from fifty brother-in-laws, by George ! growls MacWhirter.

"What ? Don't you bring me any message from him ? "

"I tell you, Tom Bunch, I want to send a message to him. Invite me to his house, and insult me and Emily when we come ! By George, it makes my blood boil ! Insult us after travelling twenty-four hours in a confounded diligence, and say we're not invited ! He and his little catamaran."

"Hush !" interposed Bunch.

"I say catamaran, sir ! don't tell *me!* They came and

stayed with us four months at Dumdum—the children ill with the pip, or some confounded thing—went to Europe, and left me to pay the doctor's bill; and now, by——"

Was the Major going to invoke George, the Cappadocian champion, or Olympian Jove? At this moment a door, by which they stood, opens. You may remember there were three doors, all on that landing; if you doubt me, go and see the house (Avenue de Valmy, Champs Elysées, Paris). A third door opens, and a young lady comes out, looking very pale and sad, her hair hanging over her shoulders;—her hair, which hung in rich clusters generally, but I suppose tears have put it all out of curl.

"Is it you, uncle Mac? I thought I knew your voice, and I heard aunt Emily's," says the little person.

"Yes, it is I, Charley," says uncle Mac. And he looks into the round face, which looks so wild and is so full of grief unutterable that uncle Mac is quite melted, and takes the child to his arms, and says, "What is it, my dear?" And he quite forgets that he proposes to blow her father's brains out in the morning. "How hot your little hands are!"

"Uncle, uncle!" she says, in a swift febrile whisper, "you're come to take me away, I know. I heard you and papa, I heard mamma and aunt Emily speaking quite loud! But if I go—I'll—I'll never love any but him!"

"But whom, dear?"

"But Philip, uncle."

"By George, Char, no more you shall!" says the Major. And herewith the poor child, who had been sitting up on her bed whilst this quarrelling of sisters,—whilst this brawling of majors, generals, colonels,—whilst this coming of hackney-coaches, —whilst this arrival and departure of visitors on horseback,— had been taking place, gave a fine hysterical scream, and fell into her uncle's arms laughing and crying wildly.

This outcry, of course, brought the gentlemen from their adjacent room, and the ladies from theirs.

"What are you making a fool of yourself about?" growls Mrs. Baynes, in her deepest bark.

"By George, Eliza, you are too bad!" says the General, quite white.

"Eliza, you are a brute!" cries Mrs. MacWhirter.

"So she is!" shrieks Mrs. Bunch from the landing place overhead, where other lady-boarders were assembled looking down on this awful family battle.

Eliza Baynes knew she had gone too far. Poor Charley

was scarce conscious by this time, and wildly screaming, "Never, never!" * * * * When, as I live, who should burst into the premises but a young man with fair hair, with flaming whiskers, with flaming eyes, who calls out, "What is it? I am here, Charlotte, Charlotte!"

Who is that young man? We had a glimpse of him, prowling about the Champs Elysées just now, and dodging behind a tree when Colonel Bunch went out in search of his second. Then the young man saw the MacWhirter hackney-coach approach the house. Then he waited and waited, looking to that upper window behind which we know his beloved was *not* reposing. Then he beheld Bunch and Doctor Martin arrive. Then he passed through the wicket into the garden, and heard Mrs. Mac and Mrs. Baynes fighting. Then there came from the passage—where you see, this battle was going on—that ringing dreadful laugh and scream of poor Charlotte; and Philip Firmin burst like a bombshell into the midst of the hall where the battle was raging, and of the family circle who were fighting and screaming.

Here *is* a picture I protest. We have—first, the boarders on the first landing, whither, too, the Baynes children have crept in their night-gowns. Secondly, we have Auguste, Françoise the cook, and the assistant coming up from the basement. And, third, we have Colonel Bunch, Doctor Martin, Major MacWhirter, with Charlotte in his arms; Madame, General B., Mrs. Mac, Mrs. General B., all in the passage, when our friend the bombshell bursts in amongst them.

"What is it? Charlotte, I am here!" cries Philip, with his great voice; at hearing which, little Char gives one final scream, and, at the next moment, she has fainted quite dead—but this time she is on Philip's shoulder.

"You brute, how dare you do this?" asks Mrs. Baynes, glaring at the young man.

"It is *you* who have done it, Eliza!" says aunt Emily.

"And so she has, Mrs. MacWhirter!" calls out Mrs. Colonel Bunch, from the landing above.

And Charles Baynes felt he had acted like a traitor, and hung down his head. He had encouraged his daughter to give her heart away, and she had obeyed him. When he saw Philip I think he was glad: so was the Major, though Firmin, to be sure, pushed him quite roughly up against the wall.

"Is this vulgar scandal to go on in the passage before the whole house?" gasped Mrs. Baynes.

"Bunch brought me here to prescribe for this young lady,"

says little Doctor Martin, in a very courtly way. "Madame, will you get a little sal-volatile from Anjubeau's in the Faubourg; and let her be kept very quiet!"

"Come, Monsieur Philippe, it is enough like that!" cries Madame, who can't repress a smile. "Come to your chamber, dear little!"

"Madame," cries Mrs. Baynes, "une mère——"

Madame shrugs her shoulders. "Une mère, une belle mère, ma foi!" she says. Come, mademoiselle!"

There were only very few people in the boarding-house: if they knew, if they saw, what happened, how can we help ourselves? But that they had all been sitting over a powder-magazine, which might have blown up and destroyed one, two, three, five people, even Philip did not know, until afterwards, when, laughing, Major MacWhirter told him how that meek but most savage Baynes had first challenged Bunch, had then challenged his brother-in-law, and how all sorts of battle, murder, sudden death might have ensued had the quarrel not come to an end.

Were your humble servant anxious to harrow his reader's feelings, or display his own graphical powers, you understand that I never would have allowed those two gallant officers to quarrel and threaten each other's very noses, without having the insult wiped out in blood. The Bois de Boulogne is hard by the Avenue de Valmy, with plenty of cool fighting ground. The *octroi* officers never stop gentlemen going out at the neighboring barrier upon duelling business, or prevent the return of the slain victim in the hackney-coach when the dreadful combat is over. From my knowledge of Mrs. Baynes's character I have not the slightest doubt that she would have encouraged her husband to fight; and, the General down, would have put pistols into the hands of her boys, and bidden them carry on the *vendetta;* but as I do not, for my part, love to see brethren at war, or Moses and Aaron tugging white handfuls out of each other's beards, I am glad there is going to be no fight between the veterans, and that either's stout old breast is secure from the fratricidal bullet.

Major MacWhirter forgot all about bullets and battles when poor little Charlotte kissed him, and was not in the least jealous when he saw the little maiden clinging on Philip's arm. He was melted at the sight of that grief and innocence, when Mrs. Baynes still continued to bark out her private rage, and said: "If the General won't protect me from insult, I think I had better go."

" By Jove, I think you had ! " exclaimed MacWhirter, to which remark the eyes of the Doctor and Colonel Bunch gleamed an approval.

" *Allons*, Monsieur Philippe. Enough like that — let me take her to bed again," madame resumed. " Come, dear miss ! "

What a pity that the bedroom was but a yard from where they stood ! Philip felt strong enough to carry his little Charlotte to the Tuileries. The thick brown locks, which had fallen over his shoulders, are lifted away. The little wounded heart that had lain against his own, parts from him with a reviving throb. Madame and her mother carry away little Charlotte. The door of the neighboring chamber closes on her. The sad little vision has disappeared. The men, quarrelling anon in the passage, stand there silent.

" I heard her voice outside," said Philip, after a little pause (with love, with grief, with excitement, I suppose his head was in a whirl). " I heard her voice outside, and I couldn't help coming in."

" By George, I should think not, young fellow ! " says Major MacWhirter, stoutly shaking the young man by the hand.

" Hush, hush ! " whispers the Doctor ; " she must be kept quite quiet. She has had quite excitement enough for to-night. There must be no more scenes, my young fellow."

And Philip says, when in this his agony of grief and doubt he found a friendly hand put out to him, he himself was so exceedingly moved that he was compelled to fly out of the company of the old men, into the night, where the rain was pouring—the gentle rain.

While Philip, without Madame Smolensk's premises, is saying his tenderest prayers, offering up his tears, heart-throbs and most passionate vows of love for little Charlotte's benefit, the warriors assembled within once more retreat to a colloquy in the salle-à-manger ; and, in consequence of the rainy state of the night, the astonished Auguste has to bring a third supply of hot-water for the four gentlemen attending the congress. The Colonel, the Major, the Doctor, ranged themselves on one side the table, defended, as it were, by a line of armed tumblers, flanked by a strong brandy-bottle and a stout earth-work, from an embrasure in which scalding water could be discharged. Behind these fortifications the veterans awaited their enemy, who, after marching up and down the room for awhile, takes position finally in their front and prepares to attack. The General remounts his *his cheval de bataille*, but cannot bring the animal to charge as fiercely as before. Charlotte's white

apparition has come amongst them, and flung her fair arms between the men of war. In vain Baynes tries to get up a bluster,
and to enforce his passion with by Georges, by Joves, and
words naughtier still. That weak, meek, quiet, henpecked, but
most bloodthirsty old General found himself forming his own
minority, and against him his old comrade Bunch, whom he
had insulted and nose-pulled ; his brother-in-law MacWhirter,
whom he had nose-pulled and insulted ; and the Doctor, who
had been called in as the friend of the former. As they faced
him, shoulder to shoulder, each of those three acquired fresh
courage from his neighbor. Each, taking his aim, deliberately
poured his fire into Baynes. To yield to such odds, on the
other hand, was not so distasteful to the veteran, as to have to
give up his sword to any single adversary. Before he would
own himself in the wrong to any individual, he would eat that
individual's ears and nose : but to be surrounded by three
enemies, and strike your flag before such odds, was no disgrace ;
and Baynes could take the circumbendibus way of apology to
which some proud spirits will submit. Thus he could say to
the Doctor, "Well, Doctor, perhaps I was hasty in accusing
Bunch of employing bad language to me. A bystander can
see these things sometimes when a principal is too angry ; and
as you go against me—well—there, then, I ask Bunch's pardon." That business over, the MacWhirter reconciliation was
very speedily brought about. " Fact was, was in a confounded
ill-temper—very much disturbed by events of the day—didn't
mean anything but this, that, and so forth." If this old chief
had to eat humble pie, his brave adversaries were anxious that
he should gobble up his portion as quickly as possible, and
turned away their honest old heads as he swallowed it. One of
the party told his wife of the quarrel which had arisen, but
Baynes never did. " I declare, sir," Philip used to say, " had
she known anything about the quarrel that night, Mrs. Baynes
would have made her husband turn out of bed at midnight, and
challenge his old friends over again ! " But then there was no
love between Philip and Mrs. Baynes, and in those whom he
hates he is accustomed to see little good.

Thus, any gentle reader who expected to be treated to an
account of the breakage of the sixth commandment will close
this chapter disappointed. Those stout old rusty swords which
were fetched off their hooks by the warriors, their owners, were
returned undrawn to their flannel cases. Hands were shaken
after a fashion—at least no blood was shed. But, though the
words spoken between the old boys were civil enough, Bunch

Baynes, and the Doctor could not alter their opinion that Philip had been hardly used, and that the benefactor of his family merited a better treatment from General Baynes.

Meanwhile, that benefactor strode home through the rain in a state of perfect rapture. The rain refreshed him, as did his own tears. The dearest little maiden had sunk for a moment on his heart, and, as she lay there, a thrill of hope vibrated through his whole frame. Her father's old friends had held out a hand to him, and bid him not despair. Blow wind, fall autumn rains! In the midnight, under the gusty trees, amidst which the lamps of the *réverbères* are tossing, the young fellow strides back to his lodgings. He is poor and unhappy, but he has Hope along with him. He looks at a certain breast-button of his old coat ere he takes it off to sleep. " Her cheek was lying there," he thinks—" just there." My poor little Charlotte! what could she have done to the breast-button of the old coat?

CHAPTER XXVIII.

IN WHICH MRS MACWHIRTER HAS A NEW BONNET.

Now though the unhappy Philip slept quite soundly, so that his boots, those tramp-worn sentries, remained *en faction* at his door until quite a late hour next morning; and though little Charlotte, after a prayer or two, sank into the sweetest and most refreshing girlish slumber, Charlotte's father and mother had a bad night; and, for my part, I maintain that they did not deserve a good one. It was very well for Mrs. Baynes to declare that it was MacWhirter's snoring which kept them awake (Mr. and Mrs. Mac being lodged in the bedroom over their relatives)—I don't say a snoring neighbor is pleasant— but what a bedfellow is a bad conscience! Under Mrs. Baynes's night-cap the grim eyes lie open all night; on Baynes's pillow is a silent, wakeful head that hears the hours toll. " A plague upon the young man! " thinks the female *bonnet de nuit;* " how dare he come in and disturb everything? How pale Charlotte will look to-morrow when Mrs. Hely calls with her son! When she has been crying she looks hideous, and her eyelids and nose are quite red. She may fly out, and say something wicked and absurd, as she did to-day. I wish I had never seen that insolent young man, with his carroty beard and vulgar blucher

boots ! If my boys were grown up, he should not come hectoring about the house as he does ; *they* would soon find a way of
punishing his impudence ! " Baulked revenge and a hungry
disappointment, I think, are keeping that old woman awake ;
and, if she hears the hours tolling, it is because wicked thoughts
make her sleepless.

As for Baynes, I believe that old man is awake, because he
is awake to the shabbyness of his own conduct. His conscience has got the better of him, which he has been trying to
bully out of doors. Do what he will, that reflection forces
itself upon him. Mac, Bunch, and the Doctor all saw the
thing at once, and went dead against him. He wanted to break
his word to a young fellow, who, whatever his faults might
be, had acted most nobly and generously by the Baynes family.
He might have been ruined but for Philip's forbearance ; and
showed his gratitude by breaking his promise to the young
fellow. He was a henpecked man—that was the fact. He
allowed his wife to govern him : that little old plain, cantank-
erous woman asleep yonder. Asleep was she ? No. He knew
she wasn't. Both were lying quite still, wide awake, pursuing
their dismal thoughts. Only Charles was owning that he was
a sinner, whilst Eliza his wife, in a rage at her last defeat, was
meditating how she could continue and still win her battle.

Then Baynes reflects how persevering his wife is ; how, all
through life, she has come back and back and back to her
point, until he has ended by an almost utter subjugation. He
will resist for a day : she will fight for a year, for a life. If
once she hates people, the sentiment always remains with her
fresh and lively. Her jealousy never dies ; nor her desire to
rule. What a life she will lead poor Charlotte now she has
declared against Philip ! The poor child will be subject to a
dreadful tyranny : the father knows it. As soon as he leaves
the house on his daily walks the girl's torture will begin.
Baynes knows how his wife can torture a woman. As she
groans out a hollow cough from her bed in the midnight, the
guilty man lies quite mum under his own counterpane. If she
fancies him awake, it will be *his* turn to receive the torture.
Ah, Othello *mon ami !* when you look round at married life,
and know what you know, don't you wonder that the bolster is
not used a great deal more freely on both sides ? Horrible
cynicism ! Yes—I know. These propositions served raw are
savage, and shock your sensibility ; cooked with a little piquant
sauce, they are welcome at quite polite tables.

" Poor child ! Yes, by George ! What a life her mother

will lead her!" thinks the General, rolling uneasy on the midnight pillow. "No rest for her, day or night, until she marries the man of her mother's choosing. And she has a delicate chest—Martin says she has ; and she wants coaxing and soothing, and pretty coaxing she will have from her mamma!" Then, I dare say, the past rises up in that wakeful old man's uncomfortable memory. His little Charlotte is a child again, laughing on his knee, and playing with his accoutrements as he comes home from parade. He remembers the fever which she had, when she would take medicine from no other hand ; and how, though silent with her mother, with him she would never tire prattling, prattling. Guilt-stricken old man ! are those tears trickling down thy old nose ? It is midnight. We cannot see. When you brought her to the river, and parted with her to send her to Europe, how the little maid clung to you, and cried, "Papa, papa !" Staggering up the steps of the ghaut, how you wept yourself—yes, wept tears of passionate, tender grief at parting with the darling of your soul. And now, deliberately, and for the sake of money, you stab her to the heart, and break your plighted honor with your child. "And it is yonder cruel, shrivelled, bilious, plain old woman who makes me do all this, and trample on my darling, and torture her !" he thinks. In Zoffany's famous picture of Garrick and Mrs. Pritchard as Macbeth and Lady Macbeth, Macbeth stands in an attitude hideously contorted and constrained, while lady Mac is firm and easy. Was this the actor's art, or the poet's device ? Baynes is wretched, then. He is wrung with remorse, and shame and pity. Well, I am glad of it. Old man, old man ! how darest thou to cause that child's tender little bosom to bleed ? How bilious he looks the next morning ! I declare as yellow as his grim old wife ! When Mrs. General B. hears the children their lessons, how she will scold them ! It is my belief she will bark through the morning chapter, and scarce understand a word of its meaning. As for Charlotte, when she appears with red eyes, and ever so little color in her round cheek, there is that in her look and demeanor which warns her mother to refrain from too familiar abuse or scolding. The girl is in rebellion. All day Char was in a feverish state, her eyes flashing war. There was a song which Philip loved in those days : the song of Ruth. Char sat down to the piano, and sang it with a strange energy. "Thy people shall be my people"—she sang with all her heart—"and thy God my God !" The slave had risen. The little heart was in arms and mutiny. The mother was scared by her defiance.

As for the guilty old father ; pursued by the fiend remorse, he fled early from his house, and read all the papers at Galignani's without comprehending them. Madly regardless of expense, he then plunged into one of those luxurious restaurants in the Palais Royal, where you get soup, three dishes, a sweet, and a pint of delicious wine for two frongs, by George ! But all the luxuries there presented to him could not drive away care, or create appetite. Then the poor old wretch went off, and saw a ballet at the Grand Opera. In vain. The pink nymphs had not the slightest fascination for him. He hardly was aware of their ogles, bounds, and capers. He saw a little maid with round, sad eyes :—his Iphigenia whom he was stabbing. He took more brandy-and-water at cafés on his way home. In vain, in vain, I tell you ! The old wife was sitting up for him, scared at the unusual absence of her lord. She dared not remonstrate with him when he returned. His face was pale. His eyes were fierce and bloodshot. When the General had a particular look, Eliza Baynes cowered in silence. Mac, the two sisters, and I think, Colonel Bunch (but on this point my informant, Philip, cannot be sure) were having a dreary rubber when the General came in. Mrs. B. knew by the General's face that he had been having recourse to alcoholic stimulus. But she dared not speak. A tiger in a jungle was not more savage than Baynes sometimes. "Where's Char ?" he asked in his dreadful, his Bluebeard voice. "Char was gone to bed," said mamma, sorting her trumps. "Hm ! Augoost, Odevee, Osho ! " Did Eliza Baynes interfere, though she knew he had had enough ? As soon interfere with a tiger, and tell him he had eaten enough Sepoy. After Lady Macbeth had induced Mac to go through that business with Duncan, depend upon it she was very deferential and respectful to her general. No groans, prayers, remorses could avail to bring his late majesty back to life again. As for you, old man, though your deed is done, it is not past recalling. Though you have withdrawn from your word on a sordid money pretext ; made two hearts miserable, stabbed cruelly that one which you love best in the world ; acted with wicked ingratitude towards a young man, who has been nobly forgiving towards you and yours ; and are suffering with rage and remorse, as you own your crime to yourself ;—your deed is not past recalling as yet. You may soothe that anguish, and dry those tears. It is but an act of resolution on your part, and a firm resumption of your marital authority. Mrs. Baynes, after her crime, is quite humble and gentle. She has half murdered her child, and stretched Philip

on an infernal rack of torture ; but she is quite civil to everybody at Madame's house. Not one word does she say respecting Mrs. Colonel Bunch's outbreak of the night before. She
talks to sister Emily about Paris, the fashions, and Emily's
walks on the Boulevard and the Palais Royal with her Major.
She bestows ghastly smiles upon sundry lodgers at table. She
thanks Augoost when he serves her at dinner—and says, " Ah,
madame, que le boof est bong aujourdhui, rien que j'aime
comme le potofou." Oh, you old hypocrite ! But you know I,
for my part, always disliked the woman, and said her good-
humor was more detestable than her anger. You hypocrite !
I say again :—ay, and avow that there were other hypocrites at
the table, as you shall presently hear.

When Baynes got an opportunity of speaking unobserved,
as he thought, to madame, you may be sure the guilty wretch
asked her how his little Charlotte was. Mrs. Baynes trumped
her partner's best heart at that moment, but pretended to
observe or overhear nothing. " She goes better—she sleeps,"
madame said. " Mr. the Doctor Martin has commanded her a
calming potion." And what if I were to tell you that somebody
had taken a little letter from Charlotte, and actually had given
fifteen sous to a Savoyard youth to convey that letter to somebody else? What if I were to tell you that the party to whom
that letter was addressed, straightway wrote an answer—
directed to Madame de Smolensk, of course ? I know it was
very wrong ; but I suspect Philip's prescription did quite as
much good as Doctor Martin's, and don't intend to be very
angry with madame for consulting the unlicensed practitioner.
Don't preach to me, madame, about morality, and dangerous
examples set to young people. Even at your present mature
age, and with your dear daughters around you, if your ladyship
goes to hear the " Barber of Seville," on which side are your
sympathies—on Dr. Bartolo's, or Miss Rosina's ?

Although, then, Mrs. Baynes was most respectful to her husband, and by many grim blandishments, humble appeals, and
forced humiliations, strove to conciliate and soothe him, the
General turned a dark, lowering face upon the partner of his
existence : her dismal smiles were no longer pleasing to him :
he returned curt " Ohs ! " and " Ahs ! " to her remarks. When
Mrs. Hely and her son and her daughter drove up in their
family coach to pay yet a second visit to the Baynes family, the
General flew in a passion, and cried, " Bless my soul, Eliza, you
can't think of receiving visitors, with our poor child sick in the
next room ? It's inhuman ! " The scared woman ventured on

no remonstrances. She was so frightened that she did not attempt to scold the younger children. She took a piece of work, and sat amongst them, furtively weeping. Their artless queries and unseasonable laughter stabbed and punished the matron. You see people do wrong, though they are long past fifty years of age. It is not only the scholars, but the ushers, and the head-master himself, who sometimes deserve a chastisement. I, for my part, hope to remember this sweet truth, though I live into the year 1900.

To those other ladies boarding at madame's establishment, to Mrs. Mac and Mrs. Colonel Bunch, though they had declared against him, and expressed their opinions in the frankest way on the night of the battle royal, the General was provokingly polite and amiable. They had said, but twenty-four hours since, that the General was a brute; and Lord Chesterfield could not have been more polite to a lovely young duchess than was Baynes to these matrons next day. You have heard how Mrs. Mac had a strong desire to possess a new Paris bonnet, so that she might appear with proper lustre among the ladies on the promenade at Tours ? Major and Mrs. Mac and Mrs. Bunch talked of going to the Palais Royal (where Mac-Whirter said he had remarked some uncommonly neat things, by George ! at the corner shop under the glass gallery). On this, Baynes started up, and said he would accompany his friends, adding, " You know, Emily, I had promised you a hat ever so long ago ! " And those four went away together, and not one offer did Baynes make to his wife to join the party ; though her best bonnet, poor thing, was a dreadfully old performance, with moulting feathers, rumpled ribbons, tarnished flowers, and lace bought in St. Martin's Alley months and months before. Emily, to be sure, said to her sister, " Eliza, won't *you* be of the party ? We can take the omnibus at the corner, which will land us at the very gate." But as Emily gave this unlucky invitation, the General's face wore an expression of ill-will so savage and terrific, that Eliza Baynes said, " No, thank you, Emily ; Charlotte is still unwell, and I—I may be wanted at home." And the party went away without Mrs. Baynes ; and they were absent I don't know how long: and Emily Mac-Whirter came back to the boarding-house in a bonnet—the sweetest thing you ever saw !—green piqué velvet, with a *ruche* full of rosebuds, and a bird of paradise perched on the top, pecking at a bunch of the most magnificent grapes, poppies, ears of corn, barley, &c., all indicative of the bounteous autumn season. Mrs. General Baynes had to see her sister return home in this elegant bonnet ; to welcome her ; to acquiesce in Emily's remark that the General had done the genteel thing ; to hear how the party had further been to Tortoni's and had ices ; and then to go up stairs to her own room, and look at her own battered, blowsy old *chapeau*, with its limp streamers, hanging from its peg. This humiliation, I say, Eliza Baynes had to bear in silence, without wincing, and, if possible, with a smile on her face.

In consequence of circumstances before indicated, Miss Charlotte was pronounced to be very much better when her papa returned from his Palais Royal trip. He found her seated on madame's sofa, pale, but with the wonted sweetness in her smile. He kissed and caressed her with many tender words. I dare say he told her there was nothing in the world he loved so much as his Charlotte. He would never willingly do anything to give her pain, never ! She has been his good girl, and his blessing, all his life ! Ah ! that is a prettier little picture to imagine—that repentant man, and his child clinging to him —than the tableau overhead, viz., Mrs. Baynes looking at her old bonnet. Not one word was said about Philip in the talk between Baynes and his daughter, but those tender paternal looks and caresses carried hope into Charlotte's heart ; and when her papa went away (she said afterwards to a female friend), " I got up and followed him, intending to show him Philip's letter. But at the door I saw mamma coming down the stairs ; and she looked so dreadful, and frightened me so, that I went back." There are some mothers I have heard of, who won't allow their daughters to read the works of this humble homilist, lest they should imbibe " dangerous " notions, &c., &c. My good ladies, give them " Goody Twoshoes " if you like, or whatever work, combining instruction and amusement, you think most appropriate to their juvenile understandings ; but I beseech you to be gentle with them. I never saw people on better terms with each other, more frank, affectionate, and cordial, than the parents and the grown-up young folks in the United States. And why ? Because the children were spoiled, to be sure ! I say to you, get the confidence of yours—before the day comes of revolt and independence, after which love returneth not.

Now, when Mrs. Baynes went in to her daughter, who had been sitting pretty comfortably kissing her father on the sofa in madame's chamber, all those soft tremulous smiles and twinkling dew-drops of compassion and forgiveness which anon had come to soothe the little maid, fled from cheek and eyes.

They began to flash again with their febrile brightness, and her heart to throb with dangerous rapidity. " How are you now? " asks mamma, with her deep voice. " I am much the same," says the girl, beginning to tremble. " Leave the child ; you agitate her, madam," cries the mistress of the house, coming in after Mrs. Baynes. That sad, humiliated, deserted mother goes out from her daughter's presence, hanging her head. She put on the poor old bonnet, and had a walk that evening on the Champs Elysées with her little ones, and showed them Guignol : she gave a penny to Guignol's man. It is my belief that she saw no more of the performance than her husband had seen of the ballet the night previous, when Taglioni, and Noblet, and Duvernay, danced before his hot eyes. But then, you see, the hot eyes had been washed with a refreshing water since, which enabled them to view the world much more cheerfully and brightly. Ah, gracious heaven gives us eyes to see our own wrong, however dim age may make them ; and knees not too stiff to kneel, in spite of years, cramps, and rheumatism ! That stricken old woman, then, treated her children to the trivial comedy of Guignol. She did not cry out when the two boys climbed up the trees of the Elysian Fields, though the guardians bade them descend. She bought pink sticks of barley-sugar for the young ones. Withdrawing the glistening sweetmeats from their lips, they pointed to Mrs. Hely's splendid barouche as it rolled citywards from the Bois de Boulogne. The gray shades were falling, and Auguste was in the act of ringing the first dinner-bell at Madame Smolensk's establishment, when Mrs. General Baynes returned to her lodgings.

Meanwhile, aunt MacWhirter had been to pay a visit to little Miss Charlotte, in the new bonnet which the General, Charlotte's papa, had bought for her. This elegant article had furnished a subject of pleasing conversation between niece and aunt, who held each other in very kindly regard, and all the details of the bonnet, the blue flowers, scarlet flowers, grapes, sheaves of corn, lace, &c., were examined and admired in detail. Charlotte remembered the dowdy old English thing which aunt Mac wore when she went out ? Charlotte did remember the bonnet, and laughed when Mrs. Mac described how papa, in the hackney-coach on their return home, insisted upon taking the old wretch of a bonnet, and flinging it out of the coach window into the road, where an old chiffonnier passing picked it up with his iron hook, put it on his own head, and walked away grinning. I declare, at the recital of this narrative, Charlotte laughed as pleasantly and happily as in former days ; and, no doubt, there were more kisses between this poor little maid and her aunt.

Now, you will remark, that the General and his party, though they returned from the Palais Royal in a hackney-coach, went thither on foot, two and two—viz., Major MacWhirter leading, and giving his arm to Mrs. Bunch, (who, I promise you, knew the shops in the Palais Royal well,) and the General following at some distance, with his sister-in-law for a partner.

In that walk a conversation very important to Charlotte's interests took place between her aunt and her father.

"Ah, Baynes! this is a sad business about dearest Char," Mrs. Mac broke out with a sigh.

"It is, indeed, Emily," says the General, with a very sad groan on his part.

"It goes to my heart to see you, Baynes; it goes to Mac's heart. We talked about it ever so late last night. You were suffering dreadfully; and all the brandy-pawnee in the world won't cure you, Charles."

"No, faith," says the General, with a dismal screw of the mouth. "You see, Emily, to see that child suffer, tears my heart out—by George, it does. She has been the best child, and the most gentle, and the merriest, and the most obedient, and I never had a word of fault to find with her; and—poo-ooh!" Here the General's eyes, which have been winking with extreme rapidity, give way; and at the signal pooh! there issue out from them two streams of that eye-water which we have said is sometimes so good for the sight.

"My dear kind Charles, you were always a good creature," says Emily, patting the arm on which hers rests. Meanwhile Major-General Baynes, C.B., puts his bamboo cane under his disengaged arm, extracts from his hind pocket a fine large yellow bandanna pocket-handkerchief, and performs a prodigious loud obligato—just under the spray of the Rond-point fountain, opposite the Bridge of the Invalides, over which poor Philip has tramped many and many a day and night to see his little maid.

"Have a care with your cane, there, old imbecile!" cries an approaching foot-passenger, whom the General meets and charges with his iron ferule.

"Mille pardong, mosoo; je vous demande mille pardong," says the old man, quite meekly.

"You are a good soul, Charles," the lady continues; "and my little Char is a darling. You never would have done this of your own accord. Mercy! And see what it was coming to!"

Mac only told me last night. You horrid, bloodthirsty creature! Two challenges—and dearest Mac as hot as pepper! Oh, Charles Baynes, I tremble when I think of the danger from which you have all been rescued! Suppose you brought home to Eliza—suppose dearest Mac brought home to me killed by this arm on which I am leaning. Oh, it is dreadful, dreadful! We are sinners all, that we are, Baynes!"

"I humbly ask pardon for having thought of a great crime. I ask pardon," says the General, very pale and solemn.

"If you had killed dear Mac, would you ever have had rest again, Charles?"

"No; I think not. I should not deserve it," answers the contrite Baynes.

"*You* have a good heart. It was not *you* who did this. I know who it was. She always had a dreadful temper. The way in which she used to torture our poor dear Louisa who is dead, I can hardly forgive now, Baynes. Poor suffering angel! Eliza was at her bedside nagging and torturing her up to the very last day. Did you ever see her with nurses and servants in India? The way in which she treated them was——"

"Don't say any more. I am aware of my wife's faults of temper. Heaven knows it has made me suffer enough!" says the General, hanging his head down.

"Why, man—do you intend to give way to her altogether? I said to Mac last night, 'Mac, does he intend to give way to her altogether? The "Army List" doesn't contain the name of a braver man than Charles Baynes, and is my sister Eliza to rule him entirely, Mac!' I said. No, if you stand up to Eliza, I know from experience she will give way. We have had quarrels, scores and hundreds, as you know, Baynes."

"Faith, I do," owns the General, with a sad smile on his countenance.

"And sometimes she has had the best and sometimes I have had the best, Baynes! But I never yielded, as you do, without a fight for my own. No, never, Baynes! And me and Mac are shocked, I tell you fairly, when we see the way in which you give up to her!"

"Come, come! I think you have told me often enough that I am henpecked," says the General.

"And you give up not yourself only, Charles, but your dear, dear child—poor little suffering love!"

"The young man's a beggar!" cries the General, biting his lips.

"What were you, what was Mac and me when we married?

We hadn't much beside our pay, had we? we rubbed on through bad weather and good, managing as best we could, loving each other, God be praised! And here we are, owing nobody anything, and me going to have a new bonnet!" and she tossed up her head and gave her companion a good-natured look through her twinkling eyes.

"Emily, you have a good heart! that's the truth," says the General.

"And *you* have a good heart, Charles, as sure as my name's MacWhirter; and I want you to act upon it, and I propose——"

"What?"

"Well, I propose that——" But now they have reached the Tuileries garden gates, and pass through, and continue their conversation in the midst of such a hubbub that we cannot overhear them. They cross the garden, and so make their way into the Palais Royal, and the purchase of the bonnet takes place; and in the midst of the excitement occasioned by *that* event, of course all discussion of domestic affairs becomes uninteresting.

But the gist of Baynes's talk with his sister-in-law may be divined from the conversation which presently occurred between Charlotte and her aunt. Charlotte did not come in to the public dinner. She was too weak for that; and "*un bon bouillon*" and a wing of fowl were served to her in the private apartment, where she had been reclining all day. At dessert, however, Mrs. MacWhirter took a fine bunch of grapes and a plump rosy peach from the table, and carried them to the little maid, and their interview may be described with sufficient accuracy, though it passed without other witnesses.

From the outbreak on the night of quarrels, Charlotte knew that her aunt was her friend. The glances of Mrs. Mac-Whirter's eyes, and the expression of her bonny, homely face, told her sympathy to the girl. There were no pallors now, no angry glances, no heart-beating. Miss Char could even make a little joke when her aunt appeared, and say, "What beautiful grapes! Why, aunt, you must have taken them out of the new bonnet."

"You should have had the bird of paradise, too, dear, only I see you have not eaten your chicken. She is a kind woman, Madame Smolensk. I like her. She gives very nice dinners. I can't think how she does it for the money, I am sure!"

"She has been very, very kind to me; and I love her with all my heart!" cries Charlotte.

"Poor darling! We have all our trials, and yours have begun, my love!"

"Yes, indeed, aunt!" whimpers the young person; upon which osculation possibly takes place.

"My dear! when your papa took me to buy the bonnet, we had a long talk, and it was about you."

"About me, aunt?" warbles Miss Charlotte.

"He would not take mamma; he would only go with me, alone. I knew he wanted to say something about you; and what do you think it was? My dear, you have been very much agitated here. You and your poor mamma are likely to disagree for some time. She will drag you to those balls and fine parties, and bring you those *fine partners*."

"Oh, I hate them!" cries Charlotte. Poor little Walsingham Hely, what had he done to be hated?

"Well. It is not for me to speak of a mother to her own daughter. But you know mamma has *a way* with her. She expects to be obeyed. She will give you no peace. She will come back to her point again and again. You know how she speaks of some one—a certain gentleman? If ever she sees him, she will be rude to him. Mamma can be rude at times—that I must say of my own sister. As long as you remain here——"

"Oh, aunt, aunt! Don't take me away, don't take me away!" cries Charlotte.

"My dearest, are you afraid of your old aunt, and your uncle Mac, who is so kind, and has always loved you? Major MacWhirter has a will of his own, too, though of course I make no allusions. *We* know how admirably somebody has behaved to your family. Somebody who has been most *ungratefully* treated, though of course I make no allusions. If you had given away your heart to your father's *greatest benefactor*, do you suppose I and uncle Mac will quarrel with you? When Eliza married Baynes (your father was a penniless subaltern, then, my dear,—and my sister was certainly neither a fortune nor a beauty,) didn't she go dead against the wishes of *our* father? Certainly she did! But she said she was of age—that she was, and a great deal more, too—and she would do as she liked, and she made Baynes marry her. Why should you be afraid of coming to us, love? You are nearer somebody here, but can you see him? Your mamma will never let you go out, but she will follow you like a shadow. You may write to him. Don't tell *me*, child. Haven't I been young myself; and when there was a difficulty between Mac and poor papa, didn't Mac write to me, though he hates letters, poor dear, and certainly is *a stick* at them. And, though we were forbidden, had we not twenty ways of telegraphing to each other? Law! your poor dear grandfather was in such a rage with me once, when he found one, that he took down his great buggy whip to me, a grown girl!"

Charlotte, who has plenty of humor, would have laughed at this confession some other time, but now she was too much agitated by that invitation to quit Paris, which her aunt had just given her. Quit Paris? Lose the chance of seeing her dearest friend, her protector? If he was not with her was he not near her? Yes, near her always! On that horrible night, when all was so desperate, did not her champion burst forward to her rescue? Oh, the dearest and bravest! Oh, the tender and true!

"You are not listening, you poor child!" said aunt Mac, surveying her niece with looks of kindness. "Now listen to me once more. Whisper!" And sitting down on the settee by Charlotte's side, aunt Emily first kissed the girl's round cheek, and then whispered into her ear.

Never, I declare, was medicine so efficacious, or rapid of effect, as that wondrous distilment which aunt Emily poured into her niece's ear! "Oh, you goose!" she began by saying, and the rest of the charm she whispered into that pearly little pink shell round which Miss Charlotte's soft brown ringlets clustered. Such a sweet blush rose straightway to the cheek! Such sweet lips began to cry, "Oh, you dear, dear aunt," and then began to kiss aunt's kind face, that, I declare, if I knew the spell, I would like to pronounce it right off, with such a sweet young patient to practice on.

"When do we go? To-morrow, aunt, n'est-ce pas? Oh, I am quite strong! never felt so well in my life! I'll go and pack up *this instant*," cries the young person.

"Doucement! Papa knows of the plan. Indeed, it was he who proposed it."

"Dearest, best father!" ejaculates Miss Charlotte.

"But mamma does not; and if you show yourself very eager, Charlotte, she may object, you know. Heaven forbid that *I* should counsel dissimulation to a child; but under the circumstances, my love —— At least I own what happened between Mac and me. Law! *I* didn't care for papa's buggy whip! I knew it would not hurt; and as for Baynes, I am sure he would not hurt a fly. Never was man more sorry for what he has done. He told me so whilst we walked away from the bonnet-shop, whilst he was carrying my old yellow. We met somebody near the Bourse. How sad he looked, and how handsome, too ! *I* bowed to him, and kissed my hand to him, that is, the knob of my parasol. Papa couldn't shake hands with him, because of my bonnet, you know, in the brown-paper bag. He has a grand beard, indeed ! He looked like a wounded lion. I said so to papa. And I said, 'It is you who wound him, Charles Baynes !' 'I know that,' papa said. 'I have been thinking of it. I can't sleep at night for thinking about it : and it makes me dee'd unhappy.' You know what papa sometimes says ? Dear me ! You should have heard them, when Eliza and I joined the army, years and years ago !"

For once, Charlotte Baynes was happy at her father's being unhappy. The little maiden's heart had been wounded to think that her father could do his Charlotte a wrong. Ah ! take warning by him, ye graybeards ! And however old and tooth-less, if you have done wrong, own that you have done so ; and sit down and say grace, and mumble your humble pie !

The General, then, did not shake hands with Philip ; but Major MacWhirter went up in the most marked way, and gave the wounded lion his own paw, and said, "Mr. Firmin, glad to see you ! If ever you come to Tours, mind, don't forget my wife and me. Fine day. Little patient much better ! Bon courage, as they say !"

I wonder what sort of a bungle Philip made of his corre-spondence with the *Pall Mall Gazette* that night ? Every man who lives by his pen, if by chance he looks back at his writings of former years, lives in the past again. Our griefs, our pleasures, our youth, our sorrows, our dear, dear friends, resuscitate. How we tingle with shame over some of those fine passages ! How dreary are those disinterred jokes ! It was Wednesday night. Philip was writing off at home, in his inn, one of his grand tirades, dated "Paris, Thursday"—so as to be in time, you understand, for the post of Saturday, when the little waiter comes and says, winking, "Again that lady, Monsieur Philippe !"

"What lady ? " asks our own intelligent correspondent.

"That old lady who came the other day, you know."

"C'est moi, mon ami ! " cries Madame Smolensk's well-known grave voice. "Here is a letter, d'abord. But that says nothing. It was written before the grande nouvelle—the great news—the good news ! "

"What good news ? " asks the gentleman.

"In two days miss goes to Tours with her aunt and uncle

THE POOR HELPING THE POOR.

—this good Macvirterre. They have taken their places by the diligence of Lafitte and Caillard. They are thy friends. Papa encourages her going. Here is their card of visit. Go thou also ; they will receive thee with open arms. What hast thou, my son ? "

Philip looked dreadfully sad. An injured and unfortunate gentleman at New York had drawn upon him, and he had paid away everything he had but four francs, and he was living on credit until his next remittance arrived.

" Thou hast no money ! I have thought of it. Behold of it ! Let him wait—the proprietor ! " And she takes out a bank-note, which she puts in the young man's hand.

" Tiens, il l'embrasse encor c'te vieille ! " says the little knife-boy. " J'aimerai pas ça, moi, par examp ! "

CHAPTER XXIX.

IN THE DEPARTMENTS OF SEINE, LOIRE AND STYX (INFERIEUR).

OUR dear friend Mrs. Baynes was suffering under the influence of one of those panics which sometimes seized her, and during which she remained her husband's most obedient Eliza and vassal. When Baynes wore a certain expression of countenance, we have said that his wife knew resistance to be useless. That expression, I suppose, he assumed, when he announced Charlotte's departure to her mother, and ordered Mrs. General Baynes to make the necessary preparations for the girl. " She might stay some time with her aunt," Baynes stated. " A change of air would do the child a great deal of good. Let everything necessary in the shape of hats, bonnets, winter clothes, and so forth, be got ready." " Was Char, then, to stay away so long ? " asked Mrs. B. " She has been so happy here that you want to keep her, and fancy she can't be happy without you ! " I can fancy the General grimly replying to the partner of his existence. Hanging down her withered head, with a tear mayhap trickling down her cheek, I can fancy the old woman silently departing to do the bidding of her lord. She selects a trunk out of the store of Baynes's baggage. A young lady's trunk was a trunk in those days. Now it is a two or three storied edifice of wood, in which two or three full-grown

bodies of young ladies (without crinoline) might be packed. I
saw a little old countrywoman at the Folkesone station last
year with her travelling baggage contained in a band-box tied
up in an old cotton handkerchief hanging on her arm; and she
surveyed Lady Knightsbridge's twenty-three black trunks, each
wellnigh as large as her ladyship's opera-box. Before these
great edifices that old woman stood wondering dumbly. That
old lady and I had lived in a time when crinoline was not; and
yet, I think, women looked even prettier in that time than they
do now. Well, a trunk and a band-box were fetched out of the
baggage heap for little Charlotte, and I dare say her little
brothers jumped and danced on the box with much energy to
make the lid shut, and the General brought out his hammer
and nails, and nailed a card on the box with "Mademoiselle
Baynes" thereon printed. And mamma had to look on and
witness those preparations. And Walsingham Hely had called;
and he wouldn't call again, she knew; and that fair chance for
the establishment of her child was lost by the obstinacy of her
self-willed, reckless husband. That woman had to water her
soup with her furtive tears, to sit of nights behind hearts and
spades, and brood over her crushed hopes. If I contemplate
that wretched old Niobe much longer, I shall begin to pity her.
Away softness! Take out thy arrows, the poisoned, the barbed,
the rankling, and prod me the old creature well, god of the
silver bow! Eliza Baynes had to look on, then, and see the
trunks packed; to see her own authority over her own daughter
wrested away from her; to see the undutiful girl prepare with
perfect delight and alacrity to go away, without feeling a pang
at leaving a mother who had nursed her through adverse illnesses: who had scolded her for seventeen years.

The General accompanied the party to the diligence office.
Little Char was very pale and melancholy indeed when she took
her place in the coupé. "She should have a corner: she had
been ill, and ought to have a corner," uncle Mac said, and
cheerfully consented to be bodkin. Our three special friends
are seated. The other passengers clamber into their places.
Away goes the clattering team, as the General waves an adieu
to his friends. "Monstrous fine horses those gray Normans;
famous breed, indeed," he remarks to his wife on his return.

"Indeed," she echoes. "Pray, in what part of the carriage
was Mr. Firmin?" she presently asks.

"In no part of the carriage at all!" Baynes answers fiercely,
turning beet-root red. And thus, though she had been silent,
obedient, hanging her head, the woman showed that she was

aware of her master's schemes, and why her girl had been taken away. She knew; but she was beaten. It remained for her but to be silent and bow her head. I dare say she did not sleep one wink that night. She followed the diligence in its journey. "Char is gone," she thought. "Yes; in due time he will take from me the obedience of my other children, and tear them out of my lap." He—that is, the General—was sleeping meanwhile. He had had in the last few days four awful battles —with his child, with his friends, with his wife—in which latter combat he had been conqueror. No wonder Baynes was tired, and needed rest. Any one of those engagements was enough to weary the veteran.

If we take the liberty of looking into double-bedded rooms and peering into the thoughts which are passing under private nightcaps, may we not examine the coupé of a jingling diligence with an open window, in which a young lady sits wide awake by the side of her uncle and aunt? These perhaps are asleep; but she is not. Ah! she is thinking of another journey! that blissful one from Boulogne, when *he* was there yonder in the imperial, by the side of the conductor. When the MacWhirter party had come to the diligence office, how her little heart had beat! How she had looked under the lamps at all the people lounging about the court! How she had listened when the clerk called out the names of the passengers; and, mercy, what a fright she had been in, lest he should be there after all, while she stood yet leaning on her father's arm! But there was no——well, names, I think, need scarcely be mentioned. There was no sign of the individual in question. Papa kissed her, and sadly said good-by. Good madame Smolensk came with an adieu and an embrace for her dear Miss, and whispered, "Courage, mon enfant," and then said, "Hold, I have brought you some bonbons." There they were in a little packet. Little Charlotte put the packet into her little basket. Away goes the diligence, but the individual had made no sign.

Away goes the diligence; and every now and then Charlotte feels the little packet in her little basket. What does it contain —oh, what? If Charlotte could but read with her heart, she would see in that little packet—the sweetest bonbon of all perhaps it might be, or, ah me! the bitterest almond! Through the night goes the diligence, passing relay after relay. Uncle Mac sleeps. I think I have said he snored. Aunt Mac is quite silent, and Char sits plaintively with her lonely thoughts and her bonbons, as miles, hours, relays pass.

"These ladies will they descend and take a cup of coffee, a

cup of bouillon?" at last cries a waiter at the coupé door, as
the carriage stops in Orleans. "By all means a cup of coffee,"
says aunt Mac. "The little Orleans wine is good," cries uncle
Mac. "Descendons!" "This way, madame," says the
waiter. "Charlotte my love, some coffee?"

"I will—I will stay in the carriage. I don't want anything,
thank you," says Miss Charlotte. And the instant her relations are gone, entering the gate of the "Lion Noir," where,
you know, are the Bureaux des Messageries Lafitte, Caillard et
Cie—I say, on the very instant when her relations have disappeared, what do you think Miss Charlotte does?

She opens that packet of bonbons with fingers that tremble
—tremble so, I wonder how she could undo the knot of the
string (or do you think she had untied that knot under her
shawl in the dark? I can't say. We never shall know). Well;
she opens the packet. She does not care one fig for the lolli-
pops, almonds, and so forth. She pounces on a little scrap of
paper, and is going to read it by the light of the steaming
stable lanterns, when——oh, what made her start so?——

In those old days there used to be two diligences which
travelled nightly to Tours, setting out at the same hour, and
stopping at almost the same relays. The diligence of Lafitte
and Caillard supped at the "Lion Noir" at Orleans—the diligence of the Messageries Royales stopped at the "Ecu de
France," hard by.

Well, as the Messageries Royales are supping at the "Ecu
de France," a passenger strolls over from that coach, and strolls
and strolls until he comes to the coach of Lafitte, Caillard, and
Company, and to the coupé window where Miss Baynes is trying to decipher her bonbon.

He comes up—and as the night-lamps fall on his face and
beard—his rosy face, his yellow beard—oh!——What means
that scream of the young lady in the coupé of Lafitte, Caillard
et Compagnie! I declare she has dropped the letter which
she was about to read. It has dropped into a pool of mud
under the diligence off fore-wheel. And he with the yellow
beard, and a sweet happy laugh, and a tremble in his deep
voice, says, "You need not read it. It was only to tell you
what you know."

Then the coupé window says, "Oh, Philip! Oh, my——"

My what? You cannot hear the words, because the gray
Norman horses come squealing and clattering up to their
coach-pole with such accompanying cries and imprecations
from the horsekeepers and postilions, that no wonder the little

warble is lost. It was not intended for you and me to hear ; but perhaps you can guess the purport of the words. Perhaps in quite old, old days, you may remember having heard such little whispers, in a time when the song-birds in your grove carolled that kind of song very pleasantly and freely. But this, my good madam, is written in February. The birds are gone : the branches are bare : the gardener has actually swept the leaves off the walks : and the whole affair is an affair of a past year, you understand. Well ! *carpe diem, fugit hora,* &c., &c. There, for one minute, for two minutes, stands Philip over the diligence off fore-wheel, talking to Charlotte at the window, and their heads are quite close—quite close. What are those pairs of lips warbling, whispering? " Hi ! Gare ! Ohé ! " The horsekeepers, I say, quite prevent you from hearing ; and here come the passengers out of the " Lion Noir," aunt Mac still munching a great slice of bread-and-butter. Charlotte is quite comfortable, and does not want anything, dear aunt, thank you. I hope she nestles in her corner, and has a sweet slumber. On the journey the twin diligences pass and repass each other. Perhaps Charlotte looks out of her window sometimes and towards the other carriage. I don't know. It is a long time ago. What used you to do in old days, ere railroads were, and when diligences ran ? They were slow enough : but they have got to their journey's end somehow. They were tight, hot, dusty, dear, stuffy, and uncomfortable ; but, for all that, travelling was good sport sometimes. And if the world would have the kindness to go back for five-and-twenty or thirty years, some of us who have travelled on the Tours and Orleans Railway very comfortably would like to take the diligence journey now.

Having myself seen the city of Tours only last year, of course I don't remember much about it. A man remembers boyhood, and the first sight of Calais, and so forth. But after much travel or converse with the world, to see a new town is to be introduced to Jones. He is like Brown ; he is not unlike Smith. In a little while you hash him up with Thompson. I dare not be particular, then, regarding Mr. Firmin's life at Tours, lest I should make topographical errors, for which the critical schoolmaster would justly inflict chastisement. In the last novel I read about Tours, there were blunders from the effect of which you know the wretched author never recovered. It was by one Scott, and had young Quentin Durward for a hero, and Isabel de Croye for a heroine ; and she sat in her hostel, and sang, " Ah, County Guy, the hour is nigh." A

pretty ballad enough : but what ignorance, my dear sir ! What
descriptions of Tours, of Liége, are in that fallacious story !
Yes, so fallacious and misleading, that I remember I was sorry,
not because the description was unlike Tours, but because
Tours was unlike the description.

So Quentin Firmin went and put up at the snug little hostel
of the " Faisan ; " and Isabel de Baynes took up her abode
with her uncle the Sire de MacWhirter ; and I believe Master
Firmin had no more money in his pocket than the Master
Durward whose story the Scottish novelist told some forty
years since. And I cannot promise you that our young English
adventurer shall marry a noble heiress of vast property, and
engage the Boar of Ardennes in a hand-to-hand combat ; that
sort of Boar, madam, does not appear in our modern drawing-
room histories. Of others, not wild, there be plenty. They
gore you in clubs. They seize you by the doublet, and pin you
against posts in public streets. They run at you in parks. I
have seen them sit at bay after dinner, ripping, gashing, tossing,
a whole company. These our young adventurer had in good
sooth to encounter, as is the case with most knights. Who
escapes them ? I remember an eminent person talking to me
about bores for two hours once. Oh, you stupid eminent
person ! You never knew that you yourself had tusks, little eyes
in your *hure ;* a bristly mane to cut into tooth-brushes ; and a
curly tail ! I have a notion that the multitude of bores is
enormous in the world. If a man is a bore himself, when he is
bored—and you can't deny this statement—then what am I,
what are you, what your father, grandfather, son—all your
amiable acquaintance, in a word ? Of this I am sure. Major
and Mrs. MacWhirter were not brilliant in conversation. What
would you and I do, or say, if we listen to the tittle-tattle of
Tours. How the clergyman was certainly too fond of cards,
and going to the café ; how the dinners those Popjoys gave
were too absurdly ostentatious ; and Popjoy, we know, in the
Bench last year. How Mrs. Flights, going on with that Major
of French Carabiniers, was really too &c., &c. " How could I
endure those people ? " Philip would ask himself, when talking
of that personage in after days, as he loved, and loves to do.
" How could I endure them, I say ? Mac was a good man ;
but I knew secretly in my heart, sir, that he was a bore. Well :
I loved him. I liked his old stories. I liked his bad old
dinners : there is a very comfortable Touraine wine, by the way
—a very warming little wine, sir. Mrs. Mac you never saw,
my good Mrs. Pendennis. Be sure of this, you never would

have liked her. Well, I did. I liked her house, though it was damp, in a damp garden, frequented by dull people. I should like to go and see that old house now. I am perfectly happy with my wife, but I sometimes go away from her to enjoy the luxury of living over our old days again. With nothing in the world but an allowance which was precarious, and had been spent in advance ; with no particular plans for the future, and a few five-franc pieces for the present,—by Jove, sir, how did I dare to be so happy ? What idiots we were, my love, to be happy at all ! We were mad to marry. Don't tell me : with a purse which didn't contain three months' consumption, would we dare to marry now ? We should be put into the mad ward of the workhouse : that would be the only place for us. Talk about trusting in heaven. Stuff and nonsense, ma'am ! I have as good a right to go and buy a house in Belgrave Square, and trust to heaven for the payment, as I had to marry when I did. We were paupers, Mrs. Char, and you know that very well !"

"Oh, yes. We were very wrong: very ! " says Mrs. Charlotte, looking up to her chandelier (which, by the way, is of very handsome Venetian old glass). "We were very wrong, were not we, my dearest ? " And herewith she will begin to kiss and fondle two or more babies that disport in her room— as if two or more babies had anything to do with Philip's argument, that a man has no right to marry who has no pretty well-assured means of keeping a wife.

Here, then, by the banks of Loire, although Philip had but a very few francs in his pocket, and was obliged to keep a sharp look-out on his expenses at the Hotel of the " Golden Pheasant," he passed a fortnight of such happiness as I, for my part, wish to all young folks who read his veracious history. Though he was so poor, and ate and drank so modestly in the house, the maids, waiters, the landlady of the " Pheasant," were as civil to him—yes, as civil as they were to the gouty old Marchioness of Carabas herself, who stayed here on her way to the south, occupied the grand apartments, quarrelled with her lodging, dinner, breakfast, bread-and-butter in general, insulted the landlady in bad French, and only paid her bill under compulsion. Philip's was a little bill, but he paid it cheerfully. He gave only a small gratuity to the servants, but he was kind and hearty, and they knew he was poor. He was kind and hearty, I suppose because he was so happy. I have known the gentleman to be by no means civil ; and have heard him storm, and hector, and browbeat landlord and waiters, as fiercely as the Marquis of Carabas himself. But now Philip the Bear was the most gentle of bears, because his little Charlotte was leading him.

Away with trouble and doubt, with squeamish pride and gloomy care! Philip had enough money for a fortnight, during which Tom Glazier, of the *Monitor*, promised to supply Philip's letters for the *Pall Mall Gazette*. All the designs of France, Spain, Russia, gave that idle "our correspondent" not the slightest anxiety. In the morning it was Miss Baynes; in the afternoon it was Miss Baynes. At six it was dinner and Charlotte; at nine it was Charlotte and tea. "Anyhow, love-making does not spoil his appetite," Major MacWhirter remarked. Indeed, Philip had a glorious appetite; and health bloomed in Miss Charlotte's cheek, and beamed in her happy little heart. Dr. Firmin, in the height of his practice, never completed a cure more skilfully than that which was performed by Dr. Firmin, junior.

"I ran the thing so close, sir," I remember Philip bawling out, in his usual energetic way, whilst describing this period of his life's greatest happiness to his biographer, "that I came back to Paris outside the diligence, and had not money enough to dine on the road. But I bought a sausage, sir, and a bit of bread—and a brutal sausage it was, sir—and I reached my lodgings with exactly two sous in my pocket." Roger Bontemps himself was not more content than our easy philosopher.

So Philip and Charlotte ratified and sealed the treaty of Tours, which they determined should never be broken by either party. Marry without papa's consent? Oh, never! Marry anybody but Philip? Oh, never—never! Not if she lived to be a hundred, when Philip would in consequence be in his hundred and ninth or tenth year, would this young Joan have any but her present Darby. Aunt Mac, though she may not have been the most accomplished or highly-bred of ladies, was a warm-hearted and affectionate aunt Mac. She caught in a mild form the fever from these young people. She had not much to leave, and Mac's relations would want all *he* could spare when he was gone. But Charlotte should have her garnets, and her teapot, and her India shawl—that she should.* And with many blessings this enthusiastic old lady took leave of her future nephew-in-law when he returned to Paris and duty. Crack your whip, and scream your *hi!* and be off quick,

---

* I am sorry to say that in later days, after Mrs. Major MacWhirter's decease, it was found that she had promised these treasures *in writing* to several members of her husband's family, and that much heart-burning arose in consequence. But our story has nothing to do with these painful disputes.

postilion and diligence! I am glad we have taken Mr. Firmin out of that dangerous, lazy love-making place. Nothing is to me so sweet as sentimental writing. I could have written hundreds of pages describing Philip and Charlotte, Charlotte and Philip. But a stern sense of duty intervenes. My modest Muse puts a finger on her lip, and says, "Hush about that business!" Ah, my worthy friend, you little know what soft-hearted people those cynics are! If you could have come on Diogenes by surprise, I dare say you might have found him reading sentimental novels and whimpering in his tub. Philip shall leave his sweetheart and go back to his business, and we will not have one word about tears, promises, raptures, parting. Never mind about these sentimentalities, but please, rather, to depict to yourself our young fellow so poor that when the coach stops for dinner at Orleans he can only afford to purchase a penny-loaf and a sausage for his own hungry cheek. When he reached the "Hôtel Poussin," with his meagre carpet-bag, they served him a supper which he ate to the admiration of all beholders in the little coffee-room. He was in gay spirits and gayety. He did not care to make any secret of his poverty, and how he had been unable to afford to pay for dinner. Most of the guests at "Hôtel Poisson" knew what it was to be poor. Often and often they had dined on credit when they put back their napkins into their respective pigeon-holes. But my landlord knew his guests. They were poor men—honest men. They paid him in the end, and each could help his neighbor in a strait.

After Mr. Firmin's return to Paris, he did not care for a while to go to the Elysian Fields. They were not Elysian for him, except in Miss Charlotte's company. He resumed his newspaper correspondence, which occupied a day in each week, and he had the other six—nay, he scribbled on the seventh day likewise, and covered immense sheets of letter-paper with remarks upon all manner of subjects, addressed to a certain Mademoiselle, Mademoiselle Baynes, chez M. le Major Mac, &c. On these sheets of paper Mr. Firmin could talk so long, so loudly, so fervently, so eloquently to Miss Baynes, that she was never tired of hearing, or he of holding forth. He began imparting his dreams and his earliest sensations to his beloved before breakfast. At noon-day he gave her his opinion of the contents of the morning papers. His packet was ordinarily full and brimming over by post-time, so that his expressions of love and fidelity leaked from under the cover, or were squeezed into the queerest corners, where, no doubt, it was a delightful task for Miss Baynes to trace out and detect those little Cupids which a faithful lover despatched to her. It would be, " I have found this little corner unoccupied. Do you know what I have to say in it ? Oh, Charlotte, I," &c., &c. My sweet young lady, you can guess, or will one day guess, the rest ; and will receive such dear, delightful, nonsensical double letters, and will answer them with that elegant propriety which I have no doubt Miss Baynes showed in her replies. Ah ! if all who are writing and receiving such letters, or who have written and received such, or who remember writing and receiving such letters, would order a copy of this novel from the publishers, what reams, and piles, and pyramids of paper our ink would have to blacken ! Since Charlotte and Philip had been engaged to each other, he had scarcely, except in those dreadful, ghastly days of quarrel, enjoyed the luxury of absence from his soul's blessing—the exquisite delights of writing to her. He could do few things in moderation, this man—and of this delightful privilege of writing to Charlotte he now enjoyed his heart's fill.

After brief enjoyment of the weeks of this rapture, when winter was come on Paris, and icicles hung on the bough, how did it happen that one day, two days, three days passed, and the postman brought no little letter in the well-known little handwriting for Monsieur Philip Firmin, à Paris ? Three days, four days, and no letter. O torture, could she be ill ? Could her aunt and uncle have turned against her, and forbidden her to write, as her father and mother had done before ? O grief, and sorrow, and rage ! As for jealousy, our leonine friend never knew such a passion. It never entered into his lordly heart to doubt of his little maiden's love. But still four, five days have passed, and not one word has come from Tours. The little " Hôtel Poussin " was in a commotion. I have said that when our friend felt any passion very strongly he was sure to speak of it. Did Don Quixote lose any opportunity of declaring to the world that Dulcinea del Toboso was peerless among women ? Did not Antar bawl out in battle, " I am the lover of Ibla ? " Our knight had taken all the people of the hotel into his confidence somehow. They all knew of his condition — all, the painter, the poet, the half-pay Polish officer, the landlord, the hostess, down to the little knife-boy who used to come in with, " The factor comes of to pass—no letter this morning."

No doubt Philip's political letters became, under this outward pressure, very desponding and gloomy. One day, as he sat gnawing his mustaches at his desk, the little Anatole enters his apartment and cries, "Tenez, M. Philippe. That lady again!" And the faithful, the watchful, the active Madame Smolensk once more made her appearance in his chamber.

Philip blushed and hung his head for shame. "Ungrateful brute that I am," he thought; "I have been back more than a week, and never thought a bit about that good, kind soul who came to my succor. I am an awful egotist. Love is always so."

As he rose up to greet his friend, she looked so grave, and pale, and sad, that he could not but note her demeanor. "Bon Dieu! had anything happened?"

"Ce pauvre Général is ill, very ill, Philip," Smolensk said, in her grave voice.

He was so gravely ill, Madame said, that his daughter had been sent for.

"Had she come?" asked Philip, with a start.

"You think but of her—you care not for the poor old man. You are all the same, you men. All egotists—all. Go! I know you! I never knew one that was not," said madame.

Philip has his little faults: perhaps egotism *is* one of his defects. Perhaps it is yours, or even mine.

"You have been here a week since Thursday last, and you have never written or sent to a woman who loves you well. Go! It was not well, Monsieur Philippe."

As soon as he saw her, Philip felt that he had been neglectful and ungrateful. We have owned so much already. But how should madame know that he had returned on Thursday week? When they looked up after her reproof, his eager eyes seemed to ask this question.

"Could she not write to me and tell me that you were come back? Perhaps she knew that you would not do so yourself. A woman's heart teaches her these experiences early," continued the lady, sadly; then she added: "I tell you, you are good-for-nothings, all of you! And I repent me, see you, of having had the bêtise to pity you!"

"I shall have my quarter's pay on Saturday. I was coming to you then," said Philip.

"Was it that I was speaking of? What! you are all cowards, men all! Oh, that I have been beast, beast, to think at last I had found a man of heart!"

How much or how often this poor Ariadne had trusted and been forsaken, I have no means of knowing, or desire of inquiring. Perhaps it is as well for the polite reader, who is taken into my entire confidence, that we should not know

Madame de Smolensk's history from the first page to the last. Granted that Ariadne was deceived by Theseus : but then she consoled herself, as we may all read in " Smith's Dictionary ; " and then she must have deceived her father in order to run away with Theseus. I suspect— I suspect, I say, that these women who are so *very* much betrayed, are——but we are speculating on this French lady's antecedents, when Charlotte, her lover, and her family are the persons with whom we have mainly to do.

These two, I suppose, forgot self, about which each for a moment had been busy, and Madame resumed :—" Yes, you have reason ; Miss is here. It was time. Hold ! Here is a note from her." And Philip's kind messenger once more put a paper into his hands.

" My dearest father is very, very ill. Oh, Philip ! I am so unhappy ; and he is so good, and gentle, and kind, and loves me so ! "

" It is true," madame resumed. " Before Charlotte came, he thought only of her. When his wife comes up to him, he turns from her. I have not loved her much, that lady, that is true. But to see her now, it is navrant. He will take no medicine from her. He pushes her away. Before Charlotte came, he sent for me, and spoke as well as his poor throat would let him, this poor General ! His daughter's arrival seemed to comfort him. But he says, ' Not my wife ! not my wife ! ' And the poor thing has to go away and cry in the chamber at the side. He says—in his French, you know—he has never been well since Charlotte went away. He has often been out. He has dined but rarely at our table, and there has always been a silence between him and Madame la Générale. Last week he had a great inflammation of the chest. Then he took to bed, and Monsieur the Docteur came—the little doctor whom you know. Then a quinsy has declared itself, and he now is scarce able to speak. His condition is most grave. He lies suffering, dying, perhaps—yes, dying, do you hear? And you are thinking of your little school-girl ! Men are all the same. Monsters ! Go ! "

Philip, who, I have said, is very fond of talking about Philip, surveys his own faults with great magnanimity and good-humor, and acknowledges them without the least intention to correct them. " How selfish we are ! " I can hear him say, looking at himself in the glass. " By George ! sir, when I heard simultaneously the news of that poor old man's illness, and of Charlotte's return, I felt that I wanted to see *her* that instant. I must go to her, and speak to her. The old man and his suffering did not seem to affect me. It is humiliating to have to own that we are selfish beasts. But we are, sir— we are brutes, by George! and nothing else."——And he gives a finishing twist to the ends of his flaming mustaches as he surveys them in the glass.

Poor little Charlotte was in such affliction that of course she must have Philip to console her at once. No time was to be lost. Quick! a cab this moment: and, coachman, you shall have an ex- tra for drink if you go quick to the Avenue de Valmy! Madame puts herself into the carriage, and as they go along, tells Philip more at length of the gloomy occurrences of the last few days. Four days since the poor General was so bad with his quinsy that he thought he should not recover, and Charlotte was sent for. He was a little better on the day of her arrival; but yesterday the inflammation had increased; he could not swal- low; he could not speak audibly; he was in very great suffer- ing and danger. He turned away from his wife. The un- happy Generaless had been to Madame Bunch in her tears and grief, complaining that after twenty years' fidelity and attachment her husband had withdrawn his regard from her. Baynes at- tributed even his illness to his wife; and at other times said it was a just punishment for his wicked conduct in breaking his word to Philip and Charlotte. If he did not see his dear child again he must beg her forgiveness for having made her suffer so. He had acted wickedly and ungratefully, and his wife had forced him to do what he did. He prayed that heaven might pardon him. And he had behaved with wicked injustice to- wards Philip, who had acted most generously towards his family. And he had been a scoundrel—he knew he had—and Bunch, and MacWhirter, and the Doctor all said so—and it was that woman's doing. And he pointed to the scared wife as he painfully hissed out these words of anger and contrition: —"When I saw that child ill, and almost made mad, because I broke my word, I felt I was a scoundrel, Martin; and I was; and that woman made me so; and I deserve to be shot; and I sha'n't recover; I tell you I sha'n't." Dr. Martin, who attended the General, thus described his patient's last talk and behavior to Philip.

It was the doctor who sent madame in quest of the young man. He found poor Mrs. Baynes with hot, tearless eyes and livid face, a wretched sentinel outside the sick-chamber. "You will find General Baynes very ill, sir," she said to Philip with a ghastly calmness, and a gaze he could scarcely face. "My daughter is in the room with him. It appears I have offended him, and he refuses to see me." And she squeezed a dry handkerchief which she held, and put on her spectacles again, and tried again to read the Bible in her lap.

Philip hardly knew the meaning of Mrs. Baynes' words as yet. He was agitated by the thought of the General's illness, perhaps by the notion that the beloved was so near. Her hand was in his a moment afterwards ; and, even in that sad chamber, each could give the other a soft pressure, a fond, silent signal of mutual love and faith.

The poor man laid the hands of the young people together, and his own upon them. The suffering to which he had put his daughter seemed to be the crime which specially affected him. He thanked heaven he was able to see he was wrong. He whispered to his little maid a prayer for pardon in one or two words, which caused poor Charlotte to sink on her knees and cover his fevered hand with tears and kisses. Out of all her heart she forgave him. She had felt that the parent she loved and was accustomed to honor had been mercenary and cruel. It had wounded her pure heart to be obliged to think that her father could be other than generous, and just, and good. That he should humble himself before her, smote her with the keenest pang of tender commiseration. I do not care to pursue this last scene. Let us close the door as the children kneel by the sufferer's bedside, and to the old man's petition for forgiveness, and to the young girl's sobbing vows of love and fondness, say a reverent Amen.

By the following letter, which he wrote a few days before the fatal termination of his illness, the worthy General, it would appear, had already despaired of his recovery :—" My dear Mac,—I speak and breathe with such difficulty as I write this from my bed, that I doubt whether I shall ever leave it. I do not wish to vex poor Eliza, and in my state cannot *enter into disputes* which I know would ensue regarding settlement of property. When I left England there was a claim hanging over me (young Firmin's) at which I was needlessly frightened, as having to satisfy it would swallow up *much more than everything I possessed in the world.* Hence made arrangements for leaving everything in Eliza's name and the children after. Will with Smith and Thompson, Raymond Buildings, Gray's Inn. Think Char *won't be happy for a long time with her mother.* To break from F., who has been most generous to us, will break her heart. Will you and Emily keep her for a little ? I gave *F. my promise.* As you told me, I have acted ill by him, which I own and deeply lament. If Char marries, *she ought to have her share.* May God bless her, her father prays, in case he should not see her again. And with best love to Emily, am yours, dear Mac, sincerely,—CHARLES BAYNES."

On the receipt of this letter, Charlotte disobeyed her father's wish, and set forth from Tours instantly, under her worthy uncle's guardianship. The old soldier was in his comrade's room when the General put the hands of Charlotte and her lover together. He confessed his fault, though it is hard for those who expect love and reverence to have to own to wrong and to ask pardon. Old knees are stiff to bend : brother reader, young or old, when our last hour comes, may ours have grace to do so.

CHAPTER XXX.

RETURNS TO OLD FRIENDS.

THE three old comrades and Philip formed the little mourning procession which followed the General to his place of rest at Montmartre. When the service has been read, and the last volley has been fired over the buried soldier, the troops march to quarters with a quick step, and to a lively tune. Our veteran has been laid in the grave with brief ceremonies. We do not even prolong his obsequies with a sermon. His place knows him no longer. There are a few who remember him : a very, very few who grieve for him—so few that to think of them is a humiliation almost. The sun sets on the earth, and our dear brother has departed off its face. Stars twinkle ; dews fall ; children go to sleep in awe and maybe tears ; the sun rises on a new day, which he has never seen, and children wake hungry. They are interested about their new black clothes, perhaps. They are presently at their work, plays, quarrels. They are looking forward to the day when the holidays will be over, and the eyes which shone here yesterday so kindly are gone, gone gone. A drive to the cemetery, followed by a coach with four acquaintances dressed in decorous black, who separate and go to their homes or clubs, and wear your crape for a few days after—can most of us expect much more ? The thought is not ennobling or exhilarating, worthy sir. And, pray, why should we be proud of ourselves? Is it because we have been so good, or are so wise and great, that we expect to be beloved, lamented, remembered? Why, great Xerxes or blustering Bobadil must know in that last hour and resting-place how abject, how small, how low, how lonely they are, and what a little dust will cover them. Quick, drums and fifes, a lively tune! Whip the black team, coachman, and trot back to town again—to the world, and to business, and duty!

I am for saying no single unkindness of General Baynes which is not forced upon me by my story-teller's office. We know from Marlborough's story that the bravest man and greatest military genius is not always brave or successful in his battles with his wife; that some of the greatest warriors have committed errors in accounts and the distribution of *meum* and *tuum*. We can't disguise from ourselves the fact that Baynes permitted himself to be misled, and had weaknesses not quite consistent with the highest virtue.

When he became aware that his carelessness in the matter of Mrs. Firmin's trust-money had placed him in her son's power, we have seen how the old General, in order to avoid being called to account, fled across the water with his family and all his little fortune, and how terrified he was on landing on a foreign shore to find himself face to face with this dreadful creditor. Philip's renunciation of all claims against Baynes soothed and pleased the old man wonderfully. But Philip might change his mind, an adviser at Baynes' side repeatedly urged. To live abroad was cheaper and safer than to live at home. Accordingly Baynes, his wife, family, and money, all went into exile, and remained there.

What savings the old man had I don't accurately know. He and his wife were very dark upon this subject with Philip: and when the General died, his widow declared herself to be almost a pauper! It was impossible that Baynes should have left much money; but that Charlotte's share should have amounted to—that sum which may or may not presently be stated—was a little *too* absurd! You see Mr. and Mrs. Firmin are travelling abroad just now. When I wrote to Firmin, to ask if I might mention the amount of his wife's fortune, he gave me no answer; nor do I like to enter upon these matters of calculation without his explicit permission. He is of a hot temper; he might, on his return, grow angry with the friend of his youth, and say, " Sir, how dare you talk about my private affairs? and what has the public to do with Mrs. Firmin's private fortune?"

When, the last rites over, good-natured uncle Mac proposed to take Charlotte back to Tours her mother made no objection. The widow had tried to do the girl such an injury, that perhaps the latter felt that forgiveness was impossible. Little Char loved Philip with all her heart and strength ; had been authorized and encouraged to do so, as we have seen. To give him up now, because a richer suitor presented himself, was an act of treason from which her faithful heart revolted, and she never could pardon the instigator. You see, in this simple story, I scarcely care even to have reticence or secrets. I don't want you to understand for a moment that Walsingham Hely was still crying his eyes out about Charlotte. Goodness bless you ! It was two or three weeks ago—four or five weeks ago, that he was in love with *her* ! He had not seen the Duchesse d'Ivry then, about whom you may remember he had the quarrel with Podichon, at the club in the Rue de Grammont. (He and the Duchesse wrote poems to each other, each in the other's native language.) The Charlotte had long passed out of the young fellow's mind. That butterfly had fluttered off from our English rosebud, and had settled on the other elderly flower ! I don't know that Mrs. Baynes was aware of young Hely's fickleness at this present time of which we are writing ; but his visits had ceased, and she was angry and disappointed ; and not the less angry because her labor had been in vain. On her part, Charlotte could also be resolutely unforgiving. Take her Philip from her ! Never, never ! Her mother force her to give up the man whom she had been encouraged to love ? Mamma should have defended Philip, not betrayed him ! If I command my son to steal a spoon, shall he obey me ? And if I do obey and steal, and be transported, will he love me afterwards ? I think I can hardly ask for so much filial affection.

So there was strife between mother and daughter; and anger not the less bitter, on Mrs. Baynes's part, because her husband, whose cupidity or fear had, at first, induced him to take her side, had deserted her and gone over to her daughter. In the anger of that controversy Baynes died, leaving the victory and right with Charlotte. He shrank from his wife : would not speak to her in his last moments. The widow had these injuries against her daughter and Philip : and thus neither side forgave the other. She was not averse to the child's going away to her uncle : put a lean, hungry face against Charlotte's lip, and received a kiss which I fear had but little love in it. I don't envy those children who remain under the widow's lonely command ; or poor Madam Smolensk, who has to endure the arrogance, the grief, the avarice of that grim woman. Nor did madame suffer under this tyranny long. *Galignani's Messenger* very soon announced that she had lodgings to let, and I remember being edified by reading one day in the *Pall Mall Gazette* that elegant apartments, select society, and an excellent table were to be found in one of the most airy and fashionable quarters of Paris. Inquire of Madame la Baronne de S——sk, Avenue de Valmy, Champs Elysées.

We guessed without difficulty how this advertisement found its way to the *Pall Mall Gazette ;* and very soon after its appearance Madame de Smolensk's friend, Mr. Philip, made his appearance at our tea-table in London. He was always welcome amongst us elders and children. He wore a crape on his hat. As soon as the young ones were gone, you may be sure he poured his story out ; and enlarged upon the death, the burial, the quarrels, the loves, the partings we have narrated. How could he be put in a way to earn three or four hundred a year ? That was the present question. Ere he came to see us, he had already been totting up ways and means. He had been with our friend Mrs. Brandon : was staying with her. The Little Sister thought three hundred would be sufficient. They could have her second floor—not for nothing ; no, no, but at a moderate price, which would pay her. They could have attics, if more rooms were needed. They could have her kitchen fire, and one maid, for the present, would do all their work. Poor little thing ! She was very young. She would be past eighteen by the time she could marry ; the Little Sister was for early marriages, against long courtships. "Heaven helps those as helps themselves," she said. And Mr. Philip thought this excellent advice, and Mr. Philip's friend, when asked for *his* opinion—"Candidly now, what's your opinion ?"—said, "Is she in the next room ? Of course you mean you are married already."

Philip roared one of his great laughs. No, he was not married already. Had he not said that Miss Baynes was gone away to Tours to her aunt and uncle ? But that he wanted to be married ; but that he could never settle down to work till he married ; but that he could have no rest, peace, health till he married that angel, he was ready to confess. Ready ? All the street might hear him calling out the name and expatiating on the angelic charms and goodness of his Charlotte. He spoke so loud and long on this subject that my wife grew a little tired ; and my wife *always* likes to hear other women praised, that (she says) I know she does. But when a man goes on roaring for an hour about Dulcinea? You know such talk becomes fulsome at last; and, in fine, when he was gone, my wife said, "Well, he is very much in love; so were you—I mean long before my time, sir; but does love pay the housekeeping bills, pray?"

"No, my dear. And love is always controlled by other people's advice:—always," says Philip's friend; who, I hope, you will perceive was speaking ironically.

Philip's friends had listened not impatiently to Philip's talk about Philip. Almost all women will give a sympathizing hearing to men who are in love. Be they ever so old, they grow young again with that conversation, and renew their own early times. Men are not quite so generous: Tityrus tires of hearing Corydon discourse endlessly on the charms of his shepherdess. And yet egotism is good talk. Even dull autobiographies are pleasant to read: and if to read, why not to hear? Had Master Philip not been such an egotist, he would not have been so pleasant a companion. Can't you like a man at whom you laugh a little? I had rather such an open-mouthed conversationist than your cautious jaws that never unlock without a careful application of the key. As for the entrance to Mr. Philip's mind, that door was always open when he was awake, or not hungry, or in a friend's company. Besides his love, and his prospects in life, his poverty, &c., Philip had other favorite topics of conversation. His friend the Little Sister was a great theme with him; his father was another favorite subject of his talk. By the way, his father had written to the Little Sister. The doctor said he was sure to prosper in his newly adopted country. He and another physician had invented a new medicine, which was to effect wonders, and in a few years would assuredly make the fortune of both of them. He was never without one scheme or another for making that fortune which never came. Whenever he drew upon poor Philip for little sums, his letters were sure to be especially magniloquent and hopeful. "Whenever the doctor says he has invented the philosopher's stone," said poor Philip, "I am sure there will be a postscript to say that a little bill will be presented for so much, at so many days' date."

Had he drawn on Philip lately? Philip told us when, and how often. We gave him all the benefit of our virtuous indignation. As for my wife's eyes, they gleamed with anger. What a man: what a father! Oh, he was incorrigible! "Yes, I am afraid he is," says poor Phil, comically, with his hands roaming at ease in his pockets. They contained little else than those big hands. " My father is of a hopeful turn. His views regarding property are peculiar. It is a comfort to have such a distinguished parent, isn't it ? I am always surprised to hear that he is not married again. I sigh for a mother-in-law," Philip continued.

"Oh, *don't*, Philip!" cried Mrs. Laura, in a pet. " Be generous : be forgiving : be noble : be Christian ! Don't be cynical, and imitating—you know whom ! "

Whom could she possibly mean, I wonder ? After flashes, there came showers in this lady's eyes. From long habit I can understand her thoughts, although she does not utter them. She was thinking of those poor, noble, simple, friendless young people ; and asking heaven's protection for them. I am not in the habit of over-praising my friends, goodness knows. The foibles of this one I have described honestly enough. But if I write down here that he was courageous, cheerful in adversity, generous, simple, truth-loving, above a scheme—after having said that he was a noble young fellow—*dixi ;* and I won't cancel the words.

Ardent lover as he was, our friend was glad to be back in the midst of the London smoke, and wealth, and bustle. The fog agreed with his lungs, he said. He breathed more freely in our great City than in that little English village in the centre of Paris which he had been inhabiting. In his hotel, and at his café (where he composed his eloquent " own correspondence "), he had occasion to speak a little French, but it never came very trippingly from his stout English tongue. " You don't suppose I would like to be taken for a Frenchman," he would say, with much gravity. I wonder who ever thought of mistaking friend Philip for a Frenchman ?

As for that faithful Little Sister, her house and heart were still at the young man's service. We have not visited Thornhaugh Street for some time. Mr. Philip, whom we have been bound to attend, has been too much occupied with his love-making to bestow much thought on his affectionate little friend. She has been trudging meanwhile on her humble course of life, cheerful, modest, laborious, doing her duty, with a helping little hand ready to relieve many a fallen wayfarer on her road. She had a room vacant in her house when Philip came :—a room, indeed ! Would she not have had a house vacant, if Philip wanted it ? But in the interval since we saw her last, the Little Sister, too, has had to assume black robes. Her father, the old Captain, has gone to his rest. His place is vacant in the little parlor : his bedroom is ready for Philip, as long as Philip

will stay. She did not profess to feel much affliction for the
loss of the captain. She talked of him constantly as though he
were present ; and made a supper for Philip, and seated him
in her Pa's chair. How she bustled about on the night when
Philip arrived ! What a beaming welcome there was in her
kind eyes ! Her modest hair was touched with silver now ;
but her cheeks were like apples ; her little figure was neat, and
light, and active : and her voice, with its gentle laugh, and little
sweet bad grammar, has always seemed one of the sweetest of
voices to me.

Very soon after Philip's arrival in London, Mrs. Brandon
paid a visit to the wife of Mr. Firmin's humble servant and
biographer, and the two women had a fine sentimental consultation. All good women, you know, are sentimental. The
idea of young lovers, of match-making, of amiable poverty,
tenderly excites and interests them. My wife, at this time,
began to pour off fine long letters to Miss Faynes, to which the
latter modestly and dutifully replied, with many expressions of
fervor and gratitude for the interest which her friend in London
was pleased to take in the little maid. I saw by these answers
that Charlotte's union with Philip was taken as a received point
by these two ladies. They discussed the ways and means.
They did not talk about broughams, settlements, town and
country houses, pin-moneys, trousseaux : and my wife, in com-
puting their sources of income, always pointed out that Miss
Charlotte's fortune, though certainly small, would give a very
useful addition to the young couple's income. " Fifty pounds
a year not much ! Let me tell you, sir, that fifty pounds a year
is a very pretty little sum : if Philip can but make three hundred
a year himself, Mrs. Brandon says they ought to be able to live
quite nicely." You ask, my genteel friend, is it possible that
people can live for four hundred a year ? How do they manage,
ces pauvres gens ? They eat, they drink, they are clothed, they
are warmed, they have roofs over their heads, and glass in their
windows ; and some of them are as good, happy, and well-bred
as their neighbors who are ten times as rich. Then, besides
this calculation of money, there is the fond woman's firm belief
that the day will bring its daily bread for those who work for it
and ask for it in the proper quarter ; against which reasoning
many a man knows it is in vain to argue. As to my own little
objections and doubts, my wife met them by reference to Philip's
former love-affair with his cousin, Miss Twysden. " You had
no objection in that case, sir," this logician would say. " You
would have had him take a creature without a heart. *You*

would cheerfully have seen him made miserable for life, because you thought there was money enough and a genteel connection. Money indeed! Very happy Mrs. Woolcomb is with her money. Very creditably to all sides has *that* marriage turned out!" I need scarcely remind my readers of the unfortunate result of that marriage. Woolcomb's behavior to his wife was the agreeable talk of London society and of the London clubs very soon after the pair were joined together in holy matrimony. Do we not all remember how Woolcomb was accused of striking his wife, of starving his wife, and how she took refuge at home and came to her father's house with a black eye? The two Twysdens were so ashamed of this transaction, that father and son left off coming to "Bays's," where I never heard their absence regretted but by one man, who said that Talbot owed him money for losses at whist for which he could get no settlement.

Should Mr. Firmin go and see his aunt in her misfortune? By-gones might be by-gones, some of Philip's advisers thought. Now, Mrs. Twysden was unhappy, her heart might relent to Philip, whom she certainly had loved as a boy. Philip had the magnanimity to call upon her; and found her carriage waiting at the door. But a servant, after keeping the gentleman waiting in the dreary, well-remembered hall, brought him word that his mistress was out, smiled in his face with an engaging insolence, and proceeded to put cloaks, court-guides, and other female gear into the carriage in the presence of this poor deserted nephew. This visit it must be owned was one of Mrs. Laura's romantic efforts at reconciling enemies: as if, my good creature, the Twysdens ever let a man into their house who was poor or out of fashion! They lived in a constant dread lest Philip should call to borrow money of them. As if they ever lent money to a man who was in need! If they ask the respected reader to their house, depend upon it they think he is well to do. On the other hand, the Twysdens made a very handsome entertainment for the new Lord of Whipham and Ringwood who now reigned after his kinsman's death. They affably went and passed Christmas with him in the country; and they cringed and bowed before Sir John Ringwood as they had bowed and cringed before the earl in his time. The old earl had been a Tory in his latter days, when Talbot Twysden's views were also very conservative. The present Lord of Ringwood was a Whig. It is surprising how liberal the Twysdens grew in the course of a fortnight's after-dinner conversation and pheasant-shooting talk at Ringwood. "Hang it! you know, young Twysden said, in his office afterwards, "a fellow must go with the politics of his family, you know!" and he bragged about the dinners, wines, splendors, cooks, and preserves of Ringwood as freely as in the time of his noble granduncle. Anyone who has kept a house-dog in London, which licks your boots and your platter, and fawns for the bones in your dish, knows how the animal barks and flies at the poor who come to the door. The Twysdens, father and son, were of this canine species : and there are vast packs of such dogs here and elsewhere.

If Philip opened his heart to us, and talked unreservedly regarding his hopes and his plans, you may be sure he had his little friend, Mrs. Brandon, also in his confidence, and that no person in the world was more eager to serve him. Whilst we were talking about what was to be done, this little lady was also at work in her favorite's behalf. She had a firm ally in Mrs. Mugford, the proprietor's lady of the *Pall Mall Gazette.* Mrs. Mugford had long been interested in Philip, his misfortunes and his love affairs. These two good women had made a sentimental hero of him. Ah! that they could devise some feasible scheme to help him! And such a chance actually did very soon present itself to these delighted women.

In almost all the papers of the new year appeared a brilliant advertisement, announcing the speedy appearance in Dublin of a new paper. It was to be called THE SHAMROCK, and its first number was to be issued on the ensuing St. Patrick's day. I need not quote at length the advertisement which heralded the advent of this new periodical. The most famous pens of the national party in Ireland were, of course, engaged to contribute to its columns. Those pens would be hammered into steel of a different shape when the opportunity should offer. Beloved prelates, authors of world-wide fame, bards, the bold strings of whose lyres had rung through the isle already, and made millions of noble hearts to beat, and, by consequence, double the number of eyes to fill ; philosophers, renowned for science ; and illustrious advocates, whose manly voices had ever spoken the language of hope and freedom to an &c., &c., would be found rallying round the journal, and proud to wear the symbol of THE SHAMROCK. Finally, Michael Cassidy, Esq., was chosen to be the editor of this new journal.

This was the M. Cassidy, Esq., who appeared, I think, at Mr. Firmin's call-supper ; and who had long been the sub-editor of the *Pall Mall Gazette.* If Michael went to Dame Street, why should not Philip be sub-editor at Pall Mall? Mrs. Brandon

argued. Of course there would be a score of candidates for
Michael s office. The editor would like the patronage. Barnet,
Mugford's partner in the *Gazette*, would wish to appoint his
man. Cassidy, before retiring, would assuredly intimate his
approaching resignation to scores of gentlemen of his nation,
who would not object to take the Saxon's pay until they finally
shook his yoke off, and would eat his bread until the happy
moment arrived when they could knock out his brains in fair
battle. As soon as Mrs. Brandon heard of the vacant place,
that moment she determined that Philip should have it. It was
surprising what a quantity of information our little friend possessed about artists, and pressmen, and their lives, families,
ways and means. Many gentlemen of both professions came
to Mr. Ridley's chambers, and called on the Little Sister on
their way to and fro. How Tom Smith had left the *Herald*,
and gone to the *Post;* what price Jack Jones had for his
picture, and who sat for the principal figures.—I promise you
Madam Brandon had all these interesting details by heart; and
I think I have described this little person very inadequately if
I have not made you understand that she was as intrepid a little
jobber as ever lived, and never scrupled to go any length to
serve a friend. To be Archbishop of Canterbury, to be professor of Hebrew, to be teacher of a dancing-school, to be
organist for a church: for any conceivable place of function
this little person would have asserted Philip's capability.
"Don't tell me! He can dance or preach (as the case may
be), or write beautiful! And as for being unfit to be a sub-
editor, I want to know, has he not as good a head and as good
an education as that Cassidy, indeed? And is not Cambridge
College the best college in the world? It is, I say. And he
went there ever so long. And he might have taken the very
best prize, only money was no object to him then, dear fellow,
and he did not like to keep the poor out of what he didn't
want!"

Mrs. Mugford had always considered the young man as very
haughty, but quite the gentleman, and speedily was infected by
her gossip's enthusiasm about him. My wife hired a fly, packed
several of the children into it, called upon Mrs. Mugford, and
chose to be delighted with that lady's garden, with that lady's
nursery—with everything that bore the name of Mugford. It
was a curiosity to remark in what a flurry of excitement these
women plunged, and how they schemed, and coaxed, and
caballed, in order to get this place for their protégé. My wife
thought—she merely happened to surmise: nothing more, of

course—that Mrs. Mugford's fond desire was to shine in the world. " Could we not ask some people—with—with what you call handles to their names,—I think I before heard you use some such term, sir,—to meet the Mugfords ? Some of Philip's old friends, who I am sure would be very happy to serve him." Some such artifice was, I own, practised. We coaxed, cajoled, fondled the Mugfords for Philip's sake, and heaven forgive Mrs. Laura her hypocrisy. We had an entertainment then, I own. We asked our finest company, and Mr. and Mrs. Mugford to meet them : and we prayed that unlucky Philip to be on his best behavior to all persons who were invited to the feast.

Before my wife this lion of a Firmin was as a lamb. Rough, captious, and overbearing in general society, with those whom he loved and esteemed Philip was of all men the most modest and humble. He would never tire of playing with our children, joining in their games, laughing and roaring at their little sports. I have never had such a laugher at my jokes as Philip Firmin. I think my wife liked him for that noble guffaw with which he used to salute those pieces of wit. He arrived a little late sometimes with his laughing chorus, but ten people at table were not so loud as this faithful friend. On the contrary, when those people for whom he has no liking venture on a pun or other pleasantry, I am bound to own that Philip's acknowledgment of their waggery must be anything but pleasant or flattering to them. Now, on occasion of this important dinner, I enjoined him to be very kind, and very civil, and very much pleased with everybody, and to stamp upon nobody's corns, as, indeed, why should he, in life ? Who was he to be *censor morum ?* And it has been said that no man could admit his own faults with a more engaging candor than our friend.

We invited, then, Mugford, the proprietor of the *Pall Mall Gazette,* and his wife ; and Bickerton, the editor of that periodical ; Lord Egham, Philip's old college friend ; and one or two more gentlemen. Our invitations to the ladies were not so fortunate. Some were engaged, others away in the country keeping Christmas. In fine, we considered ourselves rather lucky in securing old Lady Hixie, who lives hard by in Westminster, and who will pass for a lady of fashion when no person of greater note is present. My wife told her that the object of the dinner was to make our friend Firmin acquainted with the editor and proprietor of the *Pall Mall Gazette,* with whom it was important that he should be on the most amicable footing. Oh ! very well. Lady Hixie promised to be quite gracious to the newspaper gentleman and his wife ; and kept her promise

most graciously during the evening. Our good friend Mrs.
Mugford was the first of our guests to arrive. She drove "in
her trap" from her villa in the suburbs ; and after putting up
his carriage at a neighboring livery-stable, her groom volunteered to help our servants in waiting at dinner. His zeal and
activity were remarkable. China smashed, and dish-covers
clanged in the passage. Mrs. Mugford said that "Sam was at
his old tricks ;" and I hope the hostess showed she was mistress of herself amidst that fall of china. Mrs. Mugford came
before the appointed hour, she said, in order to see our children. "With our late London dinner hours," she remarked,
"children was never seen now." At Hampstead, hers always
appeared at the dessert, and enlivened the table with their
innocent outcries for oranges and struggles for sweetmeats. In
the nursery, where one little maid, in her crisp long night-gown,
was saying her prayers ; where another little person, in the most
airy costume, was standing before the great barred fire ; where
a third Lilliputian was sitting up in its nightcap and surplice,
surveying the scene below from its crib ; the ladies found our
dear Little Sister installed. She had come to see her little pets
(she had known two or three of them from the very earliest
times). She was a great favorite amongst them all ; and, I
believe, conspired with the cook down below in preparing certain delicacies for the table. A fine conversation then ensued
about our children, about the Mugford children, about babies
in general. And then the artful women (the house mistress and
the Little Sister) brought Philip on the *tapis*, and discoursed,
à qui mieux, about his virtues, his misfortunes, his engagement,
and that dear little creature to whom he was betrothed. This
conversation went on until carriage-wheels were heard in the
square, and the knocker (there were actually knockers in that
old-fashioned place and time) began to peal. "Oh, bother!
There's the company a-comin'," Mrs. Mugford said ; and
arranging her cap and flounces, with neat-handed Mrs. Brandon's aid, came down stairs, after taking a tender leave of the
little people, to whom she sent a present next day of a pile of
fine Christmas books, which had come to the *Pall Mall Gazette*
for review. The kind woman had been coaxed, wheedled, and
won over to our side, to Philip's side. He had *her* vote for the
sub-editorship, whatever might ensue.

Most of our guests had already arrived, when at length Mrs.
Mugford was announced. I am bound to say that she presented
a remarkable appearance, and that the splendor of her attire
was such as is seldom beheld.

Bickerton and Philip were presented to one another, and had a talk about French politics before dinner, during which conversation Philip behaved with perfect discretion and politeness. Bickerton had happened to hear Philip's letters well spoken of—in a good quarter, mind ; and his cordiality increased when Lord Egham entered, called Philip by his surname, and entered into a perfectly free conversation with him. Old Lady Hixie went into perfectly good society, Bickerton condescended to acknowledge. "As for Mrs. Mugford," says he, with a glance of wondering compassion at that lady, "of course, I need not tell you that *she* is seen nowhere—nowhere." This said, Mr. Bickerton stepped forward, and calmly patronized my wife, gave me a good-natured nod for my own part, reminded Lord Egham that he had had the pleasure of meeting him at Egham ; and then fixed on Tom Page, of the Bread-and-Butter Office (who, I own, is one of our most genteel guests), with whom he entered into a discussion of some political matter of that day—I forget what : but the main point was that he named two or three leading public men with whom he had discussed the question, whatever it might be. He named very great names, and led us to understand that with the proprietors of those very great names he was on the most intimate and confidential footing. With his owners—with the proprietor of the *Pall Mall Gazette*, he was on the most distant terms, and indeed I am afraid that his behavior to myself and my wife was scarcely respectful. I fancied I saw Philip's brow gathering wrinkles as his eye followed this man strutting from one person to another, and patronizing each. The dinner was a little late, from some reason best known in the lower regions. "I take it," says Bickerton, winking at Philip, in a pause of the conversation, "that our good friend and host is not much used to giving dinners. The mistress of the house is evidently in a state of perturbation." Philip gave such a horrible grimace that the other at first thought he was in pain.

"You, who have lived a great deal with old Ringwood, know what a good dinner is," Bickerton continued, giving Firmin a knowing look.

"Any dinner is good which is accompanied with such a welcome as I get here," said Philip.

"Oh ! very good people, very good people, of course !" cries Bickerton.

I need not say he thinks he has perfectly succeeded in adopting the air of a man of the world. He went off to Lady Hixie and talked with her about the last great party at which he had met her ; and then he turned to the host, and remarked that my friend, the doctor's son, was a fierce looking fellow.   In five minutes he had the good fortune to make himself hated by Mr. Firmin.   He walks through the world patronizing his betters.   "Our good friend is not much used to giving dinners,"—isn't he ?   I say, what do you mean by continuing to endure this man ?   Tom Page, of the Bread-and-Butter office, is a well-known diner-out ; Lord Egham is a peer ; Bickerton, in a pretty loud voice, talked to one or other of these during dinner and across the table.   He sat next to Mrs. Mugford, but he turned his back on that bewildered woman, and never condescended to address a word to her personally.   "Of course, I understand you, my dear fellow," he said to me when, on the retreat of the ladies, we approached within whispering distance.   "You have these people at dinner for reasons of state. You have a book coming out, and want to have it noticed in the paper.   I make a point of keeping these people at a distance—the only way of dealing with them, I give you my word."

Not one offensive word had Philip said to the chief writer of the *Pall Mall Gazette;* and I began to congratulate myself that our dinner would pass without any mishap, when some one unluckily happening to praise the wine, a fresh supply was ordered.   "Very good claret.   Who is your wine merchant ? Upon my word, I get better claret here than I do in Paris— don't you think so, Mr. Fermor ?   Where do you generally dine at Paris ? "

"I generally dine for thirty sous, and three francs on grand days, Mr. Beckerton," growls Philip.

"My name is Bickerton."   ("What a vulgar thing for a fellow to talk about his thirty-sous dinners ! " murmured my neighbor to me.)   "Well, there is no accounting for tastes ! When I go to Paris, I dine at the 'Trois Frères.'   Give me the Burgundy at the 'Trois Frères.'"

"That is because you great leader-writers are paid better than poor correspondents.   I shall be delighted to be able to dine better."   And with this Mr. Firmin smiles at Mr. Mugford, his master and owner.

"Nothing so vulgar as talking shop," says Bickerton, rather loud.

"I am not ashamed of the shop I keep.   Are you of yours Mr. Bickerton ? " growls Philip.

"F. had him there," says Mr. Mugford.

Mr. Bickerton got up from table, turning quite pale.   "Do you mean to be offensive, sir ? " he asked.

" Offensive, sir ?   No, sir.   Some men are offensive without meaning it.   *You* have been several times to-night ! " says Lord Philip.

" I don't see that I am called upon to bear this kind of thing at any man's table ! " cried Mr. Bickerton.   " Lord Egham, I wish you good-night ! "

" I say, old boy, what's the row about ? " asked his lordship. And we were all astonished as my guest rose and left the table in great wrath.

" Serve him right, Firmin, I say ! " said Mr. Mugford, again drinking off a glass.

" Why, don't you know ? " says Tom Page.   " His father keeps a haberdasher's shop at Cambridge, and sent him to Oxford, where he took a good degree."

And this had come of a dinner of conciliation—a dinner which was to advance Philip's interest in life !

" Hit him again, I say," cried Mugford, whom wine had rendered eloquent.   " He's a supercilious beast, that Bickerton is, and I hate him, and so does Mrs. M."

CHAPTER XXXI.

NARRATES THAT FAMOUS JOKE ABOUT MISS GRIGSBY.

FOR once Philip found that he had offended without giving general offence.   In the confidence of female intercourse, Mrs. Mugford had already, in her own artless but powerful language, confirmed her husband's statement regarding Mr. Bickerton, and declared that B. was a beast, and she was only sorry that Mr. F. had not hit him a little harder.   So different are the opinions which different individuals entertain of the same event !   I happen to know that Bickerton, on his side, went away, averring that we were quarrelsome, under-bred people ; and that a man of any refinement had best avoid that kind of society.   He does really and seriously believe himself our superior, and will lecture almost any gentleman on the art of being one.   This assurance is not at all uncommon with your *parvenu.*   Proud of his newly acquired knowledge of the art of exhausting the contents of an egg, the well-known little boy of the apologue rushed to impart his knowledge to his grand-

mother, who had been for many years familiar with the process
which the child had just discovered. Which of us has not met
with some such instructors? I know men who would be ready
to step forward and teach Taglioni how to dance, Tom Sayers
how to box, or the Chevalier Bayard how to be a gentleman.
We most of us know such men, and undergo, from time to
time, the ineffable benefit of their patronage.

Mugford went away from our little entertainment vowing,
by George, that Philip shouldn't want for a friend at the proper
season; and this proper season very speedily arrived. I
laughed one day, on going to the *Pall Mall Gazette* office, to
find Philip installed in the sub-editor's room, with a provision
of scissors, wafers, and paste-pots, snipping paragraphs from
this paper and that, altering, condensing, giving titles, and so
forth; and, in a word, in regular harness. The three-headed
calves, the great prize gooseberries, the old maiden ladies of
wonderful ages who at length died in country places—it was
wonderful (considering his little experience) how Firmin hunted
out these. He entered into all the spirit of his business. He
prided himself on the clever titles which he found for his paragraphs. When his paper was completed at the week's end,
he surveyed it fondly—not the leading articles, or those profound and yet brilliant literary essays which appeared in the
Gazette—but the births, deaths, marriages, markets, trials and
what not. As a shop-boy, having decorated his master's window, goes into the street, and pleased surveys his work; so
the fair face of the *Pall Mall Gazette* rejoiced Mr Firmin, and
Mr. Bince, the printer of the paper. They looked with an
honest pride upon the result of their joint labors. Nor did
Firmin relish pleasantry on the subject. Did his friends allude
to it, and ask if he had shot any especially fine *canard* that
week? Mr. Philip's brow would corrugate and his cheeks red-
den. He did not like jokes to be made at his expense: was
not his a singular antipathy?

In his capacity of sub-editor, the good fellow had the privilege of taking and giving away countless theatre orders, and
panorama and diorama tickets. the *Pall Mall Gazette* was not
above accepting such little bribes in those days, and Mrs. Mugford's familiarity with the names of opera singers, and splendid
appearance in an opera-box, was quite remarkable. Friend
Philip would bear away a heap of these cards of admission,
delighted to carry off our young folks to one exhibition or another. But once at the diorama, where our young people sat
in the darkness, very much frightened as usual, a voice from

out the midnight gloom cried out : " *Who has come in with orders from the Pall Mall Gazette?* " A lady, two scared children, and Mr. Sub-editor Philip, all trembled at this dreadful summons. I think I should not dare to print the story even now, did I not know that Mr. Firmin was travelling abroad. It was a blessing the place was dark, so that none could see the poor sub-editor's blushes. Rather than cause any mortification to this lady, I am sure Philip would have submitted to rack and torture. But, indeed, her annoyance was very slight, except in seeing her friend annoyed. The humor of the scene surpassed the annoyance in the lady's mind, and caused her to laugh at the mishap ; but I own our little boy (who is of an aristocratic turn, and rather too sensitive to ridicule from his schoolfellows) was not at all anxious to talk upon the subject, or to let the world know that he went to a place of public amusement " with an order."

As for Philip's landlady, the Little Sister, she, you know, had been familiar with the press, and pressmen, and orders for the play for years past. She looked quite young and pretty, with her kind smiling face and neat tight black dress, as she came to the theatre—it was to an Easter piece—on Philip's arm, one evening. Our children saw her from their cab, as they, too, were driving to the same performance. It was, " Look, mamma ! There's Philip and the Little Sister ! " And then came such smiles, and nods, and delighted recognitions from the cab to the two friends on foot ! Of course I have forgotten what was the piece which we all saw on that Easter evening. But those children will never forget ; no, though they live to be a hundred years old, and though their attention was distracted from the piece by constant observation of Philip and his companion in the public boxes opposite.

Mr. Firmin's work and pay were both light, and he accepted both very cheerfully. He saved money out of his little stipend. It was surprising how economically he could live with his little landlady's aid and counsel. He would come to us, recounting his feats of parsimony with a childish delight : he loved to contemplate his sovereigns, as week by week the little pile accumulated. He kept a sharp eye upon sales, and purchased now and again articles of furniture. In this way he brought home a piano to his lodgings, on which he could no more play than he could on the tight-rope ; but he was given to understand that it was a very fine instrument ; and my wife played on it one day when we went to visit him, and he sat listening, with his great hands on his knees, in ecstasies. He was thinking how one day, please heaven, he should see other hands touching the keys—and player and instrument disappeared in a mist before his happy eyes. His purchases were not all always lucky. For example, he was sadly taken in at an auction about a little pearl ornament. Some artful Hebrews at the sale conspired and "ran him up," as the phrase is, to a price more than equal to the value of the trinket. "But you know who it was for, ma'am," one of Philip's apologists said. "If she would like to wear his ten fingers he would cut 'em off and send 'em to her. But he keeps 'em to write her letters and verses—and most beautiful they are, too."

"And the dear fellow, who was bred up in splendor and luxury, Mrs. Mugford, as you, ma'am, know too well—he won't drink no wine now. A little whiskey and a glass of beer is all he takes. And his clothes—he who used to be so grand—you see how he is now, ma'am. Always the gentleman, and, indeed, a finer or grander looking gentleman never entered a room ; but he is saving—you know for what, ma'am."

And, indeed, Mrs. Mugford *did* know ; and so did Mrs. Pendennis and Mrs. Brandon. And these three women worked themselves into a perfect fever, interesting themselves for Mr. Firmin. And Mugford, in his rough, funny way, used to say, "Mr. P., a certain Mr. Heff has come and put our noses out of joint. He has, as sure as my name is Hem. And I am getting quite jealous of our sub-editor, and that is the long and short of it. But it's good to see him haw-haw Bickerton if ever they meet in the office, that it is ! Bickerton won't bully *him* any more, I promise you ! "

The conclaves and conspiracies of these women were endless in Philip's behalf. One day, I let the Little Sister out of my house with a handkerchief to her eyes, and in a great state of flurry and excitement, which perhaps communicates itself to the gentleman who passes her at his own door. The gentleman's wife is, on her part, not a little moved and excited. "What do you think Mrs. Brandon says ? Philip is learning shorthand. He says he does not think he is clever enough to be a writer of any mark ;—but he can be a reporter, and with this, and his place at Mr. Mugford's, he thinks he can earn enough to—— Oh, he is a fine fellow ! " I suppose feminine emotion stopped the completion of this speech. But when Mr. Philip slouched into dinner that day, his hostess did homage before him ; she loved him : she treated him with a tender respect and sympathy which her like are ever wont to bestow upon brave and honest men in misfortune.

Why should not Mr. Philip Firmin, barrister-at-law, bethink him that he belonged to a profession which has helped very many men to competence, and not a few to wealth and honors? A barrister might surely hope for as good earnings as could be made by a newspaper reporter. We all know instances of men who, having commenced their careers as writers for the press, had carried on the legal profession simultaneously, and attained the greatest honors of the bar and the bench. "Can I sit in a Pump Court garret waiting for attorneys?" asked poor Phil; "I shall break my heart before they come. My brains are not worth much: I should addle them altogether in poring over law books. I am not at all a clever fellow you see; and I haven't the ambition and obstinate will to succeed which carry on many a man with no greater capacity than my own. I may have as good brains as Bickerton, for example: but I am not so *bumptious* as he is. By claiming the first place wherever he goes, he gets it very often. My dear friends, don't you see how modest I am? There never was a man less likely to get on than myself—you must own that; and I tell you that Charlotte and I must look forward to a life of poverty, of cheese-parings, and second floor lodgings at Pentonville or Islington. That's about my mark. I would let her off, only I know she would not take me at my word—the dear little thing! She has set her heart upon a hulking pauper: that's the truth. And I tell you what I am going to do. I am going seriously to learn the profession of poverty, and make myself master of it. What's the price of cowheel and tripe? You don't know. I do; and the right place to buy 'em. I am as good a judge of sprats as any man in London. My tap in life is to be small beer henceforth, and I am growing quite to like it, and think it is brisk, and pleasant, and wholesome." There was not a little truth in Philip's account of himself, and his capacities and incapacities. Doubtless, he was not born to make a great name for himself in the world. But do we like those only who are famous? As well say we will only give our regard to men who have ten thousand a year, or are more than six feet high.

While of his three female friends and advisers, my wife admired Philip's humility, Mrs. Brandon and Mrs. Mugford were rather disappointed at his want of spirit, and to think that he aimed so low. I shall not say which side Firmin's biographer took in this matter. Was it my business to applaud or rebuke him for being humble-minded, or was I called upon to advise at all? My amiable reader, acknowledge that you and I in life pretty much go our own way. We eat the dishes we like because we like them, not because our neighbor relishes them. We rise early, or sit up late ; we work, idle, smoke, or what not, because we choose so to do, not because the doctor orders. Philip, then, was like you and me, who will have our own way when we can. Will we not ? If you won't, you do not deserve it. Instead of hungering after a stalled ox, he was accustoming himself to be content with a dinner of herbs. Instead of braving the tempest, he chose to take in sail, creep along shore, and wait for calmer weather.

So, on Tuesday of every week let us say, it was this modest sub-editor's duty to begin snipping and pasting paragraphs for the ensuing Saturday's issue. He cut down the parliamentary speeches, giving due favoritism to the orators of the *Pall Mall Gazette* party, and meagre outlines of their opponent's discourses. If the leading public men on the side of the *Pall Mall Gazette* gave entertainments, you may be sure they were duly chronicled in the fashionable intelligence ; if one of their party wrote a book it was pretty sure to get praise from the critic. I am speaking of simple old days, you understand. Of course there is *no* puffing, or jobbing, or false praise, or unfair censure now. Every critic knows what he is writing about, and writes with no aim but to tell truth.

Thus Philip, the dandy of two years back, was content to wear the shabbiest old coat ; Philip, the Philippus of one-and-twenty, who rode showy horses, and rejoiced to display his horse and person in the park, now humbly took his place in an omnibus, and only on occasions indulged in a cab. From the roof of the larger vehicle he would salute his friends with perfect affability, and stare down on his aunt as she passed in her barouche. He never could be quite made to acknowledge that she purposely would not see him ; or he would attribute her blindness to the quarrel which they had had, not to his poverty and present position. As for his cousin Ringwood, "That fellow would commit any baseness," Philip acknowledged ; "and it is I who have cut *him*," our friend averred.

A real danger was lest our friend should in his poverty become more haughty and insolent than he had been in his days of better fortune, and that he should make companions of men who were not his equals. Whether was it better for him to be slighted in a fashionable club, or to swagger at the head of the company in a tavern parlor ? This was the danger we might fear for Firmin. It was impossible not to confess that he was choosing to take a lower place in the world than that to which he had been born.

"Do you mean that Philip is lowered, because he is poor?" asked an angry lady, to whom this remark was made by her husband—man and wife being both very good friends to Mr. Firmin.

"My dear," replies the worldling of a husband, "suppose Philip were to take a fancy to buy a donkey and sell cabbages? He would be doing no harm; but there is no doubt he would lower himself in the world's estimation."

"Lower himself!" says the lady, with a toss of her head. "No man lowers himself by pursuing an honest calling. No man!"

"Very good. There is Grundsell, the greengrocer, out of Tuthill Street, who waits at our dinners. Instead of asking him to wait, we should beg him to sit down at table; or perhaps *we* should wait, and stand with a napkin behind Grundsell."

"Nonsense!"

"Grundsell's calling is strictly honest, unless he abuses his opportunities, and smuggles away——"

"——smuggles away stuff and nonsense!"

"Very good; Grundsell is *not* a fitting companion, then, for us, or the nine little Grundsells for our children. Then why should Philip give up the friends of his youth, and forsake a club for a tavern parlor? You can't say our little friend, Mrs. Brandon, good as she is, is a fitting companion for him?"

"If he had a good little wife, he would have a companion of his own degree; and he would be twice as happy; and he would be out of all danger and temptation—and the best thing he can do is to marry directly!" cries the lady. "And, my dear, I think I shall write to Charlotte and ask her to come and stay with us."

There was no withstanding this argument. As long as Charlotte was with us we were sure that Philip would be out of harm's way, and seek for no other company. There was a snug little bedroom close by the quarters inhabited by our own children. My wife pleased herself by adorning this chamber, and uncle Mac happening to come to London on business about this time, the young lady came over to us under his convoy, and I should like to describe the meeting between her and Mr. Philip in our parlor. No doubt it was very edifying. But my wife and I were not present, *vous conçevez.* We only heard one shout of surprise and delight from Philip as he went into the room where the young lady was waiting. We had but said, "Go into the parlor, Philip. You will find your old friend Major Mac there. He has come to London on business, and has news of——" There was no need to speak, for here Philip straightway bounced into the room.

And then came the shout. And then out came Major Mac, with such a droll twinkle in his eyes! What artifices and hypocrisies had we not to practice previously, so as to keep our secret from our children, who assuredly would have discovered it! I must tell you that the *paterfamilias* had guarded against the innocent prattle and inquiries of the children regarding the preparation of the little bedroom, by informing them that it was intended for Miss Grigsby the governess, with whose advent they had long been threatened. And one of our girls, when the unconscious Philip arrived, said, "Philip, if you go into the parlor, you will find *Miss Grigsby, the governess, there.*" And then Philip entered into that parlor, and then arose that shout, and then out came uncle Mac, and then, &c., &c. And we called Charlotte Miss Grigsby all dinner-time; and we called her Miss Grigsby next day; and the more we called her Miss Grigsby the more we all laughed. And the baby, who could not speak plain yet, called her Miss Gibby, and laughed loudest of all; and it was such fun. But I think Philip and Charlotte had the best of the fun, my dears, though they may not have laughed quite so loud as we did.

As for Mrs. Brandon, who, you may be sure, speedily came to pay us a visit, Charlotte blushed, and looked quite beautiful when she went up and kissed the Little Sister. "He *have* told you about me, then!" she said, in her soft little voice, smoothing the young lady's brown hair. "Should I have known him at all but for you, and did you not save his life for me when he was ill?" asked Miss Baynes. "And mayn't I love everybody who loves him?" she asked. And we left these women alone for a quarter of an hour, during which they became the most intimate friends in the world. And all our household, great and small, including the nurse, (a woman of a most jealous, domineering, and uncomfortable fidelity,) thought well of our gentle young guest, and welcomed Miss Grigsby.

Charlotte, you see, is not so exceedingly handsome as to cause other women to perjure themselves by protesting that she is no great things after all. At the period with which we are concerned, she certainly had a lovely complexion, which her black dress set off, perhaps. And when Philip used to come into the room, she had always a fine garland of roses ready to offer him, and growing upon her cheeks, the moment he appeared. Her manners are so entirely unaffected and simple that they can't be otherwise than good: for is she not grateful truthful, unconscious of self, easily pleased and interested in others?   Is she very witty?   I never said so—though that she appreciated *some* men's wit (whose names need not be mentioned) I cannot doubt.   " I say," cries Philip, on that memorable first night of her arrival, and when she and other ladies had gone to bed, "by George ! isn't she glorious, I say !   What can I have done to win such a pure little heart as that ?   *Non sum dignus.*   It is too much happiness—too much, by George !"   And his voice breaks behind his pipe, and he squeezes two fists into eyes that are brimful of joy and thanks.   Where Fortune bestows such a bounty as this, I think we need not pity a man for what she withdraws.   As Philip walks away at midnight, (walks away ? is turned out of doors ; or surely he would have gone on talking till dawn,) with the rain beating in his face, and fifty or a hundred pounds for all his fortune in his pocket, I think there goes one of the happiest of men—the happiest and richest.   For is he not possessor of a treasure which he could not buy, or would not sell, for all the wealth of the world ?

My wife may say what she will, but she assuredly is answerable for the invitation to Miss Baynes, and for all that ensued in consequence.   At a hint that she would be a welcome guest in our house, in London, where all her heart and treasure lay, Charlotte Baynes gave up straightway her dear aunt at Tours, who had been kind to her ; her dear uncle, her dear mamma, and all her dear brothers—following that natural law which ordains that a woman, under certain circumstances, shall resign home, parents, brothers, sisters, for the sake of that one individual who is henceforth to be dearer to her than all.   Mrs. Baynes, the widow, growled a complaint at her daughter's ingratitude, but did not refuse her consent.   She may have known that little Hely, Charlotte's volatile admirer, had fluttered off to another flower by this time, and that a pursuit of that butterfly was in vain : or she may have heard that he was going to pass the spring—the butterfly season—in London, and hoped that he perchance might again light on her girl.   Howbeit, she was glad enough that her daughter should accept an invitation to our house, and owned that as yet the poor child's share of this life's pleasures had been but small.   Charlotte's modest little trunks were again packed, then, and the poor child was sent off, I won't say with how small a provision of pocket-money, by her mother.   But the thrifty woman had but little, and of it was determined to give as little as she could.   " Heaven will provide for my child," she would piously say : and hence interfered very little with those agents whom heaven

sent to befriend her children. " Her mother told Charlotte
that she would send her some money next Tuesday," the Major
told us ; " but, between ourselves, I doubt whether she will.
Between ourselves, my sister-in-law is always going to give
money next Tuesday : but somehow Wednesday comes, and
the money has not arrived. I could not let the little maid be
without a few guineas, and have provided her out of a half-pay
purse ; but mark me, that pay-day Tuesday will never come."
Shall I deny or confirm the worthy Major's statement ? Thus
far I will say, that Tuesday most certainly came ; and a letter
from her mamma to Charlotte, which said that one of her
brothers and a younger sister were going to stay with aunt
Mac ; and that as Char was so happy with her most hospitable
and kind friends, a fond widowed mother, who had given up all
pleasures for herself, would not interfere to prevent a darling
child's happiness.

It has been said that three women, whose names have been
given up, were conspiring in the behalf of this young person
and the young man her sweetheart. Three days after Charlotte's arrival at our house, my wife persists in thinking that a
drive into the country would do the child good, orders a
brougham, dresses Charlotte in her best, and trots away to see
Mrs. Mugford at Hampstead. Mrs. Brandon is at Mrs. Mugford's, of course quite by chance : and I feel sure that Charlotte's friend compliments Mrs. Mugford upon her garden, upon
her nursery, upon her luncheon, upon everything that is hers.
" Why, dear me," says Mrs. Mugford (as the ladies discourse
upon a certain subject), " what does it matter ? Me and Mugford married on two pound a week ; and on two pound a week
my dear eldest children were born. It was a hard struggle
sometimes, but we were all the happier for it ; and I'm sure if
a man won't risk a little he don't deserve much. I know *I*
would risk, if I were a man, to marry such a pretty young dear.
And I should take a young man to be but a mean-spirited
fellow who waited and went shilly-shallying when he had but
to say the word and be happy. I thought Mr. F. was a brave,
courageous gentleman, I did, Mrs. Brandon. Do you want me
for to have a bad opinion of him ? My dear, a little of that
cream. It's very good. We 'ad a dinner yesterday, and a cook
down from town, on purpose." This speech, with appropriate
imitations of voice and gesture, was repeated to the present
biographer by the present biographer's wife, and he now began
to see in what webs and meshes of conspiracy these artful
women had enveloped the subject of the present biography.

Like Mrs. Brandon, and the other matron, Charlotte's friend, Mrs. Mugford became interested in the gentle young creature, and kissed her kindly, and made her a present on going away. It was a brooch in the shape of a thistle, if I remember aright, set with amethysts and a lovely Scottish stone called, I believe a cairngorm. "She ain't no style about her; and I confess, from a general's daughter, brought up on the Continent, I should have expected better. But we'll show her a little of the world and the opera, Brandon, and she'll do very well, of that I make no doubt." And Mrs. Mugford took Miss Baynes to the opera, and pointed out the other people of fashion there assembled. And delighted Charlotte was. I make no doubt there was a young gentleman of our acquaintance at the back of the box who was very happy too. And this year, Philip's kinsman's wife, LADY RINGWOOD, had a box, in which Philip saw her and her daughters, and little Ringwood Twysden paying assiduous court to her ladyship. They met in the crush-room by chance again, and Lady Ringwood looked hard at Philip and the blushing young lady on his arm. And it happened that Mrs. Mugford's carriage—the little one-horse trap which opens and shuts so conveniently—and Lady Ringwood's tall, emblazoned chariot of state, stopped the way together. And from the tall emblazoned chariot the ladies looked not unkindly at the trap which contained the beloved of Philip's heart : and the carriages departed each on its way ; and Ringwood Twysden, seeing his cousin advancing towards him, turned very pale, and dodged at a double quick down an arcade. But he need not have been afraid of Philip. Mr. Firmin's heart was all softness and benevolence at that time. He was thinking of those sweet, sweet eyes that had just glanced to him a tender good-night ; of that little hand which a moment since had hung with fond pressure on his arm. Do you suppose in such a frame of mind he had leisure to think of a nauseous little reptile crawling behind him ? He was so happy that night, that Philip was King Philip again. And he went to the "Haunt," and sang his song of *Garryowen na gloria*, and greeted the boys assembled, and spent at least three shillings over his supper and drinks. But the next day being Sunday, Mr. Firmin was at Westminster Abbey, listening to the sweet church chants, by the side of the very same young person whom he had escorted to the opera on the night before. They sat together so close that one must have heard exactly as well as the other. I dare say it is edifying to listen to anthems à *deux*. And how complimentary to the clergyman to have to wish that the sermon was longer! Through the vast cathedral aisles the organ notes peal gloriously. Ruby and topaz and amethyst blaze from the great church windows. Under the tall arcades the young people went together. Hand in hand they passed, and thought no ill.

Do gentle readers begin to tire of this spectacle of billing and cooing? I have tried to describe Mr. Philip's love affairs with as few words and in as modest phrases as may be—omitting the raptures, the passionate vows, the reams of correspondence, and the usual commonplaces of his situation. And yet, my dear madam, though you and I may be past the age of billing and cooing, though your ringlets, which I remember a lovely auburn, are now—well—are now a rich purple and green black, and my brow may be as bald as a cannon-ball ;—I say, though we are old, we are not too old to forget. We may not care about the pantomime much now, but we like to take the young folks, and see them rejoicing. From the window where I write, I can look down into the garden of a certain square. In that garden I can at this moment see a young gentleman and lady of my acquaintance pacing up and down. They are talking some such talk as Milton imagines our first parents engaged in ; and yonder garden is a paradise to my young friends. Did they choose to look outside the railings of the square, or at any other objects than each other's noses, they might see—the tax-gatherer we will say—with his book, knocking at one door, the doctor's brougham at a second, a hatchment over the windows of a third mansion, the baker's boy discoursing with the housemaid over the railings of a fourth. But what to them are these phenomena of life? Arm in arm my young folks go pacing up and down their Eden, and discoursing about that happy time which I suppose is now drawing near, about that charming little snuggery for which the furniture is ordered, and to which, miss, your old friend and very humble servant will take the liberty of forwarding his best regards and a neat silver teapot. I dare say, with these young people, as with Mr. Philip and Miss Charlotte, all occurrences of life seem to have reference to that event which forms the subject of their perpetual longing and contemplation. There is the doctor's brougham driving away, and Imogene says to Alonzo, "What anguish I shall have if you are ill!" Then there is the carpenter putting up the hatchment. "Ah, my love, if you were to die, I think they might put up a hatchment for both of us," says Alonzo, with a killing sigh. Both sympathise with Mary and the baker's boy whispering over the railings. Go to, gentle baker's boy, we also know what it is to love !

The whole soul and strength of Charlotte and Philip being bent upon marriage, I take leave to put in a document which Philip received at this time ; and can imagine that it occasioned no little sensation :—

> " *Astor House, New York.*
>
> " AND so you are returned to the great city—to the *fumum,* the *strepitum,* and I sincerely hope the *opes* of our Rome ! Your own letters are but brief ; but I have an occasional correspondent (there are few, alas ! who remember *the exile !*) who keeps me *au courant* of my Philip's history, and tells me that you are industrious, that you are cheerful, that you prosper; Cheerfulness is the companion of Industry, Prosperity their offspring. That that prosperity may attain *the fullest growth,* is an absent father's fondest prayer ! Perhaps ere long I shall be able to announce to you that I too am prospering. I am engaged in pursuing a scientific discovery here (it is medical, and connected with my own profession), of which the results *ought* to lead to Fortune, unless the jade has for ever deserted George Brand Firmin ! So you have embarked in the drudgery of the press, and have become a member of *the fourth estate.* It has been despised, and press-man and poverty were for a long time supposed to be synonymous. But the power, the wealth of the press are daily developing, and they will increase yet further. I confess I should have liked to hear that my Philip was pursuing his profession of the bar, at which honor, splendid competence, nay, aristocratic rank, are the prizes of *the bold, the industrious, and the deserving.* Why should you not?— should I not still hope that you may gain legal eminence and position ? A father who has had much to suffer, who is descending the vale of years alone and in a distant land, would be soothed in his exile if he thought his son would one day be able to repair the shattered fortunes of his race. But it is not yet, I fondly think, too late. You may yet qualify for the bar, and one of its prizes may fall to you. I confess it was not without a pang of grief I heard from our kind little friend Mrs. B., you were studying shorthand in order to become a newspaper reporter. And has Fortune, then, been so relentless to me that my son is to be compelled to follow such a calling ? I shall try and be resigned. I had hoped higher things for you—for me.
>
> " My dear boy, with regard to your romantic attachment for Miss Baynes, which our good little Brandon narrates to me, in her *peculiar orthography,* but with much *touching simplicity,*—I make it a rule not to say a word of comment, of warning, or remonstrance. As sure as you are your father's son, you will take your own line in any matter of attachment to a woman, and all the fathers in the world won't stop you. In Philip of four-and-twenty I recognize his father thirty years ago. My father scolded, entreated, quarrelled with me, never forgave me. I will learn to be more generous towards my son. I may grieve, but I bear you no malice. If ever I achieve wealth again, you shall not be deprived of it. I suffered so myself from a harsh father, that I will never be one to my son !
>
> " As you have put on the livery of the Muses, and regularly entered yourself of the Fraternity of the Press, what say you to a little addition to your income by letters addressed to my friend, the editor of the new journal, called here the *Gazette of the Upper Ten Thousand.* It is *the* fashionable journal published here ; and your qualifications are precisely those which would make your services valuable as a contributor. Doctor Geraldine, the editor, is not, I believe, a relative of the Leinster family, but a self-made man, who arrived in this country some years since, poor, and an exile from his native country. He advocates Repeal politics in Ireland : but with these of course you need have nothing to do. And he is much too liberal to expect these from his contributors. I have been of service professionally to Mrs. Geraldine and himself. My friend of the *Emerald* introduced me to the doctor. Terrible enemies in print, in private they are perfectly good friends, and the little passages of arms between the two journalists serve rather to amuse than to irritate. ' The grocer's boy from Ormond Quay ' (Geraldine once, it appears, engaged in that useful but humble calling), and the 'miscreant from Cork'—the editor of the *Emerald* comes from that city—assail each other in public, but drink whisky-and-water *galore* in private. If you write for Geraldine, of course you will say nothing disrespectful about *grocers' boys. His dollars are good silver,* of that you may be sure. Dr. G. knows a part of your history : he knows that you are now fairly engaged in literary pursuits ; that you are a man of education, a gentleman, a man of the world, a man of courage. I have answered for your possessing all these qualities. (The doctor, in his droll, humorous way, said that if you were a chip of the old block you would be just what he called ' the grit.') Political treatises are not so much wanted as personal news regarding the notabilities of London, and these, I assured him, you were the very man to be able to furnish. You, who know everybody,

who have lived with the great world—the world of lawyers, the world of artists, the world of the university—have already had an experience to which few gentlemen of the press can boast of, and may turn that experience to profit. Suppose you were to trust a little to your imagination in composing these letters? there can be no harm in being *poetical*. Suppose an *intelligent correspondent* writes that he has met the D-ke of W-ll-ngt-n, had a private interview with the Pr-m-r, and so forth, who is to say him nay? And this is the kind of talk our *gobe-mouches* of New York delight in. My worthy friend, Doctor Geraldine, for example—between ourselves his name is Finnigan, but his private history is *strictly entre nous*—when he first came to New York astonished the people by the copiousness of his anecdotes regarding the *English aristocracy*, of whom he knows as much as he does of the Court of Pekin. He was smart, ready, sarcastic, amusing ; he found readers : from one success he advanced to another, and the *Gazette of the Upper Ten Thousand* is likely to make *this worthy man's fortune*. You really may be serviceable to him, and may justly earn the *liberal remuneration* which he offers for a weekly letter. Anecdotes of men and women of fashion—the more gay and lively the more welcome—the *quicquid agunt homines*, in a word,—should be the *farrago libelli*. Who are the reigning beauties of London? and Beauty, you know, has a rank and fashion of its own Has any one lately won or lost on the turf or at play? What are the clubs talking about? Are there any duels? What is the last scandal? Does the good old Duke keep his health? Is that affair over between the Duchess of This and Captain That?

" Such is the information which our *badauds* here like to have, and for which my friend the doctor will pay at the rate of —— dollars per letter. Your name need not appear at all. The remuneration is certain. *C'est à prendre ou à laisser*, as our lively neighbors say. Write in the first place in confidence to me ; and in whom can you confide more safely than in your father?

" You will, of course, pay your respects to your relative the new Lord of Ringwood. For a young man whose family is so powerful as yours, there can surely be no derogation in entertaining some feudal respect, and who knows whether and how soon Sir John Ringwood may be able to help his cousin? By the way, Sir John is a Whig, and your paper is a Conservative. But you are, above all, *homme du monde*. In such a subordinate place as you occupy with the *Pall Mall Gazette*, a man's private politics do not surely count at all. If Sir John Ringwood, your kinsman, sees any way of helping you, so much the better, and of course your politics will be those of your family. I have no knowledge of him. He was a very quiet man at college, where, I regret to say, your father's friends were not of the quiet sort at all. I trust I have repented. I have sown my wild oats. And ah! how pleased I shall be to hear that my Philip has bent *his* proud head a little, and is ready to submit more than he used of old to the customs of the world. Call upon Sir John, then. As a Whig gentleman of large estate, I need not tell you that he will expect *respect* from you. He is your kinsman ; the representative of your grandfather's gallant and noble race. He bears the name your mother bore. To *her* my Philip was always gentle, and for her sake you will comply with the wishes of

" Your affectionate father,
" G. B. F."

" I have not said a word of compliment to mademoiselle. I wish her so well that I own I wish she were about to marry a richer suitor than my dear son. Will fortune ever permit me to embrace my daughter-in-law, and take your children on my knee? You will speak kindly to them of their grandfather, will you not? Poor General Baynes, I have heard, used violent and unseemly language regarding me, which I most heartily pardon. I am grateful when I think *that I never did General B. an injury*: grateful and proud to accept benefits from my own son. These I treasure up in my heart ; and still hope I shall be able to repay with something more substantial than my fondest prayers. Give my best wishes, then, to Miss Charlotte, and try and teach her to think kindly of her Philip's father."

Miss Charlotte Baynes, who kept the name of Miss Grigsby, the governess amongst all the roguish children of a facetious father, was with us one month, and her mamma expressed great cheerfulness at her absence, and at the thought that she had found such good friends. After two months, her uncle, Major MacWhirter, returned from visiting his relations in the North, and offered to take his niece back to France again. He made this proposition with the jollyest air in the world, and as if his niece would jump for joy to go back to her mother. But to the

Major's astonishment, Miss Baynes turned quite pale, ran to her hostess, flung herself into that lady's arms, and then there began an osculatory performance which perfectly astonished the good Major.   Charlotte's friend, holding Miss Baynes tight in her embrace, looked fiercely at the Major over the girl's shoulder, and defied him to take her away from that sanctuary.

"Oh, you dear, good friend!" Charlotte gurgled out, and sobbed I know not what more expressions of fondness and gratitude.

But the truth is, that two sisters, or mother and daughter, could not love each other more heartily than these two personages.   Mother and daughter forsooth!   You should have seen Charlotte's piteous look when sometimes the conviction would come on her that she ought at length to go home to mamma ; such a look as I can fancy Iphigenia casting on Agamemnon, when, in obedience to a painful sense of duty, he was about to —to use the sacrificial knife.   No, we all loved her.   The children would howl at the idea of parting with their Miss Grigsby.   Charlotte, in return, helped them to very pretty lessons in music and French—served hot, as it were, from her own recent studies at Tours—and a good daily governess operated on the rest of their education to everybody's satisfaction.

And so months rolled on and our young favorite still remained with us.   Mamma fed the little maid's purse with occasional remittances ; and begged her hostess to supply her with all necessary articles from the milliner.   Afterwards, it is true, Mrs. General Baynes * *   But why enter upon these painful family disputes in a chapter which has been devoted to sentiment ?

As soon as Mr. Firmin received the letter above faithfully copied, (with the exception of the pecuniary offer, which I do not consider myself at liberty to divulge,) he hurried down from Thornhaugh Street to Westminster.   He dashed by Buttons, the page ; he took no notice of my wondering wife at the drawing-room door ; he rushed to the second floor, bursting open the schoolroom door, where Charlotte was teaching our dear third daughter to play "In my Cottage near a Wood."

"Charlotte! Charlotte!" he cried out.

"La, Philip! don't you see Miss Grigsby is giving us lessons?" said the children.

But he would not listen to those wags, and still beckoned Charlotte to him.   That young woman rose up and followed him out of the door ; indeed she would have followed him out of the window ; and there, on the stairs, they read Doctor Firmin's letter, with their heads quite close together, you understand.

" Two hundred a year more," said Philip, his heart throbbing so that he could hardly speak ; " and your fifty—and two hundred the *Gazette*—and——"

" Oh, Philip ! " was all Charlotte could say, and then—— There was a pretty group for the children to see, and for an artist to draw !

CHAPTER XXXII.

WAYS AND MEANS.

OF course any man of the world, who is possessed of decent prudence, will perceive that the idea of marrying on four hundred and fifty pounds a year, so secured as was Master Philip's income, was preposterous and absurd. In the first place, you can't live on four hundred and fifty pounds a year, that is a certainty. People do live on less, I believe. But a life without a brougham, without a decent house, without claret for dinner, and a footman to wait, can hardly be called existence. Philip's income might fail any day. He might not please the American paper. He might quarrel with the *Pall Mall Gazette*. And then what would remain to him ? Only poor little Charlotte's fifty pounds a year ! So Philip's most intimate male friend—a man of the world, and with a good deal of experience—argued. Of course I was not surprised that Philip did not choose to take my advice ; though I did not expect he would become so violently angry, call names almost, and use most rude expressions, when, *at his express desire*, this advice was tendered to him. If he did not want it, why did he ask for it ? The advice might be unwelcome to him, but why did he choose to tell me at my own table, over my own claret, that it was the advice of a sneak and a worldling ? My good fellow, that claret, though it is a second growth, and I can afford no better, costs seventy-two shillings a dozen. How much is six times three hundred and sixty-five ? A bottle a day is the least you can calculate (the fellow would come to my house and drink two bottles to himself, with the utmost nonchalance). A bottle per diem of that light claret—of that second-growth stuff—costs one hundred and four guineas a year, do you understand ? or,

A LETTER FROM NEW YORK.

to speak plainly with you, *one hundred and nine pounds four shillings!*"

"Well," says Philip, "après? We'll do without. Meantime I will take what I can get!" and he tosses off about a pint as he speaks (these *mousseline* glass are not only enormous, but they break by dozens). He tosses off a pint of my Larose, and gives a great roar of laughter, as if he had said a good thing!

Philip Firmin *is* coarse and offensive at times, and Bickerton in holding this opinion is not altogether wrong.

"I'll drink claret when I come to you, old boy," he says, grinning; "and at home I will have whiskey-and-water."

"But suppose Charlotte is ordered claret!"

"Well, she can have it," says this liberal lover; "a bottle will last her a week."

"Don't you see," I shriek out, "that even a bottle a week costs something like—six by fifty-two—eighteen pounds a year!" (I own it is really only fifteen twelve; but, in the hurry of argument, a man *may* stretch a figure or so.) "Eighteen pounds for Charlotte's claret; as much, at least, you great boozy toper, for your whiskey and beer. Why, you actually want a tenth part of your income for the liquor you consume! And then clothes; and then lodging; and then coals; and then doctor's bills; and then pocket-money; and then sea-side for the little dears. Just have the kindness to add these things up, and you will find that you have about two-and-ninepence left to pay the grocer and the butcher."

"What you call prudence," says Philip, thumping the table, and, of course, breaking a glass, "I call cowardice—I call blasphemy! Do you mean, as a Christian man, to tell me that two young people and a family, if it should please heaven to send them one, cannot subsist upon five hundred pounds a year? Look round, sir, at the myriads of God's creatures who live, love, are happy and poor, and be ashamed of the wicked doubt which you utter!" And he starts up, and strides up and down the dining-room, curling his flaming mustache, and rings the bell fiercely, and says, "Johnson, I've broke a glass. Get me another."

In the drawing-room, my wife asks what we two were fighting about? And, as Charlotte is up stairs, telling the children stories as they are put to bed, or writing to her dear mamma, or what not, our friend bursts out with more rude and violent expressions than he had used in the dinner-room over my glasses which he was smashing, tells my own wife that I am an atheist, or at best a miserable skeptic and Sadducee: that I doubt of the goodness of heaven, and am not thankful for my daily bread. And, with one of her kindling looks directed towards the young man, of course my wife sides with him. Miss Char presently came down from the young folks, and went to the piano, and played us Beethoven's " Dream of Saint Jerome," which always soothes me, and charms me, so that I fancy it is a poem of Tennyson in music. And our children, as they sink off to sleep overhead, like to hear soft music, which soothes them into slumber, Miss Baynes says. And Miss Charlotte looks very pretty at her piano : and Philip lies gazing at her, with his great feet and hands tumbled over one of our arm-chairs. And the music, with its solemn cheer, makes us all very happy and kind-hearted, and ennobles us somehow as we listen. And my wife wears her *benedictory* look whenever she turns towards these young people. She has worked herself up to the opinion that yonder couple ought to marry. She can give chapter and verse for her belief. To doubt about the matter at all is wicked according to her notions. And there are certain points upon which, I humbly own, that I don't dare to argue with her.

When the women of the house have settled a matter, is there much use in man's resistance ? If my harem orders that I shall wear a yellow coat and pink trousers, I know that, before three months are over, I shall be walking about in *rose-tendre* and canary-colored garments. It is the perseverance which con-quers, the daily return to the object desired. Take my advice, my dear sir, when you see your womankind resolute about a matter, give up at once, and have a quiet life. Perhaps to one of these evening entertainments, where Miss Baynes played the piano, as she did very pleasantly, and Mr. Philip's great clumsy fist turned the leaves, little Mrs. Brandon would come tripping in, and as she surveyed the young couple, her remark would be, " Did you ever see a better suited couple ? " When I came home from chambers, and passed the dining-room door, my eldest daughter with a knowing face would bar the way and say, " You mustn't go in there, papa ! Miss Grigsby is there, and Master Philip is *not to be disturbed at his lessons !*" Mrs. Mugford had begun to arrange marriages between her young people and ours from the very first day she saw us ; and Mrs. M.'s ch. filly Toddles, rising two years, and our three-year old colt Billyboy, were rehearsing in the nursery the endless little comedy which the grown-up young persons were perform-ing in the drawing-room.

With the greatest frankness Mrs. Mugford gave her opinion

that Philip, with four or five hundred a year, would be no better than a sneak if he delayed to marry. How much had she and Mugford when *they* married, she would like to know? "Emily Street, Pentonville, was where *we* had apartments," she remarked; "we were pinched sometimes; but we owed nothing: and our housekeeping books I can show you." I believe Mrs. M. actually brought these dingy relics of her honeymoon for my wife's inspection. I tell you, my house was peopled with these friends of matrimony. Flies were for ever in requisition, and our boys were very sulky at having to sit for an hour at Schoolbred's, while certain ladies lingered there over blankets, tablecloths, and what not. Once I found my wife and Charlotte flitting about Wardour Street, the former lady much interested in a great Dutch cabinet, with a glass cupboard and corpulent drawers. And that cabinet was, ere long, carted off to Mrs. Brandon's, Thornhaugh Street; and in that glass cupboard there was presently to be seen a neat set of china for tea and breakfast. The end was approaching. That event, with which the third volume of the old novels used to close, was at hand. I am afraid our young people can't drive off from St. George's in a chaise and four, and that no noble relative will lend them his castle for the honeymoon. Well: some people cannot drive to happiness, even with four horses; and other folks can reach the goal on foot. My venerable Muse stoops down, unlooses her *cothurnus* with some difficulty, and prepares to fling that old shoe after the pair.

Tell, venerable Muse! what were the marriage gifts which friendship provided for Philip and Charlotte? Philip's cousin, Ringwood Twysden, came simpering up to me at "Bays's Club" one afternoon, and said: "I hear my precious cousin is going to marry. I think I shall send him a broom to sweep a crossin'." I was nearly going to say, "This was a piece of generosity to be expected from your father's son;" but the fact is, that I did not think of this withering repartee until I was crossing St. James's Park on my way home, when Twysden of course was out of ear-shot. A great number of my best witticisms have been a little late in making their appearance in the world. If we could but hear the *un*spoken jokes, how we should all laugh; if we could but speak them, how witty we should be! When you have left the room, you have no notion what clever things I was going to say when you baulked me by going away. Well, then, the fact is, the Twysden family gave Philip nothing on his marriage, being the exact sum of regard which they professed to have for him.

MRS. MAJOR MACWHIRTER gave the bride an Indian brooch, representing the Taj Mahal at Agra, which General Baynes had given to his sister-in-law in old days. At a later period, it is true, Mrs. Mac asked Charlotte for the brooch back again ; but this was when many family quarrels had raged between the relatives—quarrels which to describe at length would be to tax too much the writer and the readers of this history.

MRS. MUGFORD presented an elegant plated coffee-pot, six drawing-room almanacs (spoils of the *Pall Mall Gazette*), and fourteen richly cut jelly-glasses, most useful for negus if the young couple gave evening-parties ; for dinners they would not be able to afford.

MRS. BRANDON made an offering of two tablecloths and twelve dinner napkins, most beautifully worked, and I don't know how much house linen.

THE LADY OF THE PRESENT WRITER—Twelve tea-spoons in bullion, and a pair of sugar-tongs. Mrs. Baynes, Philip's mother-in-law, sent him also a pair of sugar-tongs, of a light manufacture, easily broken. He keeps a tong to the present day, and speaks very satirically regarding that relic.

PHILIP'S INN OF COURT—A bill for commons and Inn taxes, with the Treasurer's compliments.

And these, I think, formed the items of poor little Charlotte's meagre trousseau. Before Cinderella went to the ball she was almost as rich as our little maid. Charlotte's mother sent a grim consent to the child's marriage, but declined herself to attend it. She was ailing and poor. Her year's widowhood was just over. She had her other children to look after. My impression is that Mrs. Baynes thought that she would be out of Philip's power so long as she remained abroad, and that the General's savings would be secure from him. So she delegated her authority to Philip's friends in London, and sent her daughter a moderate wish for her happiness, which may or may not have profited the young people.

"Well, my dear, you are rich, compared to what I was, when I married," little Mrs. Brandon said to her young friend. "You will have a good husband. That is more than I had. You will have good friends ; and I was almost alone for a time, until it pleased God to befriend me." It was not without a feeling of awe that we saw these young people commence that voyage of life on which henceforth they were to journey together ; and I am sure that of the small company who accompanied them to the silent little chapel where they were joined in marriage there was not one who did not follow them with tender good wishes and heartfelt prayers. They had a little purse provided for a month's holiday. They had health, hope, good spirits, good friends. I have never learned that life's trials were over after marriage; only lucky is he who has a loving companion to share them. As for the lady with whom Charlotte had stayed before her marriage, she was in a state of the most lachrymose sentimentality. She sat on the bed in the chamber which the little maid had vacated. Her tears flowed copiously. She knew not why, she could not tell how the girl had wound herself round her maternal heart. And I think if heaven had decreed this young creature should be poor, it had sent her many blessings and treasures in compensation.

Every respectable man and woman in London will, of course, pity these young people, and reprobate the mad risk which they were running, and yet, by the influence and example of a sentimental wife probably, so madly sentimental have I become, that I own sometimes I almost fancy these misguided wretches were to be envied.

A melancholy little chapel it is where they were married, and stands hard by our house. We did not decorate the church with flowers, or adorn the beadles with white ribbons. We had, I must confess, a dreary little breakfast, not in the least enlivened by Mugford's jokes, who would make a speech *de circonstance*, which was not, I am thankful to say, reported in the *Pall Mall Gazette*. "We sha'n't charge you for advertising the marriage *there*, my dear," Mrs. Mugford said. "And I've already took it myself to Mr. Burjoyce." Mrs. Mugford had insisted upon pinning a large white favor upon John, who drove her from Hampstead: but that was the only ornament present at the nuptial ceremony, much to the disappointment of the good lady. There was a very pretty cake, with two doves in sugar, on the top, which the Little Sister made and sent, and no other hymeneal emblem. Our little girls as bridesmaids appeared, to be sure, in new bonnets and dresses, but everybody else looked so quiet and demure, that when we went into the church, three or four street urchins knocking about the gate, said, "Look at 'em. They're going to be 'ung." And so the words are spoken, and the indissoluble knot is tied. Amen. For better, for worse, for good days or evil, love each other, cling to each other, dear friends. Fulfil your course, and accomplish your life's toil. In sorrow, soothe each other; in illness, watch and tend. Cheer, fond wife, the husband's struggle; lighten his gloomy hours with your tender smiles, and

gladden his home with your love. Husband, father, whatso-
ever your lot, be your heart pure, your life honest. For the
sake of those who bear your name, let no bad action sully it. As
you look at those innocent faces, which ever tenderly greet you,
be yours, too, innocent, and your conscience without reproach.
As the young people kneel before the altar-railing, some such
thoughts as these pass through a friend's mind who witnesses
the ceremony of their marriage. Is not all we hear in that
place meant to apply to ourselves, and to be carried away for
everyday cogitation?

After the ceremony we sign the book, and walk back demurely to breakfast. And Mrs. Mugford does not conceal her
disappointment at the small preparations made for the reception of the marriage party. "I call it shabby, Brandon; and
I speak my mind. No favors. Only your cake. No speeches
to speak of. No lobster-salad : and wine on the sideboard.
I thought your Queen Square friends knew how to do the thing
better! When one of *my* gurls is married, I promise you we
sha'n't let her go out of the back door ; and at least we shall
have the best four grays that Newman's can furnish. It's my
belief your young friend is getting too fond of money, Brandon,
and so I have told Mugford." But these, you see, were only
questions of taste. Good Mrs. Mugford's led her to a green
satin dress and pink turban, when other ladies were in gray or
quiet colors. The intimacy between our two families dwindled
immediately after Philip's marriage ; Mrs. M., I am sorry to
say, setting us down as shabby-genteel people, and she couldn't
bear screwing—never could!

Well : the speeches were spoken. The bride was kissed,
and departed with her bridegroom : they had not even a valet
and lady's-maid to bear them company. The route of the happy
pair was to be Canterbury, Folkestone, Boulogne, Amiens,
Paris, and Italy perhaps, if their little stock of pocket-money
would serve them so far. But the very instant when half was
spent, it was agreed that these young people should turn their
faces homeward again ; and meanwhile the printer and Mugford
himself agreed that they would do Mr. Sub-editor's duty. How
much had they in the little purse for their pleasure-journey?
That is no business of ours, surely ; but with youth, health, happiness, love, amongst their possessions, I don't think our young
friends had need to be discontented. Away then they drive to
their cab to the railway station. Farewell, and heaven bless
you, Charlotte and Philip! I have said how I found my wife
crying in her favorite's vacant bedroom. The marriage table

did coldly furnish forth a funeral kind of dinner. The cold chicken choked us all, and the jelly was but a sickly compound to my taste, though it was the Little Sister's most artful manufacture. I own for one I was quite miserable. I found no comfort at clubs, nor could the last new novel fix my attention. I saw Philip's eyes and heard the warble of Charlotte's sweet voice. I walked off from "Bays's," and through Old Parr Street, where Philip had lived, and his parents entertained me as a boy; and then tramped to Thornhaugh Street, rather ashamed of myself. The maid said mistress was in Mr. Philip's rooms, the two pair,—and what was that I heard on the piano as I entered the apartment? Mrs. Brandon sat there hemming some chintz window-curtains, or bed-curtains, or what not: by her side sat my own eldest girl stitching away very resolutely; and at the piano—the piano which Philip had bought—there sat my own wife picking out that "Dream of Saint Jerome," of Beethoven, which Charlotte used to play so delicately. We had tea out of Philip's tea-things, and a nice hot cake, which consoled some of us. But I have known few evenings more melancholy than that. It felt like the first night at school after the holidays, when we all used to try and appear cheerful, you know. But ah! how dismal the gayety was: and how dreary that lying awake in the night, and thinking of the happy days just over.

The way in which we looked forward for letters from our bride and bridegroom was quite a curiosity. At length a letter arrived from these personages: and as it contains no secret, I take the liberty to print it *in extenso.*

"*Amiens, Friday. Paris, Saturday.*

"DEAREST FRIENDS,—(For the dearest friends you *are* to us, and will continue to be *as long as we live*)—We perform our promise of writing to you to say that we are *well*, and *safe*, and *happy!* Philip says I mustn't use *dashes*, but I can't help it. He says, he supposes I am dashing off a letter. You know his joking way. Oh, what a blessing it is to see him so happy. And if he is happy I am. I tremble to think *how* happy. He sits opposite me, smoking his cigar, looking so noble! *I like it*, and I went to our room and *brought him this one.* He says, 'Char, if I were to say bring me your head, you would order a waiter to cut it off.' Pray, did I not promise three days ago to love, honor, and obey him, and am I going to break my promise already? I hope not. I pray not. All my life I hope I shall be trying to keep that promise of mine. We liked Canterbury almost as much as dear Westminster. We had an open carriage and took *a glorious drive* to Folkestone, and in the crossing Philip was ill, and I wasn't. And he looked very droll; and he was in a dreadful bad humor; and that was my first appearance as nurse. I think I should like him to be *a little* ill sometimes, so that I may sit up and take care of him. We went through the cords at the custom-house at Boulogne; and I remembered how, two years ago, I passed through those very cords with my poor papa, and *we* stood outside, and saw us! We went to the 'Hôtel des Bains.' We walked about the town. We went to the Tintelleries, where we used to live, and to your house in the Haute Ville, where I remember *everything as if it was yesterday.* Don't you remember, as we were walking one day, you said, 'Charlotte, there is the steamer coming; there is the smoke of his funnel;' and I said, 'What steamer?' and you said, 'The Philip, to be sure.' And he came up, smoking his pipe! We passed over and over the old ground where we used to walk. We went to the pier, and gave money to the poor little hunchback who plays the guitar, and he said, '*Merci, madame.*' How droll it sounded? And that good kind Marie at the 'Hôtel des Bains' remembered us, and called us '*mes enfans.*' And if you were not the most good-natured woman *in the world*, I think I should be ashamed to write such nonsense.

"Think of Mrs. Brandon having knitted me a purse, which she gave me as we went away from *dear, dear* Queen Square; and when I opened it, there were five sovereigns in it! When we found what the purse contained, Philip used one of his great *jurons* (as he always does when he is most tender-hearted), and he said that woman was an angel, and that we would keep those five sovereigns, and never change them. Ah! I am thankful my husband has such friends! I will love all who love him—you most of all. For were not you the means of bringing this noble heart to me? I fancy I have known *bigger people*, since I have known you, and some of your friends. Their talk is simpler, their thoughts are greater than—those with whom I used to live. P. says, heaven has given Mrs. Brandon such a great heart, that she must have a good intellect. If loving my Philip be wisdom, I know some one who will be very wise!

"If I was not in a very great hurry to see mamma, Philip said we might stop a day at Amiens. And we went to the Cathedral, and to whom do you think it is dedicated? to *my* saint: to SAINT FIRMIN! and oh! I prayed to heaven to give me strength to devote my life to *my saint's service*, to love him always, as a pure, true wife; in sickness to guard him, in sorrow to soothe him. I will try and *learn* and *study*, not to make my intellect equal to his—very few women can hope for that—but that I may better comprehend him, and give him a companion more worthy of him. I wonder whether there are many men in the world as clever as our husbands? Though Philip is so modest. He says he is not clever *at all*. Yet I know he is, and grander somehow than other men. I said nothing, but I used to listen at Queen Square; and some who came who thought best of themselves, seemed to me pert, and worldly, and small; and some were like princes somehow. My Philip is one of the princes. Ah, dear friend! may I not give thanks where thanks are due, that I am chosen to be the wife of a true gentleman? Kind, and brave, and loyal Philip! Honest and generous,—above deceit or selfish scheme. Oh! I hope it is not wrong to be so happy!

"We wrote to mamma and dear Madame Smolensk to say we were coming. Mamma finds Madame de Valentinois' boarding-house even dearer than dear Madame Smolensk's. I *don't mean* a pun! She says she has found out that Madame de Valentinois' real name is Cornichon; that she was a person of the worst character, and that cheating at *écarté* was practised at her house. She took up her own two francs and another two-franc piece from the card-table, saying that Colonel Boulotte was cheating, and by rights the money was hers. She is going to leave Madame de Valentinois at the end of her month, or as soon as her children, who have the measles, can move. She desired that on no account I would come to see her at Madame V.'s; and she brought Philip 12*l.* 10*s.* in five-franc pieces, which she laid down on the table before him, and said it was my first quarter's payment. It is not due yet, I know. 'But do you think I will be beholden,' says she, 'to a man like you!' And P. shrugged his shoulders, and put the *rouleau* of silver pieces into a drawer. He did not say a word, but of course, I saw he was ill pleased. 'What shall we do with your fortune, Char?' he said, when mamma went away. And a part we spent at the opera and at Véry's restaurant, where we took our dear kind Madame Smolensk. Ah, how good that woman was to me! Ah, how I suffered in that house when mamma wanted to part me from Philip! We walked by and saw the windows of the room where that horrible, horrible tragedy was performed, and Philip shook his fist at the green *jalousies*. 'Good heavens!' he said: 'how, my darling, how I was made to suffer there!' I bear no malice. I will do no injury. But I can never forgive: never! I can forgive mamma, who made my husband so unhappy; but can I love her again? Indeed and indeed I have tried. Often and often in my dreams that horrid tragedy is acted over again; and they are taking him from me, and I feel as if I should die. When I was with you I used often to be afraid to go to sleep for fear of that dreadful dream, and I kept one of his letters under my pillow so that I might hold it in the night. And now! No one can part us!—oh, no one!—until the end comes!

"He took me about to all his old *bachelor haunts*; to the 'Hôtel Poussin,' where he used to live, which is very dingy but comfortable. And he introduced me to the landlady, in a Madras handkerchief, and to the landlord (in earrings and with no coat on), and to the little boy who *frottes* the floors. And he said, '*Tiens*' and '*merci, madame!*' as we gave him a five-franc piece *out of my fortune*. And then we went to the café opposite the Bourse, where Philip used to write his letters; and then we went to the Palais Royal, where Madame de Smolensk was in waiting for us. And then we went to the play. And then we went to Tortoni's to take ices. And then we walked a part of the way home with Madame Smolensk under a hundred million blazing stars; and then we walked down the Champs Elysées avenues, by which Philip used to come to me, and beside the plashing fountains shining under the silver moon. And, oh, Laura! I wonder under the silver moon was anybody so happy as your *loving and grateful*

                                                            "C. F."

" P.S." [In the handwriting of Philip Firmin Esq.]—" MY DEAR FRIENDS.—I'm so jolly that it seems like a dream. I have been watching Charlotte scribble, scribble for an hour past ; and wondered and thought is it actually true ? and gone and convinced myself of the truth by looking at the paper and the dashes which she will put under the words. My dear friends, what have I done in life that I am to be made a present of a little angel ? Once there was so much wrong in me, and my heart was so black and revengeful, that I knew not what might happen to me. She came and rescued me. The love of this creature purifies me—and—and I think that is all. I think I only want to say that I am the happiest man in Europe. That Saint Firmin at Amiens ! Didn't it seem like a good omen ? By St. George ! I never heard of St. F. until I lighted on him in the cathedral. When shall we write next ? Where shall we tell you to direct ? We don't know where we are going. We don't want letters. But we are not the less grateful to dear kind friends ; and our names are

" P. AND C. F.''

CHAPTER XXXIII.

DESCRIBES A SITUATION INTERESTING BUT NOT UNEXPECTED.

ONLY very wilful and silly children cry after the moon. Sensible people who have shed their sweet tooth can't be expected to be very much interested about honey. We may hope Mr. and Mrs. Philip Firmin enjoyed a pleasant wedding tour and that sort of thing : but as for chronicling its delights or adventures, Miss Sowerby and I vote that the task is altogether needless and immoral. Young people are already much too sentimental, and inclined to idle, maudlin reading. Life is earnest, Miss Sowerby remarks (with a strong inclination to spell " earnest " with a large E). Life is labor. Life is duty. Life is rent. Life is taxes. Life brings its ills, bills, doctor's pills. Life is not a mere calendar of honey and moonshine. Very good. But without love, Miss Sowerby, life is just death, and I know, my dear, you would no more care to go on with it, than with a new chapter of—of our dear friend Boreham's new story.

Between ourselves, Philip's humor is not much more lightsome than that of the ingenious contemporary above named ; but if it served to amuse Philip himself, why baulk him of a little sport ? Well, then : he wrote us a great ream of lumbering pleasantries, dated Paris, Thursday ; Geneva, Saturday. Summit of Mont Blanc, Monday ; Timbuctoo, Wednesday. Pekin, Friday—with facetious descriptions of those spots and cities. He said that in the last-named place, Charlotte's shoes being worn out, those which she purchased were rather tight for her, and the high heels annoyed her. He stated that the beef at Timbuctoo was not cooked enough for Charlotte's taste, and that the Emperor's attentions were becoming rather marked, and so forth ; whereas poor little Char's simple postscripts mentioned no travelling at all ; but averred that they were staying at Saint Germain, and as happy as the day was long. As happy as the day was long? As it was short, alas ! Their little purse was very slenderly furnished ; and in a very, very brief holiday, poor Philip's few napoleons had almost all rolled away. Luckily, it was pay-day when the young people came back to London. They were almost reduced to the Little Sister's wedding present : and surely they would rather work than purchase a few hours' more ease with that poor widow's mite.

Who talked and was afraid of poverty ? Philip, with his two newspapers, averred that he had enough ; more than enough ; could save ; could put by. It was at this time that Ridley, the Academician, painted that sweet picture, No. 1,976 —of course you remember it—' Portrait of a Lady.' He became romantically attached to the second-floor lodger ; would have no noisy parties in his rooms, or smoking, lest it should annoy her. Would Mrs. Firmin desire to give entertainments of her own ? His studio and sitting-room were at her orders. He fetched and carried. He brought presents, and theatre-boxes. He was her slave of slaves. And she gave him back in return for all this romantic adoration a condescending shake of a soft little hand, and a kind look from a pair of soft eyes, with which the painter was fain to be content. Low of stature, and of misshapen form, J. J. thought himself naturally outcast from marriage and love, and looked in with longing eyes at the paradise which he was forbidden to enter. And Mr. Philip sat within this Palace of Delight ; and lolled at his ease, and took his pleasure, and Charlotte ministered to him. And once in a way, my lord sent out a crumb of kindness, or a little cup of comfort, to the outcast at the gate, who blessed his benefactress, and my lord his benefactor, and was thankful. Charlotte had not two-pence : but she had a little court. It was the fashion for Philip's friends to come and bow before her. Very fine gentlemen who had known him at college, and forgot him, or sooth to say, thought him rough and overbearing, now suddenly remembered him, and his young wife had quite fashionable assemblies at her five o'clock tea-table. All men liked her, and Miss Sowerby of course says Mrs. Firmin was a good-natured, quite harmless little woman, rather pretty, and—you know, my dear—such as men like. Look you, if I like cold veal, dear Sowerby, it is that my tastes are simple. A fine tough old dry camel, no doubt, is a much nobler and more sagacious animal—and perhaps you think a double hump is quite a delicacy.

Yes: Mrs. Philip was a success. She had scarce any female friends as yet, being too poor to go into the world : but she had Mrs. Pendennis, and dear little Mrs. Brandon, and Mrs. Mugford, whose celebrated trap repeatedly brought delicacies for the bride from Hampstead, whose chaise was once or twice a week at Philip's door, and who was very much exercised and impressed by the fine company whom she met in Mrs. Firmin's apartments. "Lord Thingambury's card ! what next, Brandon, upon my word? Lady Slowby at home ? well, I never, Mrs. B. !" In such artless phrases Mrs. Mugford would express her admiration and astonishment during the early time, and when Charlotte still retained the good lady's favor. That a state of things far less agreeable ensued, I must own. But though there is ever so small a cloud in the sky even now, let us not heed it for a while, and bask and be content and happy in the sunshine. "Oh, Laura, I tremble when I think how happy I am !" was our little bird's perpetual warble. "How did I live when I was at home with mamma?" she would say. "Do you know that Philip never scolds me ? If he were to say a rough word I think I should die ; whereas mamma was barking, barking from morning till night, and I didn't care a pin." This is what comes of injudicious scolding, as of any other drug. The wholesome medicine loses its effects. The inured patient calmly takes a dose that would frighten or kill a stranger. Poor Mrs. Baynes' crossed letters came still, and I am not prepared to pledge my word that Charlotte read them all. Mrs. B. offered to come and superintend and take care of dear Philip when an enteresting event should take place. But Mrs. Brandon was already engaged for this important occasion, and Charlotte became so alarmed lest her mother should invade her, that Philip wrote curtly, and positively forbade Mrs. Baynes. You remember the picture "A Cradle" by J. J. ? the two little rosy feet brought I don't know how many hundred guineas apiece to Mr. Ridley. The mother herself did not study babydom more fondly and devotedly than Ridley did in the ways, looks, features, anatomies, attitudes, baby-clothes, &c., of this first-born infant of Charlotte and Philip Firmin. My wife is very angry because I have forgotten whether the first of the young Firmin brood was a boy or a girl, and says I shall forget the names of my own children next. Well ? "At this distance of time, I *think* it was a boy,— for their boy is very tall, you know

—a great deal taller——— *Not* a boy? Then, between ourselves, I have no doubt it was a———" " A goose," says the
lady, which is not even reasonable.

This is certain, we all thought the young mother looked
very pretty, with her pink cheeks and beaming eyes, as she
bent over the little infant. J. J. says he thinks there is something *heavenly* in the looks of young mothers at that time.
Nay, he goes so far as to declare that a tigress at the Zoological
Gardens looks beautiful and gentle as she bends her black
nozzle over her cubs. And if a tigress, why not Mrs. Philip?
O ye powers of sentiment, in what a state J. J. was about this
young woman! There is a brightness in a young mother's eye:
there are pearl and rose tints on her cheek, which are sure to
fascinate a painter. This artist used to hang about Mrs. Brandon's rooms, till it was droll to see him. I believe he took off
his shoes in his own studio, so as not to disturb by his creaking
the lady overhead. He purchased the most preposterous mug,
and other presents for the infant. Philip went out to his club
or his newspaper as he was ordered to do. But Mr. J. J. could
not be got away from Thornhaugh Street, so that little Mrs.
Brandon laughed at him :—absolutely laughed at him.

During all this while Philip and his wife continued in the
very greatest favor with Mr. and Mrs. Mugford, and were invited
by that worthy couple to go with their infant to Mugford's villa
at Hampstead, where a change of air might do good to dear
baby and dear mamma. Philip went to this village retreat.
Streets and terraces now cover over the house and grounds
which worthy Mugford inhabited, and which people say he used
to call his Russian Irby. He had amassed in a small space a
heap of country pleasures. He had a little garden; a little
paddock; a little green-house; a little cucumber-frame; a little
stable for his little trap; a little Guernsey cow; a little dairy;
a little pigsty; and with this little treasure the good man was
not a little content. He loved and praised everything that was
his. No man admired his own port more than Mugford, or
paid more compliments to his own butter and home-baked
bread. He enjoyed his own happiness. He appreciated his
own worth. He loved to talk of the days when he was a poor
boy in London streets, and now—" now try that glass of port,
my boy, and say whether the Lord Mayor has got any better,"
he would say, winking at his glass and his company. To be
virtuous, to be lucky, and constantly to think and own that you
are so—is not this true happiness? To sing hymns in praise of
himself is a charming amusement—at least to the performer;

and anybody who dined at Mugford's table was pretty sure to hear some of this music after dinner. I am sorry to say Philip did not care for this trumpet-blowing. He was frightfully bored at Haverstock Hill ; and when bored, Mr. Philip is not altogether an agreeable companion. He will yawn in a man's face, He will contradict you freely. He will say the mutton is tough, or the wine not fit to drink ; that such and such an orator is overrated, and such and such a politician is a fool. Mugford and his guest had battles after dinner, had actually high words. " What-hever is it, Mugford ? and what were you quarrelling about in the dining-room ? " asks Mrs. Mugford. " Quarrelling ? It's only the sub-editor snoring," said the gentleman, with a flushed face. " My wine ain't good enough for him ; and now my gentleman must put his boots upon a chair and go to sleep under my nose. He *is* a cool hand, and no mistake, Mrs. M." At this juncture poor little Char would gently glide down from a visit to her baby : and would play something on the piano, and soothe the rising anger ; and thus Philip would come in from a little walk in the shrubberies, where he had been blowing a little cloud. Ah ! there was a little cloud rising indeed :— quite a little one—nay, not so little. When you consider that Philip's bread depended on the good-will of these people, you will allow that his friends might be anxious regarding the future. A word from Mugford, and Philip and Charlotte and the child were adrift on the world. And these points Mr. Firmin would freely admit, while he stood discoursing of his own affairs (as he loved to do), his hands in his pockets, and his back warming at our fire.

" My dear fellow," says the candid bridegroom, " these things are constantly in my head. I used to talk about 'em to Char, but I don't now. They disturb her, the poor thing ; and she clutches hold of the baby ; and—and it tears my heart out to think that any grief should come to her. I try and do my best, my good people—but when I'm bored I can't help showing I'm bored, don't you see ? I can't be a hypocrite. No, not for two hundred a year, or for twenty thousand. You can't make a silk purse out of that sow's-ear of a Mugford. A very good man. I don't say no. A good father, a good husband, a generous host, and a most tremendous bore, and cad. Be agreeable to him ? How can I be agreeable when I am being killed ? He has a story about Leigh Hunt being put into Newgate, where Mugford, bringing him proofs, saw Lord Byron. I cannot keep awake during that story any longer ; or, if awake, I grind my teeth, and swear inwardly, so that I know

I'm dreadful to hear and see. Well, Mugford has yellow satin sofas in the 'droaring-room '—"

" Oh, Philip ! " says a lady ; and two or three circumjacent children set up an insane giggle, which is speedily and sternly silenced.

" I tell you she calls it ' droaring-room.' You know she does, as well as I do. She is a good woman : a kind woman : a hot-tempered woman. I hear her scolding the servants in the kitchen with immense vehemence, and at prodigious length. But how can Char frankly be the friend of a woman who calls a drawing-room a droaring-room ? With our dear little friend in Thornhaugh Street, it is different. She makes no pretence even at equality. Here is a patron and patroness, don't you see ? When Mugford walks me round his paddock and gardens, and says, ' Look year, Firmin ;' or scratches one of his pigs on the back, and says, ' We'll 'ave a cut of this fellow on Saturday ' "—(explosive attempts at insubordination and derision on the part of the children again are severely checked by the parental authorities)—" ' we'll 'ave a cut of this fellow on Saturday,' I felt inclined to throw him or myself into the trough over the palings. Do you know that that man put that hand into his pocket and offered me some filberts ? "

Here I own the lady to whom Philip was addressing himself turned pale and shuddered.

" I can no more be that man's friend que celui du domestique qui vient d'apporter le what-d'you-call'em ? le coal-scuttle " —(John entered the room with that useful article during Philip's oration—and we allowed the elder children to laugh this time, for the fact is, none of us knew the French for coal scuttle, and I will wager there is no such word in Chambaud). " This holding back is not arrogance," Philip went on. " This reticence is not want of humility. To serve that man honestly is one thing ; to make friends with him, to laugh at his dull jokes, is to make friends with the mammon of unrighteousness, is subserviency and hypocrisy on my part. I ought to say to him, Mr. Mugford, I will give you my work for your wage ; I will compile your paper, I will produce an agreeable miscellany containing proper proportions of news, politics, and scandal, put titles to your paragraphs, see the *Pall Mall Gazette* ship-shape through the press, and go home to my wife and dinner. You are my employer, but you are not my friend, and ——bless my soul ! there is five o'clock striking ! " (The timepiece in our drawing-room gave that announcement as he was speaking.) " We have what Mugford calls a white-choker

MUGFORD'S FAVORITE.

dinner to-day, in honor of the pig!" And with this Philip
plunges out of the house, and I hoped reached Hampstead in
time for the entertainment.

Philip's friends in Westminster felt no little doubt about
his prospects, and the Little Sister shared their alarm. "They
are not fit to be with those folks," Mrs. Brandon said, "though
as for Mrs. Philip, dear thing, I am sure nobody can ever
quarrel with *her*. With me it's different. I never had no education, you know—no more than the Mugfords, but I don't like
to see my Philip sittin' down as if he was the guest and equal
of that fellar." Nor indeed did it ever enter "that fellar's" head
that Mr. Frederick Mugford could be Mr. Philip Firmin's equal.
With our knowledge of the two men, then we all dismally looked
forward to a rupture between Firmin and his patron.

As for the New York journal, we were more easy in respect
to Philip's success in that quarter. Several of his friends made
a vow to help him. We clubbed club-stories ; we begged from
our polite friends anecdotes (that would bear sea-transport) of
the fashionable world. We happened to overhear the most remarkable conversations between the most influential public
characters who had no secrets from us. We had astonishing
intelligence at most European courts ; exclusive reports of the
Emperor of Russia's last joke—his last ? his next, very likely.
We knew the most secret designs of the Austrian Privy Coun-
cill ; the views which the Pope had in his eye ; who was the
latest favorite of the Grand Turk, and so on. The upper Ten
Thousand at New York were supplied with a quantity of information which I trust profited them. It was "Palmerston remarked yesterday at dinner," or, "The good old Duke said
last night at Aspley House to the French Ambassador," and
the rest. The letters were signed "Philalethes ;" and, as nobody was wounded by the shafts of our long bow, I trust Mr.
Philip and his friends may be pardoned for twanging it. By
information procured from learned female personages, we even
managed to give accounts, more or less correct, of the latest
ladies' fashions. We were members of all the clubs ; we were
present at the routs and assemblies of the political leaders of
both sides. We had little doubt that Philalethes would be
successful at New York, and looked forward to an increased
payment for his labors. At the end of the first year of Philip
Firmin's married life, we made a calculation by which it was
clear that he had actually saved money. His expenses, to be
sure, were increased. There was a baby in the nursery : but
there was a little bag of sovereigns in the cupboard, and the
thrifty young fellow hoped to add still more to his store.

We were relieved at finding that Firmin and his wife were not invited to repeat their visit to their employer's house at Hampstead. An occasional invitation to dinner was still sent to the young people ; but Mugford, a haughty man in his way, with a proper spirit of his own, had the good sense to see that much intimacy could not arise between him and his sub-editor, and magnanimously declined to be angry at the young fellow's easy superciliousness. I think that indefatigable Little Sister was the peacemaker between the houses of Mugford and Firmin junior, and that she kept both Philip and his master on their good behavior. At all events, and when a quarrel did arise between them, I grieve to have to own it was poor Philip who was in the wrong.

You know in the old, old days the young king and queen never gave any christening entertainment without neglecting to invite some old fairy, who was furious at the omission. I am sorry to say Charlotte's mother was so angry at not being appointed godmother to the new baby, that she omitted to make her little quarterly payment of 12l. 10s. ; and has altogether discontinued that payment from that remote period up to the present time ; so that Philip says his wife has brought him a fortune of 35l., paid in three instalments. There was the first quarter paid when the old lady " would not be beholden to a man like him." Then there came a second quarter—and then ———but I dare say I shall be able to tell when and how Philip's mamma-in-law paid the rest of her poor little daughter's fortune.

Well, Regent's Park is a fine healthy place for infantine diversion, and I don't think Philip at all demeaned himself in walking there with his wife, her little maid, and his baby on his arm. " He is as rude as a bear, and his manners are dreadful ; but he has a good heart, that I will say for him," Mugford said to me. In his drive from London to Hampstead Mugford once or twice met the little family group, of which his sub-editor formed the principal figure ; and for the sake of Philip's young wife and child Mr. M. pardoned the young man's vulgarity, and treated him with long-suffering.

Poor as he was, this was his happiest time, my friend is disposed to think. A young child, a young wife, whose whole life was a tender caress of love for child and husband, a young husband watching both :—I recall the group, as we used often to see it in those days, and see a something sacred in the homely figures. On the wife's bright face what a radiant happiness there is, and what a rapturous smile ! Over the sleep•

ing infant and the happy mother the father looks with pride and thanks in his eyes. Happiness and gratitude fill his simple heart, and prayer involuntary to the Giver of good, that he may have strength to do his duty as father, husband ; that he may be enabled to keep want and care from those dear innocent beings ; that he may defend them, befriend them, leave them a good name. I am bound to say that Philip became thrifty and saving for the sake of Char and the child ; that he came home early of nights ; that he thought his child a wonder ; that he never tired of speaking about that infant in our house, about its fatness, its strength, its weight, its wonderful early talents and humor. He felt himself a man now for the first time, he said. Life had been play and folly until now. And now especially he regretted that he had been idle, and had neglected his opportunities as a lad. Had he studied for the bar, he might have made that profession now profitable, and a source of honor and competence to his family. Our friend estimated his own powers very humbly : I am sure he was not the less aniable on account of that humility. O fortunate he, of whom Love is the teacher, the guide and master, the reformer and chastener ! Where was our friend's former arrogance, self-confidence, and boisterous profusion ? He was at the feet of his wife and child. He was quite humbled about himself ; or gratified himself in fondling and caressing these. They taught him, he said ; and as he thought of them, his heart turned in awful thanks to the gracious heaven which had given them to him. As the tiny infant hand closes round his fingers, I can see the father bending over mother and child, and interpret those maybe unspoken blessings which he asks and bestows. Happy wife, happy husband ! However poor his little home may be, it holds treasures and wealth inestimable ; whatever storms may threaten without, the home fireside is brightened with the welcome of the dearest eyes.

CHAPTER XXXIV.

IN WHICH I OWN THAT PHILLIP TELLS AN UNTRUTH.

CHARLOTTE (and the usual little procession of nurse, baby, &c.) once made their appearance at our house in Queen Square, where they were ever welcomed by the lady of the mansion. The young woman was in a great state of elation, and when we came to hear the cause of her delight, her friends too opened the eyes of wonder. She actually announced that Dr. Firmin had sent over a bill of forty pounds (I may be incorrect as to the sum) from New York. It had arrived that morning, and she had seen the bill, and Philip had told her that his father had sent it ; and was it not a comfort to think that poor Doctor Firmin was endeavoring to repair some of the evil which he had done ; and that he was repenting, and, perhaps, was going to become quite honest and good ? This was indeed an astounding piece of intelligence : and the two women felt joy at the thought of that sinner repenting, and some one else was accused of cynicism, skepticism, and so forth, for doubting the correctness of the information. " You believe in no one, sir. You. are always incredulous about good," &c., &c., &c., was the accusation brought against the reader's very humble servant. Well, about the contrition of this sinner, I confess I still continued to have doubts ; and thought a present of forty pounds to a son, to whom he owed thousands, was no great proof of the doctor's amendment.

And oh ! how vexed some people were when the real story came out at last ! Not for the money's sake—not because they were wrong in argument, and I turned out to be right. Oh, no ! But because it was proved that this unhappy doctor had no present intention of repenting at all. This brand would not come out of the burning, whatever we might hope ; and the doctor's supporters were obliged to admit as much when they came to know the real story. " Oh, Philip," cries Mrs. Laura, when next she saw Mr. Firmin. " How pleased I was to hear of that letter ! "

" What letter ? " asks the gentleman.

" That letter from your father at New York," says the lady.

" Oh," says the gentleman addressed, with a red face

" What then ?   Is it not—is it not all true ? " we ask.

" Poor Charlotte does not understand about business," says Philip ; " I did not read the letter to her.   Here it is." And he hands over the document to me, and I have the liberty to publish it.

New York ————

" AND so, my dear Philip, I may congratulate myself on having achieved *ancestral* honor, and may add grandfather to my titles ?   How quickly this one has come !   I feel myself a young man still, *in spite of the blows of misfortune*—at least I know I was a young man but yesterday, when I may say with our dear old poet, *Non sine gloriâ militavi.* Suppose I too were to tire of solitary widowhood and re-enter the married state ?   There are one or two ladies here who would still condescend to look not unfavorably *on the retired English gentleman.*   Without vanity I may say it, a man of birth and position in England acquires a polish and refinement of manner which dollars cannot purchase, and many a *Wall Street millionary* might envy !

" Your wife has been pronounced to be an angel by a *little correspondent* of mine, who gives me much fuller intelligence of my family than my son condescends to furnish.   Mrs. Philip I hear is gentle ; Mrs. Brandon says she is beautiful,—she is all good-humored.   I hope you have taught her to think not *very* badly of her husband's father ?   I was the dupe of villains who lured me into their schemes ; who robbed me of a life's earnings ; who induced me by their *false representations* to have such confidence in them, that I embarked all my property, and yours, my poor boy, alas ! in their undertakings.   Your Charlotte will take the liberal, the wise, the *just* view of the case, and pity rather than blame my misfortune.   Such is the view, I am happy to say, generally adopted in this city : where there are men of the world who know the vicissitudes of a mercantile career, and can make allowances for misfortune.   What made Rome at first great and prosperous ?   Were its first colonists all wealthy patricians ?   Nothing can be more satisfactory than the disregard shown here *to mere pecuniary difficulty.*   At the same time to be a gentleman is to possess no trifling privilege in this society, where the advantages of birth, respected name, and early education *always* tell in the possessor's favor.   Many persons whom I visit here have certainly not these advantages—and in the highest society of the city I could point out individuals who have had pecuniary misfortunes like myself, who have gallantly renewed the combat after their fall, and are now *fully* restored to competence, to wealth, and the respect of the world ! I was in a house in Fifth Avenue last night.   Is Washington White shunned by his fellowmen because he has been a bankrupt three times ?   Anything more elegant or profuse than his entertainment I have not witnessed on this continent.   His lady had diamonds which a duchess might envy.   The most costly wines, the most magnificent supper, and myriads of canvas-backed ducks covered his board.   Dear Charlotte, my friend Captain Clopoys brings you over three brace of these from your father-in-law, who hopes they will furnish your little dinner-table.   We eat currant jelly with them here, but I like an old English lemon and *cayenne sauce better.*

" By the way, dear Philip, I trust you will not be inconvenienced by a little financial operation, which necessity (alas !) has compelled me to perform.   Knowing that your quarter with the *Upper Ten Thousand Gazette* was now due, I have made so bold as to request Colonel ———— to pay it over to me.   Promises to pay must be met here as with us—an obdurate holder of an unlucky acceptance of mine (I am happy to say there are very few such) would admit of *no delay,* and I have been compelled to appropriate my poor Philip's earnings.   I have only put you off for ninety days : with your credit and wealthy friends you can *easily negotiate the bill enclosed,* and I *promise you* that when presented it shall be honored by my Philip's ever affectionate father,   G. B. F."

" By the way, your Philalethes' letters are not *quite spicy* enough, my worthy friend the colonel says.   They are *elegant and gay,* but the public here desires to have *more personal news* ; a *little scandal about Queen Elizabeth,* you understand ?   Can't you attack somebody ?   Look at the letters and articles published by my respected friend of the *New York Emerald !*   The readers here like a *high-spiced article* : and I recommend P. F. to put a little more pepper in his dishes.   What a comfort to me it is to think that I have procured this place for you, and have been enabled to help my son and his young family !
                                                                  " G. B. F."

Enclosed in this letter was a slip of paper which poor Philip supposed to be a cheque when he first beheld it, but which turned out to be his papa's promissory note, payable at New York four months after date. And this document was to represent the money which the elder Firmin had received in his son's name! Philip's eyes met his friend's when they talked about this matter. Firmin looked almost as much ashamed as if he himself had done the wrong.

"Does the loss of this money annoy you?" asked Philip's friend.

"The manner of the loss does," said poor Philip. "I don't care about the money. But he should not have taken this. He should not have taken this. Think of poor Charlotte and the child being in want possibly! Oh, friend, it's hard to bear, isn't it? I'm an honest fellow, ain't I? I think I am. I pray heaven I am. In any extremity of poverty could I have done this? It was my father who introduced me to these people. I suppose he thinks he has a right to my earnings: and if he is in want, you know, so he has."

"Had you not better write to the New York publishers and beg them henceforth to remit to you directly?" asks Philip's friend.

"That would be to tell them that he has disposed of the money," groans Philip. "I can't tell them that my father is a —— "

"No; but you can thank them for having handed over such a sum on your account to the doctor: and warn them that you will draw on them from this country henceforth. They won't in this case pay the next quarter to the doctor."

"Suppose he is in want, ought I not to supply him?" Firmin said. "As long as there are four crusts in the house, the doctor ought to have one. Ought I to be angry with him for helping himself, old boy?" and he drinks a glass of wine, poor fellow, with a rueful smile. By the way, it is my duty to mention here, that the elder Firmin was in the habit of giving very elegant little dinner-parties at New York, where little dinner-parties are much more costly than in Europe—"in order," he said, "to establish and keep up his connection as a physician." As a *bon-vivant*, I am informed, the doctor began to be celebrated in his new dwelling-place, where his anecdotes of the British aristocracy were received with pleasure in certain circles.

But it would be as well henceforth that Philip should deal directly with his American correspondents, and not employ the services of so very expensive a broker. To this suggestion he could not but agree. Meanwhile,—and let this be a warning to men never to deceive their wives in any the slightest circumstances ; to tell them *everything* they wish to know, to keep nothing hidden from those dear and excellent beings—you must know, ladies, that when Philip's famous ship of dollars arrived from America, Firmin had promised his wife that baby should have a dear delightful white cloak trimmed with the most lovely tape, on which poor Charlotte had often cast a longing eye as she passed by the milliner and curiosity shops in Hanway Yard, which, I own, she loved to frequent. Well ; when Philip told her that his father had sent home forty pounds, or what not, thereby deceiving his fond wife, the little lady went away straight to her darling shop in the Yard—(Hanway Yard has become a street now, but ah ! it is always delightful)—Charlotte, I say, went off, ran off to Hanway Yard, pavid with fear lest the darling cloak should be gone, found it—oh, joy !—still in Miss Isaacson's window ; put it on baby straightway then and there ; kissed the dear infant, and was delighted with the effect of the garment, which all the young ladies at Miss Isaacson's pronounced to be perfect ; and took the cloak away on baby's shoulders, promising to send the money, five pounds, if you please, next day. And in this cloak baby and Charlotte went to meet papa when he came home ; and I don't know which of them, mamma or baby, was the most pleased and absurd and happy baby of the two. On his way home from his newspaper, Mr. Philip had orders to pursue a certain line of streets, and when his accustomed hour for returning from his business drew nigh, Mrs. Char went down Thornhaugh Street, down Rathbone Place, with Betsy the nursekin and baby in the new cloak. Behold, he comes at last—papa—striding down the street. He sees the figures : he sees the child, which laughs, and holds out its little pink hands, and crows a recognition. And "Look—look, papa," cries the happy mother. (Away ! I cannot keep up the mystery about the baby any longer, and though I had forgotten for a moment the child's sex, remembered it the instant after, and that it was a girl to be sure, and that its name was Laura Caroline.) "Look, look, papa !" cries the happy mother. "She has got another little tooth since the morning, such a beautiful little tooth—and look here, sir, don't you observe anything ?"

"Any what ?" asks Philip.

"La ! sir," says Betsy, giving Laura Caroline a great toss, so that her white cloak floats in the air.

"Isn't it a dear cloak ?" cries mamma ; "and doesn't baby look like an angel in it ? I bought it at Miss Isaacson's to-day as you got your money from New York; and oh, my dear, it only cost five guineas."

"Well, it's a week's work," sighs poor Philip; "and I think I need not grudge that to give Charlotte pleasure." And he feels his empty pockets rather ruefully.

"God bless you, Philip," says my wife, with her eyes full. "They came here this morning, Charlotte and the nurse and the baby in the new—the new—" Here the lady seized hold of Philip's hand, and fairly broke out into tears. Had she embraced Mr. Firmin before her husband's own eyes, I should not have been surprised. Indeed she confessed that she was on the point of giving way to this most sentimental outbreak.

And now, my brethren, see how one crime is the parent of many, and one act of duplicity leads to a whole career of deceit. In the first place, you see, Philip had deceived his wife—with the pious desire, it is true, of screening his father's little peculiarities—but, *ruat cœlum*, we must tell no lies. No: and from this day forth I order John never to say Not at home to the greatest bore, dun, dawdle of my acquaintance. If Philip's father had not deceived him, Philip would not have deceived his wife; if he had not deceived his wife, she would not have given five guineas for that cloak for the baby. If she had not given five guineas for the cloak, my wife would never have entered into a secret correspondence with Mr. Firmin, which might, but for my own sweetness of temper, have bred jealousy, mistrust, and the most awful quarrels—nay, duels— between the heads of the two families. Fancy Philip's body lying stark upon Hampstead Heath with a bullet through it, despatched by the hand of his friend! Fancy a cab driving up to my own house, and from it—under the eyes of the children at the parlor windows—their father's bleeding corpse ejected! ——Enough of this dreadful pleasantry! Two days after the affair of the cloak, I found a letter in Philip's handwriting addressed to my wife, and thinking that the note had reference to a matter of dinner then pending between our families, I broke the envelope and read as follows!—

> *"Thornhaugh Street, Thursday.*
>
> "MY DEAR, KIND GODMAMMA,—As soon as ever I can write and speak, I will thank you for being so kind to me. My mamma says she is very jealous, and as she bought my cloak she can't think of allowing you to pay for it. But she desires me never to forget your kindness to us, and though I don't know anything about it now, she promises to tell me when I am old enough. Meanwhile I am your grateful and affectionate little goddaughter.
> "L. C. F."

Philip was persuaded by his friends at home to send out the request to his New York employers to pay his salary henceforth to himself ; and I remember a dignified letter came from his parent, in which the matter was spoken of in sorrow rather than in anger ; in which the doctor pointed out that this precautionary measure seemed to imply a doubt on Philip's side of his father's honor ; and surely, surely, he was unhappy enough and unfortunate enough already without meriting this mistrust from his son. The duty of a son to honor his father and mother was feelingly pointed out, and the doctor meekly trusted that Philip's children would give *him* more confidence than he seemed to be inclined to award to his unfortunate father. Never mind. He should bear no malice. If Fortune ever smiled on him again, and something told him she would, he would show Philip that he could forgive ; although he might not be able to forget that in his exile, his solitude, his declining years, his misfortune, his own child had mistrusted him. This he said was the most cruel blow of all for his susceptible heart to bear.

This letter of paternal remonstrance was enclosed in one from the doctor to his old friend the Little Sister, in which he vaunted a discovery which he and some other scientific gentlemen were engaged in perfecting—of a medicine which was to be extraordinarily efficacious in cases in which Mrs. Brandon herself was often specially and professionally engaged, and he felt sure that the sale of this medicine would go far to retrieve his shattered fortune. He pointed out the complaints in which this medicine was most efficacious. He would send some of it, and details regarding its use, to Mrs. Brandon, who might try its efficacy upon her patients. He was advancing slowly, but steadily, in his medical profession, he said ; though of course, he had to suffer from the jealousy of his professional brethren. Never mind. Better times, he was sure, were in store for all ; when his son should see that a wretched matter of forty pounds more should not deter him from paying all just claims upon him. Amen ! We all heartily wished for the day when Philip's father should be able to settle his little accounts. Meanwhile, the proprietors of the *Gazette of the Upper Ten Thousand* were instructed to write directly to their London correspondent.

Although Mr. Firmin prided himself, as we have seen, upon his taste and dexterity as sub-editor of the *Pall Mall Gazette,* I must own that he was a very insubordinate officer, with whom his superiors often had cause to be angry. Certain people were praised in the *Gazette*—certain others were attacked. Very dull books were admired, and very lively works attacked. Some men were praised for everything they did ; some others

were satirized, no matter what their works were. " I find," poor
Philip used to say with a groan, "that in matters of criticism
especially there are so often private reasons for the praise and
the blame administered, that I am glad, for my part, my only
duty is to see the paper through the press. For instance, there
is Harrocks, the tragedian, of Drury Lane : every piece in which
he appears is a masterpiece, and his performance the greatest
triumph ever witnessed. Very good. Harrocks and my excellent employer are good friends, and dine with each other ;
and it is natural that Mugford should like to have his friend
praised, and to help him in every way. But Balderson, of
Covent Garden, is also a very fine actor. Why can't our critic
see his merit as well as Harrocks' ? Poor Balderson is never
allowed any merit at all. He is passed over with a sneer, or a
curt word of cold commendation, while columns of flattery are
not enough for his rival."

"Why, Mr. F., what a flat you must be, askin' your pardon,"
remarked Mugford, in reply to his sub-editor's simple remonstrance. " How can we praise Balderson, when Harrocks is
our friend ? Me and Harrocks are thick. Our wives are close
friends. If I was to let Balderson be praised, I should drive
Harrocks mad. I *can't* praise Balderson, don't you see, out of
justice to Harrocks ! "

Then there was a certain author whom Bickerton was for
ever attacking. They had had a private quarrel, and Bickerton
revenged himself in this way. In reply to Philip's outcries and
remonstrances, Mr. Mugford only laughed : " The two men are
enemies, and Bickerton hits him whenever he can. Why, that's
only human nature, Mr. F.," says Philip's employer.

" Great heavens ! " bawls out Firmin, " do you mean to say
that the man is base enough to strike at his private enemies
through the press ? "

" Private enemies ! private gammon, Mr. Firmin ! " cries
Philip's employer. " If I have enemies—and I have, there's
no doubt about that—I serve them out whenever and wherever
I can. And let me tell you I don't half relish having my conduct called base. It's only natural ; and it's right. Perhaps
you would like to praise your enemies, and abuse your friend ?
If that's your line, let me tell you you won't do in the noos-
paper business, and had better take to some other trade." And
the employer parted from his subordinate in some heat.

Mugford, indeed, feelingly spoke to me about this insubordination of Philip. " What does the fellow mean by quarrelling
with his bread and butter ? " Mr. Mugford asked. " Speak to

him, and show him what's what, Mr. P., or we shall come to a quarrel, mind you—and I don't want that, for the sake of his little wife, poor little delicate thing. Whatever is to happen to them, if we don't stand by them?"

What was to happen to them, indeed? Any one who knew Philip's temper as we did, was aware how little advice or remonstrance were likely to affect that gentleman. "Good heavens!" he said to me, when I endeavored to make him adopt a conciliatory tone towards his employer, "do you want to make me Mugford's galley-slave? I shall have him standing over me and swearing at me as he does at the printers. He looks into my room at times when he is in a passion, and glares at me as if he would like to seize me by the throat; and after a word or two he goes off, and I hear him curse the boys in the passage. One day it will be on me that he will turn, I feel sure of that. I tell you the slavery is beginning to be awful. I wake of a night and groan and chafe, and poor Char, too, wakes and asks, 'What is it, Philip?' I say it is rheumatism. Rheumatism!" Of course to Philip's malady his friends tried to apply the commonplace anodynes and consolations. He must be gentle in his bearing. He must remember that his employer had not been bred a gentleman, and that, though rough and coarse in language, Mugford had a kind heart. "There is no need to tell me he is not a gentleman, I know that," says poor Phil. "He *is* kind to Char and the child, that is the truth, and so is his wife. I am a slave for all that. He is my driver. He feeds me. He hasn't beat me yet. When I was away at Paris I did not feel the chain so much. But it is scarcely tolerable now, when I have to see my jailer four or five times a week. My poor little Char, why did I drag you into this slavery?"

"Because you wanted a consoler, I suppose," remarks one of Philip's comforters. "And do you suppose Charlotte would be happier if she were away from you? Though you live up two pair of stairs, is any home happier than yours, Philip? You often own as much, when you are in happier moods. Who has not his work to do, and his burden to bear? You say sometimes that you are imperious and hot-tempered. Perhaps your slavery as you call it, may be good for you."

"I have doomed myself and her to it," says Philip, hanging down his head.

"Does she ever repine?" asks his adviser. "Does she not think herself the happiest little wife in the world? See here, Philip, here is a note from her yesterday in which she says as much. Do you want to know what the rote is about, sir?" says the lady with a smile. "Well, then, she wanted a receipt for that dish which you liked so much on Friday, and she and Mrs. Brandon will make it for you."

"And if it consisted of minced Charlotte," says Philip's other friend, "you know she would cheerfully chop herself up, and have herself served with a little cream-sauce and sippets of toast for your honor's dinner."

This was undoubtedly true. Did not Job's friends make many true remarks when they visited him in his affliction? Patient as he was, the patriarch groaned and lamented, and why should not poor Philip be allowed to grumble, who was not a model of patience at all? He was not broke in as yet. The mill-horse was restive and kicked at his work. He would chafe not seldom at the daily drudgery, and have his fits of revolt and despondency. Well? Have others not had to toil, to bow the proud head, and carry the daily burden? Don't you see Pegasus, who was going to win the plate, a weary, broken-knee'd, broken-down old cab-hack shivering in the rank; or a sleek gelding, mayhap, pacing under a corpulent master in Rotten Row? Philip's crust began to be scanty, and was dipped in bitter waters. I am not going to make a long story of this part of his career, or parade my friend as too hungry and poor. He is safe now, and out of all peril, heaven be thanked! but he had to pass through hard times, and to look out very wistfully lest the wolf should enter at the door. He never laid claim to be a man of genius, nor was he a successful quack who could pass as a man of genius. When there were French prisoners in England, we know how stout old officers who had plied their sabres against Mamelouks, or Russians, or Germans, were fain to carve little gimcracks in bone with their penknives, or make baskets and boxes of chipped straw, and piteously sell them to casual visitors to their prison. Philip was poverty's prisoner. He had to make such shifts, and do such work, as he could find in his captivity. I do not think men who have undergone the struggle and served the dire task-master, like to look back and recall the grim apprenticeship. When Philip says now, "What fools we were to marry, Char," she looks up radiantly, with love and happiness in her eyes—looks up to heaven, and is thankful; but grief and sadness come over her husband's face at the thought of those days of pain and gloom. She may soothe him, and he may be thankful too; but the wounds are still there which were dealt to him in the cruel battle with fortune. Men are ridden down in it. Men are poltroons and run. Men maraud, break ranks, are guilty of meanness, cowardice, shabby plunder. Men are raised to rank and honor, or drop and perish unnoticed on the field. Happy he who comes from it with his honor pure ! Philip did not win crosses and epaulets. He is like us, my dear sir, not a heroic genius at all. And it is to be hoped that all three have behaved with an average pluck, and have been guilty of no meanness, or treachery, or desertion. Did you behave otherwise, what would wife and children say ? As for Mrs. Philip, I tell you she thinks to this day that there is no man like her husband, and is ready to fall down and worship the boots in which he walks.

How do men live ? How is rent paid ? How does the dinner come day after day ? As a rule there *is* dinner. You might live longer with less of it, but you can't go without it and live long. How did my neighbor 23 earn his carriage, and how did 24 pay for his house ? As I am writing this sentence Mr. Cox, who collects the taxes in this quarter, walks in. How do you do, Mr. Cox ? We are not in the least afraid of meeting one another. Time was—two, three years of time—when poor Philip was troubled at the sight of Cox ; and this troublous time his biographer intends to pass over in a very few pages.

At the end of six months the Upper Ten Thousand of New York heard with modified wonder that the editor of that fashionable journal had made a retreat from the city, carrying with him the scanty contents of the till ; so the contributions of Philalthetes never brought our poor friend any dollars at all. But though one fish is caught and eaten, are there not plenty more left in the sea ? At this very time, when I was in a natural state of despondency about poor Philip's affairs, it struck Tregarvan, the wealthy Cornish Member of Parliament, that the Government and the House of Commons slighted his speeches and his views on foreign politics ; that the wife of the Foreign Secretary had been very inattentive to Lady Tregarvan ; that the designs of a Great Power were most menacing and dangerous, and ought to be exposed and counteracted ; and that the peerage which he had long desired ought to be bestowed on him. Sir John Tregarvan applied to certain literary and political gentlemen with whom he was acquainted. He would bring out the *European Review*. He would expose the designs of that Great Power which was menacing Europe. He would show up in his proper colors a Minister who was careless of the country's honor, and forgetful of his own : a Minister whose arrogance ought no longer to be tolerated by the country gentlemen of England. Sir John, a little man in brass buttons, and a tall head, who loves to hear his own voice, came and made a speech on the above topics to the writer of the present biography ; that writer's lady was in his study as Sir John expounded his views at some length. She listened to him with the greatest attention and respect. She was shocked to hear of the ingratitude of Government ; astounded and terrified by his exposition of the designs of—of that Great Power whose intrigues were so menacing to European tranquillity. She was most deeply interested in the idea of establishing the *Review*. He would, of of course, be himself the editor ; and—and—(here the woman looked across the table at her husband with a strange triumph in her eyes)—she knew, they both knew, the very man *of all the world* who was most suited to act as sub-editor under Sir John —a gentleman, one of the truest that ever lived—a university man ; a man remarkably versed in the European languages— that is, in French most certainly. And now the reader, I dare say, can guess who this individual was. " I knew it at once," says the lady, after Sir John had taken his leave. " I told you that those dear children would not be forsaken." And I would no more try and persuade her that the *European Review* was not ordained of all time to afford maintainance to Philip, than I would induce her to turn Mormon, and accept all the consequences to which ladies· must submit when they make profession of that creed.

" You see, my love," I say to the partner of my existence, " what other things must have been ordained of all time as well as Philip's appointment to be sub-editor of the *European Review*. It must have been decreed *ab initio* that Lady Plinlimmon should give evening-parties, in order that she might offend Lady Tregarvan by not asking her to those parties. It must have been ordained by fate that Lady Tregarvan should be of a jealous disposition, so that she might hate Lady Plinlimmon, and was to work upon her husband, and inspire him with anger and revolt against his chief. It must have been ruled by destiny that Tregarvan should be rather a weak and wordy personage, fancying that he had a talent for literary composition. Else he would not have thought of setting up the *Review*. Else he would never have been angry with Lord Plinlimmon for not inviting him to tea. Else he would not have engaged Philip as sub-editor. So, you see, in order to bring about this event, and put a couple of hundred a year into Philip Firmin's pocket, the Tregarvans have to be born from the earliest times : the Plinlimmons have to spring up in the remotest ages, and come down to the present day : Doctor Firmin has to be a rogue, and undergo his destiny of cheating his son of money : all mankind up to the origin of our race are involved in your proposition, and we actually arrive at Adam and Eve, who are but fulfilling their destiny, which was to be the ancestors of Philip Firmin."

"Even in our first parents there was doubt and skepticism and misgiving," says the lady, with strong emphasis on the words. "If you mean to say that there is no such thing as a Superior Power watching over us, and ordaining things for our good, you are an atheist—and such a thing as an atheist does not exist in the world, and I would not believe you if you said you were one twenty times over."

I mention these points by the way, and as samples of lady-like logic. I acknowledge that Philip himself, as he looks back at his past career, is very much moved. "I do not deny," he says, gravely, "that these things happened in the natural order. I say I am grateful for what happened ; and look back at the past not without awe. In great grief and danger maybe, I have had timely rescue. Under great suffering I have met with su-preme consolation. When the trial has seemed almost too hard for me it has ended, and our darkness has been lightened. *Ut vivo et valeo—si valeo*, I know by Whose permission this is,—and would you forbid me to be thankful ? to be thankful for my life ; to be thankful for my children ; to be thankful for the daily bread which has been granted to me, and the temptation from which I have been rescued ? As I think of the past and its bitter trials, I bow my head in thanks and awe. I wanted succor, and I found it. I fell on evil times, and good friends pitied and helped me—good friends like yourself, your dear wife, many another I could name. In what moments of de-pression, old friend, have you not seen me, and cheered me ? Do you know in the moments of our grief the inexpressible value of your sympathy ? Your good Samaritan takes out only twopence maybe for the wayfarer whom he has rescued, but the little timely supply saves a life. You remember dear old Ned St. George—dead in the West Indies years ago ? Before he got his place Ned was hanging on in London, so utterly poor and ruined, that he had not often a shilling to buy a dinner. He used often to come to us, and my wife and our children loved him ; and I used to leave a heap of shillings on my study-table, so that he might take two or three as he wanted them. Of course you remember him. You were at the dinner which we gave him on his getting his place. I forget the cost of that dinner ; but I remember my share amounted to the exact number of shillings which poor Ned had taken off my table. He gave me

the money then and there at the tavern at Blackwall. He **said**
it seemed providential.   But for those shillings, and the constant welcome at our poor little table, he said he thought he
should have made away with his life.   I am not bragging of the
twopence which I gave, but thanking God for sending me there
to give it.   *Benedico Benedictus*.   I wonder sometimes am I the
I of twenty years ago ? before our heads were bald, friend, and
when the little ones reached up to our knees ?   Before dinner
you saw me in the library reading in that old *European Review*
which your friend Tregarvan established.   I came upon an
article of my own, and a very dull one, on a subject which I
knew nothing about.   'Persian politics, and the intrigues at the
Court of Teheran.'   It was done to order.   Tregarvan had
some special interest about Persia, or wanted to vex Sir Thomas
Nobbles, who was Minister there.   I breakfasted with Tregarvan in the 'Albany,' the facts (we will call them facts) and
papers were supplied to me, and I went home to point out the
delinquencies of Sir Thomas, and the atrocious intrigues of the
Russian Court.   Well, sir, Nobbles, Tregarvan, Teheran, all
disappeared as I looked at the text in the old volume of the
Review.   I saw a deal table in a little room, and a reading-lamp,
and a young fellow writing at it, with a sad heart, and a dreadful apprehension torturing him.   One of our children was ill in
the adjoining room, and I have before me the figure of my wife
coming in from time to time to my room and saying, ' She is
asleep now, and the fever is much lower.' "

Here our conversation was interrupted by the entrance of
a tall young lady, who says, " Papa, the coffee is quite cold :
and the carriage will be here very soon, and both mamma and
my godmother say they are growing very angry.   Do you know
you have been talking here for two hours ? "

Had two hours actually slipped away as we sat prattling
about old times ?   As I narrate them, I prefer to give Mr.
Firmin's account of his adventures in his own words, where I
can recall or imitate them.   Both of us are graver and more
reverend seigniors than we were at the time of which I am
writing.   Has not Firmin's girl grown up to be taller than her
godmother ?   Veterans both, we love to prattle about the merry
days when we were young—(the merry days ? no, the past is
never merry)—about the days when we were young ; and do we
grow young in talking of them, or only indulge in a senile cheerfulness and prolixity ?

Tregarvan sleeps with his Cornish fathers : Europe for
many years has gone on without her *Review :* but it is a cer-

tainty that the establishment of that occult organ of opinion tended very much to benefit Philip Firmin, and helped for a while to supply him and several innocent people dependent on him with their daily bread. Of course, as they were so poor, this worthy family increased and multiplied; and as they increased, and as they multiplied, my wife insists that I should point out how support was found for them. When there was a second child in Philip's nursery, he would have removed from his lodgings in Thornhaugh Street, but for the prayers and commands of the affectionate Little Sister, who insisted that there was plenty of room in the house for everybody, and who said that if Philip went away she would cut off her little god-child with a shilling. And then indeed it was discovered for the first time, that this faithful and affectionate creature had endowed Philip with all her property. These are the rays of sunshine in the dungeon. These are the drops of water in the desert. And with a full heart our friend acknowledges how comfort came to him in his hour of need.

Though Mr. Firmin has a very grateful heart, it has been admitted that he was a loud, disagreeable Firmin at times, impetuous in his talk, and violent in his behavior : and we are now come to that period of his history, when he had a quarrel in which I am sorry to say Mr. Philip was in the wrong. Why do we consort with those whom we dislike? Why is it that men *will* try and associate between whom no love is? I think it was the ladies who tried to reconcile Philip and his master; who brought them together, and strove to make them friends; but the more they met the more they disliked each other; and now the Muse has to relate their final and irreconcilable rupture.

Of Mugford's wrath the direful tale relate, O Muse! and Philip's pitiable fate. I have shown how the men had long been inwardly envenomed one against the other. "Because Firmin is as poor as a rat, that's no reason why he should adopt that hawhaw manner, and them high and mighty airs towards a man who gives him the bread he eats," Mugford argued not unjustly. "What do *I* care for his being a university man? I am as good as he is. I am better than his old scamp of a father, who was a college man too, and lived in fine company. I made my own way in the world, independent, and supported myself since I was fourteen years of age, and helped my mother and brothers too, and that's more than my sub-editor can say, who can't support himself yet. I could get fifty sub-editors as good as he is, by calling out of window into the street, I could.

I say, hang Firmin! I'm a-losing all patience with him." On the other hand, Mr. Philip was in the habit of speaking his mind with equal candor. "What right has that person to call me Firmin?" he asked. "I am Firmin to my equals and friends. I am this man's laborer at four guineas a week. I give him his money's worth, and on every Saturday evening we are quits. Call me Philip, indeed, and strike me in the side! I choke, sir, as I think of the confounded familiarity!" "Confound his impudence!" was the cry, and the not unjust cry of the laborer and his employer. The men should have been kept apart : and it was a most mistaken Christian charity and female conspiracy which brought them together. "Another invitation from Mugford. It was agreed that I was never to go again, and I won't go," says Philip to his meek wife. "Write and say we are engaged, Charlotte."

"It is for the 18th of next month, and this is the 23d," said poor Charlotte. "We can't well say that we are engaged so far off."

"It is for one of his grand ceremony parties," urged the Little Sister. "You can't come to no quarrelling there. He has a good heart. So have you. There's no good quarrelling with him. Oh, Philip, do forgive, and be friends!" Philip yielded to the remonstrances of the women, as we all do; and a letter was sent to Hampstead, announcing that Mr. and Mrs. P. F. would have the honor of, &c.

In his quality of newspaper proprietor, musical professors and opera singers paid much court to Mr. Mugford; and he liked to entertain them at his hospitable table ; to brag about his wines, cookery, plate, garden, prosperity, and private virtue, during dinner, whilst the artists sat respectively listening to him ; and to go to sleep and snore, or wake up and join cheerfully in a chorus, when the professional people performed in the drawing-room. Now, there was a lady who was once known at the theatre by the name of Mrs. Ravenswing, and who had been forced on to the stage by the misconduct of her husband, a certain Walker, one of the greatest scamps who ever entered a jail. On Walker's death, this lady married a Mr. Woolsey, a wealthy tailor, who retired from his business, as he caused his wife to withdraw from hers.

Now, more worthy and honorable people do not live than Woolsey and his wife, as those know who were acquainted with their history. Mrs. Woolsey is loud. Her *h*'s are by no means where they should be ; her knife at dinner is often where it should not be. She calls men aloud by their names, and without any prefix of courtesy. She is very fond of porter, and has no scruple in asking for it. She sits down to play the piano and to sing with perfect good nature, and if you look at her hands as they wander over the keys—well, I don't wish to say anything unkind, but I am forced to own that those hands are not so white as the ivory which they thump. Woolsey sits in perfect rapture listening to his wife. Mugford presses her to take a glass of "somethink" afterwards; and the good-natured soul says she will take "something 'ot." She sits and listens with infinite patience and good-humor whilst the little Mugfords go through their horrible little musical exercises; and these over, she is ready to go back to the piano again, and sing more songs, and drink more " 'ot."

I do not say that this was an elegant woman, or a fitting companion for Mrs. Philip; but I know that Mrs. Woolsey was a good, clever, and kindly woman, and that Philip behaved rudely to her. He never meant to be rude to her, he said; but the truth is, he treated her, her husband, Mugford, and Mrs. Mugford, with a haughty ill-humor which utterly exasperated and perplexed them.

About this poor lady, who was modest and innocent as Susannah, Philip had heard some wicked elders at wicked clubs tell wicked stories in old times. There was that old Trail, for instance, what woman escaped from *his* sneers and slanders? There were others who could be named, and whose testimony was equally untruthful. On an ordinary occasion Philip would never have cared or squabbled about a question of precedence, and would have taken any place assigned to him at any table. But when Mrs. Woolsey in crumpled satins and blowsy lace made her appearance, and was eagerly and respectfully saluted by the host and hostess, Philip remembered those early stories about the poor lady: his eyes flashed wrath, and his breast beat with an indignation which almost choked him. Ask that woman to meet my wife? he thought to himself, and looked so ferocious and desperate that the timid little wife gazed with alarm at her Philip, and crept up to him and whispered, "What is it, dear?"

Meanwhile, Mrs. Mugford and Mrs. Woolsey were in full colloquy about the weather, the nursery, and so forth—and Woolsey and Mugford giving each other the hearty grasp of friendship. Philip, then, scowling at the newly-arrived guests, turning his great hulking back upon the company, and talking to his wife, presented a not agreeable figure to his entertainer.

" Hang the fellow's pride ! " thought Mugford. " He chooses to turn his back upon my company because Woolsey was a tradesman. An honest tailor is better than a bankrupt, swindling doctor, I should think. *Woolsey* need not be ashamed to show his face, I suppose. Why did you make me ask that fellar again, Mrs. M. ? Don't you see, our society ain't good enough for him ? "

Philip's conduct, then, so irritated Mugford, that when dinner was announced, he stepped forward and offered his arm to Mrs. Woolsey ; having intended in the first instance to confer that honor upon Charlotte. I'll show him," thought Mugford, "that an honest tradesman's lady who pays his way, and is not afraid of anybody, is better than my sub-editor's wife, the daughter of a bankrupt swell." Though the dinner was illuminated by Mugford's grandest plate, and accompanied by his very best wine, it was a gloomy and weary repast to several people present, and Philip and Charlotte, and I dare say Mugford, thought it never would be done. Mrs. Woolsey, to be sure, placidly ate her dinner, and drank her wine ; whilst remembering these wicked legends against her, Philip sat before the poor unconscious lady, silent, with glaring eyes, insolent and odious ; so much so, that Mrs. Woolsey imparted to Mrs. Mugford her surprise that the tall gentleman must have got out of bed the wrong leg foremost.

Well, Mrs. Woolsey's carriage and Mr. Firmin's cab were announced at the same moment ; and immediately Philip started up and beckoned his wife away. But Mrs. Woolsey's carriage and lamps of course had the precedence ; and this lady Mr. Mugford accompanied to her carriage step.

He did not pay the same attention to Mrs. Firmin. Most likely he forgot. Possibly he did not think etiquette required he should show that sort of politeness to a sub-editor's wife : at any rate, he was not so rude as Philip himself had been during the evening, but he stood in the hall looking at his guests departing in their cab, when, in a sudden gust of passion, Philip stepped out of the carriage, and stalked up to his host, who stood there in his own hall confronting him, Philip declared, with a most impudent smile on his face.

" Come back to light a pipe I suppose ? Nice thing for your wife, ain't it ? " said Mugford, relishing his own joke.

" I am come back, sir," said Philip, glaring at Mugford, " to ask how you dared invite Mrs. Philip Firmin to meet that woman ? "

Here, on his side, Mr. Mugford lost his temper, and from

this moment *his* wrong begins. When he was in a passion, the language used by Mr. Mugford was not, it appears, choice. We have heard that when angry, he was in the habit of swearing freely at his subordinates. He broke out on this occasion also with many oaths. He told Philip that he would stand his impudence no longer ; that he was as good as a swindling doctor's son ; that though he hadn't been to college he could buy and pay them as had ; and that if Philip liked to come into the back yard for ten minutes, he'd give him one—two, and show him whether he was a man or not. Poor Char, who, indeed, fancied that her husband had gone back to light his cigar, sat awhile unconscious in her cab, and supposed that the two gentlemen were engaged on newspaper business. When Mugford began to pull his coat off, she sat wondering, but not in the least understanding the meaning of the action. Philip had described his employer as walking about his office without a coat and using energetic language.

But when, attracted by the loudness of the talk, Mrs. Mugford came forth from her neighboring drawing-room, accompanied by such of her children as had not yet gone to roost—when seeing Mugford pulling off his dress-coat, she began to scream—when, lifting his voice over hers, Mugford poured forth oaths, and frantically shook his fists at Philip, asking how that blackguard dared insult him in his own house, and proposing to knock his head off at that moment—then poor Char, in wild alarm, sprang out of the cab, and ran to her husband, whose whole frame was throbbing, whose nostrils were snorting with passion. Then Mrs. Mugford springing forward, placed her ample form before her husband's, and calling Philip a great cowardly beast, asked him if he was going to attack that little old man ? Then Mugford dashing his coat down to the ground, called with fresh oaths to Philip to come on. And, in fine, there was a most unpleasant row, occasioned by Mr. Philip Firmin's hot temper.

CHAPTER XXXV.

RES ANGUSTA DOMI.

To reconcile these two men was impossible, after such a quarrel as that described in the last chapter. The only chance of peace was to keep the two men apart. If they met, they

would fly at each other. Mugford always persisted that he could
have got the better of his great hulking sub-editor, who did not
know the use of his fists. In Mugford's youthful time, bruising
was a fashionable art ; and the old gentleman still believed in
his own skill and prowess. "Don't tell me," he would say ;
"though the fellar is as big as a life-guardsman, I would have
doubled him up in two minutes." I am very glad, for poor
Charlotte's sake and his own, that Philip did not undergo the
doubling-up process. He himself felt such a wrath and surprise at his employer as, I suppose, a lion does when a little
dog attacks him. I should not like to be that little dog ; nor
nor does my modest and peaceful nature at all prompt and
impel me to combat with lions.

It was mighty well Mr. Philip Firmin had shown his spirit,
and quarrelled with his bread-and-butter ; but when Saturday
came, what philanthropist would hand four sovereigns and four
shillings over to Mr. F., as Mr. Burjoice, the publisher of the
Pall Mall Gazette, had been accustomed to do ? I will say for
my friend that a still keener remorse than that which he felt
about money thrown away attended him when he found that
Mrs. Woolsey, towards whom he had cast a sidelong stone of
persecution, was a most respectable and honorable lady. "I
should like to go, sir, and grovel before her," Philip said, in his
energetic way. "If I see that tailor, I will request him to put
his foot on my head, and trample on me with his high-lows.
Oh, for shame ! for shame ! Shall I never learn charity towards my neighbors, and always go on believing in the lies
which people tell me ? When I meet that scoundrel Trail at
the club, I must chastise him. How dared he take away the
reputation of an honest woman ? " Philip's friends besought
him, for the sake of society and peace, not to carry this quarrel
farther. "If," we said, "every woman whom Trail has maligned had a champion who should box Trail's ears at the club,
what a vulgar, quarrelsome place that club would become !
My dear Philip, did you ever know Mr. Trail say a good word
of man or woman ? " and by these or similar entreaties and
arguments, we succeeded in keeping the Queen's peace.

Yes : but how find another *Pall Mall Gazette* ? Had Philip
possessed seven thousand pounds in the three per cents., his
income would have been no greater than that which he drew
from Mugford's faithful bank. Ah ! how wonderful ways and
means are ! When I think how this very line, this very word,
which I am writing represents money, I am lost in respectful
astonishment. A man takes his own case, as he says his own

prayers, on behalf of himself and his family. I am paid, we will say, for the sake of illustration, at the rate of sixpence per line. With the words, "Ah, how wonderful," to the words "per line," I can buy a loaf, a piece of butter, a jug of milk, a modicum of tea,—actually enough to make breakfast for the family; and the servants of the house; and the charwoman, *their* servant, can shake up the tea-leaves with a fresh supply of water, sop the crusts, and get a meal *tant bien que mal.* Wife, children, guests, servants, charwoman, we are all actually making a meal off Philip Firmin's bones as it were. And my next-door neighbor, whom I see marching away to chambers, umbrella in hand? And next door but one the City man? And next door but two the doctor?—I know the baker has left loaves at every one of their doors this morning, that all their chimneys are smoking, and they will all have breakfast. Ah, thank God for it! I hope, friend, you and I are not too proud to ask for our daily bread, and to be grateful for getting it? Mr. Philip had to work for his, in care and trouble, like other children of men :—to work for it, and I hope to pray for it, too. It is a thought to me awful and beautiful, that of the daily prayer, and of the myriads of fellow-men uttering it, in care and in sickness, in doubt and in poverty, in health and in wealth. *Panem nostrum da nobis hodie.* Philip whispers it by the bedside where wife and child lie sleeping, and goes to his early labor with a stouter heart : as he creeps to his rest when the day's labor is over, and the quotidian bread is earned, and breathes his hushed thanks to the bountiful Giver of the meal. All over this world what an endless chorus is singing of love, and thanks, and prayer. Day tells to day the wondrous story, and night recounts it unto night.——How do I come to think of a sunrise which I saw near twenty years ago on the Nile, when the river and sky flushed and glowed with the dawning light, and as the luminary appeared, the boatman knelt on the rosy deck, and adored Allah? So, as thy sun rises, friend, over the humble housetops round about your home, shall you wake many and many a day to duty and labor. May the task have been honestly done when the night comes ; and the steward deal kindly with the laborer.

So two of Philip's cables cracked and gave way after a very brief strain, and the poor fellow held by nothing now but that wonderful *European Review* established by the mysterious Tregarvan. Actors, a people of superstitions and traditions, opine that heaven, in some mysterious way, makes managers for their benefit. In like manner, Review proprietors are sent to pro vide the pabulum for us men of letters. With what compla-cency did my wife listen to the somewhat long-winded and pompous oratory of Tregarvan! He pompous and common-place? Tregarvan spoke with excellent good sense. That wily woman never showed she was tired of his conversation. She praised him to Philip behind his back, and would not allow a word in his disparagement. As a doctor will punch your chest, your liver, your heart, listen at your lungs, squeeze your pulse, and what not, so this practitioner studied, shampooed, aus-cultated Tregarvan. Of course, he allowed himself to be oper-ated upon. Of course, he had no idea that the lady was flatter-ing, wheedling, humbugging him; but thought that he was a very well-informed, eloquent man, who had seen and read a great deal, and had an agreeable method of imparting his knowledge, and that the lady in question was a sensible woman, naturally ea-ger for more information. Go, Delilah! I understand your tricks! I know many another Omphale in London, who will coax Hercules away from his club, to come and listen to her wheedling talk.

One great difficulty we had was to make Philip read Tre-garvan's own articles in the *Review*. He at first said he could not, or that he could not remember them; so that there was no use in reading them. And Philip's new master used to make artful allusions to his own writings in the course of con-versation, so that our unwary friend would find himself under examination in any casual interview with Tregarvan, whose opinions on free-trade, malt-tax, income-tax, designs of Russia, or what not, might be accepted or denied, but ought at least to be known. We actually made Philip get up his owner's ar-ticles. We put questions to him, privily, regarding them—"coached" him, according to the university phrase. My wife humbugged that wretched Member of Parliament in a way which makes me shudder, when I think of what hypocrisy the sex is capable. Those arts and dissimulations with which she wheedles others, suppose she exercise them on *me?* Horrible thought! No, angel! To others thou mayest be a coaxing hypocrite; to me thou art all candor. *Other* men may have been humbugged by other women; but I am not to be taken in by that sort of thing; and thou art all candor!

We had then so much per annum as editor. We were paid, besides, for our articles. We had really a snug little pension out of this *Review*, and we prayed it might last for ever. We might write a novel. We might contribute articles to a daily paper; get a little parliamentary practice as a barrister.

We actually did get Philip into a railway case or two, and my wife must be coaxing and hugging solicitors' ladies, as she had wheedled and coaxed Members of Parliament. Why, I do believe my Delilah set up a flirtation with old Bishop Crossticks, with an idea of getting her *protégé* a living ; and though the lady indignantly repudiates this charge, will she be pleased to explain how the bishop's sermons were so outrageously praised in the *Review ?*

Philip's roughness and frankness did not displease Tregarvan, to the wonder of us all, who trembled lest he should lose this as he had lost his former place. Tregarvan had more country-houses than one, and at these not only was the editor of the *Review* made welcome, but the editor's wife and children, whom Tregarvan's wife took into especial regard. In London, Lady Mary had assemblies where our little friend Charlotte made her appearance ; and half-a-dozen times in the course of the season the wealthy Cornish gentleman feasted his retainers of the *Review*. His wine was excellent and old ; his jokes were old, too ; his table pompous, grave, plentiful. If Philip was to eat the bread of dependence, the loaf was here very kindly prepared for him ; and he ate it humbly, and with not too much grumbling. This diet chokes some proud stomachs and disagrees with them ; but Philip was very humble now, and of a nature grateful for kindness. He is one who requires the help of friends, and can accept benefits without losing independence—not all men's gifts, but some men's, whom he repays not only with coin, but with an immense affection and gratitude. How that man did laugh at my witticisms ! How he worshipped the ground on which my wife walked ! He elected himself our champion. He quarrelled with other people who found fault with our characters, or would not see our perfections. There was something affecting in the way in which this big man took the humble place. We could do no wrong in his eyes ; and woe betide the man who spoke disparagingly of us in his presence !

One day, at his patron's table, Philip exercised his valor and championship in our behalf by defending us against the evil speaking of that Mr. Trail, who has been mentioned before as a gentleman difficult to please, and credulous of ill regarding his neighbor. The talk happened to fall upon the character of the reader's most humble servant, and Trail, as may be imagined, spared me no more than the rest of mankind. Would you like to be liked by all people? That would be a reason why Trail should hate you. Were you an angel fresh dropped from the skies, he would espy dirt on your robe, and a black feather or two in your wing. As for me, I know I am not angelical at all ; and in walking my native earth, can't help a little mud on my trousers. Well : Mr. Trail began to paint my portrait, laying on those dark shadows which that well-known master is in the habit of employing. I was a parasite of the nobility ; I was a heartless sycophant, house-breaker, drunkard, murderer, returned convict, &c., &c. With a little imagination, Mrs. Candour can fill up the outline, and arrange the colors so as to suit her amiable fancy.

Philip had come late to dinner ;—of *this* fault, I must confess, he is guilty only too often. The company were at table ; he took the only place vacant, and this happened to be at the side of Mr. Trail. On Trail's other side was a portly individual, of a healthy and rosy countenance and voluminous white waistcoat, to whom Trail directed much of his amiable talk, and whom he addressed once or twice as Sir John. Once or twice already we have seen how Philip has quarrelled at table. He cried *mea culpa* loudly and honestly enough. He made vows of reform in this particular. He succeeded, dearly beloved brethren, not much worse or better than you or I do, who confess our faults, and go on promising to improve, and stumbling and picking ourselves up every day. The pavement of life is strewed with orange-peel ; and who has not slipped on the flags ?

" He is the most conceited man in London,"—Trail was going on, " and one of the most worldly. He will throw over a colonel to dine with a general. He wouldn't throw over you two baronets—he is a great deal too shrewd a fellow for that. He wouldn't give *you* up, perhaps, to dine with a lord ; but any ordinary baronet he would."

" And why not us as well as the rest ? " asks Tregarvan, who seemed amused at the speaker's chatter.

" Because you are not like common baronets at all. Because your estates are a great deal too large. Because, I suppose, you might either of you go to the Upper House any day. Because, as an author, he may be supposed to be afraid of a certain *Review*," cries Trail, with a loud laugh.

" Trail is speaking of a friend of yours," said the host, nodding and smiling, to the new-comer.

" Very lucky for my friend," growls Philip, and eats his soup in silence.

" By the way, that article of his on Madame de Sevigné is poor stuff. No knowledge of the period. Three gross blunders ın French. A man can't write of French society unless he has lived in French society. What does Pendennis know of it? A man who makes blunders like those can't understand French. A man who can't speak French can't get on in French society. Therefore he can't write about French society. All these propositions are clear enough. Thank you. Dry champagne, if you please. He is enormously over-rated, I tell you; and so is his wife. They used to put her forward as a beauty: and she is only a dowdy woman out of a nursery. She has no style about her."

" She is only one of the best women in the world," Mr. Firmin called out, turning very red ; and hereupon entered into a defence of characters, and pronounced a eulogium upon both and each of us, in which I hope there was some little truth. However, he spoke with great enthusiasm, and Mr. Trail found himself in a minority.

" You are right to stand up for your friends, Firmin!" cried the host. " Let me introduce you to——"

" Let me introduce myself," said the gentleman on the other side of Mr. Trail. " Mr. Firmin, you and I are kinsmen,—I am Sir John Ringwood." And Sir John reached a hand to Philip across Trail's chair. They talked a great deal together in the course of the evening : and when Mr. Trail found that the great county gentleman was friendly and familiar with Philip, and claimed a relationship with him, his manner towards Firmin altered. He pronounced afterwards a warm eulogy upon Sir John for his frankness and good nature in recognizing his unfortunate relative, and charitably said, " Philip might not be like the doctor, and could not help having a rogue for a father." In former days, Trail had eaten and drunken freely at that rogue's table. But we must have truth, you know, before all things : and if your own brother has committed a sin, common justice requires that you should stone him.

In former days, and not long after Lord Ringwood's death, Philip had left his card at this kinsman's door, and Sir John's butler, driving in his master's brougham, had left a card upon Philip, who was not over well pleased by this acknowledgment of his civility, and, in fact, employed abusive epithets when he spoke of the transaction. But when the two gentlemen actually met, their intercourse was kindly and pleasant enough. Sir John listened to his relative's talk—and it appears, Philip comported himself with his usual free and easy manner—with interest and curiosity ; and owned afterwards that evil tongues had previously been busy with the young man's character, and that slander and untruth had been spoken regarding him. In this respect, if Philip is worse off than his neighbors, I can only say his neighbors are fortunate.

Two days after the meeting of the cousins, the tranquillity of Thornhaugh Street was disturbed by the appearance of a magnificent yellow chariot, with crests, hammer-cloths, a bewigged coachman, and a powdered footman. Betsy, the nurse, who was going to take baby out for a walk, encountered this giant on the threshold of Mrs. Brandon's door: and a lady within the chariot delivered three cards to the tall menial, who transferred them to Betsy. And Betsy persisted in saying that the lady in the carriage admired baby very much, and asked its age, at which baby's mamma was not in the least surprised. In due course, an invitation to dinner followed, and our friends became acquainted with their kinsfolk.

If you have a good memory for pedigrees—and in my youthful time every man *de bonne maison* studied genealogies, and had his English families in his memory—you know that this Sir John Ringwood, who succeeded to the principal portion of the estates, but not to the titles of the late earl, was descended from a mutual ancestor, a Sir John, whose elder son was ennobled (temp Geo. I.), whilst the second son, following the legal profession, became a judge, and had a son, who became a baronet, and who begat that present Sir John who has just been shaking hands with Philip across Trail's back.*

* Copied, by permission of P. Firmin, Esq., from the Genealogical Tree in his possession.

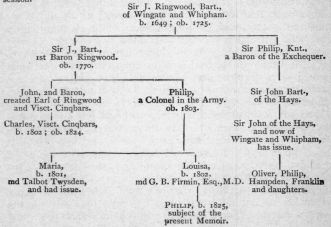

Sir J. Ringwood, Bart.,
of Wingate and Whipham.
b. 1649 ; ob. 1725.

Sir J., Bart.,
1st Baron Ringwood.
ob. 1770.

Sir Philip, Knt.,
a Baron of the Exchequer.

John, 2nd Baron,
created Earl of Ringwood
and Visct. Cinqbars.

Philip,
a Colonel in the Army.
ob. 1803.

Sir John Bart.,
of the Hays.

Charles, Visct. Cinqbars,
b. 1802 ; ob. 1824.

Sir John of the Hays,
and now of
Wingate and Whipham,
has issue.

Maria,
b. 1801,
md Talbot Twysden,
and had issue.

Louisa,
b. 1802,
md G. B. Firmin, Esq.,M.D.

Oliver, Philip,
Hampden, Franklin
and daughters.

PHILIP, b. 1825,
subject of the
present Memoir.

Thus the two men were cousins; and in right of the heiress, his poor mother, Philip might quarter the Ringwood arms on his carriage, whenever he drove out. These, you know, are argent, a dexter sinople on a fesse wavy of the first—or pick out, my dear friend, any coat you like out of the whole heraldic wardrobe, and accommodate it to our friend Firmin.

When he was a young man at college, Philip had dabbled a little in this queer science of heraldry, and used to try and believe the legends about his ancestry, which his fond mother imparted to him. He had a great book-plate made for himself, with a prodigious number of quarterings, and could recite the alliances by which such and such a quartering came into his shield. His father rather confirmed these histories, and spoke of them and of his wife's noble family with much respect; and Philip, artlessly whispering to a vulgar boy at school that he was descended from King John, was thrashed very unkindly by the vulgar upper boy, and nicknamed King John for many a long day after. I dare say many other gentlemen who profess to trace their descent from ancient kings have no better or worse authority for their pedigree than friend Philip.

When our friend paid his second visit to Sir John Ringwood, he was introduced to his kinsman's library; a great family tree hung over the mantel-piece, surrounded by a whole gallery of defunct Ringwoods, of whom the Baronet was now the representative. He quoted to Philip the hackneyed old Ovidian lines (some score of years ago a great deal of that old coin was current in conversation). As for family, he said, and ancestors, and what we have not done ourselves, these things we can hardly call ours. Sir John gave Philip to understand that he was a staunch Liberal. Sir John was for going with the age. Sir John had fired a shot from the Paris barricades. Sir John was for the rights of man everywhere all over the world. He had pictures of Franklin, Lafayette, Washington, and the First Consul Bonaparte, on his walls along with his ancestors. He had lithograph copies of Magna Charta, the Declaration of American Independence, and the Signatures to the Death of Charles I. He did not scruple to own his preference for republican institutions. He wished to know what right had any man—the late Lord Ringwood, for example—to sit in a hereditary House of Peers and legislate over him? That lord had had a son, Cinqbars, who died many years before, a victim of his own follies and debaucheries. Had Lord Cinqbars survived his father, he would now be sitting an earl in the House of Peers — the most ignorant young man, the most unprincipled young man, reckless, dissolute, of the feeblest intellect, and the worst life. Well, had he lived and inherited the Ringwood property, that creature would have been an earl: whereas he, Sir John, his superior in morals, in character, in intellect, his equal in point of birth (for had they not both a common ancestor?) was Sir John still. The inequalities in men's chances in life were monstrous and ridiculous. He was determined, henceforth, to look at a man for himself alone, and not esteem him for any of the absurd caprices of fortune.

As the republican was talking to his relative, a servant came into the room and whispered to his master that the plumber had come with his bill as by appointment; upon which Sir John rose up in a fury, asked the servant how he dared to disturb him, and bade him to tell the plumber to go to the lowest depth of Tartarus. Nothing could equal the insolence and rapacity of tradesmen, he said, except the insolence and idleness of servants; and he called this one back, and asked him how he dared to leave the fire in that state?— stormed and raged at him with a volubility which astonished his new acquaintance; and, the man being gone, resumed his previous subject of conversation, viz., natural equality and the outrageous injustice of the present social system. After talking for half an hour, during which Philip found that he himself could hardly find an opportunity of uttering a word, Sir John took out his watch, and got up from his chair; at which hint Philip too rose, not sorry to bring the interview to an end. And herewith Sir John accompanied his kinsman into the hall, and to the street door, before which the Baronet's groom was riding, leading his master's horse. And Philip heard the Baronet using violent language to the groom, as he had done to the servant within doors. Why, the army in Flanders did not swear more terribly than this admirer of republican institutions and advocate of the rights of man.

Philip was not allowed to go away without appointing a day when he and his wife would partake of their kinsman's hospitality. On this occasion, Mrs. Philip comported herself with so much grace and simplicity, that Sir John and Lady Ringwood pronounced her to be a very pleasing and ladylike person; and I dare say wondered how a person in her rank of life could have acquired manners that were so refined and agreeable. Lady Ringwood asked after the child which she had seen, praised its beauty; of course, won the mother's heart, and thereby caused her to speak with perhaps more freedom than she would otherwise have felt at a first interview,

Mrs. Philip has a dainty touch on the piano, and a sweet singing voice that is charmingly true and neat. She performed at the dinner some of the songs of her little *repertoire*, and pleased her audience. Lady Ringwood loved good music, and was herself a fine performer of the ancient school, when she played Haydn and Mozart under the tuition of good old Sir George Thrum. The tall and handsome beneficed clergyman who acted as major-domo of Sir John's establishment, placed a parcel in the carriage when Mr. and Mrs. Philip took their leave, and announced with much respectful deference that the cab was paid. Our friends no doubt would have preferred to dispense with this ceremony; but it is ill looking even a gift cab-horse in the mouth, and so Philip was a gainer of some two shillings by his kinsman's liberality.

When Charlotte came to open the parcel which major-domo, with his lady's compliments, had placed in the cab, I fear she did not exhibit that elation which we ought to feel for the favors of our friends. A couple of little frocks, of the cut of George IV., some little red shoes of the same period, some crumpled sashes, and other small articles of wearing apparel, by her lady-ship's order by her ladyship's lady's-maid; and Lady Ringwood kissing Charlotte at her departure, told her that she had caused this little packet to be put away for her. "H'm," says Philip, only half pleased. "Suppose Sir John had told his butler to put up one of his blue coats and brass buttons for me, as well as pay the cab?"

"If it was meant in kindness, Philip, we must not be angry," pleaded Philip's wife;—"and I am sure if you had heard her and the Miss Ringwoods speak of baby, you would like them, as I intend to do."

But Mrs. Philip never put those mouldy old red shoes upon baby; and as for the little frocks, children's frocks are made so much fuller now that Lady Ringwood's presents did not an-swer at all. Charlotte managed to furbish up a sash, and a pair of epaulets for her child—epaulets are they called? Shoulder-knots—what you will, ladies; and with these orna-ments Miss Firmin was presented to Lady Ringwood and some of her family.

The good-will of these new-found relatives of Philip's was laborious was evident, and yet I must say was not altogether agreeable. At the first period of their intercourse—for this, too, I am sorry to say, came to an end, or presently suffered interruption—tokens of affection in the shape of farm produce, country butter and poultry, and actual butcher's meat, came

from Berkeley Square to Thornhaugh Street. The Duke of
Double-glo'ster I know is much richer than you are ; but if he
were to offer to make you a present of half-a-crown, I doubt
whether you would be quite pleased. And so with Philip and
his relatives. A hamper brought in the brougham, containing
hot-house grapes and country butter, is very well, but a leg of
mutton I own was a gift that was rather tough to swallow. It
was tough. That point we ascertained and established amidst
roars of laughter one day when we dined with our friends.
Did Lady Ringwood send a sack of turnips in the brougham
too ? In a word, we ate Sir John's mutton, and we laughed at
him, and be sure many a man has done the same by you and
me. Last Friday, for instance, as Jones and Brown go away
after dining with your humble servant. " Did you ever see
such profusion and extravagance ? " asks Brown. " Profusion
and extravagance ! " cries Jones, that well-known epicure. " I
never saw anything so shabby in my life. What does the fellow
mean by asking *me* to such a dinner ? " " True," says the other,
" it *was* an abominable dinner, Jones, as you justly say ; but it
was very profuse in him to give it. Don't you see ? " and so
both our good friends are agreed.

Ere many days were over the great yellow chariot and its
powdered attendants again made their appearance before Mrs.
Brandon's modest door in Thornhaugh Street, and Lady Ringwood and two daughters descended from the carriage and made
their way to Mr. Philip's apartments in the second floor, just
as that worthy gentleman was sitting down to dinner with his
wife. Lady Ringwood, bent upon being gracious, was in ecstasies with everything she saw—a clean house—a nice little maid
—pretty picturesque rooms—odd rooms—and what charming
pictures ! Several of these were the work of the fond pencil
of poor J. J., who, as has been told, had painted Philip's beard
and Charlotte's eyebrow, and Charlotte's baby a thousand and
a thousand times. " May we come in ? Are we disturbing
you ? What dear little bits of china ! What a beautiful mug,
Mr. Firmin ! " This was poor J. J.'s present to his goddaughter.
" How nice the luncheon looks ! Dinner, is it ? How pleasant
to dine at this hour ! " The ladies were determined to be
charmed with everything round about them.

" We are dining on your poultry. May we offer some to you
and Miss Ringwood," says the master of the house.

" Why don't you dine in the dining-room ? Why do you
dine in a bedroom ? " asks Franklin Ringwood, the interesting
young son of the Baron of Ringwood.

"Somebody else lives in the parlor," says Mrs. Philip. "On which the boy remarks, "We have two dining-rooms in Berkeley Square. I mean for us, besides papa's study, which I mustn't go into. And the servants have two dining-rooms and——"

"Hush!" here cries mamma, with the usual remark regarding the beauty of silence in little boys.

But Franklin persists in spite of the "Hushes!" "And so we have at Ringwood; and at Whipham there's ever so many dining-rooms—ever so many—and I like Whipham a great deal better than Ringwood, because my pony is at Whipham. *You* have not got a pony. You are too poor."

"Franklin!"

"You said he was too poor; and you would not have had chickens if we had not given them to you. Mamma, you know you said they were very poor, and would like them."

And here mamma looked red, and I dare say Philip's cheeks and ears tingled, and for once Mrs. Philip was thankful at hearing her baby cry, for it gave her a pretext for leaving the room and flying to the nursery, whither the other two ladies accompanied her.

Meanwhile Master Franklin went on with his artless conversation. "Mr. Philip, why do they say you are wicked? You do not look wicked; and I am sure Mrs. Philip does not look wicked—she looks very good."

"Who says I am wicked?" asks Mr. Firmin of his candid young relative.

"Oh, ever so many! Cousin Ringwood says so; and Blanche says so; and Woolcomb says so; only I don't like him, he's so very brown. And when they heard you had been to dinner, 'Has that beast been here?' Ringwood says. And I don't like him a bit. But I like you, at least I think I do. You only have oranges for dessert. We always have lots of things for dessert at home. *You* don't, I suppose, because you've got no money—only a very little."

"Well: I have got only a very little," says Philip.

"I have some—ever so much. And I'll buy something for your wife; and I shall like to have you better at home than Blanche, and Ringwood, and that Woolcomb; and they never give me anything. You can't, you know; because you are so very poor—you are; but we'll often send you things, I dare say. And I'll have an orange, please, thank you. And there's a chap at our school, and his name is Suckling, and he ate eighteen oranges, and wouldn't give one away to anybody. Wasn't he a greedy pig? And I have wine with my oranges—I do : a glass of wine—thank you. That's jolly. But you don't have it often, I suppose, because you're so very poor."

I am glad Philip's infant could not understand, being yet of too tender age, the compliments which Lady Ringwood and her daughter passed upon her. As it was, the compliments charmed the mother, for whom indeed they were intended, and did not inflame the unconscious baby's vanity.

What would the polite mamma and sister have said if they had heard that unlucky Franklin's prattle? The boy's simplicity amused his tall cousin. "Yes," says Philip, "we are very poor, but we are very happy, and don't mind—that's the truth."

"Mademoiselle, that's the German governess, said she wondered how you could live at all ; and I don't think you could if you ate as much as she did. You should see her eat ; she is such a *oner* at eating. Fred, my brother, that's the one who is at college, one day tried to see how Mademoiselle Wallfisch could eat, and she had twice of soup, and then she said *sivoplay ;* and then twice of fish, and she said *sivoplay* for more ; and then she had roast mutton—no, I think, roast beef it was ; and she eats the pease with her knife ; and then she had raspberry jam pudding, and ever so much beer, and then——" But what came then we never shall know ; because while young Franklin was choking with laughter (accompanied with a large piece of orange) at the ridiculous recollection of Miss Wallfisch's appetite, his mamma and sister came down stairs from Charlotte's nursery, and brought the dear boy's conversation to an end. The ladies chose to go home, delighted with Philip, baby, Charlotte. Everything was *so* proper. Everything was so nice. Mrs. Firmin was so ladylike. The fine ladies watched her, and her behavior, with that curiosity which the Brobdingnag ladies displayed when they held up little Gulliver on their palms, and saw him bow, smile, dance, draw his sword, and take off his hat, just like a man.

CHAPTER XXXVI.

IN WHICH THE DRAWING-ROOMS ARE NOT FURNISHED AFTER ALL.

WE cannot expect to be loved by a relative whom we have knocked into an illuminated pond, and whose coat-tails, pantaloons, nether limbs, and best feelings we have lacerated with ill treatment and broken glass. A man whom you have so treated behind his back will not be sparing of his punishment behind yours. Of course all the Twysdens, male and female, and Woolcomb, the dusky husband of Philip's former love, hated and feared, and maligned him ; and were in the habit of speaking of him as a truculent and reckless savage and monster, coarse and brutal in his language and behavior, ragged, dirty and reckless in his personal appearance ; reeking with smoke, perpetually reeling in drink, indulging in oaths, actions, laughter which rendered him intolerable in civilized society. The Twysdens, during Philip's absence abroad, had been very respectful and assiduous in courting the new head of the Ringwood family. They had flattered Sir John, and paid court to my lady. They had been welcomed at Sir John's houses in town and country. They had adopted his politics in a great measure, as they had adopted the politics of the deceased peer. They had never lost an opportunity of abusing poor Philip and of ingratiating themselves. They had never refused any invitation from Sir John in town or country, and had ended by utterly boring him and Lady Ringwood and the Ringwood family in general. Lady Ringwood learned somewhere how pitilessly Mrs. Woolcomb had jilted her cousin when a richer suitor appeared in the person of the West Indian. Then news came how Philip had administered a beating to Woolcomb, to young Twysden, to a dozen who set on him. The early prejudices began to pass away. A friend or two of Philip's told Ringwood how he was mistaken in the young man, and painted a portrait of him in colors much more favorable than those which his kinsfolk employed. Indeed, dear relations, if the public wants to know our little faults and errors, I think I know who will not grudge the requisite information. Dear aunt Candour, are you not still alive, and don't you know what we had for dinner yesterday, and the amount (monstrous extravagance !) of the washerwoman's bill ?

Well, the Twysden family so bespattered poor Philip with abuse, and represented him as a monster of such hideous mien, that no wonder the Ringwoods avoided him. They then began to grow utterly sick and tired of his detractors. And then Sir John, happening to talk with his brother Member of Parliament, Tregarvan, in the House of Commons, heard quite a different story regarding our friend to that with which the Twysdens had regaled him, and, with no little surprise on Sir John's part, was told by Tregarvan how honest, rough, worthy, affectionate and gentle this poor maligned fellow was; how he had been sinned against by his wretch of a father, whom he had forgiven and actually helped out of his wretched means; and how he was making a brave battle against poverty, and had a sweet little loving wife and child, whom every kind heart would willingly strive to help. Because people are rich they are not of necessity ogres. Because they are born gentlemen and ladies of good degree, are in easy circumstances, and have a generous education, it does not follow that they are heartless and will turn their back on a friend. *Mois que vous parle*—I have been in a great strait of sickness near to death, and the friends who came to help me with every comfort, succor, sympathy were actually gentlemen, who lived in good houses, and had a good education. They didn't turn away because I was sick, or fly from me because they thought I was poor ; on the contrary, hand, purse, succor, sympathy were ready, and praise be to heaven. And so too did Philip find help when he needed it, and succor when he was in poverty. Tregarvan, we will own, was a pompous little man, his House of Commons speeches were dull, and his written documents awfully slow ; but he had a kind heart : he was touched by that picture which Laura drew of the young man's poverty, and honesty, and simple hopefulness in the midst of hard times : and we have seen how the *European Review* was thus entrusted to Mr. Philip's management. Then some artful friends of Philip's determined that he should be reconciled to his relations, who were well to do in the world, and might serve him. And I wish, dear reader, that your respectable relatives and mine would bear this little paragraph in mind and leave us both handsome legacies. Then Tregarvan spoke to Sir John Ringwood, and that meeting was brought about, where, for once at least, Mr. Philip quarrelled with nobody.

And now came another little piece of good luck, which, I suppose, must be attributed to the same kind friend who had been scheming for Philip's benefit, and who is never so happy as when her little plots for her friends' benefit can be made to succeed. Yes : when that arch-jobber—don't tell me ;—I never knew a woman worth a pin who wasn't—when that arch-jobber, I say, has achieved a job by which some friend is made happy, her eyes and cheeks brighten with triumph. Whether she has put a sick man into a hospital, or got a poor woman a family's washing, or made a sinner repent and return to wife, husband, or what not, that woman goes off and pays her thanks, where thanks are due, with such fervor, with such lightsomeness, with such happiness, that I assure you she is a sight to behold. Hush ! When one sinner is saved, who are glad ? Some of us know a woman or two pure as angels—know, and are thankful.

When the person about whom I have been prattling has one of her benevolent jobs on hand, or has completed it, there is a sort of triumph and mischief in her manner, which I don't know otherwise how to describe. She does not understand my best jokes at this period, or answers them at random, or laughs very absurdly and vacantly. She embraces her children wildly, and, at the most absurd moments, is utterly unmindful when they are saying their lessons, prattling their little questions and so forth. I recall all these symptoms (and put this and that together, as the saying is) as happening on one especial day, at the commencement of Easter Term, eighteen hundred and never mind what—as happening on one especial morning when this lady had been astoundingly *distraite* and curiously excited. I now remember how, during her children's dinner-time, she sat looking into the square out of her window, and scarcely attending to the little innocent cries for mutton which the children were offering up.

At last there was a rapid clank over the pavement, a tall figure passed the parlor windows, which our kind friends know look into Queen Square, and then came a loud ring at the bell, and I thought the mistress of the house gave an ah—a sigh— as though her heart was relieved.

The street door was presently opened, and then the dining-room door, and Philip walks in with his hat on, his blue eyes staring before him, his hair flaming about, and " La, uncle Philip ! " cry the children. " What have you done to yourself ? You have shaved off your mustache." And so he had, I declare.

" I say, Pen, look here ! This has been left at chambers ; and Cassidy has sent it on by his clerk," our friend said. I forget whether it has been stated that Philip's name still remained on the door of those chambers in Parchment Buildings, where we once heard his song of " Dr. Luther," and were present at his call-supper.

The document which Philip produced was actually a brief. The papers were superscribed, " In Parliament, Polwheedle and Tredyddlum Railway. To support bill, Mr. Firmin ; retainer, five guineas ; brief, fifty guineas ; consultation, five guineas. With you Mr. Armstrong, Sir J. Whitworth, Mr. Pinkerton." Here was a wonder of wonders ! A shower of gold was poured out on my friend. A light dawned upon me. The proposed bill was for a Cornish line. Our friend Tregarvan was concerned in it, the line passing through his property, and my wife had canvassed him privately, and by her wheedling and blandishments had persuaded Tregarvan to use his interest with the agents and get Philip this welcome aid.

Philip eyed the paper with a queer expression. He handled it as some men handle a baby. He looked as if he did not know what to do with it, and as if he should like to drop it. I believe I made some satirical remark to this effect as I looked at our friend with his paper.

" He holds a child beautifully," said my wife with much enthusiasm ; " much better than some people who laugh at him."

" And he will hold this no doubt much to his credit. May this be the father of many briefs. May you have bags full of them ! " Philip has all our good wishes. They did not cost much, or avail much, but they were sincere. I know men who can't for the lives of them give even that cheap coin of good will, but hate their neighbors' prosperity, and are angry with them when they cease to be dependent and poor.

We have said how Cassidy's astonished clerk had brought the brief from chambers to Firmin at his lodgings at Mrs. Brandon's in Thornhaugh Street. Had a bailiff served him with a writ, Philip could not have been more surprised, or in a greater tremor. A brief ? Grands Dieux ! What was he to do with a brief ? He thought of going to bed, and being ill, or flying from home, country, family. Brief ? Charlotte, of course, seeing her husband alarmed, began to quake too. Indeed, if his worship's finger aches, does not her whole body suffer ? But Charlotte's and Philip's constant friend, the Little Sister, felt no such fear. " Now there's this opening, you must take it, my dear," she said. " Suppose you don't know much about law——" " Much ! nothing," interposed Philip. " You might ask me to play the piano ; but as I never happened to have learned——"

" La — don't tell me ! You mustn't show a faint heart. Take the business, and do it as best you can. You'll do it better next time, and next. The Bar's a gentleman's business.

Don't I attend a judge's lady, which I remember her with her first in a little bit of a house in Bernard Street, Russell Square; and now haven't I been to her in Eaton Square, with a butler and two footmen, and carriages ever so many? You may work on at your newspapers, and get a crust, and when you're old, and if you quarrel—and you have a knack of quarrelling—he has, Mrs. Firmin. I knew him before you did. Quarrelsome he is, and he will be, though you think him an angel, to be sure.—Suppose you quarrel with your newspaper masters, and your reviews, and that, you lose your place. A gentleman like Mr. Philip oughtn't to have a master. I couldn't bear to think of your going down of a Saturday to the publishing office to get your wages like a workman."

" But I *am* a workman," interposes Philip.

" La! But do you mean to remain one for ever? I would rise, if I was a man!" said the intrepid little woman: " I would rise, or I'd know the reason why. Who knows how many in family you're going to be? I'd have more spirit than to live in a second floor—I would!"

And the Little Sister said this, though she clung round Philip's child with a rapture of fondness which she tried in vain to conceal; though she felt that to part from it would be to part from her life's chief happiness; though she loved Philip as her own son: and Charlotte—well, Charlotte for Philip's sake—as women love other women.

Charlotte came to her friends in Queen Square, and told us of the resolute Little Sister's advice and conversation. She knew that Mrs. Brandon only loved her as something belonging to Philip. She admired this Little Sister; and trusted her; and could afford to bear that little somewhat scornful domination which Brandon exercised. " She does not love me, because Philip does," Charlotte said. " Do you think I could like her, or any woman, if I thought Philip loved them? I could kill them, Laura, that I could!" And at this sentiment I imagine daggers shooting out of a pair of eyes that were ordinarily very gentle and bright.

Not having been engaged in the case in which Philip had the honor of first appearing, I cannot enter into particulars regarding it, but am sure that case must have been uncommonly strong in itself which could survive such an advocate. He passed a frightful night of torture before appearing in committee-room. During that night, he says, his hair grew gray. His old college friend and comrade Pinkerton, who was with him in the case, " coached " him on the day previous; and indeed it must be owned that the work which he had to perform was not of a nature to impair the inside or the outside of his skull. A great man was his leader; his friend Pinkerton followed; and all Mr. Philip's business was to examine a half-dozen witnesses by questions previously arranged between them and the agents.

When you hear that, as a reward of his services in this case, Mr. Firmin received a sum of money sufficient to pay his modest family expenses for some four months, I am sure, dear and respected literary friends, that you will wish the lot of a parliamentary barrister had been yours, or that your immortal works could be paid with such a liberality as rewards the labors of these lawyers. " *Nimmer erscheinen die Götter allein.*" After one agent had employed Philip, another came and secured his valuable services : him two or three others followed, and our friend positively had money in bank. Not only were apprehensions of poverty removed for the present, but we had every reason to hope that Firmin's prosperity would increase and continue. And when a little son and heir was born, which blessing was conferred upon Mr. Philip about a year after his daughter, our godchild, saw the light, we should have thought it shame to have any misgivings about the future, so cheerful did Philip's prospects appear. "Did I not tell you," said my wife, with her usual kindling romance, "that comfort and succor would be found for these in the hour of their need?" Amen. We were grateful that comfort and succor should come. No one, I am sure, was more humbly thankful than Philip himself for the fortunate chances which befell him.

He was alarmed rather than elated by his sudden prosperity. "It can't last," he said. "Don't tell me. The attorneys must find me out before long. They cannot continue to give their business to such an ignoramus : and I really think I must remonstrate with them." You should have seen the Little Sister's indignation when Philip uttered this sentiment in her presence. "Give up your business? Yes, do!" she cried, tossing up Philip's youngest born. "Fling this baby out of window, why not indeed, which heaven has sent it you! You ought to go down on your knees and ask pardon for having thought anything so wicked." Philip's heir, by the way, immediately on his entrance into the world, had become the prime favorite of this unreasoning woman. The little daughter was passed over as a little person of no account, and so began to entertain the passion of jealousy at almost the very earliest age at which even the female breast is capable of enjoying it.

And though this Little Sister loved all these people with an almost ferocious passion of love, and lay awake, I believe, hearing their infantine cries, or crept on stealthy feet in darkness to their mother's chamber door, behind which they lay sleeping; though she had, as it were, a rage for these infants, and was wretched out of their sight, yet, when a third and a fourth brief came to Philip, and he was enabled to put a little money aside, nothing would content Mrs. Brandon but that he should go into a house of his own. "A gentleman," she said, "ought not to live in a two-pair lodging; he ought to have a house of his own." So, you see, she hastened on the preparations for her own execution. She trudged to the brokers' shops and made wonderful bargains of furniture. She cut chintzes, and covered sofas, and sewed, and patched, and fitted. She found a house and took it—Milman Street, Guildford Street, opposite the Fondling (as the dear little soul called it), a most genteel, quiet little street, "and quite near for me to come," she said, "to see my dears." Did she speak with dry eyes? Mine moisten sometimes when I think of the faith, of the generosity, of the sacrifice, of that devoted, loving creature.

I am very fond of Charlotte. Her sweetness and simplicity won all our hearts at home. No wife or mother ever was more attached and affectionate; but I own there was a time when I hated her, though of course that highly principled woman, the wife of the author of the present memoirs, says that the statement I am making here is stuff and nonsense, not to say immoral and irreligious. Well, then, I hated Charlotte for the horrible eagerness which she showed in getting away from this Little Sister, who clung round those children, whose first cries she had heard. I hated Charlotte for a cruel happiness which she felt as she hugged the children to her heart: her own children in their own room, whom she would dress, and watch, and wash, and tend; and for whom she wanted no aid. No aid, *entendez-vous !* Oh, it was a shame, a shame! In the new house, in the pleasant little trim new nursery (fitted up by whose fond hands we will not say), is the mother glaring over the cot, where the little, soft, round cheeks are pillowed; and yonder in the rooms in Thornhaugh Street, where she has tended them for two years, the Little Sister sits lonely, as the moonlight streams in. God help thee, little suffering faithful heart! Never but once in her life before had she known so exquisite a pain.

Of course, we had an entertainment in the new house; and Philip's friends, old and new, came to the house-warming. The family coach of the Ringwoods blocked up that astonished little street. The powder on their footmen's heads nearly brushed the ceiling, as the monsters rose when the guests passed in and out of the hall. The Little Sister merely took charge of the tea-room. Philip's "library" was that usual little cupboard beyond the dining-room. The little drawing-room was dreadfully crowded by an ex-nursery piano, which the Ringwoods bestowed upon their friends ; and somebody was in duty bound to play upon it on the evening of this *soirée;* though the Little Sister chafed down stairs at the music. In fact her very words were " Rat that piano ! " She "ratted " the instrument, because the music would wake her little dears up stairs, And that music *did* wake them ; and they howled melodiously, and the Little Sister, who was about to serve Lady Jane Tregarvan with some tea, dashed up stairs to the nursery : and Charlotte had reached the room already : and she looked angry when the Little Sister came in : and she said, " I am sure, Mrs. Brandon, the people down stairs will be wanting their tea ; " and she spoke with some asperity. And Mrs. Brandon went down stairs without one word ; and, happening to be on the landing, conversing with a friend, and a little out of the way of the duet which the Miss Ringwoods were performing — riding their great old horse, as it were, and putting it through its paces in Mrs. Firmin's little paddock ;—happening, I say, to be on the landing when Caroline passed, I took a hand as cold as stone, and never saw a look of grief more tragic than that worn by her poor little face as it passed. " My children cried," she said, " and I went up to the nursery. But she don't want me there now." Poor Little Sister ! She humbled herself and grovelled before Charlotte. You could not help trampling upon her then, madam ; and I hated you—and a great number of other women. Ridley and I went down to her tea-room, where Caroline resumed her place. She looked very nice and pretty, with her pale sweet face, and her neat cap and blue ribbon. Tortures I know she was suffering. Charlotte had been stabbing her. Women will use the edge sometimes, and drive the steel in. Charlotte said to me, some time afterwards, I *was* jealous of her, and you were right ; and a dearer, more faithful creature never lived." But who told Charlotte I said she was jealous ? O fool ! I told Ridley, and Mr. Ridley told Mrs. Firmin.

If Charlotte stabbed Caroline, Caroline could not help coming back again and again to the knife. On Sundays, when she was free, there was always a place for her at Philip's modest table ; and when Mrs. Philip went to church, Caroline was allowed to reign in the nursery. Sometimes Charlotte was generous enough to give Mrs. Brandon this chance. When Philip took a house — a whole house to himself — Philip's mother-in-law proposed to come and stay with him, and said that, wishing to be beholden to no one, she would pay for her board and lodging. But Philip declined this treat, representing, justly, that his present house was no bigger than his former lodgings. " My poor love is dying to have me," Mrs. Baynes remarked on this. " But her husband is so cruel to her, and keeps her under such terror, that she dares not call her life her own." Cruel to her ! Charlotte was the happiest of the happy in her little house. In consequence of his parliamentary success, Philip went regularly to chambers now, in the fond hope that more briefs might come. At chambers he likewise conducted the chief business of his *Review :* and, at the accustomed hour of his return, that usual little procession of mother and child and nurse would be seen on the watch for him ; and the young woman — the happiest woman in Christendom — would walk back clinging on her husband's arm.

All this while letters came from Philip's dear father at New York, where, it appeared, he was engaged not only in his profession, but in various speculations, with which he was always about to make his fortune. One day Philip got a newspaper advertising a new insurance company, and saw, to his astonishment, the announcement of " Counsel in London, Philip Firmin, Esq., Parchment Buildings, Temple." A paternal letter promised Philip great fees out of this insurance company, but I never heard that poor Philip was any the richer. In fact his friends advised him to have nothing to do with this insurance company, and to make no allusion to it in his letters. " They feared the Danai, and the gifts they brought," as old Firmin would have said. They had to impress upon Philip an abiding mistrust of that wily old Greek, his father. Firmin senior always wrote hopefully and magnificently, and persisted in believing or declaring that ere very long he should have to announce to Philip that his fortune was made. He speculated in Wall Street, I don't know in what shares, inventions, mines, railways. One day, some few months after his migration to Milman Street, Philip, blushing and hanging down his head, had to tell me that his father had drawn upon him again. Had he not paid up his shares in a certain mine, they would have been forfeited, and he and *his son after him* would have lost a certain fortune, old Danaus said. I fear an artful, a long-bow-pulling Danaus. What, shall a man have birth, wealth, friends, high position, and end so that we dare not leave him alone in the room with our spoons? "And you have paid this bill which the old man drew?" we asked. Yes, Philip had paid the bill. He vowed he would pay no more. But it was not difficult to see that the doctor would draw more bills upon this accommodating banker. "I dread the letters which begin with a flourish about the fortune which he is just going to make," Philip said. He knew that the old parent prefaced his demands for money in that way.

Mention has been made of a great medical discovery which he had announced to his correspondent, Mrs. Brandon, and by which the doctor declared as usual that he was about to make a fortune. In New York and Boston he had tried experiments which had been attended with the most astonishing success. A remedy was discovered, the mere sale of which in Europe and America must bring an immense revenue to the fortunate inventors. For the ladies whom Mrs. Brandon attended, the remedy was of priceless value. He would send her some. His friend, Captain Morgan, of the Southampton packet-ship, would bring her some of this astonishing medicine. Let her try it. Let her show the accompanying cases to Doctor Goodenough —to any of his brother physicians in London. Though himself an exile from his country, he loved it, and was proud in being able to confer upon it one of the greatest blessings with which science had endowed mankind.

Goodenough, I am sorry to say, had such a mistrust of his *confrère* that he chose to disbelieve any statement Firmin made. " I don't believe, my good Brandon, the fellow has *nous* enough to light upon any scientific discovery more useful than a new sauce for cutlets. He invent anything but fibs, never! " You see this Goodenough is an obstinate old heathen; and when he has once found reason to mistrust a man, he for ever after declines to believe him.

However, the doctor is a man for ever on the look-out for more knowledge of his profession, and for more remedies to benefit mankind : he hummed and ha'd over the pamphlet, as the Little Sister sat watching him in his study. He clapped it down after a while, and slapped his hands on his little legs as his wont is. " Brandon," he says, " I think there is a great deal in it, and I think so the more because it turns out that Firmin has nothing to do with the discovery, which has been made at Boston." In fact, Dr. Firmin, late of London, had only been present in the Boston hospital, where the experiments were made with the new remedy. He had cried " Halves," and proposed to sell it as a secret remedy, and the bottle which he forwarded to our friend the Little Sister was labelled " Firmin's Anodyne." What Firmin did, indeed, was what he had been in the habit of doing. He had taken another man's property, and was endeavoring to make a flourish with it. The Little Sister returned home, then, with her bottle of Chloroform—for this was what Dr. Firmin chose to call his discovery, and he had sent home a specimen of it ; as he sent home a cask of petroleum from Virginia ; as he sent proposals for new railways upon which he promised Philip a munificent commission, if his son could but place the shares amongst his friends.

And with regard to these valuables, the sanguine doctor got to believe that he really was endowing his son with large sums of money. " My boy has set up a house, and has a wife and two children, the young jackanapes ! " he would say to people in New York ; " as if he had not been extravagant enough in former days ! When I married, I had private means, and married a nobleman's niece with a large fortune. Neither of these two young folks has a penny. Well, well, the old father must help them as well as he can ! " And I am told there were ladies who dropped the tear of sensibility, and said, "What a fond father this doctor is ! How he sacrifices himself for that scapegrace of a son ! Think of the dear doctor at his age, toiling cheerfully for that young man, who helped to ruin him ! " And Firmin sighed ; and passed a beautiful white handkerchief over his eyes with a beautiful white hand ; and, I believe, really cried ; and thought himself quite a good, affectionate, injured man. He held the plate at church ; he looked very handsome and tall, and bowed with a charming melancholy grace to the ladies as they put in their contributions. The dear man ! His plate was fuller than other people's—so a traveller told us who saw him in New York ; and described a very choice dinner which the doctor gave to a few friends, at one of the smartest hotels just then opened.

With all the Little Sister's good management Mr. and Mrs. Philip were only able to install themselves in their new house at a considerable expense, and beyond that great Ringwood piano which swaggered in Philip's little drawing-room, I am constrained to say that there was scarce any furniture at all. One of the railway accounts was not paid as yet, and poor Philip could not feed upon mere paper promises to pay. Nor was he inclined to accept the offers of private friends, who were

willing enough to be his bankers. " One in a family is enough
for that kind of business," he said, gloomily ; and it came out
that again and again the interesting exile at New York who
was deploring his son's extravagance and foolish marriage, had
drawn bills upon Philip which our friend accepted and paid—
bills, who knows to what amount ? He has never told ; and
the engaging parent who robbed him—must I use a word
so unpolite ?—will never now tell to what extent he helped
himself to Philip's small means. This I know, that when autumn came—when September was past—we in our cozy little
retreat at the sea-side received a letter from the Little Sister, in
her dear little bad spelling (about which there used to be
somehow a pathos which the very finest writing does not
possess) ; there came, I say, a letter from the Little Sister in
which she told us, with many dashes, that dear Mrs. Philip and
the children were pining and sick in London, and " that Philip,
he had too much pride and spirit to take money from any one ;
that Mr. Tregarvan was away travelling on the continent, and
that wretch—that monster, *you know who*—have drawn upon
Philip again for money, and again he have paid, and the dear,
dear children can't have fresh air."

" Did she tell you," said Philip, brushing his hands across
his eyes when a friend came to remonstrate with him, " did she
tell you that she brought me money herself, but we would not
use it ? Look ! I have her little marriage gift yonder in
my desk, and pray God I shall be able to leave it to my children. The fact is, the doctor has drawn upon me as usual ; he
is going to make a fortune next week. I have paid another
bill of his. The parliamentary agents are out of town, at their
moors in Scotland, I suppose. The air of Russell Square
is uncommonly wholesome, and when the babies have had
enough of that, why, they must change it for Brunswick Square.
Talk about the country ! what country can be more quiet
than Guildford Street in September ? I stretch out of a morning, and breathe the mountain air on Ludgate Hill." And
with these dismal pleasantries and jokes our friend chose to
put a good face upon bad fortune. The kinsmen of Ringwood
offered hospitality kindly enough, but how was poor Philip to
pay railway expenses for servants, babies, and wife ? In this
strait Tregarvan from abroad, having found out some monstrous
design of Russ—— of the great Power of which he stood
in daily terror, and which, as we are in strict amity with that
Power, no other Power shall induce me to name—Tregarvan
wrote to his editor, and communicated to him in confidence a

most prodigious and nefarious plot against the liberties of all the rest of Europe, in which the Power in question was engaged, and in a postscript added, "By the way, the Michaelmas quarter is due, and I send you a check," &c., &c. O precious postscript.

"Didn't I tell you it would be so?" said my wife, with a self-satisfied air. "Was I not certain that succor would come?"

And succor did come, sure enough; and a very happy little party went down to Brighton in a second-class carriage, and got an extraordinary cheap lodging, and the roses came back to the little pale cheeks, and mamma was wonderfully invigorated and refreshed, as all her friends could have seen when the little family came back to town, only there was such a thick dun fog that it was impossible to see complexions at all.

When the shooting season was come to an end, the parliamentary agents who had employed Philip came back to London: and, I am happy to say, gave him a check for his little account. My wife cried, "Did I not tell you so?" more than ever. "Is not everything for the best? I knew dear Philip would prosper!"

"Everything was for the best, was it? Philip was sure to prosper, was he? What do you think of the next news which the poor fellow brought to us? One night in December he came to us, and I saw by his face that some event of importance had befallen him.

"I am almost heart-broken," he said, thumping on the table when the young ones had retreated from it. "I don't know what to do. I have not told you all. I have paid four bills for him already, and now he has——he has signed my name."

"Who has?"

"He at New York. *You* know," said poor Philip. "I tell you he has put my name on a bill, and without my authority."

"Gracious heavens! You mean your father has for——" I could not say the word.

"Yes," groaned Philip. "Here is a letter from him;" and he handed a letter across the table in the doctor's well-known handwriting.

"DEAREST PHILIP," the father wrote, "a sad misfortune has befallen me, which I had hoped to conceal, or at any rate, to avert from my dear son. For you, Philip, are a participator in that misfortune through the imprudence—must I say it?—of your father. Would I had struck off the hand which has done the deed, ere it had been done! But the fault has taken wings and flown out of my reach. *Immeritus*, dear boy, you have to suffer for the *delicta majorum*. Ah, that a father should have to own his fault; to kneel and ask pardon of his son!

"I am engaged in many speculations. Some have succeeded beyond my wildest hope:

some have taken in the most rational, the most prudent, the least sanguine of our capitalists in Wall Street, and, promising the greatest results, have ended in the most extreme failure! To meet a call in an undertaking which seemed to offer the MOST CERTAIN PROSPECTS of success, which seemed to promise a fortune for me and my boy, and your dear children, I put in amongst other securities which I had to realize on a sudden, a bill, on which I used your name. I dated it as drawn six months back by me at New York, on you at Parchment Buildings, Temple; and I wrote your acceptance, as though the signature were yours. I give myself up to you. I tell you what I have done. Make the matter public. Give my confession to the world, as here I write, and sign it, and your father is branded for ever to the world as a —— Spare me the word!

"As I live, as I hope for your forgiveness, long ere that bill became due—it is at five months' date, for 386*l.* 4*s.* 3*d.* value received, and dated from the Temple, on the 4th of July—I passed it to one who promised to keep it until I myself should redeem it! The commission which he charged me was *enormous, rascally*; and not content with the immense interest which he extorted from me, the scoundrel has passed the bill away, and it is in Europe, in the hands of an enemy.

"You remember Tufton Hunt? Yes. You *most justly* chastised him. The wretch lately made his detested appearance in this city, associated with *the lowest of the base*, and endeavored to resume his old practice of *threats, cajoleries*, and extortions! In a *fatal hour* the villain heard of the bill of which I have warned you. He purchased it from the gambler, to whom it had been passed. As New York was speedily too hot to hold him (*for the unhappy man has even left me to pay his hotel score*) he has fled—and fled to Europe—taking with him that fatal bill, which he says he knows you will pay. Ah! dear Philip, if that bill were but once out of the wretch's hands! What sleepless hours of agony should I be spared! I pray you, I implore you, make every sacrifice to meet it! You will not disown it? No. As you have children of your own—as you love them—you would not willingly let them leave a dishonored

　　　　　　　　　　　　　　　　　　　　"FATHER."

"I have a share in a *great medical discovery*,[*] regarding which I have written to our friend, Mrs. Brandon, and which is sure to realize an immense profit, as introduced into England by a physician so well known—may I not say professionally? *respected as myself.* The very first profits resulting from that discovery I promise, on my honor, to devote to you. They will very soon *far more* than repay the loss which my inprudence has brought on my dear boy. Farewell! Love to your wife and little ones.—G. B. F."

CHAPTER XXXVII.

NEC PLENA CRUORIS HIRUDO.

THE reading of this precious letter filled Philip's friend with an inward indignation which it was very hard to control or disguise. It is no pleasant task to tell a gentleman that his father is a rogue. Old Firmin would have been hanged a few years earlier, for practices like these. As you talk with a very great scoundrel, or with a madman, has not the respected reader sometimes reflected, with a grim self-humiliation, how the fellow is of our own kind; and *homo est?* Let us, dearly beloved, who are outside—I mean outside the hulks or the asylum—be thankful that we have to pay a barber for snipping

---

[*] *Æther* was first employed, I believe, in America; and I hope the reader will excuse the substitution of Chloroform in this instance.—W. M. T.

our hair, and are entrusted with the choice of the cut of our own jerkins. As poor Philip read his father's letter, my thought was: "And I can remember the soft white hand of that scoundrel, which has just been forging his own son's name, putting sovereigns into my own palm, when I was a schoolboy." I always liked that man:—but the story is not *de me*—it regards Philip.

"You won't pay this bill?" Philip's friend indignantly said, then.

"What can I do?" says poor Phil, shaking a sad head.

"You are not worth five hundred pounds in the world," remarks the friend.

"Who ever said I was? I am worth this bill: or my credit is," answers the victim.

"If you pay this, he will draw more."

"I dare say he will:" that Firmin admits.

"And he will continue to draw as long as there is a drop of blood to be had out of you."

"Yes," owns poor Philip, putting a finger to his lip. He thought I might be about to speak. His artless wife and mine were conversing at that moment upon the respective merits of some sweet chintzes which they had seen at Shoolbred's, in Tottenham Court Road, and which were so cheap and pleasant, and lively to look at! Really those drawing-room curtains would cost scarcely anything! Our Regulus, you see, before stepping into his torture-tub, was smiling on his friends, and talking upholstery with a cheerful, smirking countenance. On chintz, or some other household errand, the ladies went prattling off: but there was no care, save for husband and children, in Charlotte's poor little innocent heart just then.

"Nice to hear her talking about sweet drawing-room chintzes, isn't it?" says Philip. "Shall we try Shoolbred's or the other shop?" And then he laughs. It was not a very lively laugh.

"You mean that you are determined, then, on——"

"On acknowledging *my signature?* Of course," says Philip, "if ever it is presented to me, I would own it." And having formed and announced this resolution, I knew my stubborn friend too well to think that he ever would shirk it.

The most exasperating part of the matter was, that however generously Philip's friends might be disposed towards him, they could not in this case give him a helping hand. The doctor would draw more bills, and more. As sure as Philip supplied, the parent would ask; and that devouring dragon of a doctor

had stomach enough for the blood of all of us, were we inclined
to give it. In fact, Philip saw as much, and owned everything
with his usual candor. " I see what is going on in your mind,
old boy," the poor fellow said, " as well as if you spoke. You
mean that I am helpless and irreclaimable, and doomed to
hopeless ruin. So it would seem. A man can't escape his
fate, friend, and my father has made mine for me. If I manage
to struggle through the payment of this bill, of course he will
draw another. My only chance of escape is, that he should
succeed in some of his speculations. As he is always gambling, there may be some luck for him one day or another. He
won't benefit me, then. That is not his way. If he makes a
coup, he will keep the money, or spend it. He won't give me
any. But he will not draw upon me as he does now, or send
forth fancy imitations of the filial autograph. It is a blessing
to have such a father, isn't it ? I say, Pen, as I think from
whom I am descended, and look at your spoons, I am astonished I have not put any of them in my pocket. You leave
me in the room with 'em quite unprotected. I say, it is quite
affecting the way in which you and your dear wife have confidence in me." And with a bitter execration at his fate, the
poor fellow pauses for a moment in his lament.

His father was his fate, he seemed to think, and there were
no means of averting it. " You remember that picture of
Abraham and Isaac in the doctor's study in Old Parr Street ? "
he would say. " My patriarch has tied me up, and had the
knife in me repeatedly. He does not sacrifice me at one operation ; but there will be a final one some day, and I shall bleed
no more. It's gay and amusing, isn't it? Especially when one
has a wife and children." I, for my part, felt so indignant,
that I was minded to advertise in the papers that all accept-
ances drawn in Philip's name were forgeries ; and let his father
take the consequences of his own act. But the consequences
would have been life imprisonment for the old man, and almost
as much disgrace and ruin for the young one, as were actually
impending. He pointed out this clearly enough ; nor could
we altogether gainsay his dismal logic. It was better, at any
rate, to meet his bill, and give the doctor warning for the
future. Well : perhaps it was ; only suppose the doctor should
take the warning in good part, accept the rebuke with perfect
meekness, and at an early opportunity commit another forgery ?
To this Philip replied, that no man could resist his fate : that
he had always expected his own doom through his father : that
when the elder went to America he thought possibly the charm

was broken ; " but you see it is not," groaned Philip, "and my father's emissaries reach me, and I am still under the spell." The bearer of the *bowstring*, we knew, was on his way, and would deliver his grim message ere long.

Having frequently succeeded in extorting money from Dr. Firmin, Mr. Tufton Hunt thought he could not do better than follow his banker across the Atlantic ; and we need not describe the annoyance and rage of the doctor on finding this black care still behind his back. He had not much to give ; indeed the sum which he took away with him, and of which he robbed his son and his other creditors, was but small : but Hunt was bent upon having a portion of this ; and, of course, hinted that, if the doctor refused, he would carry to the New York press the particulars of Firmin's early career and latest defalcations. Mr. Hunt had been under the gallery of the House of Commons half a dozen times, and knew our public men by sight. In the course of a pretty long and disreputable career he had learned anecdotes regarding members of the aristocracy, turfmen, and the like ; and he offered to sell this precious knowledge of his to more than one American paper, as other amiable exiles from our country have done. But Hunt was too old, and his stories too stale for the New York public. They dated from George IV., and the boxing and coaching times. He found but little market for his wares ; and the tipsy parson reeled from tavern to bar, only the object of scorn to younger reprobates who despised his old-fashioned stories, and could top them with blackguardism of a much more modern date.

After some two years' sojourn in the United States, this worthy felt the passionate longing to revisit his native country which generous hearts often experience, and made his way from Liverpool to London ; and when in London directed his steps to the house of the Little Sister, of which he expected to find Philip still an inmate. Although Hunt had been once kicked out of the premises, he felt little shame now about re-entering them. He had that in his pocket which would insure him respectful behavior from Philip. What were the circumstances under which that forged bill was obtained ? Was it a speculation between Hunt and Philip's father ? Did Hunt suggest that, to screen the elder Firmin from disgrace and ruin, Philip would assuredly take the bill up ? That a forged signature was, in fact, a better document than a genuine acceptance ? We shall never know the truth regarding this transaction now. We have but the statements of the two parties concerned ; and as both of them, I grieve to say, are entirely unworthy of credit, we must remain in ignorance regarding this matter. Perhaps Hunt forged Philip's acceptance : perhaps his unhappy father wrote it : perhaps the doctor's story that the paper was extorted from him was true, perhaps false. What matters? Both the men have passed away from amongst us, and will write and speak no more lies.

Caroline was absent from home, when Hunt paid his first visit after his return from America. Her servant described the man, and his appearance. Mrs. Brandon felt sure that Hunt was her visitor, and foreboded no good to Philip from the parson's arrival. In former days we have seen how the Little Sister had found favor in the eyes of this man. The besotted creature, shunned of men, stained with crime, drink, debt, had still no little vanity in his composition, and gave himself airs in the tavern parlors which he frequented. Because he had been at the University thirty years ago, his idea was that he was superior to ordinary men who had not had the benefit of an education at Oxford or Cambridge ; and that the " snobs," as he called them, respected him. He would assume grandiose airs in talking to a tradesman ever so wealthy ; speak to such a man by his surname ; and deem that he honored him by his patronage and conversation. The Little Sister's grammar, I have told you, was not good ; her poor little *h's* were sadly irregular. A letter was a painful task to her. She knew how ill she performed it, and that she was for ever making blunders.

She would invent a thousand funny little pleas and excuses for her faults of writing. With all the blunders of spelling, her little letters had a pathos which somehow brought tears into the eyes. The Rev. Mr. Hunt believed himself to be this woman's superior. He thought his University education gave him a claim upon her respect, and draped himself and swaggered before her and others in his dingy college gown. He had paraded his Master of Arts degree in many thousand tavern parlors, where his Greek and learning had got him a kind of respect. He patronized landlords, and strutted by hostesses' bars with a vinous leer or a tipsy solemnity. He must have been very far gone and debased indeed when he could still think that he was any living man's better :—he, who ought to have waited on the waiters, and blacked Boots's own shoes. When he had reached a certain stage of liquor he commonly began to brag about the University, and recite the titles of his friends of early days. Never was kicking more righteously administered than that which Philip once bestowed on this miscreant. The fellow took to the gutter as naturally as to his bed, Firmin used to say; and vowed that the washing there was a novelty which did him good.

Mrs. Brandon soon found that her surmises were correct regarding her nameless visitor. Next day, as she was watering some little flowers in her window, she looked from it into the street, where she saw the shambling parson leering up at her. When she saw him he took off his greasy hat and made her a bow. At the moment she saw him, she felt that he was come upon some errand hostile to Philip. She knew he meant mischief as he looked up with that sodden face, those bloodshot eyes, those unshorn, grinning lips.

She might have been inclined to faint, or disposed to scream, or to hide herself from the man, the sight of whom she loathed. She did not faint, or hide herself, or cry out : but she instantly nodded her head and smiled in the most engaging manner on that unwelcome, dingy stranger. She went to her door; she opened it (though her heart beat so that you might have heard it, as she told her friend afterwards). She stood there a moment archly smiling at him, and she beckoned him into her house with a little gesture of welcome. "Law bless us" (these I have reason to believe, were her very words)—"Law bless us, Mr. Hunt, where ever have you been this ever so long?" And a smiling face looked at him resolutely from under a neat cap and fresh ribbon. Why, I know some women can smile, and look at ease, when they sit down in a dentist's chair.

"Law bless me, Mr. Hunt," then says the artless creature, "who ever would have thought of seeing *you*, I do declare !" And she makes a nice cheery little curtsey, and looks quite gay, pleased, and pretty ; and so did Judith look gay, no doubt, and smile, and prattle before Holofernes ; and then of course she said, "Won't you step in?" And then Hunt swaggered up the steps of the house, and entered the little parlor, into which the kind reader has often been conducted, with its neat little ornaments, its pictures, its glistening corner cupboard, and its well-scrubbed, shining furniture.

"How is the captain?" asks the man (alone in the company of this Little Sister, the fellow's own heart began to beat, and his blood shot eyes to glisten).

He had not heard about poor Pa? "That shows how long you have been away !" Mrs. Brandon remarks, and mentions the date of her father's fatal illness. Yes : she was alone now, and had to care for herself ; and straightway, I have no doubt, Mrs. Brandon asked Mr. Hunt whether he would "take" anything. Indeed, that good little woman was for ever pressing her friends to "take" something, and would have thought the laws of hospitality violated unless she had made this offer.

Hunt was never known to refuse a proposal of this sort. He *would* take a taste of something——of something warm. He had had fever and ague at New York, and the malady hung about him. Mrs. Brandon was straightway very much interested to hear about Mr. Hunt's complaint, and knew that a comfortable glass was very efficacious in removing threatening fever. Her nimble, neat little hands mixed him a cup. He could not but see what a trim little housekeeper she was. "Ah, Mrs. Brandon, if I had had such a kind friend watching over me, I should not be such a wreck as I am!" he sighed. He must have advanced to a second, nay, a third glass, when he sighed and became sentimental regarding his own unhappy condition; and Brandon owned to her friends afterwards that she made those glasses very strong.

Having "taken something," in considerable quantities, then, Hunt condescended to ask how his hostess was getting on, and how were her lodgers. How she was getting on? Brandon drew the most cheerful picture of herself and her circumstances. The apartments let well, and were never empty. Thanks to good Dr. Goodenough and other friends, she had as much professional occupation as she could desire. Since *you know who* has left the country, she said, her mind had been ever so much easier. As long as he was near, she never felt secure. But he was gone, and bad luck go with him! said this vindictive Little Sister.

"Was his son still lodging up stairs?" asked Mr. Hunt.

On this, what does Mrs. Brandon do but begin a most angry attack upon Philip and his family. *He* lodge there? No, thank goodness! She had had enough of him and his wife with her airs and graces, and the children crying all night, and the furniture spoiled, and the bills not even paid! "I wanted him to think that me and Philip was friends no longer; and heaven forgive me for telling stories! I know this fellow means no good to Philip; and before long I will know *what* he means, that I will," she vowed.

For, on the very day when Mr. Hunt paid her a visit, Mrs. Brandon came to see Philip's friends, and acquaint them with Hunt's arrival. We could not be sure that he was the bearer of the forged bill with which poor Philip was threatened. As yet Hunt had made no allusion to it. But, though we are far from sanctioning deceit or hypocrisy, we own that we were not *very* angry with the Little Sister for employing dissimulation in the present instance, and inducing Hunt to believe that she was by no means an accomplice of Philip's. If Philip's wife pardoned her, ought his friends to be less forgiving? To do right, you know you must not do wrong; though I own this was one of the cases in which I am inclined not to deal very hardly with the well-meaning little criminal.

Now, Charlotte had to pardon (and for this fault, if not for some others, Charlotte did most heartily pardon) our little friend, for this reason, that Brandon most wantonly maligned her. When Hunt asked what sort of wife Philip had married? Mrs. Brandon declared that Mrs. Philip was a pert, odious little thing; that she gave herself airs, neglected her children, bullied her husband, and what not; and, finally, Brandon vowed that she disliked Charlotte, and was very glad to get her out of the house: and that Philip was not the same Philip since he married her, and that *he* gave himself airs, and was rude, and in all things led by his wife; and to get rid of them was a good riddance.

Hunt gracefully suggested that quarrels between landladies and tenants were not unusual; that lodgers sometimes did not pay their rent punctually; that others were unreasonably anxious about the consumption of their groceries, liquors, and so forth; and little Brandon, who, rather than steal a pennyworth from her Philip, would have cut her hand off, laughed at her guest's joke, and pretended to be amused with his knowing hints that she was a rogue. There was not a word he said but she received it with a gracious acquiescence: she might shudder inwardly at the leering familiarity of the odious tipsy wretch, but she gave no outward sign of disgust or fear. She allowed him to talk as much as he would, in hopes that he would come to a subject which deeply interested her. She asked about the doctor, and what he was doing, and whether it was likely that he would ever be able to pay back any of that money which he had taken from his son? And she spoke with an indifferent tone, pretending to be very busy over some work at which she was stitching.

"Oh, you are still hankering after him," says the chaplain, winking a bloodshot eye.

"Hankering after that old man! What should I care for him? As if he haven't done me harm enough already!" cries poor Caroline.

"Yes. But women don't dislike a man the worse for a little ill-usage," suggests Hunt. No doubt the fellow had made his own experiments on woman's fidelity.

" Well, I suppose," says Brandon, with a toss of her head, " women may get tired as well as men, mayn't they ?   I found out that man, and wearied of him years and years ago.   Another little drop out of the green bottle, Mr. Hunt !   It's very good for ague-fever, and keeps the cold fit off wonderful ! "

And Hunt drank, and he talked a little more—much more : and he gave his opinion of the elder Firmin, and spoke of his chances of success, and of his rage for speculations, and doubted whether he would ever be able to lift his head again—though he might, he might still.   He was in the country where, if ever a man could retrieve himself, he had a chance.   And Philip was giving himself airs, was he ?   He was always an arrogant chap, that Mr. Philip.   And he had left her house ? and was gone ever so long ? and where did he live now ?

Then I am sorry to say Mrs. Brandon asked, how should *she* know where Philip lived ?   She believed it was near Gray's Inn, or Lincoln's Inn, or somewhere ; and she was for turning the conversation away from this subject altogether : and sought to do so by many lively remarks and ingenious little artifices which I can imagine, but which she only in part acknowledged to me—for you must know that as soon as her visitor took leave—to turn into the " Admiral Byng " public-house, and renew acquaintance with the worthies assembled in the parlor of that tavern, Mrs. Brandon ran away to a cab, drove in it to Philip's house in Milman Street, where only Mrs. Philip was at home—and after a *banale* conversation with her, which puzzled Charlotte not a little, for Brandon would not say on what errand she came, and never mentioned Hunt's arrival and visit to her,—the Little Sister made her way to another cab, and presently made her appearance at the house of Philip's friends in Queen Square.   And here she informed me, how Hunt had arrived, and how she was sure he meant no good to Philip, and how she had told certain—certain stories which were not founded in fact—to Mr. Hunt ; for the telling of which fibs I am not about to endeavor to excuse her.

Though the interesting clergyman had not said one word regarding that bill of which Philip's father had warned him, we believed that the document was in Hunt's possession, and that it would be produced in due season.   We happened to know where Philip dined, and sent him word to come to us.

" What can he mean ? " the people asked at the table—a bachelors' table at the Temple (for Philip's good wife actually encouraged him to go abroad from time to time, and make merry with his friends).   " What can this mean ? " and they read out the scrap of paper which he had cast down as he was summoned away.

Philip's correspondent wrote : "Dear Philip,—I believe the BEARER OF THE BOWSTRING has arrived ; and has been with the L. S. this very day."

The L. S. ? the bearer of the bowstring ? Not one of the bachelors dining in Parchment Building could read the riddle. Only after receiving the scrap of paper Philip had jumped up and left the room ; and a friend of ours, a sly wag and Don Juan of Pump Court, offered to take odds that there was a lady in the case.

At the hasty little council which was convened at our house on the receipt of the news, the Little Sister, whose instinct had not betrayed her, was made acquainted with the precise nature of the danger which menaced Philip ; and exhibited a fine hearty wrath when she heard how he proposed to meet the enemy. He had a certain sum in hand. He would borrow more of his friends, who knew that he was an honest man. This bill he would meet, whatever might come ; and avert at least this disgrace from his father.

What ? Give in to those rogues ? Leave his children to starve, and his poor wife to turn drudge and house-servant, who was not fit for anything but a fine lady ? (There was no love lost, you see, between these two ladies, who both loved Mr. Philip.) It was a sin and a shame ! Mrs. Brandon averred, and declared she thought Philip had been a man of more spirit. Philip's friend has before stated his own private sentiments regarding the calamity which menaced Firmin. To pay this bill was to bring a dozen more down upon him. Philip might as well resist now as at a later day. Such, in fact, was the opinion given by the reader's very humble servant at command.

My wife, on the other hand, took Philip's side. She was very much moved at his announcement that he would forgive his father this once at least, and endeavor to cover his sin.

"As you hope to be forgiven yourself, dear Philip, I am sure you are doing right," Laura said ; "I am sure Charlotte will think so."

"Oh, Charlotte, Charlotte ! " interposes the Little Sister, rather peevishly ; "of course, Mrs. Philip thinks whatever her husband tells her ! "

" In his own time of trial Philip has been met with wonderful succor and kindness," Laura urged. " See how one thing after another has contributed to help him ! When he wanted, there were friends always at his need. If he wants again, I am sure my husband and I will share with him." (I may have made a wry face at this; for with the best feelings towards a man, and that kind of thing, you know it is not always convenient to be lending him five or six hundred pounds without security.) "My dear husband and I will share with him," goes on Mrs. Laura; "won't we, Arthur? Yes, Brandon, that we will. Be sure, Charlotte and the children shall not want because Philip covers his father's wrong, and hides it from the world! God bless you, dear friend!" and what does this woman do next, and before her husband's face? Actually she goes up to Philip; she takes his hand—and—— Well, what took place before my own eyes, I do not choose to write down.

"She's encouraging him to ruin the children for the sake of that—that wicked old brute!" cries Mrs. Brandon. "It's enough to provoke a saint, it is!" And she seizes up her bonnet from the table, and claps it on her head, and walks out of our room in a little tempest of wrath.

My wife, clasping her hands, whispers a few words, which say: "Forgive us our trespasses, as we forgive them who trespass against us."

"Yes," says Philip, very much moved. "It is the Divine order. You are right, dear Laura. I have had a weary time; and a terrible gloom of doubt and sadness over my mind whilst I have been debating this matter, and before I had determined to do as you would have me. But a great weight is off my heart since I have been enabled to see what my conduct should be. What hundreds of struggling men as well as myself have met with losses, and faced them! I will pay this bill, and I will warn the drawer to—to spare me for the future."

Now that the Little Sister had gone away in her fit of indignation, you see I was left in a minority in the council of war, and the opposition was quite too strong for me. I began to be of the majority's opinion. I dare say I am not the only gentleman who has been led round by a woman. We men of great strength of mind very frequently are. Yes: my wife convinced me with passages from her text-book, admitting of no contradiction according to her judgment, that Philip's duty was to forgive his father.

"And how lucky it was we did not buy the chintzes that day!" says Laura, with a laugh. "Do you know there were two which were so pretty that Charlotte could not make up her mind which of the two she would take?"

Philip roared out one of his laughs, which made the

windows shake. He was in great spirits. For a man who was going to ruin himself, he was in the most enviable good-humor. Did Charlotte know about this—this claim which was impending over him? No. It might make her anxious,—poor little thing! Philip had not told her. He had thought of concealing the matter from her. What need was there to disturb her rest, poor innocent child? You see, we all treated Mrs. Charlotte more or less like a child. Philip played with her. J. J., the painter, coaxed and dandled her, so to speak. The Little Sister loved her, but certainly with a love that was not respectful; and Charlotte took everybody's good-will with a pleasant meekness and sweet smiling content. It was not for Laura to give advice to man and wife (as if the woman was not always giving lectures to Philip and his young wife!); but in the present instance she thought Mrs. Philip certainly ought to know what Philip's real situation was; what danger was menacing; "and how admirable and right, and Christian—and you will have your reward for it, dear Philip!" interjects the enthusiastic lady—"your conduct has been!"

When we came, as we straightway did in a cab, to Charlotte's house, to expound the matter to her, goodness bless us! she was not shocked, or anxious, or frightened at all. Mrs. Brandon had just been with her, and told her of what was happening, and she had said, "Of course, Philip ought to help his father; and Brandon had gone away quite in a tantrum of anger, and had really been quite rude; and she should not pardon her, only she knew how dearly the Little Sister loved Philip; and of course they must help Dr. Firmin; and what dreadful, dreadful distress he must have been in to do as he did! But he had warned Philip, you know," and so forth. "And as for the chintzes, Laura, why I suppose we must go on with the old shabby covers. You know they will do very well till next year." This was the way in which Mrs. Charlotte received the news which Philip had concealed from her, lest it should terrify her. As if a loving woman was ever very much frightened at being called upon to share her husband's misfortune!

As for the little case of forgery, I don't believe the young person could ever be got to see the heinous nature of Dr. Firmin's offence. The desperate little logician seemed rather to pity the father than the son in the business. "How dreadfully pressed he must have been when he did it, poor man!" she said. "To be sure, he ought not to have done it at all; but think of his necessity! That is what I said to Brandon,

Now, there's little Philip's cake in the cupboard which you brought him. Now suppose papa was very hungry, and went and took some without asking Philly, he wouldn't be so very wrong, I think, would he? A child is glad enough to give for his father, isn't he? And when I said this to Brandon, she was so rude and violent, I really had no patience with her! And she forgets that I am a lady, and" &c., &c. So it appeared the Little Sister had made a desperate attempt to bring over Charlotte to her side, was still minded to rescue Philip in spite of himself, and had gone off in wrath at her defeat.

We looked to the doctor's letters, ascertained the date of the bill. It had crossed the water and would be at Philip's door in a very few days. Had Hunt brought it? The rascal would have it presented through some regular channel, no doubt; and Philip and all of us totted up ways and means, and strove to make the slender figures look as big as possible, as the thrifty housewife puts a patch here and a darn there, and cuts a little slice out of this old garment, so as to make the poor little frock serve for winter wear. We had so much at the banker's. A friend might help with a little advance. We would fairly ask a loan from the *Review*. We were in a scrape, but we would meet it. And so with resolute hearts, we would prepare to receive the Bearer of the Bowstring.

CHAPTER XXXVIII.

THE BEARER OF THE BOWSTRING.

THE poor Little Sister trudged away from Milman Street exasperated with Philip, with Philip's wife, and with the determination of the pair to accept the hopeless ruin impending over them. "Three hundred and eighty-six pounds four and threepence," she thought, "to pay for that wicked old villain! It is more than poor Philip is worth, with all his savings and his little sticks of furniture. I know what he will do : he will borrow of the money-lenders, and give those bills, and renew them, and end by ruin. When he have paid this bill, that old villain will forge another, and that precious wife of his will tell him to pay that, I suppose ; and those little darlings will be begging for bread, unless they come and eat mine, to which— God bless them !—they are always welcome." She calculated

—it was a sum not difficult to reckon—the amount of her own little store of saved ready money. To pay four hundred pounds out of such an income as Philip's, she felt, was an attempt vain and impossible. "And he mustn't have my poor little stocking now," she argued ; "they will want that presently when their pride is broken down, as it will be, and my darlings are hungering for their dinner ! " Revolving this dismal matter in her mind, and scarce knowing where to go for comfort and counsel, she made her way to her good friend, Dr. Goodenough, and found that worthy man, who had always a welcome for his Little Sister.

She found Goodenough alone in his great dining-room, taking a very slender meal, after visiting his hospital and his fifty patients, among whom I think there were more poor than rich : and the good sleepy doctor woke up with a vengeance, when he heard his little nurse's news, and fired off a volley of angry language against Philip and his scoundrel of a father ; "which it was a comfort to hear him," little Brandon told us afterwards. Then Goodenough trotted out of the dining-room into the adjoining library and consulting-room, whither his old friend followed him. Then he pulled out a bunch of keys and opened a secretaire, from which he took a parchment-covered volume, on which *F. Goodenough, Esq., M.D.*, was written in a fine legible hand,—and which, in fact, was a banker's book. The inspection of the MS. volume in question must have pleased the worthy physician ; for a grin came over his venerable features, and he straightway drew out of the desk a slim volume of grey paper, on each page of which were inscribed the highly respectable names of Messrs. Stumpy and Rowdy and Co., of Lombard Street, Bankers. On a slip of gray paper the doctor wrote a prescription for a draught, *statim sumendus* —(a *draught*—mark my pleasantry)—which he handed over to his little friend.

"There, you little fool ! " said he. "The father is a rascal, but the boy is a fine fellow ; and you, you little silly thing, I must help in this business myself, or you will go and ruin yourself ; I know you will ! Offer this to the fellow for his bill. Or, stay ! How much money is there in the house ? Perhaps the sight of notes and gold will tempt him more than a cheque." And the doctor emptied his pockets of all the fees which happened to be therein—I don't know how many fees of shining shillings and sovereigns, neatly wrapped up in paper ; and he emptied a drawer in which there was more silver and gold : and he trotted up to his bedroom, and came panting,

presently, down stairs with a fat little pocket-book, containing a
bundle of notes, and, with one thing or another, he made up a
sum of—I won't mention what ; but this sum of money, I say,
he thrust into the Little Sister's hand, and said, "Try the fellow
with this, Little Sister ; and see if you can get the bill from
him.　Don't say it's my money, or the scoundrel will be for
having twenty shillings in the pound.　Say it's yours, and
there's no more where that came from ; and coax him, and
wheedle him, and tell him plenty of lies, my dear.　It won't
break your heart to do that.　What an immortal scoundrel
Brummell Firmin is, to be sure !　Though, by the way, in two
more cases at the hospital I have tried that——"　And here
the doctor went off into a professional conversation with his
favorite nurse, which I could not presume to repeat to any non-
medical men.

　　The Little Sister bade God bless Dr. Goodenough, and
wiped her glistening eyes with her handkerchief, and put away
the notes and gold with a trembling little hand, and trudged off
with a lightsome step and happy heart.　Arrived at Tottenham
Court Road, she thought, shall I go home, or shall I go to poor
Mrs. Philip and take her this money ?　No.　Their talk that day
had not been very pleasant : words, very like high words, had
passed between them, and our Little Sister had to own herself
that she had been rather rude in her late colloquy with Charlotte.　And she was a proud Little Sister : at least she did
not care to own that she had been hasty or disrespectful in her
conduct to *that* young woman.　She had too much spirit for
that.　Have we ever said that our little friend was exempt from
the prejudices and vanities of this wicked world ?　Well, to
rescue Philip, to secure the fatal bill, to go with it to Charlotte,
and say, "There, Mrs. Philip, there's your husband's liberty."
It would be a rare triumph, that it would !　And Philip would
promise, on his honor, that this should be the last and only bill
he would pay for that wretched old father.　With these
happy thoughts swelling in her little heart, Mrs. Brandon made
her way to the familiar little house in Thornhaugh Street, and
would have a little bit of supper, so she would.　And laid her
own little cloth ; and set forth her little forks and spoons,
which were as bright as rubbing could make them ; and I am
authorized to state that her repast consisted of two nice little
lamb chops, which she purchased from her neighbor, Mr.
Chump, in Tottenham Court Road, after a pleasant little conversation with that gentleman and his good lady.　And, with
her bit of supper, after a day's work, our little friend would

sometimes indulge in a glass—a little glass—of something comfortable. The case bottle was in the cupboard, out of which her poor Pa had been wont to mix his tumbler for many a long day. So, having prepared it with her own hands, down she sat to her little meal, tired and happy ; and as she thought of the occurrences of the day, and of the rescue which had come so opportunely to her beloved Philip and his children, I am sure she said a grace before her meat.

Her candles being lighted and her blind up, any one in the street could see that her chamber was occupied ; and at about ten o'clock at night there came a heavy step clinking along the pavement, the sound of which, I have no doubt, made the Little Sister start a little. The heavy foot paused before her window, and presently clattered up the steps of her door. Then as her bell rang—I consider it is most probable that her cheeks flushed a little—she went to her hall door and opened it herself. " Lor', is it you, Mr. Hunt ? Well, I never ! that is, I thought you might come. Really, now "—and with the moonlight behind him, the dingy Hunt swaggered in.

" How comfortable you looked at your little table," says Hunt, with his hat over his eye.

"Won't you step in and sit down to it, and take something?" asks the smiling hostess.

Of course, Hunt would take something. And the greasy hat is taken off his head with a flourish, and he struts into the poor Little Sister's little room, pulling a wisp of grizzling hair, and endeavoring to assume a careless, fashionable look. The dingy hand had seized the case-bottle in a moment. " What ! you do a little in this way, do you ? " he says, and winks amiably at Mrs. Brandon and the bottle. She takes ever so little, she owns ; and reminds him of days which he must remember, when she had a wine-glass out of poor Pa's tumbler. A bright little kettle is singing on the fire,—will not Mr. Hunt mix a glass for himself ? She takes a bright beaker from the corner-cupboard, which is near her, with her keys hanging in it.

" Oh—ho ! that's where we keep the ginnims, is it ? " says the graceful Hunt, with a laugh.

" My papa always kept it there," says Caroline, meekly. And whilst her back is turned to fetch a canister from the cupboard, she knows that the astute Mr. Hunt has taken the opportunity to fill a good large measure from the square bottle. " Make yourself welcome," says the Little Sister, in her gay, artless way ; " there's more where that came from ! " And Hunt drinks his hostess's health : and she bows to him and smiles, and sips a little from her own glass ; and the little ʌady looks quite pretty and rosy and bright. Her cheeks are like apples, her figure is trim and graceful, and always attired in the neatest-fitting gown. By the comfortable light of the candles on her sparkling tables, you scarce see the silver lines in her light hair, or the marks which time has made round her eyes. Hunt gazes on her with admiration.

" Why," says he, " I vow you look younger and prettier than when—when I saw you first."

" Ah, Mr. Hunt ! " cries Mrs. Brandon, with a flush on her cheek, which becomes it, " don't recall that time, or that—that wretch who served me so cruel ! "

" He was a scoundrel, Caroline, to treat as he did such a woman as you ! The fellow has no principle ; he was a bad one from the beginning. Why, he ruined me as well as you : got me to play ; run me into debt by introducing me to his fine companions. I was a simple young fellow then, and thought it was a fine thing to live with fellow-commoners and noblemen who drove their tandems and gave their grand dinners. It was he that led me astray, I tell you. I might have been Fellow of my college—had a living—married a good wife—risen to be a bishop, by George !—for I had great talents, Caroline ; only I was so confounded idle, and fond of the cards and the bones."

" The bones ? " cries Caroline, with a bewildered look.

" The dice, my dear ! ' Seven's the main ' was my ruin. Seven's the main and eleven's the nick to seven. That used to be the little game ! " And he made a graceful gesture with his empty wine-glass, as though he were tossing a pair of dice on the table. " The man next to me in a lecture is a bishop now, and I could knock his head off in Greek iambics and Latin hexameters too. In my second year I got the Latin decla-mation prize, I tell you——"

" Brandon always said you were one of the cleverest men at the college. He always said *that*, I remember," remarks the lady, very respectfully.

" Did he ? He *did* say a good word for me then ? Brum-mell Firmin wasn't a clever man ; he wasn't a reading man. Whereas I would back myself for a Sapphic ode against any man in my college—against any man ! Thank you. You *do* mix it so uncommon hot and well, there's no saying no ; indeed, there ain't ! Though I have had enough—upon my honor, I have."

" Lor' ! I thought you men could drink anything ! And Mr. Brandon—Mr. Firmin you said ? "

Well, I said Brummell Firmin was a swell somehow. He had a sort of grand manner with him——"

"Yes, he had," sighed Caroline. And I dare say her thoughts wandered back to a time long, long ago, when this grand gentleman had captivated her.

"And it was trying to keep up with him that ruined me! I quarrelled with my poor old governor about money, of course; grew idle, and lost my Fellowship. Then the bills came down upon me. I tell you, there are some of my college ticks ain't paid now."

"College ticks? Law!" ejaculates the lady. "And——"

"Tailors' ticks, tavern ticks, livery-stable ticks—for there were famous hacks in our days, and I used to hunt with the tip-top men. I wasn't bad across country, I wasn't. But we can't keep the pace with those rich fellows. We try, and they go ahead—they ride us down. Do you think, if I hadn't been very hard up, I would have done what I did to you, Caroline? You poor little innocent suffering thing. It was a shame. It was a shame!"

"Yes, a shame it was," cries Caroline. "And that I never gainsay. You did deal hard with a poor girl, both of you."

"It was rascally. But Firmin was the worst. He had me in his power. It was he led me wrong. It was he drove me into debt, and then abroad, and then into qu—— into jail, perhaps: and then into this kind of thing." ("This kind of thing" has before been explained elegantly to signify a tumbler of hot grog.) "And my father wouldn't see me on his death-bed; and my brothers and sisters broke with me; and I owe it all to Brummell Firmin—all. Do you think, after ruining me, he oughtn't to pay me?" and again he thumps a dusky hand upon the table. It made dingy marks on the poor Little Sister's spotless tablecloth. It rubbed its owner's forehead, and lank, grizzling hair.

"And me, Mr. Hunt? What do he owe me?" asks Hunt's hostess.

"Caroline!" cries Hunt, "I have made Brummell Firmin pay me a good bit back already, and I'll have more;" and he thumped his breast, and thrust his hand into his breast-pocket as he spoke, and clutched at something within.

"It is there!" thought Caroline. She might turn pale; but he did not remark her pallor. He was all intent on drink, on vanity, on revenge.

"I have him, I say. He owes me a good bit; and he has paid me a good bit; and he shall pay me a good bit more. Do you think I am a fellow who will be ruined and insulted, and won't revenge myself? You should have seen his face when I turned up at New York at the ' Astor House,' and said, ' Brummell, old fellow, here I am,' I said ; and he turned as white— as white as this tablecloth. ' *I'll* never leave you, my boy,' I said. ' Other fellows may go from you, but old Tom Hunt will stick to you. Let's go into the bar and have a drink ! ' and he was obliged to come. And I have him now in my power, I tell you. And when I say to him, ' Brummell, have a drink,' drink he must. His bald old head must go into the pail ! " And Mr. Hunt laughed a laugh which I dare say was not agreeable.

After a pause he went on : " Caroline ! Do you hate him, I say ? or do you like a fellow who deserted you and treated you like a scoundrel ? Some women do. I could tell of women who do. I could tell you of other fellows, perhaps, but I won't. Do you hate Brummell Firmin, that bald-headed Brum —hypocrite, and that—that insolent rascal who laid his hand on a clergyman, and an old man, by George, and hit me—and hit me in that street. Do you hate him, I say ? Hoo ! hoo ! hick ! I've got 'em both !—here, in my pocket—both ! "

" You have got—what ? " gasped Caroline.

" I have got their—hallo ! stop, what's that to you what I've got ? " And he sinks back in his chair, and grins, and leers, and triumphantly tosses his glass.

" Well, it ain't much to me ; I—I never got any good out of either of 'em yet," says poor Caroline, with a sinking heart. " Let's talk about somebody else than them two plagues. Because you were a little merry one night—and I don't mind what a gentleman says when he has had a glass—for a big strong man to hit an old one——"

" To strike a clergyman ! " yells Hunt.

" It was a shame—a cowardly shame ! And I gave it him for it, I promise you ! " cries Mrs. Brandon.

" On your honor, now, do you hate 'em ? " cries Hunt, starting up, and clenching his fist, and dropping again into his chair.

" Have I any reason to love 'em, Mr. Hunt ? Do sit down and have a little——"

" No : you have no reason to like 'em. You hate 'em—I hate 'em. Look here. Promise—'pon your honor, now, Caroline—I've got 'em both, I tell you. Strike a clergyman, will he ? What do you say to that ? "

And starting from his chair once more, and supporting himself against the wall (where hung one of J. J.'s pictures of

Philip), Hunt pulls out the greasy pocket-book once more, and
fumbles amongst the greasy contents : and as the papers flutter
on the floor and the table, he pounces down on one with a
dingy hand, and yells a laugh, and says, " I've cotched you !
That's it. What do you say to that ?—' London, July 4th.—
Five months after date, I promise to pay to —— ' No, you
don't."

"La ! Mr. Hunt, won't you let me look at it ? " cries the
hostess. "Whatever is it ? A bill. My Pa had plenty of
'em."

" What ? with candles in the room ? No, you don't, I say."

" What is it ? Won't you tell me ? "

" It's the young one's acceptance of the old man's draft,"
says Hunt, hissing and laughing.

" For how much ? "

" Three hundred and eighty-six four three—that's all ; and
I guess I can get more where that came from ! " says Hunt,
laughing more and more cheerful.

" What will you take for it ? I'll buy it of you," cries the
Little Sister. " I—I've seen plenty of my Pa's bills ; and I'll
—I'll discount this, if you like."

" What ! are you a little discounter ? Is that the way you
make your money, and the silver spoons, and the nice supper,
and everything delightful about you ? A little discountess, are
you—you little rogue ? Little discountess, by George ! How
much will you give, little discountess ? " And the reverend
gentleman laughs and winks, and drinks and laughs, and tears
twinkle out of his tipsy old eyes, as he wipes them with one
hand, and again says, " How much will you give, little discountess ? "

When poor Caroline went to her cupboard, and from it took
the notes and the gold which she had had we know from whom,
and added to these out of a cunning box a little heap of her
own private savings, and with trembling hands poured the
notes, and the sovereigns, and the shillings into a dish on the
table, I never heard accurately how much she laid down. But
she must have spread out everything she had in the world ; for
she felt her pockets and emptied them ; and, tapping her head,
she again applied to the cupboard, and took from thence a
little store of spoons and forks, and then a brooch, and then a
watch ; and she piled these all up in a dish, and she said,
" Now, Mr. Hunt, I will give you all these for that bill." And
she looked up at Philip's picture, which hung over the parson's
bloodshot, satyr face. " Take these," she said, " and give me

that! There's two hundred pound, I know; and there's thirty-four, and two eighteen, thirty-six eighteen, and there's the plate and watch, and I wan't that bill."

"What? have you got all this, you little dear?" cried Hunt, dropping back into his chair again. "Why, you're a little fortune, by Jove—a pretty little fortune, a little discountess, a little wife, a little fortune. I say, I'm a University man; I could write alcaics once as well as any man. I'm a gentleman. I say, how much *have* you got? Count it over again, my dear."

And again she told him the amount of the gold, and the notes, and the silver, and the number of the poor little spoons.

A thought came across the fellow's boozy brain: "If you offer so much," says he, "and you're a little discountess, the bill's worth more; that fellow must be making his fortune! Or do you know about it? I say, do you know about it? No. I'll have my bond. I'll have my bond!" And he gave a tipsy imitation of Shylock, and lurched back into his chair, and laughed.

"Let's have a little more, and talk about things," said the poor Little Sister; and she daintily heaped her little treasures and arranged them in her dish, and smiled upon the parson laughing in his chair.

"Caroline," says he, after a pause, "you are still fond of that old bald-headed scoundrel! That's it! Just like you women—just like, but I won't tell. No, no, I won't tell! You are fond of that old swindler still, I say! Wherever did you get that lot of money? Look here now—with that, and this little bill in my pocket, there's enough to carry us on for ever so long. And when this money's gone, I tell you I know who'll give us more, and who can't refuse us, I tell you. Look here, Caroline, dear Caroline! I'm an old fellow, I know; but I'm a good fellow: I'm a classical scholar: and I am a gentleman."

The classical scholar and gentleman bleared over his words as he uttered them, and with his vinous eyes and sordid face gave a leer, which must have frightened the poor little lady to whom he proffered himself as a suitor, for she started back with a pallid face, and an aspect of such dislike and terror, that even her guest remarked it.

"I said I was a scholar and gentleman," he shrieked again. "Do you doubt it? I am as good a man as Brummell Firmin, I say. I ain't so tall. But I'll do a copy of Latin alcaics or Greek iambics against him or any man of my weight. Do you mean to insult me? Don't I know who you are? Are you better than a Master of Arts and a clergyman? He went out in medicine, Firmin did. Do you mean, when a Master of Arts and classical scholar offers you his hand and fortune, that you're above him and refuse him, by George?"

The Little Sister was growing bewildered and frightened by the man's energy and horrid looks. "Oh, Mr. Hunt!" she cried, "see here, take this! See—there are two hundred and thirty—thirty-six pounds and all these things! Take them, and give me that paper."

"Sovereigns, and notes, and spoons, and a watch, and what I have in my pocket—and that ain't much—and Firmin's bill! Three hundred and eighty-six four three. It's a fortune, my dear, with economy! I won't have you going on being a nurse and that kind of thing. I'm a scholar and a gentleman—I am—and that place ain't fit for Mrs. Hunt. We'll first spend your money. No : we'll first spend my money—three hundred and eighty-six and—and hang the change—and when that's gone, we'll have another bill from that bald-headed old scoundrel : and his son who struck a poor cler—— We *will*, I say, Caroline—we——"

The wretch was suiting actions to his words, and rose once more, advancing towards his hostess, who shrank back, laughing half-hysterically, and retreating as the other neared her. Behind her was that cupboard which had contained her poor little treasure and other stores, and appended to the lock of which her keys were still hanging. As the brute approached her, she flung back the cupboard door smartly upon him. The keys struck him on the head ; and bleeding, and with a curse and a cry, he fell back on his chair.

In the cupboard was that bottle which she had received from America not long since ; and about which she had talked with Goodenough on that very day. It had been used twice or thrice by his direction, by hospital surgeons, and under her eye. She suddenly seized this bottle. As the ruffian before her uttered his imprecations of wrath, she poured out a quantity of the contents of the bottle on her handkerchief. She said, "Oh! Mr. Hunt, have I hurt you? I didn't mean it. But you shouldn't—you shouldn't frighten a lonely woman so ! Here, let me bathe you ! Smell this ! It will—it will do you—good —it will—it will, indeed." The handkerchief was over his face. Bewildered by drink before, the fumes of the liquor which he was absorbing served almost instantly to overcome him. He struggled for a moment or two. "Stop — stop ! you'll be better in a moment," she whispered. "Oh, yes ! better, quite better !" She squeezed more of the liquor from the bottle on to the handkerchief. In a minute Hunt was quite inanimate.

Then the little pale woman leant over him, and took the pocket-book out of his pocket, and from it the bill which bore Philip's name. As Hunt lay in stupor before her, she now squeezed more of the liquor over his head ; and then thrust the bill into the fire, and saw it burn to ashes. Then she put back the pocket-book into Hunt's breast. She said afterwards that she never should have thought about that Chloroform, but for her brief conversation with Dr. Goodenough that evening, regarding a case in which she had employed the new remedy under his orders.

How long did Hunt lie in that stupor ? It seemed a whole long night to Caroline. She said afterwards that the thought of that act that night made her hair · grow gray. Poor little head ! Indeed, she would have laid it down for Philip.

Hunt, I suppose, came to himself when the handkerchief was withdrawn, and the fumes of the potent liquor ceased to work on his brain. He was very much frightened and bewildered. " What was it ? Where am I ?" he asked, in a husky voice.

" It was the keys struck you in the cupboard door when you—you ran against it," said pale Caroline. " Look ! you are all bleeding on the head. Let me dry it."

" No ; keep off ! " cried the terrified man.

" Will you have a cab to go home ? The poor gentleman hit himself against the cupboard door, Mary. You remember him here before, don't you, one night ? " And Caroline, with a shrug, pointed out to her maid, whom she had summoned, the great square bottle of spirits still on the table, and indicated that there lay the cause of Hunt's bewilderment.

" Are you better now ? Will you—will you—take a little more refreshment ? " asked Caroline.

" No ! " he cried with an oath, and with glaring, bloodshot eyes he lurched towards his hat.

" Lor', mum ! what ever is it ? And this smell in the room, and all this here heap of money and things on the table ? "

Caroline flung open her window. " It's medicine, which Dr. Goodenough has ordered for one of his patients. I must go and see her to-night," she said. And at midnight, looking as pale as death, the Little Sister went to the doctor's house, and roused him up from his bed, and told him the story here narrated. " I offered him all you gave me," she said, " and all I had in the world besides, and he wouldn't—and——" Here she broke out into a fit of hysterics. The doctor had to ring up his servants ; to administer remedies to his little nurse ; to put her to bed in his own house.

JUDITH AND HOLOFERNES.

" By the immortal Jove," he said afterwards, " I had a great mind to beg her never to leave it! But that my housekeeper would tear Caroline's eyes out, Mrs. Brandon should be welcome to stay for ever. Except her *h*'s, that woman has every virtue : constancy, gentleness, generosity, cheerfulness, and the courage of a lioness! To think of that fool, that dandified idiot, that triple ass, Firmin "—(there were few men in the world for whom Goodenough entertained a greater scorn than for his late *confrère*, Firmin of Old Parr Street)—" think of the villain having possessed such a treasure—let alone his having deceived and deserted her—of his having possessed such a treasure and flung it away! Sir, I always admired Mrs. Brandon ; but I think ten thousand times more highly of her since her glorious crime, and most righteous robbery. If the villain had died, dropped dead in the street—the drunken miscreant, forger, housebreaker, assassin—so that no punishment could have fallen upon poor Brandon, I think I should have respected her only the more! "

At an early hour Dr. Goodenough had thought proper to send off messengers to Philip and myself, and to make us acquainted with the strange adventure of the previous night. We both hastened to him. I myself was summoned, no doubt, in consequence of my profound legal knowledge, which might be of use in poor little Caroline's present trouble. And Philip came because she longed to see him. By some instinct she knew when he arrived. She crept down from the chamber where the doctor's housekeeper had laid her on a bed. She knocked at the doctor's study, where we were all in consultation. She came in quite pale, and tottered towards Philip, and flung herself into his arms, with a burst of tears that greatly relieved her excitement and fever. Firmin was scarcely less moved.

" You'll pardon me for what I have done, Philip," she sobbed. " If they—if they take me up, you won't forsake me ? '

" Forsake you ? Pardon you ? Come and live with us, and never leave us ! " cried Philip.

" I don't think Mrs. Philip would like that, dear," said the little woman sobbing on his arm ; " but ever since the Grey Friars school, when you was so ill, you have been like a son to me, and somehow I couldn't help doing that last night to that villain—I couldn't."

" Serve the scoundrel right. Never deserved to come to life again, my dear," said Dr. Goodenough. " Don't you be exciting yourself, little Brandon! I must have you sent back to lie down on your bed. Take her up, Philip, to the little room next mine ; and order her to lie down and be as quiet as a mouse. You are not to move till I give you leave, Brandon— mind that, and come back to us, Firmin, or we shall have the patients coming."

So Philip led away this poor Little Sister ; and trembling, and clinging to his arm, she returned to the room assigned to her.

" She wants to be alone with him," the doctor said ; and he spoke a brief word or two of that strange delusion under which the little woman labored, that this was her dead child come back to her.

" I know that is in her mind," Goodenough said ; " she never got over that brain fever in which I found her. If I were to swear her on the book, and say, ' Brandon, don't you believe he is your son alive again? ' she would not dare to say no. She will leave him everything she has got. I only gave her so much less than that scoundrel's bill yesterday, because I knew she would like to contribute her own share. It would have offended her mortally to have been left out of the subscription. They like to sacrifice themselves. Why, there are women in India who, if not allowed to roast with their dead husbands, would die of vexation." And by this time Mr. Philip came striding back into the room again, rubbing a pair of very red eyes.

" Long ere this, no doubt, that drunken ruffian is sobered, and knows that the bill is gone. He is likely enough to accuse her of the robbery," says the doctor.

" Suppose," says Philip's other friend, " I had put a pistol to your head, and was going to shoot you, and the doctor took the pistol out of my hand, and flung it into the sea, would you help me to prosecute the doctor for robbing me of the pistol ? "

" You don't suppose it will be a pleasure to me to pay that bill ? " said Philip. " I said, if a certain bill were presented to me, purporting to be accepted by Philip Firmin, I would pay it. But if that scoundrel, Hunt, only *says* that he had such a bill, and has lost it ; I will cheerfully take my oath that I have never signed any bill at all—and they can't find Brandon guilty of stealing a thing which never existed."

" Let us hope, then, that the bill was not in duplicate ! "

And to this wish all three gentlemen heartily said Amen!

And now the doctor's door-bell began to be agitated by arriving patients. His dining-room was already full of them. The Little Sister must lie still, and the discussion of her affairs must be deferred to a more convenient hour ; and Philip and his friend agreed to reconnoitre the house in Thornhaugh Street, and see if anything had happened since its mistress had left it.

Yes : something had happened. Mrs. Brandon's maid, who ushered us into her mistress's little room, told us that in the early morning that horrible man who had come over night, and been so tipsy, and behaved so ill,—the very same man who had come there tipsy afore once, and whom Mr. Philip had flung into the street—had come battering at the knocker, and pulling at the bell, and swearing and cursing most dreadful, and calling for " Mrs. Brandon ! Mrs. Brandon ! Mrs. Brandon ! " and frightening the whole street. After he had rung, he knocked and battered ever so long. Mary looked out at him from the upper window, and told him to go along home, or she would call the police. On this the man roared out that he would call the police himself if Mary did not let him in ; and as he went on calling " Police ! " and yelling from the door, Mary came down stairs, and opened the hall door, keeping the chain fastened, and asked him what he wanted ?

Hunt, from the steps without, began to swear and rage more loudly, and to demand to be let in. He must and would see Mrs. Brandon.

Mary, from behind her chain barricade, said that her mistress was not at home, but that she had been called out that night to a patient of Dr. Goodenough's.

Hunt, with more shrieks and curses, said it was a lie : and that she was at home ; and that he would see her ; and that he must go into her room ; and that he had left something there ; that he had lost something ; and that he would have it.

" Lost something here ? " cried Mary. " Why here ? when you reeled out of this house, you couldn't scarce walk, and you almost fell into the gutter, which I have seen you there before. Get away and go home ! You are not sober yet, you horrible man ! "

On this, clinging on to the area-railings, and demeaning himself like a madman, Hunt continued to call out, " Police, police ! I have been robbed, I've been robbed ! Police ! " until astonished heads appeared at various windows in the quiet street, and a policeman actually came up.

When the policeman appeared, Hunt began to sway and pull at the door, confined by its chain ; and he frantically reiterated his charge, that he had been robbed and hocussed in that house, that night, by Mrs. Brandon.

The policeman, by a familiar expression, conveyed his utter disbelief of the statement, and told the dirty, disreputable man to move on, and go to bed. Mrs. Brandon was known and respected all around the neighborhood. She had befriended numerous poor round about ; and was known for a hundred charities. She attended many respectable families. In that parish there was no woman more esteemed. And by the word "Gammon," the policeman expressed his sense of the utter absurdity of the charge against the good lady.

Hunt still continued to yell out that he had been robbed and hocussed ; and Mary from behind her door repeated to the officer (with whom she perhaps had relations not unfriendly) her statement that the beast had gone reeling away from the house the night before, and if he had lost anything, who knows where he might not have lost it?

"It was taken out of this pocket, and out of this pocket-book," howled Hunt clinging to the rail. "I give her in charge. I give the house in charge! It's a den of thieves!"

During this shouting and turmoil, the sash of a window in Ridley's studio was thrown up. The painter was going to his morning work. He had appointed an early model. The sun could not rise too soon for Ridley ; and, as soon as ever it gave its light, found him happy at his labor. He had heard from his bedroom the brawl going on about the door.

"Mr. Ridley !" says the policeman, touching the glazed hat with much respect—(in fact, in and out of uniform, Z 25 has figured in more than one of J. J.'s pictures)—"Here's a fellow disturbing the whole street, and shouting out that Mrs. Brandon have robbed and hocussed him !"

Ridley ran down stairs in a high state of indignation. He is nervous, like men of his tribe ; quick to feel, to pity, to love, to be angry. He undid the chain, and ran into the street.

"I remember that fellow drunk here before," said the painter ; "and lying in that very gutter."

"Drunk and disorderly! Come along !" cries Z 25 ; and his hand was quickly fastened on the parson's greasy collar, and under its strong grasp Hunt is forced to move on. He goes, still yelling out that he has been robbed.

"Tell that to his worship," said the incredulous Z. And this was the news which Mrs. Brandon's friends received from her maid, when they called at her house.

CHAPTER XXXIX.

IN WHICH SEVERAL PEOPLE HAVE THEIR TRIALS.

IF Philip and his friend had happened to pass through High Street, Marylebone, on their way to Thornhaugh Street to reconnoitre the Little Sister's house, they would have seen the Reverend Mr. Hunt, in a very dirty, battered, crestfallen and unsatisfactory state, marching to Marylebone from the station, where the reverend gentleman had passed the night, and under the custody of the police. A convoy of street boys followed the prisoner and his guard, making sarcastic remarks on both. Hunt's appearance was not improved since we had the pleasure of meeting him on the previous evening. With a grizzled beard and hair, a dingy face, a dingy shirt, and a countenance mottled with dirt and drink, we may fancy the reverend man passing in tattered raiment through the street to make his appearance before the magistrate.

You have no doubt forgotten the narrative which appeared in the morning papers two days after the Thornhaugh Street incident, but my clerk has been at the pains to hunt up and copy the police report, in which events connected with our history are briefly recorded.

"MARYLEBONE, *Wednesday.*—Thomas Tufton Hunt, professing to be a clergyman, but wearing an appearance of extreme squalor, was brought before Mr. Beaksby at this office, charged by Z 25 with being drunk and very disorderly on Tuesday se'nnight, and endeavoring by force and threats to effect his reentrance into a house in Thornhaugh Street, from which he had been previously ejected in a most unclerical and inebriated state.

"On being taken to the station-house, the reverend gentleman lodged a complaint on his own side, and averred that he had been stupefied and hocussed in the house in Thornhaugh Street by means of some drug, and that, whilst in this state, he had been robbed of a bill for 386*l.* 4*s.* 3*d.*, drawn by a person in New York, and accepted by Mr. P. Firmin, barrister, of Parchment Buildings, Temple.

"Mrs. Brandon, the landlady of the house, No. —, Thornhaugh Street, has been in the habit of letting lodgings for many years past, and several of her friends, including Mr. Firmin,

Mr. Ridley, the Rl. Acad., and other gentlemen, were in attend-ance to speak to her character, which is most respectable. After Z 25 had given evidence, the servant deposed that Hunt had been more than once disorderly and drunk before that house, and had been forcibly ejected from it.   On the night when the alleged robbery was said to have taken place, he had visited the house in Thornhaugh Street, had left it in an inebriated state, and returned some hours afterwards, vowing that he had been robbed of the document in question.

"Mr. P. Firmin said : 'I am a barrister, and have chambers at Parchment Buildings, Temple, and know the person calling himself Hunt.   I have not accepted any bill of Exchange, nor is my signature affixed to any such document.'

. "At this stage the worthy magistrate interposed, and said that this only went to prove that the bill was not completed by Mr. F.'s acceptance, and would by no means conclude the case set up before him.   Dealing with it, however, on the merits, and looking at the way in which the charge had been preferred, and the entire absence of sufficient testimony to warrant him in deciding that even a piece of paper had been abstracted in that house, or by the person accused, and believing that if he were to commit, a conviction would be impossible, he dismissed the charge.

"The lady left the court with her friends, and the accuser, when called upon to pay a fine for drunkenness, broke out into very unclerical language, in the midst of which he was forcibly removed."

Philip Firmin's statement, that he had given no bill of ex-change, was made not without hesitation on his part, and indeed at his friends' strong entreaty.   It was addressed not so much to the sitting magistrate, as to that elderly individual at New York, who was warned no more to forge his son's name.   I fear a coolness ensued between Philip and his parent in consequence of the younger man's behavior.   The doctor had thought better of his boy than to suppose that, at a *moment of necessity*, Philip would desert him.   He forgave Philip, nevertheless.   Perhaps since his marriage *other influences* were at work upon him, &c. The parent made further remarks in this strain.   A man who takes your money is naturally offended if you remonstrate ; you wound his sense of delicacy by protesting against his putting his hand in your pocket.   The elegant doctor in New York continued to speak of his unhappy son with a mournful shake of the head ; he said, perhaps believed, that Philip's imprudence was in part the cause of his own exile.   "This is not the kind of entertainment to which I would have invited you at my own house in England," he would say. "I thought to have ended my days there, and to have left my son in comfort—nay, splendor. I am an exile in poverty : and he—but I will use no hard words." And to his female patients he would say : "No, my dear madam !—not a syllable of reproach shall escape these lips regarding that misguided boy ! But you can feel for me ; I know you can feel for me." In the old days, a high-spirited highwayman, who took a coach-passenger's purse, thought himself injured, and the traveller a shabby fellow, if he secreted a guinea or two under the cushions. In the doctor's now rare letters, he breathed a manly sigh here and there, to think that he had lost the confidence of his boy. I do believe that certain ladies of our acquaintance were inclined to think that the elder Firmin had been not altogether well used, however much they loved and admired the Little Sister for her lawless act in her boy's defence. But this main point we had won. The doctor at New York took the warning, and wrote his son's signature upon no more bills of exchange. The good Goodenough's loan was carried back to him in the very coin which he had supplied. He said that his little nurse Brandon was *splendide mendax*, and that her robbery was a sublime and courageous act of war.

In so far, since his marriage, Mr. Philip had been pretty fortunate. At need, friends had come to him. In moments of peril he had had succor and relief. Though he had married without money, fate had sent him a sufficiency. His flask had never been empty, and there was always meal in his bin. But now hard trials were in store for him : hard trials which we have said were endurable, and which he has long since lived through. Any man who has played the game of life or whist, knows how for one while he will have a series of good cards dealt him, and again will get no trumps at all. After he got into his house in Milman Street and quitted the Little Sister's kind roof, our friend's good fortune seemed to desert him. "Perhaps it was a punishment for my pride, because I was haughty with her, and—and jealous of that dear good little creature," poor Charlotte afterwards owned in conversation with other friends :— "but our fortune seemed to change when we were away from her, and that I must own."

Perhaps, when she was yet under Mrs. Brandon's roof, the Little Sister's provident care had done a great deal more for Charlotte than Charlotte knew. Mrs. Philip had the most simple tastes in the world, and upon herself never spent an unnecessary shilling. Indeed, it was a wonder, considering her small expenses, how neat and nice Mrs. Philip ever looked. But she never could deny herself when the children were in question; and had them arrayed in all sorts of fine clothes; and stitched and hemmed all day and night to decorate their little persons; and in reply to the remonstrances of the matrons her friends, showed how it was impossible children *could* be dressed for less cost. If anything ailed them, quick, the doctor must be sent for. Not worthy Goodenough, who came without a fee, and pooh-poohed her alarms and anxieties; but dear Mr. Bland, who had a feeling heart, and was himself a father of children, and who supported those children by the produce of the pills, draughts, powders, visits, which he bestowed on all families into whose doors he entered. Bland's sympathy was very consolatory; but it was found to be very costly at the end of the year. "And, what then?" says Charlotte, with kindling cheeks. "Do you suppose we should grudge that money, which was to give health to our dearest, dearest babies? No. You can't have such a bad opinion of me as that!" And accordingly Mr. Bland received a nice little annuity from our friends. Philip had a joke about his wife's housekeeping which perhaps may apply to other young women who are kept by overwatchful mothers too much *in statu pupillari*. When they were married, or about to be married, Philip asked Charlotte what she would order for dinner? She promptly said she would order leg of mutton. "And after leg of mutton?" "Leg of beef, to be sure!" says Mrs. Charlotte, looking very pleased, and knowing. And the fact is, as this little housekeeper was obliged demurely to admit, their household bills increased *prodigiously* after they left Thornhaugh Street. "And I can't understand, my dear, how the grocer's book should mount up so; and the butterman's, and the beer," &c., &c. We have often seen the pretty little head bent over the dingy volumes, puzzling, puzzling: and the eldest child would hold up a warning finger to ours, and tell them to be very quiet, as mamma was at her "atounts."

And now, I grieve to say, money became scarce for the payment of these accounts; and though Philip fancied he hid his anxieties from his wife, be sure she loved him too much to be deceived by one of the clumsiest hypocrites in the world. Only, being a much cleverer hypocrite than her husband, she pretended to be deceived, and acted her part so well that poor Philip was mortified with her gayety, and chose to fancy his wife was indifferent to their misfortunes. She ought not to be so smiling and happy, he thought; and, as usual, bemoaned his lot to his friends. "I come home racked with care, and thinking of those inevitable bills ; I shudder, sir, at every note that lies on the hall table, and would tremble as I dashed them open as they do on the stage. But I laugh and put on a jaunty air and humbug Char. And I hear her singing about the house and laughing and cooing with the children, by Jove ! *She's* not aware of anything. *She* does not know how dreadfully the `res domi` is squeezing me. But *before marriage* she did, I tell you. Then, if anything annoyed me, she divined it. If I felt ever so little unwell, you should have seen the alarm on her face ! It was, ' Philip dear, how pale you are ;' or, ' Philip, how flushed you are ;' or, ' I am sure you have had a letter from your father. Why do you conceal anything from me, sir ? You never should—never !' And now when the fox is gnawing at my side under my cloak, I laugh and grin so naturally that she believes I am all right, and she comes to meet me flouncing the children about in my face, and wearing an air of consummate happiness ! I would not deceive her for the world, you know. But it's mortifying. Don't tell me. It *is* mortifying to be tossing awake all night, and racked with care all day, and have the wife of your bosom chattering and singing and laughing, as if there were no cares, or doubts, or duns in the world. If I had the gout and she were to laugh and sing, I should not call that sympathy. If I were arrested for debt, and she were to come grinning and laughing to the sponging-house, I should not call that consolation. Why doesn't she feel ? She ought to feel. There's Betsy, our parlor-maid. There's the old fellow who comes to clean the boots and knives. *They* know how hard up I am. And my wife sings and dances whilst I am on the verge of ruin, by Jove ; and giggles and laughs as if life was a pantomime !"

Then the man and woman into whose ears poor Philip roared out his confessions and griefs, hung down their blushing heads in humble silence. They are tolerably prosperous in life, and, I fear, are pretty well satisfied with themselves and each other. A woman who scarcely ever does any wrong, and rules and governs her own house and family, as my ——, as the wife of the reader's humble servant most notoriously does, often becomes—must it be said ?—too certain of her own virtue, and is too sure of the correctness of her own opinion. We virtuous people give advice a good deal, and set a considerable value upon that advice. We meet a certain man who has fallen among thieves, let us say. We succor him readily enough. We take him kindly to the inn, and pay his score there ; but we say to the landlord, " You must give this poor man his bed ;

his medicine at such a time, and his broth at such another. But, mind you, he must have that physic, and no other ; that broth when we order it. *We* take his case in hand, you understand. Don't listen to him or anybody else. We know all about everything. Good-by. Take care of him. Mind the medicine and the broth ! " and Mr. Benefactor or Lady Bountiful goes away, perfectly self-satisfied.

Do you take this allegory ? When Philip complained to us of his wife's friskiness and gayety ; when he bitterly contrasted her levity and carelessness with his own despondency and doubt, Charlotte's two principal friends were smitten by shame. " Oh, Philip ! dear Philip ! " his female adviser said (having looked at her husband once or twice as Firmin spoke, and in vain endeavored to keep her guilty eyes down on her work), " Charlotte has done this, because she is humble, and because she takes the advice of friends who are not. She knows everything, and more than everything ; for her dear tender heart is filled with apprehension. But we told her to show no sign of care, lest her husband should be disturbed. And she trusted in us ; and she puts her trust elsewhere, Philip ; and she has hidden her own anxieties, lest yours should be increased ; and has met you gayly when her heart was full of dread. We think she has done wrong now ; but she did so because she was so simple, and trusted in us who advised her wrongly. Now we see that there ought to have been perfect confidence always between you, and that it is her simplicity and faith in us which have misled her."

Philip hung down his head for a moment, and hid his eyes ; and we knew, during that minute when his face was concealed from us, how his grateful heart was employed.

" And you know, dear Philip——" says Laura, looking at her husband, and nodding to that person, who certainly understood the hint.

" And I say, Firmin," breaks in the lady's husband, " you understand, if you are at all—that is, if you — that is if we can——"

" Hold your tongue ! " shouts Firmin, with a face beaming over with happiness. " I know what you mean. You beggar, you are going to offer me money ! I see it in your face ; bless you both ! But we'll try and do without, please heaven. And —and it's worth feeling a pinch of poverty to find such friends as I have had, and to share it with such a—such a—dash— dear little thing as I have at home. And I won't try and humbug Char any more. I'm bad at that sort of business.

And good-night, and I'll never forget your kindness, never ! "
And he is off a moment afterwards, and jumping down the steps
of our door, and so into the park. And though there were not
five pounds in the poor little house in Milman Street, there
were not two happier people in London that night than Charlotte and Philip Firmin. If he had his troubles, our friend
had his immense consolations. Fortunate he, however poor,
who has friends to help, and love to console him in his trials.

CHAPTER XL.

IN WHICH THE LUCK GOES VERY MUCH AGAINST US.

EVERY man and woman amongst us has made his voyage to
Lilliput, and his tour in the kingdom of Brobdingnag. When
I go to my native country town, the local paper announces our
arrival; the laborers touch their hats, as the pony-chaise
passes, the girls and old women drop curtsies; Mr. Hicks, the
grocer and hatter, comes to his door and makes a bow, and
smirks and smiles. When our neighbor Sir John arrives at the
hall, he is a still greater personage ; the bell-ringers greet the
hall family with a peal ; the rector walks over on an early day,
and pays his visit ; and the farmers at market press round for
a nod of recognition. Sir John at home is in Lilliput : in
Belgrave Square he is in Brobdingnag, where almost everybody
we meet is ever so much taller than ourselves. "Which do
you like best, to be a giant amongst the pigmies, or a pigmy
amongst the giants ? " I know what sort of company I prefer
myself : but that is not the point. What I would hint is, that
we possibly give ourselves patronizing airs before small people,
as folks higher placed than ourselves give themselves airs
before *us*. Patronizing airs ? Old Miss Mumbles, the half-pay
lieutenant's daughter, who lives over the plumber's, with her
maid, gives herself in her degree more airs than any duchess
in Belgravia, and would leave the room if a tradesman's wife
sat down in it.

Now it has been said that few men in this city of London
are so simple in their manners as Philip Firmin, and that he
treated the patron whose bread he ate, and the wealthy relative
who condescended to visit him, with a like freedom. He is

blunt, but not familiar, and is not a whit more polite to my
lord than to Jack or Tom at the coffee-house. He resents
familiarity from vulgar persons, and those who venture on it
retire maimed and mortified after coming into collision with
him. As for the people he loves, he grovels before them,
worships their boot-tips, and their gown-hems. But he submits
to them, not for their wealth or rank, but for love's sake. He
submitted very magnanimously, at first, to the kindnesses and
caresses of Lady Ringwood and her daughters, being softened
and won by the regard which they showed for his wife and
children.

Although Sir John was for the Rights of Man everywhere,
all over the world, and had pictures of Franklin, Lafayette, and
Washington in his library, he likewise had portraits of his own
ancestors in that apartment, and entertained a very high
opinion of the present representative of the Ringwood family.
The character of the late chief of the house was notorious.
Lord Ringwood's life had been irregular and his morals loose.
His talents were considerable, no doubt, but they had not been
devoted to serious study or directed to useful ends. A wild
man in early life, he had only changed his practices in later life
in consequence of ill health, and became a hermit as a Certain
Person became a monk. He was a frivolous person to the end,
and was not to be considered as a public man and statesman ;
and this light-minded man of pleasure had been advanced to the
third rank of the peerage, whilst his successor, his superior in
intellect and morality, remained a Baronet still. How blind
the Ministry was which refused to recognize so much talent and
worth ! Had there been public virtue or common sense in the
governors of the nation, merits like Sir John's never could have
been overlooked. But Ministers were notoriously a family
clique, and only helped each other. Promotion and patronage
were disgracefully monopolized by the members of a very few
families who were not better men of business, men of better
character, men of more ancient lineage (though birth, of course,
was a mere accident) than Sir John himself. In a word, until
they gave him a peerage, he saw very little hope for the cabinet
or the country.

In a very early page of this history mention was made of a
certain Philip Ringwood, to whose protection Philip Firmin's
mother confided her boy when he was first sent to school.
Philip Ringwood was Firmin's senior by seven years ; he came
to Old Parr Street twice or thrice during his stay at school,
condescended to take the " tips," of which the poor doctor

was liberal enough, but never deigned to take any notice of young Firmin, who looked up to his kinsman with awe and trembling. From school Philip Ringwood speedily departed to college, and then entered upon public life. He was the eldest son of Sir John Ringwood, with whom our friend has of late made acquaintance.

Mr. Ringwood was a much greater personage than the baronet his father. Even when the latter succeeded to Lord Ringwood's estates and came to London, he could scarcely be said to equal his son in social rank ; and the younger patronized his parent. What is the secret of great social success ? It is not to be gained by beauty, or wealth, or birth, or wit, or valor, or eminence of any kind. It is a gift of Fortune, bestowed, like that goddess's favors, capriciously. Look, dear madam, at the most fashionable ladies at present reigning in London. Are they better bred, or more amiable, or richer, or more beautiful than yourself ? See, good sir, the men who lead the fashion, and stand in the bow-window at " Black's ; " are they wiser, or wittier, or more agreeable people than you ? And yet you know what your fate would be if you were put up at that club. Sir John Ringwood never dared to be proposed there, even after his great accession of fortune on the earl's death. His son did not encourage him. People even said that Ringwood would blackball his father if he dared to offer himself as a candidate.

I never, I say, could understand the reason of Philip Ringwood's success in life, though you must acknowledge that he is one of our most eminent dandies. He is affable to dukes. He patronizes marquises. He is not witty. He is not clever. He does not give good dinners. How many baronets are there in the British empire ? Look to your book, and see. I tell you there are many of these whom Philip Ringwood would scarcely admit to wait at one of his bad dinners. By calmly asserting himself in life, this man has achieved his social eminence. We may hate him ; but we acknowledge his superiority. For instance, I should as soon think of asking him to dine with me, as I should of slapping the Archbishop of Canterbury on the back.

Mr. Ringwood has a meagre little house in May Fair, and belongs to a public office, where he patronizes his *chef*. His own family bow down before him ; his mother is humble in his company ; his sisters are respectful ; his father does not brag of his own liberal principles, and never alludes to the rights of man in the son's presence. He is called " Mr. Ringwood " in

the family. The person who is least in awe of him is his
younger brother, who has been known to make faces behind
the elder's back. But he is a dreadfully headstrong and ignorant child, and respects nothing. Lady Ringwood, by the
way, is Mr. Ringwood's step-mother. His own mother was the
daughter of a noble house, and died in giving birth to this paragon.

Philip Firmin, who had not set eyes upon his kinsman since
they were at school together, remembered some stories which
were current about Ringwood, and by no means to that eminent
dandy's credit—stories of intrigue, of play, of various libertine
exploits on Mr. Ringwood's part. One day, Philip and Charlotte dined with Sir John, who was talking and chirping, and
laying down the law, and bragging away according to his wont,
when his son entered and asked for dinner. He had accepted
an invitation to dine at Garterton House. The Duke had one
of his attacks of gout just before dinner. The dinner was off.
If Lady Ringwood would give him a slice of mutton, he would
be very much obliged to her. A place was soon found for
him. "And, Philip, this is your namesake, and our cousin,
Mr. Philip Firmin," said the Baronet, presenting his son to his
kinsman.

"Your father used to give me sovereigns, when I was at
school. I have a faint recollection of you, too. Little white-
headed boy, weren't you? How is the doctor, and Mrs. Firmin? All right?"

"Why, don't you know his father ran away?" calls out the
youngest member of the family. "Don't kick me, Emily. He
did run away."

Then Mr. Ringwood remembered, and a faint blush tinged
his face. "Lapse of time. I know. Shouldn't have asked
after such a lapse of time." And he mentioned a case in which
a duke, who was very forgetful, had asked a marquis about his
wife who had run away with an earl, and made inquiries about
the duke's son, who, as everybody knew, was not on terms with
his father.

"This is Mrs. Firmin—Mrs. Philip Firmin!" cried Lady
Ringwood, rather nervously ; and I suppose Mrs. Philip blushed,
and the blush became her ; for Mr. Ringwood afterwards condescended to say to one of his sisters, that their new-found
relative seemed one of your rough-and-ready sort of gentlemen,
but his wife was really very well bred, and quite a pretty young
woman, and presentable anywhere—really anywhere. Charlotte was asked to sing one or two of her little songs after

dinner.   Mr. Ringwood was delighted.   Her voice was perfectly
true.   What she sang, she sang admirably.   And he was good
enough to hum over one of her songs (during which performance
he showed that *his* voice was not exempt from little frailties),
and to say he had heard Lady Philomela Shakerley sing that
very song at Glenmavis, last autumn ; and it was such a favorite
that the Duchess asked for it every night—actually every night.
When our friends were going home, Mr. Ringwood gave Philip
almost the whole of one finger to shake ; and while Philip was
inwardly raging at his impertinence, believed that he had
entirely fascinated his humble relatives, and that he had been
most good-natured and friendly.

I cannot tell why this man's patronage chafed and goaded
our worthy friend so as to drive him beyond the bounds of all
politeness and reason.   The artless remarks of the little boy,
and the occasional simple speeches of the young ladies, had
only tickled Philip's humor, and served to amuse him when he
met his relatives.   I suspect it was a certain free-and-easy manner
which Mr. Ringwood chose to adopt towards Mrs. Philip, which
annoyed her husband.   He had said nothing at which offence
could be taken : perhaps he was quite unconscious of offending ; nay, thought himself eminently pleasing : perhaps he was
not more impertinent towards her than towards other women :
but in talking about him, Mr. Firmin's eyes flashed very fiercely,
and he spoke of his new acquaintance and relative, with his
usual extreme candor, as an upstart, and an arrogant conceited
puppy whose ears he would like to pull.

How do good women learn to discover men who are not
good ?   Is it by instinct ?   How do they learn those stories
about men ?   I protest I never told my wife anything good or bad
regarding this Mr. Ringwood, though of course, as a man about
town, I have heard—who has not ?—little anecdotes regarding his career.   His conduct in that affair with Miss Willowby
was heartless and cruel ; his behavior to that unhappy Blanche
Painter nobody can defend.   My wife conveys her opinion
regarding Philip Ringwood, his life, principles, and morality, by
looks and silences which are more awful and killing than the
bitterest words of sarcasm or reproof.   Philip Firmin, who
knows her ways, watches her features, and, as I have said, hum-
bles himself at her feet, marked the lady's awful looks, when
he came to describe to us his meeting with his cousin, and
the magnificent patronizing airs which Mr. Ringwood assumed.

"What ?" he said, "you don't like him any more than I
do ?   I thought you would not ; and I am so glad."

Philip's friend said she did not know Mr. Ringwood, and had never spoken a word to him in her life.

"Yes; but you know of him," cries the impetuous Firmin. "What do you know of him, with his monstrous puppyism and arrogance?" Oh, Mrs. Laura knew very little of him. She did not believe—she had much rather not believe—what the world said about Mr. Ringwood.

"Suppose we were to ask the Woolcombs their opinion of your character, Philip?" cries that gentleman's biographer, with a laugh.

"My dear!" says Laura, with a yet severer look, the severity of which glance I must explain. The differences of Woolcomb and his wife were notorious. Their unhappiness was known to all the world. Society was beginning to look with a very, very cold face upon Mrs. Woolcomb. After quarrels, jealousies, battles, reconciliations, scenes of renewed violence and furious language, had come indifference, and the most reckless gayety on the woman's part. Her home was splendid, but mean and miserable; all sorts of stories were rife regarding her husband's brutal treatment of poor Agnes, and her own imprudent behavior. Mrs. Laura was indignant when this unhappy woman's name was ever mentioned, except when she thought how our warm, true-hearted Philip had escaped from the heartless creature. "What a blessing it was that you were ruined, Philip, and that she deserted you!" Laura would say. "What fortune would repay you for marrying such a woman?"

"Indeed it was worth all I had to lose her," says Philip, "and so the doctor and I are quits. If he had not spent my fortune, Agnes would have married me. If she had married me, I might have turned Othello, and have been hung for smothering her. Why, if I had not been poor, I should never have been married to little Char—and fancy not being married to Char!" The worthy fellow here lapses into silence, and indulges in an inward rupture at the idea of his own excessive happiness. Then he is scared again at the thought which his own imagination has raised.

"I say! Fancy being without the kids and Char!" he cries with a blank look.

"That horrible father—that dreadful mother—pardon me, Philip; but when I think of the worldliness of those unhappy people, and how that poor unhappy woman has been bred in it, and ruined by it—I am so, so, so *enraged*, that I can't keep my temper!" cries the lady. "Is the woman answerable, or the parents, who hardened her heart, and sold her—sold her to that——O!" Our illustrious friend Woolcomb was signified by "that O," and the lady once more paused, choked with wrath as she thought about that O, and that O's wife.

"I wonder he has not Othello'd her," remarks Philip, with his hands in his pockets. "I should, if she had been mine, and gone on as they say she is going on."

"It is dreadful, dreadful to contemplate!" continues the lady. "To think she was sold by her own parents, poor thing, poor thing! The guilt is with them who led her wrong."

"Nay," says one of the three interlocutors. "Why stop at poor Mr. and Mrs. Twysden? Why not let them off, and accuse *their* parents? who lived worldly too in their generation. Or stay; they descend from William the Conqueror. Let us absolve poor Talbot Twysden and his heartless wife, and have the Norman into court."

"Ah, Arthur! Did not our sin begin with the beginning," cries the lady, "and have we not its remedy? Oh, this poor creature, this poor creature! May she know where to take refuge from it, and learn to repent in time!"

The Georgian and Circassian girls, they say, used to submit to their lot very complacently, and were quite eager to get to market at Constantinople and be sold. Mrs. Woolcomb wanted nobody to tempt her away from poor Philip. She hopped away from the old love soon as ever the new one appeared with his bag of money. She knew quite well to whom she was selling herself, and for what. The tempter needed no skill, or artifice, or eloquence. He had none. But he showed her a purse, and three fine houses—and she came. Innocent child, forsooth! She knew quite as much about the world as papa and mamma; and the lawyers did not look to her settlement more warily, and coolly, than she herself did. Did she not live on it afterwards? I do not say she lived reputably, but most comfortably: as Paris, and Rome, and Naples, and Florence can tell you, where she is known; where she receives a great deal of a certain kind of company; where she is scorned and flattered, and splendid, and lonely, and miserable. She is not miserable when she sees children: she does not care for other persons' children, as she never did for her own, even when they were taken from her. She is of course hurt and angry, when quite common, vulgar people, not in society, you understand, turn away from her, and avoid her, and won't come to her parties. She gives excellent dinners which jolly fogeys, rattling bachelors, and doubtful ladies frequent: but she is alone and unhappy—unhappy because she does not see parents, sister, or brother? *Allons, mon bon Monsieur!* She never cared for parents, sister, or brother; or for baby: or for man (except once for Philip a little, little bit, when her pulse would sometimes go up two beats in a minute at his appearance). But she is unhappy, because she is losing her figure, and from tight lacing her nose has become very red, and the pearl-powder won't lie on it somehow. And though you may have thought Woolcomb an odious, ignorant, and underbred little wretch, you must own that at least he had red blood in his veins. Did he not spend a great part of his fortune for the possession of this cold wife? For whom did *she* ever make a sacrifice, or feel a pang? I am sure a greater misfortune than any which has befallen friend Philip might have happened to him, and so congratulate him on his escape.

Having vented his wrath upon the arrogance and impertinence of this solemn puppy of a Philip Ringwood, our friend went away somewhat soothed to his club in St. James's Street. The "Megatherium Club" is only a very few doors from the much more aristocratic establishment of "Black's." Mr. Philip Ringwood and Mr. Woolcomb were standing on the steps of "Black's." Mr. Ringwood waved a graceful little kid-gloved hand to Philip, and smiled on him. Mr. Woolcomb glared at our friend out of his opal eyeballs. Philip had once proposed to kick Woolcomb into the sea. He somehow felt as if he would like to treat Ringwood to the same bath. Meanwhile, Mr. Ringwood labored under the notion that he and his newfound acquaintance were on the very best possible terms.

At one time poor little Woolcomb loved to be seen with Philip Ringwood. He thought he acquired distinction from the companionship of that man of fashion, and would hang on Ringwood as they walked the Pall Mall pavement.

"Do you know that great hulking, overbearing brute?" says Woolcomb to his companion on the steps of "Black's." Perhaps somebody overheard them from the bow-window. (I tell you everything is overheard in London, and a great deal more too.)

"Brute, is he?" says Ringwood; "seems a rough, overbearing sort of chap."

"Blackguard doctor's son. Bankrupt. Father ran away," says the dusky man with the opal eyeballs.

"I have heard he was a rogue—the doctor; but I like him. Remember he gave me three sovereigns when I was at school. Always like a fellow who tips you when you are at school." And here Ringwood beckoned his brougham which was in waiting.

"Shall we see you at dinner? Where are you going?" asked Mr. Woolcomb. "If you are going towards——"

"Towards Gray's Inn, to see my lawyer; have an appointment there; be with you at eight!" And Mr. Ringwood skipped into his little brougham and was gone.

Tom Eaves told Philip. Tom Eaves belongs to "Black's Club," to "Bays's," to the "Megatherium," I don't know to how many clubs in St. James's Street. Tom Eaves knows everybody's business, and all the scandal of all the clubs for the last forty years. He knows who has lost money and to whom; what is the talk of the opera-box and what the scandal of the *coulisses;* who is making love to whose daughter. Whatever men and women are doing in May Fair, is the farrago of Tom's libel. He knows so many stories, that of course he makes mistakes in names sometimes, and says that Jones is on the verge of ruin, when he is thriving and prosperous, and it is poor Brown who is in difficulties; or informs us that Mrs. Fanny is flirting with Captain Ogle when both are as innocent of a flirtation as you and I are. Tom certainly is mischievous, and often is wrong; but when he speaks of our neighbors he is amusing.

"It is as good as a play to see Ringwood and Othello together," says Tom to Philip. "How proud the black man is to be seen with him! Heard him abuse you to Ringwood. Ringwood stuck up for you and for your poor governor—spoke up like a man—like a man who sticks up for a fellow who is down. How the black man brags about having Ringwood to dinner! Always having him to dinner. You should have seen Ringwood shake him off! Said he was going to Gray's Inn. Heard him say Gray's Inn Lane to his man. Don't believe a word of it."

Now I dare say you are much too fashionable to know that Milman Street is a little *cul de sac* of a street, which leads into Guildford Street, which leads into Gray's Inn Lane. Philip went his way homewards, shaking off Tom Eaves, who for his part, trotted off to his other clubs, telling people how he had just been talking with that bankrupt doctor's son, and wondering how Philip should get money enough to pay his club subscription. Philip then went on his way, striding homewards at his usual manly pace.

Whose black brougham was that?—the black brougham with the chestnut horse walking up and down Guildford Street. Mr. Ringwood's crest was on the brougham. When Philip entered his drawing-room, having opened the door with his own key, there sat Mr. Ringwood, talking to Mrs. Charlotte, who was taking a cup of tea at five o'clock. She and the children liked that cup of tea. Sometimes it served Mrs. Char for dinner when Philip dined from home.

"If I had known you were coming here, you might have brought me home and saved me a long walk," said Philip, wiping a burning forehead.

"So I might—so I might!" said the other. "I never thought of it. I had to see my lawyer in Gray's Inn; and it was then I thought of coming on to see you, as I was telling Mrs. Firmin; and a very nice quiet place you live in!"

This was very well. But for the first and only time of his life, Philip was jealous.

"Don't drub so with your feet! Don't like to ride when you jog so on the floor," said Philip's eldest darling, who had clambered on papa's knee. "Why do you look so? Don't squeeze my arm, papa!"

Mamma was utterly unaware that Philip had any cause for agitation. "You have walked all the way from Westminster, and the club, and you are quite hot and tired!" she said. "Some tea, my dear?"

Philip nearly choked with the tea. From under his hair, which fell over his forehead, he looked into his wife's face. It wore such a sweet look of innocence and wonder, that, as he regarded her, the spasm of jealousy passed off. No: there was no look of guilt in those tender eyes. Philip could only read in them the wife's tender love and anxiety for himself.

But what of Mr. Ringwood's face? When the first little blush and hesitation had passed away, Mr. Ringwood's pale countenance reassumed that calm self-satisfied smile, which it customarily wore. "The coolness of the man maddened me," said Philip, talking about the little occurrence afterwards, and to his usual confidant.

"Gracious powers," cries the other. "If I went to see Charlotte and the children, would you be jealous of me, you bearded Turk? Are you prepared with sack and bowstring for every man who visits Mrs. Firmin? If you are to come out in this character, you will lead yourself and your wife pretty lives. Of course you quarrelled with Lovelace then and there, and threatened to throw him out of window then and there? Your custom is to strike when you are hot, witness——"

"Oh, dear, no!" cried Philip, interrupting me. "I have not quarrelled with him yet." And he ground his teeth, and gave a very fierce glare with his eyes. "I sat him out quite civilly. I went with him to the door; and I have left direc-

MORE FREE THAN WELCOME.

tions that he is never to pass it again—that's all. But I have not quarrelled with him in the least. Two men never behaved more politely than we did. We bowed and grinned at each other quite amiably. But I own, when he held out his hand, I was obliged to keep mine behind my back, for they felt very mischievous, and inclined to—— Well, never mind. Perhaps it is, as you say: and he meant no sort of harm."

Where, I say again, do women learn all the mischief they know? Why should my wife have such a mistrust and horror of this gentleman? She took Philip's side entirely. She said she thought he was quite right in keeping that person out of his house. What did she know about that person? Did I not know myself? He was a libertine, and led a bad life. He had led young men astray, and taught them to gamble, and helped them to ruin themselves. We have all heard stories about the late Sir Philip Ringwood; that last scandal in which he was engaged, three years ago, and which brought his career to an end at Naples, I need not, of course, allude to. But fourteen or fifteen years ago, about which time this present portion of our little story is enacted, what did she know about Ringwood's misdoings?

No: Philip Firmin did not quarrel with Philip Ringwood on this occasion. But he shut his door on Mr. Ringwood. He refused all invitations to Sir John's house, which of course, came less frequently, and which then ceased to come at all. Rich folks do not like to be so treated by the poor. Had Lady Ringwood a notion of the reason why Philip kept away from her house? I think it is more than possible. Some of Philip's friends knew her; and she seemed only pained, not surprised or angry, at a quarrel which somehow *did* take place between the two gentlemen not very long after that visit of Mr. Ringwood to his kinsman in Milman Street.

" Your friend seems very hot-headed and violent-tempered," Lady Ringwood said, speaking of that very quarrel. " I am sorry he keeps that kind of company. I am sure it must be too expensive for him."

" As luck would have it, Philip's old school-friend, Lord Egham, met us a very few days after the meeting and parting of Philip and his cousin in Milman Street, and invited us to a bachelor's dinner on the river. Our wives (without whose sanction no good man would surely ever look a whitebait in the face) gave us permission to attend this entertainment, and remained at home, and partook of a tea-dinner (blessings on them!) with the dear children. Men grow young again when they meet at these parties. We talk of flogging, proctors, old cronies; we recite old school and college jokes. I hope that some of us may carry on these pleasant entertainments until we are fourscore, and that our toothless old gums will mumble the old stories, and will laugh over the old jokes with ever-renewed gusto. Does the kind reader remember the account of such a dinner at the commencement of this history? On this afternoon, Egham, Maynard, Burroughs (several of the men formerly mentioned), reassembled. I think we actually like each other well enough to be pleased to hear of each other's successes. I know that one or two good fellows, upon whom fortune has frowned, have found other good fellows in that company to help and aid them; and that all are better for that kindly freemasonry.

Before the dinner was served, the guests met on the green of the hotel, and examined that fair landscape, which surely does not lose its charm in our eyes because it is commonly seen before a good dinner. The crested elms, the shining river, the emerald meadows, the painted parterres of flowers around, all wafting an agreeable smell of *friture*, of flowers and flounders exquisitely commingled. Who has not enjoyed these delights? May some of us, I say, live to drink the '58 claret in the year 1900! I have no doubt that the survivors of our society will still laugh at the jokes which we used to relish when the present century was still only middle-aged. Egham was going to be married. Would he be allowed to dine next year? Frank Berry's wife would not let him come. Do you remember his tremendous fight with Biggs? Remember? who didn't? Marston was Berry's bottle-holder; poor Marston, who was killed in India. And Biggs and Berry were the closest friends in life ever after. Who would ever have thought of Brackley becoming serious, and being made an archdeacon? Do you remember his fight with Ringwood? What an infernal bully he was, and how glad we all were when Brackley thrashed him. What different fates await men! Who would ever have imagined Nosey Brackley a curate in the mining districts, and ending by wearing a rosette in his hat? Who would ever have thought of Ringwood becoming such a prodigious swell and leader of fashion? He was a very shy fellow; not at all a good-looking fellow: and what a wild fellow he had become, and what a lady-killer! Isn't he some connection of yours, Firmin? Philip said yes, but that he had scarcely met Ringwood at all. And one man after another told anecdotes of Ringwood; how he had young men to play in his house; how he had played in that very "Star and Garter;" and how he always won. You must please to remember that our story dates back some sixteen years, when the dice-box still rattled occasionally and the king was turned.

As this old school gossip is going on, Lord Egham arrives, and with him this very Ringwood about whom the old school-fellows had just been talking. He came down in Egham's phaeton. Of course, the greatest man of the party always waits for Ringwood. "If we had had a duke at Grey Friars," says some grumbler, "Ringwood would have made the duke bring him down."

Philip's friend, when he beheld the arrival of Mr. Ringwood, seized Firmin's big arm, and whispered—

"Hold your tongue. No fighting. No quarrels. Let by-gones be by-gones. Remember, there can be no earthly use in a scandal."

"Leave me alone," says Philip, "and don't be afraid."

I thought Ringwood seemed to start back for a moment, and perhaps fancied that he looked a little pale, but he advanced with a gracious smile towards Philip, and remarked, "It is a long time since we have seen you at my father's."

Philip grinned and smiled too. "It *was* a long time since he had been in Hill Street." But Philip's smile was not at all pleasing to behold. Indeed, a worse performer of comedy than our friend does not walk the stage of this life.

On this the other gayly remarked he was glad Philip had leave to join the bachelor's party. "Meeting of old school-fellows very pleasant. Hadn't been to one of them for a long time : though the 'Friars' was an abominable hole : that was the truth. Who was that in the shovel-hat? a bishop? what bishop?"

It was Brackley, the Archdeacon, who turned very red on seeing Ringwood. For the fact is, Brackley was talking to Pennystone, the little boy about whom the quarrel and fight had taken place at school, when Ringwood had proposed forcibly to take Pennystone's money from him. "I think, Mr. Ringwood, that Pennystone is big enough to hold his own now, don't you?" said the Archdeacon; and with this the Venerable man turned on his heel, leaving Ringwood to face the little Pennystone of former years ; now a gigantic country squire, with health ringing in his voice, and a pair of great arms and fists that would have demolished six Ringwoods in the field.

The sight of these quondam enemies rather disturbed Mr. Ringwood's tranquillity.

"I was dreadfully bullied at that school," he said, in an appealing manner, to Mr. Pennystone. "I did as others did. It was a horrible place, and I hate the name of it. I say, Egham, don't you think that Barnaby's motion last night was very ill-timed, and that the Chancellor of the Exchequer answered him very neatly?"

This became a cant phrase amongst some of us wags afterwards. Whenever we wished to change a conversation, it was, "I say, Egham, don't you think Barnaby's motion was very ill-timed; and that the Chancellor of the Exchequer answered him very neatly?" You know Mr. Ringwood would scarcely have thought of coming amongst such common people as his old schoolfellows, but seeing Lord Egham's phaeton at "Black's," he condescended to drive down to Richmond with his lordship, and I hope a great number of his friends in St. James's Street saw him in that noble company.

Windham was the chairman of the evening—elected to that post because he is very fond of making speeches to which he does not in the least expect you to listen. All men of sense are glad to hand over this office to him: and I hope, for my part, a day will soon arrive (but I own, mind you, that I do not carve well) when we shall have the speeches done by a skilled waiter at the side table, as we now have the carving. Don't you find that you splash the gravy, that you mangle the meat, that you can't nick the joint in helping the company to a dinner-speech? I, for my part, own that I am in a state of tremor and absence of mind before the operation; in a condition of imbecility during the business; and that I am sure of a headache and indigestion the next morning. What then? Have I not seen one of the bravest men in the world, at a City dinner last year, in a state of equal panic?———I feel that I am wandering from Philip's adventures to his biographer's, and confess I am thinking of the dismal *fiasco* I myself made on this occasion at the Richmond dinner.

You see, the order of the day at these meetings is to joke at everything—to joke at the chairman, at all the speakers, at the army and navy, at the venerable the legislature, at the bar and bench, and so forth. If we toast a barrister, we show how admirably he would have figured in the dock: if a sailor, how lamentably sea-sick he was: if a soldier, how nimbly he ran away. For example, we drank the Venerable Archdeacon Brackley and the army. We deplored the perverseness which had led him to adopt a black coat instead of a red. War had evidently been his vocation, as he had shown by the frequent battles in which he had been engaged at school. For what was the *other* great warrior of the age famous? for that Roman feature in his face, which distinguished, which gave a name to, our Brackley—a name by which we fondly clung (cries of "Nosey, Nosey!") Might that feature ornament ere long the face of—of one of the chiefs of that army of which he was a distinguished field-officer! Might—— Here I confess I fairly broke down, lost the thread of my joke—at which Brackley seemed to look rather severe—and finished the speech with a gobble about regard, esteem, everybody respect you, and good health, old boy—which answered quite as well as a finished oration, however the author might be discontented with it.

The Archdeacon's little sermon was very brief, as the discourses of sensible divines sometimes will be. He was glad to meet old friends—to make friends with old foes (loud cries of "Bravo, Nosey!") In the battle of life, every man must meet with a blow or two; and every brave one would take his facer with good-humor. Had he quarrelled with any old schoolfellow in old times? He wore peace not only on his coat, but in his heart. Peace and good-will were the words of the day in the army to which he belonged; and he hoped that all officers in it were animated by one *esprit de corps*.

A silence ensued, during which men looked towards Mr. Ringwood, as the "old foe" towards whom the Archdeacon had held out the hand of amity: but Ringwood, who had listened to the Archdeacon's speech with an expression of great disgust, did not rise from his chair—only remarking to his neighbor Egham, "Why should I get up? Hang him, I have nothing to say. I say, Egham, why did you induce me to come into this kind of thing?"

Fearing that a collision might take place between Philip and his kinsman, I had drawn Philip away from the place in the room to which Lord Egham beckoned him, saying, "Never mind, Philip, about sitting by the lord," by whose side I knew perfectly well that Mr. Ringwood would find a place. But it was our lot to be separated from his lordship by merely the table's breadth, and some intervening vases of flowers and fruits through which we could see and hear our opposite neighbors. When Ringwood spoke "of this kind of thing," Philip glared across the table, and started as if he was going to speak; but his neighbor pinched him on the knee, and whispered to him, "Silence—no scandal. Remember!" The other fell back, swallowed a glass of wine, and made me far from comfortable by performing a tattoo on my chair.

The speeches went on. If they were not more eloquent they were more noisy and lively than before. Then the aid of song was called in to enliven the banquet. The Archdeacon, who had looked a little uneasy for the last half hour, rose up at the call for a song, and quitted the room. "Let us go too, Philip," said Philip's neighbor. "You don't want to hear those dreadful old college songs over again?" But Philip sulkily said, "You go, I should like to stay."

Lord Egham was seeing the last of his bachelor life. He liked those last evenings to be merry; he lingered over them, and did not wish them to end too quickly. His neighbor was long since tired of the entertainment, and sick of our company. Mr. Ringwood had lived of late in a world of such fashion that ordinary mortals were despicable to him. He had no affectionate remembrance of his early days, or of anybody belonging to them. Whilst Philip was singing his song of " Doctor Luther," I was glad that he could not see the face of surprise and disgust which his kinsman bore. Other vocal performances followed, including a song by Lord Egham, which I am bound to say was hideously out of tune; but was received by his near neighbor complacently enough.

The noise now began to increase, the choruses were fuller, the speeches were louder and more incoherent. I don't think the company heard a speech by little Mr. Vanjohn, whose health was drank as representative of the British Turf, and who said that he had never known anything about the turf or about play, until their old schoolfellow, his dear friend—his swell friend, if he might be permitted the expression—Mr. Ringwood, taught him the use of cards; and once, in his own house, in May Fair, and once in this very house, the " Star and Garter," showed him how to play the noble game of Blind Hookey. "The men are drunk. Let us go away, Egham. I didn't come for this kind of thing!" cries Ringwood, furious, by Lord Egham's side.

This was the expression which Mr. Ringwood had used a short time before, when Philip was about to interrupt him. He had lifted his gun to fire then, but his hand had been held back. The bird passed him once more, and he could not help taking aim. "This kind of thing is very dull, isn't it, Ringwood?" he called across the table, pulling away a flower, and glaring at the other through the little open space.

"Dull, old boy? I call it doosed good fun," cries Lord Egham, in the height of good-humor.

"Dull? What do you mean?" asked my lord's neighbor.

"I mean you would prefer having a couple of packs of cards, and a little room, where you could win three or four hundred from a young fellow ? It's more profitable and more quiet than 'this kind of thing.'"

"I say, I don't know what you mean !" cries the other.

"What ! You have forgotten already ? Has not Vanjohn just told you, how you and Mr. Deuceace brought him down here, and won his money from him ; and then how you gave him his revenge at your own house in——"

"Did I come here to be insulted by that fellow ?" cries Mr. Ringwood, appealing to his neighbor.

"If that is an insult, you may put it in your pipe and smoke it, Mr. Ringwood !" cries Philip.

"Come away, come away, Egham ! Don't keep me here listening to this bla——"

"If you say another word," say, Philip, "I'll send this decanter at your head !"

"Come, come—nonsense ! No quarrelling ! Make it up ! Everybody has had too much ! Get the bill and order the omnibus round !" A crowd was on one side of the table, and the other. One of the cousins had not the least wish that the quarrel should proceed any further.

When, being in a quarrel, Philip Firmin assumes the calm and stately manner, he is perhaps in his most dangerous state. Lord Egham's phaeton (in which Mr. Ringwood showed a great unwillingness to take a seat by the driver) was at the hotel gate, an omnibus and a private carriage or two were in readiness to take home the other guests of the feast. Egham went into the hotel to light a final cigar, and now Philip springing forward, caught by the arm the gentleman sitting on the front seat of the phaeton.

"Stop !" he said. "You used a word just now——"

"What word ? I don't know anything about words !" cries the other, in a loud voice.

"You said 'insulted,'" murmured Philip, in the gentlest tone.

"I don't know what I said," said Ringwood, peevishly.

"I said in reply to the words which you forget, 'that I would knock you down,' or words to that effect. If you feel in the least aggrieved, you know where my chambers are—with Mr. Vanjohn, whom you and your mistress inveigled to play cards when he was a boy. You are not fit to come into an honest man's house. It was only because I wished to spare a lady's feeling that I refrained from turning you out of mine.

Good-night, Egham!" and with great majesty Mr. Philip returned to his companion and the Hansom cab which was in waiting to convey these two gentlemen to London.

I was quite correct in my surmise that Philip's antagonist would take no further notice of the quarrel to Philip personally. Indeed, he affected to treat it as a drunken brawl, regarding which no man of sense would allow himself to be seriously disturbed. A quarrel between two men of the same family :—between Philip and his own relative who had only wished him well ?—It was absurd and impossible. What Mr. Ringwood deplored was the obstinate ill temper and known violence of Philip, which were for ever leading him into these brawls, and estranging his family from him. A men seized by the coat, insulted, threatened with a decanter! A man of station so treated by a person whose own position was most questionable, whose father was a fugitive, and who himself was struggling for precarious subsistence! The arrogance was too great. With the best wishes for the unhappy young man, and his amiable (but empty-headed) little wife, it was impossible to take further notice of them. Let the visits cease. Let the carriage no more drive from Berkeley Square to Milman Street. Let there be no presents of game, poultry, legs of mutton, old clothes, and what not. Henceforth, therefore, the Ringwood carriage was unknown in the neighborhood of the Foundling, and the Ringwood footmen no more scented with their powdered heads the Firmins' little hall ceiling. Sir John said to the end that he was about to procure a comfortable place for Philip, when his deplorable violence obliged Sir John to break off all relations with the most misguided young man.

Nor was the end of the mischief here. We have all read how the gods never appear alone—the gods bringing good or evil fortune. When two or three little pieces of good luck had befallen our poor friend, my wife triumphantly cried out, "I told you so! Did I not always say that heaven would befriend that dear, innocent wife and children ; that brave, generous, imprudent father?" And now when the evil days came, this monstrous logician insisted that poverty, sickness, dreadful doubt and terror, hunger and want almost, were all equally intended for Philip's advantage, and would work for good in the end. So that rain was good, and sunshine was good ; so that sickness was good, and health was good ; that Philip ill was to be as happy as Philip well, and as thankful for a sick house and an empty pocket as for a warm fireside and a comfortable larder. Mind, I ask no Christian philosopher to revile at his ill fortunes, or to despair. I will accept a toothache (or any evil of life), and bear it without too much grumbling. But I cannot say that to have a tooth pulled out is a blessing, or fondle the hand which wrenches at my jaw.

"They can live without their fine relations, and their donations of mutton and turnips," cries my wife with a toss of her head. "The way in which those people patronized Philip and dear Charlotte was perfectly intolerable. Lady Ringwood knows how dreadful the conduct of that Mr. Ringwood is, and—and I have no patience with her!" How, I repeat, do women know about men? How do they telegraph to each other their notices of alarm and mistrust? and fly as birds rise up with a rush and a skurry when danger appears to be near? All this was very well. But Mr. Tregarvan heard some account of the dispute between Philip and Mr. Ringwood, and applied to Sir John for further particulars; and Sir John—liberal man as he was and ever had been, and priding himself little, heaven knew, on the privilege of rank, which was merely adventitious—was constrained to confess that this young man's conduct showed a great deal too much *laissez aller*. He had constantly, at Sir John's own house, manifested an independence which had bordered on rudeness; he was always notorious for his quarrelsome disposition, and lately had so disgraced himself in a scene with Sir John's eldest son, Mr. Ringwood, had exhibited such brutality, ingratitude, and—and inebriation, that Sir John was free to confess he had forbidden the gentleman his door.

"An insubordinate, ill-conditioned fellow, certainly!" thinks Tregarvan. (And I do not say, though Philip is my friend, that Tregarvan and Sir John were altogether wrong regarding their *protégé*.) Twice Tregarvan had invited him to breakfast, and Philip had not appeared. More than once he had contradicted Tregarvan about the *Review*. He had said that the *Review* was not getting on, and if you asked Philip his candid opinion, it would not get on. Six numbers had appeared, and it did not meet with that attention which the public ought to pay to it. The public was careless as to the designs of that Great Power which it was Tregarvan's aim to defy and confound. He took counsel with himself. He walked over to the publisher's, and inspected the books; and the result of that inspection was so disagreeable, that he went home straightway and wrote a letter to Philip Firmin, Esq., New Milman Street, Guildford Street, which that poor fellow brought to his usual advisers.

That letter contained a check for a quarter's salary and

bade adieu to Mr. Firmin. The writer would not recapitulate the causes of dissatisfaction which he felt respecting the conduct of the *Review*. He was much disappointed in its progress, and dissatisfied with its general management. He thought an opportunity was lost which never could be recovered for exposing the designs of a Power which menaced the liberty and tranquillity of Europe. Had it been directed with proper energy that *Review* might have been an ægis to that threatened liberty, a lamp to lighten the darkness of that menaced freedom. It might have pointed the way to the cultivation *bonarum literarum*; it might have fostered rising talent, it might have chastised the arrogance of so-called critics; it might have served the cause of truth. Tregarvan's hopes were disappointed: he would not say by whose remissness or fault. He had done *his* utmost in the good work, and, finally, would thank Mr. Firmin to print off the articles already purchased and paid for, and to prepare a brief notice for the next number, announcing the discontinuance of the *Review;* and Tregarvan showed my wife a cold shoulder for a considerable time afterwards, nor were we asked to his tea-parties, I forget for how many seasons.

This to us was no great loss or subject of annoyance: but to poor Philip? It was a matter of life and almost death to him. He never could save much out of his little pittance. Here were fifty pounds in his hand, it is true; but bills, taxes, rent, the hundred little obligations of a house, were due and pressing upon him; and in the midst of his anxiety, our dear little Mrs. Philip was about to present him with a third ornament to his nursery. Poor little Tertius arrived duly enough; and, such hypocrites were we, that the poor mother was absolutely thinking of calling the child Tregarvan Firmin, as a compliment to Mr. Tregarvan, who had been so kind to them, and Tregarvan Firmin would be such a pretty name, she thought. We imagined the Little Sister knew nothing about Philip's anxieties. Of course, she attended Mrs. Philip through her troubles, and we vow that we never said a word to her regarding Philip's own. But Mrs. Brandon went in to Philip one day, as he was sitting very gravè and sad with his two first-born children, and she took both his hands, and said, "You know, dear, I have saved ever so much: and I always intended it for —you know who." And here she loosened one hand from him, and felt in her pocket for a purse, and put it into Philip's hand, and wept on his shoulder. And Philip kissed her, and thanked God for sending him such a dear friend, and gave her back her purse, though indeed he had but five pounds left in his own when this benefactress came to him.

Yes: but there were debts owing to him. There was his wife's little portion of fifty pounds a year, which had never been paid since the second quarter after their marriage, which had happened now more than three years ago. As Philip had scarce a guinea in the world, he wrote to Mrs. Baynes, his wife's mother, to explain his extreme want, and to remind her that this money was due. Mrs. General Baynes was living at Jersey at this time in a choice society of half-pay ladies, clergymen, captains, and the like, among whom I have no doubt she moved as a great lady. She wore a large medallion of the deceased General on her neck. She wept dry tears over that interesting cameo at frequent tea-parties. She never could forgive Philip for taking away her child from her, and if any one would take away others of her girls, she would be equally unforgiving. Endowed with that wonderful logic with which women are blessed, I believe she never admitted, or has been able to admit to her own mind, that she did Philip or her daughter a wrong. In the tea-parties of her acquaintance she groaned over the extravagance of her son-in-law and his brutal treatment of her blessed child. Many good people agreed with her and shook their respectable noddles when the name of that prodigal Philip was mentioned over her muffins and Bohea. He was prayed for ; his dear widowed mother-in-law was pitied, and blessed with all the comfort reverend gentlemen could supply on the spot. "Upon my honor, Firmin, Emily and I were made to believe that you were a monster, sir," the stout Major MacWhirter once said ; "and now I have heard your story, by Jove, I think it is you, and not Eliza Baynes, who were wronged. She has a deuce of a tongue, Eliza has : and a temper—poor Charles knew what *that* was ! " In fine, when Philip, reduced to his last guinea, asked Charlotte's mother to pay her debt to her sick daughter, Mrs. General B. sent Philip a ten-pound note, open, by Captain Swang, of the Indian army, who happened to be coming to England. And that, Philip says, of all the hard knocks of fate, has been the very hardest which he has had to endure.

But the poor little wife knew nothing of this cruelty, nor indeed of the very poverty which was hemming round her curtain ; and in the midst of his griefs, Philip Firmin was immensely consoled by the tender fidelity of the friends whom God had sent him. Their griefs were drawing to an end now. Kind readers all, may your sorrows, may mine, leave us with hearts not embittered, and humbly acquiescent to the Great Will !

CHAPTER XLI.

IN WHICH WE REACH THE LAST STAGE BUT ONE OF THIS JOURNEY.

ALTHOUGH poverty was knocking at Philip's humble door, little Charlotte in all her trouble never knew how menacing the grim visitor had been. She did not quite understand that her husband in his last necessity sent to her mother for his due, and that the mother turned away and refused him. "Ah," thought poor Philip, groaning in his despair, "I wonder whether the thieves who attacked the man in the parable were robbers of his own family, who knew that he carried money with him to Jerusalem, and waylaid him on the journey?" But again and again he has thanked God, with grateful heart, for the Samaritans whom he has met on life's road, and if he has not forgiven, it must be owned he has never done any wrong to those who robbed him.

Charlotte did not know that her husband was at his last guinea, and a prey to dreadful anxiety for her dear sake, for after the birth of her child a fever came upon her ; in the delirium consequent upon which the poor thing was ignorant of all that happened round her. A fortnight with a wife in extremity, with crying infants, with hunger menacing at the door, passed for Philip somehow. The young man became an old man in this time. Indeed, his fair hair was streaked with white at the temples afterwards. But it must not be imagined that he had not friends during his affliction, and he always can gratefully count up the names of many persons to whom he might have applied had he been in need. He did not look or ask for these succors from his relatives. Aunt and uncle Twysden shrieked and cried out at his extravagance, imprudence, and folly. Sir John Ringwood said he must really wash his hands of a young man who menaced the life of his own son. Grenville Wool-comb, with many oaths, in which brother-in-law Ringwood joined chorus, cursed Philip, and said he didn't care, and the beggar ought to be hung, and his father ought to be hung. But I think I know half-a-dozen good men and true who told a different tale, and who were ready with their sympathy and suc-cor. Did not Mrs. Flanagan, the Irish laundress, in a voice broken by sobs and gin. offer to go and chare at Philip's house for nothing, and nurse the dear children? Did not Goodenough say, "If you are in need, my dear fellow, of course you know where to come;" and did he not actually give two prescriptions, one for poor Charlotte, and one for fifty pounds to be taken immediately, which he handed to the nurse by mistake? You may be sure she did not appropriate the money, for of course you know that the nurse was Mrs. Brandon. Charlotte has one remorse in her life. She owns she was jealous of the Little Sister. And now when that gentle life is over, when Philip's poverty trials are ended, when the children go some times and look wistfully at the grave of their dear Caroline, friend Charlotte leans her head against her husband's shoulder, and owns humbly how good, how brave, how generous a friend heaven sent them in that humble defender.

Have you ever felt the pinch of poverty? In many cases it is like the dentist's chair, more dreadful in the contemplation than in the actual suffering. Philip says he was never fairly beaten, but on that day when, in reply to his solicitation to have his due, Mrs. Baynes's friend, Captain Swang, brought him the open ten-pound note. It was not much of a blow; the hand which dealt it made the hurt so keen. "I remember," says he, "bursting out crying at school, because a big boy hit me a slight tap, and other boys said, 'Oh, you coward.' It was that I knew the boy at home, and my parents had been kind to him. It seemed to me a wrong that Bumps should strike me," said Philip; and he looked, while telling the story, as if he could cry about this injury now. I hope he has revenged himself by presenting coals of fire to his wife's relations. But this day, when he is enjoying good health, and competence, it is not safe to mention mothers-in-law in his presence. He fumes, shouts and rages against them, as if all were like his; and his, I have been told, is a lady perfectly well satisfied with herself and her conduct in this world; and as for the next——but our story does not dare to point so far. It only interests itself about a little clique of people here below—their griefs, their trials, their weaknesses, their kindly hearts.

People there are in our history who do not seem to me to have kindly hearts at all; and yet, perhaps, if a biography could be written from their point of view, some other novelist might show how Philip and *his* biographer were a pair of selfish worldlings unworthy of credit: how uncle and aunt Twysden were most exemplary people, and so forth. Have I not told you how many people at New York shook their heads when Philip's name was mentioned, and intimated a strong opinion that he used his father very ill? When he fell wounded and bleeding, patron Tregarvan dropped him off his horse, and cousin Ringwood did not look behind to see how he fared. But these, again, may have had their opinion regarding our friend, who may have been misrepresented to them——I protest as I look back at the past portions of this history, I begin to have qualms, and ask myself whether the folks of whom we have been prattling have had justice done to them; whether Agnes Twysden is not a suffering martyr justly offended by Philip's turbulent behavior, and whether Philip deserves any particular attention or kindness at all. He is not transcendently clever; he is not gloriously beautiful. He is not about to illuminate the darkness in which the people grovel, with the flashing emanations of his truth. He sometimes owes money, which he cannot pay. He slips, stumbles, blunders, brags. Ah! he sins and repents —pray heaven—of faults, of vanities, of pride, of a thousand shortcomings! This I say—*Ego*—as my friend's biographer. Perhaps I do not understand the other characters round about him so well, and have overlooked a number of their merits, and caricatured and exaggerated their little defects.

Among the Samaritans who came to Philip's help in these his straits, he loves to remember the name of J. J., the painter, whom he found sitting with the children one day making drawings for them, which the good painter never tired to sketch.

Now if those children would but have kept Ridley's sketches, and waited for a good season at Christie's I have no doubt they might have got scores of pounds for the drawings; but then, you see, they chose to improve the drawings with their own hands. They painted the soldiers yellow, the horses blue, and so forth. On the horses they put soldiers of their own construction. Ridley's landscapes were enriched with representations of "omnibuses," which the children saw and admired in the neighboring New Road. I dare say, as the fever left her, and as she came to see things as they were, Charlotte's eyes dwelt fondly on the pictures of the omnibuses inserted in Mr. Ridley's sketches, and she put some aside and showed them to her friends, and said, "Doesn't our darling show extraordinary talent for drawing? Mr. Ridley says he does. He did a great part of this etching."

But, besides the drawings, what do you think Master Ridley offered to draw for his friends? Besides the prescriptions of medicine, what drafts did Dr. Goodenough prescribe? When nurse Brandon came to Mrs. Philip in her anxious time, we know what sort of payment she proposed for her services. Who says the world is all cold? There is the sun and the shadows. And the heaven which ordains poverty and sickness sends pity, and love, and succor.

During Charlotte's fever and illness, the Little Sister had left her but for one day, when her patient was quiet, and pronounced to be mending. It appears that Mrs. Charlotte was very ill indeed on this occasion; so ill that Dr. Goodenough thought she she might have given us all the slip: so ill that, but for Brandon, she would, in all probability, have escaped out of this troublous world, and left Philip and her orphaned little ones. Charlotte mended then: could take food, and liked it, and was specially pleased with some chickens which her nurse informed her were "from the country." "From Sir John Ringwood, no doubt?" said Mrs. Firmin, remembering the presents sent from Berkeley Square, and the mutton and the turnips.

"Well, eat and be thankful!" says the Little Sister, who was as gay as a little sister could be, and who had prepared a beautiful bread sauce for the fowl; and who had tossed the baby, and who showed it to its admiring brother and sister ever so many times; and who saw that Mr. Philip had his dinner comfortable; and who never took so much as a drop of porter—at home a little glass sometimes was comfortable, but on duty, never, never! No, not if Dr. Goodenough ordered it! she vowed. And the doctor wished he could say as much, or believe as much, of all his nurses.

Milman Street is such a quiet little street that our friends had not carpeted it in the usual way; and three days after her temporary absence, as nurse Brandon sits by her patient's bed, powdering the back of a small pink infant that makes believe to swim upon her apron, a rattle of wheels is heard in the quiet street—of four wheels, of one horse, of a jingling carriage, which stops before Philip's door. "It's the trap," says nurse Brandon, delighted. "It must be those kind Ringwoods," says Mrs. Philip. "But stop, Brandon. Did not they, did not we?—oh, how kind of them!" She was trying to recall the past. Past and present for days had been strangely mingled in her fevered brain. "Hush, my dear! you are to be kep' quite still," says the nurse—and then proceeded to finish the polishing and powdering of the pink frog on her lap.

The bedroom window was open towards the sunny street: but Mrs. Philip did not hear a female voice say, "'Old the 'orse's 'ead, Jim," or she might have been agitated. The horse's head was held, and a gentleman and a lady with a great basket containing pease, butter, greens, flowers, and other rural produce, descended from the vehicle and rang at the bell.

Philip opened it ; with his little ones, as usual, trotting at his knees.

"Why, my darlings, how you air grown !" cries the lady.

"By-gones be by-gones. Give us your 'and, Firmin : here's mine. My missus has brought some country butter and things for your dear good lady. And we hoped you liked the chickens. And God bless you, old fellow, how are you ?" The tears were rolling down the good man's cheeks as he spoke. And Mrs. Mugford was likewise exceedingly hot, and very much affected. And the children said to her, "Mamma is better now : and we have a little brother, and he is crying now up stairs."

"Bless you, my darlings !" Mrs. Mugford was off by this time. She put down her peace-offering of carrots, chickens, bacon, butter. She cried plentifully. "It was Brandon came and told us," she said ; "and when she told us how all your great people had flung you over, and you'd been quarrelling again, you naughty fellar, I says to Mugford, 'Let's go and see after that dear thing, Mugford,' I says. And here we are. And year's two nice cakes for your children" (after a forage in the cornucopia), "and, lor', how they are grown !"

A little nurse from the up stairs regions here makes her appearance, holding a bundle of cashmere shawls, part of which is removed, and discloses a being pronounced to be ravishingly beautiful, and "jest like Mrs. Mugford's Emaly !"

"I say," says Mugford, "the old shop's still open to you. T'other chap wouldn't do at all. He was wild when he got the drink on board. Hirish. Pitched into Bickerton, and black'd 'is eye. It was Bickerton who told you lies about that poor lady. Don't see 'em no more now. Borrowed some money of me ; haven't seen him since. We were both wrong, and we must make it up—the missus says we must."

"Amen !" said Philip, with a grasp of the honest fellow's hand. And next Sunday he and a trim little sister, and two children, went to an old church in Queen Square, Bloomsbury, which was fashionable in the reign of Queen Anne, when Richard Steele kept house, and did not pay rent, hard by. And when the clergyman in the Thanksgiving particularized those who desired now to "offer up their praises and thanksgiving for late mercies vouchsafed to them," once more Philip Firmin said "Amen," on his knees, and with all his heart.

CHAPTER XLII.

THE REALMS OF BLISS.

You know—all good boys and girls at Christmas know—that, before the last scene of the pantomime, when the Good Fairy ascends in a blaze of glory, and Harlequin and Columbine take hands, having danced through all their tricks and troubles and tumbles, there is a dark, brief, seemingly meaningless, penultimate scene, in which the performers appear to grope about perplexed, whilst the music of bassoons and trombones, and the like, groans tragically. As the actors, with gestures of dismay and outstretched arms, move hither and thither, the wary frequenter of pantomimes sees the illuminators of the Abode of Bliss and Hall of Prismatic Splendor nimbly moving behind the canvas, and streaking the darkness with twinkling fires—fires which shall blaze out presently in a thousand colors round the Good Fairy in the Revolving temple of Blinding Bliss. Be happy, Harlequin! Love and be happy and dance, pretty Columbine! Children, mamma bids you put your shawls on. And Jack and Mary (who are young and love pantomimes) look lingeringly still over the ledge of the box, whilst the fairy temple yet revolves, whilst the fireworks play, and ere the Great Dark Curtain descends.

My dear young people, who have sat kindly through the scenes during which our entertainment has lasted, be it known to you that last chapter was the dark scene. Look to your cloaks, and tie up your little throats, for I tell you the great baize will soon fall down. Have I had any secrets from you all through the piece? I tell you the house will be empty and you will be in the cold air. When the boxes have got their nightgowns on, and you are all gone, and I have turned off the gas, and am in the empty theatre alone in the darkness, I promise you I shall not be merry. Never mind! We can make jokes though we are ever so sad. We can jump overhead and heels, though I declare the pit is half emptied already, and the last orange-woman has slunk away. Encore une pirouette, Colombine! Saute, Arlequin, mon ami! Though there are but five bars more of the music, my good people, we must jump over them briskly, and then go home to supper and bed.

Philip Firmin, then, was immensely moved by this magna-nimity and kindness on the part of his old employer, and has always considered Mugford's arrival and friendliness as a special interposition in his favor. He owes it all to Brandon, he says. It was she who bethought herself of his condition, represented it to Mugford, and reconciled him to his enemy. Others were most ready with their money. It was Brandon who brought him work rather than alms, and enabled him to face fortune cheerfully. His interval of poverty was so short, that he actually had not occasion to borrow. A week more, and he could not have held out, and poor Brandon's little marriage present must have gone to the cenotaph of sovereigns—the dear Little Sister's gift which Philip's family cherish to this hour.

So Philip, with a humbled heart and demeanor, clambered up on his sub-editorial stool once more at the *Pall Mall Gazette*, and again brandished the paste-pot and the scissors. I forget whether Bickerton still remained in command at the *Pall Mall Gazette*, or was more kind to Philip than before, or was afraid of him, having heard of his exploits as a fire-eater; but certain it is, the two did not come to a quarrel, giving each other a wide berth, as the saying is, and each doing his own duty. Good-by, Monsieur Bickerton. Except mayhap, in the final group, round the FAIRY CHARIOT (when, I promise you, there will be such a blaze of glory that he will be invisible), we shall never see the little spiteful envious creature more. Let him pop down his appointed trap-door; and, quick fiddles! let the brisk music jig on.

Owing to the coolness which had arisen between Philip and his father on account of their different views regarding the use to be made of Philip's signature, the old gentleman drew no further bills in his son's name, and our friend was spared from the unpleasant persecution. Mr. Hunt loved Dr. Firmin so ardently that he could not bear to be separated from the doctor long. Without the doctor, London was a dreary wilderness to Hunt. Unfortunate remembrances of past pecuniary transac-tions haunted him here. We were all of us glad when he finally retired from the Covent Garden taverns and betook himself to the Bowery once more.

And now friend Philip was at work again, hardly earning a scanty meal for self, wife, servant, children. It was indeed a meagre meal, and a small wage. Charlotte's illness, and other mishaps, had swept away poor Philip's little savings. It was determined that we would let the elegantly-furnished apartments on the first floor. You might have fancied the proud Mr. Firmin rather repugnant to such a measure. And so he was on the score of convenience, but of dignity, not a whit. To this day, if necessity called, Philip would turn a mangle with perfect gravity. I believe the thought of Mrs. General Baynes's horror at the idea of her son-in-law letting lodgings greatly soothed and comforted Philip. The lodgings were absolutely taken by our country acquaintance, Miss Pybus, who was coming up for the May meetings, and whom we persuaded (heaven be good to us !) that she would find a most desirable quiet residence in the house of a man with three squalling children. Miss P. came, then, with my wife to look at the apartments ; and we allured her by describing to her the delightful musical services at the Foundling hard by ; and she was very much pleased with Mrs. Philip, and did not even wince at the elder children, whose pretty faces won the kind old lady's heart : and I am ashamed to say we were mum about the baby : and Pybus was going to close for the lodgings, when Philip burst out of his little room without his coat, I believe, and objurgated a little printer's boy, who was sitting in the hall, waiting for some " copy " regarding which he had made a blunder ; and Philip used such violent language towards the little lazy boy, that Pybus said " she never could think of taking apartments in that house," and hurried thence in a panic. When Brandon heard of this project of letting lodgings, she was in a fury. *She* might let lodgin's, but it wasn't for Philip to do so. " Let lodgin's, indeed ! Buy a broom, and sweep a crossin' ! " Brandon always thought Charlotte a poor-spirited creature, and the way she scolded Mrs. Firmin about this transaction was not a little amusing. Charlotte was not angry. She liked the scheme as little as Brandon. No other person ever asked for lodgings in Charlotte's house. May and its meetings came to an end. The old ladies went back to their country towns. The missionaries returned to Caffraria. (Ah ! where are the pleasant-looking Quakeresses of our youth, with their comely faces, and pretty dove-colored robes ? They say the goodly sect is dwindling—dwindling.) The Quakeresses went out of town · then the fashionable world began to move : the Parliament went out of town. In a word, everybody who could, made away for a holiday, whilst poor Philip remained at his work, snipping and pasting his paragraphs, and doing his humble drudgery.

A sojourn on the sea-shore was prescribed by Dr. Goodenough, as absolutely necessary for Charlotte and her young ones, and when Philip pleaded certain cogent reasons why the family could not take the medicine prescribed by the doctor, that eccentric physician had recourse to the same pocket-book which we have known him to produce on a former occasion; and took from it, for what I know, some of the very same notes which he had formerly given to the Little Sister. "I suppose you may as well have them as that rascal Hunt?" said the Doctor, scowling very fiercely. "Don't tell *me*. Stuff and nonsense. Pooh! Pay me when you are a rich man!" And this Samaritan had jumped into his carriage, and was gone, before Philip or Mrs. Philip could say a word of thanks. Look at him as he is going off. See the green brougham drive away, and turn westward, and mark it well. A shoe go after thee, John Goodenough; we shall see thee no more in this story. You are not in the secret, good reader: but I, who have been living with certain people for many months past, and have a hearty liking for some of them, grow very soft when the hour for shaking hands comes, to think we are to meet no more. Go to! when this tale began, and for some months after, a pair of kind old eyes used to read these pages, which are now closed in the sleep appointed for all of us. And so page is turned after page, and behold Finis and the volume's end.

So Philip and his young folks came down to Periwinkle Bay, where we were staying, and the girls in the two families nursed the baby, and the child and mother got health and comfort from the fresh air, and Mr. Mugford—who believes himself to be the finest sub-editor in the world, and I can tell you there is a great art in sub-editing a paper—Mr. Mugford, I say, took Philip's scissors and paste-pot, whilst the latter enjoyed his holiday. And J. J. Ridley, R.A., came and joined us presently, and we had many sketching parties, and my drawings of the various points about the bay, viz., Lobster Head, the Mollusc Rocks, &c., &c., are considered to be very spirited, though my little boy (who certainly has not his father's taste for art) mistook for the rock a really capital portrait of Philip, in a gray hat and paletot, sprawling on the sand.

Some twelve miles inland from the bay is the little town of Whipham Market, and Whipham skirts the park palings of that castle where Lord Ringwood had lived, and where Philip's mother was born and bred. There is a statue of the late lord in Whipham market-place. Could he have had his will, the borough would have continued to return two Members to Parliament, as in the good old times before us. In that ancient and grass-grown little place, where your footsteps echo as you pass through the street, where you hear distinctly the creaking of the sign of the "Ringwood Arms" hotel and posting-house, and the opposition creaking of the "Ram Inn" over the way —where the half-pay captain, the curate, and the medical man stand before the fly-blown window-blind of the "Ringwood Institute" and survey the strangers—there is still a respect felt for the memory of the great lord who dwelt behind the oaks in yonder hall. He had his faults. His lordship's life was not that of an anchorite. The company his lordship kept, especially in his latter days, was not of that select description which a nobleman of his lordship's rank might command. But he was a good friend to Whipham. He was a good landlord to a good tenant. If he had his will, Whipham would have kept its own. His lordship paid half the expense after the burning of the town hall. He was an arbitrary man, certainly, and he flogged Alderman Duffle before his own shop, but he apologized for it most handsome afterwards. Would the gentlemen like port or sherry? Claret not called for in Whipham · not at all: and no fish, because all the fish at Periwinkle Bay is brought up and goes to London. Such were the remarks made by the landlord of the "Ringwood Arms" to three cavaliers who entered that hostelry. And you may be sure he told us about Lord Ringwood's death in the post-chaise as he came from Turreys Regum; and how his lordship went through them gates (pointing to a pair of gates and lodges which skirt the town), and was drove up to the castle and laid in state; and his lordship never would take the railway, never; and he always travelled like a nobleman, and when he came to a hotel and changed horses, he always called for a bottle of wine, and only took a glass, and sometimes not even that. And the present Sir John has kept no company here as yet; and they say he is close of his money, they say he is. And this is certain, Whipham haven't seen much of it, Whipham haven't.

We went into the inn yard, which may have been once a stirring place, and then sauntered up to the park gate, surmounted by the supporters and armorial bearings of the Ringwoods. "I wonder whether my poor mother came out of that gate when she eloped with my father?" said Philip. "Poor thing, poor thing!" The great gates were shut. The westering sun cast shadows over the sward where here and there the deer were browsing, and at some mile distance lay the house, with its towers and porticos and vanes flaming in the sun. The small gate was open, and a girl was standing by the lodge door. Was the house to be seen?

"Yes," says a little red-cheeked girl, with a curtsey.

"No!" calls out a harsh voice from within, and an old woman comes out from the lodge and looks at us fiercely. "Nobody is to go to the house. The family is a-coming."

That was provoking. Philip would have liked to behold the great house where his mother and her ancestors were born.

"Marry, good dame," Philip's companion said to the old beldam, "this goodly gentleman hath a right of entrance to yonder castle, which I trow, ye wot not of. Heard ye never tell of one Philip Ringwood, slain at Busaco's glorious fi——"

"Hold your tongue, and don't chaff her, Pen," growled Firmin.

"Nay, and she knows not Philip Ringwood's grandson," the other wag continued, in a softened tone, "this will convince her of our right to enter. Canst recognize this image of your queen?"

"Well, I suppose 'ee can go up," said the old woman, at the sight of this talisman. "There's only two of them staying there, and they're out a-drivin'."

Philip was bent on seeing the halls of his ancestors. Gray and huge, with towers, and vanes, and porticos, they lay before us a mile off, separated from us by a streak of glistening river. A great chestnut avenue led up to the river, and in the dappled grass the deer was browsing.

You know the house of course. There is a picture of it in Watts, bearing date 1783. A gentleman in a cocked hat and pigtail is rowing a lady in a boat on the shining river. Another nobleman in a cocked hat is angling in the glistening river from the bridge, over which a post-chaise is passing.

"Yes, the place is like enough," said Philip; "but I miss the post-chaise going over the bridge, and the lady in the punt with the tall parasol. Don't you remember the print in our housekeeper's room in Old Parr Street? My poor mother used to tell me about the house, and I imagined it grander than the palace of Aladdin. It *is* a very handsome house," Philip went on. "'It extends two hundred and sixty feet by seventy-five, and consists of a rustic basement and principal story, with an attic in the centre, the whole executed in stone. The grand front towards the park is adorned with a noble portico of the Corinthian order, and may with propriety be considered one ot the finest elevations in the ——.' I tell you I am quoting out of Watts's 'Seats of the Nobility and Gentry,' published by John and Josiah Boydell, and lying in our drawing-room. Ah, dear me! I painted the boat and the lady and gentleman in the drawing-room copy, and my father boxed my ears, and my mother cried out, poor dear soul! And this is the river, is it? And over this the post-chaise went with the club-tailed horses, and here was the pigtailed gentleman fishing. It gives me a queer sensation," says Philip, standing on the bridge, and stretching out his big arms. "Yes, there are the two people in the punt by the rushes. I can see them, but you can't; and I hope, sir, you will have good sport." And here he took off his hat to an imaginary gentleman supposed to be angling from the balustrade for ghostly gudgeon. We reach the house presently. We ring at the door in the basement under the portico. The porter demurs, and says some of the family is down, but they are out, to be sure. The same half-crown argument answers with him which persuaded the keeper at the lodge. We go through the show-rooms of the stately but somewhat faded and melancholy palace. In the cedar dining-room there hangs the grim portrait of the late earl; and that fair-haired officer in red? that must be Philip's grandfather. And those two slim girls embracing, surely those are his mother and his aunt. Philip walks softly through the vacant rooms. He gives the porter a gold piece ere he goes out of the great hall, forty feet cube ornamented with statues brought from Rome by John first Baron, namely, Heliogabalus, Nero's mother, a priestess of Isis, and a river god; the pictures over the doors by Pedimento; the ceiling by Leotardi, &c.; and in a window in the great hall there is a table with a visitors' book, in which Philip writes his name. As we went away, we met a carriage which drove rapidly towards the house, and which no doubt contained the members of the Ringwood family, regarding whom the porteress had spoken. After the family differences previously related, we did not care to face these kinsfolks of Philip, and passed on quickly in twilight beneath the rustling umbrage of the chestnuts. J. saw a hundred fine pictorial effects as we walked; the palace reflected in the water; the dappled deer under the chequered shadow of the trees. It was, "Oh, what a jolly bit of color," and, "I say, look, how well that old woman's red cloak comes in!" and so forth. Painters never seem tired of their work. At seventy they are students still, patient, docile, happy. May we too, my good sir, live for fourscore years, and never be too old to learn! The walk, the brisk accompanying conversation, amid stately scenery around, brought us with good appetites and spirits to our inn, where we were told that dinner would be served when the omnibus arrived from the railway.

At a short distance from the "Ringwood Arms," and on the

opposite side of the street, is the " Ram Inn," neat post-chaises
and farmers' ordinary ; a house, of which the pretensions seemed
less, though the trade was somewhat more lively.   When the
tooting of the horn announced the arrival of the omnibus from
the railway, I should think a crowd of at least fifteen people
assembled at various doors of the High Street and Market.
The half-pay captain and the curate came out from the "Ringwood Athenæum."   The doctor's apprentice stood on the step
of the surgery door, and the surgeon's lady looked out from the
first floor.   We shared the general curiosity.   We and the
waiter stood at the door of the " Ringwood Arms."   We were
mortified to see that of the five persons conveyed by the 'bus,
one was a tradesman, who descended at his door, (Mr. Pack-
wood, the saddler, so the waiter informed us,) three travellers
were discharged at the " Ram," and only one came to us.

"Mostly bagmen goes to the ' Ram,' " the waiter said, with
a scornful air ; and these bagmen, and their bags, quitted the
omnibus.

Only one passenger remained for the " Ringwood Arms
Hotel," and he presently descended under the *porte-cochère;* and
the omnibus—I own, with regret, it was but a one-horse machine—drove rattling into the court-yard, where the bells of the
" Star," the " George," the " Rodney," the " Dolphin," and so
on, had once been wont to jingle, and the court had echoed
with the noise and clatter of hoofs and ostlers, and the cries of
" First and second, turn out."

Who was the merry-faced little gentleman in black, who got
out of the omnibus, and cried, when he saw us, " What, *you*
here ? "   It was Mr. Bradgate, that lawyer of Lord Ringwood's
with whom we made a brief acquaintance just after his lordship's death.   " What, *you* here ? " cries Bradgate, then, to
Philip.   " Come down about this business, of course ?   Very
glad that you and — and certain parties have made it up.
Thought you weren't friends."

What business ?   What parties ?   We had not heard the
news ?   We had only come over from Periwinkle Bay by chance,
in order to see the house.

" How very singular !   Did you meet the—the people who
were staying there ? "

We said we had seen a carriage pass, but did not remark
who was in it.   What, however, was the news ?   Well.   It
would be known immediately, and would appear in Tuesday's
Gazette.   The news was that Sir John Ringwood was going to
take a peerage, and that the seat for Whipham would be vacant.

And herewith our friend produced from his travelling bag a proclamation, which he read to us, and which was addressed—

"To the worthy and independent Electors of the Borough of Ringwood.

"*London, Wednesday.*

"GENTLEMEN,—A gracious Sovereign having been pleased to order that the family of Ringwood should continue to be represented in the House of Peers, I take leave of my friends and constituents who have given me their kind confidence hitherto, and promise them that my regard for them will never cease, or my interest in the town and neighborhood where my family have dwelt for many centuries. The late lamented Lord Ringwood's brother died in the service of his Sovereign in Portugal, following the same flag under which his ancestors for centuries have fought and bled. My own son serves the Crown in a civil capacity. It was natural that one of our name and family should continue the relations which so long have subsisted between us and this loyal, affectionate, but independent borough. Mr. Ringwood's onerous duties in the office which he holds are sufficient to occupy his time. A gentleman united to our family by the closest ties will offer himself as a candidate for your suffrages——"

"Why, who is it? He is not going to put in uncle Twysden, or my sneak of a cousin?"

"No," says Mr. Bradgate.

"Well, bless my soul! he can't mean me," said Philip. "Who is the dark horse he has in his stable?"

Then Mr. Bradgate laughed. "Dark horse you may call him. The new Member is to be Grenville Woolcomb, Esq., your West India relative, and no other."

Those who know the extreme energy of Mr. P. Firmin's language when he is excited, may imagine the explosion of Philippine wrath which ensued as our friend heard this name. "That miscreant : that skinflint : that wealthy crossing-sweeper : that ignoramus who scarce could do more than sign his name! Oh, it was horrible, shameful! Why, the man is on such ill terms with his wife that they say he strikes her. When I see him I feel inclined to choke him, and murder him. *That* brute going into Parliament, and the republican Sir John Ringwood sending him there! It's monstrous!"

"Family arrangements. Sir John, or, I should say, my Lord Ringwood, is one of the most affectionate of parents," Mr. Bradgate remarked. "He has a large family by his second marriage, and his estates go to his eldest son. We must not quarrel with Lord Ringwood for wishing to provide for his young ones. I don't say that he quite acts up to the extreme Liberal principle of which he was once rather fond of boasting. But if you were offered a peerage, what would you do ; what would I do ? If you wanted money for your young ones, and could get it, would you not take it ? Come, come, don't let us have too much of this Spartan virtue! If we were tried, my good friend, we should not be much worse or better than our neighbors. Is my fly coming, waiter ? " We asked ·Mr. Bradgate to defer his departure, and to share our dinner. But he declined, and said he must go up to the great house, where he and his client had plenty of business to arrange, and where no doubt he would stay for the night. He bade the inn servants put his portmanteau into his carriage when it came. " The old lord had some famous port-wine," he said ; " I hope my friends have the key of the cellar."

The waiter was just putting our meal on the table, as we stood in the bow-window of the " Ringwood Arms " coffee-room, engaged in this colloquy. Hence we could see the street, and the opposition inn of the " Ram," where presently a great placard was posted. At least a dozen street-boys, shopmen, and rustics were quickly gathered round this manifesto, and we ourselves went out to examine it. The " Ram " placard denounced, in terms of unmeasured wrath, the impudent attempt from the Castle to dictate to the free and independent electors of the borough. Freemen were invited not to promise their votes ; to show themselves worthy of their name ; to submit to no Castle dictation. A county gentleman of property, of influence, of liberal principles—no WEST INDIAN, no CASTLE FLUNKEY, but a TRUE ENGLISH GENTLEMAN, would come forward to rescue them from the tyranny under which they labored. On this point the electors might rely on the word of A BRITON.

" This was brought down by the clerk from Bedloe's. He and a newspaper man came down in the train with me ; a Mr.——."

As he spoke, there came forth from the " Ram " the newspaper man of whom Mr. Bradgate spoke—an old friend and comrade of Philip, that energetic man and able reporter, Phipps of the *Daily Intelligencer*, who recognized Philip, and cordially greeting him, asked what *he* did down here, and supposed he had come to support his family.

Philip explained that we were strangers, had come from a

neighboring watering-place to see the home of Philip's ancestors, and were not even aware, until then, that an electioneering
contest was pending in the place, or that Sir John Ringwood
was about to be promoted to the peerage. Meanwhile, Mr.
Bradgate's fly had driven out of the hotel yard of the " Ringwood Arms," and the lawyer running to the house for a bag of
papers, jumped into the carriage and called to the coachman to
drive to the Castle.

" *Bon appétit!* " says he, in a confident tone, and he was gone.

'Would Phipps dine with us ? " Phipps whispered, " I am
on the other side, and the ' Ram ' is our house."

We, who were on no side, entered into the " Ringwood
Arms," and sat down to our meal—to the mutton and the cat-
sup, cauliflower, and potatoes, the copper-edged side-dishes,
and the watery melted butter, with which strangers are regaled
in inns in declining towns. The town *badauds*, who had read
the placard at the " Ram," now came to peruse the proclamation in our window. I dare say thirty pairs of clinking boots
stopped before the one window and the other, the while we ate
tough mutton and drank fiery sherry. And J. J., leaving his
dinner, sketched some of the figures of the townsfolk staring at
the manifesto, with the old-fashioned " Ram Inn " for a back-
ground—a picturesque gable enough.

Our meal was just over, when, somewhat to our surprise,
our friend Mr. Bradgate the lawyer returned to the " Ringwood Arms." He wore a disturbed countenance. He asked
what he could have for dinner ? Mutton, neither hot nor cold.
Hum ! That must do. So he had not been invited to dine at
the Park ? We rallied him with much facetiousness on this
disappointment.

Little Bradgate's eyes started with wrath. " What a churl
the little black fellow is ! " he cried. " I took him his papers.
I talked with him till dinner was laid in the very room where
we were. French beans and neck of venison—I saw the housekeeper and his man bring them in ! And Mr. Woolcomb did
not so much as ask me to sit down to dinner—but told me to
come again at nine o'clock ! Confound this mutton—it's neither
hot nor cold ! The little skinflint ! The glasses of fiery sherry
which Bradgate now swallowed served rather to choke than
appease the lawyer. We laughed, and this jocularity angered
him more. "Oh," said he, " I am not the only person Woolcomb was rude to. He was in a dreadful ill temper. He
abused his wife : and when he read somebody's name in the
stranger's book, I promise you, Firmin, he abused *you*. I had

a mind to say to him, 'Sir, Mr. Firmin is dining at the "Ringwood Arms," and I will tell him what you say of him.' What india-rubber mutton this is! What villanous sherry! Go back to him at nine o'clock, indeed! Be hanged to his impudence!"

"You must not abuse Woolcomb before Firmin," said one of our party. "Philip is so fond of his cousin's husband, that he cannot bear to hear the black man abused."

This was not a very brilliant joke, but Philip grinned at it with much savage satisfaction.

"Hit Woolcomb as hard as you please, he has no friends here, Mr. Bradgate," growled Philip. "So he is rude to his lawyer, is he?"

"I tell you he is worse than the old earl," cried the indignant Bradgate. "At least the old man was a peer of England, and could be a gentleman when he wished. But to be bullied by a fellow who might be a black footman, or ought to be sweeping a crossing! It's monstrous!"

"Don't speak ill of a man and a brother, Mr. Bradgate. Woolcomb can't help his complexion."

"But he can help his confounded impudence, and sha'n't practise it on *me*!" the attorney cried.

As Bradgate called out from his box, puffing and fuming, friend J. J. was scribbling in the little sketch-book which he always carried. He smiled over his work. "I know," he said, "the Black Prince well enough. I have often seen him driving his chestnut mares in the Park, with that bewildered white wife by his side. I am sure that woman is miserable, and, poor thing——"

"Serve her right! What did an English lady mean by marrying such a fellow!" cries Bradgate.

"A fellow who does not ask his lawyer to dinner!" remarks one of the company; perhaps the reader's very humble servant. "But what an imprudent lawyer he has chosen—a lawyer who speaks his mind."

"I have spoken my mind to his betters, and be hanged to him! Do you think I am going to be afraid of *him*?" bawls the irascible solicitor.

"*Contempsi Catilinæ gladios*—do you remember the old quotation at school, Philip?" And here there was a break in our conversation, for chancing to look at friend J. J.'s sketch-book, we saw that he had made a wonderful little drawing, representing Woolcomb and Woolcomb's wife, grooms, phaeton, and chestnut mares, as they were to be seen any afternoon in Hyde Park during the London season.

Admirable! Capital! Everybody at once knew the likeness of the dusky charioteer. Iracundus himself smiled and
sniggered over it. "Unless you behave yourself, Mr. Bradgate, Ridley will make a picture of *you*," says Philip. Bradgate
made a comical face, and retreated into his box, of which he
pretended to draw the curtain. But the sociable little man did
not long remain in his retirement; he emerged from it in a
short time, his wine decanter in his hand, and joined our little
party; and then we fell to talking of old times; and we all
remembered a famous drawing by H. B., of the late Earl of
Ringwood, in the old-fashioned swallow-tailed coat and tight
trousers, on the old-fashioned horse, with the old-fashioned
groom behind him, as he used to be seen pounding along
Rotten Row.

"I speak my mind, do I?" says Bradgate, presently. "I
know somebody who spoke *his* mind to that old man, and who
would have been better off if he had held his tongue."

"Come, tell me, Bradgate," cried Philip. "It is all over
and past now. Had Lord Ringwood left me something? I
declare I thought at one time that he intended to do so."

"Nay, has not your friend here been rebuking me for
speaking my mind? I am going to be as mum as a mouse.
Let us talk about the election," and the provoking lawyer
would say no more on a subject possessing a dismal interest
for poor Phil.

"I have no more right to repine," said that philosopher,
"than a man would have who drew number *x* in the lottery,
when the winning ticket was number *y*. Let us talk, as you
say, about the election. Who is to oppose Mr. Woolcomb?"

Mr. Bradgate believed a neighboring squire, Mr. Hornblow,
was to be the candidate put forward against the Ringwood
nominee.

"Hornblow! what, Hornblow of Grey Friars?" cries Philip.
"A better fellow never lived. In this case he shall have our
vote and interest; and I think we ought to go over and take
another dinner at the 'Ram.'"

The new candidate actually turned out to be Philip's old
school and college friend, Mr. Hornblow. After dinner we
met him with a staff of canvassers on the tramp through the
little town. Mr. Hornblow was paying his respects to such
tradesmen as had their shops yet open. Next day being market-
day, he proposed to canvass the market-people. "If I meet
the black man, Firmin," said the burly squire, "I think I can
chaff him off his legs. He is a bad one at speaking, I am told."

As if the tongue of Plato would have prevailed in Whipham and against the nominee of the great house! The hour was late to be sure, but the companions of Mr. Hornblow on his canvass augured ill of his success after half-an-hour's walk at his heels. Baker Jones would not promise no how: that meant Jones would vote for the Castle, Mr. Hornblow's legal aide-de-camp, Mr. Batley, was forced to allow. Butcher Brown was having his tea,—his shrill-voiced wife told us, looking out from her glazed-back parlor: Brown would vote for the Castle. Saddler Briggs would see about it. Grocer Adams fairly said he would vote against us — against *us ?*—against Hornblow, whose part we were taking already. I fear the flattering promises of support of a great body of free and unbiassed electors, which had induced Mr. Hornblow to come forward and, &c., were but inventions of that little lawyer, Batley, who found his account in having a contest in the borough. When the polling-day came—you see I disdain to make any mysteries in this simple and veracious story — Mr. Grenville Woolcomb, whose solicitor and agent spoke for him—Mr. Grenville Woolcomb, who could not spell or speak two sentences of decent English, and whose character for dulness, ferocity, penuriousness, jealousy, almost fatuity, was notorious to all the world—was returned by an immense majority, and the country gentleman brought scarce a hundred votes to the poll.

We who were in nowise engaged in the contest, nevertheless found amusement from it in a quiet country place where little else was stirring. We came over once or twice from Periwinkle Bay. We mounted Hornblow's colors openly. We drove up ostentatiously to the "Ram," forsaking the "Ringwood Arms," where Mr. Grenville Woolcomb's Committee Room was now established in that very coffee-room where we had dined in Mr. Bradgate's company. We warmed in the contest. We met Bradgate and his principal more than once, and our Montagus and Capulets defied each other in the public street. It was fine to see Philip's great figure and noble scowl when he met Woolcomb at the canvass. Gleams of mulatto hate quivered from the eyes of the little captain. Darts of fire flashed from beneath Philip's eyebrows as he elbowed his way forward, and hustled Woolcomb off the pavement. Mr. Philip never disguised any sentiment of his. "Hate the little ignorant, spiteful, vulgar, avaricious beast? Of course I hate him, and I should like to pitch him into the river." "Oh, Philip!" Charlotte pleaded. But there was no reasoning with this savage when in wrath. I deplored, though perhaps I was amused by, his ferocity.

The local paper on our side was filled with withering epigrams against this poor Woolcomb, of which, I suspect, Philip was the author. I think I know that fierce style and tremendous invective. In the man whom he hates he can see no good : and in his friend no fault. When we met Bradgate apart from his principal, we were friendly enough. He said we had no chance in the contest. He did not conceal his dislike and contempt for his client. He amused us in later days (when he actually became Philip's man of law) by recounting ancedotes of Woolcomb, his fury, his jealousy, his avarice, his brutal behavior. Poor Agnes had married for money, and he gave her none. Old Twysden, in giving his daughter to this man, had hoped to have the run of a fine house ; to ride in Woolcomb's carriages, and feast at his table. But Woolcomb was so stingy that he grudged the meat which his wife ate, and would give none to her relations. He turned those relations out of his doors. Talbot and Ringwood Twysden, he drove them both away. He lost a child, because he would not send for a physician. His wife never forgave him that meanness. Her hatred for him became open and avowed. They parted, and she led a life into which we will look no farther. She quarrelled with parents as well as husband. "Why," she said, "did they sell me to that man?" Why did she sell herelf? She required little persuasion from father and mother when she committed that crime. To be sure, they had educated her so well to worldliness, that when the occasion came she was ready.

We used to see this luckless woman, with her horses and servants decked with Woolcomb's ribbons, driving about the little town, and making feeble efforts to canvass the townspeople. They all knew how she and her husband quarrelled. Reports came very quickly from the Hall to the town. Woolcomb had not been at Whipham a week when people began to hoot and jeer at him as he passed in his carriage. "Think how weak you must be," Bradgate said, "when we can win with this horse! I wish he would stay away, though. We could manage much better without him. He has insulted I don't know how many free and independent electors, and infuriated others, because he will not give them beer when they come to the house. If Woolcomb would stay in the place, and we could have the election next year, I think your man might win. But, as it is, he may as well give in, and spare the expense of a poll." Meanwhile Hornblow was very confident. We believe what we wish to believe. It is marvellous what faith an enthusiastic electioneering agent can inspire in his client. At any rate, if Hornblow did not win this time, he would at the next election. The old Ringwood domination in Whipham was gone henceforth for ever.

When the day of election arrived, you may be sure we came over from Periwinkle Bay to see the battle. By this time Philip had grown so enthusiastic in Hornblow's cause—(Philip, by the way, never would allow the possibility of a defeat)—that he had his children decked in the Hornblow ribbons, and drove from the bay, wearing a cockade as large as a pancake. He, I, and Ridley the painter, went together in a dog-cart. We were hopeful, though we knew the enemy was strong; and cheerful, though, ere we had driven five miles, the rain began to fall.

Philip was very anxious about a certain great roll of paper which we carried with us. When I asked him what it contained, he said it was a gun; which was absurd. Ridley smiled in his silent way. When the rain came, Philip cast a cloak over his artillery, and sheltered his powder. We little guessed at the time what strange game his shot would bring down.

When we reached Whipham, the polling had continued for some hours. The confounded black miscreant, as Philip called his cousin's husband, was at the head of the poll, and with every hour his majority increased. The free and independent electors did not seem to be in the least influenced by Philip's articles in the county paper, or by the placards which our side had pasted over the little town, and in which freemen were called upon to do their duty, to support a fine old English gentleman, to submit to no Castle nominee, and so forth. The pressure of the Ringwood steward and bailiffs was too strong. However much they disliked the black man, tradesman after tradesman, and tenant after tenant, came up to vote for him. Our drums and trumpets at the "Ram" blew loud defiance to the brass band at the "Ringwood Arms." From our balcony, I flatter myself, we made much finer speeches than the Ringwood people could deliver. Hornblow was a popular man in the county. When he came forward to speak, the market-place echoed with applause. The farmers and small tradesmen touched their hats to him kindly, but slunk off sadly to the polling-booth, and voted according to order. A fine, healthy, handsome, red-cheeked squire, our champion's personal appearance enlisted all the ladies in his favor.

"If the two men," bawled Philip, from the "Ram" window, "could decide the contest with their coats off before the market-house yonder, which do you think would win—the fair man or the darkey?" (Loud cries of "Hornblow for iver!" or "Mr. Philip, we'll have *yew*.") "But you see, my friends, Mr. Woolcomb does not like a *fair* fight. Why doesn't he show at the 'Ringwood Arms' and speak? I don't believe he can speak—not English. Are you men? Are you English-men? Are you white slaves to be sold to that fellow?" (Im-mense uproar. Mr. Finch, the Ringwood agent, in vain tries to get a hearing from the balcony of the "Ringwood Arms.") "Why does not Sir John Ringwood—my Lord Ringwood now —come down amongst his tenantry and back the man he has sent down? I suppose he is ashamed to look his tenants in the face. I should be if I ordered them to do such a degrad-ing job. You know, gentlemen, that I am a Ringwood myself. My grandfather lies buried—no, not buried—in yonder church. His tomb is there. His body lies on the glorious field of Busaco!" ("Hurray!") "I am a Ringwood." (Cries of "Hoo—down. No Ringwoods year. We wunt have un!") "And before George, if I had a vote, I would give it for the gallant, the good, the admirable, the excellent Hornblow. Some one holds up the state of the poll, and Woolcomb is ahead! I can only say, electors of Whipham, *the more shame for you!*" "Hooray! Bravo!" The boys, the people, the shouting are all on our side. The voting, I regret to say, steadily continues in favor of the enemy.

As Philip was making his speech, an immense banging of drums and blowing of trumpets arose from the balcony of the "Ringwood Arms," and a something resembling the song of triumph called, "See the Conquering Hero comes," was per-formed by the opposition orchestra. The lodge-gates of the park were now decorated with the Ringwood and Woolcomb flags. They were flung open, and a dark green chariot with four gray horses issued from the park. On the chariot was an earl's coronet, and the people looked rather scared as it came towards us, and said—"Do'ee look, now, 'tis my lard's own post-chaise!" On former days Mr. Woolcomb, and his wife as his aide-de-camp, had driven through the town in an open barouche, but, to-day being rainy, preferred the shelter of the old chariot, and we saw, presently, within, Mr. Bradgate, the London agent, and by his side the darkling figure of Mr. Wool-comb. He had passed many agonizing hours, we were told subsequently, in attempting to learn a speech. He cried over it. He never could get it by heart. He swore like a frantic child at his wife who endeavored to teach him his lesson.

"Now's the time, Mr. Briggs!" Philip said to Mr. B., our lawyer's clerk, and the intelligent Briggs sprang down stairs to obey his orders. Clear the road there! make way! was heard from the crowd below us. The gates of our inn court-yard, which had been closed, were suddenly flung open, and, amidst the roar of the multitude, there issued out a cart drawn by two don·keys, and driven by a negro, beasts and man all wearing Woolcomb's colors. In the cart was fixed a placard, on which a most undeniable likeness of Mr. Woolcomb was designed: who was made to say, " VOTE FOR ME ! AM I NOT A MAN AND A BRUDDER ? " This cart trotted out of the yard of the " Ram," and, with a cortège of shouting boys, advanced into the market-place, which Mr. Woolcomb's carriage was then crossing.

Before the market-house stands the statue of the late earl, whereof mention has been made. In his peer's robes, a hand extended, he points towards his park gates. An inscription, not more mendacious than many other epigraphs, records his rank, age, virtues, and the esteem in which the people of Whipham held him. The mulatto who drove the team of donkeys was an itinerant tradesman who brought fish from the bay to the little town ; a jolly wag, a fellow of indifferent character, a frequenter of all the ale-houses in the neighborhood, and rather celebrated for his skill as a bruiser. He and his steeds streamed with Woolcomb ribbons. With ironical shouts of " Woolcomb for ever ! " Yellow Jack urged his cart towards the chariot with the white horses. He took off his hat with mock respect to the candidate sitting within the green chariot. From the balcony of the " Ram " we could see the two vehicles approaching each other ; and Yellow Jack waving his ribboned hat, kicking his bandy legs here and there, and urging on his donkeys. What with the roar of the peeple, and the banging and trumpeting of the rival bands, we could hear but little : but I saw Woolcomb thrust his yellow head out of his chaise window—he pointed towards that impudent donkey-cart, and urged, seemingly, his postilions to ride it down. Plying their whips, the postboys galloped towards Yellow Jack and his vehicle, a yelling crowd scattering from before the horses, and rallying behind them, to utter execrations at Woolcomb. His horses were frightened, no doubt ; for just as Yellow Jack wheeled nimbly round one side of the Ringwood statue, Woolcomb's horses were all huddled together and plunging in confusion beside it, the fore-wheel came in abrupt collision with the stonework of the statue railing : and then we saw the vehicle turn over altogether, one of the wheelers down with its rider, and the leaders kicking, plunging, lashing out right and left, wild and maddened with fear. Mr. Philip's countenance, I am bound to say, wore a most guilty and queer expression. This accident, this collision, this injury, perhaps death of Woolcomb and his lawyer, arose out of our fine joke about the Man and the Brother.

We dashed down the stairs from the " Ram "—Hornblow, Philip, and half-a-dozen more—and made a way through the crowd towards the carriage, with its prostrate occupants. The mob made way civilly for the popular candidate—the losing candidate. When we reached the chaise, the traces had been cut : the horses were free : the fallen postilion was up and rubbing his leg : and, as soon as the wheelers were taken out of the chaise, Woolcomb emerged from it. He had said from within (accompanying his speech with many oaths, which need not be repeated, and showing a just sense of his danger), " Cut the traces, hang you ! And take the horse away : I can wait until they're gone. I'm sittin' on my lawyer ; I ain't going to have *my* head kicked off by those wheelers." And just as we reached the fallen post-chaise he emerged from it, laughing and saying, " Lie still, you old beggar ! " to Mr. Bradgate, who was writhing underneath him. His issue from the carriage was received with shouts of laughter, which increased prodigiously when Yellow Jack, nimbly clambering up the statue-railings, thrust the outstretched arm of the statue through the picture of the Man and the Brother, and left that cartoon flapping in the air over Woolcomb's head.

Then a shout arose, the like of which has seldom been heard in that quiet little town. Then Woolcomb, who had been quite good-humored as he issued out of the broken post-chaise, began to shriek, curse and revile more shrilly than before ; and was heard, in the midst of his oaths, and wrath, to say, " He would give any man a shillin' who would bring him down that confounded thing ! " Then scared, bruised, contused, confused, poor Mr. Bradgate came out of the carriage, his employer taking not the least notice of him.

Hornblow hoped Woolcomb was not hurt, on which the little gentleman turned round and said, " Hurt ? no ; who are you ? Is no fellah goin' to bring me down that confounded thing ? I'll give a shillin', I say, to the fellah who does ! "

" A shilling is offered for that picture ! " shouts Philip with a red face, and wild with excitement. " Who will take a whole shilling for that beauty ? "

On which Woolcomb began to scream, curse, and revile more bitterly than before. " You here ? Hang you, why are you here? Don't come bullyin' me. Take that fellah away, some of you fellahs. Bradgate, come to my committee-room. I won't stay here, I say. Let's have the beast of a carriage, and——Well, what's up now? "

While he was talking, shrieking, and swearing, half-a-dozen shoulders in the crowd had raised the carriage up on its three wheels. The panel which had fallen towards the ground had split against a stone, and a great gap was seen in the side. A lad was about to thrust his hand into the orifice, when Woolcomb turned upon him.

"Hands off, you little beggar!" he cried, "no priggin'! Drive away some of these fellahs, you postboys! Don't stand rubbin' your knee there, you great fool. What's this?" and he thrusts his own hand into the place where the boy had just been marauding.

In the old travelling carriages there used to be a well or sword-case, in which travellers used to put swords and pistols in days when such weapons of defence were needful on the road. Out of this sword-case of Lord Ringwood's old post-chariot, Woolcomb did not draw a sword, but a foolscap paper folded and tied with a red tape. And he began to read the superscription—"Will of the Right Honorable John, Earl of Ringwood. Bradgate, Smith and Burrows."

"God bless my soul! It's the will he had back from my office, and which I thought he had destroyed. My dear fellow, I congratulate you with all my heart!" And herewith Mr. Bradgate the lawyer began to shake Philip's hand with much warmth. "Allow me to look at that paper. Yes, this is in my handwriting. Let us come into the 'Ringwood Arms'—the 'Ram'—anywhere, and read it to you!"

* * Here we looked up to the balcony of the "Ringwood Arms," and beheld a great placard announcing the state of the poll at 1 o'clock.

> WOOLCOMB   .   .   216
> HORNBLOW   .   .   .   92

"We are beaten," said Mr. Hornblow, very good-naturedly. "We may take our flag down. Mr. Woolcomb, I congratulate you."

"I knew we should do it," said Mr. Woolcomb, putting out a little yellow-kidded hand. "Had all the votes beforehand—knew we should do the trick, I say. Hi! you—What-do-you-call'im—Bradgate! What is it about, that will? It does not do any good to *that* beggar, does it?" and with laughter and shouts, and cries of "Woolcomb for ever," and "Give us something to drink, your honor," the successful candidate marched into his hotel.

And was the tawny Woolcomb the fairy who was to rescue Philip from grief, debt, and poverty? Yes. And the old post-chaise of the late Lord Ringwood was the fairy chariot. You have read in a past chapter how the old lord, being transported with anger against Philip, desired his lawyer to bring back a will in which he had left a handsome legacy to the young man, as his mother's son. My lord had intended to make a provision for Mrs. Firmin, when she was his dutiful niece, and yet under his roof. When she eloped with Mr. Firmin, Lord Ringwood vowed he would give his niece nothing. But he was pleased with the independent and forgiving spirit exhibited by her son; and, being a person of much grim humor, I dare say chuckled inwardly at thinking how furious the Twysdens would be, when they found Philip was the old lord's favorite. Then Mr. Philip chose to be insubordinate, and to excite the wrath of his great-uncle, who desired to have his will back again. He put the document into his carriage, in the secret box, as he drove away on that last journey, in the midst of which death seized him. Had he survived, would he have made another will, leaving out all mention of Philip? Who shall say? My lord made and cancelled many wills. This certainly, duly drawn and witnessed, was the last he ever signed; and by it Philip is put in posses-sion of a sum of money which is sufficient to ensure a provision for those whom he loves. Kind readers, I know not whether the fairies be rife now, or banished from this work-a-day earth, but Philip's biographer wishes you some of those blessings which never forsook Philip in his trials: a dear wife and child-ren to love you, a true friend or two to stand by you, and in health or sickness a clear conscience, and a kindly heart. If you fall upon the way, may succor reach you. And may you, in your turn, have help and pity in store for the unfortunate whom you overtake on life's journey.

Would you care to know what happened to the other per-sonages of our narrative? Old Twysden is still babbling and bragging at clubs, and though aged is not the least venerable. He has quarrelled with his son for not calling Woolcomb out, when that unhappy difference arose between the Black Prince and his wife. He says his family has been treated with cruel injustice by the late Lord Ringwood, but as soon as Philip had a little fortune left him he instantly was reconciled to his wife's nephew. There are other friends of Firmin's who were kind

enough to him in his evil days, but cannot pardon his prosperity. Being in that benevolent mood which must accompany
any leave-taking, we will not name these ill-wishers of Philip,
but wish that all readers of his story may have like reason to
make some of their acquaintances angry.

Our dear Little Sister would never live with Philip and
Charlotte, though the latter *especially* and with all her heart
besought Mrs. Brandon to come to them. That pure and useful and modest life ended a few years since. She died of a
fever caught from one of her patients. She would not allow
Philip or Charlotte to come near her. She said she was justly
punished for being so proud as to refuse to live with them. All
her little store she left to Philip. He has now in his desk the
five guineas which she gave him at his marriage ; and J. J. has
made a little picture of her, with her sad smile and her sweet
face, which hangs in Philip's drawing-room, where father,
mother, and children talk of the Little Sister as though she
were among them still.

She was dreadfully agitated when the news came from New
York of Doctor Firmin's second marriage. "His second?
His third?" she said. "The villain, the villain!" That
strange delusion which we have described as sometimes possessing her increased in intensity after this news. More than
ever, she believed that Philip was her own child. She came
wildly to him, and cried that his father had forsaken them. It
was only when she was excited that she gave utterance to this
opinion. Doctor Goodenough says that though generally silent
about it, it never left her.

Upon his marriage Dr. Firmin wrote one of his long letters
to his son, announcing the event. He described the wealth of
the lady (a widow from Norfolk, in Virginia) to whom he was
about to be united. He would pay back, ay, with interest,
every pound, every dollar, every cent he owed his son. Was
the lady wealthy ? We had only the poor doctor's word.

Three months after his marriage he died of yellow fever, on
his wife's estate. It was then the Little Sister came to see us
in widow's mourning, very wild and flushed. She bade our
servant say, "Mrs. Firmin was at the door ;" to the astonishment of the man, who knew her. She had even caused a
mourning-card to be printed. Ah, there is rest now for that
little fevered brain, and peace, let us pray, for that fond faithful heart.

The mothers in Philip's household and mine have already
made a match between our children. We had a great gathering

the other day at Roehampton, at the house of our friend, Mr. Clive Newcome (whose tall boy, my wife says, was very attentive to our Helen), and, having been educated at the same school, we sat ever so long at dessert, telling old stories, whilst the children danced to piano music on the lawn. Dance on the lawn, young folks, whilst the elders talk in the shade ! What ? The night is falling : we have talked enough over our wine : and it is time to go home ? Good-night. Good-night, friends, old and young ! The night will fall : the stories must end : and the best friends must part.

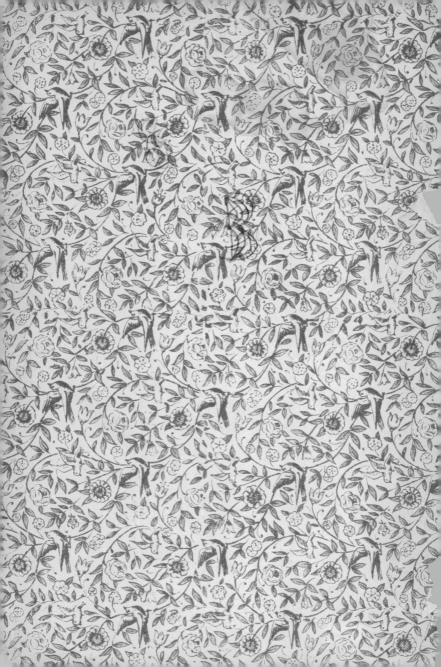